SETTLERS LANDING

A NOVEL

TRAVIS JEPPESEN

ITNA PRESS
Los Angeles, CA
www.itnapress.com

Settlers Landing. -- 1st ed.
ISBN 978-0-9976432-8-2

Library of Congress Control Number: 2023939880

The author would like to thank the International Writers' and Translators' Centre of Rhodes for their generous support during a key phase of this novel's development.

"It is always hard like this, not having a world,
to imagine one, to go to the far edge
apart and imagine, to wall whether in
or out, to build a kind of cage for the sake
of feeling the bars around us, to give shape to a world.
And oh, it is always a world and not the world."

—William Bronk, "At Tikal"

"No one dreams of being Faust anymore and everyone dreams of being king."

—Jean-Luc Godard, *Le Livre d'image*

BOOK ONE

PART ONE

CONFUSION

1.

WELL, LET'S JUST say there was a confusion of ideals. No one could quite determine the exact tenor of the era, though that did not prevent the many from their efforts at articulation, damned though they might be. A whole new phraseology was required—the old language just wouldn't do. Everything was simplified into neo-this, alt-that; post- seemed much too complex and worrisome a prefix. The world was posh and impoverished—somehow both at once. Violence so tightly woven into the fabric of the daily, hardly anyone noticed real instances of mass murder anymore. Far too frequent, they had become the norm. Stains on the carpeting. Drops of blood running down. The news, anyhoo, was left to be categorized as *real* or *fake*. What to believe? The real: what's that? We couldn't quite figure it out; perhaps we didn't genuinely want to. So comfortable in this state of confusion had we ultimately settled, been settled. Buying things helped. Certainly made us feel better. The algebra of want and need had become so variegated, so sophisticated in its molding by internal forces, so as to resemble a sort of arcane calculus. Suddenly we felt the acute bodily *need* for things that hadn't even existed five years prior, attachments and extensions to our being, without which, we might very well fail to endure. More than anything, you could say, the thing we *needed* was for all that pain to disappear. Why did the chicken cross the road? To reach the other side of the void. People began doing heroin—and not even rock stars. Hicks and suburban-ites. High school kids. Housewives. The emptiness was vast, enswathing an entire generation. A *de*-generation—a degeneration of ideals, yes. *What the fuck,* we might imagine a future historian throwing their hands in the air and asking—were we to sincerely fathom such a thing as a future, much less come to dwell in one.

The headlines were no longer epigrammatic and inferential, deferential to the readers' presumed intelligence, in the seductive way of years long past, but written in blunt declarative and often instructive sentences, rife with skepticism about its intended audience's literacy level and attention span—and for good reason, in all likelihood.

> *It's not about fun. It's about survival.*

Or:

> *Here's the real reason X did Y.*

Or:

> *Reading this will make you...*

...laugh? Cry? Moan? Squeal? Puke? Yes, they also had a whiny undertone, so as to appeal to that anxious malaise everyone was pressed into absorbing by the mediated noise machine surrounding. No room for subtle metaphor or poetic evocation here. Just the cold cruel bitter bluntness that might stand some chance of rippling the synapses of the overly medicated.

To live in a state of perpetual anxiety was to be *engaged.* Just look at Harold Hull over there, tweaking out in front of his MacBook at Belle Encoding, ensconced (encoded?) in the drab windowless confines of one decrepit office tower in the middle of one island, the "island of many hills," according to one etymological investigatory work that pinpoints its name as a derogation of the Lenape-language word *Mannahatta.* One of countless such humble, near nameless enterprises on this fine island of many more near-spirits cloaked in human bodies than actual hills, and Harold has been incentivized into its shadows and beyond, his talents rewarded of late with the bestowal of Motherfucker of the Month—a title with which he has been enshrined, some might say burdened, for no less than three months and five days, which was the last time a meager representative from the home office deigned to stick their toe in the door.

What exactly Harold does in front of the dim glow of his screen for nine, ten, twelve hours each day—well, it's a bit complicated in many senses. Technically, spiritually, legally... I myself don't pretend to understand half of it. Oh, *encoding,* for sure, as the name of the business would imply. But what, exactly, does that entail? What does it mean? It's a question I thought to ask Mrdok on many occasions. But it's also the type of question best not to ask Mrdok. For it is sure to yield a most unpalatable response. And so I never did. Ah, the complexities of our era! The talents of a young programmer like Mister Hull! From what I can gather, he is a problem solver of sorts. Or rather: problem cleanser. Some people have problems with their money. It gets dirty somehow. It requires a good rinse in order to continue circulating without jamming the circuitry, the disorderly flow of the system. Well, think about that problem on a much larger, twenty-first century sort of scale. Infinite as the world of finance and markets has now become, there are some individuals—some *entities,* let us say—who need not just their money, but their entire business enterprise scrubbed! Can you imagine? Me, a lowly personal assistant, I don't pretend to understand the nuances of all this. All I have been told is that Mister Hull and his colleagues at the enterprise christened Belle—after Mrdok's favorite adult film star, one Belle Amie (not her real name, I presume)—*encode transactions.* That is their main task. Purification through datafication!—or *data optimization,* I believe is the official name of the service offered by this particular branch of Mrdok's overall enterprise, which extends as far and wide as the very outer reaches of the globe.

Belle Encoding: merely a sign on an office door. An identificatory marker. You won't find any mention of it on the World Wide Web. It exists in some public registry, somewhere—city hall, perhaps? Otherwise, not the sort of enterprise that requires—or would even benefit from—much publicity. With the exception of Belle's neighbors in the corridor—a *software development extravaganza* run by two perpetually absent Chinese gentlemen and a *maintenance organ* (for these are how the signs on the respective doors designate what lies beyond them on the otherwise vacant fluorescent-sterile hallway) whose sole employee appears to be a middle-aged woman speaking heavily Russified English, who once politely inquired of Harry as to the location of the restroom (he thinks) when they chanced to cross paths in the hall one morning.

Now, I have often heard it said that the best stories begin with endings. Or, wait… Was it that the best stories end with new beginnings? Or that the beginning of the ending marks a new beginning? No, that last one makes no sense at all, does it? Let me slow down: There is Harry in one location on the island, while a few miles away, in another part, Central Park, to be precise, is Mrdok. The part of the story where Harry is will come to an end very soon. But where we are, it is just beginning. In the middle. Where all good stories start. Mrdok walking. Me beside him.

There has now been a long silence to accompany our jaunt, Mrdok reveling in the display of autumnal foliage. Autumn, he says, is his favorite season because everything looks more beautiful when it begins to die. I happen to be of a much more traditional and romantic temperament, I suppose, in my preference for spring, a season synonymous with revivification, when the world emerges from cold darkness only to shimmer anew. But it could be asserted, not unreasonably, that my enduring tenure as Mrdok's assistant has its roots in this very temperamental complementarity, the force of the cosmos having rendered us a most compatible pair.

We pass by a homeless couple sitting on a bench. The woman is making a grab for the paper bag in the man's hands.

—Don't be takin no sip of my beer, baby, I don't wanna catch the AIDS!

—You simple ass muthafucka, you already got the AIDS. Just look at yo hair!

At that, I had to quietly snicker. His hair, after all, did look rather AIDSy.

—Shut up, gurl, he snaps back. Yo hair aint even real. Damn bitch got the corona in her cooter, her armpit got the AIDS, bird flu in da thorax… You aint takin no sip of *my* beer, bitch.

—Gordo, Mrdok suddenly grabs my wrist, and I already know what will come next: How much am I worth?

The smartphone, so named because it knows so much more than I do, is at my fingertips before he even arrives at the question mark. A few clicks later, the eleven-digit number has flashed across the screen. At these moments, the toughest challenge is getting a good estimate on the final five to six digits, which tend to fluctuate rapidly according to the current seizure rhythms of the global markets. I have come to learn how to zero in on the best guesstimate, a skill Mrdok cherishes, I know, even though he cannot often find the words to convey such a common sentiment as gratitude.

I have a way of reciting such numbers that instantly calms Mrdok's nerves. Unlike the pleasant sedation of a Valium, however, the mathematical anesthesia wears off within seconds.

—Give me the phone.

—Shouldn't I call for you…?

—Fucking cocksuckers. What am I even *helping* these assholes for?

I was rather under the impression that it was they who were helping him by not sending Mrdok to a place where the wardrobe's entire palette is restricted to an orange hue. Though I don't dare bring such a thought into the open air.

–I think we might wait just a minute. It would be best, no? That bench over there, a perfect place from which to admire the sky. The trees, the autumn foliage—

–Gordo, you fat fuck: Phone. Now.

Swallowing the demon swelling in my throat, the phone goes into his outstretched hand.

–Dima, darling, he barks into the receiver, a sardonic emphasis on that *darling*. What the fuck?

High in the windowless office tower near the bottom of the island, Dima's response less of a bark than a whispery affirmation.

–Do you really want everyone to hear?

–I can't get through my day until this is taken care of. I've got my intestines wrapped around my sphincter here.

–What do you want me to do? Take a laxative.

–Funny.

–You think I got a direct line to your guy? It's you who set this up. Not me. All I'm supposed to do is call you once it's happened. That's the thing I'm supposed to do.

Mrdok not knowing exactly how to reply to that. One of those frustrating moments when the universe appears to be running on someone else's clock.

–Well… Fucking call. Or else.

Click.

On second thought, as we find ourselves turning from the 85th Street pathway on to the Great Lawn, there's something else in the air bothering him. The green oddly desolate, even for a midday just after lunch, just a series of tourists taking selfies while ignoring each other's presence spread across the lawn, an old homeless granny muttering to herself upon a bench, the odd jogger passing through the scene.

–Whattaya think, Gordo? he suddenly lets blurt. This fed fuck. He a rat?

Rat-sniffing being something of an obsession, a sport in Mrdok's universe. Find the rat, win a prize. But my answer, as always, is as frank as I can let myself be.

–We're on safe ground, I assure him. He has too much at stake in the operation to allow it to go in any direction other than the one we've all agreed to.

Mrdok grimaces.

–I don't know. Something stinks.

I raise my nose to the air to confirm my hunch that Mrdok isn't speaking of any actual olfactory sensate matter: a sort of hazy, tree-laced tire smell, the same lacing the air throughout mid-Manhattan in seeming perpetuity.

I try to think of a sentence that might both respond to his olfactory commentary—which I am now quite sure was a reference to a larger ecology we now find ourselves in, rather than merely the task at hand (across town) or our current physical station in the park—and simultaneously calm my boss's muddled nerves. As I struggle in silence, Mrdok himself finally arrives at a placation.

–Fuck it, says he. Let's go get a snow cone.

2.

OH, MRDOK. MRDOK in his park, the Central one. No etymology required of that one! Mrdok in his collector's edition Converse, designer black sunglasses blocking out the lights of this world. Mrdok in his world, his island—the island world he has created and carries with him, wherever he may roam. His empire, Mrdpire: world-within-this-world. World that *eats* this world.

Mrdok and his millions. Well, billions, actually. But the billions Mrdok's made aren't good enough. He needs more. I say *need* rather than *want*. Because that is what it is, in all simplicity. How else to understand the nature of his movements, constant, if not for impulse? For sure there is a thing called mere *want*. We all know what that is. Need: something *entirely* different. A savage beast with no understanding of the concept of limitation. Therefore, the moment a limit is imposed, he must immediately find a way to bust right through it: hence, the source of Mrdok's genius. Well, a good part of it, at least. Want: passive; need: active.

A man of enviable qualities—that's my perspective, of course, spilling out inelegantly across the page. No way to contain the spillage in this case. Mrdok a man I have been fascinated by, a man I have studied long before I began working for him. A man constantly surrounded by people, so no need to feel lonely. (Though *does* he ever feel lonely? An intriguing question. No idea; his inner life a mystery, shrouded from the inquiries of others: the savviest of businessmen.)

Your face in the mirror each morning: That is want. In a very basic, crude sense. Something that's just *there*: every man has it. To preserve it, or destroy it, or change it somehow, whether surgically or through other means; the will to alterance. The face of a beautiful woman, a body you wish to possess, a body outside your own: well, that is need. It presses on you. It isn't just inward; outward necessity comes into play. The quest to conquer that which is truly outstanding in its otherness.

I would know. I have needed Mrdok in my time more than he ever needed—or wanted, for that matter—me. Though I have stuck through it all, the good times and the bad. Not just from a sense of devotion, but because (I admit) I am eager to see how it will all turn out. And because I *believe*. Not necessarily in the man *per se* but in the feeling that possesses him. It is a very American feeling, I would say: that sensation that one is on top of the world. That the world springs out from under you like the tentacles of an octopus. Mrdok's tentacles are far reaching, and they have taken me to many distant places, places I'd never have considered going on my own. And here I am:, still going.

I myself could only ever appear as a minor character in any major account of such a great man's largesse and ambition, though I am hoping that the uniqueness of my access to his minor foibles and major soarings will be of value on the level of pure perspective. For as physically close as I have been allowed to get to Mrdok, the greater the distance I have tried to keep in analyzing just what it is that propels him forward. Only through that distance can one begin to fathom the mechanics of such an unparalleled engine.

Fat fuck: that's one of the things he calls me. Gordo, another. Neither is my real name. Mrdok has ones for us all. They're frequently not the names our mothers gave. But it's all okay. And if it weren't, we likely wouldn't tell him.

I prefer *Gordo*.

There are moments, I am afraid, when omniscience will have to take over—after all, you can't avoid it—it's everywhere! Ha, but seriously, it is an inevitability in accounts such as these, when it is simply impossible for a body (notably a body as girthy and stout in stature as my own) to be physically present, when the godmind will have to suffice. I don't mean to put on airs. It is just that to forgo the opportunities that access brings would be to put on a show of false modesty. Even when I am far away from Mrdok—when work dictates that I occupy a distant continent while he is off charting new courses—we are still in constant contact via the wonders of digital technology, and so there is some truth in the assertion that I am always with him. The liberties I take in *playing God* are unique to our era, and since not even the women in his life have come as close as I have to fully inhabiting the genius that is Mrdok, you will have to excuse the liberties I have had to take in order to arrive at the truth.

Forget third person, first person; let's just call it the *no-person.*
Which, troublingly, is a bit uncomfortably similar to the *everyperson,*
an inclusivity that doesn't fit well with the particularities of our—that
is to say, *Mrdok's*—project. For you cannot pursue the line of endeavor that Mrdok has with a desire to accommodate the wishes, the
wants—the *needs*—of everyone. Or anyone, even. As a matter of
truth, one of the distinguishing features of Mrdok's journey is its singularity. As anyone who has been drawn to Mrdok, attracted by his
wealth and fame, could tell you, there is an aura of intrigue surrounding the man that no one has quite reached the bottom of—yet. The
modest effort made here amounts to an omniscience for those excluded from the direct tumult of Mrdok's day-to-day, and a portrait
of perhaps the most virile ambitionist of our era.

3.

A SEAMLESSNESS TO his occupancy—the spaces he fills, the
moments he feels himself to be *at home.* Those moments, few and far
between, he sits or stands still. Now, his Long Island abode, it is to
be specified. Shelter Island, to be even more precise. Home. Place of
relaxation and retreat for most; for Mrdok, an anxiety magnet: the
place where he feels the needing the most. That relentless crave. You
don't need to position yourself too far away to smell it. Wafts off
him, onionlike, ornery, swelters through the open pores on his ageless face whenever he thunders his way into a room, all primed for
completion. Mrtol watches, her face encrusted with a permanent
pained disgust. It is all deals, deals, deals, all the time—that's the way
it sounds to her. Mrdok can never rest unless there are several hundred occurring at once, until he can get lost in the flow of *deals,* his
staff on hand to anchor him. There was a raunchy malfeasance to his
perspect that left them all gloating. Adrift at sea, like the captain in
his favorite novel, the abridged version he read as a young toss and
made an indelible mark on him. Deals snaking out from him Medusa-
like. Mrdok never gave much thought to where all the flying dirt
landed, that bottomless pit that formed the core. Mrdok, his self, is
a mobile wall of holes.

    –These things don't matter, his wife now pronounces, picking up
an onion distractedly and wielding it before her face as though about
to perform an inspection. She didn't inspect it. She didn't even look
at it. She was looking at, speaking to: him. Mrdok. The other onion.

    –What matters then? he asks, leaking exasperation.

–Distance! she nearly belches back at him. (Undoubtedly it would have been a belch scented with Chardonnay.) Where have you been this entire conversation, Elias?

(For Elias is the name she calls him when she *really* wants to get his attention. That first name that not even friends and familiars have permission to use. The weight of MRDOK is enough for the world; he had decided this early on…)

–You know, Mrtol, I'm in the middle—

–of an important deal, yes, I know this, I—

–So why can't you handle it on your own then?

–I handle *everything* around here.

–That one again. Well, you have a lot of help. And let me tell you, Mrtol, you do a damn fine job of it.

–Mrdok.

She sets the onion down on the kitchen counter. Black marquina marble. Even allows it to roll a little. Then pours herself another glass.

–So you want more distance, he falters. So what? Call the travel agent. Take the house in the Keys for a week.

She shakes her head, starts to say something. Falters.

–I forgot. It's hurricane season. So then Maui. Come on, Mrtol, you love the ocean. Salt air, sand in your bathing suit. Always does the trick.

–I want something more permanent, Mrdok.

Now, a curl of the stomach. Painfully familiar sensation.

–You leaving me?

–Mrdok, of course not. We have a pre-nup. Besides, I'm not Krstal.

A relaxation of the esophagus. Stifled belch.

–Why do you always compare yourself to her.

Truth is, Mrtol does look a bit like Krstal. But then, nearly all the women Mrdok has enjoyed have had a similar look. Thick, plump, perhaps, though not so robust as to be classed as *busty*—a word Mrdok despises. The blonde-reddish thing going on. The pouty lips. But it's not as though he has a set criteria. More like a list of qualities he avoids. And yes, most of the women he met had at least one of these off qualities. The psychology of desire often boiling down to a no-go list. Of course, if it was just to be a one-off fuck, that was different. Then any old whore would do—the more variety, the better. All those trips to Asia, sampling the local barbeque. Paying the safest option. Some distance between himself and the game. That way, he could always be sure he wasn't being used. When you pay, they always go away.

—Venice? he now whimpers.

He doesn't really want her going to Venice. Not now. Venice is his place. But he's running out of options here.

Mrtol relents. At least her shoulders.

—I don't want to live the rest of my time as some Upper East Side Hausfrau. Or stashed away up in Greenwich, faghag of some closeted talk show host. Gossip girl for some D-list soap star. Gucci-leaking tropical fish expert. Country club salad shitter.

—Enough, says Mrdok. I'll get you the dog.

—What am I, twelve? I don't want a goddamn animal.

—I thought…

—What, Mrdok? What did you think? I need *long-term release*, okay? Look at this. A big prison, is what this is.

—This is a fucking *Shelter Island mansion*, Mrtol—

And it was. With the North Fork front, the rolling lawns, the winding drive, manicured fields, the sculpture garden, the Persian rugs, the art collection, the yacht. The rooftop heliport, so necessary for the commute from Manhattan. All the clichés required to land a feature in *Architectural Digest*. But not enough for Mrtol, apparently.

—I drive through one gate to leave my house, a second to leave the estate… You get it? I'm trapped here. Wilting.

—You've been back on Shelter Island for a week now, Mrtol. Where do you want to go? I mean, if none of the other palaces're good enough for you, I'm always happy to buy more.

—I've been through it all in my mind. The palazzo is only good in the spring—in the summer, you can't go anywhere because of all the tourists, and in the winter, Venice floods. You don't want me going back to the chateau again in France, though I told you over and over again I'm not remotely interested in even *looking* at that bricklayer anymore—

—Can you not mention the fucking short-dicked teenage fucking juvenile delinquent bricklayer, please?

Clenched teeth.

—Okay, first of all, he was twenty-three, Mrdok. And secondly, you were the one who insisted on building that fireplace. I was perfectly fine with the gas heating—

—You just *love* the taste of that cheesy frog cock, don't you?

—Ribbit. Ribbit.

—Fucking whore.

–It was a joke, Mrdok. No need to talk that way. And, besides, it was a one-time thing. You just happened to walk in at the wrong time.

–One-time thing. That fucking blowjob nearly ruined our marriage.

–And how many sluts have you stuck it in since we got married?

Now Mrdok's had enough. Lets her know with one of his looks. A look that simultaneously gives her permission to go on.

–Maui is tacky, she continues. Monaco overcrowded. The trashy people in Key West? Please, don't make me regurgitate, I had octopus salad for lunch.

–Maybe something… urban, then.

–Oh, Mrdok, please. All I have to do is queef and I'm back in Manhattan. It's *boring*.

She swings her glass of wine around now, spilling a few drops on the counter.

–London? Paris? Dare I say… LA?

At that, Mrdok's mobile suddenly goes into spastic convulsion on the dining room table.

–Look! That's a sign. Go to LA. You can check in on Bobby while you're at it. We haven't done that in a while—

–*You* haven't done it—

–We'll discuss it over dinner, Mrtol. Tell Juanita to do that Colombian thing, you know, with the spicy soup. I've got a conference call at nine, though, so early.

Mrdok, exhausted: and yes, his exhaustion the very thing that feeds him. The cravings. It comes from always being in the middle of things and never really satisfied until he can see them through. Till he can see through them. Inspecting each rest stop along the way. Till the endgame. Hey, it's *all* a game. Isn't it?

Ring ring. Vibrate vibrate. Here's Rick on the line yapping about a new building in Berlin. Rick looks over all the medium-small projects, as Mrdok has classed them.

–Berlin? Do tourists even go there anymore? I thought it was Munich we were eyeing.

–Lotsa yids now going to Berlin from Israel. Y'know. All the historical shit they got over there. Hitler or whoever.

Rick doesn't know his goddamn history from his mother's asshole. All Rick knows is numbers numbers numbers. Rick had been trained by Mrdok, plucked right out of sophomore year City College as his chosen ingenue. A no-name family. Perfect, in other words. When hunting protégés, Mrdok knows better than to hobnob with the high-end crowd. Desperation's something you can bend like a fork. Numbers numbers numbers. Kid can worry about history once he's in the bathrobe-and-cigars phase.

–So we've got eight apartments spread over four floors? I don't know, Ricky. Are we gonna flip it? Cos if not, I think we're gonna have to break em up, divide em. Which is hard in Europe, with all the historical regulation bullshit they got goin over there.

–It's new. There's actually six, but two are penthouses on two stories. So yeah, I've already divided those up for you to make eight.

–How much we talkin.

–Twelve.

–Twelve?! Who we dealin' with here. They Jews?

–Naw. Not just Jews. Real hardcore ones. Israelis. The ones they got the permed sideburns and everything.

–Tell em we'll do nine.

–I've already got em down to ten five.

–Oh, you're starting to turn me on, baby. Tell em we'll go nine and not a penny higher.

–Shouldn't be a problem. Berlin aint as broke as she used to be, but the market there's a joke. Unbelievable, the numbers I've been finding in that city.

–Sounds like we still have some minutes left on the clock, am I right? Tell em we have some other shopping to do. Cut the call real short, tell em you got another property on the line. That should expedite things.

He can hear Rick smile through the phone.

–Got it, boss. And how's the lady doing? You with her right now?

By which he means, most likely, Bev. Always screws up Mrdok's women in his head. Rick's adulation can be annoying. That and his penchant for pussy. Not so distant from Mrdok's own, but still. He didn't want to be confronted by it in other men. Particularly not those he works with. He doesn't hire people to hold a mirror up to his being. If anything, there needs to be a little bit of friction there, to spur the momentum onward. Somehow hadn't been able to instill that in the kid. Yet. Too much reflection, you wind up stalled. Mired in shit and grinning like an ape.

But he could always just hang up the phone. Nowadays you don't even have to; a tiny little button does the trick. He presses it, the red one. There's something there he can't fully trust. Problem is, that's the same quality you look for in every useful person, every high earner. Kid could wind up the next big shit on the block. Safer to keep ones like that close to you. You let them go, they come back twice as tall with the aim to stomp.

Phone still in his hand. Who should he call? Dinner, that's right. Fuck. Have to sit across from Mrtol's impromptu freak-out. She'll be shit drunk by then. At least think of someone, anyone to call, put some distance between himself and that onslaught. Block the time between now and the night's conference call.

Here comes Jaco bumbling into the room, juggling his screens. Little wide-eyed tot still in his white sweater, St. Anne's Academy crest neat on his chest.

–Yo, how's it going, Jaco?

Kid can't pry his eyes from the glow.

–Not good, Daddy, in his trademark monotone.

–No? What happened?

Looks up now as though stunned by Daddy's not knowing the obvious.

–Ellen got shot at school.

–Oh. Oh no.

Ellen is a guy. Jaco's imaginary friend.

–You mean the doctor gave him a shot?

–No. I mean he got shot. By a bad man. A criminal.

–Well. I'm sorry to hear that.

–He'll be okay.

His eyes go back to the screen, he wanders into the pantry, calling Juanita's name. Time for after-school snack. For some reason, every exchange these days concerns Ellen. Nothing about what's going on in school. Maybe nothing is. Kid plays no sports, no hobbies. Doesn't even get into music. Has no real friends. Just stares at that goddamn phone half the time, tablet the other half. When he does enter the real world, it's to do with Ellen, who doesn't exist. Never an actual human relation. Has to be something wrong there. Should talk to Mrtol about it, find out why the fuck *she* hasn't done something already. Then again, it would only provoke another—No, not tonight.

Mrdok standing there, staring at his phone. Common twenty-first century imagery. Pixels on the screen forming shreds, bytes they call it. *All information is useful information.* Mrdok slowly recites this old cliché aloud, temporarily lost in the numbers. For a minute, he lets them become just numbers and nothing else—raw data, detached from any IRL signified. Usually it's Gordo who looks after all this shit. But Gordo's not here right now. Proctologist appointment downtown. Something like that. The fat fuck. With no Gordo here, with no one around, he finds himself lost, not sure what it is he wants. His first free moment in the entire day. Suddenly, he panics. No calls coming in. No texts. No e-mails… Wait, *no e-mails?* He opens his server, refreshes. *You're all done for the day!* Shit. Something wrong. Call Manhattan Marcia, see what's up with the server. At least it'll kill time.

No. Fuck it. Let the world collapse. All of it. Mrdok removes his coat, tosses it on the dining room table: weak gesture of defeat. Juanita'll see it, hang it up before dinner. Up the stairs for some quality time with the widescreen. Turn the silencer on, let em text if they need something. Mrdok asleep in his tower within the half hour, denizens and employees of the household immersed in their stirrings in the down below and surrounding.

4.

LET US NOW press the rewind button on that ancient relic known as the VCR. To watch a scene starring the adolescent Mrdok, whence we might gain some understanding of our man in his hour. Lest I be accused of painting a picture with an excess of rose upon my palette, it must be said that one's adolescence is often the chapter in one's life narrative that harbors treacherous secrets of the darkest shadings. Luckily, as the scene about to play out will show, Mrdok was able to briskly overcome those early impulses that once threatened to imprint an unfortunately permanent smudge upon his biographical odyssey.

Here's Mrdok, fifteen years of age, impressionable and eager to please, perhaps a little lost, having been shuttled to and fro throughout childhood owing to his father's volatile line of work, landing his sophomore year at a shiny brand new high school in a Long Island suburb whose name is less important than the fact that it was much like every other bastion of slight privilege upon that island and that Mrdok hardly knew a soul there. Most of his days spent alone, fantasizing what life in more glamorous climes, such as nearby New York City, must be like.

A young man in such a pitiable state naturally finds himself in a vulnerable position before much worldlier, nefarious types. At this stage in life, situated precariously on the precipice of adulthood, one naturally wishes to find appeal in the eyes of anyone older, wiser, craftier—*cooler,* in the parlance of today's youth. Young Mrdok found himself the human Play-Doh of a couple boys his senior, Malik and

Morton, types of the lowest sort, really, who nonetheless were engaged in a very profitable game that Mrdok, in his inexperience, found fascinating and very much wanted to play.

The endgoal of this game was the liberation and subsequent sale of apparel and accoutrements from certain middle-to-high-end retailers. Diesel, Calvin Klein, DKNY, Ralph Lauren… All the flashy labels that imbue the wearer with a certain degree of luxury that connotes style and commands respect. His traineeship was long and drawn-out. The two boys who took him on started him off on the silk circuit. The magic of silk is its *délicatesse,* its scrunchability. Can be made to disappear so readily in one's palm, and just as readily up the sleeve.

Cut to the interior of a luxury brand retailer in Your Town, USA. A well-dressed lone customer enters mid-morning, not long after opening, peruses the shirts/pants/suits for a while, then asks the lone clerk on duty whether they happen to have a particular ready-to-wear suit in his size. Clerk retreats to the stockroom to check, and in the interim, well-dressed young man quickly stashes any number of goods in dressing room #2. Enter second customer, who asks to try a shirt on. While well-dressed young man is taking his time trying on that suit in dressing room #1, second customer goes into dressing room #2, where all the goodies have been stashed. He slashes the security tags, stuffs the clothing into his bag, then returns the shirt to the clerk—*Sorry, boss, just not my style*—then exits. Shortly thereafter, well-dressed young man will make a similar apology as he returns the suit to the clerk and makes his way out the door.

And so on.

As a team, they were all but impossible to catch. Mrdok's apprenticeship took him through the full range of tactics, beginning with preliminary casing of the joint, primitive sleeving, and slowly building up to myriad variations of stash 'n' grab.

Along the way, Mrdok learned many a valuable lesson about security. A subject that has stuck with him up until this very day. The most important being that security is always, in its inherent nature, an illusion. For nothing is secure.

–The moment you put something out on display, it is an open invitation for someone to come and grab it, explained Morton, who, being the eldest, was the self-appointed theoretician of the gang.

You cannot guard against such an impulse. To grab what is dangling right there in front of you, make it yours. Fuck the notion of exchange, the nibbling middleman that seeks to arrest or delay the entire process, pervert it into artifice. Let *being* finally unite with *becoming,* like some German philosopher might say.

Psychologically, the premiere barrier is already shattered in the very instant of display. Display is always inherently pornographic, in that it is meant to evoke wild cravings in the viewer. There is a perversity of display; a perversity in objects, now that I think of it. That is indeed something to contemplate: this pornographic affect that drives people to buy and to steal.

That need is well sensed, and so an entire industry must evolve to guard against the effects of that impulse's erupting in others. From a distance, this guarding, this act of *security,* of securing, is in actuality just another performance—much like the stealing. A game.

They became so adept, young Mrdok and his co-conspirators, even in large retail outlets where there were security cameras, that they might emerge with anywhere between $15,000 and $25,000 in merchandise on a single day's swoop. Cocky from victory, it rather got to the point where they deliberately *chose* shops with security cameras—originally because they relished the challenge, then later because they had grown so accustomed to them, they had over time tailored their techniques to accommodate this precise tool of the authorities.

Each of the three had his own particular role in the endeavor—and costume to go along with it. Malik's naturally dark skin allowed him to play up to the security teams' inevitable inborn racial biases (for those who did not have them were not typically considered qualified to work as security guards.) Though in daily life, Malik preferred to go around in tailored suits—the lone student in their high school, heck, in any Long Island high school probably, to maintain such a strenuous and studied daily grooming habit—for these operations, Malik would *dress down* in order to become the object of suspicion straight out of central casting: the Thug.

There goes the Thug, wandering around the goods splayed out all lustily in the aisles, deliberately playing to the cameras that the trio located on a prior scouting mission (naturally attired in completely different garb.) Malik picks up as many different items as he can, inspecting them closely, looking *nervously* over his shoulder, back and forth and forth and back, mimicking the motions of a deranged crackhead, then *pretends* to pocket an item here or there. Always in camera view. This performance would continue on for a long, suspense-building while, until all security cameras had zoomed in on the Thug, the security personnel's gaze fully occupied, adrenaline rising in the apes as they anticipate their nab of the day.

Meanwhile, young Mrdok, adorned in All-American Boy Scout Jamboree wholesomeness, would be making his way round the store with a tiny de-tagger cupped in the palm of his hand—snip snip, as the security tags come off, only to be inserted in some opportune layaway pile. A good distance behind him, a third customer has now entered the premises. None other than the third member of the triple-M gang, sticky-fingered Morton, portraying an older gentleman of the white collar besuited variety (his intimidating stature, at nearly six feet eight, allowed this illusion to come to pass), employing his heightened power of corner-of-the-eye farsight to observe each and every item Mrdok has freed from the store alarm's recognition device.

As soon as the Thug makes his exit, the store's entire security personnel would invariably come streaming out of the back office. Outside, Malik is tackled, enduring varying degrees of violence, to the ground. Shortly thereafter, the Gentleman, behooved in the whitest of privilege—and with many layers beneath his suit as he emerges from the dressing room—calmly makes his way out the door, casually and detachedly observing the struggle on the street as the security personnel attempts to wrench the combative and protesting Malik back into the shop.

Mrdok was always the last to leave. Theoretically empty-handed, save for those occasions when he was feeling particularly cocky and the timing was right, when he would feel emboldened enough to engage in the old tactic of *sleeving*, as they call it in that profession's parlance. A rather primitive method whereby an individual might take advantage of the shoulder height of the security gates by stuffing a piece of tagged merchandise up one's sleeve, then raising one's arm in a yawning stretch or headscratch that is timed to coincide with the moment one bypasses the barriers upon exiting.

Meeting up later at the private residence of one or the other of the triple-M gang, depending on who had the house free—often Mrdok, as his father was perpetually absent due to work commitments, his mother having departed the narrative early on—perhaps hours after the heist, depending on how long it took them to release Malik following the string of recriminations and subsequent apologies from management once it became clear that the young man had stolen nothing and he began issuing not-so-coded threats inclusive of terms such as *racial profiling* and *my lawyer father.* The boys would then divvy up the merchandise to sell at huge profit through an older gentleman Morton knew—as that gentleman happened to be *his* father.

The important thing, according to both Malik and Morton, was to buy nothing. It was, Mrdok soon realized, a principle of ethics more than anything else. An ethics of nihilism. To buy anything was to let them win. A compromise; and true artists never compromise.

Amateurs were fine with compromise. Buy a little something to mask the pocketing of the something big. Ward off suspicion rather than cause a distraction. The Triple M Gang *cruised* distraction. You could say they were addicted to it. Above all, they deigned to *craft* distraction, until it rather became an artform.

All was well and fine in Sherwood Forest, with the boys raking in thousands of dollars a day, having all but retired from their high school careers in order to take up the game full-time. Then one day, Malik didn't come back.

This put the two remaining M's in an odd position. They sat in the basement of Morton's house, gazes shifting nervously between the pile of acquired goods from that afternoon's endeavor spread on the floor and each other's eyes. Neither quite knew what to say. Or what to do. Whether, for instance, to stash the clothing somewhere else, perhaps dig a hole in the backyard. Failure had never been in the master plan. There was no Plan B or C. It's not that they were thoughtless, reckless in their endeavor. Every facet of the operation, after all, had been so well planned, it just never for a moment occurred to any of the three that they might one day experience such a shortcoming.

It was to be one of Mrdok's first big lessons in business: Always Plan For Just-In-Case.

Finally, the silence was broken by Morton.

—I think he's not coming.

Mrdok snorted his agreement, then verbalized it.

—I think so too, said in a fathomless daze.

And so it was that the whole operation was busted into smithereens over the course of a single afternoon. It was a disastrous affair—and, in particular, for Malik, who had become the tragic victim of a trigger-happy security guard's illicit weapon. The guard had always told the colleagues who nervously espied it resting on his desk in the back office that it was a toy gun. Others recalled him saying it was a taser. The point is, it shouldn't have been there; legally, there were no grounds by which a private security guard might carry a loaded weapon in the line of duty (*in the line of duty* perhaps an overstatement, given that rent-a-cops are not actual cops; more like hired toughs masquerading as cops.) The point is, in the process of dragging Malik back into the store, the guard *accidentally*, he and his colleagues later claimed, dislodged a bullet into the young man's skull, culminating in an awful waking death—a paralysis from which he would never recover.

For Mrdok, suddenly sensing that very afternoon when Malik didn't return that things very well might have taken a turn for the worse, decided to do what any soul, we might conjecture, would do in the same situation.

One need not be born with a strong sense of integrity in order to develop it later in life. To really grasp the proprieties of honesty, one must first fall afoul of them.

Mrdok did not immediately run to the authorities. He at least discussed the matter in some detail with his father, who, quite preoccupied at the time with his fledgling real estate business, had no prior inkling as to his son's shenanigans. The father, in turn, immediately brought his son before his lawyer, the infamous Antony Fatobello, who never once lost a case and would eventually come to serve as a sort of early role model for the precocious Mrdok.

After listening patiently to his young client's narration, Tony Fatballs, as his clients were wont to call him, advised Mrdok and his father to go to the authorities right away. Not just any branch of the authorities, however, but to one police captain in particular, in a precinct confusingly distant from Mrdok's own, the captain's name now forgotten, though Mrdok can retrospectively swear it ended in a vowel sound quite similar to Mister Fatobello's.

The captain chain-smoked for the entirety of the session as Mrdok regaled him of his sorrowful adventures, admitted his moral culpabilities, even shed a few tears of shame—the latter coaxed out of him by the admonitions of his lawyer, who was naturally on hand for the entirety of the submission.

–Let me see if I got this straight, said Mister Police Captain, stubbing out his sixth cigarette. You're saying, you and your friends— you were a part of this little...

–It wasn't a *gang*, Mister Fatobello cut in for clarification's sake.

–This *operation*. But, uh, you yourself never stole nothing? You were just there to, uh, distract, while the other boys were the ones who lifted the merchandise?

Mrdok nodded his head in agreement, his face painted with the same doe-eyed innocence he'd put on with his Scout uniform each time they were on their way to a new job.

It may not have been *precisely* true, not in the exact way in which the police captain had phrased it. But after a firm sideways glance from Tony Fatballs, Mrdok knew better than to amend this loose summary of his alleged contribution to the conspiracy.

–I have here, Fatballs now signed in, written testimonies from three of Mister Mrdok's teachers, his guidance counselor, and his vice-principal. I am telling you, Captain, in my decades-long career dealing with adult and juvenile offenders alike, I have never before encountered such a sheer quantity of individuals willing—trampling over one another, really—to, at a moment's notice, to vouch for one young man's moral rectitude. It really was a bit emotionally overwhelming. Not to mention the kid clearly has an enviable homelife. His father, after all, is one of our county's outstanding business leaders. Why, his firm just last year made a very generous contribution to the Police Veterans Fund, as I have it in my records right here? While nobody in this room is denying that a heinous, *hei-nous* series of crimes has taken place, we, as the adults in this situation, must use our judgment wisely here in determining whether we really and truly think it is right to dash away the promising future of a bright and socially upright young man who was clearly misled by elements of a criminal nature?

A few more tears were then required of Mrdok. With them, he would pay his penance. Morton, who was unlucky enough not to have the services of Mister Fatobello at his disposal, did not fare quite as well. Being two years older than Mrdok, he was placed in the legal category of adulthood. Even though it was his first offense, the court found that the severity of his crimes lay in their great frequency, especially when the amount of wealth attained by he and his father— who had placed the blame solely on his son—was enunciated. That the year-long operation had come to a spectacularly bloody end made the verdict clear: with Mrdok removed from the legal equation, and with Malik in his permanently pickled state, someone had to confront the weight of blame.

About what became of Morton in later years, very little is known. Suffice it to say that by the time Morton was released from serving his sentence, Malik had passed away and Mrdok had by then advanced to much more successful, legal ventures.

It was Tony Fatballs who corrected Mrdok's moral failings. He suggested that Mrdok invest his significant earnings from his illicit adventure into a philanthropical endeavor. Thus Mrdok's next significant dosh stash was earned out of an act of pure naked unadulterated generosity: lending to those in need. As the youngest ever CEO of what was to become America's most coveted and respected payday loan chain—with branches in low-income neighborhoods across the nation—Tony would teach Mrdok a valuable life lesson: that it is best to help others by helping oneself.

And that is precisely what Mrdok did. Until the day came a couple years later when it was decided by Tony—who had by this point become a makeshift father figure, having essentially bought out Mrdok's biological father—that the time would be ideal for Mrdok to dissolve operations of his successful loan company and devote himself to higher educational endeavors across the pond. (It has been surmised by one yellow journalist that this moment coincided with the entrance of certain actors from the Security and Exchange Commission, who felt—wrongly, it must be said—that they were deserving of answers to certain niggling questions regarding the business and its assets; though in actuality, the two events had nothing to do with each other; Mrdok had in fact been longing to study abroad for quite some time, as has been well documented.) That, in fact, is where us two jolly expats would first cross paths: at uni in merry old England. But that, I'm afraid, is a tale we will have to reserve for another day.

5.

–THIS AUTUMN FUCKIN' SUCKS! Mrdok exudes. Look at the leaves! Usually you get a nice variety of yellow. This year: shit brown! All of 'em. What is this shit? Can't we do something about this?

–It isn't like the autum we witnessed last year, I timidly concur. It is almost as though the season has given up on itself. Though autumn, I find, tends to be the most volatile of seasons, particularly here in the city. Moreso than spring, even which, by popular opinion—

–Shut the fuck up, Gordo. Just shut up.

–All right…

–I need to know…

–The data is safe.

–I know the motherfuckin data is safe! Why are you always telling me shit I already know? You think I pay you to, to—

–We have the deal set in stone. The federal agents have agreed not to investigate further. With the apprehension of Mister Hull—

–I told him from the beginning. Whatever you do, as my employee, you *do not* leave our footprints all over the web. And what does he do?! How much was I payin that fuck anyway?

Mrdok spits.

–I mean, when you work for me, you get treated so fuckin well. Like a fuckin prince! All I require is a thin *modicum* of anonymity.

He uses three fingers to model thinness. Then he plucks up a leaf of the yellowest hue, really an anomaly from the brown detritus that had accumulated beside the bench.

–So all the files are on a cloud now anyway, I intone, attempting to calm his fraying nerves. And it's a fair trade, really.

Or it seemed so to me, at least. A deal I had engineered almost single-handedly on my own and am still feeling most proud of: for I had, in a sense, saved Mrdok in more than one sense. Though it must be said that Mrdok had not had much personal contact with Harry Hull—he had been discovered by a distant associate of ours through something called the dark web with which I am only faintly familiar—Mrdok had merely facilitated the nurturing of his unique talents through the auspices of Belle Encoding. True, the one aspect of the business—its front-of-the-house operation, shall we say—was this cleansing and encoding of data that I mentioned earlier—way too complex for such a feeble mind as my own to comprehend in all its particulars—though also fully licit in all its machinations, I might add. However, using many of the metrics gleamed from these powerful clients as a plug-in, Hull had also invented a unique algorithm-oriented web-sweeping software device that enabled him to collect huge swaths of data according to user-written perimeters that could be easily altered. The software could get past virtually any paywall, any secure server, vacuuming up anything desirable to know about an individual—anything from appearance and biological facts and overall physical and psychological health to credit rating to household income to items purchased online over the course of one's life, to more specific data sets, such as the number of Dostoevsky novels read compared to the number of *Keeping Up with the Kardashians* episodes streamed—and amalgamating that data into a highly accurate Ultimate Worth rating on a scale of one to ten, with anyone rating seven and up a surefire go, anyone falling below four probably deserving to be preemptively arrested, and those falling in the middle safe to ignore. A veritable reading machine!

Well, Hull *had* been slightly reckless in that he had allowed himself to get caught. The technology itself did not violate any laws; what the FBI objected to was the unlawful way Hull had gone about collecting private citizens' data. This data was meant to be stored—or, in Mrdokian parlance, harvested—in a future project, whose exact nature had yet to be intuited.

What it came down to, of course, was that the federal agents in the hacking division were jealous in the extreme of Hull's awesome skills: not necessarily his technical know-how—any run-of-the-mill thief could hack into a website and wreak havoc; but what could only be deemed his design-savviness; when combined, these two skill sets fit the psychological profile of genius—or at least came awfully close.

In exchange for Hull, then, it was agreed that Mrdok would evade all legal culpability, but also (and this is where certain aspects of the agreement assumed a peculiar shade of gray) have the question of Mrdok's access to the cloud storing the data remain unasked; though the operations of Belle Encoding must also be quietly dissolved. The raid of Belle Encoding's office will be undertaken under the pretense that Mrdok is collaborating with the Feds on turning in this rogue employee who had exploited his clients' trust in what would be publicly described as a quote-unquote data leak, the exact particulars of which would never be publicized.

Well, it is the exact sort of win-win situation that, not to brag, I have become something of an expert in fomenting over the years. Hence my slight dismay at this current display of Mrdok's discomforts.

—I've gotta go in there.

—… Where?

—Into the office.

—Into the…? What office?

—Belle. Belle Encoding. You moron. Which office did you think I meant?

—Yes, but… Why… Everything will go according to plan, Mrdok. You don't need your, your *image* getting muddled up in this… These agents don't even know what you look like!

Buzz buzz.

—Shit. It's them. It's the Feds. Give it to me.

—No, let me answer—

—Fuck. This is it. They're going in. The phone! Now, Gordo!

I compromise by pressing the speaker button.

—This line safe? asks the voice on the other end.

—What do you mean, *is it safe?* I thought you guys were supposed to be the experts here.

—Just thought I'd check. The operation's about to be carried out.

—Finally.

—Thought you might like to come along with us.

—Come along?

—Well, actually… I've been advised against turning on the camera. But I can keep you on the line, allow you to hear everything as it unravels, if you'd like.

—Yes. I mean…

Mrdok glances at me to read my face's opinion. He finds no objection; I myself am more than vaguely curious.

—… I'd like that.

—Okay then. Here's where we're at: On the street, staked-out across from One West 43rd Street. An address you're familiar with, I take it.

—He is not at liberty to respond to that assertion, I interject.

—Well. I hope so. Cos it's where we're about to pull the operation.

—You… Look, what's my liability here? I need you to be honest with me.

—I thought you'd already been over that with the home office.

—No. I'm not talkin about that. I'm talkin right here, right now. Like, if I stay here on the line while you do this…

—It's the same as you discussed before. No changes.

—Good.

—Mister Hull won't be told anything from our end, either.

—Okay, okay. Cos I don't like last minute changes.

—Your legal counsel made that abundantly clear. Eighth floor, right? We're in the elevator now.

—Yo Gordo. What floor is Belle on? Eighth?

I nod my head.

—Okay… Here we are. You think we should knock first, guys?

—That's no fun.

—Hey Mrdok, comes another voice. You aint got nothin invested in this here door, am I correct?

—What, like you want to break it down?

—Yeah.

—Pff. Go ahead. I could give a fuck.

Bam, goes the sound.

—FBI! Stay on the ground!

—What the—

—Okay, Mister Mrdok, you there? You're not going to believe this.

—What the fuck? Did you guys do it? Are you in there?

—Are you Harry Hull?

—Yes! I mean, no! I mean… What the fuck?!

—You are not going to believe this shit—

—Believe what?! What the fuck is goin on?

–Hey Barnes, check this shit out. You're gonna love this.

–Oh god. Not again!

–This is the second time she's—

–The last raid we did, the guy was also jerkin off. You remember?

–It's because Vanzetti's here! They love to show off to the girls!

–Hey! shouts Mrdok now, startling a nanny pushing a stroller past us towards the Ramble. Can you *please* tell me what the fuck is goin on over there?

–Your employee, Mister Mrdok, has his pants down around his ankles. It seems as though he was… pleasuring himself when we entered the premises.

–What the…

–Who the fuck are you?

–FBI, kid. Stay down. Barnes, pull his fuckin pants up. I don't need to see this.

–Pull em up yourself.

–Don't touch me!

–You're coming with us, kid.

–Unbe-fucking-lievable. Hey, you. Whatever your name is. Give him the phone. Put him on the line.

–I'm afraid it's against protocol, sir. We cannot allow you to speak—

–I don't give a flying fuck. He's my employee still, is he not? Put him on. I want to have a word with him.

–We'll put you on speaker… Go ahead, Mister Mrdok.

–Hey. Hey. You. You hear me? You know who this is?

–Uh, yeah. They just told me. What is going on?

–This. This is what's going on. This is what happens when you de-fraud our clients. You filthy piece of shit.

–What? What the fuck are you talking about? I…

–And another thing. I don't pay you to jack off.

–Hey. Hey! Fuck you. I never de-frauded anybody. I—

–Okay, that's it. Get him out of here, Barnes.

–What? We're federal agents. You're in our custody now. Zip his fly, Vanzetti.

–Ouch. Fuck!

CHAPTER TWO

CATALINA

1.

WHEN SHE ACTUALLY does make it out here—and it's not often—Mrtol is wont to select Catalina or one of the surrounding oceanic splotches in the channel versus LA proper. Bored to death of all the mainland crowds, the smog, the scent of marijuana in the air everywhere, the Hollywood pricks, the fakes, the rich hippies of Malibu… What else is there? *The Real Wives of Beverly*? She's done it all enough times to say no thank you please. Funny, she can remember a time when LA used to matter to Mrdok. Now he won't even get on a plane. Still, there's Bobby. A problem that has to be looked in on from time to time. Looking about all that is left. And might as well do the Krstal plumage while she's at it. To ensure there *really* won't be any cheery memories to look back on this time…

LA: where the American Dream never dies—it just slowly rots…

Even before, the only real reason to come was for the shopping. Where else is it better? Of course, the biggest problem with LA is always lunch—not where to have it, but who to have it with. Choosing Catalina at least alleviated that strain. Even Krstal has a house out here now. Even Krstal is withdrawing from the mainland. Scarce the chances she'd ever admit it out loud, though.

Krstal the sort of nouveau riche trash you only hang around with out of desperation, loneliness, fascination, disgust… Pick and choose. In Mrtol's case, it's because she was once married to Mrdok. Let the gods ponder the mystery of that one. Maybe she was different before. As long as Mrtol had known her, she was the same predictable sort of Beverly Hills social climber that seems as native to Los

Angeles as that mossy fungus that grows on the trunks of palm trees. She'd started out small, one of the Big No Ones that form the city's underlying white migrant social class, but had Moved On To Bigger And Better Things, as the more attractive climbers of that class constantly struggle to do. The plastic surgeon she used to fuck gave her her first titjob when she was twenty-three. Up soared her rocket. Culminated in her first McMansion with a producer of reality TV shows. A period in New York, where she started out with Mrdok, two sons, before convincing him it really was so much better out here. Three husbands later, she is currently wedded to the producer of the last three films of a certain Latin martial arts *actor*—one can only use the word pejoratively in his case. A close personal friend of the Governator. In Krstal's peroxide world, she's about as high up the ladder as you can get without risking missing a step and falling headfirst into a drained pool.

Though spawned in a trailer park in one of those middle American states Mrtol had certainly heard of but would have difficulty placing on a blank map, Krstal had taken well to southern California's brainless sensibility. Had mostly gotten rid of the accent, too, except for those not-so-rare moments when she had imbibed one too many glasses of sparkly, though sometimes she laid it down out of habit, as she knew a certain kind of man found irresistible that twang of mo-lass ass sass that people where she grew up paraded as a substitute for cleverness. Poor Krstal. You could almost feel sorry for her—were there anything there to feel sorry for. Laser eye surgery had taken care of the lazy gaze. Have we already mentioned the drop dead tits? Well, surely you noticed them yourself already. Finally, she had changed the C in her first name to a K and dropped the Y in the deluded belief that it made her seem more *unique,* another of those words that gave away her real class background whenever she deployed it. Krstal Mrdok; for of all the husbands, his was the last name she chose to keep. So much of LA, Mrtol reflected, is projecting an image of yourself that is essentially a fantasy, then having the audacity to believe it's real. At least no one around you will question its authenticity—they're far too busy projecting their own delusional construct.

Lunch winding down, Krstal's been blabbering on and on about the perfectly curved cock of the fifteen-year-old Mexican pool boy she's been fucking out here for the past two weeks while Mrtol diddles with the olive in her empty martini glass.

–Oh, I know it sounds filthy, Beverly—

–Fuck, Krstal. It's Mrtol, not Beverly. Got it?

Clearly a provocation. Bev is the name of Mrdok's current maî-tresse-en-titre.

–Gosh, I am so sorry. But anyway, I'm not *normally* attracted to them, you know. They're just a bit too diminutive in stature for my tastes. This little guy, though… Well, Mrtol—*squeezing her hand from across the table*—it turns out he's not so little. Now I know what you're thinking. Jésus is different from most of them, though. For one thing, he's not so brown. Really quite pale skin, which is a wonder, given that he's outside under that glaring sun all day long. And omigod, the great thing about having a lover this young is that they can go three or four times in one afternoon.

–Jesus fuck.

–*Jésus*. Not Jesus.

–He's younger than your son, Krstal. Both of them. Speaking of which—

–They don't get tired from it the way a man does. It's still a new thing for them. I mean, not *that* new… Jésus told me his first time was when he was eleven with his cousin. Can you imagine? I mean, really, when was the last time you've been fucked royal like that?

Said with an edge of genuine curiosity. Which Mrtol takes to mean: Does Mrdok still do her after all these years?

Mrtol staring at a tiny yellow foam of almond butter in the upper right hand corner of Krstal's lip throughout much of her discourse. Now, expected to contribute, she is finding it difficult to peel her eyes off it.

–I don't know, Krstal. There's not much action on Shelter Island, if that's what you're asking. And the wives there are so gossipy. For the past three years, the showerhead has been my most reliable com-panion.

–Oh honey, believe me, the girls talk in Beverly Hills too. It's just a different kind of talk out here. We're just a little bit looser when it comes to our secrets—

–Not only your secrets, apparently…

–Georgie has his affairs, and they're what protect mine. If it ever comes down to divorce, he'd never think of playing the adultery card against me or else I could go and do the same. And everyone knows the judges are more prone to rule in the wife's favor. Especially with knockers like these. I'd walk away with goddamn just about every-thing!

Krstal manhandles her so-called knockers, then flaps her arms through the air wildly in a sort of half-stretch, as though it all, every-thing, already belonged to her through default. And, in a sense, it did.

–Why don't you come back for a dip in the pool? I think Jésus is there this afternoon, I'd love for you to see him, check out the merchandise, if you know what I'm sayin…

She snorts out some godawful laugh, nearly sending Mrtol's nerves over the edge of the rooftop and into the bay down below. Why the fuck did she decide to come to Catalina? Fucking Mrdok.

–Jesus, Krstal—

–*Jésus* is his name, sweetheart—

–Whatever. Can you keep it down, or do you really want all of Avalon to hear about your whore escapades?

–All three of them? Hahahaha. I know the owners of this place. They're all gays, honey, and bigger whores than I am. But okay, lady. Mercy me, someone is uptight today! You sure you don't need a screw, honey? I thought that's what you came to the West Coast to do. I know this top notch escort service in Santa Monica, I mean these guys are all models moonlighting as dicks-for-hire. Not like the limpwrists and retirees around here! I swear, this place is turning into a second-rate Palm Springs. We can get one of them helicoptered out here for you, if you want.

–Thanks, doll, but if I wanna get laid, I can fly to Rio anytime I want and get fucked by a proper stud, not some greasy pre-pubescent illegal.

–Oh, come on—live a little!

–I'm here strictly for the fall/winter collections, Krstal. Maybe buy a little art for the South Beach property—we're thinking of subleasing it to my ex-mother-in-law for the winter. This buffalo milk is as risqué as it's gonna get for me this time around. And, in case you didn't notice, it's finished. Check, please!

After lunch, a short jaunt past the Catalina Casino, its Mediterranean Revival façade always shuttling Krstal off into some Andalusian daydream—a little slice of Granada in California—elegant as ever. In the water, kayakers paddling their way toward the clock tower. The ladies catch a golfcart limo up to the house.

Krstal occupies the home of a former chewing gum magnate. A rental, for sure—it's almost impossible to buy anything on Santa Catalina. The mansion is elevated on a hill with a wraparound view of the ocean. The décor leaves something to be desired, Mrtol feels— well, a lot to be desired, actually—but it is a rental, after all, and getting anything from the mainland up this hill is a logistical nightmare, so Krstal gets a pass on this one.

There had been a small debate between Krstal and her hubby. Krstal favored Palm Springs, despite her frequent outbursts of derision for the place; but Georgie insisted on Catalina—in Palm Springs, after all, he was bound to know every other person they came across, so in his world, that didn't make for much of a retreat. In the end, it was pointless anyway, because she comes here more often than he does—and when he does manage to make it out here, he spends most of his hours puttering off the shore in his little submarine. Krstal's peregrinations lead her mainly between the house and bars along the pier. Everywhere else you have to get by golf cart—and she doesn't want to be seen driving one, even though it's how most of the locals get around. Hiking the rugged mountains, another favored local activity, is not the sort of endeavor Krstal'd ever considered with a half-ounce of seriousness.

Now they're on the top floor by the infinity pool sipping cocktails. Mrtol dozing while Krstal continues to run her lewd mouth.

–Anyways, Don, I mean Georgie, my husband—I don't know why I thought of Don all of a sudden, Don's my lip guy in the Valley who I've never fucked before, even though he clearly wants to fuck me—Georgie, *Georgie* would *never* divorce me. I told him when we got hitched that he ever even dared contemplate it, the only way I'd do it is on one of his reality TV shows for the world to see! Even wrote it into the pre-nup. I can't believe he actually agreed. So, unless his career really starts to go down the drain, there's no way in hell this marriage is going to catapult.

–Well, cheers to reality TV. Now get your tit out of my martini, Krstal.

Krstal blabbed on unconscionably.

–And I'm glad, too. Georgie, he might have his shortcomings, but he's a keeper. Unlike the one you got stuck with! How is the old bastard anyway?

–Well…

–Say, you think I need another waxjob? I think I spy a stray hair down there…

Just to tease pour pathetic Jésus, jerkily trimming bushes on the other side of the pool, Krstal had elected to sunbathe nude. She spreads her legs and stares down, much to Mrtol's disgust, as she is now being asked to look in the same place.

–Gee, I don't know, Krstal. How does Jésus like it? Bald? Or did he vote for Bush? Wait, I forgot—he's too young.

–Jésus, honey, you can come over here and trim my bush anytime you want!

The boy blushes and feigns concentrated interest in his work.

–Oh don't worry, he don't ah-blah een-gless… Aint that right, Jésus? El gringa es loca! Woo hoo!

–Just shut the fuck up, Krstal. No one wants to hear about you and your natty cunt. God. Can't you behave like a decent human being for once in your life?

–Honey, I don't live in a decent world. This here is La-La-Land. We live in a whirr of delusion out here. And we broadcast those delusions far and wide, for all of America and the rest of the world to chow down on with a side of nachos. And it ain't half bad, when you get right down to it. It's a world where sex and love are much the same. Where even the lesbians are photogenic. Where anyone with a story to sell can see their name in lights. Where glamour rules over everything and common vulgarity has no place.

Mrtol snorted. This again.

–Don't you just *love* it? Why you and that *trillionaire* ex-dick of mine ought to get yourselves a slice of this. I mean, everyone else is out here at least part of the year. I don't see why you shouldn't be. You *belong* here, Mrtol.

–I don't *want* to belong here, Krstal.

Mrtol finishes her drink, spits a cube back into the glass.

–Where the hell is Bobby, Krstal? Would you say *he* belongs out here?

There it is. The one place Krstal isn't willing to go.

–You know, I changed my mind. I think we won't be having dinner tonight.

And she dives right into the pool.

2.

THAT'S A NEEDLE, all right, going right into his vein. What can I say? I'm standing here right outside seeing it. Clearly my timing isn't great today. This whole trip's been a disaster. First Krstal and her disgusting theatrics, now this. And what am I to do? He's not even my son. Who am I kidding? Mrdok's barely my husband.

I start to tiptoe away. Then I feel his eyes on me. Too late. So I turn back to the door, *knock knock,* a cutesy expression. He puts the needle down. One of those thin hypodermic syringes.

Things weren't all that different in the past. Not from what I can remember. I never wanted to play stepmother. Not to anyone's child, let alone these two nightmare concoctions of Krstal and Mrdok's.

The air in Los Angeles is so dry. I know we're not in LA proper. But even here, on this island, surrounded by water. I've been drinking like a shark ever since we got here. Probably make my skin even drier, but who cares? Seeing Bobby like this, I'm more sober than I have been in weeks. Which makes me tremble for another drink.

–You coming in or gonna stand there and creep me out all day with your creepy glares, he wavers.

The screen door snaps behind me. He disappears into the living room, obviously expecting me to chase him in there. When he lived on the mainland, it was in one of those prefab dingbats oh so common to the wretched Hollywood landscape. Place where you could picture some unsuccessful screenwriter drinking himself into blacklisted oblivion back in the old days. But it was still better than this dump.

Well, the truth is I feel awkward. Because I don't really know how to talk to someone who's on heroin. Bobby and I don't have any kind of relationship, none to speak of. Which makes it all the more awkward. But Mrdok expects this whenever I come out here, even if he doesn't explicitly ask for it. If he knows I've been to La-La-Land, then I have to drop in on Bobby. Deliver some sort of report. Along with the receipt for everything I've bought, since these are inevitably shopping sojourns. A fair exchange, even if I'm dreading it now.

The cottage looks like it was dropped at the end of this cactus-lined barely paved road leading out of Avalon, into what I guess is the wilderness part of the island. Okay, so maybe I'm being harsh. I suppose the place did have some promise, once, maybe back in the 1950s, when some Hollywood type constructed it as his weekend getaway. It was never supposed to be lived in—not for this long. The front garden, which had once been a haven of azalea bushes, has all gone to rot, is overgrown with weeds. Well, big surprise, all the money Mrdok's sending him isn't going toward gardening.

He sprawls nodding on the beige couch, a color I'm pretty sure the interior designers are now calling *cosmic latte*. He has no shirt on, his torso is all mottled with a kind of interesting arrangement of scars where I guess he scratched himself, since he's actually scratching one of them now just below his ribcage. A tuft of faded turquoise hair capes his pinpoint colorless eyes, burning Marlboro hanging off the pierced lip of his thin skull, the smoke stinking up these squalid environs of a room once meant for living. A bong sits on the cracked glass coffee table, rimmed with splotches of what looks like either candle wax or dried sperm, cigarette ashes graying the horrid sickly couch, surf magazines on the floor. An unplugged television set, I'm guesstimating it at circa 1997, certainly a boxy pre-digital relic, faces the entrance to the living room next to an electric guitar plugged in to a small Peavey amplifier.

–Well I see you've pulled off a faithful re-creation of your teenage bedroom, I offer. Bobby? Oh god. I didn't bring any Narcan…

–Maid's on vacation, Bobby now jolts awake.

He says it in a way that is meant to express his total indifference to every aspect of my materialization.

I start to wonder what time's the last flight at LAX and how long it will take me to get there. Then I shake myself out of that funk. I figure I have to give this at least fifteen minutes in order for it to really count. If nothing comes of it by then, I can excuse myself out of the situation and plot my way back to LAX.

–Well, aren't you going to offer me something to drink?

–Oh, golly, I'm terribly sorry, he says in a sort of fake British accent. Would you like a glass of my piss? It'll be warm, but there's some cubes in the freezer.

–Bobby. Is that really necessary?

–What, the ice cubes? You can also leave.

I sit myself on the Peavey amplifier and hold my bag in my lap, so as to not let it touch the grimy carpeting.

–Doesn't it get old after a while, Bobby? I mean, you're not exactly a child anymore. You've been in rehab now how many times? Don't they ask you to come up with… I don't know, a life plan or something?

–You don't have the brains to process it. Any of it. You're just some cunt from Long Island. Some lousy cunt who married a rich asshole, who—

–Oh right, I get it. None of us—me, your father, your mother— we none of us are on a par with the great genius that is Bobby Mrdok.

He perks up through the haze at the mention of his mother. Breakthrough.

–She's in Catalina, isn't she?

–We had lunch.

–Ha. I'm sure it was a *riveting* conversation.

–Bobby, can I just… The walls. Why this puke green?

–Psilocybin Summer Citrus is I believe what they call it. What did she say?

–It would have been better, well, more *tolerable*. If you had *at least* finished the job. Now there's still that patch of ugly wallpaper beneath—

–C'mon, Mrt. You're a mother. You don't think it's at all strange that we're both here, this tiny ass island, she doesn't even poke her head around to say hi? You know how long it's been since she last spoke to me?

Hazarding those kinds of guesses aren't really in my domain. Instead I take my eyes away from the walls, the carpet, in other words from the entire interior of this depressing shack, over to the pale desolate light making its way in through the porch's screen. He has to at least have something, I don't know, vodka or brandy. Or is he one of those pure heroin addicts that doesn't touch alcohol? I don't even know.

Bobby plugs in the TV, snaps on the remote to distract himself from my presence. A rerun of some ancient cop show. Good cops chasing bad cops.

–Can I ask how you get it?

–Get what.

–You know. The stuff.

Bobby sighs like I'm the stupidest person on earth. I've seen his father do the same to other people. Not to me. At least not all that often.

–Ever heard of the dark web? You can get it sent. In the mail. Delivered to your door.

–Really? They deliver heroin in the mail these days?

–Come on. You're not *that* old.

I'm about to ask if he's heard from Stevo Rey, but then think better of it. It's like a wall of sore points with Bobby. Anything you bring up has the potential to cause offense.

–I'm guessing your mother doesn't see you because she's scared. She knows what kind of shape you're in, and she doesn't want to see it. Not after last time…

–Well I don't want to see her either! Bobby coughs, turns the TV off, then lifts himself off the couch and wanders into the kitchen area. It's getting late, isn't it, he says behind his back. And you're ruining my afternoon nod.

Poor kid. I mean, I can't help but feel sorry. It's like his entire family has abandoned him. Well, in the case of Mrdok, okay, it's justified. He's busy, after all. With Krstal, okay, it's a little cruel, but also a coping mechanism. Stevo Rey's the one I can't figure out. Okay, so they barely know each other now. Stevo Rey was sent off to boarding school when they were just kids. They grew up in different worlds: East Coast, West Coast. Bobby came out here, then Stevo Rey went off to Japan. To pursue his music career, or whatever it is he does.

–Look, I might not be as smart as you, Bobby. I might not have the brains to process much of anything. But I'm part of your story now, whether you like it or not. What your father, and probably your mother as well, what they want is for you to get back to your old self again. He doesn't come out here because he doesn't want to see you like this.

–Tell him I said thanks for the money. And to keep it rolling in.

–I mean, do you even *want* to clean up?

–Right now? Right now I want you to leave.

–So what would it take to persuade you? Look, we know how it is. There's an *epidemic* out there…

–Out there?

–Well. In here, too.

–First thing you need to understand is, I'm fuckin old school. Okay? I don't have anything to do with those, those pharma people. Those pill heads who, who can't get their Oxy no more so they turn to junk. That, that fentanyl shit. Those poor people. The addicts today, man, they don't know what they're doing. They're all posers. They're *imitating* people like me… Or at least they would be if they knew who I was.

–Wow. What a speech. What do you want? An A for authenticity?

–I'm gonna ask you real nice—

–I'm leaving. I just wanted to stop in. Obviously I'm not welcome. Your father misses you.

–Bullshit.

–The old you, I mean. Okay, so maybe not. But he makes a gesture now and then. And I happen to be one of them.

–Here's a gesture for both of you.

On the main street of Avalon, there's the daytripper crunch on Crescent Avenue. The scent of frying fish fills the air. I know it's late, but I don't feel like crawling back on the boat quite yet, so I make my way down along the water toward the yacht club. The deep blue waters of Avalon Bay, the boats floating placidly, it's a nice scene, maybe I should just spend the night. That would entail the risk of running into Krstal again. And Jaco's waiting for me back East—even if he doesn't realize it…

Yacht club's closed for some reason, so that means I'll have to go even farther, to the casino, for a drink. So be it.

I should have known he was back on drugs the minute he started taking Mrdok's handouts. For a long time he didn't. Whatever Krstal had been giving him was enough. Not like there's much to spend it on out here.

Instead of going into the casino, I decide to continue on. There's a little resort up ahead, with this charming field, at least there was years ago, I want to see if it's still there. Overhead, a cloud formation has amassed, the whole So Cal Endless Sunshine stereotype's about to be flushed into the Pacific. Well, dock's not far.

–Hey little doe!

In the field, this cute little deer is standing right there, plucking at the grass. And I have it all to myself—well, if you ignore the couple taking photos on the deck of their cabin.

Bambi being one of the first movies my parents took me to. When I was, how old. Probably Jaco's age now?

I'm losing track of the time, and I'm not even drunk yet. Should've asked Bobby, Krstal, someone when the last ferry goes. Well, dock's not far. Maybe I can get a cocktail to go from the casino? Are there open container laws in California?

I check my phone: tremors on the mainland, 3.5 on the Richter scale. All flights from LAX canceled. I look up. Now it's the deer that's staring at me.

3.

THE PROBLEM IS life on an island. Well, he could complain about the constipation too. Been a few days since he laid a log. But now he can't piss neither. Just shot up, what, thirty minutes ago. Those moments the junk freezes you. What did he, a smoothie for breakfast. Neighbor's suitcase, purse dog yapping. As soon as he can get some piss out, go back to bed again. That crumpled curl at the bottom of the mattress. Calls out to him. When he finally does shit, it's gonna be like giving birth. Split his asshole open. He used to care. No wait that's a lie. Can't remember. The dope started to get bad, what, two months ago. Third time out of rehab, said he'd never go back. That this was it. Embarrassing. There are better ways of wasting dad's hard stolen money. Just ask the expert. Krstal slapped him in the face. Well, he knew a thing or three. Full-on Beverly Hausfrau, teenage Mexican jammed in her puss. You call that a mom? He couldn't feign respect for something that wasn't even there. Go out back to puke. Call John tomorrow to fix the toilet. Again. Next time wait at least half hour to fix after breakfast. Or vice versa. Look on the internet, Reddit. Find new means of clouding the morning pangs. Swimming pool out back a good place to barf in. A few droplets squeezed from the tip. This fucking sun.

SOUTH BEACH

IT IS TRUE, somehow, owing to a mystery perhaps enshrouded in those hurricane winds blowing in off the mid-Atlantic, Miami is a place where Mrdok is often able to *resolve* things, harvest wholly fresh ideas. Much of the time they come to him when he is engulfed in one or a larger number of hedonistic pursuits. Well, one would be wrong to impose a harsh sentence of judgment on a man simply for allowing his defenses to drop to a level low enough to accommodate certain sultry vices every now and again. Throughout the history of genius, countless examples persist of men whose positioning on the precipice of greatness has gone unquestioned, who nevertheless have required moments of salubrious *re-fueling,* as it were, in order to keep their engines revved up and in gear (if that is the proper metaphor…)

–Woo-hoo!—Mrdok's voice comes thundering in from the enclosed patio.

Myself, I tend to remain embedded within my suite of rooms on these South Beach excursions. I've never taken well to the searing heat of the tropics, and, though Mrdok always requires me to be present during these refueling/brainstorming sessions in Miami, I usually elect not to partake in the preferred activities designated by the locale. The chief reason being, of course, that duty preserves me from such indulgences; while Mrdok has his own particular way of working on these occasions, another hand, and frequently another mind, is required to fulfill the feats of divinated inspiration that often arise. Since I am not nearly as talented as Mrdok when it comes to fully containing myself in certain situations, I find it best to absent my participation so as to remain busy with more practical affairs.

In the day's case, I was just putting the finishing touches on one of those niggling Manhattan matters, namely the dispersal of Belle Encoding's diminished assets into—

–Gordo, get in here! Mrdok interrupts. Get that lard ass in here!

I follow the scented trail of the boss's voice. Mrdok, in polka dotted boxer shorts, is surrounded by three lesser-clothed ladies whose names I've long forgotten and Mrdok himself likely never learned, met at a club off Millionaire's Row earlier in the evening's festivities, courtesy of Nell…

–That's Gordo—pointing at me—and this fat fuck, he can fart the entire soundtrack to *The Sound of Music.*

Oh, not this again.

Two of the whores erupt in giggles; the third, dazed in a drunken drugged oblivion, forgets to laugh. Or else never learned how.

–C'mon, Gordo. Give it a go! Then I gotta tell you an idea. *Sniff.* Our new city. Girls, did you know we, I am building a whole new city? Yeah yeah. It's gonna be named after me. Mrdokia. It's gonna be the Tokyo of North America! Doesn't that sound good?

The whores seem unimpressed.

–Go on, Gordo. Let's hear Edelweiss. From the ass horn. Your favorite instrument.

–Well, I…

–These ladies *love* the musicals, don't you, girls? I swear, this is gonna be like Broadway in Miami!

Blushing, for, I must admit, modesty has always delayed me in unleashing these displays. My failure at *impromptu* perhaps derailing me from a fully formed career in the business of show…

–I'm serious. He's the Miles Davis of flatulence! And you can quote me on that… Hey, turn that shit off!

Jean-Pierre, our handsome Benneton-attired Haitian butler, taps the iPad in his hand and the thumpity hip-hop belching from the hidden speakers sputters off, returning the room to its dim blue glow of high octane silence. The chill lighting suddenly imbuing the stale sex atmospherics with air-conditioned anticipation of the command performance.

–Mrdok, I'm afraid I haven't really prepared…

For, in truth, it is a rather discreet talent, one that I tend to preserve among equals and intimates. While it might sound rather unique to amateur ears, *pétomanie,* as it has been deemed in the Gallic tongue, is an ancient, venerated, and much storied art form—well, art with a capital F, if you'll allow me… No less a figure than Saint Augustine (about whom I authored an incomplete dissertation) wrote, in his *City of God*, of ancient practitioners of the craft, performers endowed with *such command of their bowels, that they can break wind continuously at will, so as to produce the effect of singing*. Later in the medieval period, the court of King Henry II in England played host to Roland the Farter, a court jester whose flatulence performances fulfilled his Christian duty in keeping His Royal Highness merry throughout the annual Christmas celebrations. While I do not wish to subject the reader at present to an entire historical treatise, which anyway would require several volumes, suffice to mention one final, more recent example, named by an eminence no less grise than Salvador Dalí as the second greatest artist of all time (the first being, naturally, himself), as it gives us a deeper, more modern insight into the scientific facet behind this age-old phenomenon: Joseph Pujol. Pujol made, at an early age, the same discovery as I slightly later in life: that he had the natural ability to breathe through his rectal cavity. Indeed, for such divinated gentlemen (for I have yet to read of any ladies endowed with such a gift), the rectal opening serves as a second mouth, through which Nature broadcasts her opera. Through a rigorous self-discipline, Pujol endeavored to develop this precocious talent, taking in up to two quarts of air at a time. By moderating the force through which it was expelled, he could sustain musical notes of varied timber and pitch. Eventually, he was able to develop an entire repertoire that would keep the crowds at no less an esteemed venue as the Moulin Rouge rolling in the aisles in performances that could last up to ninety minutes. By one account, a poor soul in the audience even died of a heart attack while witnessing one of these shows; you can't buy much better publicity than that! It is true, and somewhat surprising, that no one of prominence in the Americas has risen to contribute to the prolongation of this form of entertainment. After all, America being the entertainment capital of the entire world, one would think that in the hallowed halls of Radio City and/or the Hollywood scene, such a performer could be found. But none has graced the stage or the silver screen over the past hundred years. While I myself never harbored the ambition to, like Monsieur Pujol, turn this modest ability into a professional career, I did make this idiosyncratic talent of mine known early on. In my sophomore year of high school, I won second prize in the annual talent contest for my solo rendition of I'm Proud to be an American—an accolade that brought with it a certain amount of controversy, as one of the judges objected that I had neglected to include one of the verses (the lesser known one that starts *From the lakes of Minnesota to the hills of Tennessee...*), a rather debatable claim, considering I had the entire audience on my side (they had been clapping in rhythm throughout, mesmerized), that nonetheless robbed me of first prize. And in my acquaintanceship with Mrdok, my discreet talent has naturally brought countless hours of delight. On this particular night, however, it has been many moons since I've practiced, and so I fear that I might not have the endurance required to sustain my way through the entirety of Rodgers and Hammerstein's famed classic. For just like any other wind instrument, the anus must be kept properly oiled and taut in order to be played at random. This is something that professionals like Monsieur Pujol were fully cognizant of, their organic horns maintained in stupendous condition through a dedicated regimen of strenuous exercise, massage, and pampering.

–Just shut up and fart! bellows Mrdok through his cocaine mustache, impatience furrowing his brow. We wanna hear it! Fart, you fat fuck, fart!

The whores begin to chant in unison. Mrdok commences to sing along his own variation on the lyrics:

–Dyke! A queer, a female queer—

With his vocal encouragement, the wind begins to break in accompaniment:

Pfff. Pf pf. Pf pf pf pf. Pfffrp—

–Ray! A drop of golden cum—

–Mrdok, I think I may need a microphone to continue—

–Fag! A name you call yourself—

The whores hysterical flabbergasted laughing now—

Pfffffffffffffrrrrrrrrrprffffffffffppppppppppppppppp—.

And with that, I'm afraid my overworked, ill-prepared sphincter gave out, letting one go that was so enormous, so large and loud, that it very well might have stirred both Rodgers *and* Hammerstein from their graves. The room deflated. The hills were no longer alive.

–Well. Thank God we're not in an enclosed space.

The Black whore emits a loud cackle that bounces off the chrome bar and echoes throughout the lounge. I go out past the pool, now craving the beach's nighttime quietude. Thankful to get it at this time of the year; Mrdok will sometimes insist on coming down here at spring break, teenagers recklessly braying and snotting and belching and puking and fucking upon the shores, not a moment of silence passes the week's entirety. In lieu of shells, a long piece of dental floss embedded in the dark sand. Turning away from the crashing waves, the orange lamps alighting the shore, an insistent ugliness to their glow's endurance, as though brattily denying the very force of night. Old man saunters forth, Hawaiian shirt unbuttoned, flapping in the wind. He holds a stick in his hand, German Shepherd trots past eagerly, dipping its snout in at the lip of the water then hastily retreating back to its master on semi-dry sand. I trail behind them mindlessly for a while, toward the neon sleaze up ahead. Suddenly find ourselves, myself, wandering up Ocean Drive. Still shoeless in the shoeless night. But who cares? It's Florida. Sand gives way to concrete. Feet hardly notice. Mind lost in the night's tropical mindlessness. My wanderings take me up Millionaire's Row. Lured off the main stretch by the palm trees down Española Way. It's a breezy, empty night. South Beach feels nearly abandoned. Down past American Apparel, its fall window display meant to evoke a sleazy shack lifestyle, so distant from the Miami Beach aesthetic as to be incomprehensible. Through the open doors of a bar, I hear the unmistakable sound of Miles Davis's horn. I drift inside. Despite my barefoot state, the gruff bouncers standing guard outside don't say anything. Perhaps they are too bored to notice or care.

The place is nearly empty. The slim, waifish Cubano bartender, hair dyed in blue and red shades of cotton candy, asks what'll it be—then, to my surprise, calls me *handsome*. Grapefruit and Absolut, comes his rhyming answer. Behind the bar, a mishmash of lighted shelves extending up to the ceiling contains a display of the bar owners' collection of weird memorabilia—ram's head with a hand-sized mirrored disco ball hanging off one of its horns, plastic pink flamingo (for those who reach a state of drunkenness which requires a visual reminder of where they are, one surmises), shark head with a wig hanging out of its mouth—along with the expected amalgamation of bottles. Hanging from the ceiling upside down throughout the interior, an array of mannequins in costumage, from hip rock 'n' roll all the way up to Bruce Lee. Even one in full astronaut regalia. A sole young lady sits at the end of the bar smoking. Dress stretched stripish to reveal a magnificent muscled form, earlobes stretched in concert with thick black implements denoting the era's transgressive youth, face painted gothically in rouge et noire extremis. *Mind if I join you?* I feel compelled to ask.

–Whatever you want, dude, comes coughing in response an unmistakably male voice.

–Oh, I'm sorry—*taken aback*—I didn't realize...

–What? You never seen a beautiful woman before?

S/he blows smoke at the model airplane hanging over the bar.

–Well... I really happen... not to mind...

–Ohhh, thank *Jesus* for that! I have no idea what I would do, how I would be able to cope, if you *minded*.

Exhalation of sarcasm fills the entire bar.

—Well, are you gonna sit there and bore me to tears all night or are you gonna buy me a drink? Carlos!

The young bartender wanders over.

—Yes, mama?

—Granma needs a drink. And this faggot wants to buy her one.

—The usual?

—Yeah. With extra spice this time.

Feeling compelled to introduce myself at this juncture, I tell the creature my name.

—Pleased. I'm Harry Mary, it responds without extending a hand.

—I do believe, I speak in to her produced cloud, that this is from *Bitches Brew*. If I'm not mistaken.

—Close, but no Tom of Finland cigar, responds the drag queen. It's the album that came after. *Jack Johnson.*

—Jack Johnson I've certainly heard of. He was the famous boxer. They made a movie about him. *The Great White Hope,* starring James Earl Jones. But who is this Tom of Finland you refer to? Oh wait… Is he the one playing those fabulous guitar lines?

Harry Mary spits a mouthful of drink across the bar.

—Carlos, this fucking queen is out of her mind! Which sand dune did you dig this one out from?

—Did I say something amusing…?

—… Wait, are you actually *serious*? Haha. Well, fuck a duck. Where do you come from, honey? Jacksonville? Daytona?

—Well, if you really want to know…

—Trust me, I don't.

I'm Jack Johnson heavyweight champion of the world. I'm Black alright and they'll never let me forget it—

—I mean, you do realize you're in a gay bar, don't you?

—Well… Not exactly, no.

—It's not exactly a gay bar, you mean? Or else you weren't exactly aware?

—Well. Both, I suppose.

—Aha, stop it. This queen's *killing* me.

—Don't you worry, honey, says Carlos the bartender. Everyone's welcome at Kill Your Idol.

—Kill Your… ?

—Idol.

—That's a funny name for a bar!

—What happened to your shoes, sweetheart?

—I must have left them behind… At the house…

–Queen's in a daze.

–You know something about dazes, don't you?

–Hail Mary.

Now we are joined by a young man with glasses and beard in a sequined miniskirt and ripped t-shirt with the Turkish flag on it.

–This here's Brianna Häagen Dazs. Heiress to the Häagen Dazs fortune.

–Really?

Sensing a networking opportunity, I begin feeling around my pockets for my card.

He shakes his head.

–This girl's full of shit.

–Harry Mary wraps herself around his waist nonetheless.

–She be my pimp daddy. My main squeeze. So if you want some action, Miss Gordina, you're gonna hafta go through this bitch.

–Well, I wasn't... planning for any *action* tonight... I mean, I really...

–Haha, don't look so serious, sweetheart. She's only joking. She'll do you for free! You want another drink, Marybeth? I know. It's a slow night. Why don't we all do a round of shots?

All of these young men, it seems they know each other quite well, without knowing me at all. Still, temporarily at least, in this very moment I start to feel as though they've accepted me as one of their own——even though I have nothing to do with this particular community. Yet this feeling is precisely, I suddenly realize, what is needed after the evening's travesty; for when I walked into this bar, I felt something less than human. And it would require a great deal more than just a lone alcoholic beverage to return my diminished powers to a functional state. I simply cannot go back to the house and face Mrdok in this condition. I am, I silently ruminate, attached to Mrdok; not so much like an appendage; I feel myself more a kind of organ, without which, the vital juices may very well fail to flow. At the same time, were I to sever myself from Mrdok's person, then I would become little more than a curiosity to be glossed once over before being tossed in the discard heap; for devoid of my function, what use am I? It is true that I am typically kept so busy in the performance of my duties that I scarcely have time to consider these matters in such depth. But here I am, in the pit of humiliation, drink in hand, mixing my metaphors into a most putrid and inedible stew. It isn't just the evening's failed performance that brings me down to such a low level. That has almost certainly brought it on. But now there is something else. It is as though an abyss of rank dread has been hit upon in some excavation of my soul, only to open up and overtake me through my exposure to its radiation. It is not that I am *afraid* of Mrdok; it is more that, at times such as these, I am struck with a fear that is inadvertently *refracted through* the person of Mrdok; a paralyzing fear of *failure*. There, now I've said it. Measured next to a man whose omnipotence simply dwarfs me, I can only move through life by ignoring those parts of my being that simply don't stand up to his measured greatness. Mrdok is, in a sense, not merely the man I am destined to serve, but simultaneously my safety net. This puts us in a peculiar status as to one another. I know he could, more or less, venture forward without me, continue to prosper. But were I to fall—to let Mrdok down, to let myself down—to cause some unprecedented disaster that would prove to be the undoing of either or both of us— this would be a devastation I could not fathom to endure. Just as my very personal conception of success in the worldly sphere is indelibly tied to, epitomized by Mrdok, so I cannot conceive of failure in a personal sense, and the sudden realization of this frightens me beyond any coherent act of reckoning.

Of course, I cannot even pretend to articulate such anxious thoughts to my new companions—undoubtedly they would have a hard time understanding me were I to attempt it. And so I settle upon second best, and proceed to get roaring drunk.

Before I myself am fully aware what is happening, I'm on the bar, my t-shirt tied around my neck, kicking aside glasses as I shuffle my way down to the other end.

–Oh yeah, Miss Thing! Go, girl!

–Go Jiggly! Go Jiggly! Go Jiggly!

Totally oblivious, I am, to the sound of glass bottles breaking on the floor, my companions dispersed across the space in an equal state of willed reckless disregard. Even Carlos, the bartender, has neglected his duty in favor of the dance floor, demonstrating a rather recent dance move they inform me is known as the Twerk, and involves a swift demonstrative movement of the flabbergasted buttocks. Meanwhile, the lone bouncer sits by the entrance with a sort of impervious grin smeared across his face. It is hard to decipher what his new job is in the evening's reversion to a state of anarchy. Certainly no new customers are coming in, the night has reached its expiration. He seems hardly bothered by it, a rather amused spectator to this Dionysian outburst of degeneration.

–Shake dat ass, Jiggly! Shake dat jiggly ass!

I oblige the young creatures of the night, although I'm still not sure why they have taken to calling me Jiggly all of a sudden, when I already introduced myself as Gordon. One name I have bluntly omitted from the night's conversational proceedings is Mrdok's, since above all else I have an ethical obligation to never mention my boss's name unless I am operating in an environment in which I have been explicitly ordained to do so. And it is freeing!—so few questions of a personal or professional sort posed, thankfully, as the *queens,* as they refer to one another, prefer instead to engage in a sort of playful banter, a back-and-forth of sexual insult and innuendo that becomes more outrageous with each fresh drink poured.

–Throw yr hands in the fuckin air! Wiggle yr jiggle like you just don't care!

Eventually, even the bouncer reaches his peak of tolerance. Assuming a parental role, he makes a watch gesture at Carlos.

–Okay, kittens. One more drink and it's closing time. Daddy says so.

By the time I make my way back to the house, after promising my young companions I'll return to the bar on my next business trip to Miami, the moon has already begun its retreat. Rather than confront the security regiment at the front entrance—which would be rather embarrassing, given my shoeless state—I opt to re-trace my steps on the beach and enter through the back lounge area.

Most of the security apparatus is in the lounge at this point anyway, as I soon discover.

–Here comes Gordo, announces one guard to another. Instantly I feel a pang of remorse and guilt for having stayed away for so long.

–About time, comes the second's confirmation.

–What happened?

–He must've done about ten grams of blow in one night. Man, I've lived in Miami for a long time, I aint never seen nothin like that.

–But that's not all, resounds the deep voice of the first.

–Well… What? What is it?

–… He done lost his hand.

–… What?

Without waiting for their response, I make my way into the lounge. The three hookers are scattered about the room, nervous expressions as though trying to ignore the situation going on around them. Mrdok, coked up beyond all coherence, still in the boxers I'd left him in earlier, is walking directionlessly around the room muttering to himself, the stump at the end of his right arm indeed naked beneath the soft light.

–Keith Richards the gi-tar player from the Rolling Stones say if the coke is good, you only need to do one line for the entire night, then you good to go.

I turn around to face the baboon.

–I know who Keith Richards is, I tell him sternly, and if you intend to hold on to your job, I'd advise you to refrain from any further commentary and find that hand.

The guard walks backward toward the pool, hands in the air.

It takes a minute or three for Mrdok to register my tired presence.

–These whores… Gordo… Look!… My hand… I don't know… where… Hand—gone!… See? They took my… I can't find… I called security I—

–Did you take it off at some point, Mrdok?

–I… off? What the… No! No off!

He recommences pacing.

–Mrdok. Be still a moment.

He goes over to the bar, grabs the silver card in his good left hand, begins to make a line from the forlorn pile.

–No more blow, Mrdok! Not now. We've got to find your hand first.

–… My hand?

Looking down at the stump.

–What happened to my hand?

Goodness gracious. I turn to the one security guard still standing in the room.

–Did you check all the bathrooms?

–We did a pretty thorough sweep.

–It's time for round two. Mrdok, sit still for a minute. Over here, on the love seat.

I go over to the girls. The Black one and the Latin one sit across from one another before the fake fireplace, staring mesmerized into the flames being broadcast across the screen.

–Any idea where his hands might have gone, ladies?

–Shit, says the Black one. I didn't even know that thing was fake till it done came off.

–Most people don't. That's the point. When did it come off?

–He was in da hot tub in da bafroom wif J-Nell over there. That's when she start screamin. We din't know what the hell. Ran inside, even though wed been told not to. Hell, we just wanted to make sure he wuddnt killin her or nuffin. Sho nuf, bodyguards got there before we did. J-Nell come runnin out all covered in suds. I don't know where he went, the guards told us don't come in there and so me and J-Nell come back in here.

—Gordo! Mrdok's voice suddenly comes bellowing from across the room. The whores stole my hand! Whores stole my—

—Shut yo ass up, comes J-Nell's response. What the hell use I got for a extra hand? Thing aint even real.

The security guard steps over and places his fingers lightly on Mrdok's chest to keep him seated.

—These fuckin goons stole it, he now announces. Security goons! Can't trust any of these fuckers down here. Fuckin south Florida. Fuckin bunch of crooks.

—And you the biggest one of all, whispers the goon.

—What was that?!

—Nothin.

So I decide to go check out the scene in the master bedroom for myself since this little interrogation is going nowhere. Guilt evaporated, as I reason that my being present in the house undoubtedly would not have prevented the mishap from occurring. I certainly would have absented myself in my own rooms for most of the night, which would have granted them the same amount of time required to lose the hand. Sobered by the hour of crisis, there is no doubt that the hand will reappear, and likely in one of the most predictable pockets—no pun intended. They don't call me Mrdok's second mind for nothing.

The scene in the bathroom predictable enough. Half-full tub, spillage of water and suds upon the floor, underclothes strewn about, bottles of champagne and shampoo competing in the disarray. No hand in sight, none in the by-now cold water as I swish my hand around then quickly wipe its potential sewage off with the nearest towel. I do notice something odd, though: the light in the walk-in closet is on. Nobody ever goes in there except for Mrtol on those rare occasions she deigns to visit, usually separate from Mrdok, as it contains her Miami wardrobe. I step inside, half-expecting to catch one of the hookers red handed in the act of plunder. But, alas, save for a wettened bathrobe lying upon the floor, it appears as though nothing has been disturbed by any human—or, in the whores' case— subhuman entity.

It is the same bathrobe that Mrdok always wears around the Miami property, and I can swear I saw him wearing it earlier in the evening, the day… I pick it up, check the two deep pockets. No hand. Nothing other than a cigarette lighter, which is strange, since Mrdok only smokes on the rarest occasion…

I carry the robe slung over my shoulder into the lounge as a thought occurs to me.

—Mrdok, I say, did you go anywhere else this evening?

Mrdok too busy grinding his jaw to respond.

—Girls, you can answer the question.

The one called J-Nell grunts.

—Where the hell would we go, him coked up like that? Motherfucker cuddnt even get uh 'rection.

—There are plenty of places in South Beach where a gentleman in Mrdok's state might find entertainment.

—Honey, you can do a fuckin full cavity search, nameless Latin whore interjects. You aint gonna find nothin on dis ass.

—For real, though… Can we go now? It must be getting on six in the motherfuckin a.m.

—You can go once we've found the hand, I tell them sternly.

—How the hell we gon help you find it when we cant go inside the house? This shit is unfair, man.

—I know. It's like I in prison all over again.

—Here. Keep yourselves entertained.

I slide over a tray of Colombia's finest.

—Drinks at the bar.

—Shit, says J-Nell, then snorts up a line for the hell of it.

A full scan of the house. Sans my suite of rooms, of course, since only I have the key to those—there's no way the hand might have landed there.

Down the hallway, past the family photos (current: Mrtol and Jaco, previous wives and sons conspicuously absent), plus extended family, namely, Tony Fatballs, closer to Mrdok than his own father. I enter the code to the master bedroom on the electronic lock. It looks relatively untouched, having been cleaned after the previous night's debaucheries and not slept in since.

(—Sides, the white whore could be heard to break her silence in the other room, he seems to know so much, why don't he just fart out the answer?

(Her outburst met by a chorus of cackles, a veritable witches' coven. As soon as the hand is found, I will put those whores back out on the street where they belong, and Mrdok to bed.)

Conchita has done a rather desultory job of making the bed, I see, with a couple of creases on the silk coverlet visible without any real strain of the eye. I make a mental note to reprimand her for this error. All that money spent on tuition at the local hospitality academy wasted, it seems. That's the problem with Floridians. Swamp people.

Always seeking out new ways to disappoint their generous benefactors.

Lackluster, the effects of sleeplessness suddenly pressing down upon me. I make my way into the west wing, its crown being the octagon-shaped office, where Mrdok conducts some of his more important work when in Florida. I cast my eyes up and down the floor-to-ceiling black walnut with silver crestings pronouncing the built-in bookcases with fake ancient volumes and glassed-in displays holding a handful of Mrdok's most prominent awards, trophies, and honorable degrees—still no hand. Out onto the porch, overlooking the stretch of private beach in the near distance, and, in the foreground, a garden of silver—yes, more silver—fountains and cobblestone walkways amongst the lovingly tended foliage. Well, at least the gardeners are still up to the task. Though no hand in sight.

Down the marble staircase to the front entrance, where arriving guests are greeted by a seventeen-foot silver mermaid sculpture by a renowned Danish contemporary artist whose name escapes me at this exhausted hour. I make my way up into the common areas, reminding myself to skip over the four remaining bathrooms (with travertine floors and showers, just FYI), since the security personnel has already agreed to review those. It is a shame, it suddenly occurs to me, that these areas do not see more in the way of entertainment and visitors. But Mrdok, a man of habit and insistence, is wont to conduct the great majority of his affairs in the comparatively banal, though no less comfortable environs of the lounge whenever this Miami estate calls out to him. There are practical reasons for this, as the nature of the current night's company makes shimmeringly crystalline.

Past the abandoned ballroom, with nearly four thousand square feet of chiseled marble floors in which is reflected the burning rays of the mammoth antique chandelier hovering above, I make my way into the kitchen. While I realize the chances of Mrdok's having trespassed its grounds within the past twenty-four are slim to nil, I find myself in dire need of refueling. With its fittings for the most sophisticated of gourmands, the kitchen happens to be my favorite room on the entire property. (The smallish kitchenette in my own quarters, in its reduced modesty, does not even rate a comparison, I am sad to report.) Its marble floors give the slippered feet a sensation of sweeping elegance as they glide across the sapphire-inspired elegance, the façades of all the furnishings, fittings, and appliances custom molded to elicit a most irrepressible sheen that just barely overenunciates a sense of dignified, well-earned superiority. Beneath these glimmering moldings, one finds outstanding custom cypress cabinets and a full range of Wolf appliances. I enter the code on the electric lock and the pantry door opens before me. Among its perks, a walk-in refrigerator whose temperature gradually drops into a deep freeze, stocked with every item one might expect to find in a supermarket (to accommodate any late night whim that might come the maestro's way) in addition to a number of imported items—Russian caviar, Korean ginseng, rhino horn, and, frighteningly and somewhat inexplicably, the frozen head of a jaguar—not likely to be found in even the more upmarket outlets of our otherwise fine country.

I remove from the shelf a box of Triscuits, then put it back, opting instead for a collection of white cheddar Cheez-Its. Then a jar of gourmet peanut butter from the shelf holding some two dozen unopened spreads of all sorts. I then dash into the fridge, where my trusty can of whipped cream is retrieved from its usual hiding spot.

I then set about making myself a most salubrious (if I am using the word right) hors d'oeuvre, one that my mother engineered especially for me in my youth, with each tiny cracker slathered with a good delectation of that thick brown gook and crowned with a spot of sweet white foam. The admixture of salted cheesiness, nutty richness, and a dose of naughty sugary splat nearly impels the imbiber to stomp his feet upon the marble, so scrumptious is the munching. I find myself getting carried away as my enjoyment increases, discarding the butter knife altogether and simply dipping the crackers one after another into the jar, littering them into my wide open gorge, and spraying increasingly liberal effusions of white foam down my throat.

As I proceed to desiccate and masticate my way through to the bottom of the Cheez-Its box, all that chewy crunchy deliciosity, I become more and more oblivious to all else that is happening around me. Losing myself, I come to feel as though I've been found. Bits and pieces flying out of my mouth, I have no idea where they might land—I can't stop the munching. I don't want to. I loosen my belt, my pants fall down around my ankles. Before I know it, I have the frying pan out, melting what must be half a pound of butter, into which I drop a Tupperware container full of tagliatelle I retrieved from the fridge, and relish the soundtrack of the sizzle as I splatter some oil and hot sauce on to the pasta and attack the smoking mass with gleaming spatula...

Back in the lounge, Jean-Pierre gently turns on the radio. The summer's hit R&B love jam comes jiving through the speakers, crooned by a Grammy-winning pop star renowned for her ability to hit notes so piercingly high that at outdoor stadium concerts, birds have been known to come tumbling out of the sky:

> I want a real Dutch lover
> Who won't blow my cover
> A real Dutch lover
> I won't accept another

The ladies of the night set to finishing off the coke and talk at each other while Mrdok sits grinding his jaw on the white leather loveseat.

–He be bein all weird n shit, mackin on my feet lak he done want to eat my toes or sumfin. I'm lahk I don't care, man, as long as dey pay, I'm happy jest to make it outta there without havin to traffic in too fine a line a work, you know what I'm sayin?

–Yeah, I get it.

–See, girl, I from Montgomery—

–Where dat at.

–Alabama.

–Oh.

–And up there, once you trick with all the police chiefs, the politicians, they lawyers, folks start gettin real nervous. Start lookin fo ways to run yo ass outta town.

–That's how you wind up here?

–Sho nuf.

–Thass some small town shenanigans.

–Like you only good for one season.

–Aint you have any regulars up there?

–Course I got regulars. Some of em high up too. I don't know. It's a different scene. Different scene.

–High up in Montgomery aint shit next to high up in Miami.

> Yeah I was feelin down, needed to get away
> I went to Amsterdam to smoke some big fat jays
> And look at pretty tulips growin by the big canal
> That's when I saw him come walkin out of Café Royale

–See, the thing about Miami is—

–You don't have to tell me, girl. Born and raised.

–Naw, but the thing is, Miami's vacationland. I got regulars here alright. But half my regulars don't even live in Miami.

—Me too. Like this dick over here. I bet this mofo don't spend more than three nights a year in this house. No offense, baby.

—Were you out there last Sunday when Laronda got jumped outside the Fontainebleau?

—Say what?!

—Laronda. Got her ass beat.

—What you talkin bout?

—Oh there was some rapper and his crew.

—What rapper?

—I forget his name. One of those out of town niggas always in Miami.

—Lil Bigfoot?

—Yeah, that it.

—Mm damn. I remember when he drop that track *Outta Space Niggas*. I was like, *what?!*

—See, they was like five girls already up in that shit. Motherfucker got a damn Tesla—

—What?!

—Model X.

—Rented no doubt.

—See, the thing is, he already had Laronda. Been partyin with her for days before those other bitches showed up. Tell her he's gonna put her in his next video, all that shabazz.

—Aint we all heard that shit before.

—How many videos you been in, girl?

—Girl, I aint out to be in no videos. Them broke ass muthafuckas. They all for show.

> It wasn't that kinda spot, if you know what I mean
> There weren't no colored lights, neither red nor green
> But the beating of my heart went thumpity-thump
> I knew in a sec I had just fallen for this lump
>
> I need a real Dutch lover
> Not some lousy glue huffer—

—When'd you get started up in Montgomery?

—Fourteen.

—Fourteen?!

—Girl, no fuckin way…

—Girl, I looked *older* for my age…

—At that age…

–What happened to Laronda?

–Say what?

–Laronda.

–Got her ass jumped.

–That's what you said.

–Some other hos come down, they be from Little Haiti or some shit, I don't know. They was some tough ass hos, what I heard. She tryin to get in the car, these other bitches said no way, it's our turn to party. Dey cussin n screamin on the avenue. One of em throwed a punch. It ended with Laronda in the middle of the damn street.

–Shit.

Gravity yanks the coke booger off J-Nell's Lee Press-on Nail. She stares half-absently at the floor, wondering where it has gone, then gives up and cuts herself another line.

–Lord, I tell you, were I to do it all over again…

–You wouldn't be on the game?

–Now I didn't say that, girl…

–Oh, don't go there, mi amour.

–Would you, though?

Fielding anxiety, the whore called Santana sings along to the last verse.

> He took me to his houseboat right across from a windmill
> We ate some cheese and talked all night upon the water still—

–Do what?

–You think it's gonna get better? Any of it?

–Worse places to be than Miami.

–Montgomery?

–Never go back there again.

–Wait a minute. How you tellin me that in this day and age, the twenty-first motherfuckin century, they can go and run a white girl out of town? I mean *any* town. Dat's some wild west shit up in there.

–First off, I aint white.

–Like hell you aint.

–Nope.

–What is you then, gringa?

–I'm Native.

–The fuck.

–What tribe.

–I'm Creek.

–That a thing? No shit.

–I shit yo skanky ass not. Born on a reservation outside Montgomery.

–From the reservation to the escort agency. That's some American Dream Come True shit right there.

–Creek… ?

–Creek Indians of Alabama. Used to be the whole state was our land. Alabama is an Indian name. Means *Here We May Rest.*

At that, Mrdok suddenly rouses from his zombification.

–Here we may rest! Hey! I like that!

The whores eye their client despicably, then silently and communally agree to ignore his outburst.

–That's crazy, girl. How you get turned on to the ho game all the way out there in the wilds of Alabama?

–A man.

–Of course.

–White man.

–Mm hmm.

–Guess you could call him a boyfriend. Though that's more how I felt *at the time.*

–It sho do fly by quick, don't it.

–Not fast enough.

–This white guy called AJ. Shaggy blonde ass motherfucker. He done made all these promises.

–Cos that's what a man do.

–Man, I thought he had all the answers. That he was gonna rescue me out of that shit. Cos you know our reservation wasn't nothin but a damn trailer park by this point. Buncha drunk half dead Indians wanderin around.

–I thought they done turned them all into casinos. At least get the money from them white muthafuckas.

–Naw. Village elders. Didn't want it. Say it aint the right thing to do. I don't know, man. I just wanted outta that junk.

–So what'd this AJ do.

–Thought he was different from all the white men used to come on the reservation. Cops and whisky sellers. We barely left with nothin, save for our misery. They damn try and come steal that away too.

AJ different. Got a tattoo of a spine on his spine. Runnin down the length of it. I thought that was real neat. Certainly cooler than the goddamn roses and dragons I seen on most white men's skin.

AJ liked to talk real sweet. And I wasn't a virgin or nothin. Lost that at twelve. Thought it was supposed to be somethin real special, it wasn't. But we don't talk about that.

He like to party, AJ. At first it was the usual. Smoke, pills. We moved on up the ladder. Then one day he's all like, *We out in the boondocks, girl. Let's move to the city. Montgomery's where it's at. We can stay with my cousin till we find a job.*

I say what the hell. Aint no use rottin on the reservation. Course we argued, me and my ma. *Don't go, don't go.* But I went anyway. I knew a lot for sixteen. Thought I did. But obviously what I knew didn't cover it. Not for what was about to come.

Montgomery aint that far. But it's actually another world. I mean literally. For us, it's technically another country. I'd say it wasn't what I was expectin. His cousin, for one thing, livin in a Motel 6. We supposed to share the other bed. His cousin this big ol redneck name Lewis. Try to tell me he an expert on Indians, but he don't know shit. He just like to talk. Say the white man did us all a big favor teachin us how to get civilized and shit. I say my civilization is older than yours, asshole. I ask him where his folk come from, he say he don't know. Europe, Spain or some shit. England. He don't even know, he just throwing names of countries out in the air. That's white people in the twenty-first century for you. They don't even know where their damn people come from half the time, yet they think that gives them a right to rule over everything. I told him he can say anything, but one thing we Indians have proved time and time again is we don't cheat. We don't steal. We don't lie. It aint part of our culture, our heritage. And they done all that to all of us. Killed us too. That's why we are the way we are today. All fucked up like.

Anyway. Turns out, Lewis likes to party too. Even moreso. Worked out like this. Lewis was our supplier. The one with the connections. He could do the trade, get the gear. AJ served as the boss, then. That left me to be the worker, the earner. I think you know where this is going…

At the time, I didn't like to look at it that way like. I mean, by then I had a habit to feed. That and AJ loved me. That makes a difference. Well, things got desperate. I got sick. Started to feel things again. Once you start to feel things, after livin that way for so long, bein so numb, you start to realize things too. Reality hits, and it's painful. Like. Certain kinds of love just aint real, turns out.

That's when I started to leave. It was a process. One of my johns, he helped. Gave me a place to go and get clean. Once the junk got out of my system, I said I aint workin the motels, the streets no more. Gettin out of the west side of town. That's where all the junk is in Montgomery. Was. (I don't know about now.) And I knew Lewis and AJ, they was out lookin for me. They was gonna bring my ass back in. I made it easy for em. Without me, how they gonna get the money they need to pay for the room, the money they need to score.

But I didn't want to go back to the reservation neither. How'm I gon face my ma after all that? So I went exclusive. Hooked myself up with a agency. Just like y'all do it down here. Got to see how it works. High end. Better than the online profile thing. You get the johns who're willing to pay for that extra layer of protection like. Protects your ass, too, from all the bums and psychos.

—My best friend a gay boy, goes J-Nell, got into this fancy college up in NYC. One night we get drunk, we trippin on acid, we decide, I gon come up there live with him. Seemed natural at the time. Lotsa odd things do, when you trippin. We get up there, we livin in some mangy ass dorm room, I sleepin on the floor. I said shit, gotta get my ass a job. Y'know, like, shit just got real. I'd been doin phone sex work down here in Miami, thought it was real easy, y'know. Any bitch with a first grade education and a lil bit of imagination can drag that shit right outta the bag.

—Mm hm. Those were the days.

—Phone sex? That even a thing anymore?

—Girl, you'd be surprised. Some of these old timers who growed up with it can't let it go.

So I look on Craigslist, start goin to all these interviews. Turns out, nary a one of them is for actual phone sex. NYC, baby, they got all sortsa scams runnin up there, I'll tell you. I was like, I aint gonna do no porno, I aint gonna be doin no prostitution, and like, you want me to actually pay to rent a booth in this shit? I'm like, hell no.

Finally, the most honest place I go to, it turns out to be this dungeon, run by this woman called Lee Ann.

—A *dun*geon?

—Like, house of horrors n shit?

—No, dummy. Like SM. You know, they got all these Wall Street muthafuckas up there all into this kinky ass shit.

—Like bein spanked and stuff. I done that before.

—I done had to fist a nigga's ass once.

—Oh girl, worse. I had this one man come in, his teeth be all rotten. Come in, start pullin out a motherfuckin wrench outta his briefcase. I'm like, whatchu want me to do? He's all like, baby, I want you to pull my teeth out, one by one, while I jerk off.

–*Say what?*

–That's what I said. More precisely, I said there aint no W to the A to the motherfuckin way I be goddamn pullin that dental shit. I don't care how much you thinkin to pay me.

–Ahahahaha! He done thought he was gonna save money going to your ass insteada the dentist—

–What did your girl Lee Ann say?

–Oh, she cool. I actually enjoyed working there. Never made us do a goddamn thing we didn't feel comfortable with. She said *Girls, you got to set your own limits.*

–I aint never heard of no woman pimp before. How much the house take?

–Fitty cent.

–Say what?

–Lee Ann'd come in, be all like *Where my fitty cent at?* At first I tried to resist it, be like uh-uh, aint no such thing as fitty cent in dis whirl. But then I got to thinkin that it's fair tho. When you think about it. Dey got NYC rents to pay. Shit aint cheap.

And when you think, we wuddnt doin all dat much. Some days you just sittin there bored, no customers comin in. Lee Ann real nice, for a white bitch. Might buy us Chipotle those slow days. Always try to look out for me. Give me the real good clients. I was like her daughter or sumfin.

See, the thing is, there were no actual sex. I didn't feel myself to be a actual prostitute. That's what made the job nice. Also what kept the cops away. She didn't even hafta bribe em like a regular house would. She used to tell me, don't let em touch you, girl. We aint covered.

Still. There were the occasional nastiness. I damn knowed lotsa stuff. How to tie the men up. Hot wax. CBT.

–What that?

–Cock and ball torture.

–Girl…

–I know. They was even a bathtub. I aint gon tell you what that was for.

But I's good. Got me a bit of a followin, had my regulars. My favorite client, he a rich dude from New Jersey. His whole thing be like public humiliation. Liked to take me shopping, Saks Fifth Avenue, I mean fancy ass bling shit. Buy me diamonds, haute couture. Goddamn anything I pointed at—pricier, the better.

–Girl where'd he get all that money from?

–Girl, I never asked. Probly a mafioso. Lots of thems into that kinky shit, y'know. So he'd take me shoppin, buy me all this bling. This was *ontoppa* my hourly rate of two-fitty, mind you.

–Damn!

–We get up to the cash register to pay, I just have to start rippin on him right there in front of the sales girl. Bein all, *you filthy pig, you so disgustin, I'm likin to puke right now lookin at your ugly face, you Dumb Broke Pathetic Bitch Ass Muthafucka…*

The girls all come from the same agency, Nell's Girlz. Nell, not to be confused with J-Nell, is a forty-five-year-old man who doubles as an agent in the adult film world, with which there is unsurprisingly much overlap. Mrdok employs Nell's services often when he is in Miami, though he never takes the same girls twice—more of a security precaution that I myself insist on, lest word break out and a scandal—no, we can't even think about that, it's far too awful to consider…

–Took me three fuckin times—the Cuban whore, now throwing her story into the barrel, cos at this time of night (or is it morning already?), who really cares, might as well tell everything—three motherfuckin times. This goddamn ocean. You grow to hate it. Growin up down there. It surround you, you can never get away. Up here, everyone think—these Miami Cubanos, they think down there, it's the government that's oppressive. But it's not. It's the ocean. The ocean that imprisons us. That ocean, the puta madre of us all. We all hate it. Stuck on that island. No hope there. So what do we do? We spend all our time scheming ways to get off it. Attach yourself to a tourist, tryn get married. Me and my friends, we used to hang out by the ATM machine in Havana Old Town. That's how desperate we were. How obvious. We didn't know any better. Those days, there was only one CUC-dispensing ATM in all Havana. Now, I heard there's more. Used to run out of money round three in the p.m. Can you imagine? Course, foreigners were the only ones ever used it. It was like a money supply for the tourists. Had to think of ways to approach em, get between them and that cash, real subtle-like. Me, I could speak good English. Learned at university. Was studying science, biology. I dropped out, cos what's the point in Cuba. Wasn't all that hard to get money outta them. A certain kind of man. You get to figuring it out over time. They come to Cuba all alone, by themselves, ninety percent chance they're there for one thing. Pussy or dick. More often pussy. You'd take em to places. Feed em some line. Say *hey I know where they got the best rum. Not this Hemingway tourist shit, baby. You go there, they gonna rip you off. Come with me, papi, I got the place.* You'd be surprised how much money you make. Problem is, place like Cuba, there aint nothin to spend it on. So you're left, at the end of the day. With your dream. Cos that's all there is.

–How'd you get out of there?

–Those dreams. They lead to something eventually. Dreams and money, that leads to action. Boats leave all the time. Go to Cuba today, talk to any random person on the street. I'll bet you right now fifty dollars they'll have someone in their family who's over here, that left on one of them boats. It's just a thing they have. People wanna leave.

Like I said, took me three times. Leave and never come back. You get fed up, the boredom. Every day the same damn thing, nothin changin. When you're young, you want adventure. Down there, it's not just bein poor. That's only a small part of it. The main thing is: no chance of adventure. And the same ol same ol is so *tiring*.

First time, coast guard caught us. We was barely across anyway, just a few hours. Caught and sent back.

Second time was awful. We got misdirected, there was an argument on board over who was really supposed to be doin the navigatin. So stupid. We ended up drifting towards Mexico. People were dehydrated. One guy fell in the water, almost got his leg ate off by a shark. Finally, after couple days this insanity, a boat came and rescued us. Awful. I still shudder when I remember that one.

Third time, what can I say. I'm here, aint I? Fucking big fat American dream. See, thing about us Cubans is, we naïve. Think America's the big answer. Like we gonna live in one of them music videos we see, drive a Benz truck, live in some mansion. That it's all just yours for the taken.

I told myself I was gonna do real work when I got here. Something respectable. I don't know what. Just somethin. Live a decent life. See, the thing is, when I was in Cuba, I didn't even think of myself as a prostitute. I mean, I did what I did. But it wasn't like: this is my *job*. This is my destiny. It was more like... I don't know what. That just wasn't it.

I got to America, what happens. Ha. Well. Here, at least, I know what it is I am. You figure that out real quick. Over here, there aint no blurry middle ground, no ma'am. If you're a whore, then that's just what you are.

Into the room I stumble, hunger finally satiated—but still having failed at the task at hand—which is, in fact, the retrieval of a hand. With my own I point and let out a yelp.

–Cat! Cat! Cat!

So engrossed were the hookers in their incessant mindless babble, they and Jean-Pierre alike had failed to notice the entrance of a stray pussy with mangy fur, who is bent over one of the silver plates licking at the cocaine residue.

At this, the three erupt in unanimous laughter.

–Well I be goddamned!

–Mierda!

–A crackhead cat! Hahahaha—

As I chase the filthy creature out into the night…

That's when I see it. The waters of the pool, shimmering in their multi-hued underwater lighting display, programmed by one of America's top fireworks specialists (whom we also hired out at Shelter Island for Mrtol's annual birthday celebration.) I have to blink twice to ensure it isn't a digestion-induced mirage. For didn't I walk past the pool on the way back from the bar? Hadn't the security personnel, now nowhere in sight, been standing by the pool when I returned? The same pool that Mrdok had installed *to look at,* above all, for others' enjoyment, for him to watch others enjoying themselves in. The same pool whose waters he had not bothered to part since acquiring the property some six years ago. For there, in the midst of its waters, came floating: Mrdok's artificial limb.

I sidle back into the lounge, silently extending hand to master. He stares emptily at it for half a minute or so, as though struggling to register what it is, who it belongs to. When the circuitry finally connects, he takes it and quickly reconnects it to the stump on his right arm, then looks up at me.

–Where'd you find it?

Before I can answer, the hookers have risen, stretching, heading toward the main entrance.

–Time to get paid.

–And we need taxis, hon. If your chauffeur aint given us a ride.

Hand in place, Mrdok rises revivified.

–Wait! No! Don't leave!

I stifle a sigh, rest my exhausted posterior upon a barstool.

–We still have more coke! More jams… More money!

The whores look at one another groggily, then at Mrdok, then at me.

I rest my chin in my hands, trying not to sob.

–Hey, Gordo! Mrdok shouts too loud. Tell these bitches how much I'm worth right now.

J-Nell unfastens her bikini top, liberating her triple D's.

I take out my phone, dutifully, only to find another piece of bad news, a text message from the home office: Lallyburt says no.

EMPTY FUCKING NOTHINGNESS

1.

TO EXPLAIN TO you who Lallyburt is, I must first rewind the tape a bit—for those still aware of what a VHS tape is and the rewind command associated with it—and reinsert us back in the office in Manhattan where, prior to our little sojourn in Miami, Mrdok had me summoned...

–You see that?

–Ah yes! It's a map.

–Yes, I know it's a map, you idiot. What the fuck you think I am, retarded or somethin?

–Of course not, sorry, I…

–Look at where my finger is pointing.

–Ahhh. I see.

–Do you?

–Yes!

–And what is it you see?

–I see… Empty space.

–Precisely. You know what that is?

–I… You know, I'm not *too* familiar with the region.

–Nothing. That's what that is.

–Ha! Emptiness.

–Derelict empty fucking nothingness.

–Though nothing is ever *really* empty. I mean, there must be *something* there.

–Something?

–Well... Abandoned buildings, houses... Some wild animals, perhaps...

–You ever been out there?

–Me? Well no, of course not.

–Way you're talkin now, makes you out to be some sort of expert on nothingness.

–Oh Mrdok, you're the only expert on nothingness I've ever known! I am only a lowly apprentice.

–Tell me something. What's this? Look down here, to where my finger's pointing, dingus.

–Why that's the city, of course.

–Very very good. Now, let's measure the distance between the two points: nothing and the city.

–...

–You starting to see what I'm getting at?

–Ah yes! A picture is starting to form. I think...

–All that nothing. Unmarked territory. Un*used*... What a waste.

–Yes...

–It's like an island.

–Yes! An island... surrounded by land.

–All that city over there.

–City...

–That bumbling, overcrowded, stinking mess of a city. And this pristine slice of nothingness right next to it.

–Well, we don't know how *pristine* this nothingness might be...

–Gordo. It's pristine if I say it's pristine. And if it's not, we'll make it that way. Cos that's how I envision it.

–It could be... a dumping ground. Polluted. So close to the city, surely there must be some *reason* behind its abandonment.

–Do you know who owns it.

–No. Who?

–Some lowlife development corpo. No-namers. Hicks. Been sitting on it for years, not doing anything with it. Waiting for the land to appreciate.

–Shitballs?

–Not shitballs.

–Mob?

–No mob. I had them checked out. Just some Texas cowboy speculator fuck. Waiting for it to *appreciate*.

–As though that will simply happen on its own!

–No initiative, these people. No game. God, I can't *stand* developers like that. Time-mongerers, that's what they are.

–Time-mongerers! That's a nice way to put it. As though clinging to the slow passage of time were some sort of salvation!

–Yeah? I don't know what the fuck you're saying right now… The waiting game. Blind to the fucking gold lying under their feet.

–Right! All one needs to do is dig a little.

–Oh, we're gonna dig, Gordo. That much is for sure. We're gonna dig so deep, we'll reach the front door to hell before we stop.

–Your ambition overwhelms me!

–Shut up. You sound gay.

–Ahahahaha. Mrdok. What a wit!

–Let's call em up. Start the digging already.

–What are you envisioning, if I may ask? I imagine some high-end housing, perhaps a shopping complex of some sort in the center… Are we thinking one architect for the project or many? We could have a contest…

–Architect? I'm gonna need more than a fuckin architect. I want a planner.

–Planner?

–Urban planner, Gordo. Person who makes maps like these.

–You want… ?

–No need to be modest, is there? We've done housing developments, suburbs. We've done quarters of cities—city extensions, really…

–I was thinking that's what you had in mind for this one. A whole new quarter. Expanding the city—I mean, I can see it now, this project really has your name written all over it.

–Make sure you don't give anyone my name. Not at first. They don't need to know our intentions, either. All I want is a price tag.

–A no-name buyer. Right.

2.

THE OWNER OF the so-called development company, a Texan. Lallyburt Edison Dryer III—yes, he of the toilet paper and paper towel empire. Texans everywhere these days, seems. It's true that the Lone Star State always had a disproportionate share of shitballs. Oil-drunk crackers in cowboy hats rolling around in armadillo shit beneath the desert's harsh moon glare. Mrdok standing there listening to this one rattle on like, well, a rattler.

–Ah wuz ovuh in Greece ona vaycayshun last summuh, he's droning on in his Texasized sing-song. Ah staht feelin a little homesick aftuh a week uv all that souvlaki, so I done decahd to go to whuh they call un Ay-merican restrawnt. You shoulda seen thuh dam Cobb salad they trahd to serve me. Witha *peetuh* bread on the sahd!

I study Mrdok's face, its unconcealed boredom, a *why is he telling us this?* expression barely concealed. It's a windy day, the wind ruffles his black-brown hair. Not that brutal Manhattany wind, wherein you get that tunnel effect through the skyscrapers that knocks you down when you're making your way up the avenue. More an inland swoop, a diagonal blowing whose lightness is somehow disorienting, as all inclement displays of shallowness—be they meteorological or other-wise—ultimately are.

–Well ah jesta bit dam near shat mahseylf when ah saw whut they done did with the ungyun rangs...

–You got a well or somethin? Mrdok interrupts this drone.

–A wayuhl?

Lallyburt checks his belt buckle, as though it contains the answer to Mrdok's question, then brushes a hunk of black soil off the rattle-snake skin of his left boot.

–Ah got it. So you dun want mineral rahts. But theyuh aint no oil here. Aint nothin of valyoo in this heyuh soil.

–Nonono, continues Mrdok, like how do you get water here?

–Wahtuh?

–Say I wanted to build something.

–You want to biyuld? Awn this heyuh shithole? Wah ah do deklayuh.

Lallyburt—known as Burt to his friends and colleagues, Lally to his current and ex-wives—looks at the scape before them question-ing. Mrdok bites a chewy mint off a roll, spits out the paper.

His incredulity is not hard to fathom. Even for Mrdok, who will later confess to me that the landscape here rather reminds him of the tormented skin of an old man he once knew; its pockmarked invari-ability. It must have been an old man in the late stages of skin cancer. The shrubbery somehow black, toxic—even though on closer in-spection it turns out to be a mere healthful dark forest green. It's the distance that confounds. Not quite wasteland material, since the brackish soil appears rich enough in mineral to support all kinds of industrial farming initiative, which is what Lallyburt seems to pre-sume we want it for. Lallyburt is sure to stress that the land is available *for long-term lease,* even though, as the conversation wore on, he revealed that he hadn't until recently been aware that he even *owned* this piece of black hole real estate, it having apparently been acquired in the era of Lallyburt Edison Dryer the *First.*

An old man's skin. With lotsa holes. Some of these holes must be wells. Or at least hold the potential. How can they not; what else can they be? What kind of name is Lallyburt anyway? Holes in the landscape. Pour concrete in, you've got a foundation. Perfectly rounded, peglike, as though a giant had stubbed its toe repeatedly into the earth. What are they there for? Where there is lack, there is always gain. Something that old man with the pockmarked skin used to always say. Before he won another case. Nothing like an indentation into the earth's guilelessness. We dig them for bodies, too, to get rid of the dead ones. Mrdok knew a few of those who ended up in concrete. Rumors thereof. Fatballs liked to tell him things, then dispel of them. Little yellow tale inklings etched across cocktail napkins, scrunched up and pocketed in suit vests, to be discarded on the next trip to the john.

–I think it's got good potential, I say in an attempt to revive the flagging conversation. But yes, we rather are in the business of building.

–We're not lookin to *lease* nothin, either, Mrdok adds. I was thinkin this mother is for sale.

Lallyburt thinks that over. Can't seem to remember now why he agreed to take this meeting. A gut instinct thing, perhaps; the need to get away from the home office for the afternoon. But now these damn fast-thinkin yankees're chewin his nail. In a minute, they're going to try and force him to make a decision—he can feel that one creeping up. He has to at least pretend to have something in mind when that moment arrives. Yankees're like robots, Lallyburt the Second always said. It was something of an off-the-cuff, he'd never really explained what he meant by it, but it had always stuck with Lallyburt. He and his daddy and granpappy—all the Dryers, going back however long the family historian had managed to dig—had been secessionists at heart, nostalgists for that happy brief reign of the Lone Star Republic. When the buffalo knew its place, the skies remained open, the borders closed. These days, all these goddamn nachos pouring in, and right into the heart of ol' TX. These boys from New York City aint got the faintest the problems confronting this country—they don't see it up there with their own eyes in the everyday the way *we* do. Yankees're like robots. He supposes it meant they were programmed like, that despite the nice storefront, you never really get to see the man in back operating the controls.

–This armadillo humper doesn't have the faintest clue, whispers Mrdok, and I don't want him getting in on it, either. It has to be a clean sale. Otherwise it's gonna turn into a fuckin square dance, with all his cowboy friends reddening their necks around the fire—

–But Mrdok, what are we supposed to—Can we even build infrastructure here?

–Anything, anything. I know. Tell him we wanna build condos. Office buildings. Sounds boring enough, he'll think we're just crazy—

–Not a fail-safe venture—

–We're big enough to fail. He knows that much about us.

–Here he comes, ssssshhh—

Lallyburt sauntering over.

–So you boys're thinkin youd lahk to take this here betty offah mah hands lahk.

–Indeed, we were considering making an offer, I began.

–So you're saying, no wells. No water. No infrastructure, really.

That's Mrdok, lowering the price before the negotiations have even begun. A tactic he has long refined: esteem-bashing, of a sort. Make the other guy feel real little, super small, before even getting into the real mathematics of the scheme. That way, he feels foolish trying to start off with a high number. Psychological warfare. And it works every time.

How to win enemies and destroy people. It's all part of the board game.

–You say agriculture, I pick up where Mrdok's left off. But to me, it seems more like this was designed to be a dumping ground.

–How far is the city dump from here, anyway, Gordo?

–Oh, I checked that out before we got here, boss. Just seventeen miles to the north.

I gesture—northward, though very much a guess—at a narrow clearing between two accidental rows of bushes I can very well imagine being cleared into a regal avenue. Towers along the periphery, or perhaps ringing its boundaries, demarcating inner city from outer. We haven't really begun working on the plan yet. Still, images are erupting mound-like into my mind, having grown from the seedish clues of Mrdok's out-loud dreaming and scheming.

Lallyburt thinking. He knows from word-of, from the business tabloids what kind of tawdry reputation this Mrdok enjoys—or rather, suffers. If he and his ass bandit assistant are really here to just, quote unquote *make him an offer,* as they say in robotspeak, it is more likely their real intentions are somewhere off-field. That they are

here, in fact, to bait the frog, as Lallyburt II was so fond of saying—
that is, to catch the frog in order to get the gator. Or some such. No
idea why daddy's voice keeps coming into his head whenever he
looks over at this Mrdok figure, but that's the voice he hears all right,
may god rest his long-punished soul.

–Ah happen to know a thing or three about you, Mister Mrdok.

–Apparently not the most important thing: no mister. Never mister. Just Mrdok.

–Weyl aw raht. Mur-dawg. And ahll tell you somethin. Ah got a
friend down in Amarillo, teaches at the real estate school they got set
up down thar. Made himself a bundle then lost it. That's whah he's
teachin. Wah how'd he done do that, you maht pass muster. Well, he
was fallin in the footsteps of a well-known thief. Now, down in mah
hometown bah the borduh, we aint got no problem with thieves,
long as they got the raht coluh to their skin—that is to say, no coluh
at all. Was a thief, after all, laid next to Chrahst on the cross-next-
door. Uh thief ah can always forgive. Granted he can say in all honesty whut it is he is.

–Mister Dryer, I interrupt, sensing a tone of unnecessary desperation to the proceedings—

–Hold it, Fanny Pack, he holds out his hand to me, then continues to address Mrdok: This pal o mahn was a discahple, of sorts, of
yrs. An expert, so called, in the sahence of flippology. Even wrote a
big article bout you in our little real estate gazette, *The Texas Maverick*.

Mrdok smiles grimly.

–Wow, I had no idea. In between fuckin your relatives, you all
found time to learn how to read and write?

Lallyburt spits a calm wad on to the soil, marking his territory.

–See, ah have no problem getting rid uv a piece of shiyit slahce
of mudpah. That aint mah worry. Hell, worry aint even thuh wurd.
Ah got pieces of tumbleweed down in mah home state worth more
than this shiyit pahl. What ah wanna know is—

–Condos, I tell him, we're going to build condos.

–Oh, condos mah ass, says the cowboy, tired now of this fairy's
mouth and unafraid to show it with a pointed glare. A glare that tells
Mrdok he'd better speak up, and fast.

–I'm sorry that I don't enjoy the pristine reputation of your family, Dryer, going back generations, to… Dryer… That's a German
name, aint it? So nice of you, then, selling those fighter planes to your
ancestral brethren during the Second World War through your family's banking subsidiary in, uh, Holland, was it?

–Excyuse me—

–Oh, and your valiant oil deal with those Saudi bastards, who, speaking of airplanes—

–E-nuff! Aw raht, ah see we know each othuh; Mistuh Mur-dawg. But whut ah really wanna know, fore we start talkin wells nd numbuhs nd acreage nd all that, is who the real buyuh is. Cos ah don't believe for won hot dam minute that you and Miss Pansy Ass ovuh here have any real intention uv plantin a dam thing on this here marsh.

Mrdok has to laugh.

–So that's what this is all about? You afraid—sorry, *afeard*—that I'm operating some cheap ass ponzi gimmick on your failed landfill? Baby, I don't know where you Texas cowpokes get your news from, but I haven't been in the flippin business since the last time you got a hard-on without Cialis.

Now I have to laugh. Good one, boss!

Both turn to me sharing a shut-the-fuck-up expression. A small moment of unity that enables the conversation to move forward, proving my usefulness, so now I feel a bit less guilty about my transgressive outburst.

A few minutes later and Lallyburt and Mrdok are playing minigolf at a nearby highway rest stop, the intensity of the landscape (and minor junkie enclave embedded within) having caused the conversation to stall. I'm standing in the shadow of a ceramic life-sized brontosaurus in need of a refreshed coating of paint, pretending to be engrossed in some urgent matter on my iPhone while covertly recording the entire conversation for future parsing.

Lallyburt's back to boring us on more fun-fact-filled details about his recent trip to Greece, as though Mrdok and I haven't been to that country and its islands collectively more times than I have fingers and toes to count on.

–So on mah third day, ahma thinkin, do ah really wanna trah nd get uh haircut? Ah mean the dam language barriuh nd all.

–Yeah, says Mrdok, they probably only understand *proper* English.

Lallyburt knocks his orange ball up the seventy-five degree incline towards the iguana's open mouth. The ball stops on the AstroTurf just at the tip of the tongue, but Lallyburt doesn't seem too upset about this near win, as he goes right on blabbing.

–… nd all thuh houses on the hill, whaht as day, evry single wun. Ah mean, lookin up at the village from thuh beach, lookt jest lahk uh set uh jagged teeth…

–I'm really really good at golf, says Mrdok. I mean you're gonna be real sorry you ever played me. You'll never win.

Carefully placing his yellow ball on the tee in the AstroTurf, Mrdok assumes his hunched position, lifting his club before bringing it swinging down and clunking the ball with just a tad of overexertion; the ball flies into the parking lot, whence an alarm soon sounds.

–That one didn't count! I was distracted. Gordo!

I dutifully produce another yellow ball. Always prepared, I managed to procure a whole pocketful from one of the young men working at the entrance in exchange for a Ulysses S. Grant, which swiftly quelled his reluctance to cooperate since, perhaps owing to the run-down nature of the place, golf balls are apparently a rather limited commodity here.

–... fer sum reason, whenevuh I heauh that phrase *jagged teeth*, it always makes me think uh Mick Jagguh...

Cowboy has had a piece of lint stuck to his mustache all along, which he suddenly takes notice of. The mustache is of medium-average girth, length running to either side of the lips, since too-short mustache always come across to Texan society folk as suspiciously faggoty, while an abundant bush upon the lip makes it hard to talk proper without a stray hair or two going up your nose and tickling the inner nostril.

–... thing is, uh cowerse, his teeth aint even jagged. Ah happun to no his Ay-merican dentist. Yussed to play tennis with him down in Key Weyest. Cuz, y'know, them Brits aint got the nahcest teeth, if'n they can afford it, they come ovuh here n get em fixed up real good, 'merican stahl...

Finally, a yellow ball rolls into a hole. Mrdok, triumphant, beams up at the cowboy hat.

–See? I told you so. Clearly I'm winning. You keeping points, Gordo?

–Sixty four millyen years nd we're still fascinayted.

–What?

–The dahnosawers.

Looking around. The replicae all around us.

–So what?

–Jest thank. How is it man came to be so obsessed with sumthin we aint even wonce got a chayence tuh see.

–Lots of people don't have this obsession. God, for instance. You think God cares about the dinosaurs? He don't give a shit. Never has.

—Ah aint talkin bout Gahd, dummy. Gahd we all know exiyists. It's the decorousness of mattuh that fascinaytes. Even in the Bahble lahk, in Gyenesiyis, where it says on thuh fifth day, Gahd done created all thuh sea dragons. Clearly a reference to the dahnosawers. Yearnin not just fer meanin. But fer soul. That's whut.

—Huh?

—Which wus yer favrit as a yung man?

—My favorite?

—Favrite dahnosawer, dummy. Duhh. Come on. We all had wun. Mrdok regards a cloud questioningly.

—Pterodactyl, I guess.

—Terodactyl! Wuhl ahl be damd. That do say a lot. Lallyburt sets up a ball and prepares to swing.

—And what exactly does it say?

Lallyburt swings. Ball flies into an upside down piranha's upturned mouth, swishing around the bladed teeth before gurgling down into esophageal oblivion.

—Carnivorous, of course. But then it's got un advantage othuh flesheatuhs dont got. That protects it from bigguh, mo powehful flesheatuhs: wangs. It can swoop down on, say, uh big snahlin nasty T-rex. Eat its ahballs raht outa its heyad, say goodbah lahk tomorro aint even uh day. T-rex is growlin nd screamin, but its tahny ahms dont even reach all that hah. Kinda retahded lahk, when you think uv it; lahk, whut wuz thuh Lawed up to theyuh? Caint no longuh thank to see. Wunce thuh terruh uv thuh layend, devoid uv its chief seyense, now reduced to uh piece uv pray.

Othuh thang about terodactyls. How in thuh heck they managed to go extinct lahk all thuh othuhs? Youda thunk, whutevah disastuh Gawd threw down 'pon thuh urth, terodactyl up thar in thuh skahd manage tuh escape it. 'Stead, they all s dead as thuh day. Proves sumthin, at least, to all them doutin thomases out thar. When Gahd wants sumthin, he makes dam sure to make it happen.

Mrdok, now strangely fascinated, has upturned his club, rests on it like a cane in the shade.

—And what kind of dinosaur was *your* favorite? he asks the cowboy with a thin strain of skepticism acidly stratifying the mucus at the back of his throat.

—Oh, that's easy, says Lallyburt, adjusting his hat and nodding once. Brontosaurus. Thuh christian dahnosawer.

3.

–OH AND ANOTHER thing. What the *fuck* is going on with nucleite futures?

–I'm sorry… Nucleite?

–Gordo. Open the fuckin commodities register. Right now… I'll tell you what's happening. Smart phones. Smart cars. Smart animals. Smart people. Smart this and that. All got one thing in common. What is that?

–Well, I'm no expert. Though I would hazard to guess that they all involve nucleite somehow.

–Look at the numbers. Nucleite's been flat for *years*. Now, all of a sudden, I mean, I'm lookin at the commodities charts this morning and everything else is flat as balls, then all of a sudden, there's this big hard-on stickin up towards the sky. And look and it's—

–Nucleite.

–Bing bing. Yes. Nucleite. Now, what I wanna know is: What the fuck? Get on that right away. Get back here in fifteen minutes and I want to know everything there is to know.

So you're probably asking me, how on earth does one go about fitting the acquisition of such in-depth knowledge about one of the world's more obscure commodities in such a slim window of fifteen minutes? Well, there's a very simple answer to that, my dears: you don't. What you can do, however, is take a page out of Mrdok's book. It happens to have been ghost written, it is true, but the advice is sage nonetheless: never let on that you have no idea what it is you are talking about. In the fine art of business and finance, there is really only one skill that one needs to have a pass at success: confidence. Confidence, here, may be defined as the *appearance* of knowledge. To facilitate the construction of this appearance, I open up my browser and commence a thorough study of the charts: the one thing in this world, perhaps, that never betrays the truth. What I am able to gage in the fifteen minutes allotted to me, I can then build on and elaborate with my stashed supply of confidence, which, *voilà*, will thus lead to a convincing display of knowledge.

Nucleite does have a rather peculiar history, from what I am able to gather in the search results. It is some noxious stuff. A form of coal. Actually has the same composition as diamond, though not its properties—and certainly not its worth. Worth, however, can always be adjusted… Now, charts… I'm not seeing the boner Mrdok described, so I will have to zoom out a bit on the timeline, let's get back to—what was it he said? World War the Second… Ah yes. From this vantage point, the erection stands out quite nicely. Now how could that be… Click on *News*…

Since gold tanked many moons ago, Mrdok has been in search of a new substance. Some mineral, some naturally occurring *thing*—certainly not oil, heavens no, anyone with eyes can see how much of a mess *that* market is in—with which to occupy a new avenue of interest (if putting it thusly doth not mixeth the metaphors too savagely.) He likes the ever-evolving geometry of his portfolio. A programmer devised an inventive series of displays in a unique app that he habitually plays around with, everything from a spider web to a tubular maze to a color-coded curvilinear mass resembling fishnet stockings. These displays provide him with novel means of visualizing his worth, a much more stimulating way of gaging his position at any moment than raw spoken data might elicit. Printouts of these experiments in chartography adorn the walls of his Manhattan office, and he often peruses them when speaking on the phone, rarefied works of conceptual art that spur his creativity, often giving rise to fabulous new schemes for shifting his wealth in the most improbable and ingenious ways. They also enable him to uncover gaps and inconsistencies that might otherwise remain hidden to his assorted brokers and managers, ensuring that he is always a few paces ahead of them, often startling wealth management professionals with his insights. It is less a means of *thinking outside of* than Becoming One with the proverbial box.

Natural commodities are such a slippery thing, the markets all lop-sided and highly angular, one might say—a beguiling complexity of movements inexplicable to outsiders—which is why in depth knowledge about any particular one is really required before anything remotely resembling a wise investment might be made…

–Hello, Mrdok. Yes, nucleite… Let's see… Well, you know, nucleite is used in many things. Many, many things. A bit like oil, really. Unlike oil, however, nucleite is dry. In fact, they call it a *dry lubricant.* Which, you know, it doesn't sound all that useful to me, rather oxymoronic, if I am to be honest. But it *is* used in pencils, which infers it might not be the wisest investment at the moment. I mean, who uses pencils anymore?

–I don't give a shit what it's *used* for, you fat fuck. Give me some fuckin data!

–By which you mean numbers.

–By which I mean fuckin data!

–Well, okay… Nucleite, it seems, well, it reached its heights in the late '80s, when… in East Asia, there was a big demand, a major stimulation of all the steel markets, really, precious metals… Though is nucleite really all that *precious?*

–Don't bullshit me, Gordo. Who the hell do you think you're talkin to, the media? Look, lithium's already shot up way too high and it aint lookin to get much higher—too late to float on that barge. Nucleite, I don't know. But I've a hunch. And you know *my* fuckin hunches.

–Why of course! I mean, if it's anywhere *near* the angle of hunch you got in the early aughts around those Chinese tech stocks—

–Gordo, Gordo. Look. First, you're gonna shut the fuck up. Second, you're gonna shut the fuck up again until I finish telling you what you're gonna do. Next, you're gonna call Abe, you're gonna tell him to buy a million in shares of Oostern Nucleite. That will give us a nice juicy share of the company—four percent, more or less. That'll get their attention. Then, you're gonna book me a flight to Madagascar.

–… Why Madagascar?

–Cos that's where they mine it, you fuckin fat fuck. Oostern. They just dug a huge fuckin hole there, in the middle of the island. No, wait… Where is it?... *Three* mines, Gordo. They've cleared three motherfuckin mines in the last month. We're on the late end of receiving that little tidbit. When you call Abe, you can ask him why the fuck that is. Why am I finding this out on my own. He should've been on to this three weeks ago, I could've had my name all over that shit right now. What, he think he's the only hot shit portfolio manager out there?

–So Madagascar. The capital, I presume… Whatever that might be, hahaha. And, um, a driver…

–I wanna go there next Tuesday. Check out the sights, the mines, whatever the fuck, get back to New York after the second night, by Friday at the latest, before I catch ebola or whatever the fuck it is they got down there.

–Meetings with the gentlemen of Oostern, I presume?

–All the suits. But wait, don't set that up until *after* the deal goes through. Call Abe first. Quick and discreet. I don't want my name popping up on their radar until they read it in the papers. Give em a nice little jolt with their morning espresso.

–I'll book the flight this morning.

–Fuck. The thought of chartering again just made me lose my erection. Where are we on the 727 search?

–Oh, that reminds me! A piece last week in *Business Insider* caught my eye. The new management at SunEye Corp—they're introducing major cutbacks.

–Right.

–I mean, they have to. Under the last CEO, they were nearly driven into the ground. It's inevitable! These punks have been living like kings and queens. This lavish spending, and not even on clients—their entire executive team, rolling around like the Princes of Persia—five-star glamour, limousines, every single perk you can imagine.

–Perks over profits. I see what you're…

–The company plane. They're gonna have to liquidate it! I mean, there's no way…

–Right. Fuck! Brilliant. Actually, let me take this. Get me the number of Louis—what's his last name again? The new CEO?

–Farquahson.

–Right. I wanna make this move directly. I've got an instinct on this one.

–Good move. He'll be most impressed to hear from you personally.

–A Good Guy move. I can do them a huge favor by taking it off their hands!

–And you'll get it for nothing.

–Don't jinx my game. I've gotta play it first.

Sip.

–What is this, by the way? It's delicious.

–You like it? It's dragonfruit, imported from Taiwan, with a dash of ginger ale thrown in. Gives it a nice, foamy froth, I find.

–Well done. Get me more of it.

–Right away.

Buzz buzz.

–Louis, this is Mrdok calling. I've been meaning to get you on the ringer for ages to congratulate you on the appointment. The board made a brilliant move, I feel. With you at the helm, SunEye will be out of arrears in no time. Matter of fact, I'm actually considering buying some shares.

–Is that so? Mrdok, I'm speechless. That would be wonderful. Would you mind if I pass that tidbit on to my PR and Marketing team?

–Aha. I'd rather you wait till I actually buy the shares.

–Right. Right. We don't want the huge spike to occur till *after.* Ahahaha.

–That's right. Hahahaha. But look, Louis, I'm calling for another reason. I read about the company's, uh, former excesses. And your intention to curb all that. And from what I gather, there was even a 727…

–That fucking plane. It's gonna have to be the first thing to go, I'm afraid, much as we all love it.

–I'm so sorry to hear that.

–And yet you're not… Because you're going to offer to take it off my hands.

–Well, now, don't put words in my mouth…

–At least that's what I'm hoping is happening here, if I am to be fully honest. It's not like the market for these things is so huge.

–Aha. Well, whatever I can do to help!

–Where are you right now?

–NYC, baby.

–Tell you what. I could send up the plane for you to take a look at. Could get it to you by early tomorrow, easy. Fly right into LaGuardia.

–You getting this, Gordo?—Sounds good. We'll talk in the afternoon then.

–Mrdok…

–Yes?

–Just… Thank you.

Click.

–Gordo, come look at this shit.

Mrdok with a page displayed from the Thames & Hudson volume he was flipping through on that last call: *Dark Nostalgia: Faultlessly Stylish Interiors for Business, Pleasure, and Leisure.*

–I see. Paneled ceilings… How elegant!

–Not that one, you fairy. This! The opposite page!

–Ahh…

–This dropped seating area… The general effect… I'm thinking… Maybe we could recreate it, something like it, for the lounge at the South Beach place?

–You mean the house or the hotel?

–The house, of course. Why? Something wrong with the lounge in the hotel?

–No.

–Don't lie.

–Certainly not.

–I'm just thinking… different levels. I don't know… Could make the lounge just so much more…

–Loungy.

–Yes! Exactly the word I was looking for.

–I'm also quite loving this wall screen, I have to say.

–I know, can you believe this shit? Says here it was salvaged from an old building façade in France. Fuckers ripped it right off with a crowbar and stuck it on the wall in their bar. Classy, no?

–Must have been a huge grille. They were able to fit it so that it takes up precisely the space of the wall. Impressive.

–We should get someone to go scavenge shit like that for us.

–I think we could easily do that. But going back to the decline…

–I mean, I like it in the photo—obviously, with a drop like that, you fill it with… just… coziness. Pussy pillows and all that.

–… Pussy pillows?

–Y'know. For the ladies. Something soft to elevate em. Or for them to lean on, to grasp on to, when I'm bangin em from behind.

–Aha! Pussy pillows. Yes!

–Or, you know, like stuffed animals and shit. Only, like, *elegant.* With the architecture being kinda like… chaise lounges, only *built in* to the wall, the structure—

–So when approaching from above, one can *descend* via the stairs in the center, but perhaps on the sides, you could just—drop, really. Collapse.

–Like, boom. Yeah. Somethin like that. Very Miami, y'know? We're shitfaced drunk when we're down there half the time anyway. And this *is* the lounge we're talkin bout.

–Well there are a couple ways we might go about it. The easiest, I think, would be to raise the entire lounge by a few feet. Either via steps or—I'm just thinking out loud here, but I'm thinking it could be more graceful lifted as a gradual incline, leading off from the dining area, perhaps even beginning by the pool… Then a sudden and dramatic *woosh!*

–Yeah. Woosh. We could raise the floor. Or we could just blast a fuckin hole in the ground.

–That too. But before we go any further—and I know you're not going to want to hear this, but…

–Mrtol.

–I think there's no other way. Miami: it's sensitive.

–Get me Mrtol on the line.

–She's…

–Shelter Island.

Buzz buzz.

–Dragonfruit, huh? What kind of tree does dragonfruit come from anyway? Dragon trees?

–*Bueno.*

–Fuck. Rosalita? What did I tell you? You're in America now. What do we say in American when we pick up the telephone?

–Hell-o.

–Sí, hello. Muy bien. Now can you please get me Missus Mrdok? She at home?

–Un momento, por favor.

–This bitch. I've told Mrtol a million times, she needs to speak English when Jaco's at home—

–Hello?

–Mrtol, love, how's it?

–Well, you know… You at the office?

–I is. Look, Gordo's here with me, we just came up with the most *brilliant* idea for the lounge in South Beach. You're gonna love this…

–Oh. You mean your South Beach *fuckpad?*

–Now there's no need to be vulgar, Mrtol!

–Shut up, Gordo.

–Mrtol, what are you talking—?

–What's the idea.

–What?

–Your *brilliant fucking idea,* Mrdok. What is it?

–What about, in the center, if we were to have a *decline.* Like a dropped seating area.

–A what?

–A de—

–You mean like a pit?

–Kind of. But like a square. With seating around it.

–You mean like a fuckpit? Where you can spitroast your bikini'd bimbos?

Mrdok mouthing the words *She's drunk.*

–Mrtol…

–What kind of *pit,* Mrdok?

–I didn't use the word—did I say *pit?*

–She did.

–You hear that? You did, Mrtol, you said *pit.* I never said *pit.*

–So you want to put a hole in the ground? And what's going to be in the hole, Mrdok?

–Not a hole. Like a, it will be shaped like a square. With seating around it. Comfy. Loungy, is the word Gordo came up with.

—You want… and in the *center* of the lounge? I'm just trying to picture it, I can't. How is this gonna work, Mrdok?

—I mean, there are a couple of ways…

—We just finished remodeling. Emphasis on the word *finished*.

—It's a work in progress.

—No it aint. You're gonna drill a huge hole in the middle of the lounge? What are you, out of your fucking mind?

—Mrtol, maybe, the thing is, you're not seeing the picture I'm looking at right here. I'm looking in this interior design book right now, I'll bring it home later. Or—no, you know what—Gordo, take this page, scan it. Send it to Mrtol right now.

—Mrdok, two words: no and no.

Click.

—Scan it anyway. Just email it to her. She'll change her mind once she sees it, trust me. I didn't describe it well. She's thinkin… like a barbeque pit or some shit. You know, because the lounge is partially outdoors, so she thinks—

—I don't think she believes it will be used for barbequing…

—Gordo—just take the book and scan it, please.

—Right.

Pffffffffffrp.

—Sorry, I'm having post-Sichuanese, um, issues.

—Now for the next order of business. A reporter from *New York* magazine called and—

—No media.

—But Mrdok—

—No interviews. You know the rule.

—I thought—

—How much am I worth?

—Wha, now?

—Get out the iPad. I want numbers.

—Yes yes. Just calculating—

—Better yet, don't tell me. Give it to the reporter.

—… You want me to give the reporter our numbers?

—Well what else are they trying to find out?

—Some sort of feature, I believe. *The 10 Richest People in Manhattan.*

Pffffffr pffft.

—There's my answer.

—Right. No interview.

—What is it Tony Fatballs used to always say?

—*Never talk to the media.*

–That's right. A brilliant man, Tony. Brilliant. I *still* miss him each and every day.

–Rest in peace... Another idea is to lie.

–What? How do you mean?

–Like we get someone to play you. An out-of-work actor.

–Why would we do that?

–Well, it could be rather funny. I mean, just on the telephone, of course. Everyone knows what you look like. Even though most of them have never heard your voice.

–You mean to like feed them some bullshit information?

–To, in a sense, *instrumentalize* the media, to use a rather academic term. Could employ some tricks to make this nucleite deal go quicker, if you know what I mean.

–I don't want to talk about nucleite right now. Now I'm horny about the plane. You think we can get it?

–It sounded like it's already a done deal. They're so desperate.

–Can you imagine? Never having to charter again?

–The question is whether we'll like it. The plane, I mean.

–Everyone else has one. Gates got one. Walls has two. It's embarrassing that I don't have one yet.

–Even Hall has one. Though I don't believe his is a 727.

–Hall's don't count. That's some dinky single engine piece of shit.

–I thought Hall and Walls had the same model as Gates.

–No. You're confused.

–Mrdok, before I forget, let us return to the empty space.

–... What?!

–You know, the map you showed me. The mysterious gap.

–Oh yeah. The space of nothingness. With my name all over it.

–Precisely.

–That's what we do, Gordo. We look for holes. And then we fill em.

Mrdok grabbed his bulge and shook it.

–Yessir. The... hole. The circle. Or more like a, slice of, sludge, really. Sludge slice. Outside the city.

–Got my name written all over it.

–Precisely.

–Mrdok's hole.

Pfffffr*p*.

–Crispy.

–That one had a nice pop on the end, didn't it.

–Ahahaha—But the hole... I mean the map hole. What you just showed me.

–For sure you don't want to see the other one right now.

–How shall we go about it? How do we wrest it out of Lallyburt's hands?

–He's gonna do it. I can tell. I mean, he has no reason not to. He's in Texas. He don't give a fuck about the rest of the country. Why should he?

–He did seem rather… skeptical of our intentions.

–Our intentions are not even worth explaining to him. He wouldn't get it. He's a daddy's boy. An oilman. He belongs to the last century. Not this one.

–Indeed, he lacks your—

–And you know what we're gonna do, Gordo? Once we get that plane, once we ink this deal with the cowboy, we're gonna celebrate. We're gonna—no, fuck Miami, we were just there. Let's go back to Cuba.

–It has been a while. And quite the celebration will be called for. I mean, an airplane *and* a new Mrdok development!

I emit a yelp as Mrdok grabs me by the back of the skull and pulls my face toward his. I can smell the remnants of the pu pu platter on his breath.

–It's not going to be a *development*, Gordo.

–Oh… sorry! Then a, uhm… extension.

Mrdok shaking his head.

–A… suburb?

Wrong again.

–A city… within… the city…

Floundering, running out of real estate vocab.

–Well, what then?

Mrdok gives his condescending grin. That grin that spells thinking so big it has yet to find the correctly sized container.

–A new city, he replies. One that bears *my* name.

PART TWO

AN ISLAND NONETHELESS

1.

WHAT A PLEASANT SURPRISE.

A pleasant surprise. For it was, at least, a surprise. A big one. And he had given it to them, all wrapped up with a pretty little bow. But as to the degree of its pleasantness—that, of course, was the less-than-sincere bit.

A pleasant surprise. Not just words to be greeted with, words that he would be surrounded by throughout his visit to this island, the world's fourth largest in geographical mass. Some call it the world's eighth continent—not because of its size, but because of its unusually vast array of flora and fauna. Ninety percent of these plant and animal species exist nowhere else, a fact that endows the place with a biospheric autonomy for the rest of the world's envy. This came about through a gradual process of geological evolution, when, 150 million years ago, the island ever so slowly commenced to break off from the super continent Gondwana, whose parts once comprised what is now Africa, Antarctica, and the Americas. Drifting off into the turquoise waters of the Indian Ocean, increasingly oblivious to the tumult and tyrants of the main lands, an overlooked sliver where nature could pursue its own course.

Walking the streets of the capital Antananarivo, the scent of simmering yam and coconut oil swimming through the parched air. Overlooked by life. Overlooked by time and space. Halfway round the world, long journey to land. Mrdok hums to himself the tune played through his headphones.

Refreshed from his midday jetlag nap (always required to sleep off the massive quantities of Valium ingested to overcome a mild fear of flying), his *pleasant surprise* host from the mining concern is eager to transport him to their local base of operations on the east coast of the island. The driver, however, is clearly running on Malagasy time: thirty minutes late, still no show. Waiting beneath the KODAK *Labo Couleurs* sign of the photo shop across from his hotel where they'd arranged to meet, Mrdok can't get his local SIM card to work for some reason, so he's said fuck it, opted to wander the stalls of a nearby market as he waits for his airport greeter to rearrive. The locals swarm past as he idles through the market at a sluggish pace, eyes behind deep black shades taking in all the barrels of spices, veggies of the deepest and purest hues of red yellow green. A single live duck sits in a basket, passively awaiting its fate, as its matriarchal caretaker sits idly by, chatting with a neighboring vendor. The faces of the people remark their mixed heritage gifted by the island's unique geographical situation, a mixture of all the settlers and long-term passersby that have deigned to leave their genetic imprint and help forge the unique ethnic legacy that is summed up in the name Madagascar. Arabic, East African, Indian, Chinese, yielding a fluctuating quotient that has further tribalized itself into some eighteen distinct ethnic affiliations. Faces that invariably turn to take in Mrdok's white one as he passes them by. That foreignness. Not many travelers make it to this corner of the globe. Even fewer, perhaps, care to.

Local color. Holding a strange orbular yellow thing in his hand, trying to gage whether it might be a squash or a bell pepper, or perhaps some mistaken genetic hybrid that had squeezed its way into existence—though most likely something completely other, a something to proclaim the exoticness of the locale. A morphing of a vegetation Mrdok has never before seen or tasted. An albino youth in an Osama bin Laden t-shirt struggles past, eyeing Mrdok with a vapid smile. Mrdok stares back at him blankly, then is startled by a tap on his shoulder. He turns around to see the face of his driver.

—*Je suis très desolé.* I am sorry, monsieur. Traffic—very bad today.

Mrdok nods and silently puts down the fruit, the vegetable, whatever it is, follows his guide through the crowd.

—You enjoy your sleep, monsieur?

Mrdok, sensing he is being spoken to, removes his headphones.

—Sleep? I slept, yes.

In truth, he hadn't—not much anyway. He'd spent most of the late morning and early afternoon on Skype with Gordo trying to sort through the messy aftermath of the Belle office's Manhattan disbursement and the removal of its digital files to some tropical locale where they might attain a nice tan that would render them unrecognizable to certain inquiring eyes attached to federal bodies. What he wound up getting was a mere thirty-minute catnap that nevertheless energized him to the degree required to move forward into the day—figuring, in the back of his unpronounced thoughts, that he might catch a few more winks on the ride over.

What he didn't anticipate is that the roads here are paved in mud and dotted with enough potholes to syncopate a journey with back-breaking regularity. It takes them a long while to make it out of town—clearly the driver wasn't fibbing about the traffic. Antananarivo streets a chaos of motorcycles, bikes, cars, rickshaws interweaving, frustrated forward by a craving for momentum but no clear path for attaining it. The seatbelts in the back of the SUV all busted to shit, and within minutes out of town, he can clearly see why, as the steel monster rages and flies over each jagged indentation.

A pleasant surprise!

Weaving through reddish brown lanes surrounded by rich tangles of overgrown forest, they reach the bloodied waters of a tributary of the Mangoky River, across which half a dozen shirtless youths attempt to direct a water buffalo. The vehicle speeds along this smooth stretch and they are quickly past it, back into the bumpity bump of the forest's air-quoted roads anew. Lanes, really: savage chopways baked into a flawed clayishness that glows golden brown beneath the midafternoon glare. Surrounding, indubitably engorged trunks of baobab, trunks that look fake, made of steel, and tall in the afternoon light, crowned with trees of trees, older than all life around them, and still bristling, brushing up against the heavens. Beneath them, women returning by foot from the capital's markets, effortlessly balancing all sorts of things on their heads—one, what appears to be the severed branches of an entire bush. Houses, huts really, roofed with husks of corn.

Finally, after a couple hours of this mean jostling that threatens to renew Mrdok's faith in the chiropractic arts, they arrive at a slash-and-burn operation in the middle of what was once forest. The workers, in their sweatstained fake Reebok and Adidas logo'd made in China t-shirts, pause with machetes still in hand to eye the new arrival. Mrdok climbs out of the vehicle, stretching his arms to the sky in an effort to untie the knotted mass that has been made of his spine. A gentleman in loosened tie and rolled-up sleeves approaches with outstretched hand.

–Nothing like the smell of burning timber, Mrdok remarks to no one in particular.

–Mister Mrdok! You've arrived! How was your journey here?

Mrdok looks at him.

–You know damn well how my journey was. You told him to take that route, didn't you?

The man laughs.

–It's true the roads around here probably aren't what you're used to.

–For one thing, they're not even roads.

–Haha, good one. We have, actually, begun to invest in infrastructure. But let's not go into too much detail on these particulars right now; I'm afraid that's above my pay grade. Our General Manager inside the plant is, uh, *craving* to make your acquaintance.

Thick tube ejaculating black sludge into concrete vat. Stuff is viscous, though without fat. What was it called by G—dry lubricant—though this you could most certainly drown in. To climb into that vat, lay beneath the tube, and let it bury you. Cystic variability. No chance you would come out a winner. Liquid nucleite up your nostrils. Plugging your ears into eternal deafness.

–Is it hot, burning? Mrdok asks, voice crisp with anxiety.

–This is actually the waste stream, Mister General Manager—Mrdok has already forgotten his name—responds. As you can see, the rock in this part of the island is black as tar. We grind it to shit, liquefy it, really. As you can see…

As he could see: demon semen leaking out of the great god Pan's prick. All the liquefied waste matter that yields no good, no value, no beneficence to the circulatory flow of the world out there, up above, and its ever vicious cycle of need. And the sound—a hollow thrush that reverberates all around. Shout through the mask to make yourself heard. For everyone here—save for a couple of workers who, the Mister informs Mrdok, have willingly chosen to go without.

–I don't know, says the Mister with a shrug, some of them just don't like the mask. Say it suffocates em. Others claim it interferes with their work.

–Imagine that.

Mrdok had witnessed a similar lazy indifference to occupational hazards in certain mines he had site-visited in West Africa. Though here, he was a bit more willing to buy the sincerity of the Mister's assertion, given that there did indeed seem to be a generous supply of available safety equipment spotted on the way in, and not merely a pile haphazardly assembled for the benefit of the afternoon guest's surprise appearance.

–Must be boiling hot, Mrdok continues to probe, with regard to the sludge.

–Looks a bit like coal, doesn't it? responds the mister by way of agreement.

–I'm impressed. When I think nucleite… Somehow I thought it'd all be done by hand.

–There is a crude way of extracting it. That's how it started actually. Some enterprising locals. Y'know how it works. Yokel with a pickaxe comes along. Not much else to do round here, might as well waste time, play in the dirt. *Hey, what have we here?*

–So you set up shop.

–With our machines, we can get the high grade stuff. I'm talking, three hundred fifty feet down there in the earth.

–The earth's bowels.

–This is what you get.

–What's the concentrate?

–We regrind and float. Regrind and float. Seven times over.

–These pipes ever stop excreting?

–It's part of the process. Purification. Nice and sweet.

–Then, back down into the earth.

–Once we've liberated the good stuff, of course.

–How good we talking?

–Eighty to eighty-five percent carbon, on the whole.

–Really? *All* of it?

–Good ol' Madagassy. You try the zebu yet?

–The what?

2.

A MYSTERY OF isolation. The name lemur means spirits of the dead. Everything here has evolved in its own way. Take the lemur. Almost a hundred different kinds, and all here.

These ring-tailed ones live in the mountains. A troupe of them congregates here, beneath the morning sun. Thick gray coats, raccoon eyes, black-and-white striped tails. Staring up into the light, knowing no diffidence. Open their arms to the sun, white bellies absorb those rays. Sunbathing after a night spent huddled in some freezing crevice, only their thick coats and each other's warmth. Love the sun so much, want to eat it. Birds tweet. Bite on a cactus to get some moisture. Later, eat some dirt. Helps with digestion, parasites. High up enough that nobody bothers em. The ideal spot in which to be a lemur, some might argue. You are a bit exposed up here. Sometimes a buzzard swoops down, carries one off. But as soon as one of the troupe senses the thwap of those wings, 'll start shrieking—that crude monkeyish lemur bark alerts his clan. Wa wa wa wa. Jump real far, from one mountain crag to the next. They've got the sky to compete with. The southernest sun. Freezing at night here in the mountainlands, so hot during the day. Buzzard flies right through it, that punishment sun, but won't land today. Off into the smoke, the fog of morn. The lemurs too fast for an early morning breakfast demise.

Run away, lemur, the other side of time. Mountains don't erode. Forests do. Some of your brothers and sisters out there won't have a home much longer. Farmers moving higher. The forest groans, the trees shriek.

Scream at the buzzard as she flies away. You dirty fucker. Ringtailed lemurs as suited to life on the ground as in the trees. The most adaptable of your genus. Some might say. Others can eat cyanide. Lovin the highlands. The smoke, fog. Take shelter in those trees. The morning fog condenses on the leaves, lick it off to quench your thirst. Ringtail like a question mark behind you as you walk along the rock, pause to scratch your head with your back foot. Goddamn crows over there need to get away, daddy lemur scare them off cos here comes mama with babes on her back. Twins, they grab on to mama as she leans over the water deposit alongside the other mothers, laps it up with elongated tongue. Twin mother retreats to a nice spot in the sun, babies finish milking and hop off, wrestle each other before joining the other lemur babes in their kittenlike games.

Later in the day, hopping along the broken landscape. Best rock climbers in eastern Madagascar, it's like they're floating. These crags their sphere, they have memorized entire mountains. Trees surrounding. Boys go on high for the canopy fruits. Twin mother stays low, goes for the fresh leaves. Carrying two a bigger burden, doesn't want one to drop off, splat on the mountain below.

Now for the soil. After the crunch of those leaves, some flavorless roughness to smooth the inner ride. Babies dive in too, their little noses deep in the dirt. Feels so good, the earth down your snout, lining the stomach walls.

A day through which to dance. It's an easy life, so much stuff to eat up here. But they're marooned and in danger, they don't even know. Some hunt them for the taste; others destroy them in less obvious ways, making it difficult for them to exist in this terrain—not just the one they prefer, the only one they recognize.

Buzzard swoops down and carries a squawking lemur off. That lemur was your friend and now you will never see it again. Who knows where the buzzard will take it? Into its beak to die. Buzzards have no feelings, no social life like the lemurs do. The buzzard just wants to eat. Needs to eat and survive. That's all. Lemurs got community. They like to socialize on the mountainside each morning, frying beside each other in the morning sun. A sort of communal cleansing by light, natural. One less furred body to keep you warm at night when you're huddled up sleeping. These goddamn birds—crows, buzzards. Cos the crows'll go for the babies if they're left alone. Baby always sticks beside mother, mother can't be too far. The fathers only have their chance once a year—the only time the lemur likes to breed. They'll leave their signs behind on the trees for the boys to scent, that's when they get the signal. Once, maybe twice a year, that's all. Much more important things to do than making babies. A question mark in the sun.

Trees're money. They cut em down to make it. Of course it's illegal, but what can you do. Human desperation knows no law. The tree that the lemur lives in, all fall down. No more trees surrounding. No more squawk to warn of the encroaching birds. Why not knock those birds out of the sky the lemur asks. But he gets no answer. Very few speak the lemur's language. Even fewer, it seems, want to learn.

The adults, too, they love to play. Love to groom. The sun a gift of the gods each morn. It enables us to dry out, to absorb. Feeds the things we like best to munch on. The trees that know us better than the birds we may chase away. They might know how we taste, but we can outsmart em at any time. We just need one more chance. A chance to jump across the sun. Across the mountain. Question marks floating higher and higher.

3.

GRIND GRIND GRIND. The refinery. Or wherever. Place where magic gets made.

—You really want a piece of all this? This filth?

The Mister is joshing. All elbows now, and buddy-buddy. Though behind that, hidden blade that makes itself felt. Perhaps the blade of a pickaxe; Mister here's the opening act.

—I'm just a shareholder on vacation, says Mrdok. Thought I'd stop in for a tour.

Transparently disingenuous bullshit. Mrdok doesn't care. A shoot of the breeze. The breeze above the shit. The blackish diarrhea. Bullshit corporate hazing ritual. Save the real lovey-dovey convo for the suits over dinner.

4.

RIVER BLOOD RED. SHIRTLESS boys crossing the cattle, horned heads ducking up over water's horizon. On the banks, farmer ladies stooped over, planting, hats shading faces from the sun. Nothing belongs to anyone here. It is all nature's feast, soon to be forgotten. Riverside market beneath the shadow of some trees. Fish strung up on a line for sale or barter. Boy backflips into the redwaters. Corn, pistachio nuts, shrimp. Get what you can, while it is lasting. Childhood fears come undone so fast, drink your way through this absence. Red river red river, where all ye crabs crawl, be my home, be my home.

Ducks quack at the woman with no lips, arriving in the back of a rickshaw being run by her brother-in-law. Hops out, dressed prim for the market, with a whole house behind her to feed. Get to those ducks before the other hatted women. Engorged baobab pink the day's failing light—one last chance to fish for a bite.

From the shores of a beach, the waters of the Indian Ocean pale green. Adolescent fishing party wades its way into this liquid, six pairs of little hands gripping a meter-wide net. A circle in the fish-filled waters formed, this hour of feeding. Splash their hands around to scare little fishies into net, which they close ever so slowly, a deceptive death grip. Jump splashing, kids screaming their excitement out in rhythmic yelps while older siblings bark their commands on down. Little sister holds a bucket that the bunch'll get stuffed in—enough to feed the entire village this night.

5.

–WHAT ARE THOSE little furry fucks called?

The creature stares at him with the widest of deerdumb gazes, curlicue tail question marked behind as it strengthens its clutch upon the tree.

–That, says the Suit, is Madagascar's most famous specimen: the lemur.

–Really? You eat those things?

The Suit laughs.

–Some people do. But it's not on tonight's menu, I can assure you.

Mrdok's only asked because of where they're at, a glass-encased box in the middle of the forest that is the company's private restaurant. A great idea, Mrdok has to admit—observe the green wonders of your surroundings without wasting a fret on their malarial contents. Such concerns don't usually bode well for the digestion process.

–What else you got here? No apes, I hope.

–Haha. No. No apes in Madagascar. Not for many years, at least.

–Good. I hate apes.

Wine sucked up. The jungle. Wild nature. Mrdok could get used to this. Why not?

–Of course during the rainy season, it's a whole other picture, I can assure you.

–You have to quit mining then?

The Suit laughs for an uncomfortably prolonged spell before spitting out an *of course not.*

The lemur watches. All this fucking blanket cordiality. When what he really wants to get to the bottom of is Mrdok's will. His intentions. His naked greed. The brazenness of this man, showing up on the scene like this, unannounced. Still, timing is everything. Here comes more wine.

–I'll try the red this time. Thanks.

–Your shares climbed six percent today.

–You think this is news to me?

–Mister MacAfee told me you were having problems with your phone earlier.

–That's all fixed now.

–With this market, they'll be at eight by the end of the week.

–You reckon?

–Come on, Mister Mrdok…

–Just Mrdok is fine. No mister necessary. We're partners now.

–Well, *partners,* I mean… Haha… That's quite a strong word…

–You're nervous because you don't know who I am. What I'm up to. All kinds of speculation swilling around in your mind right now.

–Well, uh, it's not that, precisely…

–You're thinking, What is this fucking guy doing with our company? With *my* company? Cos, for all I know, you probably think of it more in proprietary terms. And, I mean, you should. You developed this all on your own. Moved in here minutes after the first illiterate migrant farmer struck black gold.

Mrdok stabs at his meat with the fork.

–I *have* been in Madagascar for many years now, if what you're implying—

–No need to be modest. I've read up on you. Well, I mean, I don't read, but I've had my associates read up for me.

–Very reliable associates.

–I mean, I'm just a guy who happens to like nucleite a whole lot.

–Is that so?

–Mmm hmm. The fucking jungle, too. All this apeless muck. This is some tasty shit here, by the way. So… Tell me what the future holds.

–Well, two things, really: infrastructure and expansion.

–Right.

–Infrastructure comes first, of course. We need to continue to produce the kind of output you witnessed today. That means modernizing—

–The roads to start with.

–Well…

–I'd imagine… I'd *hope.*

–Yes, the whole area. It requires investment capital, it is true. But more than anything, it's an issue of *time.* For the workforce here…

–They're running on Malagasy time.

–Precisely.

–How to speed up the clock.

–In case you have some magic solution in mind for that one, I'm all ears.

–Tell me about expansion.

The suit produces a brochure from his inner pocket, hands it to Mrdok. *A CAUSE FOR MUCH EXCITEMENT* reads the front cover in an embarrassingly bubbly font. Mrdok takes one look at the brochure then tosses it on the table between them without deigning to open it up.

–I'm sorry. Do I have the word *idiot* branded across my forehead in big letters?

Staring lemur squawks a wordless answer. Maybe it's the wine starting to take effect. The humidity. The jet lag. Likely, some toxic combo of the three. Whatever it is, formality falls to the wayside as Mrdok no longer feels the need to mask his agitation.

The Suit makes a mental note to fire the copywriter as he wipes his fingertips on the cloth napkin.

–I apologize, Mrdok. This is simply the prospectus we like to show *all* our potential investors.

–Too bad for them. I don't like to read. And I'm *not* a potential. I'm already in the game, baby. You!—*to the Bow tie*—more wine.

–At this facility, we're currently mining twenty-four thousand tons per annum…

Fluster. Buster.

–Right. And what happens when that runs out? Where's the sequel happening? Or is there even one in the works? Outside of your gay little brochure, I mean.

–We have our eyes on a piece of land in the southeasterly region. Bluster-fluster?

–Yeah? And what's the yield like down there?

The Suit laughs.

–It's not all about nucleite here. You do know that, don't you, Mrdok?

–No.

–Well it's not.

–What are we talking about then? Lithium?

–We are, in fact, pursuing lithium. Already started. I don't mean to tantalize you too much, Mrdok, but you're not going to find better lithium reserves anywhere else than this magic little island. But then there's something else. Something even more precious than lithium.

–I'm listening.

–A magic substance called ilmenite.

–Ah. The white stuff.

–You're familiar with ilmenite, I take it?

–Sure. Toothpaste. Sunscreen. Gives everything a nice white sheen.

–Precisely. The illusion of purity!

–Oh yes. Consumers love it. The whiter, the better.

–Screams: buy me, buy me!

–Where exactly does it come from? It's in the rainforest here?

–Haha, no. Ilmenite is found in the sand. There're huge quantities of it, ripe for the taking.

–What's your relationship with the locals like?

–The locals?

–I mean the ones who pretend to hold power. The government.

–Very good, in fact.

–How good?

–They own twenty percent.

–Did you just say twenty?! You've gotta be fucking kidding me. The World Bank in on this?

–We definitely have their support. Their contribution to the negotiations and the initial investment capital has been, let us say, a big help.

–Who you selling to?

–The black stuff or the white stuff?

–White stuff.

–China, mostly.

–Figures.

–And, Mrdok? Do you like ilmenite as much as you like nucleite?

–Black and white happen to be my two favorite colors.

Dessert is brought to the table, a yellowish sludge in tiny ornate dishes of gold-rimmed china. Sprig of something green on top. That reminds Mrdok.

–That yellowish vegetable they got here… I saw one today, in the market. Never seen anything like it before. What the hell is that?

–A yellow vegetable? repeats the Suit, spooning the glop.

Mrdok tries to describe the shape of the thing, but his brain is skewered with the bottle and a half he has already imbibed, and so he reverts to replicating the form with his hands.

–That must be an ambarella that you're describing. And a misshapen one, at that. It's not a vegetable. It's a fruit.

–Am…

–Ambarella. June plum, they also call it.

–June…

–Plum. June plum. A true Malagasy delight. You must try it.

6.

BUZZ BUZZ.

—Hey babe.

—Mrdok what the—Where the fuck are you Mrdok? I've been calling—

—My phone barely works in this shithole country.

—Oh Mrdok. Are you back in Monaco?

—Madagascar.

—… What?

—I've got business here. It's a long story.

—Well, anyway, it's Jaco. He was in the hospital today.

—He… What the fuck, Mrtol?

—I got a call from the school…

—Is he okay?

—The nuns at school called. They took him to the emergency room at Saint Anne's.

—Saint Anne's? Why that shithole? Why not the Mayo Clinic?

—He ate paint, Mrdok.

—What?

—It was in art class… It was mauve. Acrylic. Mrdok…

—Who the fuck gave him paint to eat, Mrtol? Which one of those lesbian cunts?

—Now Mrdok, is that any way to talk about the sisters of god who are instructing our son?

—You call that headmistress right now and tell them I will *destroy* them—

—Mrdok, don't you even care what happened to your son?

—Yes, I… Tell me what happened to him.

—They pumped his stomach. As soon as I saw it I knew. It couldn't have just been mauve. It was *glittering*. There must at least have been some silver, maybe something copper, in there. It was *a lot*, Mrdok. A lot of paint.

—Why the fuck did he eat paint?

—It was a bet with Ellen. Something. I don't know, Mrdok.

—What the… I told you, Mrtol, the kid needs to see someone—

—They ran blood tests. There was no lead poisoning.

—So he's okay, then?

—Mrdok, I told Gordo to call you. Why didn't he call you, Mrdok?

–I've been—I've had reception issues this whole trip, Mrtol. Is he okay?

–Yes, he's fine. He's home now. I'd put him on the line, but he's in bed already, I don't want to wake him.

–Goddamn nuns.

–Mrdok! You know I'm Catholic.

–I never wanted him going to that school. I told you from the beginning. I never trusted them. They fuck kids up, Mrtol.

–Mrdok. We all of us in my family went to Catholic school.

–Yeah. And you're all equally fucked up.

–Excuse me. *We're* fucked up?

Dreary spiritual matters again. Mrdok mouths the words *why me?* Takes another sip of the room service champagne. Crass.

–You really believe in heaven and hell, all that shit? he suddenly asks her, genuinely curious.

–Yeah, she says, I do. So what?

–It's just… We just never discussed it in all that much detail, is all.

–Well, it's not the sort of topic we get on that often, is it?

–You know what I think, Mrtol?

–No. What.

–I think it's all a bunch of BS.

–What is.

–God. The devil. Heaven. Hell. Limbo. Whatever the fuck.

–Well. I can't say I'm too surprised.

–Does that make you a bad Catholic? Being married to a man like me?

–It makes *you* a bad Catholic.

–But I just told you. I'm not a Catholic at all.

–It just means you're going to hell, Mrdok.

–Well, sounds like it'll be a great party.

–Look at the way you live your life, Mrdok.

–I think I'm doin just fine. You don't seem to mind. You're not set up so bad yourself, you know.

–I'm not talking about material things. Give some thought to your soul for once.

–My soul.

–Yeah.

–See, the thing is, I mean, the soul? Where exactly is it, Mrtol?

–Where is… Where is your soul or where is my soul?

–Either. I mean: Where in the human body does the soul reside?

–… What are you talking about, Mrdok?

–I mean, doctors, scientists of, like, anatomy and shit, they cut up bodies, don't they? How come they never once found a soul in any of those bodies? I'll tell you why, Mrtol. It's cos it's not there.

–What time is it over there, Mrdok?

–Late. Middle of the night.

–And you're still up?

–Can't get to sleep.

–You said you were in—

–Madagascar. You even know where that is? It's an African country, Mrtol.

–When you coming back? You haven't seen us in… what's it been, three weeks going on now.

–I've been busy.

–So what. You gonna stay a month in Madagascar.

He flips the TV on then abruptly off again.

–I'm definitely not sayin that. I'm back in Manhattan again, what is it, day after tomorrow.

–Well, thank god for that. You need to see your son.

–The paint-eater.

–Yeah. The paint-eater. Who could've died, Mrdok, if the nuns hadn't seen it and saved him. And we need to talk. About the other one.

–Oh right. We haven't spoken since you came back from LA. How was that?

–What do you want me to say?

–You see Krstal? How's she lookin these days?

–Like a whore, Mrdok. Like the fucking whore she always was. You want me to sugar coat things for you like Gordo does? You know I won't do that, Mrdok. I always tell you the truth. And it isn't good.

–Bobby.

–Smacked out of his brain.

–Oh lord. Again?

–That's right. It's moments like these we really do need the Lord. Because it's a desperate situation.

–Jesus, Mrtol, lay off it.

–He's been in rehab now how many times already? He's done the methadone cure, the Subutex cure. None of it's working, Mrd. We're running out of options. The kid is all alone out there on that shitty little island. Krstal doesn't see him, refuses to. I don't see it ending well. No happy ending in the works here.

–Did you give him the money?

—Jesus, Mrdok. Is that all you care about? What's that gonna do? Yes, I gave it to him, Mrdok. But he's just gonna use it to get high. That's all he's doing these days. Dopin and mopin. The I Hate Dad thing.

—You're confusing him with the other one. Anyway, he's just mad that I got remarried. Don't take it personal.

—Oh, I think it might be a tad more complicated than that.

—Whatever, Bev. I've gotta go.

—Wait. What is it you just called me?

—Mrtol, I need to—

—No no no, you just called me Bev. I heard it, Elias.

—Let me go.

—You need to let that *slut* go. Is that what this trip is about? She there with you right now in the hotel?

—Goodbye, Mrtol. I'll see you back in New York.

—Goddamnit Mrdok, don't you hang up on me—

Click.

7.

NEXT MORNING, THE puke gray dawn. Struck him with a thought:

Where there's fear, there's possibility. Something Tony Fatballs once said that always stuck with him. That has motivated, really, a lot of his investment activity, wily and otherwise, throughout the years. Right? That nasal weasel, voice echoing in the membranes of memory. *Listen here, kid...*

To see himself in the most unexpected locales. Places where no one he knows goes, who knew him previously, so that means no one. Who could ever picture this. Walking down the street here in Tana (for that is how the locals refer to their capital, he has learned), the noise of the streets, the incomprehensible gibberish. The sizzle, the sleaze. He can feel danger resounding with each step. At the mine yesterday, as well.

Fear equals possibility. Possibility means *take action.* Unstick your ass cheeks from that fake leather sofa. Action required. Something violent's gonna jeppen. He felt it even before he could articulate it to himself. As one always does. When that *one* happens to be him.

To be scared. That, in a word, is what excites him the most. Where there's fear, there is a gap to be filled. Opportunity. Money. Slash and burn. Take it and run. Though it is not, in the end, so much about the money, the quick fix, as it is the megalith. All the emotions surrounding in the moment of exchange, of attainment—that swirl.

The island of magic substance. Magic substance and flexible purpose. Substance black and white, beneath the glowing redbrown, ripe for the taking. Mountain forests haunted by lemurs, those bright eyes keeping watch over their own steady extinction as the precious filth holding the trees they grasp on to is dug up and violently decimated. The grounds giving this place its juicy dimensionality. A flavorful filth you can truly lick. It doesn't take long for Mrdok to read a place—to latch on to that innate magic that spells brilliant opportunity. The chance to re-make a sliver of the world, to cast your image across a highly localized stream. Last night at dinner, the suit had showed him a 10,000 note of the local currency. Worthless shit, despite its high denomination—inflation in these shithole countries always renders the paper more valuable than the worth it is purported to hold, something better employed wiping your ass or blowing a wad of snot into. But the point is, the image on that 10,000 note. Is of mining trucks in a desolate treeless landscape. The Suit found this hilarious, couldn't keep snorting over it as he presented one for Mrdok's inspection. Meant, of course, to entice Mrdok. The implication being: where the government goes so far as to *publicize* its own corruption, surely an investment in such a locale is a safe and winning proposition.

But Mrdok had another take on that note. The Suit's implied conclusion to the message was far too simple. He didn't perceive the inherent vulnerabilities announced by that image. He was right that it wasn't intended for domestic consumption. The government's crass disregard for its own citizens was hardly shocking: it was the same crass disregard virtually every government in the world over has for its own peoples, the difference being that in these shithole countries, they feel a little less wary about broadcasting those sentiments. Obviously, the suit has never been anywhere but here and Belgium, or whatever Eurotrash outlet it was he said he came from. What kind of investor was too dim to perceive the redhot FOR SALE sign flashing across that 10K bill?

… Or did he know something Mrdok didn't know?

Likely. And for certain, he'd never share. But Mrdok has other means for attaining those golden nuggets.

He plucks the phone off his nightstand.

8.

–SO THE COPS are busting a brothel, Mrdok is saying to the Suits the next day. They've got all the whores lined up outside. A little old lady comes walking along, I mean she's old as fuck, all her teeth have fallen out, she says to one of the whores, *Whatsch goin on here?* The whore says to her, *Ah, don't worry about it, lady. They're just, uh, giving out free candy. Yeah, that's it! Free candy…* So the old lady gets in line! The cops're movin down the line, askin everyone for IDs. They get to the old granny. One of em says to her, *Excuse me, ma'am, but aren't you a little old for this?* She looks right back at him all indignant. *Well, I can schtill schuck on em, can't I?*

Oh Mrdok, what a wit! The Suits all in stitches, loosened up. Then, a rapid-fire switch. The sewage of his brain hardens into a rock. He hurls it at their faces in a sock!

–You've cleared, what, three mines in the last month, if I'm not mistaken?

Laughter evaporates. A fine rainforest mist.

When no one reaches in to fill the silence, Mrdok takes aim anew.

–We're on an island, aren't we?

–Madagascar is one of the world's largest—

–But an island nonetheless.

Mordant-pathologist-into-the-mindways Mrdok. Know your destination to make the arriving all the more supple. A dream inheritance: this joy in destructing the ivory wall, hammering at the besmirchments to presage the Whole's final debasement.

–Remember last night's dinner through your hungover haze? Cos I do. (I also drank twice as much as you did. But that's another story.) You tried to lure me in with lithium, ilmenite…

–*Lure* is a rather strong verb here—

–No it aint. Cos I know exactly what your game plan is here. You're not operating in some solitary, disconnected sphere. You're part of an oligopoly. Or at least you want to paint yourself that way. It's all rather textbook, I'm afraid.

–Okay, Mrdok. Enough of the economics lecture. I think we've been perfectly hospitable to you since you've arrived here, despite some pretty objectionable behavior on your part. Now level with me: What do you plan on doing with your shares?

Mrdok stifling a theatrical laugh.

–This was an impulse buy for me, alright? And the thing about my impulses is, they almost never turn out to be wrong. In this case, well. I'm fearing it may be one of the exceptions. And when those exceptions *do* arise, it's usually cos there's an awful lot of fish in the pond. In fact, too many.

–Bullshit.

–For one thing, you're not working with the right materials. You might've thought you were in the beginning. But it takes time to learn from our mistakes. There's something a little off in the refinement process, right? Well, more than a little off. I couldn't quite put my finger on what that might be, so I had my guy in Hong Kong check you guys out. Turns out you're not yielding the sort of high concentrate sludge the Chinese are really going for—and can get for much cheaper from half a world away, in South America. They're canceling orders left and right. Where does that leave you? To play the distraction game with your investors while you locate your asses. What I've sampled here is just a tiny dose of the flagrant filth you're flapping, and let me tell you, I know toxicity when I taste it.

–Careful.

–Let me finish… Cos your moves are so much more obvious than you even realize, I feel like I'm doing you a huge service by spelling them out for you.

Now you're trying to turn your investors' gaze away from your failing nucleite operation by starting in on lithium. What the fuck, man? I mean, desperation wears many guises—we all know that. But the lithium you're gonna get out of this stinkhole aint gonna be worth a pig's ass in a kosher butchery.

–You don't know what you're talking about. And I'm Jewish, by the way.

–And the government knows it, too. That 10K note you showed me last night? That you thought was so hilarious? With the dump trucks and the mining shit all over it? The joke's on you, bub. They're up there in Antananarivo right now laughing their asses off.

–Look, you…

–There are no brine deposits here. Chile, Argentina, that's where the good lithium comes from. The good shit requires the evaporation of highly concentrated brine. You're playing a smoke-and-mirrors game with your investors. And I have a right to know this. After all, I'm one of them.

–You're out of line, sir.

–And I'm not even gonna start in on the fantasy fart you fed me about ilmenite. Cos we both know that aint happening. I'm guessing you have all sorts of dirty tricks you're trying out, mulling over to try and fix your faulty product up. But there's no outsmarting the

Chinese, who, after all, are kings of the con. Sooner or later, your little popsicle-stick mansion is gonna come splintering down.

The Head Suit takes out an electronic cigarette and takes a long suck on it. The vapor from his mouth a snake that disappears as it unfurls.

–So I'll tell you what I'm gonna do. Because I wanna get out of this floating shithole before it gives me—or my money—AIDS. I'm gonna lay out the terms for what I like to call a soft fuck. Just as the name suggests, it's gonna feel real good for me, and only hurt you a teeny bit. You dig?

(To bend desirous before any mention of freedom: this wasn't in Mister Suit's choreographic repertoire. But then, the commands spewing forth from the Mrdokian gorge before him were coming at such a rapacious flow, the droplets would have been absorbed or else fallen between the cracks of his fingers had he raised a hand to try and catch them at this most unfortunate moment. Little more could he do than don his best poker face and assume the passive position while the lone wolf lapped at the door.)

–I'm a numbers man, the Suit finally interrupts after a particularly lengthy chain of insults. Why don't you just spit it out what it is exactly you want from me and we'll go from there?

Mrdok concurs, pronouncing a ten-digit figure with a spitting emphasis on the *b* consonant.

The Suit laughs, then quickly handkerchiefs away a bead of sweat that has suddenly manifested upon his baldness.

–Now don't get scared. What I'm giving you is an options agreement. What you'll get in return? The best motherfucking janitorial service ever fathomed in the history of this cunting world, Mister See Ee Oh. You know my precious metals list, don't you?

Indeed, every Suit west and east north and south of here did. Everyone subscribed who could. But only the worthiest of blue-chippers managed to score a subscription. An open secret in the world of high-end traders. Mrdok's e-newsletter, the ingenious concoction of a team of lawyers and PR folk and the requisite economist hack, offers weekly tips and articles, and is regarded as the Next Best Thing to illicit insiderdom in the biggest and baddest of games.

–Options? asks the Suit wearily.

–To buy back my shares, Mrdok answers. At their current price, of course. Cos frankly, after the hospitality I've received on this visit, I've begun to regret my investment. But since I'm such a nice guy, I'm not gonna cause you any chaos. I aint gonna just dump em. I mean, I could. But what would be in it for me?

My team'll decide on the timeline once I get back to civilization. But I'm gonna guesstimate it at three months. That's all I need, more or less. We'll have a contract. Encrypted, naturally. Unscreenshotable. My tech guys'll take care of it. You won't be able to share it with anyone, and it'll be built to disintegrate on the day it expires and the shares revert back to you. In the meantime, you're gonna be the most hyped precious metals biz on the globe, my friend. Ha. I bet we'll even have your Chinese friends fooled for a minute or three. Might see some of those canceled orders coming back in. Yeah. Three months. I like the sound of it, don't you? Odd numbers're a sort of superstition of mine.

Mrdok picks up his phone, texts the word *NOW* to his driver.

—In short, I'm gonna save your ass—enrich it, even—rather than bury it. Though if you'd prefer the latter to happen, I can't do that personally. Instead, I'll call my press people, splash some headlines around, sit back and watch your investors pick up their shovels. If the regulators don't get out here first... Really, it's your decision. I mean, no pressure.

The Boss, rendered inarticulate by this dissection. Be very careful what you do with arms and hands in such delicate binds. They can inadvertently give away much more than mere acquiescence; the soul is also at risk. Just ask one Herr Doktor Faust.

But Mrdok is no petty demon crawled up from the underworld. His joviality proves he is genuine!

Slapping the Suit upon the shoulder.

—*I can schtill schuck on em, can't I?*

But the Suit's no longer laughing.

9.

ON THE BANKS, straw-hatted women bend over the soil, planting. A pleasant surprise. A ride to the airport on sudden bump-free terrain. Must be a new road. Mrdok's back says thank you, Mister Driver.

Suddenly, he remembers something. Barks out an order. A market. Any market.

Tin-roofed open air, the one they arrive at. Not the choicest specimen, in the way that Antananarivo markets go. But authentic—in that Mrdok feels himself to be the sole foreigner upon its grounds. Makes his way past a stall packed with hundreds of bananas, the merchant's sole product. Wholesaler. Choice selection of food wares.

Including that thing from the other day, what's it called again? Driver follows close behind, nervous. They've got a schedule to keep, and the ax'll undoubtedly fall on him if the white man misses his flight.

—What you looking for, monsieur? Maybe I ask—

—Anything like ceramics? Clothes? Jewelry? Something my wife would like, you know. Only it has to be local—nothing Chinese.

—Local?

—Yeah, like, uh… Some kind of local specialty. Like… Madagascar vanilla! Isn't that a thing?

The driver politely conceals a smirk.

—No, monsieur. This is not real. It is, how should I say… A thing for the tourists.

The driver says something to a knife merchant in the local language. Mrdok runs his index finger lightly over a blade. The good hand.

Mrdok can feel the guy behind him even before he opens his mouth to speak.

—You speak English, right?

Mrdok daren't turn around.

—That was a lucky guess.

Figuring he's about to get the hard sell, Mrdok turns around to display a deranged smile and the knife in his hand.

A near-wizened face behind an unkempt beard, graying past middle age into tribal elder character actor, Mrdok concludes hastily.

—You were in the forest yesterday. The nucleite mines.

Mrdok twirls the knife in his fingers, never taking his eyes off the blade.

—Deep in the lemur-haunting mountains of Madagascar, Mrdok intones, you find nucleite, it is true. All kinds of minerals, in fact…

—Metals, minerals. Yes. We have everything here, it is true. What we don't have a lot of is time.

—Oh yeah? What a coincidence. Me too!

The driver interrupts.

—Monsieur, I think I know where we can find—

—You mind if I tag along? the stranger asks. I will only take a minute.

—I barely have a minute to spare.

—That company you are doing business with, he says. Do you know they're destroying us?

—Yes. I might've noticed.

—I used to be a farmer. That land they're on. I was forced off it. Yes, they paid me something. But what they paid me, it is, how you say, crap compared to what they are now earning. Paid me and relocated me. You know where they relocate me? I cannot farm there. The soil is exhausted. Has been for many years. I have no choice now. I cannot make a living no more, doing the only thing I know how to do. So what I do? I go back to my land. Where the mine now is. I hang around. I watch and I see. And I think. I talk to the foreigners who come. Men like you. Interested in my country, in all its *great riches*. Men like you. Who come to destroy. You take and you take. You do nothing to help the people out.

–That's not my role here. I haven't taken anything. And I'm leaving now.

–What is your role then? You think only of yourself, don't you. What you can get from this. This ground beneath our feet. Tell me, why you want to work with these monsters?

–Haha. Truth is, I don't. I don't wanna work with anyone.

–Then what you doing here in Madagascar, monsieur.

–Why don't you tell me who you are? I think I've told you enough.

–My name Simon.

–Simon?

–From the Bible. An apostle. I live here. I from here.

–I figured.

–I watch my country—beautiful land—go to waste. First the logging, now the mines. You get that? First above ground, then under the ground. What will they take next from us? Destroy our waters? Our sky?

–I'm sure if someone can figure out a way, then yes.

–All I ask you, monsieur, is for your small help. Justa one thing.

Here it comes. Over the years, Mrdok has engineered a unique skill set through which to avert the sort of risks that your average investor must weather on an hourly, minutely basis. In short, his master tactic can be summed up in a single word: slipperiness.

–So what is it? Mrdok asks.

–Leave Madagascar, Simon says.

Mrdok laughs, thinking it must be a joke.

–That's it? That's all?

–Leave here. Don't come back. Don't remember us, even. Don't do any business with those men you saw yesterday. They are evil. And if you do do business with them, I tell you one thing: it will blacken your soul.

Mrdok in his whimsical silence, pauses in the market as the hordes swarm past. Considers. Then starts to remove his wallet from his inner pocket. Simon stops him.

—Nonono. I no want your money.

Then, just as quickly as he appeared, Simon evaporates into the human flow.

Throw all your doubts their way, see what they come up with. As the old lawyer man used to say. One of any number of impenetrables he used to like to fling Mrdok's way, back when he was still alive. Full of life, he was—maybe *alive* isn't—wasn't—good enough in its me-reness.

He would still have to wait and see what they would come up with. But Simon needn't worry. Mrdok isn't worried either. Mrdok is going to do much more than merely leave them alone to stew in their sea of black; he is going to sink the fucking ship. He has them fucked every which way. The Mrdok organization, unbeknownst to them, large enough to weather any typhoon that might brew in these tropical winds. The newsletter, through which he'd pump their stock to heights of near ridicule, was only the one enunciated element. The second, which they'll never see coming, hidden from the purview and buried beneath a morass of names, is the short sell. That's where Mrdok, already filthy in his richesses, is about to become an abomination: betting against himself. Betting on the thing he is now most certain of: Oostern Nucleite's inevitable failure. But, first, in order to fail properly, expansively, he would have to come to own it.

Yes, Simon will be fine. In a year from now, that sludge pit'll be dryer than the desert wind sweeping its way from the continent next door.

10.

—WHAT THE HELL is this thing, Mrdok?

Mrtol holds the orb out at a distance, studying it beneath the lamplight.

—Guess.

—I have no fuckin idea. That's why I'm asking you.

—It's a giant turtle egg.

—…the fuck?

—It's considered to be a major luxury item. In Madagascar, at least.

–Yeah, but what am I supposed to do with it, Mrdok? I'm not in Madagascar.

–It's meant to be for decoration. I don't know. It's like a, like a souvenir.

–I see. So I'm meant to put this tacky fuckin thing out on display.

–Yeah. I thought. You know, it could look nice if we find a nice metal or iron stand for it. It could be like a bookshelf piece. Or for the cabinet in the living room.

–A turtle egg?

–They're worth a lot of money, Mrtol. You don't know what I had to go through to find this. They're illegal to sell now. You know what that means. Very valuable.

Mrtol looks at Mrdok skeptically, then looks back at the egg.

–I hate it, she concludes.

He kisses her forehead.

–I knew you would.

SKY HIGH

—AH SHIT. MRDOK scratching himself. I fuckin love corporate America.

Said as though it were a country unto itself. Which—in this century of ours—it very much is. Save for the issuance of passports and the need for an army (though with plenty of armies at its disposal, were an old-fashioned battle ever called for), CorpAm more compelling a land, in its narrative of success and failure, as this mass marked by ever tenuous geographic borders—rivers and oceans and walls and such.

That grin far and white and wide. How could Mrdok *not* smile? These shitballs had overdone it in a way that only *real* shit knows how. Were there such a thing as *oversight* in this world—*their* world— a lengthy prison sentence would have been the obvious consequence. But not. Instead, they've landed in Mrdok Land. Or at least their plane has.

The 727, like others in its class, had been designed to cram in a couple hundred passengers. But the SunEye execs, in conspiracy with their interior designer and team of engineers, had reconfigured the passenger area to accommodate a lavish party of fifteen max— and Mrdok doubted that even that number of cowboy hats had ever been hung on the silver rack at any one stage in its possession by the Texan corporation. Wear and tear so minimal, it could pass as new. Even some vague vestige of the new plane smell, Mrdok could swear, imagination doing acrobatics behind those shades. In the commanding center, a masterwork of executive realness to stimulate the salivatory glands of every jackass from here to the Valley of Silicone who's ever donned a suit, a custom-made mahogany desk, gleaming thanks to the kiss of sun leaking in through the paneled windows, built-in silver (silver!) lamp for those sleepless round-the-globe night flights, drawers fitted with old-fashioned skeleton key locks so as to preserve the hour's business from any prying eyes that happen to have slipped on board prior to departure or post-arrival...

Mrdok, beaming through it all, repeating the word *Shitballs* over and over, beneath his breath. All the warbling stresses of late—Mrtol's seemingly aimless restlessness, the uncertainties of nucleite and Madagascar, the pit in Miami, the done deals that got done without him—suddenly evaporated in the ebulliatory gold dust of a new toy. This vibrant reminder of who he is, this phallic denial of second-bestness. Shooting off from the shallow shores.

—This thing land in water, too?

He flows back, toward the rear. You press a button on the wall, automatic door opens, a bedroom. King-size, its fit so precise—like the desk, must be custom made. Palish mood lighting, with a reading lamp Mrdok will never require. The best part: a mirrored ceiling. Makes sense, shitballs also love to fuck.

—Oh... my... lord, comes Gordo's squeal.

—What is it? You got your period?

—Come! Mrdok, look at *this!*

Goes. Okay, then the squeal is justified. Mrdok's seen a lot of things. It's the first time he's ever seen a full bathtub on a plane.

There are still other things to see. Near the cockpit, a sort of faux viewing deck has been installed, with an expanded window through which to gaze out at the blue bliss from one of two chaises lounges. Mrdok could just picture a couple of shitballs sitting there, ties loosened, chewing on their cigars, remarking on the cloudshapes. The former CEO had been an aficionado, some say addict, of the Oreo brand; next to one of the armchairs, a silver cookie dispenser extends at yawn's reach from the ceiling.

So maybe it is a bit more plane than Mrdok really needs. So what? He would be batshit crazy to walk away from this. And hey, Gordo is here at his side to remind him, this is just the thing to present to Mrtol at this rocky juncture in the marriage narrative.

Back at the midtown office, crunchy crunchy. Mrdok sitting gurulike at his desk, eyes shut, numbers flashing across the screen of his mind. Thirty million would be the brand new of the thing. All those, zero zero zero zero zero zero zero. Turn it vertical, what've you got. A tower. Dip it upside down, you've got a spoon. Taste the sweet honey, the nectar a reminder of, what? Sweet tooth vitality. Flavor of dragonfruit like, come roaring at the established world.

Mrdok a victor of the excluded. How he's always seen himself. Not a shitball. Never saw a need to wear a suit. Way too cool, too *outside* to play their game. Not that it's a corruption. Wouldn't go that far. The world is corrupt. More a transcendence of their game. Who he is, who they are. He'll show them corruption *beyond* corruption. That's what he likes to do. That sweet flavor. Flavor that can only be conjured. Has tried, at times, to describe it to various cooks. None of them can take it out of his mind, create it in life. And so there it always remains. To be conjured. Not actually tasted.

Zero zero zero zero zero zero. Cut some of those zeroes off. Give them a taste of *his* preferred sensation. No one plays a game like Mrdok. Especially in such a favorable scenario. When you can practically smell the desperation leaking out of their pores. Like the sweat that must be just pouring out of them beneath that broiling Texas sun this morning. Oh yes—weather, climatic conditions must also be taken in. Positionality, we'll call it. North and South. Not just who I am, but that which I could never be. Zero zero zero. Show them the true meaning of. The way the dirt turns up to cover their faces. It's time for a new bath. Whole other form of water...

—What is this shit? We out of Evian?

Gordo skitters over.

—This is a new experimental vegan organic water, imported from Peru. It has electrolytes meant to—

—I want some Evian. Throw this shit away.

—I—

—Shut up for a minute, will you? I'm processing.

Reclose the eyes. A shipyard. Odd—there's supposed to be a plane there. Doesn't know what else there could be. I mean, how many people are *really* in the market for a 727? He'd heard the current president, before being elected, had acquired a G4 second hand for just under eighteen. But a G4 must be, what, a quarter size of this thing. This fuck is a monster. But downplay that, of course. They're desperate. What can they say. You really got a lot of buyers knocking at your door, Louie-boy? Now about those stocks... Ha. Yeah right. Like he needs any piece of that mess. Company's already crashed; let the plane soar from its ashes, phoenix-like.

Pure odd number crystallizes in his brain. He'll come in at five. That's right. They'll be shocked, but he'll show some swagger, some aggro. They'll come quivering back. Won't take long. When they say ten, he'll have to breathe hard to hold in the laughter. Wherever it goes from there, he'll not only have a plane. He'll have a story, by which to humiliate the fuckers, the shitballs, for life. What he gets, what they get, well. It's in the law of... What do you call it again, when you deserve something. Is that fate, Gordo? Anyway, get em to deliver it. The landing strip on Long Island. They'll say ten, we'll go to eight.

(It doesn't matter. It's just a number that will never actually be paid.)

CHAPTER THREE

CUBA

1.

... A FUZZY SORT of dream that was, and now that daylight is doing its thing, waiting for the extra-strength ibuprofen to kick in, he tries to sift through, put the puzzle pieces together, but the final picture, he knows, will be splattery and abstract, as it usually is, his dreams being always an overlapping insensate mess—too many shards, fragments of fragments of substance—to cohere into anything resembling a clear narrative, let alone a sole scene any first-, second-, or third-rate shrink would ever deem interpretable. Something about a, what was it, a man he had known, in his childhood, a man he had known and sort of looked up to, he was an artist, of sorts—used to draw the ads for that indie record store, back when such a thing as indie record stores still existed, Insatiable Recs it was called, for the local alt weekly *Artful Loitering,* back when such a thing as alt weeklies still existed—but the guy had been mostly a bum, bum with a black beard, painted or dyed black, for his hair was white, somewhere in his mid-forties still living at home with mom. That contrast—black beard, white hair—it infested the patina of the whole dream, until it was, yes, he had actually *dreamed* in black-and-white. Back in his hometown—not really, for he had no real home—town where he'd spent most but not all of his adolescence, suburban coffeeshop, where the wannabes hung out alongside the tried-and-failed NYC exiles. Young Mrdok hadn't been a regular, being far too busy with more lucrative activities even at that age, but he chanced to spend a few hours there in pursuit of one young lady with boho aspirations. That's where he'd met the bearded cootz, whose name he can't even recall right now, but in the dream, for one reason or another, it was something weird and biblical, something like Zacharias. He was back on Long Island and this specter from his adolescence *Zacharias* was being treated for brain cancer, and Mrdok had somehow wound up his caretaker. That was the gist of it at least, and though there was obviously more, much more, he can't recall much other than being led to believe that in addition to the cancer, *Zacharias* was also now a paranoid schizophrenic with a propensity for verbally lashing out at the female nurses and receptionist in the doctor's office when she took too much time locating his file. The rest of the time he spent asleep on a ratty couch in some lower-middle class interior that looked like the house of any number of kids Mrdok might have grown up with, or rather, details culled from all and put together into a rather banal assemblage... and so what does it all mean?? Could it be he himself has it?? Cancer? Must get Gordo to make an appointment, get that checked out, once we get back—*if* we ever get back...

He had woken up in Havana that morning barely cognizant of where he was, how he got there. *Pan's Ashtray,* a paperback beneath his bed lamp, cracked halfway though he can hardly remember the plot, if he'd even read three lines. He realized his immediate surroundings first, since he had stayed here before in the Presidential Suite of the Hotel Nacional, and as daylight groaned through the half-shut blinds, confusion gave way to the drudgery of pre-caffeinated consciousness.

He knows he has a meeting, first thing, 9 a.m., with the Cubans downstairs on the patio. Clockwork routine of each and every visit to the Capital of the Revolución, always the same welcome wagon. Both named Renaldo—probably not their real names, probably chosen an identical moniker to make it easier for Mrdok—and themselves—to remember. Were there to *welcome* the señor back to Cuba, always presented the señor with their cards bearing the name of some fictional government tourism office, fifteen minutes or so of banter, make sure the señor has everything he needs and should he think of anything...

It was a shakedown, of a very polite sort, with a faint treble of hope in the background, a nerved aspiration that never deigned to enunciate itself, always hoping Mrdok would be the first to break through that purposely poorly built wall, the hope growing into a sort of eagerness with each visit (maybe *this* will be the time, ... finally!... Etcetera.)

Mrdok always skips the Hotel Nacional breakfast—no one comes to Cuba for the food. This morning, there's no time anyway, seeing as he's already late for his 9 a.m. appointment. Get this over with and, what? Call Gordo, the driver, a ride through the city. A walk. See what variance has been underway since—what was it? Three years ago?

Downstairs, morning sun bakes the back patio, its colonial grace. Waiters in white jackets and bow ties bustle back and forth. Midwestern tourists pick out cigars from the glass box at the bar. *Oon q-ba leebray, por favor.* In the garden, the resident male peacock spreads its feathers for a group of tourists' social media feeds. Performance finished, he closes his plumage and saunters away.

The first one rises, the second follows, as they mark his approach.

–El señor!

–Welcome back to Cuba, Mrdok!

–Renaldo and Renaldo. How'm I ever gonna tell you two apart?

–Haha, señor.

–Very funny man! Very very funny man!

As soon as their respective buttcheeks hit the plush, a waiter appears and slides three espressos across.

At the next table, Mrdok recognizes Cuba's most famous dissident artist, Cassandra Ramos, being interviewed by a visiting journalist hungry for a Cuba-is-poor-oppressive-and-dirty story.

–In Cuba, everything is intense, and you have to be intense as well—in order to compete with the reality here. Back in the '90s when I was growing up, people were losing their sight from vitamin deficiencies, their muscles were atrophying—a lot of weird stuff started happening. It was hard. But still, Cubans never lose their sense of humor. Every time there was a blackout, a certain neighbor would shout, *Viva Fidel! Viva la Revolución!*—and everyone would laugh. I was really young, but I thought, *That's how I want to work as an artist!*

–Your… plane, says Renaldo 1. It is yours?

–Ah. You noticed. New purchase. Fell into my hands.

–I see, says Renaldo 1.

–If only a plane would fall in my hands, jokes Renaldo 2, lamely.

–I thought, why not? Thanks for clearing us to land, by the way. Though I guess my pilot must've already thanked your boys at José Martí. Making all further thanks rather redundant.

–It was not the easiest thing, securing that position.

Renaldo 2 stares out at the garden landscaping pensively. Mrdok watches him, then thinks: he probably designed it himself. Just like their old driver here had been a rocket scientist.

—… but of course, the necessary corners were cut. Only for you, señor.

—We *like* you!

—Her first trip abroad. Well, at least since she's been in my hands. Maybe I should give her a Cuban name in honor. How about Valentina?

—It was just for a few hours, continues Cassandra at the next table. They took me outside the city, disrupted my life. Then they drove me back. Even with all of this, they treated me as special. In the little room, the guy from the secret police said, *Oh, we know you're renovating your house with your own money.* I said, *Great, I wish you would say that in public. Because in public, you said I was working for the CIA. So I hope that you also make a video to clean up my image, since you created all this mess.* You see, they did this video saying that I wanted to overthrow the government, that I was CIA, all this crap. The problem right now, if I look at this as an outsider, is a lot of dysfunctional methodologies. The temporality, the speed of certain things, is too slow, and they need to catch up to the alternatives that Cuban society is proposing. So the police, for example, tell me, *Oh, your head is very hard.* I say, *No, it's not that my head is hard—it's that your methods are wrong.* So there are all these clashes—even aesthetic clashes. I believe in saying everything out in the open, and they don't want me to say anything at all.

—Valentina! We like, says Renaldo 1, feigning excitement.

Renaldo 2 raises his finger and spits something out in rapid fire at the waiter, who hustles his way into the kitchen and reappears a minute later with three more espressos and a plate of cinnamon rolls, which everyone at the table promptly ignores.

—Many many times in Cuba now.

—You must really love our country.

—There is much to love here. It is true.

—Oh yes.

—I can see why—

—Keep coming back.

At a certain point, the Renaldos like to complete each other's sentences. Perhaps, muses Mrdok, they really are the same person. Siamese twins, separated by one of the island's countless doctors and bequeathed a top notch appointment at the spy agency by Fidel, gifted out of pure amazement at this walking medical marvel times two.

–I'm already defined as a C.R.—that's *counter-revolutionary*. Which is unfair, because what I'm actually trying to do is to implement the Revolution here. Cuba says to the world, *We are different from America, we can survive by understanding each other.* So I say, *Okay, let's not just* say *that to the outside world, let's actually* do *it here.* But in fact, that's not possible. They brag, *Yeah, we respect everybody's opinion.* Okay, so let's do it here. *Oh no, that's not possible.* So what I'm doing is simple, a form of aesthetic play. They claim that what they say is the total truth, so I'm going to believe it as the total truth. Let's implement it and see if it works. I think *they* are the counter-revolutionaries. Because they're the ones who want everything to remain the same… At the beginning the interrogations were more about who I was working with and whether I knew about something connected to something else. And I said no to everything. *I'm not talking.* Now, it's different. It's been very weird. The secret police even invited me for lunch— and they paid! I'm writing a text about it because it's so disturbing.

The Renaldos pretend not to hear or otherwise just don't notice Cassandra's presence right beyond their shoulders. And who knows, maybe they don't. She's someone else's target today. Place always has so many undercover cops combing the grounds, there's no point in trying to make sense of what the local clientele is doing here. Not to mention all the waiters, half of them working for the fuzz, the other half on the payroll of the Americans. Goddamn Hotel Nacional. Where, like the rest of Cuba, nothing ever changes.

–Of course, says Renaldo 2, SunEye is a very interesting company.

–We had no idea you were working with them, adds Renaldo 1.

Mrdok sips his espresso, knowing not to show surprise or any other emotion.

– Let's just say my activities endear me to clients worldwide. Not that that's any of your business, Mrdok monotones. They sold me the plane. That's all.

–Yes, says Renaldo 1, but—

–The registration, Renaldo 2.

–It's all very complicated—

–The registration is still in their name.

–Well isn't that funny, deadpans Mrdok. You Cubans are so smart. Too bad you're also so poor.

–Cuba is a sacrosanct virgin to the international left—even when she's having a lot of sex, people don't want to see it, Cassandra blabs on. They want to keep her as a virgin. My new piece is in part a critique of the international left's tendency to be blind. Make no mistake, I am not against the entire project of the Revolution—I'm a Revolutionary. I'm against the repression of free speech. I could criticize other stuff as well. But I decided to focus on censorship in my recent work.

The problem with criticizing Cuba is that you are not allowed to criticize just one aspect. People are completely polarized in their thinking. Therefore, if you question one aspect of the Revolution, it is as though you are condemning the entire Revolution.

Sometimes, the international leftists try to salvage a political project because it's good for their own needs and their own conscience. So they overlook things they might not forgive in their own countries, because the experiment as a whole is a good example, something to show. But when you actually have to live here, under these conditions, then it becomes a different story.

–We have our pride, señor.

–Yeah? Where is it?

–That is something maybe hard for an Americano to understand.

–Haha. Good one, Renaldo.

–Cuba is a paradise that should be enjoyed by everyone, señor.

–We think you must agree with us after all this time.

–You've seen much of our island. Is it not a beautiful place?

–That is why we, uh, no cause a problem for you, your plane landing yesterday.

–Of course, many foreigners wish to have joint venture—

Renaldo 2 shushes Renaldo 1.

–We think of you as friend to the Cuban people. Not like your president.

–I sure do appreciate that: Mrdok, glumly.

–Which is why—

–Anything you need, while you are here—

–Be sure it is us you call.

–Because, as I'm sure you understand, Cuba expert that you are. You must be a bit careful on our island—

–… because by now we have two, even three generations of people born with fear already wired in their DNA. A lot of people don't even notice that they're afraid, because it's their natural state. If you are young in your house and you want to speak out, your father will say, *Sssshh! Don't say anything! The neighbors are going to hear!* Or: *Shut up! You're going to lose your place at university!* If you live that way constantly, you get used to it. My battle right now is to not get accustomed to what's happening to me. Because, as time goes on, you can get used to the secret police coming to see you. You can adjust to anything.

It becomes a habit. The habit in Cuba is to be afraid and not even tell anybody about it. Right now, people are in Fear 2.0, which is self-censorship. That's why we don't have a lot of young people. Everybody's leaving.

—Our people are good. Honest, most of them—

—Most of them, yes.

—But we are poor, we must admit, as you say—

—And the way we do things—

—We need to make sure it benefits *all* the people—

—Yes. Here in Cuba, we are very resourceful.

—We look for partners—

Renaldo 2 suddenly raises his hand to silence his twin.

—… the other day, the secret police said to me, *Yeah, but look, today the American police were beating people up in the street!* I said, *Great, of course I think this is wrong. But let me ask you: why, because they did it, does that make it okay for you to do it? What does that have to do with Cuba?* Now the government wants to be like everyone else, but they look at *everyone else* only when they're doing bad things—not good things. *Oh, they beat people. So now we have to do it too!*

—We don't want to further interrupt your vacation, señor.

—Coffee is on us.

—One more thing, leaning in for a whisper. Be careful with girls, if you know what I say.

—Right now, chlamydia big problem in Cuba.

—Very many girls, shaking his head sadly. It is true.

—If you want…

—Renaldo, you have the card—

Renaldo 2 hands Mrdok a card with just a phone number printed on it in plain Times New Roman script.

—Call this number.

—Best girls!

—Clean. No disease. Safe.

—And sexy. Don't forget sexy.

—Mulattas. Negras. Chinese, even. Any kind of señorita you need, señor. My cousin's business.

—And please. Only for you.

—Don't tell anyone.

—We could get in big trouble. Is only for friends.

Mrdok pockets the card in his breast, nodding his head in an exaggerated display of interest. He's never seen such a bad set-up for a honeypot scenario in all his years. These clowns. Ah well, the day's entertainment.

–Hasta luego, señor!

The Renaldos are all smiles and buddy-buddy winks as they sleaze their way toward the lobby.

–Creeps, utters Mrdok under his breath as he smiles and waves them off.

2.

MRDOK HIMSELF DOESN'T know why he keeps coming down, what is it, now his thirty-seventh visit to the blighted island? He'd have to count the passport stamps. Inwardly, a sense of fascination. I mean, how the hell did they manage it? Tiny little fucking speck of land floating in the ocean, big shark USA not ninety miles away. And the CIA had tried and failed to kill Castro *how many* times?

Lest he be accused of slumming—an activity, it is true, many of the money'd class are known to indulge in, but certainly not Mrdok—I should re-iterate here that he tries to spend as much time among *ordinary* people down here as he can. In this sense, Cuba gives Mrdok the rare opportunity to engage with the lower rung of the global caste system, as he is otherwise obligated, for professional reasons, to mingle solely with the movers and shakers of this world, CEOs and prime ministers and presidents and high-ranking officials and bank chiefs and financial advisers and, well, other vital interests.

There is, for example, his driver Ricardo, his main man in Cuba, who not only gets him to places, but gets him both access and information, the two most valuable commodities, since in Cuba, there are no real goods to be had. Ricardo, unlike his parents and sister, has never gotten to go anywhere, and dreams of building a house and finding a rich man to marry one day, a man who will take him off this island for good. Ricardo who, for although he is his driver, Mrdok cannot walk down the street with, as the police will within seconds to a minute stop them and attempt to detain Ricardo as a probable *jinetero*, no matter the protestations both make, an occurrence now so regular that one can't help but conclude that this has more than just a little to do with the dark brown shade of Ricardo's skin, thus putting to challenge the Cuban government's claim that the *revolución* put an end to racism, among other forms of institution-alized forms of oppression; cops that Mrdok can no longer bribe because of a recent anti-corruption campaign, which was, from Mrdok's perspective, the government's convenient way of quaffing out a symptom without addressing the real causes of the disease.

There are the unemployed middle-aged men, driven half-crazy by the poverty and the equally inescapable heat, who will follow behind him as he walks the streets of the Old Town, shouting out incomprehensibilities in Cuban Spanish even as he swats them away, their profanities directed more at the sun's glare than Mrdok himself, not even remembering what it was they were asking the obviously rich foreigner for—money friendship diamonds fuck my sister marry my sister, mister, why don't you—men who trail behind and then just as easily fall off the trail, down some other side street, where barbershops and rotting colorless yank tanks and fruitsellers and hookers and barefoot bare-chested youth sweat out their days aimless and tourists snap photos of it all, where time continues to do its fade into stasis, sea-salted air pummeling the buildings into dust and the scent of sweat and desperation mixes with the flavorlessness of root vegetables and rice and beans.

He always dreams real vivid down here, and it's because of all this stuff, he knows, as there's no way he could dream without it. Yes, a man dreams in Cuba. That's what one goes there to do. The colors, sights, smells bleed into an unseemly unsightly whole as his sleep-addled brain tries to mold some sense out of it. (Impossible task, yes, but where there is love...) Yellow school bus parked outside the Museo de la Bellas Artes decrepit in its rundown servitude. Voices exclaiming pure joy, constant going. One's life depends on never finding. Ricardo who's never been anywhere he goes he leads on the other side of the street, however he can find a way. No one knows anything, but this whore of a world is here to stay. To not go anywhere. Like the people stuck in it. A spider's web of never-changing.

Every once in a while. A new car to add to the confusion, the unbearable heat of midday, need to catch the wind to endure it, open-top vehicle a true necessity, next stop outside Museo de la Revolución. Follow the life down, the sweat lining the intimacy in your pocket, *it is impossible to stay celibate in Cuba* says the guidebook. Dandy dials up the brightness; put a coin in his hand. In Vedado, late at night, even the bartender flirts with you. Place where dreams're always found wanting. *Where will you go next, sir?* Tomorrow, find a beach, drown these troubles away.

–Where I find myself next, say.

3.

I MEET MRDOK on the beach the next day just outside Havana. We arranged to arrive in separate cars since, for whatever reason, Mrdok prefers not to let on to the Cuban G-men that he travels here in the company of a staff member, preferring, I suppose, to give the impression of a man on vacation. Which, fair enough. I have grown quite accustomed to my digs at the Hotel Inglaterra in the Old Town. We rather behave like spies on a mission. It is quite fun, although the heat always turns me into a sticky ball of lint—I must always bring a small suitcase full of handkerchiefs with me on these Havana sojourns.

What is today—oh yes, the last of September. Only a dog can find any joy in this heat. Were there any dogs left. I'm sure the Cubans would have eaten them by now.

It is not that I have anything against them, the Cubans. I have nothing but sympathy, the dire straits they find themselves in, that they've been finding themselves in for some time now, since those men with the unkempt unruly beards took over. Strange, isn't it, how men with unkempt unruly beards seem to seize control over so much of the uncivilized world. One would think presentation matters in such endeavors, and perhaps it does. Perhaps the unruly unkempt are attracted by those who most resemble them outwardly—though I see no reason why they should.

Suddenly a storm creeps upon us, darkening the day's spirit. Seagull squeals, vomiting a piece of sky. As the first cloud breaks, the smattering of beachgoers makes a run for the decrepit shell of a hotel, Streamline Moderne ruin. I open a large umbrella over Mrdok and myself. But soon after, the great god of thunder claps his hands in the sky above us, and we have no choice but to follow the others in their dash toward the hotel.

In the lobby, fat mulatta behind the desk stares at me surly when I ask to use the phone. Mine's not getting a signal out here—anyway, Mrdok discourages me from using it, as he refrains from using his, paranoid the government is listening in (and they most likely are.) After I get off the line with Ricardo, Mrdok grabs the receiver and asks if he might make an international call. Surly Cubana just stares. He slides a fifty-euro note across the counter. Surly Cubana pockets it, shrugs her shoulders, hands him the ancient consul across the desk and disappears into the back office.

–Hello?

–Bev.

–Mrdok?

–I…

–Where the hell are you?
–Cuba. Havana.
–What are you… ?
–It's raining here.
–Oh yeah?
–Stupid, I know.
–To… what?
–To say. Weather talk and all that. What are you… ?
–I'm gettin my nails done.
–Yeah?
–You know. Same place. Upper West Side.
–I'm comin back soon.
–How soon?
–… I'll let you know tomorrow.
–… Okay.
–You know, I've been thinkin.
–… Yeah?
–Nevermind.
–Bout what?
–Just…
–Spit it out.
He feels her smiling on the other end.
–Just… You know.
–Man-of-action Mrdok!
–Haha… Okay. What color are your nails?
–Mrdok… I'm getting annoyed now.
–What color?
–Cotton candy.
–Bullshit.
–So what are you thinkin, baby?
–Was thinking of… getting us a place, is all.
–… You mean midtown?
–I was thinkin of more like… Somewhere else.
–You still haven't invited me down to Miami.
–I was just there.
–Mrd… You *promised*.
–I'm talkin our *own* place. Miami is difficult. You know, Mrtol's
got all her shit there.
–Mmkay.
–Bev.
–Mrd.
–You're the only one I let call me that.

–I know.
–Our own little… place somewhere. Just you and me.
–Where?
–I don't know yet.
–Mmkay.
–I've got a hunch.
–What?
–Nothing.
–No. What?
–Something might go funny soon.
–What are you talking about?
–You've got a passport, don't you?
–No…
–Get one.
–Why'd you go to Cuba of all places?
–Cos we can. We have a fucking plane now.
–… What?
–A plane. I bought a plane.
–Wow. Really?
–Yeah.
–Mmkay.
–So why not? We have a fuckin plane now, we can go anywhere.
Haha.
–I… Mrd, is something wrong?
–With you, baby, it's always all alright.
–Aww, Mrd. Do you miss me?
–You bet I do.
–You thinkin bout me lots? You jerkin off with that good hand
o yours?
–Aha it's the only way I know how.
–Haha.
–When I get back to Manhattan, I'm gonna stick it to you so
good, you're gonna cum for days.
–Mrdok…
–Block off next week on your calendar.
–Mrd…
–I've gotta go.
Click.
–Thanks, Señora.
He throws down another fifty. Ricardo is standing at the en-
trance, keys in hand.

4.

IN THE CAR back to Havana.
 –Did you call Mrtol?
 –Yes.
 –How is she?
 –Drunk, as always.

5.

IT IS ONE of those days that turns everyone gay. Satan screams, *Get out of my way!* By the time we get back to the city, the rain has ceased, the evening sun dank in the sky. In the street, a little dog barking at Mrdok's ankles. This whory swirlish heat, no wonder everyone's horny.

People in Havana fuck a lot as there's nothing else to do. People prefer sex to making sense of things, their lives, and who can really blame them? At sunset, they gather at the sea wall. The sofa of Havana, as Malécon is popularly referred. Hungry, they'll drink instead. Bottles plastic and glass, most filled with liquid brown and amber (depending on which light is cast upon them), the fade to morrow begins. Most will remain out here until then. Some get dressed up, strut along. People get territorial. The homosexuals down at the Vedado end, beneath the Hotel Nacional; the reggaeton guys over here, the prostitutes over there. Staking out a space, night after night, always know where your people are. Mrdok glides along. Best part of being a visitor is not belonging. You can treat it all as a show, while stopping when the impetus takes you to become a part of it all. The scenery. Ocean roaring down below. Some windy nights, it is true, the crash is like an echo, a vibration occurs. Though nothing ever shatters. Here, yank tanks honking by, you can somehow feel yourself apart from the city. Lifts a little bit of that pressure off from above the eyes. Open wider to see the colors. Dressed up and sauntering. Wandering troubadour guitar in hand scours the crowd with his eyes as he strums out an acoustic version of the local hipshake hit:

> Loca María!
> Bevando tanto sangría!
> Paga con tarjeta bancaria!
> Monta su burro a la veterinaria!

... Es una loca octogenaria!

Night and its miseritude. Its miracles, its mysteries. Staring out at the sky there is nothing there. Try to remember things, like your childhood after the rain. Vacant mind-wandering poise, the teenage children who shake their asses jokingly to the twang of the guitar. People are sexualized from birth here. It's in the culture, a part of it. Which is why selling yourself to a tourist is no big deal, whether male or female or in between. Especially when you have nothing but your body to share.

There are the high-end clubs in Miramar, where all the government bigwigs dwell in the big colonial mansions. Places where the hipsters, the well-dressed kids of the politburo and their moneybag cronies, like to drink and dance the night away. Mrdok used to go to these places, but after a time grew sick of them. They ignore him, mostly, because he is not recognized. In order to distinguish themselves from the desperation displays of the peasantry, the high-end Habaneros intentionally shun all foreigners as a sign of proud prestige.

So he's left with the ones on Havana's sofa. The hurlyburly ones, the *jineteros* and the disenfranchised young and the permanently idle. And he's better for it, yes he is. *Hey Gordo, come look at this!* Man with a parrot on his shoulder and a stogie sticking out of his knuckles, shuffling his feet, showing like a wise guy. Night's turpitude, the glowing. Teenage rumpshaker mocks the alcoholic twisting and writhing upon the sidewalk, trying to finagle a couple pesos out of a fellow drunk. Sofa but also a stage. Where people live their dreams out loud. Hola chico, stop busting my, you stole my seat, maricón. See what I can—no, never. Never be a part of all this, no matter how I try, not my legacy, where I come from; still, the drift. It's like you have to fill the night with something, or else the silence will overtake, suffocate us all. Eye contact with the red t-shirt one, cut-off shorts proud owner of a flabby slappable bubble. What the Spanish must have thought when they came over here, the fire in these people, the rust is everywhere, the cars the buildings, never within. Sing a song tomorrow's late arriving, they can teach the rest of the world how to live. Rest of the world's forgotten; too preoccupied with doubt to ever go back to it. You show off what you have here, every foreign eye a potential buyer. It's all about laughter, screaming through the dream. Becoming rather than having. Desperate need to, to hurry up and get past the stringencies of the moment, lest they catch you. The ones you've grown up with all around you, except for the ones who've gone away. The strangers all ready enough to be recognized, floating in this tub with their uncertainty out on display. It's not all about salvation. Even the chance to watch TV in an air-conditioned room. Your soul jacks off in the street. Thin branch of neverance protrudes from bright sugar-rum blur. This is the night before it ate us. Circumstance that seems least exotic when one dives in for the sway.

6.

THE GREAT THING about staying at the Hotel Nacional is that you can get FaNN on the widescreen, despite the embargo. The Factual News Network has long been Mrdok's news network of choice; at one point, he even considered investing in them, before he recalled Tony Fatballs's advice to avoid direct contact with the media to the fullest extent possible. But still, in hotel rooms, he tends to keep it on constant, when he's in a place where it's actually possible to do so (in Madagascar, for instance, it wasn't.) So all Mrdok has to do when he gets homesick is to zap on the tube to feel like he's back in the good ol'.

On this next episode of Eat Your Way East, *we travel to a shitty resort town in an economically disenfranchised Latin American country at the end of the season—and see if it's actually possible to get a decent meal.*

—Whoa, this should be good, grunts Mrdok, curling up in the silk coverlet to protect his freshly showered body from AC overload.

On screen, Bradford Ambrosio, the bad-boy celebrity chef whose peregrinations form the crux of *Eat Your Way East,* is licking a speckled colorless concoction off a plastic fork.

—It tastes like batshit dipped in honey, he verdicticizes.

Mrdok doubles up in laughter.

The phone next to his bed rings. Mrdok picks up, half-expecting more room service upselling.

—Yes.

—Mrdok? What the fuck.

—Who is this.

—My voice doesn't sound familiar to you?

—Why should it.

—It's Louis, Mrdok. Louis Farquahson. SunEye Corp? You know, we sold you the goddamn plane?

—Oh, Louis, hello.

–The plane that you then flew, still registered in our name, to Cuba, a move that puts us in violation of the Trading With The Enemy Act?

–Haha, Louis…

–A *private* plane, Mrdok. Owned by a *publicly traded company.* How the fuck did they even, did you get permission from the Cubans to land?

–Connections, Louis, connections.

–You're lucky you didn't get shot down by those fucking commies.

–Whoa, easy there, boy, easy.

What an idiot. Obviously the line is tapped.

–Do you have *any idea* how this looks? What they could potentially do to me?

–Lou-is…

–My lawyers have been on the phone with Washington all morning.

–No…

–The fucking *FBI* might be investigating us now.

–No way.

–At the very least, we're looking at a hefty fine here. A big one, Mrdok.

–Aww, really?

–Fucking moron.

–Hey!

–I should've known. I should've *listened.* Everyone told me not to trust you. *Everyone.*

–Now let's not get overly excited and spoil a mutually beneficial relationship, shall we, Louis?

–And what happens if I tell the feds it's you, Mrdok. What then?

–Haha, Louis…

–What then, you bastard?

–Well, then. I suppose you'd need the paperwork to back that one up.

–Which we… Wait a minute. Didn't they… ?

–Y'know. I told your folks to forward it on to my folks. I have no idea why you're even calling me. Gordo's supposed to be taking care of it. How'd you get my number anyway?

–I called the front desk, you asshole.

–And they gave it to you? How'd you know where I was staying?

–Where else would you be staying in Havana, Mrdok?

–Oh. Well. Goodbye, then!

—Wait! Mrdok! You fuck—

Click.

Bradford Ambrosio is drunk, slurring his speech over the meal of roast pig innards garnished with a side of broiled salt-cured palm tree trunk, the local specialty of the blighted region.

—Well, I dun know why they say it's dangerous over here, Bradford sways toward his two dining companions, it's the most welcomin country in Latin America *I've* ever been to. And *I've* been to *all* of em!

That awkward silence among his dining companions that so often arises during these crude displays of over-eagerness, typically by Americans, to embrace the local culture and identify with it, usually by bashing their own, to which the locals more often than not aspire or at the very least share varying degrees of envy over; through its infinite exportability, they have a better understanding of America than most Americans do, given their ability to see it for what it is from the outside.

Mrdok picks up the phone, dials.

—Hey Fatty.

—Hahaha.

—Fatty fat fuck.

—What is it, Mrdok?

—Guess who just called?

—Is it Mrtol? Or wait… You called her from the beach hotel… I mean, you did, didn't you?

—Wrong. But yeah, I mean, I called her. Sort of.

—Well… I don't know who else it could be then.

—Remember our friend Louis Farquahson?

—Oh yes. Are they hounding us for the payment *already*? Well they're just going to have to hold their proverbial horses.

—You do anything with the papers yet?

—No, I—There simply hasn't been time. I have the papers here in my bag.

—Good. Don't.

—What was the nature of the call, exactly?

—Customer satisfaction survey.

—Oh dear.

—They're pissed we're in Cuba.

—Oh…

—Must be jealous. Such a beautiful country.

(Mrdok now, too, suddenly mindful of whoever-it-is likely listening in. Renaldo and Renaldo or perhaps their triplet?)

–But troubled in its relations with ours.

To put it mildly. Then again, the same could be said for most nations.

–You know, I didn't even stop to think…

–The registration.

–Oh dear.

–He called me an asshole.

–… How could he *dare*.

–And a moron too.

–The… terrible bastard.

–Well, they're about to find out just how much of an asshole moron I really am. And a bunch of other things, too.

The reception is crinkly, as always when calling domestic, but Mrdok can still make out the sound of Gordo cracking his knuckles on the other end of the line.

–Do you want me to call—

–Leave the Cubans out of this. These SunEye fucks are on the line with the feds.

–What on earth are they thinking?

–It's clear. They're thinking of their own asses. How to save them.

–Vile creatures. Just vile.

–So we do nothing.

–… I see. Well, that's one thing we're good at!

–Except one thing.

–Which is… ?

–I'm a man of my word. I made them a promise, didn't I?

–Well, we made them a few, if I recall…

–I'm not talkin bout the plane. The other promise. Stocks.

–Ah yes.

–Call up Abe. Tell him to fuck em up real good.

–Yes… I'm writing it down.

–Write: *Fuck em where it hurts.* I mean, *ruin* the bastards.

–*Ruin… the…* Right. I've got it.

–Buy up a scary amount of that company, their stocks, then wait till the press gets on it. It'll be a two day story: Day One, Mrdok appears to be the new owner. They'll be clamoring the New York office for quotes. Don't give em any. Day Two…

–Bye bye SunEye.

–Precisely. We dump em all. Turn into pennies as they hit the floor. By the time they remember the exact location of their assholes, they won't even know how to use them anymore, they're gonna feel themselves so full of shit. I mean, they're gonna explode. And I'm gonna watch it, jerking off on all this grandeur. Ha! I mean, by the time this all blows over, they're not even gonna remember the bit about the plane, hahaha…

–Hahahahaha. Brutal, boss, brutal! But brilliant, nonetheless…

–This is how we deal with shitballs, isn't it, Gordo? Fuckin feds my ass.

Click.

On-screen, suddenly Bradford Ambrosio projectile vomits into the pig's blackened carcass, then collapses off his stool into a sweat puddle on the grimy nocturnal street where farm animals compete with prostitutes.

–Do I keep filming? a voice says off-camera after an uncomfortable pause.

–Haha! I love this guy, Mrdok chortles.

CHAPTER FOUR

SHAVED E

—AND WHAT, EXACTLY, did the title Motherfucker of the Month *mean* to you?

–Um. Nothing much, actually.

–Don't give me that horseshit.

–Well what do you—

–I'd think, with an obnoxious title like that, that implies you were the Star Employee.

–Um. I was the *sole* employee. Least as far as I could tell.

–The *sole employee*. Awfully curious.

–Well…

–How exactly would you characterize your role at Belle Encoding, Mister Hull?

–I would characterize it as busy. Very busy.

–I'm not looking for an adjective, smart stuff.

–I gave you much more than that. You also got an adverb.

–What was your job description, Mister Hole?

–Motherfucker of the Month.

–Allow me to rephrase the question.

The fed smacks him across the face.

–What the fuck?

Smacks him again.

–I'm the one asking the—

–Questions around here. I got it. What are you, a walking cop cliché?

Smack.

–Jesus fuck.

–Tell me your official job title.

–Encoder. The company's called Belle Encoding. I'm the sole employee. So that's what I do. Duh.

–Did.

–I think I'm entitled to a phone call.

–No you're not. Not on the federal level. Not when your crime concerns national security. You're being held, Mister Hull, under suspicion that you've committed a violation that clearly falls under the purview of the MASA act.

–The MASA act?

–Making America Safe Again. That's the mission of my office, and, as it so happens, also my personal worldview. If you're truly interested in the prospect of saving yourself, Mister Hull, and ever having the freedom to jack off in front of another glowing screen, I'd suggest you get to describing your job duties and responsibilities, official and unofficial, and pronto.

–Mainly, I harvest people's data.

Smack. (More like a wallop.)

–Fuck!

–Feels good, don't it? Or at least it will in a moment. Around the eighth or ninth hit, you cross over. Start to savor it somehow. You can't even imagine how many of those I had to endure when I was undergoing my training here. Smack smack smack. It's the only way, really, to become an effective interrogator: you've gotta first see how it feels to be in the suspect's seat… It hurts the first few times, it's true. But we should be glad we were both born when we were, since the Bureau's real strict about it nowadays. Only openhand slaps is the rule. Forty years ago, you wouldn't've been so lucky.

–This is illegal, you know.

–Boo hoo hoo.

–We encode people's data.

–Before you said you *harvest* it.

–Yeah. So?

–Curious choice of verb. To harvest would imply that you're gathering it for some future use… What, then, would that future use be?

–I don't know. That's above my pay grade. All I can tell you… It's the twenty-first century, man. It's all about data. It's more important than money… It *is* money.

–Would you say that this year's was a *successful* harvest?

–Forget data harvesting, okay? Call it a memory landscaping business. It's more about maintenance, okay? Making sure all the offshore numbers look good to the IRS. And I'm not at liberty—

–Samsonian0956onxy.

–…

–That's right. Let that sink in for a minute.

–How did you… ?

–Oh, that's only one of your passwords we happen to have in our magic little file right here.

–I'm not—

–Would you like to hear some more? Because I have a whole list I could recite. Might get boring after a while.

–So what is it you want, exactly? And: aren't you supposed to offer me a cigarette or something?

–There's no smoking in the building.

–We provide services to firms. Okay, to the wealthy. To the über-über-wealthy. I can't even pretend I understand the world these people come from, what motivates them to do the things they do. It's all numbers to me. Simple numbers: I'm a math guy, not a finance wizard. A simple programmer. All I know is coding, okay? It might be a complex art to lesser minds, but once you master it—

–Oh you can do all sorts of things. I happen to know a thing or two about computers myself, Mister Hull. You can spare me the lecture.

–Call me Harry.

–Harry.

–It's my real name.

–It's not that we've been following *all* your movements…

–Yeah, that would be impossible.

–There are some gaps we would like to fill in.

–Why don't you ask the real guy responsible. The big boss. I'm just a simple employee.

–Oh we'll get to that. This is just the beginning, you understand. These things take time.

–Can I call my lawyer? You can't detain me—

–Shall we start with the letter e?

–… Excuse me?

–You seem to have a special affinity for the letter e. Lower case.

–… I thought this was about the rich people.

–There are many letters in the alphabet. *Harry.* Twenty-six of them. Why e? I'm curious, more than anything.

–You could be speaking Azerbaijani to me right now, for all I—

–Of course it would have to be a vowel, since vowels are the most frequent occurrence in *any* language, particularly on the Anglicized,

Americanized web. Why not, say, i. That's a good one. Shave a little length off that stem. Make the dot smaller.

–Should I be pretending to understand what you're talking about? Is that how the game works?

–We cover some pretty high tech shit here. Fuckin towelheads—sorry, *Islamic radicals*—hacking into CIA databases, wreaking all kinds of havoc. Virtual bank heists, the North Koreans. Down to the more petty and banal shit, Nigerian spammers scamming old ladies. Not to mention your boss's little money laundering shitshow. That's my everyday, Harry. But I'm surprised, I guess you could say. Surprised and amused. Impressed—that wouldn't be too much of an overstatement. I mean, this is a whole other category: font terrorism.

–Hey. Watch your language.

–But isn't that what you would call it? Has a nice ring to it. Don't you think? Well, I reckon that's the name I'm gonna give it. After all, it was me who discovered it. That's right. I'm the one who found you. In case you're wondering. That means I'm the one who gets to apply the label to this folder right over here.

–You sure do talk big for a guy who has next to nothing.

–Do I?

–Look, you've got the wrong guy. You should be talking to Mrdok. Let me talk to him. I'll wear a wire for you, I'll bring him in.

The fed leans in.

–Mrdok doesn't wanna talk to you. He wants nothing to do with you.

–Scum.

–What was that?

–Human scum.

–Is that any way to talk about your boss? Seems you won't be getting another promotion this year.

–I wasn't talking about him. I was referring to you.

Wallop.

–Ooh, drew a little blood there. It stop hurting yet?

–What I meant is that you don't have to be a great genius to figure any of this stuff out.

–Genius would certainly be an overstatement. Whether applied to you, your boss, or his faggot friend. What's he called again? Oh, right. Gordon Abu Lary Whiteman. Goes by Gordo, if I'm not mistaken. We have a file on him, too.

–That sniveling little sycophant. Why don't you go after that putz? He's the one with all the dirt on Mrdok. *How much am I worth? How much am I worth?* Mrdok's always asking him. Even though it's

Gordo who really wants to know. Apparently when it gets to a trillion, Mrdok's promised to buy him a Ferrari.

–I mean, I'm torn here. Why didn't one of *our* guys figure this out first? Shave a tenth of a millimeter off that tail at the end of the e, that makes a new letter, you've got a whole new link there, don't you? A bogus site. Poor victim clicks on it, goes to a site with the identical address—save, of course, for a single letter change in the address, with that shaved e, which not even twenty-twenty vision would catch... Incredible. You created so many goddamn backdoors, all of them undetectable. Or nearly so, I should say...

–Yeah, so I've done you a favor. You can go sell it to any security firm out there, clear a million easy. That or use it for yourselves. Give it to the NSA. Just imagine what they could do with it. America'll be the envy of every police state in the world.

–We already are. And I'm not in the business of *clearing millions*, as you put it.

–I'm afraid your clip-on already gave that away.

–I'm gonna let that one go, out of pity. Once we get done with you, there's not a cybersecurity firm in the world that'll ever take you or your little gimmick seriously.

–I thought—

–What, smartass? That we're gonna turn around, wipe your ass for you, give you a little desk in some cubicle? Maybe turn you loose on the network news interview circuit, repent your sins for all of America and the world to watch, show how we turn the bad guys good? Another foot soldier in the never-ending cyber war? I've got geeks down there who wouldn't bother flossing their teeth with you. You're so sure as shit, so full of yourself, but what are you at the end of the day? A goddamn one-trick pony. That's what you are. So you merge and cut and copy and grab and put back and rearrange and do it all so nice it might take em a bit of time to figure it all out, by which hour it's too late... So what? I've got guys developing new algorithms on a freakin *hourly* basis. You aint got game, son.

–I've got something more valuable than game.

–In your mind you do.

–But I aint giving it up until we can have a proper conversation.

–Hell, I don't think I've met anyone who's bored me as much as you do.

–Okay. What do you need me to say so that I can get the fuck out of here?

–A number.

–... Say what?

—You know. A simple number.

—A number.

—That will give us access. The access we have been seeking.

—Access.

—Access which I am 110 percent confident only you have.

The fed removes a sheet of paper from the folder.

—This list look familiar?

—It's the list of companies—

—Shells.

—Huh?

—Shells. All of them. Not a single one a real company.

—I'm sure.

—Each one even less of a company than the one you ostensibly work for. Worked for.

—I'll still work there when this is all over.

—Ha. Sure you will. Only it won't be the same company. And your boss will no longer be Mrdok.

—Whatever. You can't hold me responsible for the legitimacy of the firms we do business with.

—Cayman Islands. Cyprus… You ever been to Cyprus?

—No.

—My wife and I, we went there for vacation last year—

—I work from the office. Always.

—From the office. Which we've had bugged for months now. We think it's a number…

—A number?

—The password to the cloud.

—Which cloud?

Wallop.

—The cloud you send the data to. You want me to spell it out? These scumbuckets whose accounts you were scrubbing, making look all clean and shiny across the board. Criminal in and of itself, okay, but dubiously so. Hard to track. But that's not all you would do, was it? You needed something else. *Kompromat,* I believe is what the Russkies call it. Compromising info. To protect your ass—yours and Mrdok's—in case something went wrong. In case they turned on you. In case something like *me* forced them to turn on you.

—I'm bleeding over here.

—So you figured out a way, not just to get the good dirt. But to get *everything.* Must be millions of pages of files, Harry.

—Get me a handkerchief or something.

–We have your laptop. We'll get all the malware codes you've written. We already know which one you were using that you didn't write. You wanna know why? You wanna know how I found you? The mimiketz malware you were using. The keystroke logger that you installed once you had broken in. The logger that enabled you to get all those passwords, all the *really* valuable data. Guess who wrote that, Harry? We did.

–I'm thirsty.

–More than four hundred accounts. They were yours. Now they're gonna be mine. You weren't *harvesting people's data,* Harry. This is a clear-cut case of exfiltration. Rhymes with masturbation! Apparently your other favorite pastime.

–It's sweeping the nation.

Wallop.

–That's for insulting our country.

–Fuck. Okay. So what exactly is it you want to hear?

–I want a number, Harry. I want that cloud.

–I write that down on a piece of paper for you, I can get out of here?

–I'm afraid it's not that simple.

–I'm liking you less and less.

–The feeling is mutual.

CHAPTER FIVE

MRDOK MAPGAZER

THE THICK, STEWY broth brewing in Mrdok's brain during this most fortuitously fruitful period—well, I myself was scarcely aware of it at the time, embroiled as I was in the affairs of the day to day. Though, in retrospect, there were certain indelible signs, deep in the great man's character, that might have given rise to such cognizance, were I the perceptive creature I have at times dreamed of becoming. There was the morning, not long after our return to Manhattan from Cuba, I walked into the office to find Mrdok still in pajamas, gazing at maps, black-brown hair ruffled, evidently sleepless. Now, it is true that Mrdok has long been a mapgazer—a habit acquired, so I've garnered, in his youth and that has endured well into adulthood. Oddly, as much as he travels, it seems to be that he enjoys this perusal of the world in graphic format much more than he does the actual physical act of voyage. He has acquired, over the years, a great number of these territorializations, many of an antique vintage, some dating back prior to the discovery of the New World of which we are so indelibly a part, many others when the countries and designated territories were marked with names quite other from the ones that we know them as today. Much can be thought and said of these mappings of worlds known and unexplored; beyond their interest as geographical artifacts, there also leaves much speculatory space for the dreamer, for whom such maps, it often seems, are really made. Dreams of antique ships, driven by rows of slaves, drifting across oceans, red-haired aristocratic Spaniards standing before the mast, gaze turned skyward, thoughts overflowing with the gold-rimmed treasure chests of worlds as yet unknown, but fathomed through the opaque mysteries of intuition. Why, it is enough to send any vaguely imaginative being reeling through the cosmos of night into that veritable other side of new beginnings. While one does not necessarily require a map on the traversal toward discovery—I believe the man of genius possesses his own inner compass to steer himself through the murkiest and cloudiest of terrain—such territorial portrayals might serve as an impetus. For one thing, they help to make the world—as vast and unruly as it happens to be—a much more manageable, conquerable space.

It isn't odd to find Mrdok in his pajamas. Behind the bookcase in the front office, after removing a fake but convincing antique volume of *Gulliver's Travels,* one could discover a keypad that recognized only the print of Mrdok's left thumb. Once scanned, the bookcase door unclicked to reveal a small cell containing a single bed where Mrdok elects to spend certain of his nights. What is odd, I find, is the length of time he has now spent away from Mrtol and little Jaco out on Shelter Island.

The safety valve of a dream is, of course, the awakening. We seed ourselves into a vision, allow the ideality of that vision to take its course. Embedded within that ideality, however, is a certain darkness—one that often makes itself felt before it yet appears. A darkness that, when ignored, grows like a toxic cancerous cell, eventually engulfing the sheen that, once enticed, leaves little behind but the growing risk of a total engulfment. But how to dam such a tide? The operation of agency is, after all, severely compromised in the dream state. And even when it does so function, it scarcely shows any relation to the operation of agency as it occurs in waking life, when cool consciousness guides each fluctuation; rather, it seems to occur outside of our selves, in a way, such that upon waking, we are inevitably left with some variant of the question, *why did I do that?* What the dream makes us realize, inevitably, is that we do not really know ourselves, not as fully as we might wish to—as we might crave...

Speaking of dreams in the aspirative sense—the realm of desire, we might re-phrase it as—when we are more fully able to apply our gifts of reason to the live equation, we are similarly blinded by our need to attain the object of our waking dream which is called life. Need makes itself felt in the crudest way, and the sense we might apply to temper this sensate quivering is cast aside into blindness, leaving us probable victims of our very dreaming selves—that inner beast whose very nature refutes all attempts at domestication.

My reasoning for detouring thus takes the form of a tripartition. There is, of course, the sleepless state we find Mrdok in, morning raggedness oblivious to the hour, having entered into a waking dream state through his mapgazing (for I did not mention the sheer number of overlapping sheaths and *feuilletons* crowding on his desk in silent competition for his attention, which shifted between them according to his peculiar and inaccessible dream logic.) There is the object upon these maps that will soon emerge apparent as the subject of Mrdok's next waking dream—his most ambitious to date—of which, there is plenty more to come. But, finally and somewhat post-hastily, there is the dream of love, which, now, it is clear by Mrdok's concentrated avoidance of domesticity and all its commitments, has reached a point of extinguishment-by-shadow, as Mrtol's role has gradually shifted from one of beacon to burden, with little to no hope of renewal.

There was a time when everything made much more sense than we wanted it to. Mrdok's engagement with Mrtol had been rocky, but out of necessity. It was, after all, predicated on the break up of his previous entanglement with Krstal, a once-former would-be ac-tress whose star had not risen, in spite of serial attempts. Her clinging to the wastrels of the Hollywood system put her in a league far out-side of our Mrdok's pedigree. Chasers of the Hollywood dream often have little on the brain besides the attainment of this bottomless de-lusion (an affliction often aided by an intentional neglect of carbohydrates in the diet); Krstal was no different. The only thing that distinguished her from countless others is that she had Mrdok to back her up, to cushion her inevitable falls from grace—if grace be not too lofty a characterization of the platforms upon which she rode. In clawing her way to the top—or what she thought was the top—Krstal would often forget who her husband was, and how the storied little company town in which they had embedded themselves loved to talk. Her actions, then, were not only noticed but frequently remarked upon, which, though he never said so, was I suppose a source of personal humiliation for Mrdok. (That her involvement in these pursuits of rather vulgar ambitionism disabled her from per-forming the normal duties of motherhood is perhaps yet a further destination for complaint; their sons, Bobby and Stevo Rey, were largely left to be raised by a confluence of nannies and domestic staff, and, in Stevo Rey's case, boarding school.) As the Manhattan office kept him away from the left coast for weeks at a time, it became something of a refuge and a base for disassembling himself from the LA scene with its sordid implications—a place from which Mrdok might pen yet another opening chapter, so to speak.

That chapter would inevitably have one woman's name as the title, but the prologue was stitched with the names of many. Fitful spates of lovemaking. Mrdok, after some eight years of marriage, needed to remind himself that he was, after all, a man. The self that he had been, at the beginning of their courtship, needed recharging.

At a certain point, the multitudinous affairs became too much to manage. And not only for Mrdok—even I was being sucked into the morass, charged with the scheduling and the keeping-up of lies—as Mrdok was never the type of man to attract mere weekend warriors. Owing to his status, his prestige, Mrdok drew women of the bright, beautiful, ambitious sort—and he loved them right back. All of them. Temporarily, at least. And when he was done with them, well, it was often left to me to settle the bill.

Now, Mrtol: could anything be further from blonde Southwestern trailer trash Krstal? Half-Italian, half-Jewish—a show-stopping Jewoppy. (That's how she jokingly referred to herself, lest someone reading this accuse me of racism.) She was a Long Island native, like Mrdok, and with quite the mouth on her. Here, it seemed as though Mrdok had met his proverbial match. While she certainly did not peddle an artificially enhanced appearance, she had no real need to do so; and what little she lacked in looks, she more than made up for in her fiery charisma. At times, she could demand too much of Mrdok—at least that's my private thought on the matter. She has a mouth, and yet she is obviously quite nice. This multi-layeredness— certainly it's a thing that attracted Mrdok to her. But ultimately, I feel he was rather looking for a way out of the LA trap in which Krstal had ensnared him. He needed a good reason to never go back there. There was the matter of the two sons, from whom he was also growing somewhat distant as the end of the marriage approached. The oldest, Stevo Rey, had already jumped ship, gone to study in Tokyo, at what at first was meant to be a one-year Japanese language course; but from there he never returned, and made clear his disdain for his father in a very public way, through a series of crude blog posts. The younger, Bobby, proceeded to drift into a world of heavy drug use— at first, it just seemed like normal partying, the stuff that all teenage kids, at least all teenage kids growing up in that milieu, seem to inevitably flirt with; and then it became something quite else, a something that frightened both ma and pa alike, and so Krstal and Mrdok both made the unspoken decision to simply distance themselves from it to the fullest extent possible.

So Mrtol was there at a key moment in Mrdok's life, to rescue him from all these unpleasant aspects. And now, it appears to me that he has begun to question whether that rescue operation is really all there has been to their romance, now that an even greater distance than the one that had been put between he and Krstal—a span that engulfed the entirety of the country, really, from New York to Los Angeles—seems to be separating them.

Nowadays, one need not be a Columbus to discover new lands. I stand by the door, watching Mrdok, who is all but oblivious to my appearance in the office. Stand there waiting—for what, I hardly know. He holds a yellow aged map up to the light, zeroes in on a splotch of land surrounded by a near-Far Eastern sea. Grabs the magnifying glass off his desk, print too tiny to read its name with the bare eye. *Sagosia,* he whispers aloud. He puts the map down and looks up, noticing my appearance in the room for the first time. Without saying a word, he picks up the landline and dials.

PART THREE

ANOTHER ISLAND

SHE'S FAMOUS FOR playing someone's famous mom on TV. She comes rolling by all fresh air, tray of drinks in hand and looking all micro-dubious at the scene jutting out behind the trailer: sunset on ice. Someone had set the blanket alight, and now a curtain of fire hangs from the clothesline, its flames crackling out at the crowd of children like a dragon's tongue, daring any one of them to come near and let him lap up a miniscule lash of human flesh. Nearly causes her to drop the damn refreshments, but instead she comes forward with a screech of terrorized serendipity as she lurches the tray, glasses and all, toward the fiery evil, at the same time flying backward to avoid smashing into it, ending up with her skates high up in the air, a crowd of children surrounding with cruel laughter.

Time was always doing its thing, rubbery and loose, and Saturdays are never very nice. Gut sticking out of his bathrobe, husband pops out of the trailer door to ask what the hell is going on in that native tongue of the pre-colonial era, words nobody in earsight could make out besides her. The children turn to give him a good WTF staredown. Why bother making those sounds that had been phased-out so long ago? She remains splayed to the sky, awaiting its instructions. A white rooster vogues by, grazing her forehead with its pale plumage.

—Roast those damn vegetables, spits Martinique, whose fire she finds herself haunting later that night, too exhausted after putting out her own. Red spots have been manifesting up and down her arms for three weeks now, and a state of fatigue had accompanied the arrival of the strange symptom, wearing her down into the thin dusty substance that the sand has become on this part of the island.

Martinique had told her to go visit the doctor, knowing full well she wouldn't. There is scarcely a white man on the island she won't go out of her way to avoid. Her whole goddamn livelihood is this avoidance. With their taxes and tariffs, white people just cost too much money to be around, live around, and they never give all that much in return. Doctor no different. If anything, he'll just make you sicker so as to keep you coming back, fatten his bill.

Martinique tends the fire, suspiciously eyeing the spots on Lucia's arm as she peels an onion unawares.

TV left on most hours of the night and day. Satellite. It spells out presence and is rarely acknowledged. It needn't be. It serves its purpose of wieldy engulfment: a moodtrack.

Cool in the Pseudotropics this time of year, at least at night, when a smart breeze replaces the sun and a brilliant moon shimmers in the waters visible from all around, thanks to the strategic elevation on the island that had allowed the quasi-natives a pristine view of the arrival of their colonizers a couple centuries prior. Now, times are no longer as tough as they had been back when they'd been driven into the sand face-first like human tractors to install the cracker barrel infrastructure—though much had been lost in the interim. That infrastructure, the bones of their ancestors, now well in the process of decay. Storms kept coming, but nowadays, whoever wasn't killed by them briskly got a new trailer to replace the old. Words like progress always have a wavering, elusive definition on an island, geographical mass defined by circularity; place where the cyclical nature of time is less an abstraction than a reality too obvious to even mention.

–I know your damn son started that fire.

Martinique's voice rises above the din of the TV.

–Vincent.

–Not Vincent. Your other son. The one with no sense left.

–His name be Prince.

–Prince. Prince of what? Poop? Your damn boy'll be the death of us all. Runnin round, settin alight all the things in sight. They gonna fly over us one day in a chopper, see a big black mess of smoky charcoal smolderin outta the sea. Say, that was Sagosia, wasn't it? Till some young lad decided to put a flame to it... I mean *reckless,* and Lucia no control over the boy. You don't take a goddamn vine to his ass, I'm about to.

The islanders didn't have last names. It wasn't who they were. There was no need to articulate familial alliance. Everyone knew their lineage and everyone else's—why imprison patrimony in a proper noun. Lest any confusion arise, the wise women could always keep track. When the white settlers came, they imposed family names on the locals. That was how colonization happened. But it was just on paper. Nobody uses them otherwise. Papers most had long ago discarded, though copies remain, it is true, in some filing cabinet in the island's main administrative building on the second highest hill, just beyond Baldheaded Mountain. The same hill that holds the chateau of Nelson Rodgers, current director of operations at First Sagosia Bank and, per chance, the island's colonial administrator. His a face rarely seen among the quasi-natives. His presence makes itself felt constant, though, with that house overlooking the everything down below.

Vincent didn't come home for dinner that night. Lucia hadn't expected him; he'd left on a boat that afternoon, before the blanket fire incident, to go to work. He'd be back the next morning, in all likelihood. He was a wild cannon, that boy, and neither he nor Martin had the will to try and furrow that energy. Anyway, it mostly went toward good ends. Unlike his brother Prince.

Order has to be imposed from without; it never comes from within. An inadequate means of trying to put into words the island philosophy, a summary that would only come out of a foreign mouth like that of Mister Rodgers, and so not to be trusted. All the so-called gifts that had been offered over the years. There were tactics of survival and then there was this thing called civilization; frankly, Sagosians had had both, with no need to call it that before the foreign settlers came and claimed the island for their own. They had had to import everything to build a life here—couldn't make do with fish and bamboo, as the Sagosians had done for centuries, instead desperate for the ways of the world they had left behind. Where's the valor there? was the common thought. Though in the violence of articulating it, they had lost a lot more than they had gained. Now, they lived in a far more quiet state, one that breathed silence beyond dignity, rejecting as many of the settlers' advances as they could so as to avoid the stigma that came with sharing in their so-called logic. After bitterness comes a drawn-out fatigue.

Dinner spread across two plates, Lucia rises without a word. She's had enough humiliation from Martinique for one evening. And anyway, her man's hungry.

Martinique continues to stir the fire in glum silence. Damn em all to hell, she whispers to herself, picking up her own dish.

As she makes her way back to the trailer, skillfully balancing the two plates heavy with fish and seaweed, Lucia lets one eye dart around the path. She half hopes Prince'll appear, though of course senses it unlikely. After a silent dinner, her husband'll sit in front of a televised sermon, nodding off with beer can in hand as the holy man tells his audience what it means to repent in a world where any kind of living could get you into deep water. She'll do the same thing she does on most nights after dinner, go out walking along the shore. Sometimes she'll find Prince out there shrieking with his pack. She'll scold him, raise her finger, tell him to go home get into bed. Other nights she'll see young couples out there walking slowly arm in arm or else caught up in conversation seated on some convenient grassy slope perched not too high above the sea's lapping. Nothing to do and no need for distraction.

But tonight Lucia has it all to herself, sea moon and three stars that can be counted. She stares out into the sheet of shimmering blackness where the night meets the horizon, her bare feet finding the cool wetness beneath the first layers of sand. If she strains hard enough, she can nearly make out the lights of a ship somewhere out there, though maybe that's just her brain playing tricks on her.

CHAPTER TWO

VACAY

1.

HARD AS HE has been working of late, this vacation is well earned. I am determined to make the most of it for him, my beloved master; an overworked Mrdok, after all, is not a creature that will bring the world much of the benefit he might otherwise bring. Ensconced in a private villa, the requisite infinity pool forming an undefinable horizon line against the sea, I am presently being castigated for my failure to recruit poolside guests to alleviate Mrdok's boredom with the present company. With us, for reasons unknown, Rick Stewart from the home office. Of a rather moronic disposition—an opinion I have carefully kept to myself, as such candor would most certainly earn Mrdok's disapproval—I must keep my bristling to a minimum. An incorrigible suck up and an imposter to boot, one need not look far beyond his handsome blonde sculpted features to unfurl the truth of a rather middling accounts man with an overinflated sense of self-worth, brimming with the replacement envy that so commonly afflicts those of his generation, yet with none of the feigned sensitivity that is meant to come along with it as a charm substitute.

Tricky Ricky. Icky, sticky, tricky Ricky.

Sensing my disapproval of his presence on this trip and his existence in general, Rick has taken to ignoring me most of the time, and I return the favor. Mrdok doesn't seem to notice the mutual antipathy, or if he does, then he doesn't much care; he has far more pressing matters with which to concern himself.

–Might I offer you a line of Bolivian cocaine? It's vegan.

To which request Mrdok and Rick promptly reply with nods in the assertive, following the dainty bikini'd Swede into a unisex cubicle, only to emerge minutes later with synapses freshly abuzz, ready to tackle the next round of craft cocktails. Oh, I forgot to mention that we've left the villa—we're now in some techno cave across from the beach listening to DJ Disaster Area spin house music to the assorted Eurotrash who congregate here each summer for their annual fix of hedonism and sunburn. After exhausting themselves grooving on the dance floor to Yesterday's Big Thing, we move on to the next club, then the ad nauseam next, until finally, only 11 p.m., we find ourselves bleary eyed in some dismal comedy club catering to the British expats and tourists haunting or polluting (depending on one's vantage point) the island. An American entertainer, marketing himself as the World's Worst Comedian, has lately commenced his act.

—Don't you hate it when you think you're gonna fart, but instead... you shit?

The haphazard crowd of some two dozen lightly or else miserably intoxicated sunburnt bodies largely ignores the performance, rousing out of their combined stupor only on occasion to heckle the bespectacled dweeb in a hopelessly out-of-date smoking jacket—no doubt intended as part of the routine.

—Rick, what is it exactly you do for me again?

—I'm your deal finder, Mrdok. Well... One of them.

—... especially sucks when it happens in the swimming pool. Man, I once shut down my local watering hole for two whole weeks. Why, they didn't have enough chlorine in the entire state of Wyoming...

The audience issues a collective groan.

—Get off the bloody stage, you twat! some inebriate strains.

—We should've got more blow from that Danish chick, says Rick.

—I believe she was in fact Swedish.

—Yeah. Aren't they the same?

—... It also happened to me once when I was riding a motorcycle... Boy was the driver of that car behind me unhappy...

Mrdok suddenly awakens to a bright idea.

—Hey! I know. We're in Spain, right? Let's buy Gordo a whore!

—Oh, really, Mrdok, that's okay.

—Haha, I love it, says Rick. I bet this fatso hasn't been laid in... Well, when was the last time you slapped the flab against some tender puppymeat, big boy?

I glare at Rick with all the inner vile my eyes might puke forth. He looks away.

—Definitely! Let's go find a whore for Gordo.

—... Do you guys have Taco Bell over here? Do you know what Taco Bell is?... Anyone?... Okay. So the other day, I was eating at Taco Bell...

I excuse myself to go to the restroom, where I hope to plot some sort of exit strategy from this escapade. Unfortunately, no fresh ideas are coming to mind, and so I realize the need to go along with the matter temporarily and hope to improvise my way out of it eventually.

When I return, the World's Worst Comedian is reciting a rolodex of You Know You're A Pedophile If... jokes.

—I *am* feeling rather peckish, I begin in timid earnesty.

—What? You want to peck someone?

—Speak English, Gordo.

—Is anyone feeling hungry? I translate.

—Fat fuck looks like he never stopped eating. How could you be hungry?

—I know. Let's get some tapas.

—Very good, Ricky.

—Yeah. I know. Spain, man. That's all they really eat here, right? Those little... bar shits.

—... It's like when you use the same razor to shave your face right after you've shaved your balls. Like, woops...

—Are you sure we can't get more coke?

—Let's eat first. Then find some.

—Yeah. We've gotta find those Scandinavian bitches. With Bolivia's finest.

—And Gordo a whore.

—Hey! You, mate! Cum ovuh heuh!

A burley Australian bloke accosts us as we're making our way toward the exit. Mrdok assumes he's the object of a tirade, while Rick steps up to bat defensive.

—Yeah? What is it, you fancy English motherfucker?

—Oy aint a Brit, mate. Imuh ozzie. An oy aint talkin bout you, its him, youh mate ovuh theuh oym aftuh.

He points his fat index finger in the direction of my chest.

—That fat one, ovuh theuh. He royt grabbed moy arse jes now, when oy wuz havin uh slosh.

Mrdok turns to look at Rick.

—Do you understand what the fuck he's saying?

Rick shakes his head helplessly.

—Woy oy wuz jes now at thuh dunny, doin a wee, wen thes fat bloke come royt up behind me and had imself a grab of moy arse.

—I'm afraid you're sorely mistaken.

–Well it aint sore, but oy em a bit offended, mate. Don't get me wrong, aint got nuthing against em queeuhs, long as dey keep theuh distance frum moy arse. En you aint kept it, mate.

–If anything, I brushed up lightly against you as I was going past…

–Yee, you is a royt loyt brushuh, aint you?

Now Mrdok is riled to stand up in my defense.

–What did you just call him?

–Oy sez hezuh royt fairy dustuh, your mate is.

–Mrdok, I protest, you have no idea how small the restroom is. In order to get from the door to the other free urinal, I had no choice but to move past—

–Enough. I understand the situation. And think this Australian motherfucker does, as well.

Mrdok spits on the floor menacingly. I suddenly recall Mrdok's deep-seated prejudice against Australians. Stemming from many years ago in Sydney, where he and Krstal had been at some yacht party off Scotland Island in the colorfully named bay of Pittwater, when a coal industry baron (who would later go on to become prime minister) made a pass right in front of Mrdok. To this day, Mrdok still isn't entirely sure whether the two of them managed to fuck once he was out of sight, but the suspicion has endured, ultimately surviving even the termination of their marriage. As a result, Mrdok carries within him a virulent hatred and disgust of all things Australian—be it kangaroos, crocodiles, or beef—but, most especially, Australian human beings of the male sex.

–I believe my friend here has made it perfectly clear that it was a brush—not a grab. For some reason, you just can't get that through your thick Aussie head, now can you? What the fuck does he have to do—tell the same goddamn story two, three times? Even if he was a fuckin queer—which he most certainly is not—why would he want to have anything to do with you? Not even the most desperate, dick-starved fag on this island would want to have anything with a whiny Australian *bitch*.

The Aussie swings at Mrdok, who immediately ducks, allowing the fist to land on Rick's face. Rick emits a piercing womanly yell, which stuns the Aussie into immobility, an immobility that perfectly suits Mrdok, who now brings his own hand against the Aussie's cheekbone; whether by accident or pure stroke of inborn genius, Mrdok applied his right, mechanical hand to the task, artificially inflating the hit and the impact in a superhuman way, sending the

Aussie flying across the room and crashing into a cocktail display upon the bar.

Well, we don't wait around to find out what will happen next.

2.

INSTEAD, RETREATING TO a nearby restaurant, Rick holding a bag of ice to his face, which is swelling by the minute—much to Gordo's unvarnished delight.

Gordo gloating, Mrdok musing—half aloud, half to himself—on what a trashy, washed-up place Ibiza has become. Nothing like the '90s. Why had they come here again? Oh right, it was his idea. Why hadn't one of these imbeciles talked him out of it. Wasn't it their job, after all? Or at least part of their job?

Why does he bother paying anyone, he now wants to know.

Ricky and Gordo exchange glances, as though hoping to find the answer written on the other's face.

Rick figures he'd better come up with something real fast. He's never heard Mrdok talk about money this way before—the idea of not paying people. Something about it just puts him off. He can't really articulate what. His face hurts too much to articulate much of anything. In lieu of answers, he looks around the room, now desperately wishing the Scandinavian babe with the blow would rematerialize.

The bad fucking techno, the trashy Brits everywhere. The ugly architecture, the overfried tasteless food. No quality anywhere you look. Cockroaches in the kitchen of the rented villa, the lazy butler and cleaning staff who don't do anything about it. Girls all too drugged up to properly fuck.

Waitress comes over to take their order. Mrdok asks for fish. Gordo looks surprised.

—But Mrdok, you *hate* seafood.

And it is true—he normally does. But now he wants to prove something. To himself and all the others. What this is, he barely knows himself. He articulates it all the same:

—Sometimes in life, you have to become a completely different person. So as to not bore yourself to death.

Gordo and Rick contemplate that one for a while. Or at least appear to.

—Besides. If I don't like it, I can always feed it to the dogs after.

Siren sounds. An ambulance drives past the window, stops just beyond the wall where they're seated. Mrdok stands up to better see what's going on, walks out on to the terrace.

A woman with beach-matted hair in a bikini is standing over a man splayed out on the pavement.

—He's not high, I swear! He just has epilepsy.

He had fallen off his skateboard and now he was going to the hospital.

The girl is probably German. That's what her accent sounds like. The medic bends down, sticks his gloved fingers in the guy's mouth. When was the last time he had a seizure, he asks her.

Mrdok loses interest, goes back in. Of course the guy took too many drugs, he thinks. At the table, tinto de verano is served; Gordo says he'll stick with water. When Rick asks why, he starts telling everyone about his recent diabetes diagnosis. He's meant to limit his sugar intake, or else he'll die. Alcohol has a lot of sugar in it. Especially those Spanish punches.

Rick says having diabetes is worse than having HIV now. Not that he has either. But a cousin of his got it, the HIV, and told him that. Apparently they got all these medications now that can make you live a real long time. It aint like the olden days, when the homos were dropping like flies. That's why there are so many of em on TV now. As long as you don't forget to take the meds, you can live like a normal person, be on TV. Can't even transmit it, even if you do it in the behind without a rubber. Now diabetes, that's somethin else. Can do all sorts of things to you. Make you go blind, lose a limb—

(Gordo supposes Rick has no idea that Mrdok's an amputee and is certainly not going to mention it—)

Even die. That's tough, Rick says, eyeing Gordo maliciously. And not so easy to get rid of, either. Does Gordo have hope that they'll come up with a cure for diabetes now that they got one for AIDS?

The waitress brings their food. Gordo followed Mrdok's lead and ordered a calamari salad. Rick's not eating. His jaw still hurts. Mrdok squirts some lemon juice on to his fried fish then throws the rind at Rick. It hits him in the swollen jaw. Gordo chortles. What a wit, what a wit! Rick calls Gordo a shit. Mrdok tells them both to simmer down. He looks pissed off that the fish doesn't taste that good. One more thing to add to his list of things he hates about Ibiza. The new Ibiza. It was never like this before. At least not a few years ago, the last time he was here.

Mrdok asks Gordo when was the last time they were in Ibiza. Gordo tells him the year. It wasn't like this then, he says. Gordo shakes his head to show agreement.

Mrdok doesn't want to finish his fish. It tastes like ass—and not in a good way, he adds. Now it's Rick's turn to laugh. Hey, speaking of ass—weren't we meant to get some for ol' diabetes breath over here? That is, if the insulin aint kickin in.

That made no sense. The drugged-out epileptic German is being carried on a stretcher past their window into the waiting ambulance. Gordo asks Rick whether he might not want to rush out and ask the paramedic if they can fix his face. Rick ignores the suggestion. I'll feed it to the dog back at the place, Mrdok's saying. There's a dog at the villa next to theirs. A friendly dog—always comes out to greet them whenever they return.

Gordo doesn't want a whore. Gordo wants to be left alone.

They go to a whorehouse. Or, to be precise, a strip club where the girls are said to offer extra favors, quote unquote. Most of the girls working inside are from Eastern Europe. Maybe some of them are Spanish. It's hard to tell.

The girls dance around the men, jiggling their titties to the bad Euro house music. Rick has gone off to the toilets to look for more blow. He promises to bring back a gram for himself and Mrdok, should he be so lucky. A whore with an Adam's apple jiggles next to Mrdok. Move on down the road, honey, you're not the one for me.

Mrdok asks Gordo what he looks for in a whore. Gordo replies he doesn't know, he's never really gone looking for one. Mrdok asks if he's serious, and when he sees he is, shakes his head—not disparagingly, but in a perplexed way, like he still doesn't understand who Gordo is after all these years. Unless he gets some coke and fast, he'll be too tired and groggy to press much further.

America has the best whores, Mrdok now says. It's one of the rare things he can get fairly patriotic about. He's been everywhere, after all, tried out all sorts of whores in many foreign distant lands. There are some close calls, but none he's had have ever quite come close. It's not just a question of variety, but also performance. Maybe it's because Americans work harder for their money in general. He's not completely sure. But he's always felt deep in his soul that America has the best whores, and presently, there is no one seated at this table who can either agree or disagree with this loud assertion. Rick hasn't traveled enough and Gordo, apparently, doesn't fuck.

One of the girls has this sideways glare. She keeps looking at their table from the side of her face instead of dead on. Almost like she doesn't want them to notice her looking. Or like she has a lazy eye. Almost like a shy man does, to a beautiful woman in a bar he just can't work up the gall to approach, and no amount of liquid confidence will rise it up in him.

Mrdok notices. Hey sweet thing, he beckons her over. She winds her way around the clutter of tables till she reaches theirs. Hey baby, you want a private dance? No but my friend here does. Gordo visibly blanches. Sure, honey. That'll be a hundred fifty euros up front for the dance, you want something else we'll discuss it back there.

Mrdok peels off five hundred euro notes. I want you to take this fat fuck all the way. Give him the time of his life. He works hard. He deserves it.

The girl takes Gordo by the paw and leads him into the back. Mrdok watches another girl mount the pole. She's wearing nothing except for an orange g-string that barely conceals her shaved slit. Pole clenched between her fists, she raises her feet above her shoulders, then over her head until she's upside down. Then she wraps her legs around the pole's height. Once secured, she releases her hands and twirls around with arms extended, then slides her way vaginally down to the pole's culmination.

Rick returns, nostrils twitching. You find some? Mrdok asks him. Yeah, see, the thing about it is... Mrdok already knows he's not gonna like what he's about to hear.

A nervous smile spreads across Rick's dumbfuck features.

—I was just fuckin with you, boss.

Then he slaps his open palm against Mrdok's chest. A gesture Mrdok feels slightly disgusted and offended by, till he discerns the little plastic baggy full of white powder between Rick's hand and his left tit.

—You sonuvabitch. Let's go do some.

—I just did. You go ahead. There's a little surprise waiting in there for you.

There is indeed a hot little honey in the men's single stall toilet waiting when he opens the door.

—Are you Mrdok?

She must be the one who sold Rick the blow. She is one of the types he would normally go for—petite, pert tits, pointy, sculpted facial features bordering on the verminesque—but he doesn't feel like doing anything sexual, so he dismisses her with the possibility of a private dance later. He snorts two thick lines and then takes an enormous splattery shit.

When he returns to the table, Rick looks coked up and/or pissed off. Why didn't you do anything with her? You could have at least let her blow you. Mrdok says he wasn't in the mood. But I already gave her the money. I mean, extra, on top of the money for the blow. Was supposed to be my treat for you. It's not like I can get the money back now.

Mrdok's surprised the bitch even reported this back to Rick. I guess in these higher class places, the whores are less discreet. Well, it *is* Europe.

They talk some more, but it's not really chatty coke—it rather has a strong anesthetizing effect on both of them. They're wired, but they don't feel like talking. More like grinding their jaws, watching in silence the girls on the stage.

After a while, Gordo and the girl reemerge from the back, join them at the table. Gordo sits in his former seat, the girl pulls a chair from the empty table next to theirs. They sit like that for a while, being all quiet, Rick and Mrdok high and distracted, Gordo and the girl bored and with nothing rich to say.

Finally Mrdok turns his head, registering their presence for the first time. So how was he, Mrdok asks the girl, how was the fat fuck? The girl sighs. He's fat all right, but not much of a fuck. Your Gordo's a homo.

Rick and Mrdok find this hilarious—especially Rick, erupting in laughter. Gordo blushes, says something about mechanical failure under conditions of high exertion, but their laughter drowns him out.

Gordo sits there wondering where it all went wrong. Meaning: this trip. It was supposed to be a fun vacation, a little away time for he and Mrdok. Then Rick had to attach himself, ruin everything. Well—as long as Mrdok's having fun. Which apparently he is. At Gordo's expense. There's nothing else Gordo can really say about it. And so he keeps his mouth shut and allows them to laugh.

Rick is thinking of lines: like, whether it's time to do another. Or maybe that girl over there. Twitchy. The twerps in the office're gonna be so jealous when they hear about this. No one ever gets to go any-where with Mrdok except for Gordo—not even his wife Mrtol. It was a spur of the moment thing, he'll tell them, feigning modesty. Just happened to be in the office late on Friday when Mrdok came out, struck up a conversation. Come on, Mrdok, we're going to be late, Gordo had said. So Mrdok said Rick what are you doing this weekend. And here I am. Here we all are.

They're leaving. It's time to call it a night. Rick and Mrdok agree the coke is bunk. They'll yell at the stripper who sold it to them if they see her on their way out. They don't see her. Can't be bothered to look. Gordo is just exhausted. He wants to sleep and sleep and sleep. Maybe eat something on the way. Mrdok says something about his friend with the yacht. Maybe he could call him to rescue them. Take them away from all this bullshit, to somewhere classy. Venice or else Mykonos. Tells Rick he has a place in Venice, nothing fancy, a little palazzo. Anywhere would be better than this, all these ugly fuckin people, he shouts into the night. Somewhere where the whores don't sell bad cocaine. The night is cobalt blue, the Mediterranean glistens. Ghost of a dead sailor moves past them. Rounding a corner, Mrdok commands Gordo to check and see how much he's currently worth.

CHAPTER THREE

MORMONS ON METH

THIS PAST AUTUMN, *Williamsburg Ovo-Lacto Fruitarian*'s own Hipster Metal columnist Seymour Kindness had the rare opportunity to speak with Stevo Rey of legendary noise outfit Mormons on Meth. Né Stevo Rey Mrdok (he foregoes the use of his last name, out of a professed lifelong hatred of his father, billionaire Elias Brynn Mrdok, who is also known for shunning the media—like father like son?), he moved to the Japanese capital when he was only nineteen, fresh out of a prolonged stint at boarding school. Since then, he has been as prolific as he is reclusive, opting to limit his verbal communications with the outside world to his blog, which has garnered a massive readership of extreme music fans on both sides of the Pacific for its boggling nihilistic ramblings.

If that's not enough to wrap your wonder around, there's also the astounding quantity of vinyl, cassette, and compact disc recordings he's released over the years, mainly with Mormons on Meth, but in an unquantifiable array of side projects as well (a partial discography appears below the interview.) Not only does he pummel the depths of unlistenability on these punishing amplifications of his tortured conscience, Stevo Rey purposefully eschews the accessibility of the digital era by refusing to release any of his music online in an effort to keep his demonic momentum pure and chock full of ear-splitting integrity. As Stevo Rey himself once wrote: *Purity knows no foundation; it is always just pure.*

Known throughout the noise scene as much for his prickly persona as for his shocking onstage antics—Mormons on Meth shows have routinely featured live Botox injections, simulated toenail clipping, surgical acrobatics, and pyrotechnical ball shaving (don't ask)—

not to mention that time Stevo Rey jumped onstage in the middle of a Merzbow concert and de-feathered a parakeet, causing the famously vegan noisician to storm off stage in protest in a punishing sea of feedback which the sound engineer couldn't figure out how to turn off for the following sixteen-and-a-half hours—Stevo Rey nonetheless made a gracious exception to his *No Interviews Ever* rule to sit down with Kindness over brewskies at his favorite Tokyo watering hole, the Empty Shark, on the eve of the release of the Mormons' latest—and, according to some fans, most brutal—release, *You Make Me Shit Like a Natural Woman.*

WILLIAMSBURG OVO-LACTO FRUITARIAN: Stevo Rey, tell us about the new album.

STEVO REY: I'd rather not.

WOLF: I think it's your most difficult work to date. And I mean that as a compliment. And a double album. Like, wow.

SR: Yeah, well...

WOLF: Your first album-length vinyl with the Mormons, *Gay Rotten Teeth,* famously consisted of just two side-long compositions: *Loose Tooth* and *Busted Nut.* The follow-up, *Methlehem,* was just one track extended on to four sides. *Shit Like a Woman* has like actual songs, traditional two to three minutes a slice. Would you say that Mormons on Meth have entered a new phase with this release?

SR: No.

WOLF: Your involvement with the Japanese noise scene over the years has reached new heights, to quote a recent review of the album on the influential website Black Metal Songstress...

SR: You came all the way to Tokyo to tell me this? We have the internet here, you know.

WOLF: Tell me about it! This place is like so high tech, dude. How is it living here? Have you been to that robot restaurant yet? I'm going there tonight with my girlfriend!

SR: So?

WOLF: So… I was wondering about the influence of like Japanese aesthetics on your like sound.

SR: It's something you shouldn't even bother trying to understand.

WOLF: Well why not?

SR: It's far too complicated a subject for you. You're just a tourist.

WOLF: I read somewhere that it's like because they lost the war and they're like all bent out of shape about it.

SR: … That has to be the dumbest fucking thing I've ever heard.

WOLF: Well what's your take on it? You know, as like, an insider and all.

Stevo Rey ignores the question and orders another Asahi.

SR: You get all sorts of dumb foreigners here, thinking they can adopt to the Japanese way of life. The reality is, they're all like you. They don't know shit.

WOLF: Well, I know a little, at least. Like about the Japanese noise scene…

SR: No you don't.

WOLF: Well, uh…

SR: Because there is no *scene*, as you put it. If you knew as much as you think you do, you never would've phrased it that way. There's Osaka, there's Kyoto, there's where we are now. Tokyo is actually the least interesting of the three, in terms of what you call noise. There's us and a couple of other people. You should really go to those other cities, if that's what you're interested in. You'll find much more of a so-called scene there, if such a thing can even be said to really exist. Go to Amami Oshima. They have a really great pink noise scene, as well as a lot of poisonous snakes.

WOLF: I'm curious about the title of your new album.

SR: *You Make Me Shit Like a Natural Woman.*

WOLF: Yeah. I mean, like, wow.

SR: Before you start going and saying it's misogynistic, I should tell you it's Makiko who came up with it. She's big into Aretha. She meant it as a sort of tribute.

WOLF: Your girlfriend, Makiko Kawasaki. Lead singer of the legendary Japanese grindcore band Derogated Necroplastic Gore Hooker.

SR: Man, why does everything have to be Japanese this and Japanese that with you? It's a grindcore band that happens to consist of four hot Japanese chicks, okay? Get the fuck over it.

WOLF: I'm just so excited being here. It's my first time in Japan.

SR: Yeah? Well guess what? It's not that great.

WOLF: But better than America, right?

SR: Anything's better than that rotten toxic shithole. I'll never go back there.

WOLF: Just curious: How much of America did you get to see outside of that boarding school you went to in northern California?

SR: A lot. Too much.

WOLF: Why do you hate it so much?

SR: Political correctness, for one thing. I complain a lot about Japan, but at least I don't have to contend with all that shit over here. They haven't even heard of it. I tell people the title of our new album, no one even blinks an eye. They know exactly what I'm talking about. It's like I speak their language. Even though I don't really. The American music press, man, that's all they do is bitch and complain about it. You know what it is, man? It's a form of censorship is what it is. The American form of censor*shit* for the twenty-first century. You're supposed to internalize it, self-censor…

WOLF: You clearly don't buy into it.

SR: Naw. Fuck that. You ask a Japanese person about political correctness, they won't even know what you're talking about.

WOLF: So what is it that brought you to Japan in the first place? Were you listening to like Merzbow and the Boredoms, stuff like that before you got here?

SR: I came here first to study. Well, it was more an excuse to get away from my family…

WOLF: Your father is like this famous rich guy.

SR: People call me an asshole. It's no secret. What they usually don't realize is everyone in my family is an asshole. Once you're brought up that way, you really have no choice.

WOLF: Okay. That makes sense.

SR: I've always been a nihilist, man. Deep down inside. It's like the fundamental core of who I am. Noise is not music—

WOLF: Yeah, dude! It's like raw sound. Sonic aggression. Like, harshness.

SR: Beyond all that, it's an expression. It's how I'm able to externalize my sophisticated worldview.

WOLF: Speaking of your father, you have this blog, *Thoughts from the Mind of a Son in Cruel Revolt*. A lot of it seems to be about him.

SR: Oh? If you say so…

WOLF: I believe you started the blog around the time your former band Pungent Uterus was breaking up.

SR: First off all, Pungent Uterus didn't break up.

WOLF: … You didn't?! Omigod. That's fucking awesome. Can fans expect a new album?

SR: I didn't say we're still together, you dimwit. What I said is that we didn't break up.

WOLF: Oh…

SR: We *de-materialized*. Okay? We were never really a band, in like the proper sense of the term. More like an *operation*. We fulfilled a certain needed function at a particular time in the evolution of the Tokyo sound. Once that moment was finished… well, we were, too.

WOLF: I know Kasuke Hiromito went back to his act Zero Zero Love Troll, you restarted Mormons on Meth.

SR: Yeah. It was around the time we did *Methlehem*. After we finished recording that album, man, I was ready for a long break. That album nearly killed me, in all honesty…

WOLF: It's a fucking brutal album. And a double album, on top of it! I mean, never before in the annals of noise has an album come this close to de-throning Merzbow's *Venereology*.

SR: Yeah, well, whatever. I don't go in much for comparisons. Neither does Masami, as far as I know.

WOLF: There's so much saturated filth in the mix—

SR: That's because we recorded initially using analog tapes. Then we put the tapes in the washing machine using a high-grade bleach to essentially destroy them. Destroyed the washing machine, too. What you're mistaking as grain is actually pure chemical smoothness: the whitest of white noise. After we pried the tapes from the inside of the washer, which was all melted, we kept the bleachy chemical water and used it to cook up a batch of meth, which we then smoked—so essentially our bodies ingested the noise, which had come out of our bodies—like a circular process. We were on that stuff for like six days while we were doing the final master, until we pretty much collapsed. Kiyoshi ended up in a mental institution for a few months, Makiko had to lock me in the bathroom, I spent a couple weeks just sitting in the bathtub drooling… Listening to it today, I mean, I know many consider it to be our masterpiece, and in a way, I'm not gonna lie, that's what we intended it to be: our *Trout Mask Replica*, our *Twin Infinitives*, our *20 Jazz Funk Greats*. But to me, I don't know, it just sounds unfinished, incomplete. I try not to listen to it anymore. Too many memories…

WOLF: I know before you got to Tokyo, you played bass in the Serial Nothings—

SR: That was just basic three-chord punk shit, man. It was another life. You can't compare anything I'm doing now with what I was doing back then.

WOLF: Was that the only proper band you played in?

SR: Well. I did play the jew's harp in Jesus and the Jizz Junkies.

WOLF: That's right, I forgot about that one… Well is there any chance you'll tour America with the new album?

SR: There's a better chance of us touring Antarctica, playing for a bunch of fucking penguins.

WOLF: So your true fans will have to travel all the way to Japan if they harbor any hopes of ever getting the full-on Mormon experience.

SR: I almost forgot to mention the other thing I hate about America: the sound in the clubs. By that I mean both the sound system and the engineers. And I'm not unique in that. Ask any of the bands over here who've played America, they'll tell you the same thing. Or just experience a show here for yourself, then compare. The level of quality and the connoisseurship just can't be beat. People over here really know what the fuck they're doing when it comes to processing this kind of sound through a mixing board. In America, I don't know, maybe they're just not used to it. They treat it like they're doing the controls at a fucking Bon Jovi concert or some shit.

WOLF: I wanted to ask you about side four on *Methlehem*. I read somewhere that during the mixing of that track, a rat got into the recording studio and started chewing on a live wire and was electrocuted. Apparently there happened to be a mic nearby that recorded the whole thing. You guys slowed the recording down to twenty-five minutes, ran the delay through I-don't-know-how-many layers of distortion, and used it as the core underlying sound—hence, the brutality, the harsh anti-euphoria of a live death caught on tape. Was that before or after the incident with the bleach you described earlier?

SR: Uhh, can you repeat the question? I wasn't listening.

WOLF: Maybe we should go back to the blog. Do you consider it more of an art project or more like therapy?

SR: What's the difference? *Thoughts from the Mind of a Son in Cruel Revolt* is like live documentation of my ongoing collapse. It's like… the soundtrack to the music, if that makes sense.

WOLF: I have to ask: does your father know about it?

SR: It doesn't matter. Everyone in my family, we have our own ways of coping. Like my brother Bobby, he's a full-on junkie. Last I heard, he was in rehab for like the fifteenth-and-a-half time.

WOLF: Bummer. If you don't mind, I'd like to quote a passage from your blog. It's an entry dated January 5th of this year. Title: The Hairy Black Hole of My Antipathy. Quote: *The world I have seemingly left behind is one I still carry with me. It's like a loogie, a ball of saliva that trails behind you, attached to an invisible thread, even after it's been spat out. If I could kill my father, then I'd finally be the son he truly deserves. I kill him with words, over and over again, and yet it's insufficient. By constantly acknowledging his sticky foundational presence in my life, I'm doing him a tremendous disservice by per-mitting him to exist on a plane that he really never did anything to deserve. What's stupendous about this, about him in general, is that the misanthropy he subsides on is really what birthed me. By embroiling me in hatred from a young age, he formed me as an extension of his worldview. Looking at me, he knows this, and it's why he can't stand me. Saturated in the indifference in which I was bred, I really have no option other than to act out. Others might have a more simplified means of dealing with this walking piece of excrement that is my father, like calling him a capitalist pig or whatever. I speak a language he can actually understand, even while realizing he never reads this, never listens to me—he'd never give me that satisfaction. Still, a part of me always fantasizes looking up and seeing him at one of my concerts. Not because I want him to be proud or feel shocked or uncomfortable or even understand. I guess I just want a wall to throw all this hate up against. He's a person that can't be confronted—like most things evil in this world. So I'm thankful, at least, that I had this model, this under-standing of what evil was from a young age. To have this symbol, this vessel through which to channel my joy and my rage…* I'm like, whoa, dude.*

SR: Well, yeah. So at least now you know where my sickness lies.

WOLF: So the writing on your blog is, like, the underlying message of your music.

SR: There is no underlying message, sweetheart. It's just junk. Noise for the sake of sound. Okay, so it's also a language. Of sorts. That's one place where the category of Japanoise, much as we all hate it, makes some kind of sense.

WOLF: Is Japanoise—so-called—different from noise produced elsewhere? How so? And if it is, how do you fit into it, being American?

SR: Interesting question. Listen to Hijokaidan and Harry Pussy side by side, there are some similarities. Maybe the connection lies in these universal emotions that the sound sets out to express. Emotions that, in the workaday world, are certainly transmitted through culturally specific forms of mediation. We try to, like, make those forms of mediation go away. Go beyond the need for translation of cultural specificities. At the end of the day, a scream is something we can all relate to.

WOLF: How would you characterize the Mormons on Meth sound?

SR: I like to think of our latest music as avant-shit. Our first two albums were more pink noise.

WOLF: What's up next? Another Mormons record?

SR: Oh I'm branching out. Right now I'm collaborating with Stu Membrane, the vibraphonist of an Osaka bossa nova quintet, Inbred Monkey. I can't say it's gonna be noise, per se. Not as it's traditionally constituted—or de-constituted. Maybe some people'll like it nonetheless.

WOLF: Well I for one am looking forward to it. You know, man, once you get to know you, you're not such an asshole after all.

SR: Yeah? Well guess what. You don't know me. I doubt you know much of anything. So go eat shit and die.

WOLF: Spoken like a true legend.

<u>Stevo Rey: a partial discography</u>

w/ MORMONS ON METH
Gay Rotten Teeth (Hairy A.F. Recordings)
Methlehem (Hairy A.F. Recordings)
You Make Me Shit Like a Natural Woman (Hairy A.F. Recordings)

w/ PUNGENT UTERUS
Nurse with Hard-on (Toxic Grove)
Shit Upon the Fabric of Force (Broken Nun)
Dick Rider in the Sullen Allegory (Inappropriate Soundscapes)
Mamaliga in my Megalith (Partial Lightning Recordings)
Dead Every Morning, Somewhat Alive in the Afternoon (Toxic Grove)
A Fuckface from Mallorca (Toxic Grove)
Uncle Brownstain (Lead Us Off the Rails)

w/ MASAKO "CHRIST" KAWANUCHI
Pretty Rape Machine (Goretron Fabrics Limited Edition)
I want to build a shelter for all the perverts of the world to die in (Limited Ltd.)
Groovy Jack-a-lantern (Invitation to a Beheading Records)

w/ GERMOPHOBE
Japanese Wire Lady (Goretron)
Smell My Titties (Free Jazz French Fries)
Around the World in 15 Minutes (Armfist Deluxe)
The Future in My Toilet Bowl (Fear as a Nuclear Weapon)

w/ AMAMI OSHIMA LUBE CHOIR
Virulent Splat (No Bone Recordings)

w/ LO-BLO RIDER
The Internet of Dings (Destitute Sounds)
A Faint Stirring in My Nothingness (Youth in Asia)

w/ JESUS AND THE JIZZ JUNKIES
No Holes Barred (Youth in Asia)
Mega-Smell (Gay Mushroom Cloud)
Anal Holocaust (End of the Road Recordings)
Assburger Syndrome (Terminal Okay Records)

Upside Down Antenna (split 7" w/ Side 999, self-released)
Funky Jerk-off Sounds (Hairy A.F. Recordings)
The Nestings: Lost Recordings (Toxic Grove)

CHAPTER FOUR

LONDON

THE ANNOUNCEMENT OF the new real estate campaign had been greeted with much relish among the more competitive eager beavers of the lower divisions. Deals were being struck left and right, solid patches of land exchanged for digitized numerical amounts in currencies that were traded for other currencies at day rate before the sunset in whichever continent the deal was struck. Mrdok took on the more lucrative deals or else the deals that just appeared confusing or troubling or worrisome, which is why he now found himself in London, where he was to finish procuring a couple of parking lots—some junior agent's latest hot sell, and, given the price of real estate in central London potentially a career-making deal, though because of his junior status, he hadn't managed to quite tighten all the loose ends, leaving enough question marks dangling to necessitate yet another transatlantic intervention.

He had barely arrived when the call came in from the home office: Jaco had eaten paint. Again. This time, he was in intensive care.

London: Always happy to visit; even happier to leave.

Out of fairness, one couldn't readily expunge the city from Mrdok's biography. That shitless attitude he carried with him—he had partly learned it from Tony Fatballs, it is true; but he had also learned it from here. All those years back... Well, let's look at time and what it does to you. A most unpleasant task or, more literally, prospect. Hair stands on end, you're thinking it's a forest. You have your doubts, but there are enough minutes and seconds in this life to conspire into eliminating every last one of them: hairs and doubts the same. It turns gray, falls out. One's pecker no longer retains the same tremulous timber. Youth boils itself down in the pit of the stomach, singing its lining; the pain of holes. Acidic matter erupts through the throat like lava, burning twice as hard when you're forced—whether by location or circumstance—to swallow it back down.

He lived in the East End in those days, Shoreditch when it was still bleak, just as those packs of hipsters and art students followed by moneyed fashion victims were beginning to arrive in an unwitting collective effort to remake those brick building'd industrial streets into something even less desirable and even more expensive. Taking the bus home from his classes at the London School of Economics through slow-moving traffic, past the skyscrapers of bankland and into the dilapidation of those eastern territories. Sometimes he'd get held up at knifepoint. At times he'd run, at others he'd surrender over what little he had—a lesson in ownership and dispossession with which to supplement his studies, I suppose...

Lived, for a time, with art students, in a shared house that was a study in urban decay. Cheap and dangerous, then; unlike today, when it's just expensive and dangerous. Somehow less fun. If you were poor and newly arrived, that is simply where you lived.

I've gotta get the fuck out of here. I can remember Mrdok saying those very words to me one day while we waited to cross the street, struggling to digest a lunch of grease-fried chicken bits from a corner shop. It was a secret about Mrdok that no one else knew at the time, save for me. While for the art students, it served as a sort of badge of honor, living in this gang-infused battleground of abandoned warehouses squatted by faded pink-mohawked heroin addicts, for a student of the prestigious London School of Economics, it was certainly an article of shame. He hid it behind the Savile Row suits, a display of valor. Some still viewed him with suspicion—his rough way of talking. A strange and vulgar tinny twinge to the oh-so-refined ear of the English landed gentry. Who was he, dumb American, to be soaking all this up? Ambitioning to join the ranks of the so-despised legion of Bankers, who even then were distrusted, who even then were credited with every single rotten thing going wrong in London life, from the traffic to each and every five-p increase in the price of chips at the corner fry shop.

London in the nineties. The era of Brit pop, the YBAs, the not-so-great economy. How did Mrdok, of all people, end up here? As with so many key events in Mrdok's early biography, the decision was less his own than the followed advice of Anthony Fatobello, known popularly as Tony Fatballs, whose surrogacy had been rather cemented by this point, Tony having located in the person of young Mrdok a rather ideal specimen of protégé. *Go to London and find yourself*, Tony had advised him shortly after his full name had been splashed in the national media below headlines that invariably contained the phrases *predatory lending* and *pending indictment*, and, with the pull of a few strings, Mrdok found himself placed in the first year class of the world's most prominent university dedicated to the study of the flow of money and materials.

Nor did Mrdok attain much in the way of friendship with the artists with whom he first squatted (in an even more derelict building farther north in Dalston), with whom he then later moved into a legal, slightly better dwelling in Whoreditch, as it was then sardonically deemed. They came from different worlds. Like many a London art student at the time and ever since, most of them were descended from the upper echelons, posing as the working class in order to fit a predefined model of cool. To them, there was no shame in living in such squalor, surrounded by the bums, the immigrants, the neverending stench of frying meat coated in strange exotic spices—rather, it was a romantic adventure. It was Mrdok who was secretly ashamed, offended, disgusted by all this living putrefaction surrounding. It was Mrdok who was proud enough to wish to rise above all this. While the others, viewing the experience as an extended holiday (in the British sense of the term), seemingly never wished to leave, but to dwell in it in perpetuity—until they themselves were well fried.

They used to make fun of him, his flatmates, behind his back. This he knew. After a few bitter efforts, he gave up trying to be friends with them. Their irony-drenched dialogue strewn with cultural references that flew way over Mrdok's head—it frustrated and filled him with self-pity. He knew better than to mistake himself as part of their parceled world. In a sense, they were equally pathetic, Mrdok (and only in this particular phase of his life, indeed!) and the art brats, yet in opposing ways. They were relatively rich and wanted to be poor, he was relatively poor—as he, at the time, owing to a civil war in the island nation where the great bulk of his father's finances were stored, had no access to the funds put aside by his father with the help of Tony Fatballs for his education; Fatballs was in turn funding said education, quite generously—and wanted desperately to be rich. To have access to all that wealth to which he tragically and veritably was entitled.

Viewed together from the outside, they were all a group of imposters. And they viewed his hunger with derision. It was a knowing derision. They with their posh accents, Mrdok with his neutral American crackerjack. Lying on his back in bed at night in his tiny box of a room, through the toilet paper-thin walls he'd listen to them giggling, playing their indie pop, smelling their marijuana, knowing they despised him, that he was little more than a bizarre punchline to their weak jokes. And it felt, on some nights, as though the entire world despised him.

No, he would never truly understand *their* world. But he had other things to do with his life—there were other things London was good for. He was fascinated, above all, by money. How it flowed. How it operated. He was going to build things, big things. He just didn't know what. Not quite yet.

This shell. He had to crawl out of it. Reach the ceiling, become a king.

I suppose it is inevitable that Mrdok and I first met under these circumstances. We were, after all, both outsiders, in our varied ways. Searching for our space among people who didn't much look or sound like us—who, as a matter of truth, probably would have preferred our not being there. Our show of strength is that we stayed… Well, we stayed for as long as we could.

I had entered LSE myself as a slightly older student—at twenty-eight, I appeared even older than that age, and certainly more weathered than many of my fresh-faced undergraduate classmates. I had long held a certain esteem for English literature—well, for English society in general, I suppose. Something I had long fantasized and romanticized from afar, with perhaps only a naïve understanding of the demands such a society makes upon its inhabitants. The point is, in actually going so far as to relocate there for the purposes of further study, I was effectively launching myself into the orbit of a second life, so different from my first.

About that first life—well, what can I say? The path that I was pushed toward, by certain overeager family members—in particular, a stepfather with whom I am no longer in contact—turned out to be quite the wrong one for me. I found myself, at twenty, enrolled in a small-town theological seminary somewhere in the deepest recesses of Texas, a place of tumbleweed and armadillos and not much else, save for the froth-mouthed adherents to the faith. Shaking a tambourine, ebulliating the praises of The Lord Our Savior From On High. In classes such as Snakehandling for Beginners, where we learned to hone our craft, converting the heathens and scaring the world into saving itself from sin. Scaring and scarring ourselves, really, in a prolonged process of existential flagellation. If it sounds a bit much, that's because it, in fact, was. I stuck out from the start, as I was the sole student coming from a more academic state of mind.

I asked too many questions. I had, after all, spent the two years since my high school graduation locked away in my room in our small home upon the prairie, reading voraciously and strenuously avoiding contact with my mother and stepfather, about whom the less said the better.

I wish I could claim to have left the theological seminary—nay, bible college—under quieter circumstances than I did. But my exit was marked by a scandal loud and flamboyant enough that I felt it best to not only leave the state of Texas, but the United States of America… Suffice to say that the Lord's work was not for me. No need to say much more than that. For there is hardly a necessity to go digging into the deep recesses of the past, when we can all acknowledge, in unison, that truth—the ultimate goal of such excavations—is endlessly malleable—hence, the frequency of such cliché utterances as *he said, she said* (though in this case, it was more of a redundant *he said, he said*)—and indeed, often retrieved or else subsequently presented in twisted format so as to defame the innocent (who are never truly presumed as such.)

When I met Mrdok, I knew from the start that I could do great things by him, with him, for him. There is the old saying, behind every great man stands a good woman—or some such. Well, I would change that. Behind every great man stands another, perhaps not so great, but strong and sturdy, man. Or perhaps we were just drawn to each other for our own complex set of reasons. While Mrdok boasts any number of great talents, the task of writing and any kind of schoolwork in general is quite beneath him. He required, from early on, and especially while at LSE, an assistant to help toward the completion of certain tasks—a role I turned out to be quite suited for and pleased to perform. I had found my purpose.

Mrdok, after all, is a genius motivated by reflex and intuition. He is not the type to waste time sitting around, stewing, reflecting. It is perhaps a less methodical mode of genius than that to which the world is accustomed. But it is a mode of genius nonetheless—that must be asserted at every turn. There are times, it is true, when I attempted to stir up some torrent of focus in him, when we were at work on a term paper, for instance. We had both enrolled in the same seminar on Marxist economics, taught by one tweed bow tied don by the name of Professor Oliver Liveright-Hutchinson. Among our assignments in this ambitious year-long undertaking was to read the entirety of *Capital,* all three incomplete volumes, and find at least one thing wrong on each page of the treatise. Only through such a methodological index of fault-finding, Professor Liveright-Hutchinson assured us, could we truly come to understand the depth of flaw that mired the entirety of Marxian economics—the entire Marxian worldview, really—and thus come to appreciate with the proper amount of hatred befitting a duty-bound, steel-coated capitalist.

There was a bit of a contrast in the manner in which each of us pursued the assignment. I must admit that mine was endowed with a certain relish (and not the kind normally applied to American hot dogs!) There we were, after all, *in Marx's city,* the very place where much of *Capital* had been composed. London, the city of bankers! Like Herr Doktor Marx, I myself would while away many of my afternoons, post-class, huddled among the shelves of the British Library, deep in studious attention amongst a sprawl of books and scholarly journals, charting my path of understanding through this perilous world. An understanding of ideology—even such a vile ideology as that promulgated by Marx and his fellow degenerate Engels—while burdensome, is nonetheless necessary to acquire at the outset of any battle. Was it not Sun Tzu who declared *know thy enemy* at the very start of his *Art of War*? I can no longer recall such learned particulars, it is true, embedded as I have long been in the world of more practical affairs, yet they have been grounded somewhere deep in the arsenal.

Mrdok's approach to the subject, on the other hand, was more restrained.

–What the fuck is he talking about? I recall him asking, utilizing the rather pointed phraseology that he has since become known for in certain circles, throwing the book down in disgust. What is this shit? Sum it up for me in, uh, fifteen words or less.

I sat before him, pensively embroiled, staring down at the slab of desk between us, upon which rested Mrdok's hands. Mrdok always had the loveliest, in a masculine sense, of hands, but especially now, when he was in the very fertile prime of his life. Neither stout nor frail, each finger extended bluntly with a manly girth, culminating in manicured cuticles—so one would think, though an actual manicure was hardly necessary, as Mrdok himself was quite skilled with the clippers, with an eye to detail that rivaled Michelangelo himself—and on the toes, as well. What's more, he kept them impeccably clean— not the easiest task in a city as filthy as London in those years, and East London in particular, awash in germy junky homelessy immigrant swill. With only two or occasionally three blue veins impressing themselves upon the surface just below the slightly swollen knuckles, the hands were a study in sculptural perfection, the likes of which even Bernini failed to attain in his intricate studies of masculine prowess and refinement.

–I think, I began with a certain amount of apprehension, the essence of Marx's theory is that in the ideal scenario, the workers should come to own the means of production.

Mrdok stared at me open-mouthed.

–Is *that* what this is all about?

I nodded.

–In essence. Slightly distilled essence… Yes.

Mrdok shook his head.

–That's the dumbest fuckin idea I've ever heard in my life.

–Yes, I assured him. I think Professor Liveright-Hutchinson would agree with the spirit, if not the exact wording, of that remark.

–And so then what are people like us supposed to do? Under Marx's theory.

–Well, I said, under Marx's theory, people like us shouldn't exist.

–Ha! That's great. I love it. Write that down!

–I…

–That's going to be the theme of my term paper.

–You…

–*People like us shouldn't exist.* You just said it. You know what that means? Marx's theory is a violation of human rights. You can't have Marxism without violating the rights of people like us to exist! Without *killing off* people.

–Well. Now that you put it that way, there actually are a number of examples of regimes inspired by Marxian principles that *did* kill people.

–Great. Put it all in there. Have it on my desk by Monday.

Notice how just in a few words, Mrdok was able to so eloquently grasp the entire flawed nature of communism, its barbaric disregard, masquerading beneath a deceptively all-encompassing admiration for mankind, for all human life. The ideology that gave rise to, enabled and sustained, the bloodied legacies of Stalin, Mao, Castro, Pol Pot, of so many cruel murdering tyrants, all of whom were wont to proclaim, without the faintest whiff of irony, their love and admiration for the common man. Unlike mere mortals such as myself, true visionaries like Mrdok need not waste hours of their time ensconced in books and learned matters in order to apprehend both the flaws and potentials of the universe of mankind.

And with that, Mrdok was gone—for the weekend, I should qualify—where to, I seldom knew. Though his absence was merely physical, I must add. Because thoughts of him by necessity remained with me throughout the weekend as I silently completed this and certain other of his assignments. It was a unique opportunity to, in a sense, *become* Mrdok, temporarily relinquishing the exigencies of self-hood, or else *infuse* my self with his—for, in order to write as Mrdok, as I very often do, I had to in effect channel the very essence of his being—a task, it turns out, I was innately suited for.

We were able to keep it up for a time, our London ruse. Mrdok loves to tell people, self-disparagingly, that he flunked out of college. It is also, by now, something of a point of pride, a victory over the London School of Economics and the veneer of institutional respectability that it boasts. In truth (and I do not think Mrdok would mind too much my writing it here, since it makes little difference in the grand scheme of how things in the end turned out), he was expelled. I—though I was implicated in the affair—was somehow not. Though we had both by then proven, in our own ways—he in London, me in rural Texas—that neither of us was really fit for the conventional academic life. I had a choice to make: was I to continue with my wayward studies in London or would I follow Mrdok back to New York, where he promised me, in exchange for dropping out of LSE, the position of Number Two man in a start-up he promised would come to alter the very world as we know it? Well, as you can readily imagine, I did not need to hesitate for long before reaching my decision.

I think both of us were happy to leave. But the London of those years was a very different place than it is today. The nocturnal London that Mrdok now looks down upon, from his tower high up.

A well of conflicting emotions for our man. Happy, of course, that he now has a good excuse to leave. But, pragmatist that he is, Mrdok faces one seemingly insurmountable issue: he has just arrived. It is nighttime. And the business he has endeavored to undertake cannot be completed until morning. What to do. Lead poisoning no laughing matter. Brain damage, all sorts of damage, may well be on the horizon. Mrtol panicking on the phone, demanding that he get back to the city at once. And the prospect of it indeed unnerving. Where would that lead him in his Rolodex of progeny? One son a junkie, the other a hateful wretch, now the third, what, a potential vegetable?

He had to put a stop to this. Already the home office was dealing with the medical side of things, flying in the best surgeons and specialists. The lights upon the city at this hour always put him in a melancholic mood. He hates certain of the buildings, towers that have been erected in his time away. In his time there, as well. Perhaps the most reprehensible skyline mutilator was 30 St Mary Axe, commonly known as the Gherkin—although Mrdok, among his few friends here, famously branded the building King Kong's Dildo. A characterization that viscerally evokes the sheer perversion of the thing, its curvilinear protrudence into the night sky. Though now it has been dwarfed by much taller buildings, Mrdok has always secretly harbored a wish that it might some day form the target of a 9/11-style attack, thus ridding the London skyline of such a blighted monstrosity. Far from inflicting any real or lasting damage on the discipline of architecture, such that it has become in this century of ours, such an act might come to redeem it, Mrdok reasons.

Most annoyingly, its position is now blocking Mrdok's view, further befouling his mood. Confusion is not a state that befits Mrdok's person, particularly when exacerbated by jetlag. He hesitates, then picks up his phone, hits a button that instantly connects him to the home office across the pond.

–Marcia, get me the parking lot guy on the line… What's his name again?

Ring ring.

–Mister Mrdok.

–Just Mrdok.

–Mrdok, on behalf of Patel Limited Enterprises, I wish to welcome you to London. How was your flight, sir?

–Hasty. And it's gonna get hastier, I'm afraid.

–Why might that be, sir? We are still meeting tomorrow, I hope?

–The deal is set in stone, you don't have to worry. But I have an emergency back at home that popped up when I was in the air. Literally. It sucks. But I have to get back.

–Does this mean—

–Look, I'm still taking your parking lots. No need to sweat. But I'm gonna have to send someone out tomorrow to take a look at them. I'm assuming that's all right with you.

–But of course, sir. It has always been a dream of mine to meet you. But I can accept that now is not the time.

–I'm just… Fuck. You know what I'll do? I'll look at the paperwork remotely, when I'm on the plane going back tonight, tomorrow. Whatever the fucking time's gonna be over the Atlantic. I'll look at the papers and I'll… When I send my guy over there tomorrow, I'll have him conference me in, we'll do a video conference, so I'll be able to see and, just… *involve* myself with the process. I mean, I wanted to be physically there. But now we'll have to settle for the pixelated me.

–I hope it is nothing dire, sir.

–It, well… It is what it is.

–If you want, we can move the time—

–It doesn't matter. I'm not going to sleep on the plane anyway. We'll keep the original time. Gordo, my assistant Gordo is going to call you now to make all the further arrangements.

–Yes. Gordo. I will tell my personal assistant to expect his call.

–Well, look me up when you come to New York, Patel. I don't think I'll be back in London for some time.

London Eye spinning slowly on the other side of the Thames. He'll take a whisky, swallow a pill, get the driver to take him back to Heathrow. Bye bye London. This city.

When will Mrdok have a city of his own?

That's the burning question. The only question of any pertinence occupying his mind of late. Fucking parking lots. Why were they even selling. Fuckers must be desperate for cash. Mrdok would've been willing to pay twice what they were asking. Central London, the most traffic-clogged artery in the western world. The most expensive place to park your car. He sees the money in the form of numbers, digital numbers blinking in orange on the back of his eyelids. The money he'd triple within the year.

CHAPTER FIVE

BABYS FOR SALE

1.

WHAT IS ALL this waking up into and for? Where is my phone? Rosalita too. Beeping noise sounds real strange. Can't move my head now it's shifting seems like what I'm starved no there are tubes. Ralph is in the corner watching. Got tired of being called Ellen now he's Ralph. I'm not stupid I know no one else knows he is there. Ralph, Ellen, Ralphellen bring me my phone I want to say or else should but I can't say much of anything or make a noise even this tube going down my throat. This tube of daddy. Daddy coming mommy says. But I don't want daddy. When did I see daddy last I don't even know. No way of knowing. Daddy is the tube going down my throat. Mommy whispers there is food in there gonna make you strong again goddamnit Jaco in the very next breath how could you have. And of course I am relieved from having to say anything back. The tube again. Tube at the top. Little baggy at the other end. What would happen if. Ralph playing doctor comes over adjusts something on the monitors. What if Ralph were to come punch mommy in the face: something I fantasize daily. Too much maybe. Don't tell Missus Gardenia about it, will get in so much trouble. She wouldn't even notice. Ralph is lucky, he can get away with anything. Even the time that lightning struck him in half, the next day he was fine, back to-gether again. The static hum like one time I had my headphones on and my phone stopped working. Mime holding my phone in my hand so mommy'll bring it. Mommy shakes her head no, turns on TV instead. TV is so boring. Daddy'll be here soon, says. I don't want daddy, I want my phone. Why does mommy always have to be so mean? Mean to Rosalita, too, not just me and Ralph. Tubes stop me from puking. Nurse comes and adjusts lower tube, where my pee comes out of. Mommy says when is Doctor Silverstein coming back in, it's been all of two and a half hours. I was asleep when he came in here before. It's cos I wanted the colors inside me. Sister Rose says it is bad, only meant to look pretty on the outside. Why am I not allowed to? Mommy has her colors, Daddy has his brightness. Some days daddy is at home all I see are the bright lights. That's cos the colors on my cosmic. Phoneglow in the dark under the covers at night. I like to watch all sorts of things. Not just animated, either. Screen different from the sun, but only a little. The soldiers're trying to find a terrorist in creepy-looking abandoned house could pop out at any moment with full-on ammo machine guns and tut-tut-tut-tut-tut-tut-tut the good guys dead oh no what will we do next. Daddy said once there are no more wars we should start some. Once I go into the house, I can make anything happen on the screen. Ralph doesn't like going outside. He says the stratosphere melting. I think Ralph cares for the environment. Sister Megan doesn't. She says it's all a lie of the global elites. Ralph knows global warming is real, that the TV is wrong. The man on the TV said. Mommy gets to talk on her phone. Saying yes it was critical but now thank god they say he is going to pull through. I knew, wasn't going anywhere. Ralph there in the corner the whole time. If I stopped seeing him, then I'd know. Daddy bought an airplane mommy said. When I get bigger we can ride in it. One day when I'm big enough he'll even let me fly it. The beeping sounds like data. In my internet class, Sister Richard said that soon the flow of information will surpass the speed of light. I wish the curtains wouldn't be so open here all the time. Makes it hard to sleep. Mommy says I'm not supposed to sleep. Ralph says it's okay, he'll watch over. Wake me up in case anything exciting happens. Ralph has brown hair and a red plaid skirt. He's like those ones on TV. Maybe I can get a new phone. When something happens I always get something. Wouldn't it be cool if I got to have two. Icked-out waste that comes out of me here. TV now and there's nothing else to look at, so I have to. Man crawling through a tube. The tube that comes out of me. Tube of night. Man on the TV screen says silk road. That is so cool it means there was once a road made out of silk. You could like crawl on it and it wouldn't even hurt your knees. Mom changes the channel to two men yelling at each other. This is the news. Television is the most powerful force in the world the bald man shouts at the haired man. Commercial comes on and we've gotta run toward the danger. I don't want to watch the news it is loud and boring and I can't even say this to mommy so. Sometimes TV is so stupid, where is my phone. I can't even see it. I bet Mommy forgot to take it to the hospital, probably. Tell Ralph to go get it. Doctor Silverstein's breath smells like old farts. I want him to take the tube out. Paint doesn't taste that bad. Everyone on TV talks the same. The same voice. Saying the same type of things. He says sepic shock. Septic? Skeptic? Doctor Silverstein. I like the way those words sound. Tell Ralph to remember them. Pretty soon the arrows. Time to go outside. As soon as daddy comes in, I'll pretend to be asleep. Mommy changes the channel. More screaming men. I don't think she knows what she is looking for. Most grown-ups don't. Ralph already fallen asleep in the corner. I don't care if I never go home.

2.

SHE'S ON HER way to the Staten Island Ferry. As she's crossing the Bowery, she sees a lesbian beating up her girlfriend, who's cowering up against a building. The one who's hitting her has cornrows that seethe with anger.

–Come on, bro, we goin home! Now! We goin home, bro!

Just pummeling the poor girl, who clearly doesn't want to go home. At least in public it won't be so bad. She looks insane. Is she a lesbian or could it be a man? A fourteen-year-old boy. Or one of those… Bev can't tell. It is upsetting to her, disturbing to watch. She is unsure whether to do something, interfere. Try to stop this violence from happening, getting worse even. If they go home, she will probably kill her. Maybe she should do something. If she were sure she wouldn't get hurt herself. The lesbian or whatever could turn around, beat *her* up instead. Bev just got her hair and nails done. Like she does each Sunday.

There's a tall hipster, a white guy. He and his girlfriend. Like Bev, they're just standing there looking. Not interfering. Two traffic cops standing in the middle of the intersection directing traffic. Seem not to notice, and if they do, don't care. Bev can't stand it anymore. Walk signal comes, so she crosses the street. The two lesbians cross as well. At first they're behind, they quickly overtake her. Walking at this furious pace. Cornrows keeps addressing her girlfriend as bro. When they get to the other side, she suddenly turns and punches the girl in her face. Something goes flying across the sidewalk. Bev thinks it might be her glasses, or else a clip in her hair. She looks on the ground but it all happened so fast, and is still happening, she can't find the object, determine what it was.

Now cornrows has her girl up against the building by the skull. Could it be she's having a psychotic episode? The hipster and his girlfriend are standing there watching, nobody moves, nobody knows what to say or do. Arrested by conscience. This is New York City, everyone's afraid of violence. You're not supposed to see things like this anymore in New York City, it's not like it's the '70s. The traffic cops keep on ignoring the scene, or else they're preoccupied, though it's hard to believe, there's barely any traffic. They probably figure it's just a couple crackhead lezzers, who cares. Let them fight it out. Bev is scared. She doesn't know what to do.

Suddenly a third girl appears, just as cornrows begins dragging her girlfriend down the sidewalk. She appears to know the couple, but she also might not.

–Yo, you buggin, bro! You buggin! What the *fuck* you do?

She's screaming in cornrows's crazed foaming face, as though trying to compete with the rage. Cornrows pushes her girlfriend away. Girlfriend starts walking down Broome Street.

–You get back here, bro! We goin home! We goin home!

The third lesbian screams at the top of her lungs in cornrows's face, trying to scare some sense into her. Bev is scared. She can't understand what the third girl is yelling, it is just so loud and angry, she crosses to the other side, even though the light is red, it is New York City so who cares. One of the traffic cops blows his whistle at her.

–Hey! Excuse me? Which part of a red light is it that you don't understand?

–I'm sorry, I...

–No. No room for sorries today, Miss. I'm writing you a ticket.

–What about—these girls. They're tearing each other apart over there.

–That's none of my concern. Yours, either.

They watch, unconcerned. The third girl grabs the angry violent lesbian, rips the cornrows out of the back of her head. She screams, punches the girl in the face in the exact same way that she punched her girlfriend a minute ago. The girl grabs decrowned cornrows, puts her in a headlock, wrestles her down to the pavement.

–Now that's what I call a catfight! says the traffic cop with a crude chortle.

–Are you serious? You're just going to... to like sit here and watch?

–Of course not. I'm writing you a ticket. For jaywalking.

–OMG. Write *them* a ticket.

–They're not disobeying traffic laws.

–Are you even for real? Who ever heard of getting a ticket for jaywalking in New York City?

–Yeah, well. It just happens to be your lucky day. Now you can pay this online, by going –

–Can you just do your like civic duty as a police officer by like stopping this godawful fight? Just… Arrest that girl, actually. The one with the cornrows. She's the one who started it, she's been beating up that poor –

–Miss, that's not my job. I am a traffic officer. Now if you'd like to call the metropolitan police –

–This is like the wrongest thing ever.

But, ticket in her pocket, she keeps moving, which is what you do, after all, in New York. What other way forward could there be? All she'd wanted was a nice long walk after her salon visit. She won't let the weirdness of the day ruin it for her.

Unseasonably warm for October, though that's the New Normal. I mean, global warming and all, but that's not the worst thing ever when it comes to like basic comfort. She really needs to stop with that, though. She almost has. Her last boyfriend, the guy she dated before she met Mrdok, was a social linguist. He'd written his thesis on the overabundance of the superlative in the contemporary American vernacular. God, what a mouthful. Anyway, long story short, the whole time they'd been dating, he'd been using Bev as a case study without her even knowing. How ethical is that? Okay, he changed her name in the dissertation. But still. I mean, what is she *supposed* to talk like anyway? Ever since then, she becomes self-conscious whenever she hears it leeching back in. Talk about a toxic creep. Nothing like Mrdok, who—okay, it's not ideal, he's married, he can't fully commit, *at this moment*—but at least he isn't like secretly monitoring the way she talks.

Fuck it. After that shitshow, she no longer feels much like walking. She gets out her phone, will take an Uber instead.

This airy fairy morning, warm but gray. Helicopter whirring up ahead. Wonder if Mrdok's in it. Could be. He just bought a plane, apparently. Soon he'll own the whole city. The skies over it, too. Wouldn't be surprised. Life with him could be the best thing ever. Like, wow. As for now, can't really tell anyone. Let it get too loud, and ouch. I wonder what he's doing right about now.

It's raining by the time she reaches the South Ferry port. The waters separating Manhattan from Staten Island are brown and green. She puts in her earbuds, R&B streaming radio. On the upper deck, her gaze shifts between her cotton candy colored nails and the brown-green waters, the city above, its brown orifice in the musty rain. It is one of those rains that will never stop, she can already tell, and she has forgotten her umbrella. Pouring down, Statue of Liberty stabs at the sky with her torch. Fall down, evil sky, cover this city up with your clouds. Suffocate it, so that all its evils will lift up and be swallowed by the heavens.

Now, as though responding directly to her thoughts, the rains are released from the skies in torrents, pounding the grottiness of those upper bay waters like they're some sort of exotic marble rather than the accumulated filth of days. Across the aisle, guy in a Camel cigarettes t-shirt gives her the hairy eyeball. Once she starts to feel it, she looks down at her nails. To be alive in autumn already means to be half-dead, one must admit. Glances are things to be avoided, her mom'd always taught her. Particularly ones coming from men. Particularly ones coming from men in the city. The city a vile place that we nonetheless rely on. Everyone in the outer boroughs forced into a sort of parasitical existence upon the Manhattan nucleus. Men in the city are all rapists. Or at least potential rapists. That's what mom said. It's partly because she grew up in a different era, when the city was different, when this was somewhat true. She had once felt the sharpness of a knife stabbing into her. Bled out on a street corner, knew what color night was. City night, with all its broken light. Bev always suspected it was a drug deal gone horribly wrong, but when pressed, her mother never elaborated. Those were her wild years, details of which would leak forth every now and then, off hand and the cuff, without much detail gone into. Bev gathered that her mother wanted to protect her, but from what, she couldn't gage. From knowledge? Some hideous awareness of mom's adolescent past? It was more like mom didn't want her to wind up going down that road herself. But if that's the case, why not feed it to her as a warning parable?

Bev just doesn't get mom sometimes. But that's fine. She won't be living with her much longer anyway. Mrdok's promised to get her a place in the city, right in midtown. Now that'll be a life changer.

Moving up in the world. The rain won't let up. Staten Island hasn't been spared from the wet avalanche, and she doesn't feel like going home right away anyway, so she ducks into a coffee shop near the ferry port, just beyond the vast forever parking lot. She orders a green skinny chai latte and settles into a seat in the corner. She takes out of her Fendi bag the new featherweight MacBook Pro Mrdok bought her. A synthesized Muzak version of *Born to Handjive Baby* plays in the background. Bev hums along mindlessly. Opens up her browser and googles *babys for sale*. Google auto-corrects her. She always forgets to do the *ie* instead of the *y*. Somehow always slips her mind when she sits down to type. Thank god for auto-correct.

Outside, the wind's turned furious. Ugh. You have to like really comb the search results to find the ones you're looking for. The ones you want. The real ones. There is, surprisingly, a market for this kind of thing, though perhaps only a highly specialized one. The thing is, she's barren. She still wants one, though. What woman doesn't? She knows it's not politically correct to say, but she just can't see how any woman could harbor the ambition to evade the maternal duty. I mean, heck, even the gays are finding ways to have babies these days.

She thinks the time will come with Mrdok, eventually, when the need for the conversation will arise. So it never hurts to do some research in advance. Best place in the world to buy a baby from these days is Malaysia, it seems. That's what she keeps seeing in the search results. Apparently you can get one for as little as $450, though it's best to spend more up in the $7,000 range. And with her and Mrdok's budget, they can certainly afford that, if not a bit extra. Quality control and all.

This little baby is so cute. The mother only wants $700 for it. A little baby girl called Samantha. Samantha was always a pretty name, Bev thinks. Although from what she understands, there is some flexibility on the name thing. She supposes that once you buy one, you can name it whatever you want. It's only fair. You are the one paying for it, after all. I mean, why should someone else tell her what to name her own baby? That would be like if we were living under communism or something. Is that even a thing anymore? Bev isn't sure. Maybe in Malaysia. Chinese babies are the most expensive. She's not sure why that is. Mostly it's Filipino and Indonesian babies she sees online. The mothers are migrant workers who go there and they're not allowed to have babies as part of their job. Some of them get pregnant anyway, they don't know what to do about it. Selling their babies is a way out. That way, they don't get into trouble, and get some money on top of it. So there's like nothing wrong with doing it, Bev reasons. Especially if the baby is going to a nice American family, where it is bound to have a good life.

She's still not sure if she wants a boy or a girl. She figures she ought to wait and discuss it with Mrdok first. In a way it would make it easier, to be able to narrow her search results. But it's fine. He might not want another boy, he's already had three, and at least two of them, she knows he's not that happy with. Maybe it's time for a girl. Bev doesn't mind either way. But they should decide this together. When the time is right for her to bring it up.

Speaking of time. Mom's gonna get bitchy if Bev doesn't get home soon. Rain still not letting up, so time to brave it. Or else call another Uber. The grotty rain. She shuts her MacBook, carries her weight toward the door. It keeps pouring down, but she suddenly doesn't care anymore. This life is about to end for her. She's going to be a wife and a mother soon, she can just tell.

3.

THE BEST PART was when he was good and loaded up—though not so loaded as to be half dead—that he could lie very still in bed at the end of the day and feel the world drift away from him. Moments like these are what a junkie lives for. Arms wrapped around a pillow or, less often, an actual person glowing with warmth, the great buzzing non-feeling of near paralysis and near consciousness as you drift through the forever of never-morning.

Bobby always sleeps on his left side. Can be dangerous. Sometimes too relaxed, forget to breathe, wake up gasping for air. Wake up itching when you're fine—salted reflex impelled by the dirt beneath the skin. Inside the veins. Flowing through all the circuitry. You're filthy on the outside, too, of course, but you don't even care. So many things in this world for other people to worry about, that's what they were designed for—those things and those people. Worry vessels. Often those things *are* people. People just as good as things. And not even, in most examples. Bobby sees them and thinks, *A temple of worry right over there.* That's it. For what does any of it have to do with him, when he's found a way to float without water.

Now Bobby can't float. That wooden sense. It's like he's had enough, but still can't get there. Another shot now, no, would take him over the edge. Knock him out. Not that he's totally against it. What disgusts him is the knowledge that it would be days, maybe weeks, before he'd stink enough to be found.

He makes his way to the window, bare feet sticky across the floor. Look out the window, past own reflection. Down on the shore, a gay wedding is taking place. The grooms wear matching suits, dark blue bowties, the one blonde and gleaming, the other an almond-shaped head, glasses square to accentuate emerald eyes. Bobby cries. Rare, these moments when feeling breaks through. It's an ugliness the dope is meant to annihilate. One strong sign it's no longer working.

Cries and he can't know why. Crowd of some two dozen in light formal wear, hipster beards and fake flowers, the Californianized blur of human foliage so rarely seen out here, distant from the crowded shores of urban blight. How it used to call out to him—no—more like once embedded—early strain of what he once was. What he could've turned out to be. Back when he still had promise…

Feel yourself mutating—different angles. Hiding out for so long, and what for? Some distant drama, by now can hardly remember the source. Constant getting-away-from, yeah. When there's no such thing as even a trophy. Just a blaze to make you think of it. Strokey-stroke.

4.

–ISN'T THAT—?

–Mrdok's wife. What's her name again?

–Mrtol.

–That's right. Mrtol Mrdok.

–What on earth is she –?

–Ssssh, Diane, she can hear us.

–All alone. And with a drink in her hand, of course.

–Stop!

–Well, it *is* very nearly cocktail hour.

–Muffy van Damme! Have you lost your senses? It's three o'clock. Cocktail hour doesn't start for at least another hour!

–… So it's true then.

–Of course it is.

–Could it be their marriage?

–Well, it's rude to speculate. But being married to a man like that, it can't be easy.

–No simple joyride.

–What about her, though? Do you think she has a lover?

–She did just get back from somewhere, one of the girls was saying. Palm Springs, was it? Somewhere out there.

–Alone?! You think she goes out there to…

–I don't think she's had any work done. At least not lately. Look at her.

–God. It is a sad sight, isn't it?

–Don was telling me Mrdok –

–She just sits there all alone. Don't you think it's *weird?*

–Well, she does have that drink to keep her company.

–It's almost like she's depressed.

–Maybe we should go over there.

–Muf, you're hil*ar*ious!

–Glug glug glug.

–Stop it!

–Mrtol the juicer. Mrtol the lonely old juicehead!

–Oh Muff. Who are we to laugh at others' misfortune?

–Those who've never known it…

–… shouldn't disown it.

–That's right!

–It must be hard.

–A man like Mrdok? Why?

–All that ambition. Working all the time. Never at home.

–Oh please. You could be describing any one of us.

–No, really.

–Diane. That's just how men *are*.

–Some women, too…

–Yes, but let's get real.

–Could you imagine anyone being *jealous* of her?

–Well, I mean, come on…

–I mean, she is married to—

–You really think he's the biggest shark swimming in these waters? I mean here at the club.

–Oh, think it? Come on, Muf. I *know* it.

–Yeah, but so what? I mean, what's a few million extra? What more can you spend it on?

–It's not about that…

–Well, I could think of a few things…

–I mean, look at *her*. Certainly not happiness.

–You know what they're like. The men, I mean. They can't keep it in their pants—

–That's it. Mine's that way, so are all of yours. It's not even about the money –

–Does Jake go whoring?

–Not my Jacob.

–I'm pretty sure Grayson does.

–Well, as long as we don't end up like—Oh. Look at her. She's getting up now. Where's she going? Oh, of course.

–Time for a refill.

–No shame, that woman, no shame.

–I mean, does she even *realize* how she is *representing*… Do you think *Mrdok* knows?

–You know I've never seen him here. Never once.

–That's because he never comes.

–No?

–The club just isn't his world. Sigh.

–Not even to play golf?

–Oh honey. If that man wants to play golf—

–I mean, there's a certain *whorishness* to how she behaves. I know it sounds harsh. I just can't think of any other word for it. Drinking in plain sight of everyone at three in the afternoon!

–I know exactly what you mean.

–I mean, brazen.

–Not just drinking. Plastered.

–Smashed.

–Do you think she carries a flask in her purse?

–I won't be surprised if she starts bumping into things.

–Now wouldn't that be the show.

–How I'd *love* that.

–Blurred vision. Bumping around. Glug glug glug.

–Like a fish.

–What about—?

–She must get around. If you get what I mean.

–Well, we all know Mrdok does.

–Oh, do we? Come on. You can't leave it at that!

–Spill spill.

–Well, there's this place I go in the city to get my nails done…

–Mm-hm.

–So I'm sitting next to this… Well, what should I call it? This *girl*. This *creature*. She couldn't've been a day over, well… I don't know. Twenty-three?

–Go on.

–And, it's not like I'm eavesdropping—

–No, of course not—

–But I can't help but overhear the conversation. She's on the phone with him!

–Who?

–Who do you think? Mrdok.

–But how do you know it's him?

–Oh, come on, Muffy. How many Mrdoks can there be in New York City? In this world, even?

–You're right. What a name.

–Slavic, I think.

–Something. That's for sure… And so what was she saying?

–It sounded filthy.

–… Really?

–I mean, I can barely bring myself to say it.

–Really?!

–Right there in the nail salon on East Seventy-Third Street. I mean, okay, most of the girls working there probably don't understand English. But it was full of customers.

–So it was really filthy?

–Something about… jerking off.

–Oh. My. God.

–It was major OMG. I mean, I just sat there trying to look immersed in something on my phone.

–You're sure it was him?

–Yes, I'm sure. It was so gross.

–Omigod.

–And anyway. We're so bad. We need to stop this.

–Look! What's she doing?

–She's taking out her phone.

–Is she going to call someone?

–Changed her mind, it looks like.

–Poor thing.

–No one to call.

–Stop.

–Probably feels self-conscious.

–I mean, I would too. Drinking all alone in the club in the middle of the afternoon.

–So sad.

–Pathetic, even.

–I wonder what she's drinking.

–I kind of hate to say it…

–It does look good.

–Did you know they have a brand new cocktail menu?

–I did not know that.

–Well, Mamie comes here for dinner sometimes with her husband. Said something about a new selection of craft cocktails. Apparently they hired some celebrity bartender from Brazil. That's the only way I know.

–Oh really? I never come at night.

–Me neither.

–It's hard when you have kids.

–Apparently not when you're Mrtol Mrdok!

–Oh, stop.

–Do you think it's one of the new concoctions?

–You know, it could be. I can't recognize what it is from here.

–Could be anything.

–It does look good, though. Not that I'm an expert when it comes to cocktails!

–Diane. Are you thinking what I'm thinking?

–Well. What time is it?

–But we couldn't! I mean, it's way too early.

–If Mrtol Mrdok can do it...

–Oh gosh. Well... Okay. I'm game if Muffy is.

–We can at least ask to see the new menu.

–That's it. We don't have to actually *order* anything.

–Research, darling, research!

CHAPTER SIX

FATBALLS VS. SHITBALLS

AS TONY FATBALLS used to say. It's a refrain that has been heard constantly throughout this meandering little piece of reportage, and has begun to feel, I'm afraid, like a desultory deference to a dusty éminence grise. We must now pause to parse (if you will excuse the momentary lapse into homonymous indulgence) his legend. For although he has indeed gained entrance to that far superior kingdom beyond the clouds, the traces he has left behind here on Earth live on, in many ways, in the person of Mrdok. Some would go so far as to assert that Mrdok would scarcely be the man he is today without the beneficial interference of Anthony Fatobello early on in his life, in the rather risqué incident I took pains to describe earlier. Given the absence, bordering on neglect I might proffer, of Mrdok's own father throughout his early adolescence (his mother abandoned the family early on; Mrdok hardly met her), the arrival of this swarthy mustachio'd pockmark'd man of the world not only served as a convenient father substitute; Tony truly paved the way for Mrdok's entrance into the rarefied world of Manhattan.

It is a world, after all, that quavers at the prospect of opening its gates to the many, preferring—historically and in seeming perpetuity—to contain the boundlessness of the privileged few. Call it a shortcoming or a benefit, natural or civilized; what it is, in fact, is an enduring feature of meritocracy that recognizes men (and, on occasion, women) of talent. Some of these individuals, however, require elevation in the form of a human platform in order to make their presence known. Using his mental divination rod, Tony arrived at a realization upon meeting Mrdok that the future was sitting right before him in the form of his pudgy fifteen-year-old shoplifter. He must have intuited in Mrdok some semblance of himself at that vulnerable age, when fortune's smile and the nurturance it brings are most required.

How fortunate Mrdok was to become his protégé. Throughout his long and distinguished career, Fatballs, as his clients affectionately called him, was known for taking on cases considered, at best, lost causes; cases that, if any other lawyer were to take them on, would be the equivalent more or less of committing career suicide. Not only did Tony take these cases on, he was known for astonishingly winning them, each and every time. Of his controversial skill set, much scandalous ink has been spilled on Tony's cultivation of what the Chinese call *guanxi*; as Tony himself was apt to remark, *I don't care what the law is, just tell me who the judge is.* But networking wasn't Tony's sole talent—he rather had a way of turning the tables against any and every opponent, often in the most ruthless and dehumanizing manner. He earned such a reputation that, increasingly in his career, he graced seldom a courtroom with his fearsome presence. The opposing side, upon hearing who they were up against, would rather go in for a detrimental settlement than endure the tactics for which Tony Fatballs was known.

This arsenal of tactics would call for a modern day revision of the *Art of War*—one in which loss and failure, in their conventional forms, do not figure in, where the only form of dignity—and a defiant one at that—belongs to the victor. His largest and most abusive tactic was a mere change of the subject, a diversionary gaze back at the accuser. Always kept well attuned to the tonalities and dissonant harmonies of the zeitgeist, Tony knew how to draw ire out of a jury while simultaneously flattering them into submission, leading one of his begrudging admirers to comment that Tony played a jury like an accordion. He made sure, in both opening and closing deliberations, to make eye contact at least once with each and every juror. In addition, in composing his missive, he would be sure to drop at least one reference to the professional or personal attributes of each individual serving on the jury, whose curricula vitae were well researched in advance, so that each woman and man felt as though he were addressing them directly. If a client of his was, in fact, guilty, as they most often were, he would unearth any number of darknesses and misdeeds from the opposing party's past and smear them with it in the most artfully humiliating fashion, all the while presenting himself as a polite and well-intentioned man of the people—no easy task, given that Tony himself was not so easy on the eye. Then again, his was an ugliness that the everyman could relate to—so one could speculate that even this worked somehow in his favor. What one couldn't argue with was that the theater Tony invoked in the courtroom rapidly became a one man piece of performance art; there simply wasn't room for any additional cast members once Tony took to the stage.

Mafiosos, televangelists, the wealthy and the celebrated, the wealthy and the unknown all formed his friend and client base. Operating on the outer fringes, disgraced former politicians, muckraking journalists, offshore bankers, police captains of towns small and large across America—all of them were somehow in the shifting employ of Mister Fatobello. There was, in fact, no better man to introduce Mrdok into the reality of the daily machinations of Manhattan, an isle in which what certain critics decry as cronyism, but which I prefer to think of as nepotism, necessitates a certain investment in social circles of seemingly divergent orientations within the upper echelons. Flowers of self-doubt cannot, by natural law, bloom at such heights; one must maintain a certain assertive proprietary flow in accordance with the wind's ever-shifting coordinates.

With Fatballs on one's dial, one needn't bother boring oneself to death pouring over the pages of some Ayn Rand novel. He distilled it all down to its very golden essence. The rule of the game, he explained, is actually very simple: any person or entity (in the case of corporations, by and large treated as individuals according to US tax law) that does not have your money is your enemy. You might pretend to be their friend at certain moments, but such pretense is always a means to an end. It was Tony who inserted the term *shitballs* into Mrdok's vocabulary to distinguish all those who, potentially at least, had more money than he. The goal was, has always been, to separate the shitball from as much of its (or his or her, for those wont to view these entities as something akin to human) money as possible and make it one's own. If it sounds cruel and heartless to the more sensitive reader, well, all I can say is that making money has never coincided—in any civilization that I am aware of—with the making of friends. Tony instilled a tough discipline in his young disciple more akin to the drill sergeant's relation to a new recruit. Add to that the tough love that served as a substitute for a perpetually absent father—verbally and colorfully berating Mrdok when he fell aslight of expectation; granting him subtle rewards at moments unexpected—and you have the sort of rigorous mentorship that would turn even a dullard into a genius. Of course, there have been rather unfair speculations that Tony's early interest in young Mrdok was more Socratic in nature. Given his well-known predilection for keeping the company of young, slightly post-adolescent men, Mrdok certainly fit the mold. As an expert on the subject, however, I can assure anyone and everyone who deigns to read this that such speculations are unfounded, and malicious for even being uttered aloud. For whatever might be said of Tony—and, as the record elsewhere has shown, many unfortunate statements have been uttered by his numerous earned enemies—his interest in Mrdok can only be characterized as passionately Platonic, if one would be so kind as to excuse this minor indulgence in consonance.

The flows of money. An abstract subject as ever there was, and hardly one that would fit the understanding of the teenager at his first encounter with the lawyer. Tony taught him all he would need to know in order to master the subject; to become a master of it; the master he now is. It was Tony who first taught Mrdok those three magical letters: LLC. Limited Liability Corporation: Is there a sweeter set of three words in the English—in *any* language? Certainly, to become a master in the fine art of plutonomy, one must first possess a firm understanding of this clever human device and its rich bouquet of potential. What is key here—from a legal standpoint—is separability. There is Mrdok and there is the Mrdok organization. Though the two might be conflated in people's minds, in actuality, they are two separate beings. Mrdok's responsibility, his *liability*, for the debts of the Mrdok organization, is *limited*. Were one of Mrdok's business enterprises to fail, it is only the assets that would be at risk— not Mrdok's personal assets. Who, then, is responsible for the Mrdok organization's debts? Society. This, in a nutshell, is the essence of an LLC. And once Tony enlightened Mrdok thus, his mind was set ablaze.

I'm surprised some enterprising book publisher hasn't undertaken the task of compiling a compendium of aphorisms uttered over the years by the late great Tony Fatballs. Among the many ringers Tony instilled in Mrdok, one favorite of mine: *The only difference between us and politicians is that we don't have to pretend to worship Christ.* (This is not altogether true, by the way. Mrdok believes in God all right—it's just that his happens to be a lower-case god.) Ironically, it was Tony who would introduce Mrdok to one of his earliest investments post-Owl Lending, the Reverend Billy Ray Taggerston III. Taggerston had taught himself to use the internet very early on in creating a website for his rapture-based ministry, the Ministry of the True Christ and Guiding Principal (sic) of Everlasting Eternal Light. At the time, the ministry, so-called, was rather more of a one-man show. But, the internet being what it was in those tender emergent years, he steadily began to attract a congregation to his garage on Sunday mornings in the rural town of Nickelsville in the great state of Nevada. In positing an evaluation of this anomaly Tony had chanced to discover on public access television early one morning after an all-night Vegas binge, he warned Mrdok that he had yet to determine which of the Holy Trinity mattered most to Taggerston: money, the net, or Jesus. Mrdok gregariously assumed it to be some odorific swill of all three, and proceeded—cautiously—accordingly. Having honed his skills, The Taggerston, as he came to be known in Mrdok and Tony's world, was now also running an incorporation business, offering a great variety of privacy packages for fellow shitballs in need of making their assets appear less shitty. For a couple hundred dollars, he would sell you a company registered in that great state with its unusually generous privacy and tax laws. For a further two hundred, The Taggerston would provide the newly minted company with a Nevadan Nominee Officer, a resident who would serve as the nominal head of the company—particularly useful for those who did not wish their own names to come attached to the endeavor. For only a thousand dollars, one could attain the heights of privacy—one's very own company, no name attached, with its very own Nevadan bank account.

The print in the books was a bit blurry, but the two enterprises appeared to be fueling one another. The Taggerston's faith in Jesus was akin to the heroin addict's love of the needle; the real substance was something else, something contained; it was the tool, the vehicle, that really mattered. At a time when all spiritual values had been lost in America—all values, period, really—Mrdok spotted something in The Taggerston that no one else had: opportunity. And so it was he managed to ingratiate himself to The Taggerston by elevating him to the big time, through one of Tony's contacts at a California cable network specialized in religious programming, while at the same precise moment acquiring a sizeable share in the preacher's business in Nevada.

Given my own personal background, The Taggerston wasn't exactly an anomaly to me. He had been something of a staple on local television for years when I was growing up. I dimly recall the first time I happened to discover him when I was switching channels—though that memory, I must confess, might likely be conflated with any number of subsequent viewings—as I was a much more avid television-watcher in that early period of my life than I am now. He was a girthy man in those years, yet to reach the elephantine stature he was to attain later in life. He always opened his sprawling sermons as though he were in mid-speech, mid-sentence. That is because his show, in a sense, never ended. It was like an ongoing epic.

–This morning, the thought occurred to me, struck me down in a way that I knew, oh yes, I knew, could've only come from somewhere far far above, if you *truly* understand what it is I'm sayin: all the insects around me—around us—around *you*—have turned gay. This is something I've been noticing more and more. This is *at least* true in the grand state of Texas, ladies and gentlemen, where we are now broadcasting from.

(This, incidentally, as I would later come to find out, was a mild exaggeration on Taggerston's part; in point of fact, the studio was situated in Burbank, California—although, it is true, Taggerston and many of his guests closely resembled Texans in dress and appearance.)

–Why just the other day, I saw a male caterpillar crawling upon another male caterpillar. I won't go into graphic detail here, describing what it is I'm pretty sure they were doing. This, after all, is a family broadcast. We've got children out there watching. Children here in the audience, even. Children whose *future* belongs to no other being than the Lord Jesus High in Heaven. And I know this because He told me so. That's right, ladies and gentlemen. You don't have to listen very hard if you want to hear the word of the Lord. I hear it, I hear it all the time. Even when I'm sleeping. And I transmit it. All you have to do—if you want to hear God's word—is to tune in to this, to the Ministry of the True Christ and Guiding Principal (sic) of Everlasting Eternal Light. But if you want to keep hearing the message, well, then, I'm real sorry to have to be the one to tell you. But we can't do this without you. In America today—the land where devils roam free—I'm talking true agents of the dark lord, of Satan himself—there is only one true God. And it is a false God. And everyone has been corrupted by it. The politicians you vote for. The people you watch on TV. Your boss. Maybe, just maybe even people in your friendship circle. In your immediate family. The name of this false god is money. I mean, the Jews have known this for some time. That's how they became masters of it. This is why they own every bank in America. Every newspaper, too. Even every television station, ladies and gentlemen. And this new thing they've got on every computer, that everyone's talking about: the internet. Jews own the internet! Yes, they do, brothers and sisters. I'm afraid I heard it direct from the mouth of Jesus Christ himself. And you heard it here, too. Right here. And we are all victims of it, the filthy Jewish pornography that is the internet. I'm a victim of it myself. (Not the porn, but the internet part of it, of course.) Why, you see these bright lights all around me? I mean, take a minute here and look around. Look at this stage. Look at the band up here. Look at all these lights, this microphone. You think any of this comes for free? You think the Jews who own this station, they just come to me and say, Hey Billy, we're gonna give this all to you, so that you can spread the word of Jesus to all your devoted followers, maybe even convert a few of our people, bring them into the fold of Heaven? Even though we hate Jesus, even though we, our people, *raped* and *murdered* Him upon that cross, even though us *Jews went and gangbanged Jesus on that cross until he died*, in the words of the Old Testament, we're just gonna give you this little old station for free to spread the holy word!... I don't think so, brothers and sisters, fathers and mothers. Any day now, these lights are gonna go out. And you know what will happen then? No more miracles. No more word of God being transmitted, direct from here, my heart, into your living room.

What's more, you need to cleanse yourself of this evil that is polluting your souls. That is poisoning the heart of America. Devils in the White House. Devils on Main Street USA. Devils in the banks. Even devils in the natural order. The animal kingdom. The insect kingdom. What is the one thing that can stop all this evil from spreading?

I'm gonna tell y'all something. Something I aint never told no one, even my mee-maw. The Lord is watching us. He is watching our every move. That's because, he's startin to realize, we've got things wrong down here. We have taken the world in the wrong direction. We are engulfed in a spiritual battle. The agents of Satan have been sent to Earth in order to contaminate it. And they've contaminated everything. Contaminated the drinking water, even. The frogs in the sewer, the caterpillars crawling in the grass—they have stopped reproducing. And why is that? I will tell you why, brothers and sisters. One word is all you need to know: homosexuality. It's a big, long word, I know, but you might as well learn to fit it all in your mouth right now. There is a conspiracy afoot among the Jews and the homosexuals. They are in it together. What do they want? They want to turn all of America into a bastion of faggotry. To defraud us, to put us off the path to true salvation. Just like they did to Jesus Christ, they are coming for your children next. And I heard that straight from the mouth of the Man Himself. There is an intergalactic invasion going on right here, right now—and the aliens are using the bodies of homosexuals and Jews as vessels, using those bodies to contaminate the earth. I mean, look at all the filth, all the diseases that are engulfing us right now. Just look at the AIDS! Do you honestly think that came from, from where, what do they say? Africa? That was a disease sent here by God, to try and kill off the demons from Hell. The gay Jewish lizard demons that have not even—they're in the White House, brothers and sisters fathers and mothers! These politicians you see on the TV… Do you really think for one frickin second that any of them are human?

If you do not pick up the telephone, at this very and instant, and *stop them, stop these lizard people from taking over our country, over our lives,* well. I can't guarantee that you won't be next. What can stop them? There's only one thing. Money. Your money. It's filthy, it's dirty, ladies and gentlemen brothers and sisters boys and girls. And that's why you need to get rid of it. Oh I hate this, asking for money which is so filthy and I so despise, I hate it I do, but sadly that does not change the fact that if you do not pick up the phone right this instant, and pledge a *minimum* of two hundred fifty dollars—then I cannot *personally* guarantee your safety and salvation. Two hundred fifty dollars is all it takes to secure a place for yourselves on the ship of safety. To insulate yourself, your family, from these Jew lizard people, from these insects crawling all around us, that are going to turn the rest of the civilized world gay. That are trying to turn your children gay. That are even trying to circumcise your pets and turn them gay…

If I quote so extensively here, it is only to inject in the reader a firm sense of what The Taggerston's shows were really like. The seeming endlessness of it was very much the key ingredient.

Was Billy Ray Taggerston III himself a shitball? Of course, it needn't even be articulated, I think, that Mrdok did not believe in one tiny fraction of any of The Taggerston's spoutings. He didn't need to have faith in such ridiculous pseudo-doctrine; what Mrdok had faith in, has always had faith in, is the People. That gelatinous mess of sweaty obese human flesh that comprises the multitudes. And he knew that the People—or at least a sizeable enough sum of it—would deem The Taggerston shepherd worthy and come flocking.

And so they did. At least for a few years. Well, it worked until it stopped working. There are, of course, sins of a spiritual nature. But then there is also another sort of sin, one that is situated firmly and decidedly in the Earthly realm.

—People are stupid, I remember Mrdok pontificating after I questioned him on this curious investment of his. It's because God is stupid. He fucks up a lot.

This could, in a sense, be seen as a summation of Mrdok's religious proclivities. Stupidity extended to encompass quite a lot of troubling phenomena of the day to day. The poor are also stupid, and thus deserve to be poor. Nature is imperfect; she makes mistakes all over the place. It is rare that a genius like Mrdok comes along to correct those mistakes; but when he does, the world is left a better place for his having waved his proverbial wand.

Which is all to say that as an investment, The Taggerston began to lose him money. The problem was that as he got deeper and deeper into the religion business, he began to neglect the incorporation enterprise, which, to Mrdok's mind, was the surefire thing. The Taggerston also broke the golden rule one night, after a particularly grueling six-hour-long broadcast, when he slipped and mentioned Mrdok's name on the air.

Ever since the tumults of his adolescence, Tony had instilled in Mrdok one particularly firm lesson: never talk to the media. Best to not even let them know who you are, that you exist, if you can help it. Of course, such anonymity is increasingly hard to come by in today's world, cycling swiftly toward the apocalypse, where, to pervert the famous Warhol quote, everyone is now destined to be *anonymous* for fifteen minutes.

But in the nineties, there was still some hope left otherwise. And so Mrdok had little choice but to cut The Taggerston loose. Mrdok, for his part, was philosophical about the whole thing. He remembered something Tony Fatballs had told him, when he was defending one particularly notorious shitball, a billionaire who, in the midst of a heated argument, had accidentally thrown his wife off the back of his yacht onto the motor, which severed her head and turned the rest of her body into a scattered pile of pulled pork. *He might have done it,* Tony had said; *but he's not guilty.*

The gentleman was in the end acquitted of homicide and manslaughter and womanslaughter and all other slaughters, thus proving Tony right (once again.) Staring into the yellow eyes of God's countenance, Tony's gift was to spring arrival on to the world with each fresh juxtaposition. Innocence and violation, fraud landing generosity, love and violence… Well, the list might also be expanded here to include the likes of greed and loyalty, in the particular case of the Reverend Billy Taggerston III. The question could be asked: What was a redneck TV preacher doing getting mixed up with the likes of two big city movers and shakers? Two serious men: for, whatever else you might think of them, this is what in fact Mrdok and Fatballs were.

Actuality is one thing; the law is quite another, an abstraction. The benign hunger of clarification in such matters is best left to those deemed to possess some professional expertise—but just as often, as the example of Tony Fatballs proves, it is left more as an exercise in transformation, a magician's act: to turn the innocent into the guilty. To move the horizon forward just an inch, without the burden of the rest of the world's notice.

The Taggerston was brought to understand the scope and expanse of the mess he had made with Mrdok's finances. Credit had been generously and graciously extended, and it was eventually brought to Mrdok's notice by Tony that The Taggerston appeared to have little comprehension of the nature of those loans.

And so the Big City Boys eventually had to step in and take control of the situation. Well, they would end up taking a little bit more than just control. Mrdok would eventually acquire the entirety of The Taggerston's incorporation business. In doing so, he simultaneously acquired control over all of the individual businesses it contained— owing to a loophole in state law that Tony ingeniously honed in upon. Much to the surprise of those who thought that those businesses and their offshore accounts would eternally belong to them, they could do little but stand by and watch as Mrdok systematically liquidated all of their assets and dissolved them under the auspices of Tony, now practicing in his guise as a certified lawyer on the Caribbean island nation of Saint Kitts and Nevis…

Well, it is quite a story! Of course The Taggerston went through all the pathetic motions, initially splaying himself at Mrdok's feet and begging forgiveness, then, when none such was forthcoming, attempting to destroy Mrdok in court—a comical sight that was! Granted, The Taggerston *had* been rather shortsighted—some might even say stupid—in the handling of every aspect of both his businesses. The lights in the television studio quickly dimmed and the set was struck. He attempted, at a certain desperate point, a comeback on YouTube once the internet had evolved, but at that point, he was in such a state of ruin—physically, mentally, and financially—that not even his most ardent supporters from the past could take his new incarnation seriously. The Taggerston faded faster than the melody to a one-hit wonder.

In one of those near unbelievable escapades of serendipity, Mrdok would chance to encounter him once again years later, when he accompanied his first wife Krstal and son Bobby to a safari theme park on a remote island in the Indian Ocean, where fate's winds had blown the Taggerston shortly after his erasure in his home country, unbeknownst to Mrdok. I am not at liberty to reveal the name of the island, owing to an ongoing litigation dispute that Mrdok is still embroiled in, but it is one in which, like many African nations, there is lax legislation in certain tourism establishments, allowing brave individuals to come into closer contact with formerly wild animals than would otherwise be allowed here in the land of the brave and the litigious. Imagine Mrdok's surprise, then, when he met the eyes of the haggard obese man vending peanuts behind a stall, all alone save for the electric fan fruitlessly attempting to cool down the slovenly slumped figure beside. The Taggerston himself was so startled, he raised his visor to make sure it wasn't the merciless rays of the sun subjecting him to yet another hallucination. The Taggerston accepted Mrdok's rupees and could scarcely think of a thing to say when the man who had once played such a pivotal role in his existence instructed him to keep the change.

To continue, it was on this same visit that Mrdok would have yet a further beastly encounter, this one rather more literal. Mrdok, in a show-offy move, opted to enter what was known as the Jungle Cage while Bobby and Krstal sat outside with their ice creams watching. These were the days before virtual reality arrived to provide a rather safer substitute for such thrill-seeking adventurers, and anyway, Mrdok has always been one who craves the authenticity of experience that others might deem dangerous, even reckless.

–Daddy, look out! suddenly screamed little Bobby.

But it was too late.

Gizmo the gorilla had already made off with both the bag of peanuts and the small hand in whose tight clutch it now lost its former protection, leaving behind a bloody stump attached to a shrieking eminence.

CHAPTER SEVEN

DOTS IN THE AIR

1.

TAXI SPEEDBOAT WHIZZING by. The green whirr of the canal, stink of the thing. Lose yourself in that ripple. Zero-in on the motion, the centuries. To distract yourself from the pastel boggle that surrounds. Even night is red.

Coco snorted a line and farted: 

—How I love-a the taste-a of cocain-uh in the morning-uh.

Brushing her nostrils feverishly with her right index finger.

—It's not morning, Coco.

Mrdok prolongs his stare at the canal. The filthy canal.

—And that's not coke. It's ketamine.

—Oh sh-sh-sh-sh-sh-tt-tt-t-tt-tt…

Now it's not the post-taxi whirlpool of the fetid liquid comprising the canal but the whirl in Coco's brain. The massage of the synapses that precedes the nodal vibration.

The stale bread that served as the bruschetta on the evening's antipasto. Something about it, the yeast perhaps, not sitting well in Mrdok's stomach. Stomach curls.

—Yo Coco. Did I send Maria-Lucia home yet?

—

—Yo! Maria-Lucia!—shouting in the direction of the kitchen. Window still open on this crisp autumn night. You in there?!

No answer.

—Fuck me. Lazy fuckin—I should fire that bitch. Send her ass home to the volcano, to fuckin… Wait, where is it again Maria-Lucia is from? Was it Naples?

—

—Yeah. Somewhere down there anyways.

Suddenly Coco releases herself from the rococo garden seat upholding her, arms jerking in slow motion.

–M-m-m-mrdocco, you piece of sheetuh. You…you..you caynot… f-fire… *Maria-Le-Le-Looo…*

–And why the fuck is that, Coco? Mrdok arranges a line with his American Express gold card, snorts it through a silver straw. I believe—*snort*—last time I checked… that I am entitled to do practically whatever the fuck I want here in the Venetian Republic.

–Mrdocco, no! No… no… no!—stabbing the air with her imagined cigarette. Maria-Lucia is… *mia famiglia…*

–She is not your fam–

–In *mia famiglia!*

–Oh, bullshit! Never confuse the help with your own family, Coco. Weren't you ever taught that? Shit, some of the things you say really make me question the way you were brought up.

–Has worked for my family since I… a child. Avanti! My… whole..

Her jaw quaking now.

–Before you fucking put me to sleep, I'm gonna help you out here, baby. You see, the coke… is on *this* tray… *Not* that one. Silver: the coke platter; the brass: that animal tranquilizer shit that makes you retarded. You got it? Here, let me make you a line. Chop-chop-chop. Make you *coherent* again.

It's not that he minded these spasmodic spells of nightly stupefaction. With Coco, it had come to spell Venice for him. With Coco, he'd learned to put up with all of it—*but only in this specific setting.* Anyway, it's not like had much of a choice. When he was in Venice, it was between Coco and the fucking pigeons.

Snort, Coco, snort.

–Maria-Lucia…

She pounds her chest for the old broad.

–I don't care what you say, Coco. Her cooking is shit. And this is supposed to be Italy. It's really unacceptable.

–Maria-Lucia… My brother and mio… *Raised* on her food-uh. I tell you something about-a Maria-Lucia…

Go right ahead, Coco. Mrdok's not listening. There he goes into the palazzo, socks sliding across the tiles. Leaves the door wide open while he's taking a piss, candlelight gleaming off the silver-encrusted bidet. Just the beginning of the renovation, much-needed upgrade to this old dump. He can still hear the Sotheby's agent's nasal fucking parrot voice rattling off in his brain. A Jacopo Sansovino overlooked masterpiece yadadadada blab-blah-bullshit. A dump inside, floor tiles scoffed and cut to shit, the plumbing a mess. But the façade, the palatial size of the thing, enough of a wonder to wow Krstal, which is all he bought it for. Only to have the cunt stay here for a grand total of once before she divorced his ass, moved out to La La Land with a settlement of five point three and a cool fifth of his investment portfolio. Mrdok spits in the silver-plated sink. At least he's got the bathroom fixed up right. The estate agent jabber, trying to force *his* architect on to me, all his bullshit about maintaining the *Venetian heritage*, whatever the fuck that is. Gordo makes sure he's far from Venice—far from the continent—whenever the people from the preservation committee stick their noses in, lest Mrdok threaten to break those very noses. Should have seen that red flag from the very beginning, but he was still green in those days. It all went downhill from there. But soon, we'll get this place fixed into a real palace. Soon, everything'll be fuckin coated in *silver.*

–Silver, silver, silver. I want it all plated in *silver…*

Mrdok is prone to repeating the two syllables like a tic when he's feeling particularly excited, turned on, or just coked up. He also has a tendency to overenunciate when he's intellectually stimulated, coked up, or horny. Or some combination thereof. Why silver? Because it's not gold, for one thing. Gold is *tacky.* The gold standard something he stopped believing in, when? Decades ago now. It is not only that the appearance of the precious metal appeals to his aesthetic sensibility, with its cold cutting denotation of hardness. He also has this irrational belief that the value of silver is one day bound to be somehow greater than any other substance in the world, as gold was nearing its apocalypse. That crypto bullshit? Forget it. Silver was the thing. Soon, there would be none left, and in a world bereft of gold, well. You were left with second best, and nothing more.

Now he was doing lines just to get that fishy sludgy canal smell out of his fucking nostrils. If only there were such a simple remedy.

–You okay, kid?

Shakes Coco. Looks her up and down. Yeah, she's okay. With a capital K. Eyes bright yet unblinking. Clearly she was dipping back into the brass dish while Mrdok was having a whiz. Now she's entered that inevitable evening apex where she can no longer speak. Mrdok throws a blanket on her and ambles toward the garden.

What is it that the garden suddenly reminds him of tonight? Total déjà vu here—oh shit, yeah: the back garden of the Hotel Nacional in Havana. The fucking peacock walking around! Fuck, he's gotta get one of those for this place. Gotta tell Gordo next time he calls. They got peacocks in Venice? Racks his brain, but can't pull anything out of it from his last few visits here, save for the nightly palazzo get-togethers with just him and Coco.

But oh, how has his garden grown. At least one thing he can look at in this dump that doesn't make him vomit. Sage, thyme, chamomile. *Do you maybe wanna get out of my fucking face for two seconds so that I can actually breathe?* The kind of sentence he was used to uttering whenever he was back here, usually said to Coco, flailing her hyperactive shitshow before him. Poor kid. Yeah, part of him felt sorry. The other part, the large part, felt annoyed.

Somehow, this so-called friend, the sole one here, was also the biggest reminder of all his failings. He'd come to Venice with big plans—this was back when he was still with Krstal—his first property in Europe, really—first BIG ONE at least—thought it'd be a real splash. He certainly *made* a big splash in the banks. Entire fucking real estate market stood up and took notice. He made his entrance—thought he'd say *Here, Krst, Venice is all ours now.* Found out not long after—when they publicly and privately shit on him—that it aint so easy. It's a shitshow, alright—just not his kind of shitshow. The Venetians, they're a hateful, a protective bunch. Not too fond of strangers who march in, carve out a claim for themselves. As though he were expected to bow down before the old guard, kiss their aristocratic asses. Ask permission. *Permesso.* For what? To blow his wad in *their town*? Fucking pricks.

He walks through the garden. *His* garden. *His* fucking masquerade. Of greenery. He planted it. Well no, that's not entirely true—the gardener planted everything. But he hired the gardener. Well no, that's not completely true, either—Gordo did. But he did tell the son of a bitch what to plant, worked the entire architecture out beforehand. This was something he definitely wanted to be involved in. Had to have the Mrdok touch. Or else: *nothing.* Nada. Niente.

Dots in the air. That's the name of his favorite plant—at least the translation from Latin—this frilly thing with tiny brownish buds extending. Then there are lemon trees. Fans. Lilies, roses. Tobacco plants. This one looks like cacti, but is actually quite soft to the touch: horsetail, it's called. Elephant ear. Mrdok says the names aloud as he passes each one by, less to remind himself than to make sure everything is still here and in full bloom, as they all should be at this time of year. A whole range of berry bushes... Mrdok and his bushes, mosquitos fluttering about, Mrdok slaps one out of range, they rabidly dive toward anything of flesh at this point in autumn, desperate for one last bit of human DNA to stash away in the winter nest. Flora, fauna, and fucka.

Coco, too, one of these old money scions, though rejected by them like Mrdok. None could stand to be around her. Ashamed by her excesses, her craziness, her unpredictability. Not the kind of element you could introduce into very many scenes, particularly not here, where you were expected to carry yourself with a certain longitudinal sway. Though she was—for certain, Gordo had had her checked out—descended from the Grimani clan, a lineage that had included several doges and a cardinal. The same Grimanis of the palazzo in Santa Maria Formosa, a lineage that no Venetian, past or present, could scoff at. Most of the Venetian elite carried themselves with a certain degree of discretion—required it, really—that needless-to-articulate decree of quiet sophistication that seems to naturally arise when money is passed down, scattered across so many generations that it would require a full-time economic historian to keep track of its many peregrinations.

Coco was the cog that threatened to derail that passage. No one really knew where she got it from, though it was certainly some gene long forgotten that was supposed to have died out three centuries prior, its last carrier some syphilitic libertine that was previously and mistakenly thought to have spared the family the taint of procreation. The one who got outrageously drunk in the first hour of the dinner party and commenced screaming and insulting whichever guests she'd caught giving her the sideways glare. Was it bipolar disorder? The doctors couldn't give a firm diagnosis, no matter how much they paid them. To save embarrassment, they'd tried the usual trick of putting as much distance between themselves and *la pecora nera*—boarding school in the UK, rehab in the US, then, when she insisted on returning to Italy, a villa in Rome, an apartment in Milan—but she'd somehow wound up back in Venice, where she'd been stashed in some luxury attic near San Marco owned by a distant uncle.

Of the Venetian elites, she was the only one who paid Mrdok the slightest attention, the only one *open minded,* or oblivious enough, depending on who you'd ask, to entertain the new money trash that had either bribed or conned its way into the auction house and a slice of primo palazzo paradiso. The only one with no reputation to tarnish, for she had managed that already some years ago, years stretching back to adolescence...

Besides their shared love of certain substances, Mrdok actually felt a little sorry for Coco. Sure, she was a fuckup on a grand scale, one with no inkling of a path through life, no conception of a future, and probably didn't care for one all the same—this was nothing new. Some are simply born to be mistresses of oblivion. Sure, he'd stuck it in her once upon a time, but that was only once, and anyway, it was years ago, an eventless occurrence now forgotten by both. The big difference between Mrdok and all the people that had rejected Coco is that for him, she was paradoxically easy to deal with. All those qualities that frightened and repelled the others, Mrdok found to be, if not intriguing, then at least entertaining. In the way that a bullfight or a really dangerous boat race was fun to watch from a distance, even if you didn't want to be a direct participant. And Mrdok, unlike these people, still had game. They were content to stew in their wealth, be fermented in it. Mrdok was out for gain. Motion. The lifestyle that came along with it. Coco could always be counted on for some action. He didn't need her for anything more or less. And the minute he left Venice, he'd instantly forget about her. Hence, the greatness of Coco. Her innate stashability. She was easy that way.

That genus of clannishness that had resulted in the exclusion of both Mrdok and Coco was, of course, the logical result of the kind of place Venice is. It's not like Mrdok's posturing as a middling Casanova was anything the Venetians hadn't witnessed before. And, as in the case of Mrdok, buying a slice of the Venetian dream was more often than not a desperate bid on behalf of the buyer for some damsel's affections. It hardly ever lasted. Essentially, these men—because they always, inevitably, were men, and usually Americans to boot, or before them the Japanese, more recently the Chinese, who remained invisible to most because of their ethnicity and their inability to speak anything other than their own hometown dialect—represented the highest end of the tourist class, but were considered tourists nonetheless. Their *palazzi* remained empty for most of the year, and when they were in town, they couldn't even secure a canalside table at the favored ristorante, since nobody knew who they were and those who did didn't care. It is for the same reason that the *nouveau riche* who came for the opening of the Biennale every two years always arrived in yachts that they parked outside the Giardini. Of course it was a prized opportunity to flash their wealth in the faces of the ever impressionable denizens of the art world. But it also saved them the embarrassment of being snubbed by the local patrician class, its bratty descendants, who wouldn't be caught dead in public with any of them. No invitations were ever offered—even in those cases where mutual business interests would have made such encounters fortuitous for both parties. Rather, the Venetians would take pains to place themselves out of town during the opening week and the arrival of the collector hordes with the attached art circus. A face-saving gesture of convenience. (Mrdok, it should be mentioned, was not himself immune to these displays. Everyone who attends the Biennale still remembers the year he drunkenly attempted to buy an Agnes Martin from the Guggenheim Collection. *Come on,* he'd drunkenly harangued the collection's director, *everyone has their price—it's like Larry says…*)

Dots in the air. Probably what Coco is now seeing. Of course, the real reason Coco so vehemently objected to his proposed firing of Maria-Lucia was that the old hag had been providing her with drugs practically since she was in diapers. Okay, so maybe that's unfair, but very few knew to credit the family's Sicilian cook with Coco's being shipped off to boarding school at the age of fourteen to rid her of a nasty coke habit. Turned out Maria-Lucia was counted as a member of more than just one *famiglia.* When she wasn't steaming up the kitchen, Maria-Lucia was organizing the transfer of kilos of various substances from that island at the toe of the boot to the ones padding the ass cheek—at least partially disproving the myth that Venice's maritime commerce was a mummified affair of yore.

There are worse places. Mrdok's been to most of them. Standing beneath the archway of the door leading out to the canal, he studies the dance of the streetlamps upon the water. Looks almost like gold in there. It's different during the day, when the sunlight hits the canal, afflicting it with a green iridescent glow. Swampy and putrid. Water's not supposed to look that way. Still, he can't bring himself to sell the place. Not just because of Krstal, all the memories associated with that brief crazed chapter of his life. More because, well, it would mean letting go of Coco. He knows that if he left, he'd never see her again. It'd mean leaving her here, to wander in her Venetian haze, into the midwinter mist…

It was a mystery to some why he seemed to care so much about Coco. It infuriated Gordo, among others, ragingly jealous, like a woman… Gordo more a woman than Coco, now that he thinks of it… Even gets mistaken for one on the telephone every now and then.

Some nights he'll walk through the empty city, a fogged half-moon retarded in the sky above him. He'll get Vittorio, the chauffeur, to drive him in the water limousine to a quiet spot in Dorsoduro, just old-timers living there and hardly a tourist in sight, wander those empty alleyways to feel like it's his own private playground—the whole fucking package. Even leave his phone be-hind in the boat to get the full isolation padding. Just Mrdocco and the ancient façaderria, wander down the narrowest of alleyways, only one person can fit. Thinks: as a joke, should make Gordo go down one of these some day. Ha ha ha fucking lard ass'd never be able to get out. Have to demolish the building to save him. Yeah. Demolish it all. If only. Rebuild the whole from scratch. Crest it all in silver. A Venice of the mind. The only Venice worth inhabiting. Spits beneath a streetlamp, waddles back toward Vittorio and the limo on the canal.

CHAPTER EIGHT

PIRATE'S BAY

1.

AS I INSCRIBE these words into the record, I cannot help but feel something is missing. Assertions of the backward sort come, in their cool eventuality, to accumulate a tangled mass of narrative implications; from which the reader is compelled to extract the main thread. Suffice to say that the ongoing saga of a creation like Mrdok must require the spillage of much ink in order to breed a proper understanding of the sage's true character. For that reason, I will spill onward, in search of that absent *je ne sais quoi*, withholding nothing from here on out to the reader—who, after all, has stuck with us so far on this at times confused course; a course that is even confusing to me upon occasion, but which I have no doubt will eventually result in the most satisfying of resolutions; had I the least bit of doubt, I can assure you I would have personally ceased following Mrdok's trails long ago.

The other night, I was discoursing on this philosophical matter and related, though more practical subjects, with Joanne, my long-suffering wife. Now it might seem odd to the reader that I would describe her as thus. Such judgments are typically applied by outsiders looking in at the marriage; a certain pride (rightly, I might add) prevents the married spouse from describing their partner in unfavorable light, casting as it does implicative shadows on themselves in the process. But, in my many years in Mrdok's employ, I have learned to extinguish those interfering flames of the ego, so as to better perform all the multitudinous tasks that are daily entrusted to me. It is precisely the number and complexity of those tasks that keep me separated from Joanne for weeks at a time. I have to say, for most wives, such long separations would put such a major strain on the marriage that it would, in the end, be regarded as hardly sustainable. Lucky was I, then, to have met such a kind, understanding creature as Joanne turned out to be. Our arrangement is that she accepts the consequences of my profession with a generous heart and a stoic mind. My salary keeps her in superlative comfort in a colonial manor in a small-town up in Connecticut, close enough to the city that she can come down, when loneliness gets the best of her, to spend a night or two in my Manhattan apartment. No big fan of city life, however, Joanne only deigns to visit on the rarest of occasions.

Still, in spite of the idiosyncrasies of our arrangement, neither of us, when pressed, would characterize it as an unhappy marriage. She quite enjoys the pastoral scene of semirural Connecticut, much as I relish accompanying the jet-set existence that Mrdok leads and with which he has, in a sense, blessed me in return. She works—not out of financial necessity, mind you, but out of an inner desire to occupy her time with more than just the running of the household (for which anyway we have Sarita, our live-in maid)—part-time at the local library, just two or three days a week, fulfilling in turn her sense of civic duty, while conveniently keeping her abreast of all the latest town gossip, which tends to flourish in such scenarios. She has her intimate circle—notably Dot, the mail lady who, after finishing her morning shift, will come spend many an afternoon at the manor—afternoons, I am told, that will often extend into the later hours of the evening…

I am always delighted to have Joanne visit me in the city. Although such occasions are of late quite rare, these marital reprieves tend to replenish me, even when I am not feeling particularly low. By reconnecting me to some semblance of normal life—a life one can hardly lead when immersed vicariously in another's—I often very nearly come to feel that living such a life might one day be desirable.

Unfortunately, this time Joanne's arrival coincided with a rather delicate and trying moment for us. To summarize: there is the matter of the insolvency of Belle Encoding—a company that cannot, in actuality, be merely dissolved, given its prominent role in the overall portfolio of the Mrdok organization, its interconnectedness in the larger internet of things, as well as the moral obligation Mrdok has to his clients, many of whom are quite prominent individuals; as a result, the project has emerged to reformulate the company formerly known as Belle Encoding in a new geographical context; there is the ordeal with Mrdok's private plane, which was unfortunately seized on a recent trek to Cuba—a conspiracy launched by the disgruntled execs at SunEye, no doubt, with a need for complex negotiations in order to get it out; there is the deal with nucleite, which may now be a deal with ilmenite, or some other substance also ending in -ite, but in order for me to elaborate further, I would have to first locate and then consult my notes on the subject; then there are the issues of a more personal nature, namely Mrdok's need to satisfy Mrtol's recently announced desire to move elsewhere (without knowing exactly where), as well as the ongoing saga with his mistress Bev; finally, there is the upcoming trip to Sagosia to arrange—not the most accessible place in the world, so the private plane would come in handy, but first we must retrieve it from the Cubans, which will be, well… I thus have any number of Sisyphean tasks before me, which I was enumerating to Joanne as best I could in abbreviated form (for, as I discovered early on in our marriage, Joanne did not share the same intellectual fascination with all things Mrdokian as I), when she raised her hand to interrupt me with an alarmed expression across her indelicate features.

–Gordon, sorry as I am to interrupt, she started off sincerely enough, but could you tell me when this trip to, where was it, Sagosia? When is that meant to take place?

I replied, in turn, that I was in the midst of planning it, but that it would likely take up much of the latter half of February, since this was meant to be more serious, perhaps, than a mere site visit.

–Gordon. That's our anniversary.

–Why yes! Of course! I said, now improvising because, to my great misfortune, I had simply forgotten the date, so caught up in the neverending motions and action of the day-to-day as I had been.

–February twenty-fifth. To refresh your memory…

–Of course, Joanne. There's really no need! How could I forget such an important date? Why, it's inscribed into the permanent diary of my memory.

–Well, it seems like it's not.

–Joanne, darling. You understand that this job, at times—very often, really, robs me of my autonomy. It really is very busy, dare I say chaotic, at the moment. I cannot know for sure, but chances are leaning in the direction that I will either have to be in Cuba or Sagosia during that period.

–One night, Gordon. It's all I ask of you. Just one night in Middleton, then off you go, back to all of this…

She looked around her disgustedly.

–… This life you are leading. Need I remind you that you have yet to spend a single night in Connecticut this entire year.

–Through no fault of my own, Joanne. And certainly through no choice of my own… Look, may I confess something to you? I believe we are just a step or two away from something quite major—

–You know how much I hate it when you talk about your work in front of me. When you… try to sell what you do… Like I'm some sort of *client* or something.

–Mrdok has in his sight a most lucrative real estate deal that could drastically change—

–One. Night. Gordon, it's all I'm asking.

I studied Joanne from across the table. Outside, the dimming light of day, combined with the first enunciation of neon across the sidewalk, giving the city its magic hour glow.

–Aren't we at the point now in our lives that a change might do us both some good?

–Gordon… What on earth are you—?

–I am talking about a veritable *upgrade* of our lowly existence, Joanne.

–Excuse me, Gordon? What right do you have to characterize *my* existence as lowly? Speak for yourself if you're going to talk that way.

–It's all relative, my dear. Of course we are quite *comfortable,* the way we are now. We certainly don't have it *all.* But we do have quite a lot.

–You know how I feel about that vulgar man—

–*Don't…* Joanne… You. Ever. You know, not just what he means to me, but what he means to *us.* That house up in Connecticut that you hold so dear, this, everything around us, really—it is all thanks to him!

–Yes, I know how you feel about him, Gordon. I—

–We have the chance to really upgrade our lives. To live almost a parallel existence to the kind of life Mrdok—

–I know I don't want that.

–Well what is it exactly that you do want, Joanne? To simply go on and, I don't know, *expire* in that wilting old manor in Connecticut?

A shocked expression now took possession of her features.

–I happen to like our house. A lot. There is nothing wrong with it, Gordon. It's a beautiful house. And I, for one, have put a lot of effort—

–I like it too, Joanne. But we could have so much more. Think: exotic shores. Sandy beaches. Year-round sunshine.

–… Are you thinking of *relocating,* Gordon?

–Well. The idea did not originate with me. I must confess, I, too, at first—

–No. Gordon. No. The answer is no, okay?

–But Joanne—

–I happen to be perfectly happy with my life in Connecticut, eager as you are to paint such a dismal picture of it. I mean, who are you, anyway? I truly don't recognize the man you're turning into.

At which point in the conversation, I had to give pause. For it was true that I had, of late, felt a change of an unnamable sort coming over me. Much as Mrdok's inner compass was shifting toward a center that positioned our current location at its outermost circumference, I found myself oddly growing distant from the self I had just been, well, not too long before. Perhaps my inner geography, programmed as it had been so long ago to align with Mrdok's, was now shifting.

Shifting, in truth, to a locale in one of the more obscure regions of the globe, the Pseudotropics. The island of Sagosia, which Mrdok had lain on my desk to research not long after that morning I'd walked in to find him still in his pajamas mapgazing, was but a speck in the region's main liquid body, known as the Brown Sea, so-called because the iron ore deposits that once greatly encircled the coasts of the gallant Seashell Islands had, once upon a time, contributed their dark copperish hue to the waters surrounding.

Geography has never been my strong suit, at any point in my studies. As a lifelong English literature fanatic, I have enmeshed myself in tales of adventure at high sea, though when it comes to pinpointing the settings of these stories and novels on actual physical maps, I am always at a loss; this is one of many areas where Mrdok's talents heavily outweigh my own.

Of course, my position in the organization has brought with it myriad opportunities to expand this embarrassingly paltry patch of my learning, and so I have pursued it in earnest.

When its first colonizers, a renegade band of Portuguese buccaneers, ruefully adrift in the battered waters of the Brown Sea in the midst of the summer season's cruel cyclonic beatings, set foot upon the island that would eventually come to be known as Sagosia, there was actually very little that could be properly colonized. The largely forested island had evolved up to that point without the benefit of a single human inhabitant. Landing on the powdery sands of what is now known as Pirate's Bay (and is designated thus with a modest stone inscription fronting the entrance to the forested park behind, according to a photo on Wikipedia), the buccaneers were instead greeted by a family of waddling wingless creatures that appeared to one of them as a cross between a bat, a duck, and a baboon. In addition to its absurd appearance, its mauve, wingless plumage, the quasimammal further distinguished itself by its curiosity—a quality now regarded as poignant, given its fate—and apparent friendliness or at the very least lack of reserve before human presence. For as the first roving marauder stepped on to dry sand, the ass monkey, as the creature's genus would soon come to be christened, waddled right up to him in greeting. And when that bestial man swung his machete and beheaded the poor creature, none of its companions made the slightest bray or effort to run away, but rather stood there regarding the entire scene with the same expression of entranced curiosity with which they had regarded the ship in its initial process of arrival, much to the buccaneers' amusement. So the creature earned its name— dumb as an ass, and with a utilitarian value somewhat equal to said creature, for while the ass monkey was not of much use in the transporting of man and goods, its flesh was said to be as rich in flavor and satisfying in texture as venison. Its earnestness swiftly paved the way to its extinction; the hungry sea rovers, sickened by then by a diet of food extracted from the sea, proceeded to eat their way through the island's habitat. Experts in thievery and the assessment of gold and jewels though they might have been, zoologists the buccaneers were not. After studying its fossils, experts would later conclude that the ass monkey, so-called, was neither donkey nor monkey, but rather a species of flightless bird rare enough to call only the island of Sagosia its home. And the blame for its extinction cannot be attributed alone to the error of human intervention, but also to certain shortcomings in nature. For the females of the ass monkey species were so stubborn as to lay only a single egg each year. These eggs were rarely hidden well, but usually covered with a few flings of sand upon the shore, leaving them vulnerable prey to rats, serpents, and other hungry creatures, who would often discover them prior to the hatch. In short, the ass monkey was not intended as a victor in the world according to Darwin. Still, naturists have clung to the fate of the ass monkey as an allegory of the deleterious effects of human intervention in the animal kingdom—and for good reason, it turns out. The intrusion of human life on to the pristine shores of Sagosia would aid the extinction of numerous other plant and animal species, though it is the legendary demise of the ass monkey that has proven to endure in the popular imagination, which is why illustrations of the creature are promoted throughout the island. Its likeness even appears on the back of Sagosia's paper currency.

Now, according to islandological science, there are said to be two sorts of islands. Continental islands are those which once belonged to a larger land mass, but, over the centuries, have broken off or were otherwise severed by the intrusion of sea and ocean, thus endowing them with a seemingly organic autonomy. The second type, oceanic islands, are those whose organicity is scarcely an illusion. For they, in fact, managed to enunciate themselves on their very own through the deepest depths of the sea, via volcanic eruption or other natural forms of assertion. Victor, then, over the sea's violence, its attempts to cover them up; no one can deny the triumph of their eventual vertical reign. It is to this latter type that Sagosia belongs.

The original buccaneers did not remain for long. The life of a pirate, after all, is dictated by a certain inner *néomanie*. And what a lonely life it can be! Devoid of all certainty, with your immediate companions your only real source of comfort—whose proximity eventually makes them into something of an extension of your very own being—well, boredom and an internal restlessness come to preside. After a few years spent denuding the island of its trees and foliage, hatcheting pathways with their sharpened blades that would eventually become the island's premier roadways, the pirates abandoned the place, in search of new shores to raid. (They would find success in launching a micro-colony in the nearby atoll known today as the Seashell Islands. There, the native populace was immediately subordinated by the conquerors, fomenting the grisly beginnings of the legacy of slavery in the Brown Sea.)

A couple decades blew past in the pseudotropical breeze, and history entered into the Golden Age of Piracy. Somewhere in the early years of the eighteenth century, yet another gang of pirates would reach a landing on the southeastern coast near the present day Pirate's Bay, which would eventually evolve into the island's first real settlement. Unlike the Portuguese buccaneers who had essentially been sea thieves-for-hire, this particular gang of pirates was a mixed Venetian, English, and Caribbean fleet of some eighty men and women, led by the legendary Creole pirate captain John Bogatty. The pirates were coming off a series of successful raids in the Brown Sea and were, it seems, simply looking for a spot to settle down, some permanently, others temporarily. The island thus served initially as a reprieve, a sort of retirement center for elder pirates looking to enjoy the fruits of their amassed bounty somewhere remote enough from the prying eyes of the law or else revenge-seeking corsairs. Following the unfortunate example set by their brethren on the Seashell Islands, and, dare we say, the trend of the era, slaves were soon to be imported from Africa. Further explorations of the island soon led to additional settlements. Meanwhile, as the pirate settlers began to bequeath further generations, a unique patois slowly evolved that was all but impenetrable to outsiders, a mixture of Italian, Slavic, Creole, Dutch, and English; this language was further enriched by the contribution of an admixture of Fujian dialects and Korean, brought by yet a further band of renegade settlers, a large pirate ship freshly arrived from some origin in the South China Sea. Led by the legendary female pirate Chuang Xin, this gang of pan-Asiatic seafarers harbored a cultic devotion to the Warring States philosopher Yang Zhu. Yang had essentially been a Hedonist, in the ancient Greek sense of the term, with his purported belief that the privileging of the individual self, the pursuit of pleasure, and the general preservation of the delights of the body over those of the mind should be the sole mission in one's life. Individuals, so the philosophy went, cannot possibly order the world, and any effort to do so inevitably results in failure. What's more, such efforts do irreparable damage to the individual self; anyway, if one is properly attuned to the primary task of self care and the pursuit of pleasure, hardly any time would be left over for such grand pursuits as war and government. Above all, Yangists valued life over things; the latter only had any use in that they might be deployed to nourish, enhance, preserve, or otherwise benefit the former. In this, the Yangist philosophy not only pitted the pirates directly against the authority of the emperor (whom their philosophical rivals the Confucianists so venerated) back home, it also fit right into the anarcho-individualism practiced by so many Western pirates in the Golden Age, with a general scorn for work, a disregard for all manifestations and expressions of statehood, and an ethos of collectivity (wherein the captain's role was not merely to represent the will of the collective, but also to share his own personal bounty with all others; it is for this reason, a general distrust of authority, that the captain of pirate fleets often shifted over time, and served more a practical function, since each pirate by and large shared the same quotient of authority—which is to say, none at all, in principle.)

The arrival of the Yangist pirates at first threw the island into chaos. Given the inability of the new arrivals to effectively communicate—for no one on the island spoke their language; and, given the range of geographies represented, the islanders had trouble enough just communicating with each other—conflict was inevitable. For the Yangists actually had no idea that the island's settlers were themselves the descendants of pirate brethren, and proceeded to perform their standard act of sodomy and plunder upon them. Naturally, the original settlers fought back. The conflict eventually welled into battle, culminating in what would become known in history as the Sagosian War. It had the dual honor of serving not only as the sole war in the entire history of Sagosia, but also the shortest war in history, its entire length occupying a full seven minutes, its culminating moment arriving when the cannon of the settlers' army misfired, causing an explosion that decimated half their soldiers. (For this reason, it has been recorded by some historians as the Seven Minute War.) The Yangists, who had been firing from their anchored ship, soon made their way to the shore to investigate the tragicomical scene. They had among their number many who were trained in the science of traditional Chinese medicine, and they swiftly commenced doctoring to the needs of the injured settlers. This goodwill gesture, followed by a round of mutual drinking, effected a truce and endeared the two parties to one another. The Yangists were able to join the settlers in residing on Sagosia, gradually began to fornicate with them, and, though never able to make themselves sufficiently understood in their own tongue (in fact, it took several generations for the language barriers to wither down to the extent that both parties would discover that they were borne of pirate ancestry), contributed to the evolution of the unique hybrid language that would come to be called Sagosian, as well as its spiritual and cultural life—though, to this day, only a single dusty dove-shaped Yangist temple remains on the island.

Well, after several generations, the Sagosians were pirates no longer. They had become by and large citizens of a country that was, at least, recognized as one by its neighbors. The pirates' progeny became, let us say, complacent, and adapted the slow, laid-back lifestyle for which islanders in this part of the world are known. While slavery continued, one cannot say that Sagosia played much of a role in the slave trade; for after the initial importation of the first band of slaves, who were then allowed to reproduce freely, there was no need of bringing more or else exchanging them with other lands, self-sufficient as the island had briskly become. What's more, the legacy of slavery lasted a mere five or six decades. There was only one slave revolt, early on, at which point the settlers, listening in earnest to the slaves' demands, acquiesced to all of them, effectively setting them free. Many of the former slaves returned to their former masters, this time as paid employees, while others, relishing their freedom, embarked upon their own careers, intermixing with the patrician class and contributing yet further to the island's intrigue of mixed ethnicities, fully enjoying the rather relaxed lifestyle increasingly seen as a hallmark of Sagosian life.

Little surprise, then, that when, in the middle of the nineteenth century, British fleets suddenly surrounded the island one night, there was little fight to be given. The British were, of course, seeking a stronghold in the maritime trade route that engulfed much of the Brown Sea in this period, and Sagosia seemed readily within grasp (the neighboring Seashell Islands had already been divided up in an alliance between the Dutch and the French.)

The natives—or quasinatives, as they have come to be called, in deference to the fact that Sagosia was originally uninhabited and thus, in a sense, belonged to no one—who had made much of their riches as a result of those early years of slave labor, found themselves in the ironic position as slaves of the British. They were made to work the sugar cane fields and, while by and large able to continue with fishing, were forced to surrender a certain quantity of their catch at the end of each day. The British, it must be said, held very little interest in these activities as profit-earning endeavor; their aim in submitting the quasinatives was rather more to prevent any kind of revolt and to establish a hegemony over the island, whose chief importance was its strategic location, from which British fleets could readily engage in maritime trade. By the end of the nineteenth century, with that hegemony firmly in place, the British rulers could relax their stance toward the quasinatives, begin to pay wages, and release a certain number into the freedom to engage in private enterprise—mirroring, in a sort of light way, the Sagosians' own earlier process of disenslavement. No real industry (save for the Rodgers Biscuit Factory) was established by the British themselves, nor did they seem to have any real interest in the seeking out and taming of natural resources (though they did greatly enjoy at least one domestic product that pre-dated their arrival: Sagosian rum.) The island was able to develop as an unraped paradise, unknown by the vast majority of the planet's human populace.

This idyllic state endured into the middling years of the twentieth century, when, following the tumult of the Second World War, an anti-colonial movement began to gain ground back in England. So as to prevent the revolutionary fervor spreading over much of the world from ever reaching local shores, the colonial administrators of Sagosia devised a strategy. To deprive Sagosia of its colonial status, the island would be leased—for the symbolic sum of one pound a day, for a contractual period of 999 years—to another Brown Sea island in which the British held some stake, Pembroke. Pembroke itself no longer held colonial status, but was officially a British overseas territory—meaning it retained autonomy of governance, though the British handled its overseas affairs, the currency was the pound, and the official language spoken English. It is for this reason that the British are known today as quasicolonials—since, technically, the island is a territory of Pembroke, though it also retains autonomy in certain of its affairs—though it is true the situation remains somewhat murky to outsiders.

Today's status quo has been maintained in a state of relative bliss. Fishing and agriculture comprise the vast majority of the island's economy, with fish and bamboo serving as the chief exports, followed close behind by sugar cane. Many, if not most of the former British ruling class have decamped back to the United Kingdom or elsewhere, though those who remain, in the homes around where Nelson Rodgers resides in Olde Colonia in the island's administrative (and geographic) center, behave charitably toward the quasinatives, providing them with new homes along the coast whenever they are destroyed by the latest tropical storm.

Somewhat amazingly, this paradisiacal isle has yet to be discovered by the tourist hordes—or seemingly anyone, for that matter. In their strenuous efforts to keep the islands isolated from public discourse, the British have endeavored to avoid publicizing it as a tourism destination or building the needed infrastructure. Among a certain global elite class, rumors of the island's salability have occasionally emerged over the years, though have never been confirmed, nor, it seems, deeply investigated—until now…

—As fascinating as this all is, Joanne regains, you're not only putting me to sleep, Gordon, you're sidelining the entire point of the conversation.

–… But don't you see, Joanne? Sagosia could be our very own slice of paradise. We could live like, like kings and queens, we could—

–What the hell are you talking about, Gordon? I don't harbor those kinds of ambitions. I don't even like to travel to Manhattan. I'm a simple woman. And you were a simple man. At least the man I married was.

–Well. There is no need to let such simplicity *mar* us. We must continue to evolve as humans. Don't you think?

–No, I don't, Gordo. And I don't want you to think that way, either. Who do you—

–I am trying to make you, to *help* you to understand—

—I think it is getting time for you to make a decision, Gordon. A serious decision. Not just about us. But about yourself. About the life you wish to lead. Because, I have to tell you: what you're doing now, it's not living.

—Is it not? Ha.

—No, Gordon. It's not. Now, I understand your Protestant work ethic, your devotion to—

—To what, Joanne?

—To… to… this *cause*. If we can call it that. This *man*.

—Yes. It is my life's calling.

—Well, your life's calling is starting to interfere—

—Excuse me? I thought we had an understanding.

—We do have an understanding, Gordon. And our understanding does, in fact, transcend geographic barriers. But, with this, I don't even know what it is. But I'm starting to fear that you are, I don't know, about to test the boundaries of that understanding.

—What I'm doing is *expanding*—

—No, you're not, Gordon. You're testing.

—Joanne—

—To be *arrogant* enough to make these kinds of assumptions. This was not the man I married, that I decided to devote my life to.

—You have your own life, Joanne. We each do. This was the gist of our agreement. To have our own lives, and then our life together, which is by necessity separate.

—It's going to be very separate if we're not even on the same continent. Don't expect me to be there with you on this one. On this little journey of yours, Gordon. I feel like…

—What? What is it that you feel?

—I feel like you've chosen *him*. Over me.

Gordo sighs.

—It is not a question of choosing, Joanne. At least… This is not something one can choose.

—What is it, then?

—This is a thing that chooses you.

—A thing?

—Yes. A force.

—It's a person, Gordon. A man.

—No. He is not just that.

—What is he then?

—Something more. And I have to go there. To find out what that thing is. It's the only way.

Joanne begins to gather her things from the space in the booth next to her.

–I'm not staying in the city tonight, Gordon. Needless to say.

–Joanne.

–What?

–Just… We do not know the dates yet. For the trip. I will see you next weekend, nonetheless.

–No. You won't. I have something planned with Dot. Stay here, Gordon. I'm sure you can find some excuse. Your work, after all, never ends. In that, it's so different from other things in this life.

And with that, she is gone. For now, at least.

2.

TOUCHING DOWN AT Pirate's Bay, we arrive at the throat of the world. The anemic shores with their waves tonguing the pellets of dead reef strewn across rust sand. Reminds him of a place he forever arrives at, like an airport. Or summer. Only it's not. It's a shore. Distant, with all that entails. Sullen life. Had to dope himself up again to get here—paranoia of flying—doesn't always get it, more like wells up from time to time, like a bout of acid reflux. Whatever summer can be—well, it's an ugly thing. On this hemisphere it is. Vincent jumps into the water with rope in hand, guides the boat to shore. Standing there with nightblack sunglasses on, staring through them. Distant chance of arriving. He thinks: maybe. The island doesn't exactly come alive. Not like on other places one might happen to land. What is this, boat scraping against the reef. Sullen glance to Armageddon sitting next to you over there. There's a chance of getting made, of nailing all your fears into the sand here. Vincent calls out: it's okay now, boat is steady. Please disembark. Follow Gordo, big dunk in the water. Inner program that's made to rot and then. What am I supposed to do with my shoes—Here, I'll hold them. Someone's laughter is seeing them through binoculars, scan the shore and try to shake off the Xanaxized haze.

We—what is this—no grand ceremony of arrival? Day's haze. Dry antiphony. It is true how in the beginning you often end up this way. No grand ceremony of arrival—but of course!—I love it! For in these instances awareness is the big gift. Ability to suddenly register. Opposite side of the globe, this is. Sand on the hand, brush off. Lapping lightly at the shore. Feeling you get when there's not much left to die for.

That tree looks something other than palm; what might we call it?

The inspiration comes to name everything anew. No more use for the old language. Mostly it's the framing of the thing we have to get right. Here comes an old man in Hawaiian shorts a pitbull-looking breed of a beast on a leash. Vincent says something to him—the local lingo—or maybe it's English—too early to tell. Too, something, to say anything. Gordo looking concerned. Coffee is on the way.

Child crawls out of the water choking. Coffee's on its way. What are they gonna bring it, right here?—Right here, boss, right here. While the tide is medium low, anything might happen. Indeed, tuxedo'd waiter appears from out of seeming nowhere, single cup of espresso on gleaming silver tray.

Old man's dog's name is Silence. Silence doesn't keep silent all of the time. Silence is a dog that speaks in rhyme.

Let me tell you a tale of ol' Sagosia Quay
Now leased to the isle of Pembroke for one pound a day
A lease said to endure for 999 years
To appease the Brits of all their fears
That the quasis might grow restless from the strain
Of unequal life beneath the rage of a hurricane
Life smooshed up against a window pane!
There goes by a young bloke I know well
Name is Vincent, never gives the hard sell
Even gives me a tasty freebie now and then
Of an entire fish still intact with fin
While the rest of the fishers might throw me guts or a bone
Vincent'll toss me a most delectable loan
I never have to pay back
Fresh from the sack
Otherwise I'm forced to subsist
On a diet not even a pig would enlist
Nelson's dog biscuits, the pride of Sagosia
Taste like brine, I shoulda told ya
Before you gave me one just now
I forgot to mention it somehow
Earlier in my rhyme
But that's okay, we have time

Let's return to our former subject
Before my aging mind rejects

What is left of this memory and it vacates my brain
No amount of sorry would I then be able to feign—

Now Vincent's far from lazy
Though his brother's a little crazy
If you don't understand the sacred role of fire in our island's lore
I'd be happy to tell you all about it now for sure
Back in the day when the new settlers had found
This precious lil island to dig their spikes in the ground
It was a pseudotropical paradise, they were overjoyed
They just needed something to fill the spiritual void
A certain je ne sais quoi as they jumped from belief to belief
Like some sort of desperate confused thief
What they really needed
In this new world undefeated
Was a figure like god
To focus their thought
The opposite of water they sought
For it was what surrounds
They needed to cut those bounds
To the very ends
Find something that would cleanse
Their fears and doubts
One night a young settler began to spout
Flames from his mouth after drinking a near gallon
Of the locally made fun
And imbibed each night so they could sleep in their graves
Fire became the thing for their worshipful glares
Also the thing that warmed their lairs
At night when the biggest fire of all made its descent
Leaving them to feel all frigid and spent

Temples were erected, though they weren't overly devout
These were, after all, former pirates we're talking about
It was more ceremonial, a ritual bout
That over time commenced to die out

Eating fire is an art no more
Along Sagosia's desolate shore
Or so it would appear
But as in most places these days, alternative facts draw near

You see Vincent has a brother
From the very same mother
His name is Prince and he wields the flame
To him it's a little more than a juvenile delinquent's game
Pyromania inborn it seems
But to investigate further would send beams
Of shiver and suspicion down the spine
Because this kid's a veritable mine
About to explode the whole island one might suspect
His obsession is much more than what you'd expect
Of a kid just thirteen and hardly aware
Of all the life that's left to live out there
Poor Vincent and his mom, try as they might
Cannot keep wild Prince within their sight
He runs with his gang setting things alight
Mainly abandoned lots scarred by an old hurricane
With admittedly little to offer the quasis—still, it's insane
The extent to which their game does go
Anything, it seems, to watch that glow
And to feel the glare of the flames at night
Lapping the skin, oh, it gives me a fright
For I am only a dog and can't do more than bark and rhyme
At this dangerous endeavor which must surely be a crime
In places where law and order rule
But that's not Sagosia, don't be a fool

Now here on the rust colored shores of the Brown Sea
Arrives a stranger the likes of which we never see
With a funny-sounding name and an unusual smell
Why a suspicious glance on my owner just befell
What could such a walking worldvoid want
With this indelicate seaside haunt?
There is a lot of danger
In trusting such a stranger
As all islanders well know
He's on his way to the chateau
Of Nelson Rodgers
That wry ol' dodger
King of the quasicolonials
A role that is now largely ceremonial
But still we must bow when we see him pass by
Once his back is turned toward us, middle fingers point to the sky

Just as Prince's fires at night set the island ablaze
Igniting mixed feelings that evade paraphrase
So me and my master now feel a concern
That more than old houses here soon shall burn

Expand the horizon, birds're chirping. The field that lies just beyond those trees that no one has yet arrived to give a name to. First taste of that grainy black bitterness on the tongue awakens you to the awful reality of morning. Ask Gordo the schedule, a note of dread. Waiter disappears back where he came from. What is it, a resort over there. No, sir. No resorts anywhere on the island.

—Yet, Gordo adds; yes-man of the ages.

And so Mrdok doesn't bother to hush him up. There's no one around, after all, that matters at this very instant. Soon there will be. Though then, he'll know to watch his tongue.

Coffee waking him to the blue matter of day. Somehow thought the waters'd be brown here (Brown Sea.) Instead, a crystalline blue. Azurial, he thinks is the word for it. Hafta ask Gordo. Later. Now Gordo's conversing with Vincent, the boatswain, Mrdok moves closer to the shore. Some fisherboats coming in. Climbing off, they eye the foreigners with more curiosity than anything else. Almost want to say something, not sure what there is to say. Clear they don't come from this world, what is their language? The one off by himself lookin fancy somehow. Must be a rich man, but comin here, why. What is there to want.

It's the question of the hour, the one everyone's asking. Lagoonar. Bats in the sky—in the morning? Must ask about that. Bats instead of airplanes. Lusty youths and their phone-blared music upon the shore. Is this really morning?

—Hey Vincent, let me ask you something.

—It's the middle of the afternoon, sir, Vincent responds. Three o'clock.

—Was that a fuckin bat I just saw flyin overhead?

—The bats fly around here all day. Not like your bats, North American bats. Only come out at night. These are fruit bats. They're on the constant prowl. Hang upside down, just like normal bats. Only no daytime allergy.

They almost went extinct once. Challenges to the habitat posed by human life. They adapted, got used to it. Had to reorient a thing or three. New habits of mating, hanging, nesting, all that. They got used to it. They're among the lucky ones. Not so the ass monkey. You won't be seeing no ass monkeys on Sagosia no more, that much for sure. But still. All kinds of animals and plants, mister. It's an un-discovered paradise here. Just wait till you meet Mister Rodgers. He can tell you more.

–When do we meet Mister Rodgers? I somehow thought he'd be meeting us here.

–Haha. He don't come down to this shore so often. He like… He like his place up in the hills. You'll see.

There are reasons for that. Climate, for one. Every student in Sagosia learns in history class about the cataclysmic hurricane of 1895, which decimated all the island's settlements, its delicate infrastructure. They come each year, during cyclone season, in varying shades of blue to black. Living inland, of course, is no guarantee against the threat posed by this meteorological unpleasantness—but it does curb your chances. The houses on the coast don't have any. No hope to survive, once those angry winds start whipping the waters and debris into a froth against them. And so they collapse, cave in. Few die by now, as most know to abandon them toward some inland shelter, one of the many concrete façades that have been set up for these emergencies by the quasicolonial administration. And so it is around the coast that the quasinatives have traditionally made their homes. There is certainly a visible class ascendancy, the further inland and uphill you go.

Sagosia, as Mrdok and I would come to understand, is essentially a failed colony. Those attempting to preserve its ties to the dwindling empire are in point of fact fighting a losing battle. Its current colonial administrator, this Nelson Rodgers, currently serves the highest authoritative role on the island. He is one of the few white men still left, with most of the other colonizers long ago having abandoned camp for either nearby islands or else returned to the larger land mass from which the colony is ostensibly administered.

Rodgers himself is a native of Sagosia. Save for a brief spell at Oxford, he has lived on the island his entire life, and thus possesses a keen understanding of its dynamics and potentials, if not its immediate future. Like most of the *grano wango blankos,* or, roughly, princely precious whites, as they were deemed in the local language nearing extinction, Rodgers's homestead was on the island's inner plateau, away from the coast, so as to be protected from the inevitable rise of the surrounding waters, not to mention the inclement weather—the cyclones the one half of the year, the extreme piercing heat of the latter half—for in the upper regions of the island's center, the air is cool and dry.

Nelson is a descendant of a long line of British colonists, owners of the island's esteemed Rodgers Biscuit Factory. Using a secret family recipe passed down over generations—but believed to make gratuitous usage of the waters of the Brown Sea and locally grown sugarcane in equal measure—the biscuits produced here are appreciated and much adored by dogs everywhere, but in particular the dogs on the island, both of the domestic variety and the numberless strays who are known to wander its streets in seeming desperate search of them.

Less famously, the Rodgers Biscuit Factory also made tea biscuits for human consumption—using, it is said, a slight variation on the same ingredients—though given that much of the British population would abandon the island throughout the dwindling years of the twentieth century, leaving it mostly barren of its colonial invaders by the arrival of the twenty-first, the practice of taking afternoon tea is but a quaint historical relic; the biscuits began to crumble.

As we make our way slowly into the island's depths, with Vincent at the wheel of our ancient Jeep and Mrdok and myself in the backseat, we pass any number of houses covered in a strange web of black graffiti. At casual glance, it nearly manifests itself as scrawl, or tags, as I believe the amateur version of graffiti is called—wherein the inexperienced uses the spray can to crudely plaster their initials or some barely legible phrase across an architectural surface. As more of this strange pseudowriting appears, however, it begins to look purposeful, nearly systematic, although each is idiosyncratic enough in appearance to assure that it was all done by hand, rather than mass produced by some mysterious stencil.

–Look at that.

–It boggles the mind, Mrdok says. I've never seen anything like it before.

–You like it, sir? It is our local language!

Then Vincent laughs, in an unmalicious way, so as to let us all know he's just made a joke.

–First thing this place is gonna need is an airport, says Mrdok in the front seat, seemingly oblivious now to all that scrawl.

–An airport?! Vincent says in disbelief. Then he laughs like it's the funniest thing he's ever heard in his life.

–What's so funny?

–I'm sorry, it's just… Nobody ever leaves Sagosia, sir. We have no need for any airport.

–It's not for people to leave. It's so that people can come here.

–Here? To Sagosia?

Vincent has to pause at the idea. It's not like he hasn't considered it before. Sometimes rich people will show up in helicopters, though it's not very often. Usually some quasicolonial business or other. As the island's sole tour guide—or, rather, the closest thing the island has had to a tour guide, considering the paltry number of visitors it receives each year (you couldn't even call these visitors tourists, since there's nothing really *to do* here in Sagosia)—Vincent had little reason to consider that the tides might some day change—that life might one day become something different than what it currently is, what it has always been. When he isn't guiding visitors around the island—and that's most of the time—if *guiding* isn't the wrong verb here—more providing transportation in his own boat or whatever borrowed Jeep that could be scrounged up—he makes his living fishing, and since that doesn't take up many hours of the day, he fills in at home for Mama while she's off filming her stories. She is famous throughout the island for her supporting role on *Lives of the Innocents,* Sagosia's premiere—well, one and only—daytime soap opera. She plays Hornby, the mother of Rae, the lead character played by the astoundingly beautiful Maria, whose litany of affairs, substance abuse, rehabilitations, marriages, divorces, and metamorphoses forms the main crux of the show's plot. In addition to dishing out worldly wisdom to her daughter and other characters, she is known on the show for being something of a witch doctor, able to heal with herbs, potions, and chants. For this reason, some Sagosians, when they spot her in real life, confuse her likeness with her character on the show, and, convinced by her depicted powers, come to her with the expectation that she will be able to heal their ailments, be they physical or otherwise. Lucia, who is atypically shy for an actress, will often roll right away from them before they even complete their implorement; when she's not on-screen, she prefers to get around the island on rollerblades, and has them on almost all the time. They allow not just for her to get her errands done at rapid speed, to get to work and home while subverting the traffic caused by the island's problematic roadways, but as an escape module from this rather unwelcome side of celebrityhood.

Save for the same black graffiti'd scrawl covering its white surface that we'd seen on the other houses along the way, Nelson Rodgers's home reveals itself as a typical specimen of mid-nineteenth century colonial mansion, though, it must be said, in a rather weathered and dilapidated state. A spacious two-story rotting monstrosity surrounded by a rather idyllic overgrown garden—lush with azaleas, poinsettias, leafy palms, and dozens of pseudotropical plants I have not yet managed to acquire in my vocabulary—all the doors have been lazily and thoughtlessly flung open to the elements surrounding. The house, with its entrance on ground level, is ringed by an unenclosed patio that descends on to the veranda. At the rear of the house—which is where the entrance is—there is a small cottage at a few steps' remove which is still used as a kitchen. Peeking inside to investigate the source of the most savory scent hovering through the air, an exotic avalanche of spicery grounded in what must be some variation on sweet potato, we discover a scene that must have endured for well over a hundred years now, three large-boned women in aprons and hairnets busy stirring the broth, cutting vegetables, gathering the settings for the table... Only now, of course, the women are gainfully employed in their positions.

Nelson Rodgers has yet to appear, so we are able to sniff our way about the ground floor without feeling intrusive about it; all the doors, after all, have been flung open in a welcoming gesture, as though the house were waiting for our casual inspection. It appears to us as a quaint historical relic, quite othertimely, with only a few accessories thrown in to remind us of the current century. Most of the furniture, all quite old, has been carved out of blackwood, which is plentiful on the island. The ground floor consists of a living room, a dining room, and two bedrooms; neither appear to have been recently used, crammed with dusty antique furnishings and framed photos on the wall of presumed ancestry in ancient garb, so one is a guest room, I gather, while the second is for a child.

As we take our seats on the back veranda overlooking a small spice garden, a stone sculpture of a man appears before us.

—I suppose it would not surprise you to hear we're not very accustomed to receiving visitors.

Nelson Rodgers has a shock of blonde hair sprouting from the top of his round head and eyes of the darkest and most ponderous blue. He looks to be somewhere in his mid 40s—and he is, exactly, forty-five, according to my research. The island's chief British quasicolonial administrator, which means he does very little other than hold a symbolic role of power, since Sagosia is now only a British territory in the vaguest sort of way—the island has long been leased to the neighboring island of Pembroke some thousand kilometers away. The Pembrokians mostly use Sagosia as a fishing port. Beyond that, much of the economic arrangement remains a mystery to us; it is a mystery we are here to solve. Nelson Rodgers is the place to start.

He serves us water in glazed white cups bearing the same graffiti we'd seen on the houses coming into the island's interior. This finally gives me the opportunity to ask him about the source of these strange markings.

—Well, it helps to know something about pirates. Their ways and means.

Nelson Rodgers glances at Mrdok's face so as to study its response to this strange comment, then quickly looks away, as though deciding against the idea. Then he looks at me, gets up and makes his way into the small study just off the patio, removing a volume from the bookcase, which he then places on the table before us. *History and Anthropology of Sagosian Markmaking: PhD by Thesis, Nelson Rodgers, MPhil,* reads the cover.

—At first, I wanted to do something else, something not at all related to Sagosia. I've lived here my entire life, so by the time I got to Oxford, I was quite ready to explore and learn more about the world, other places. I took classes in many subjects, but History of Art was what ultimately called out to me in the end.

—How curious! The two of us also studied in England, I start to say, but am interrupted by Mrdok's foot beneath the table.

—For my master's work, Rodgers continues, I chose Cyprus. I wrote my thesis on fourteenth century glazed sgraffito ware with floral motifs. That monograph was also published, but I'm afraid I no longer have any available copies to offer. I quite took to the academic life. When it came time to submit a topic for my doctoral research, coming back to Sagosia was an obvious choice. I already knew a lot about the subject, having grown up here, and I knew that no one in academia had ever seriously written on it. I was a natural fit for the task. Markmaking. It ties in to the island's history, but also its geology. The idea that this island is totally organic, well... It depends on how far back you want to go, really. A few years ago, we had some scientists come in, they were doing some research here. Geologists, studying the ancient rock, the stuff they found in the sand... They found evidence of ancient continental crust beneath the island. That white sandstone you see everywhere, the surface of the markmaking? That rock and the ligand they use to write on it both contain ancient zircons that are more than three billion years old. Ever heard of Gondwana? The ancient continent? This was a part of it, they concluded. Though others disagree... The tribulations of ancient history, I suppose...

The markmaking itself came into practice by way of a geological oddity unearthed by divers in their plunges to the Brown Sea's sandy depths: that shiny black seastone that has come to be known as ligand.

In the island's preliterate days, the early settlers, in states of drunken revelry (for they figured out quite early one intoxicating usage to which the wild sugar cane growing all over could be put), they would break off pieces of ligand to write furiously, rapturously, illegible scrawl upon surfaces of ivory white sandstone, mocking the scholarly endeavor of civilized man, much to the amusement of their fellow illiterate pirate-cum-settlers. In the morning, they would awaken with zero recollection of the night prior's activities, so potent was the rum, and stare in amazement at this tangled mass of pseudo-writing on all the stone surrounding them. One settler became convinced it was a message from the gods who were attempting to communicate with them. So persuasive was he in his argument that an entire clan came to believe in the veracity of this myth. It was only when the last of the settlers was finally roused from his two-day-long hangover slumber, who, upon hearing this bit delivered as though it were a piece of factual news, emitted a loud guffaw before reminding the others of the drunken night's entertainment, which he alone seemed to recall in vivid detail, having more masterfully digested the homemade punch. As so often happens in these remote situations, the truth arrived a few minutes too late, as the settlers seemed to prefer by then the more glamorous explanation of divine intervention. It is not that they disbelieved, then discarded Pirate John's more rational explanation of what he had seen take place nakedly (both literally and figuratively) in front of his admittedly hazy vision two nights before; he was, though just as illiterate as they, also respected as one of the brainier former captains to have helped settle Sagosia. Somehow—as often happens in the group activity that is mythmaking—the story went that those pirates who had been so inspired as to make all this delirious scrawl had, in fact, been captive to the gods' bequest—that they had in fact been possessed at the moments the marks had been made.

Perhaps for want of any other form of entertainment—well, we could debate the reasons why endlessly without ever arriving at any firm conclusion—the making of marks—proceeding ceremoniously from the imbibing of much of the local rum until the markmaker arrived at the required trancelike state—became habitual practice on the island, surviving the introduction of learning and literacy and into the present day.

It has evolved into a fully fledged art form, as my thesis demonstrates. While it might look like just a tangle of childlike scrawl to the untrained eye, connoisseurs can make out an entire range of nuance in the individual styles—and the Sagosians, the quasinatives—they're *all* connoisseurs. They might not talk about it much themselves. But when gently pressed...

Rodgers speaks in the soft humble neutrality of someone who had once had a strong accent but has since, after many years of living in distant exile, lost it in the waves.

—It all has to do with gesture, you see. The marks that are the most basic, the most minimal—the most rudimentary, we might say—are also often charged with the strongest emotion, once we take the time to study them properly—to *read* them, as the Sagosians put it. Vincent, who brought you here to me today, he's a master of what they call the angry style. Now his marks aren't minimal at all, but very detailed, yet severe in their execution. They take on the tangled appearance of cursive script, but the gestures at the same time are absolutely controlled—unsurprising, given that it stems from a boatswain's wrists.

Now Vincent has a younger brother, Prince. He's only thirteen, but has already come up with his own very masterful style that is quite distinct from Vincent's. At first, it looks almost primitive. No curls at all, none of that quasicursiveness. His marks are more like primal, primitive stab marks—there's a syncopation there—they're mainly vertical, though to give it some denseness, some texture, he'll thrown in a horizontal diagonal here and there. Even some circles and dots—though never a perfect circle, no. More like the willed inference of a circle.

—So do all of the Sagosians engage in this activity? I feel compelled to ask.

—All of them, more or less. It's the one activity that men and women alike will partake in.

—And is the ingestion of rum always included in the practice?

—More or less always. This is a ceremony, mind you. Not something that they do every day. We call it an art form, us quasicolonials and you outsiders, because as non-participants, that is how it appears to us. But for them, it is a religious practice—their chance to commune with the gods they hold so dear.

It is not like other polytheistic religions—the Greeks and Romans you might have studied in school. Their gods don't have names. They have no use for them. They don't embody lofty principles, ideas. The gods—plural—it is more like they comprise a single entity—a singular godforce. In that regard, the division between monotheism and polytheism kind of loses its meaning here. If divisions can be said to hold meanings...

–In concert, then, with the development of markmaking came with it the island's own fledgling religion. Fascinating!

–How come there's no airport? Mrdok impatiently interrupts.

Nelson Rodgers looks over at him with those icy eyes.

–Vincent was telling us on the way over no one wants to come to Sagosia. I'd say the only reason that is is because nobody's heard of it. Why is it you've never tried to promote the place? I mean, you've got a pristine slice of pseudotropical paradise pie here. You could literally be making billions off this shit. Instead, you're sitting around, writing treatises on scrawl. I mean, come on; what is it? Is it an investment problem? Because surely, I know some people...

Mrdok's voice trails off, confused by having spoken so long without encountering any real interruption from Nelson Rodgers, neither in the form of word nor glance.

–We're not opposed to what you would call development projects, Nelson finally answers. Of course the thought has occurred to us, it's been discussed with my superiors back on Pembroke, in Westminster as well. There is an allocation of funds, if you truly wish to know. But there have been complications.

–What kind of complications?

–Complications, mainly, of a political sort. Within the parties and the highest echelons—by which I mean the monarchy—there has been a debate for some time now, about both the logistics and the moral implications of continuing to maintain certain, well, shall we say, overseas territories.

–Colonies, in other words.

–Well, we no longer call them that. But the term colony, yes. It is still commonly used on the island. We are a bit... distant from those debates.

–And so your position is...?

And now, three servants arrive carrying large trays bearing platters of steaming meat and fish and vegetables which they set down upon the table in front of us.

–I hate to appear old-fashioned, gentlemen, but I suggest we save business for after supper.

And so we munch, largely in silence, a silence that would maybe have appeared awkward from the outside, but, given our state, jet lagged exhaustion with an accompanying hunger that we did not realize had afflicted us until the moment the food arrived, I think Mrdok is secretly rather thankful that the topic at hand has been postponed.

After dinner, tea and biscuits are served.

—I take it these are the famous Rodgers biscuits? I offer.

—They are indeed.

I plop one into my mouth. Unfortunately, I find it has the consistency of cardboard. And the taste, well… Not much better.

—Goes well with tea, I try, meekly.

—You got anything stronger? Mrdok asks, ignoring the biscuits. Let's sample some of that Sagosian rum.

—I'm afraid not, Rodgers replies. I'm a teetotaler now for some thirteen years.

—Great—Mrdok, beneath his breath.

—So before that rather delicious meal, I begin, we were about to enter into a discussion of Sagosia's relations with Pembroke, if I'm not mistaken.

Rodgers sips his tea pensively.

—I'm afraid the system is going to appear rather bureaucratic to your American eyes. But my official position here, despite the fact that I do consider myself to be properly Sagosian, is as Pembroke's Quasiimperial Partial Representative of Her Majesty's Unofficial Presence. While that sounds as though I have a certain degree of autonomy when it comes to decision making, unfortunately there are limits as to what I can do. I am happy to field any proposals you might have. If there are any that I think might be of interest, then I am happy to advocate on your behalf to my colleagues in the administration in Pembroke.

—… who, what, in turn have to present it to the authorities back in England?

—Well, it's not quite that complicated. There are certain things I am able to do alone here. Building permits, things like that…

Rodgers's dog Milo sits in the corner licking his penis.

—If I could do that, I'd never leave the house, remarks Mrdok.

Rodgers appears annoyed by the comment.

—If you don't mind my saying so, I interject, attempting to salvage what is left of the conversation, it seems you have the temperament of a great romanticist in certain ways, Mister Rodgers. (Or is it Lord Rodgers?) In this, I see some deep similarities between you and Mrdok. Mrdok does have some idealistic pursuits in mind that we think will greatly benefit Sagosia.

—Yes, that's fine.

Clearly Rodgers is not in the mood for hearing much more tonight. The moon all bloody and cruel, it allows for no clarity. The kind of haze that typically obscures it in polluted or overlit places like cities completely absent in this searing blood-tasting night, filled with the caws of exotic birds commentarying on the sun's languorous disappearance into nocturne.

—I suppose I will ask Sulawesi to lead you to the guest house, says Rodgers disinterestedly. I'm afraid I will have to retire for the rest of the evening.

—Oh, we weren't planning on staying on the island tonight, I begin.

—That sounds fine, Mrdok interrupts. Then he gives me a *why not?* look.

The maid leads us down a hill at the end of the gravel driveway. The house at the bottom is not at all unpleasant, a bit too large, with its two sets of floors, to be characterized as a cottage, but retaining the quaintness of one. Although it is scarcely eight o'clock by the time we arrive there with our luggage, we are both feeling winded by the journey and mainly keep to our separate rooms. I'm dozing in bed with an open copy of Boswell's *Life of Johnson* nestled upon my chest when I hear a knock at the door.

—Come in!

Mrdok sticks his head halfway through the open door.

—Get up and call Marty, he says. Tell him to file for divorce.

3.

THAT NIGHT WE were both to have very strange dreams that left strong impressions upon waking. My dreams are very often the stuff of horses and priests—not always in a conflationary sense, but often enough so. Dream matter, I suppose, that points to a particularly trying episode in my young life that I have spent much of my adult existence trying to overcome. In my home state of Texas, I spent some time as a young parson visiting elderly and sick patients who dwelled within and upon the outskirts of my parsonage. There were quite a few ranches, or remnants of ranches past, as often, the elderly cowboys who had failed to bequeath the dream to their offspring would find themselves alone and unable to manage the daily chores of keeping their properties going. Once I had to visit an old man with Alzheimer's. He had gone crazy that morning and shaved his pony. When I asked him what had happened, why he'd done it, he looked at me and told me that the pony was his grandson. I explained to him that this couldn't be, because his grandson was, in fact, dead. I didn't know this for a fact at the time; well, I believed that the grandson was dead, for that is what his son, who owned a nearby ranch, had told me; what I later came to find out, however, is that the grandson wasn't dead, he had merely had a sex change and was living as a woman; a fact that, in the eyes of the father, made the son dead, since it did not conform to the father's conception of Christian ideals with which he and all of us in that community were burdened to live. All this to say that the horse that I rode in my dream was transsexual. It must have come from this lived experience I'd had, of seeing the old man with the shaved pony and later hearing about his dead transsexual grandson who wasn't actually dead, unbeknownst to him, he had merely swapped sexes and was living, probably in Houston or some other transgressive sodomite paradise as we then conceived it, as a woman. How did I know my horse was transsexual? Because in the middle of the dream, its thing disappeared—how would you call it on a horse? Its manhood? Strange that that's the term that came to me upon waking, since *manhood* would normally only be attributed to a human male; his horsehood, then. But that's exactly what happened: upon waking, I had had the realization that the horse, when I disembarked, was missing a piece that had been in its possession when I first got astride the saddle. Thus, I could only conclude that the horse had had a sex change while I was in the process of riding it from point A to point B. Other than riding the horse, nothing much seemed to happen in the dream. Perhaps that is why it frightened me so. For I am accustomed to dreaming *something*, but in the case of that dream that first night on Sagosia, what I woke up with was a big fat lack.

Mrdok's dream concerned a dead dog on the opposite side of the road from which he was standing. A static image, or so it seemed at first; almost as though he were staring at a photograph, but he was actually there (in terms of the dream's *there*), he was a child again, he knew this because he had a sense of sorrow at the sight of the poor animal that he would no longer have now, as a grown man. A vulture flew down and started eating the dog's corpse—that's how he became aware that what he was seeing through those sepia tones was actually real, quote unquote, rather than a photograph. He wanted to cross the street, to *save* the dog. By the childish logic that he had reverted to in the dream, the dog could somehow be made alive again if he were able to get there and save it from the vulture's hungry jaws. But he was unable to cross the street. Unable, and he could not discern why—that's what was so frustrating about it, what made him toss and turn so. It's not like there was a din of traffic, cars dashing to and fro, providing a dangerous moving barrier between his childhood likeness and the dead-undead dog across the way. It was because he was confused as to *where* to cross. Because he could not determine the *where,* he also could not figure out the *how.* He was walking back and forth, trying to find the crosswalk. Even though the streets were empty and bereft of traffic, for reasons that only made sense in the dream's logic, he was unable to find the right place to cross. It's not that crossing otherwise, jaywalking, that he had some fear of legal repercussion; rather, it was that he was somehow physically unable to cross the street to get to the dog on the other side...

When we left the guest cottage, we saw across the garden Nelson seated upon the terrace drinking his morning coffee. Fully dressed, he was waiting for us to join him before breakfast. He asked how we liked our eggs; I replied mine scrambled, Mrdok's sunny side up. Before they arrived, business was already being discussed without much pretense toward an introduction.

–There have been rumors that this place has a price tag on it, Mrdok was the first to speak up.

–I presume you're not referring to my house, Nelson replied gallantly.

–Ha. You think I don't have enough houses already?

–A man like you could always use more.

–A man like me. I could see us working well together. Being partners.

–Are there any alternatives?

–Well, I don't know how comfortable you are here, really...

–If you're seeking comfort, sir...

–Call me Mrdok.

–... then I'm afraid you've come to the wrong place. Between the weather, the climate—we have incredibly bad cyclones that come year round, they're not confined to a single season in this part of the world. The wreckage they do to the infrastructure... I'm sure you have no idea. We spend half our time rebuilding, only to have to build again when the next storm comes.

–Why not use better materials? Storm-resistant ones?

–Because the storms always manage to outsmart our materials. I know it sounds ridiculous, unbelievable, even. But, whether it's due to climate change or some other force of nature beyond scientific understanding, the storms only seem to increase in severity.

–Doesn't seem like they've done much damage to your house.

–Olde Colonia is situated in the middle of the island—if you haven't checked your GPS already. The severity of the storms is felt less here. Though we still have problems from time to time.

–Must crunch your budget. Having to rebuild after every storm.

–Fantasy and reality.

–… What?

–A delicate balance. Tough to maintain.

–I'm not sure I follow you.

–I mean you might entertain certain dreams, ideals, Mister Mrdok—

–Just Mrdok. No mister.

–Fine. Mrdok. You perhaps have certain fantasies in your mind about this place.

–I'm not the fantasizin type. Look, I don't know who the fuck you think I am. But I've been everywhere, okay? I mean everywhere. Gordo can back me up on this.

–It's true.

–Shut up, Gordo. I know what this is, what this place is. It's not some third rate third world stinkhole. Every place has its problems, okay? No place is perfect.

–A delicate balance, Mrdok. That's what we're constantly trying to maintain here. A delicate balance. And it's not easy.

–How so?

–There's the weather, the climate, as you've already heard. That's roughly, oh, I'd say, forty-six percent of it. The other, what, fifty-four percent? Can you take a guess as to what that might be?

–I don't know. Money?

–The people, Mrdok. The people. Have you given any thought whatsoever to them?

–Yeah. I've got people up the wazoo. Talented, capable people, ready to move here and help you out. To, to actually *build* things. Things that will last. Not this crumbling shit on the coast you got— what is it, a bunch of trailer parks? I mean, that's really how you deal with the—

–I'm not talking about people in a utilitarian sense. And by the way, is that the only way you are capable of viewing the human beings surrounding you?

–You know I didn't come here to get my eyes checked.

–We happen to have a structure here. We have elected officials. We have elections.

–Yeah? You think we don't got elections where I come from? In America? For your information, we invented them.

–I somehow don't believe that to be the case.

–And you know who gets my vote, each and every time?

–Let me guess.

–Yeah. That's right. Whichever one pays me for it. That's the one I endorse.

–Well, now that your politics are on the table…

–The people I bring here are going to make your people, the people living here, into dwarfs. Very comfortable dwarfs.

–And you think that's going to work? That they're going to just sit back and take it? Do you have any idea who you're dealing with? The problems that afflict our population that, that you think you're going to come in here and, what? *Solve,* in your weird way? There are tensions here, Mrdok. Severe, historical tensions, between us and them. Tensions that are always on the brink of exploding into something violent, something that has the potential of causing lasting damage. Human lives we are talking about. The quasinatives are always on the verge of revolting against us quasicolonials, while the quasicolonial indeed can be said to exploit the quasinatives—

–Look, you wanna know something? I'm gonna level with you, cos that's the kind of guy I am. I didn't even have to come here, to have this conversation with you. Okay? I could've gone to Pembroke, worked this all out with them up there. You wanna know why I did this? Because I love this place—

–You've been here for a grand total of one night.

–Yeah? And you know what? That's enough for me. That's all I need to know whether or not I like a place.

–You just said you *love* it.

–Laugh all you want. What I'm saying is, I could've gone to Pembroke and negotiated with them. Thrown your ass out of this house and into the sand. Did I do that? No, I didn't. Why? Because that's not part of my vision.

–Your vision?

–Yeah. That's right. I've got a vision.

–Mrdok *is* a visionary. That's not our words. According to a number of prominent periodicals—

–Shut up, Gordo. My vision is to include you in on this.

–What is this you want to *include me in on*?

–Well, you can call it an investment opportunity. What it is, in fact, is the opportunity of a lifetime. Do you have any idea how much I'm worth? Gordo, tell him how much I'm worth.

–Immediately, boss. Let me just get the numbers—

–I'm going to put every single penny I have into this island. That's right. I'm not gonna save any of it for myself.

–So that this will become, what, your little fiefdom? Your offshore kingdom?

–Well, there's a democratic way of doing this. One that fulfills the standards of international law.

–Something tells me you not only have no respect for international law, you don't even have any understanding of it.

–And you. You're going to have a leadership role in this.

–I already have a leadership role. I'm the bloody head of Sagosia!

–And you will continue in that capacity. Only it's gonna be more of, uh, an honorary thing from here on out. But don't worry. You're going to have anything, everything you could possibly want and need. And more.

Nelson laughs.

–And what are you going to have, Mrdok?

Mrdok gives him a pitying glance. Until he finally stops laughing.

SHUFFLING THE DECK

NOW, IN THE rather perverse and adroit way life has of directly addressing, nay, assaulting our fears, of tactlessly tackling them head-on, and thus encouraging us, in an odd way, to heal ourselves before a disaster far worse than what we fantasize actually afflicts us, a balance among nature's various forces has commenced to accrue, sending us reeling past those petrified doubts now forming some semblance of a museum—if only we would be so lucky as to assume the role of mere spectators. Caught unawares, I must admit, when, shortly after our return to Manhattan from Sagosia, two gentlemen from the Federal Bureau of Investigation suddenly barged their way past security and into our office on an otherwise dour and sundry Tuesday afternoon. I presumed their visit a mere formality, in relation to Harry Hull and/or the Belle Encoding affair more generally; for what else would this most estimable, if at times troublesome bureau possibly want with our Mrdok? We had, in fact, purposefully endeavored to maintain cordial, even amiable relations with the Feds going back many years; in fact, it was an initiative that had been presented to me practically in my first official meeting with the Mrdok organization.

Mrdok shared a similar relaxation at the prospect of this unannounced—though not reasonably unexpected—visit, sending a *send em right in* through the intercom as I announced their sudden and improbable materialization in the office. In all likelihood, we could only assume they were there to advise Mrdok as to the status of Mister Hull, in whose trust Mrdok had been so tragically betrayed.

Yet, well, what do I really know about the science of intuition? Really, I have next to none when it comes to my own affairs. When it comes to Mrdok's, however, a certain quantity of foreboding has been instilled within me—nearly a motherly instinct, it could be defined as. An instinct that was suddenly aroused in me some five minutes into the meeting. Granted, I had no idea what was going on behind that closed door. But an eerie silence that, well, normally filled the room, but now felt suddenly, I don't know, unfounded… Well, a certain mood crept upon me. There is a key on the callboard next to my desk that allows me to listen in on the goings-on in Mrdok's office. It is not a key I often press, of course—our man requires his privacy. Only when he explicitly asks me—or else at moments such as these, when a nagging concern rises to the surface and must be squelched, suffocated, so as to avert any further danger. It is my duty, after all…

–What do you mean *data fraud?* came Mrdok's voice booming into my ear.

–Our further investigation into the affairs of Belle Encoding has yielded—

–Jesus Christ, what *further investigation?* Nothing you are saying right now makes any sense to me. We had a deal. This was all worked out thoroughly in advance with your superiors. I mean, what the fuck are you even talking about? I gave you the kid, did I not? Frankly, I'm a little offended I'm not talking to Tim Buckminster right now. Why the hell did he send a bunch of his minions to my office…?

And so it went on. Something about how that earlier part of the investigation, that had resulted in the arrest of Mister Hull, did not automatically preclude further investigation by other departments of the bureau… The abusive language of federal law enforcement, let loose to bully some innocent citizen: we have all heard this before, and yet it still comes as a shock to those with some semblance of idealism left regarding one's inalienable right to privacy as an intrinsic marker of freedom.

So my anxiety in this instance was validated. But as I continued listening in on the offensive inquisition, the tightness in my stomach did not unfurl; it rather grew tighter, the more I was reminded of the Salem witch trials. (And to think, I had had the most innocent lunch that afternoon!) It is true, this was not a conversation I was officially meant to be hearing. But as my position has always required me to be, in some sense, at least three steps ahead of whatever it is that is actually happening at any given moment, I had no choice but to act. It was a compulsion that overtook me, one that simply had to be given in to.

First, I made a call to a certain storage facility on the lower end of the island where many of our organization's more sensitive documents are stored. When the gentleman who manages that particular archive picked up the phone, I uttered to him a numerical code that only he knew and that meant only one thing.

A stunned silence on the other end of the line.

–You sure about that? came his voice finally.

–Unfortunately yes, I uttered, before hanging up.

As I had just given him the cue to have that entire archive incinerated, I had to emotionally distance myself somewhat from this drastic action while simultaneously following coldly through protocol. While whatever it was that was going on was clearly a misunderstanding on the part of the Feds, it also became clear to me that in situations such as these, they often tend not to let it go until they get the person they are targeting. Harry Hull obviously was not enough for them, for someone in the bureau—whoever it was now controlling our Mrdok's fate. (We thought that we had been in contact with that person, though in these labyrinthine bureaucracies, it is common for interests to shift—and with them, personnel.)

In a way, what came to happen next could be viewed as merely the acceleration of a process that had already begun. Despite the awkwardness of our meeting with Nelson Rodgers, one meeting we did have shortly afterward in Sagosia went rather well. That was our meeting with the general manager of the island's bank—which Nelson is the ostensible head of, though clearly he is not as involved in its day-to-day operations as he perhaps should be. By transferring the majority of our assets into that bank, we came to understand, we would effectively come to control it. This was made perfectly clear to us, and, as a fact, was nothing to scoff at. It only meant that we would be on more certain footing at our next, at all our future meetings, with Nelson Rodgers—and anyone else, frankly, who had any interest or concern in Sagosia.

And so, in my next calls, I proceeded to do precisely that: derailing Nelson's fiefdom. Then I called good old Abe, our commodities broker, and asked him to transfer all our concerns abroad. Increasingly many of our investments in recent years have been outside the country; again, the time had come to solidify a thing that had already long been in the works—to push the penguin down the hallway, in a sense. I was operating on more than just instinct here. I was firmly embedded in Mrdok's mindspace. I felt the acute need to prove this to him—to prove it to myself, as well.

Next came a series of calls: to our real estate man, then our London property lawyer, followed by our Cypriot banker, after which I had to dial the after-hours number of our Mauritian mortgage officer, who advised me in turn to contact our antique rugs dealer and precious stones financier who is based in Luxembourg. The gentleman who takes care of our British PR concerns was, I was informed, presently in Saint Kitts and Nevis taking care of some pertinent business; thankfully I was able to reach him using encrypted software so as to arrange, through his associates, the implantation of a story in a UK tabloid that would purport to tell a rather distorted version of the goings-on then currently underway in Mrdok's office sure to get many of the details wrong, which will then allow us to take advantage of the UK libel laws and sue. Ultimately, for the purpose of brevity and the need for accelerated liquidity (since most funds in our UK accounts were used up recently in the purchase of Eurobonds), our solicitors will broker a settlement which will restore our prominence in the UK (our current presence there is extranominal, in that it is represented mainly by offshore real estate interests that we do not technically own), where we will need a stronghold in order to secure our position in Sagosia to polish off all that post-colonial sawdust. As a backup, I phoned in a small (for us) Maltese real estate investment that will afford passports for both Mrdok and myself from that delightful island nation that either of us has yet to visit, but certainly intend to some day in the near future, perhaps as a vacation when all this is behind us.

By the time the two agents left the office with haughty grins upon their faces, all this was complete: we were, in effect, liquefied—no longer there, in spite of our physical presence.

—Call Marty immediately, Mrdok buzzed into my office.

I did not have to suppress my grin. For one, there was not a soul in the room to see it; for another, I had indeed earned it!

—Marty is no longer a part of the Mrdok organization, I plainly replied. He is part of the nonessential personnel. That part of the organization has already been dissolved.

A slight pause.

—What are you… What the… Gordo, what the *fuck* have you done?

He then rushed into my office. I was all too happy to provide him with a rote summary of my actions. Very coolly, I accompanied this summary with a detailed reasoning. Although it had never been stated baldly, it had seemed clear to me that a shutting down of our Manhattan operations had been well in the works now for some time. That I had essentially made lemonade out of the afternoon's misfortune, accelerating the process that would transfer the brain-center of the Mrdok organization to the newly discovered paradise, where Mrdok himself could serve as a sort of sovereign and thus put an end to the incessant worries that had been occupying us so unjustly of late.

Mrdok listened to all of this in what can only be described as a stunned silence. Little had he known, prior to this moment, what stores of initiative I contained within me. However, as I prattled on, a sinking appearance of gloom and doom gradually overtook his face, and that knot in my stomach returned. My speech began to slow, in expectation of some interruption on Mrdok's part, yet none came. And so I made it to the end of my prattle, and a crisp silence enshrouded us.

—Gordo, came Mrdok finally, do you even realize what you have just done?

I had and I hadn't. In retrospect, the decision to take such drastic action was perhaps a bit rash on my part. But desperate situations require desperate actions—or some such saying.

—Sagosia was a project for down the line. Like, months or years from now. I wasn't seriously… I mean, fuck. I was *speculating*. Not acting on it. It was all bluster. It's part of my process. What the fuck am I going to do now?

—Do you not see? I asked—now, in some sense, pleading for my very life. Sagosia is all ours now! All yours. All I have done is cement the deal. Really, you don't even have to thank me; it's the cursed Feds who have done it! I really—Mrdok, let me assure you, I had zero plans, no intention whatsoever, to—to do *any* of this. It's just… We were being attacked. I mean, *you* are being attacked. I am the first line of defense, the infantry—

—So you go and fucking… burn everything down? Gordo, do you realize—That's not the way to, to fucking *do things*…

—Oh, Mrdok! Don't *you* realize? Maybe I'm a few steps ahead of you here, it is true. But that does nothing to discount the fact that this is the direction you've been going. All I've done—

—I mean, I have a fuckin *family* here, okay?

—You're divorcing her! You told me last week to put it in motion. The papers are right here! Here, look!

—I'm not getting divorced, Gordo. That was a momentary… lapse of judgment.

—But I'm getting a divorce, as well, Mrdok. I mean… It is an odd coincidence, I'll admit, but Joanne and I, we were just talking, and—

–Sagosia is just one opportunity among many, Gordo.

–Oh, no. No no no no no no. Do you not see? Sagosia is more than just an opportunity, boss. Sagosia is, in fact, The Answer. To *everything*.

–Have you lost your fucking shit?

–Hear me out, I beg of you. Then, you can fire me if you think what I'm saying makes no sense.

Do you remember Lallyburt? The Texan redneck. The city project we were meant to do. Think of it in those terms, Mrdok. With Sagosia, we could have our very own… well, island. I mean, come on, Mrdok… We've been doing offshore now for years. In that, we're hardly original. I mean, everyone does offshore. Practically the entire world is floating, floating capital! With Sagosia, we are no longer merely floating. We're not just *doing* offshore anymore. We *are* offshore. Do you not get the full implications of all this? Being versus doing? We are going to become the eighth continent!

Mrdok pondered all that I was saying with a concentration, a seriousness I had rarely seen him hold. That I had had to get this attention by essentially doing away with everything, by completely upending his life as he had known it, that gradually began to matter less to him than the promises of a veritable new world now dangling before his eyes.

–I love you.

I don't know how, but the words suddenly leaked through my lips in the most vulgar fashion. Did I even know what I was saying in the moment? Did Mrdok even hear, even understand the words? Apparently he was as shocked as I was.

–… What did you just say? came his response.

And yet the words, the emotions they expressed, could be contained no longer.

–I… I have felt it for some time now, Mrdok. It's this feeling I… Look… The moment you told me you were going to divorce Mrtol, I just thought… This is our chance… Sagosia…

Mrdok raised his hand before I could even coherently articulate, apply some structure to this excess verbiage panting out of me that was but an accurate expression of my emotional turmoil.

–Look, Gordo. I've known for some time you was a homo. We all have. And you know what? I don't really care. I'm cool with it. I mean, to my thinking, these days, it's even kind of trendy, isn't it? To have a fag, I'm sorry, a homosexual working in the organization. I mean, they have one on all the TV shows lately. It's getting to be kind of a normal thing. But if there's one thing I learned from Tony

Fatballs—well, there's several things I learned from Tony Fatballs, actually…

–I know, Mrdok, I know. Never mix business with pleasure. But…

–That's not what I was going to say, Gordo. It's something else. It's: Never let anyone in through the back door. Do you get what I'm saying, Gordo?

–Well, there are at least a couple ways that might be interpreted.

–It has nothing to do with assfucking. All that shit, you can keep to yourself—and no pun intended. What concerns me here is not your emotions, okay?—I'm a businessman, not a therapist—it's that you, your excitement or delusion or whatever the fuck it is apparently caused you to go and make an executive decision that is like way outside your purview, not to mention your paygrade—

–May I please just interrupt here? Because I feel, in a very respectful way, that perhaps the situation has been slightly misapprehended.

–Jesus, can you talk American, please?

–Mrdok, you are accusing me of a most heinous crime. When in fact it was you who made this decision, not me.

–… What?

–My role here, as your personal assistant, as your right-hand man, is just to help you accept it.

–Accept the fact that, what, that all this is gone?! That I'm about to move to an island in the middle of nowhere, a place I know next to nothing about, and, and… And what, Gordo? Be ass bandits together with you? I have a wife here. A son. A mistress, too.

–None of it is gone. It has all just… been airlifted to a far more beautiful scene. And you don't need to know anything about Sagosia, Mrdok. That is *my* role. I have become a virtual expert on the place. Any fact you need to know at any given moment, all you need to do is ask me. I'm here to provide you with knowledge so that you can make all the expert decisions. And we haven't gotten rid of *all* the personnel. All the most valuable members of the team will be going with us—or else working remotely. And those we had to divest ourselves of, in order to protect the company's interests, its very infrastructure—well, they can be replaced. Again, leave it to me. You need to concentrate on your new role, Mrdok. Your position is going to be expansive—*formidable,* as the French would say.

Mrdok looked at me. Then he walked behind his desk, peering down at the city streets below him. Our tower casts a long shadow on those streets, and the sentiment that comes attached to that shadow is a most difficult thing to separate oneself from. Not impossible, though.

—That project we tried to do with Lallyburt. The city project. You know what we did wrong with that, Gordo?

—We were… too ambitious.

—No. Nonono. See, that's why you're you and I'm me. Actually, we weren't ambitious enough.

—Yes. Yes, I can see that! How… How short-sighted I am.

—Well. We're going to need other investors if this is going to work. I mean, I'm just going through the math right now in my head…

—Most certainly! And that's one domain in which you excel.

—What do you think of that Lallyburt fuck? I mean, I know things didn't end well with him. But now that you mention his name… I'm just thinking out loud here.

—We'll certainly have him on the list. He's worth… having another conversation with. At the very least.

—You know who else I'm thinking? Barbra Browneye.

—Brunnei. Right. She's spending a lot of time in Tokyo these days…

—Yeah. I mean, it's an excuse to see the kid, right?

—It is.

—That little shit.

—Well. He certainly doesn't deserve you, in my oh so humble opinion.

—Maybe it is a good decision.

—Any decision you make is a good one. Not only that: in this case, it was the *right* decision.

—Right.

—The right decision for this precise moment. As Tony himself would say—

—We can't let this get out until we're fully gone.

—The wheels are already spinning.

—Man, this is gonna be hilarious. Wait till the Feds find out.

—Haha! Yes. The joke's on them. A brilliant move on your part. Bye bye birdy!

—Wait a minute. Just… Just wait.

I hesitated. Something in the air suddenly changed; perhaps, it suddenly occurred to me, I had overstepped my bounds. In one way or another. Was I about to be fired, demoted, removed from my post?

—How much am I worth? Right now.

Relieved, I got out the iPad to see the final results of the complex deconstruction job I had just completed. Relieved again, I was, to see the assertion of a truth long known: numbers do not lie.

Not to boast, but, the answer is rather obvious: Roughly twice the amount that he had been earlier that morning.

CHAPTER TEN

MEXICAN OMELETTES

–GOOD MORNING.

   –You're awake?

   –Wide awake. Ready for the day.

   –I don't wanna…

   –Mrtol.

   –Yes?

   –You hungover again?

   –No I am not, Mrdok.

   –Don't you wanna hear my dreams?

   –Your dreams make me sick.

   –We used to tell each other our dreams. Every single morning. Upon waking. It was like a ritual. Sometimes, I know, we'd wait until breakfast, coffee. Tell each other as we were reading the paper. But always our dreams. We'd pick through them together, laugh. Try to uncover the little mysteries. Now, it's a miracle if I get a single word out of you in the morning before I leave for the day.

   –It's called marriage, Mrdok. It's what happens. You've been through it before, with whatshername. The cunt, as you always like to call her.

   –Krstal? I never called her a cunt. Even though we're divorced. She's still my friend.

   –Ha. Don't make me laugh. You don't have any friends, Mrdok.

   –With Krstal, it was always the same dream. I never even had to ask. All she wanted was to get famous. That cunt, she was so wrapped up in her little Hollywood fantasy. She didn't even know what a dream was. Instead of a dream life, she just had a warped sense of reality.

–Whatever. I was out there recently, let me remind you. I think she's long since given up on those fantasies.

–Yeah. So you said.

–Now she's more just fulfilling her, well, everyday needs. Wants. I don't see her harboring any grand ambitions. She's given up on all that.

–Glad to hear. You know I've been back two nights now. Slept here both nights. Not one word about *How was your trip, Mrdok?* Not one ounce of curiosity from you.

–Mrdok I don't even know where you've been this time. I can't keep track of you anymore. I gave up trying long ago. You're never here. Not really. Even when you are here. In a larger sense, you're not.

–The thing about you, Mrtol, is you have no appreciation—

–You think I don't know what's going on, Elias?

–Don't call me that. I hate it when you fucking—

–It's your name. Your real name. You think I'm totally fucking clueless, that I don't hear the word on the street?

–What street, Mrtol? You haven't stepped foot on any street in probably twenty-five years.

–The club, for one.

–The club? Ha! That's hardly a street. More a manicured garden.

–How old is she, Mrdok? Your little brat. Twenty? Nineteen? I mean, what's it gonna be next. You gonna buy yourself a little Ferrari? A racing car? A nice little fucking midlife crisis mobile?

–Come on, Mrtol, you know me a little better than that. What do you think I am, a walking cliché?

–At times, I feel you're something worse.

–Come on. You trying to make me feel bad now? There are always rumors floating around about me. Always have been, always will be. It's because they're all jealous. I mean, how do you think it makes me feel? I hear things, too, Mrtol. From what I hear, you're pissing it up. Daytime drinking. I mean, it's getting messy, hon. You're certainly not keeping up appearances. And that does damage to me, too. To my brand.

–I'm not going to plead with you to stop seeing her. I won't endure that kind of humiliation… That would be even more humiliating than having to endure it, to hear about it, which is where I'm at now.

–Mrtol. Stop crying.

–I'm not crying, Mrdok. I am trying to tell you. For some time now, I have come to think of myself, first and foremost, as a mother.

I don't even think of myself as a wife anymore. As a woman, even. That part of me died a long time ago. Now, for me, it's all about Jaco.

–Jaco and the booze, maybe.

–Will you shut the fuck up, please?

–No, you need to shut the fuck up. Mrtol. You want to feel like a woman again? You know what to do. Call the plastic surgeon. Anything you want, I'll pay for it.

–The point is, I know the drinking is a problem, Mrdok. I'm not dumb, okay? I am trying my best to get it under control, without even a modicum of support from you—

–Yes, from me, who is working his ass off, let me remind you, trying *single-handedly* to support his family and enabling the exorbitant lifestyle you are privileged to enjoy—

–I'm not complaining, okay? I'm really not. All I ask, really, is that you—

–I get it. You're miserable here. I get it, okay? But I have news for you, Mrtol. I have not been neglecting my duties as a husband or a father. I've been listening to you all this time and looking for a solution. And you know what? I happen to have found one.

–What are you talking about?

–You want to get away from Shelter Island, away from the city—

–Yes. Yes. Thank you. I hate all of it.

–Away from the club. Away from this house, even.

–Mrdok, I am so sick… Even the, even Jaco, the nuns at school. He's *miserable* here, Mrdok. The paint-eating, the imaginary friend, the nonstop screen time—it's all a cry for help. We need a change. It doesn't have to be a big one. Just *something*.

–Oh, it's gonna be big alright. I wouldn't have it any other way. We're moving our base of operations, Mrtol. Overseas.

–… What?

–I've found a place. A most beautiful place. That most of the world doesn't even know about. In the Pseudotropics. Undiscovered.

–What is this place?

–It's an island. Secluded. Sagosia, it's called. And it's for sale. And it's about to become all mine. All *ours*. We're taking it over. Our own slice of paradise. A place to begin anew. Us. Our family.

–I… I don't even know what to say, Mrdok. I… Where's my phone? I need to look, I don't even know where this place is… Sagosia, was it?

–You're gonna be astounded. Such a gorgeous fucking place. It's like… How do I describe it? It's like… the end of the world. Only better.

–I think you mean the ends of the earth.

–Yeah… I mean, it's the same thing, isn't it?

–Not quite.

–What I'm really talking is, you know, beyond the, the business opportunity this represents for me, this could be a new beginning for *us*. For you and me and little Jaco. Starting over. Our very own pristine slice of paradise.

–Yes, it's… I see. I mean, it's a beautiful sentiment, Mrdok. I don't know, it's just… So big. So sudden. Can I just think about this for a minute?

–There's no need to think, Mrtol. That's what I'm here for. I've done all the thinking for you. That's my role.

–I understand. It's just… It's a lot to digest. And I haven't even had my morning latte.

–I'm calling Rosalita. I'll have her bring it in for you.

–Thank you.

–Better yet, let's… We haven't done this for a long time. Let's have breakfast in bed. Shall we?

–That would be… cute.

–I could… Let's have Mexican omelettes. And mimosas! To celebrate. To new beginnings.

–Let's…

–Sssssh, Mrtol. No more talking. I'm calling Rosalita now. You want yours with egg whites, am I right?

PART FOUR

JUST THE TIP

1.

—I HEREBY CALL this meeting to session.

–Gordo, don't be so fuckin formal about shit. You sound like a faggot.

–He is a faggot now.

–Shut up. My brother a faggot.

–My sister too.

–His mother and father, also.

–Oh right. I forgot.

–His brother's a famous drag queen from New Mexico. I saw him the other night on the TV. Georgia O'Queef.

–Shut up.

–Ahem. The purpose of this meeting—

–There is lots on the agenda. As you know, we've acquired an island… Thank you, thank you. I know. This is a very big moment for us. And, well… I wanna start this meeting off with a question. For all of you: What do you need to start a country?

–Diplomats!

–An army!

–A bank!

–A stock market!

–Nuclear weapons!

–Okay, very good, very good. Well, let me tell you: We're going to have all of those things. It's in the works right now. But, first, we've gotta take care of what we've, what we've inherited, in a sense. Now, the first thing that's gonna hafta go—

—It seems that half the staff has already gone.

—The important ones are all here. You're the ones we need. You're the future of the organization. Now the first thing—okay, the *second thing* that's going to have to go is the name.

—The name?

—Yeah. The name. Of the island. Sagosia. It sounds too, too *exotic* or something.

—Ethnic, he means.

—Yeah. Too ethnic. It's gonna put people off.

—By people, you mean...?

—Our investors. So, as a lot of you probably don't realize yet, we are currently in negotiations with the colonial administration of the island, as well as the authorities in the UK. If all goes according to plan, the island will be fully ours by year's end.

—That's not the way I heard you're going about it—

—Shut up, Rick.

—Can you clarify what you mean by *fully ours*?

—I mean that, according to our plans, if everything goes as expected, Sagosia will no longer be Sagosia.

—It's going to be Mrdokland!

—Thank you, Rick. But no thanks. I'm not so vain, contrary to what some of you might think, as to name an island, a country after myself.

—A country?

—The subject of sovereignty is something to be discussed later. For now, the topic at hand is rather cosmetic, rather—dare I say— fun!

—Yeah, we know what kind of fun *he* likes to have.

—Enough. Haven't you fuckin heard, Rick? It's the twenty-first century. Bein a faggot—sorry, homosexual—is fuckin cool. Alright?

—They don't call themselves that anymore. Now it's supposed to be *queer*.

—That's retarded.

—You can't say retarded anymore either.

—Fine, then: *cretinously deranged*.

—Yeah, alright. He's a fuckin queer then, okay? Alright? Now I don't want to hear another word about this. Or else you're fired.

—...

—Now for the matter at hand...

—Well, there are several matters. Several hands, as well...

—So, the thing is, we can't do this one alone. We need fellow travelers, as it were. Investors. Settlers. So me and Gordo were brainstormin last night—Gordo, open up the PowerPoint—and what we came up with, is this.

–...

–...

–...

–... Settlers Landing?

–O... kay...

–We feel it packs quite the punch. It will appeal to the more WASPish sentiments of a certain patrician class, rile ancestral memories of the pilgrims' adventure in the New World, while imbuing a delicate reminder that that world is no longer New. That there are still adventures to be had—new, well, *settlements* to settle.

–Subtle-like.

–I don't get it.

–It does feel like it's missing something.

–Yeah. Like an apostrophe.

–Oh, I know exactly where it should go...

–It should go after the second s, Mrdok. Settlers' Landing.

–No, I don't think...

–I know where you put the motherfuckin apostrophe in motherfuckin settlers landing, alright. You think I aint had a fuckin eighth grade education or what? It goes after the r, fucker.

–Easy, easy.

–Hmm..

–But then that would make it singular. As though... only one settler has landed. If you put it after the s, then it becomes plural. Like it belongs to *all* the new settlers.

–Actually, between the r and the s, it would be more possessive. Like, one settler *owns* the, uh... landing.

–Yeah, that's right. Cos it's *my island*, bitch. That settler is me. Get it?

–So wait then... Is *landing* meant to be a verb or a noun here?

–From a PR perspective, it's going to be hard to find an angle if the apostrophe goes between the r and the s. Like, this is one man's island, but others are welcome here?

–I get it, Mrdok, I do. And I mean no offense by it—*of course* it's your island. But the point is, you're trying to attract *other* settlers at the moment. Settler-investors, that is. You want them to feel welcome, don't you?

–They can feel however the fuck they want. As long as they give us their money. Aint that right, Gordo?

–I would like to think—

–The settlers will feel *very* welcome, no matter what we end up calling the place. This is not a dictatorship, after all.

–It's not?

–What about a *developmental dictatorship?* I'm not sure what it means, but I hear that's a hot new thing right now.

–All this *welcoming…*

–I think Murray has a point. Putting the apostrophe at the end, thus making settlers plural, gives the project an air of inclusivity. You know, like everyone's welcome.

–Oh fuck that. I hate inclusivity. *An air of inclusivity:* that's everything that's wrong with the world today. That's the world that's been left behind. The old world. A world we want to *escape* from.

–That our settlers should want to escape from, as well.

–Yeah. The motherfuckers. And if that's not what the shitballs want, then we don't want *them.*

–You're saying, then, that by putting the apostrophe between the r and the s, by, like, affirming the, uh, *singularity* of the place, the mission, that might work to subliminally attract the type of investor we want to have and leave out the more, uh, shall we say—

–Very good, fuckface. It appears you're finally learning something after all these years of eating up my payroll.

–More like *eating out* his payroll…

–But why a, why an island? Why right now?

–Haven't you heard? The Feds are after us.

–Ssssshhh.

–This has nothing to do with the Feds, you imbecile. I practically *own* the Feds, okay? I'm tired of jacking off in paradise. It's time for me to… for my seed to grow.

–What if we just, like graphically, have a very tiny apostrophe, like an inference of one rather than a full-bodied…?

–Yeah. I mean, I'm afraid if there's no apostrophe at all, then it's just like, the settlers… plop! It don't feel right somehow.

–That plopping sound. Was that like a toilet reference?

–Well he does like to call them shitballs…

–Yeah, but do we want them to know that? I vote for putting the apostrophe back in.

–Putting it to a vote! That's a good idea. I mean, if Mrdok approves, of course…

–Jesus H. Christ. Let's just drop the fuckin apostrophe bullshit for right now. We'll come back to that later. Like I pay you people to sit around all day and discuss punctuation. I mean, really, who gives a—

–Yeah! When are we gonna talk about the whores?

–Say what?!

–Prostitution is gonna be legal on the island, isn't it? At least that's what I heard.

–So I guess your mother is gonna be moving there with us.

–Fuck you, ass bandit.

–Hey, stop it with the homophobia already!

–Prostitution is not on today's agenda, Rick. Right now, I wanna talk about what the Ministry of the Interior is workin on to make this place look good for investors.

–Settlers, you mean.

–Yeah, whatever.

–Ministry of the Interior?

–I believe that's Marcia, isn't it?

–That's right. What kind of portfolio do you have laid out that might make our settler-clients—

–Shut up, Gordo. The fact is, we're down three point two eighths of a percentage point the last time I checked on the numbers. That was… when, Gordo?

–Five and a half minutes ago.

–And I don't even wanna know what's happened in the interim… What I wanna know is what the fuck is up with that. Specifically, I wanna know how come nobody told me the minute that figure started to drop.

–It's back up again.

–What was that you just said?

–Three-eighths of a percentage point regained. The numbers are moving upward it looks like. Albeit a slow climb. Slow but steady, I'd say.

–Alright, smartass. You're fired.

–… What?!

–Out! Now!

–Mrdok, as your primary market analyst—

–You thought, what, *you were just doing your job?* You know what? People like you make me want to puke my fuckin guts out and feed em to the homeless. I mean, before you walk out that door for the final time, to your pitiful uncertain future, I want you to tell me just one thing: Where in the hell did *you* of all people get the idea that you understand the numbers better than I do?

–I…

–Don't answer me just yet, okay? I'm not finished. Or—do you know what? I'm gonna do you and everyone else here a favor and *give* you the answer, okay? I don't need to be told why the numbers are going up. I don't need that kind of false optimism contaminating my reality. I understand the numbers better than any single person sitting in this room—or working remotely, for that matter. You wanna know why that is?

—Yes!

—Of course you do. It's because it is men like me who actually *control* the numbers. We say jump and the numbers jump. We say fall, bend down, roll over, the numbers follow our command. *My* command. Men like me who direct its flows, who manage to surrender their own individual frequencies to, to… *control* the effin data. To dictate the, the *vertices* of the numbers. Okay? You might think you learned a lot at Wharton or Harvard Business School or wherever the fuck it is you went to rim Robert Shiller or whoever the fuck— that you have this fuckin fancy paid-for Ivy League education you bring with you into my office. Well I'm gonna tell you this one last time: before you come in here, leave that shit at the door. We don't need no motherfuckin education here. To quote the Pink Floyd. Okay? When I say something is the way it is, that's because it *is* that way. Because *I* made it that way. And no other.

—Can I go clean out my desk now?

—No, you can't. Now sit the fuck down.

—Now that that's cleared up…

—…

—… One thing we could offer to entice our settler-investors is attractive diplomatic posts. That way they don't even have to *live* on the island if they don't want to.

—Why the fuck would they not want to live on the island? That makes zero sense to me. They're going to pour money into the thing, build a house, a business, then go away?

—Surely you can't be so… I mean… I defer to your genius in helping me to revise my understanding of the exact nature of the project. Apparently, with my, um, admittedly paltry understanding of the world of offshore…

—Yeah. So that's something I need to make clear once and for all. Gordo, can you, please, the PowerPoint, I think it's the third slide? There. As you can see, Settlers Landing, first and foremost, IS NOT an offshore finance project. This is the key thing we want to emphasize—

—I thought with Belle Encoding—

—In a minute, please! The key thing we want to emphasize—especially in our PR materials—this is most definitely *not* an offshore.

(Be sure to get that down right now, Sandy, sweetheart.) Gordo? What. You look like I just dug up your dead sister's corpse and fucked it.

–I just… Who am I to utter any words that might be construed as detracting from your genius—

–Just get to the point, dickbreath.

–It's just that the new century is so much about… Working re- motely. *Living* remotely.

–Is the century really all that new?

–The fudge packee has a point. The investors we're looking to attract don't necessarily want to *settle*. They're looking for a place to park their money, give it a good rinse. Okay, maybe get a passport, maybe take a nice sunbath once or twice a year. But, like, base them- selves there? I mean, who in the hell do we know who actually spends more than one month at a time in the same place?

–What did Susan say just a minute ago?

–Well, I didn't get a chance to finish before I was interrupted. I was starting to suggest that Belle—

–Exactly. The data we harvested with Belle Encoding over the years—well guess what? It's finally coming into season. That is, we've figured out what to do with it.

–Finally.

–Not that we weren't doin nothin with it before.

–Certainly not.

–It's just that the data is now being redirectionalized.

–Quite a savvy way of putting it.

–If I do say so myself.

–You don't. You didn't. He did.

–You see, we happen to have all the metrics in our files for the fifty richest men—and, in a couple of cases, women—in the world.

–Just fifty?

–Well, a much larger number than that, of course. But it's the fifty we wanna zero in on. From those metrics, we've extracted the following data set, which we will use to manipu—*persuade*—*incentivize* them. Into coming in as settlers.

–Can my office get a copy of this data set? Strictly for internal use—it can even be a printout or temporary dissolve file—

–Ask Marcia or Gordo to get that for you. I believe the files have already landed safely in Sagosia, Gordo?

–That's right.

–What we want to begin with, according to Mrdok's master plan, is a core of, say, around five investors. Those will be called senators, and they will have a certain degree of legislative power...

–What does that mean?

–They will have a say in the laws being written.

–Laws?

–Yes. A constitution.

–Perhaps now is the time to turn our attention to the topic of sovereignty.

–Not a subject easily attained.

–I beg your pardon?

–I mean, realistically speaking—

–Let me stop you right there. In terms of deals, yes, this is very big. Perhaps even the deal of the century. But it is also quite logical, for those of us who have been with Mrdok for as long as Gordo and myself—

–I believe I've been with him longer—

–and watched him progress—

–Yes. Have you ever seen Mrdok *fail* at making a deal?... That's exactly what I thought. Mrdok is an artist; the deal is his medium. Haven't you read his book?

–Sure. I think every one of us here has. But wresting the sovereignty of an autonomous nation—

–It's not fully autonomous.

–is a bit different than, say, wresting control of a nucleite mining operation or a data company.

–But is it, really?

–The point is, with the founding settlers—I mean, who would *not* want to be one? We're talking, this is the global elite of the world, okay? And us here, we're the, the *brains* of the operation. We are finally giving these people, these elites, the one opportunity they have all been waiting for, searching for, but not able to find—not anywhere they've been. A place where they can actually live and *make* the law, rather than having to spend their entire lives running away from and around it.

–So this is going to be a parliamentary democracy of sorts.

–Yeah. I mean, I don't know what that means. But it sounds good.

–I've heard of that. That's what they got in Sweden.

–Write that down.

–I will. How do you spell *parliament* again?

–Yeah, Sweden. That's a good model for us. Except we're gonna be a lot richer than them.

–Mrdok. You're worth a lot. You're not worth more than Sweden.

–Yeah? Well guess what. I have no interest in Sweden. Sweden's not an island. It's just, they're just a bunch of Scandinavian cocksuckers over there. Now Norway—that's a country. Rich in oil, hardly any people. That's the trick—make it so that so few can afford it, that way it don't ever get too crowded.

–You know what those Norwegian fuckers did? This is brilliant. They got an island up there in the Arctic Circle, the northernmost inhabited place on earth. There are more polar bears than there are humans there. You know what they did, the Norwegians? They built an art museum on that island. That's right. A fuckin art museum. For the polar bears.

–Now that takes balls.

–All those fuckin polar bear fucks lookin at art. Now that's my type of island!

–Let's get back to *our* island. Now the other settlers—

–How selective will we be in deciding who settles?

–With the data we've mined—sorry, *harvested*—we already have a complete biometric portrait of every single human being who might possibly apply.

–Yeah, Marko's right. All we have to do is bring up that data, which our programmers in Sagosia are decoding at this very moment, enter their name into the system—

–We can see every single icky little move they've ever made—

–From cradle to grave—

–Well, from cradle to present. Most of them aren't in the grave. Yet.

–And we make our decision according to that algorithm. Well, we don't make the decision. The algorithm actually decides. It's all automated, you see. The world's first fully automated democracy. Whoever is algorithmically correct gets to come. And their reward is to live in the twenty-first century's first surveillance-free state.

–We're… ?

–That's right. No surveillance, anywhere, on the island. True freedom! Not the fake kind they got over here.

–How in the hell are we going to—

–So the rule is—

–I thought the senators were the ones who made the rules?

–Well, in a way, yes. I mean, they'll be making *most* of the rules. But we can't just have a free-for-all going in, then it'll be chaos.

–There needs to be a governing structure.

–Oh there will be. You know, we have experience in this arena. Running a country is essentially a form of real estate management.

–There needs to be *value*. Quality assurance.

–Exactly.

–Write that down.

–The main thing is, settlers will have to earn their way toward non-taxation, at which point a title will be bestowed. Everyone got that?

–So it's not going to be a tax-free haven.

–Tax haven, is what I think you're trying to say.

–No, of course not. That would make it look offshore. This isn't an offshore scheme. For the tenth fucking time. This is a functioning, uh, democratic country, with laws and such.

–What about companies? Corporations?

–Corporations are like citizens, settlers—only better. Super-individuals. They're all tax free. We want as many as possible, naturally.

–What about the people currently living in Sagosia? What kind of say will they have in all this?

–Uh, we'll deal with that one later.

–So how do they *earn* their way toward non-taxation? And what are the taxes gonna be?

–Not that high. Not that low, either. But the thing is, most of the high caliber people we're talking about here, it will only take them a couple years, at most, to reach that point of non-taxation.

–Based on investments made. Good deeds performed that will benefit the entire populace.

–You're talking about an institutionalized form of graft.

–How I hate that word.

–Talk dirty to me.

–Anyway, this system, we're putting that into place for very practical reasons. More than anything. If we just opened our doors to everyone, said *Come live here, tax free,* then all of America would wanna come—along with half of Europe, maybe most of China. We're just a tiny island!

–Not *that* tiny.

–We have to be selective in who we invite. We want to give our new citizens *rights,* we want to give them a reason to look forward to their lives here. But we can't do it all at once. People have to *earn* their rights. If we just *gave* them their rights for free, then it wouldn't be much of a country, would it? Founding a new republic, it has to happen in baby steps.

—Baby steps. That's right. That's exactly what we intend to do, in this Settlers Landing project.

—Walk like a baby… I'm writing this down…

—What we really want to do is not just build a country. We want the island to be more than just a mere nation. It's going to be a showcase.

—A showcase for what?

—Well. I'm not quite ready to talk about that. For now. And I don't want anyone to speculate too much, either—

—So wait wait wait, let's back up for a minute here. So we have the senators, who will be the first settlers—these are the big shot shitballs, the people ready to sink, like, a buttload of money into the boat—

—And to stay on board. We will have to have a residency requirement. Say, ten months out of the year.

—I still think ten months is too long—

—Well, this is how we filter out undesirables: those who are *less* committed.

—Alright. So do these people have non-taxation status from the beginning?

—Yes. And then, the others, the regular citizens, they have to earn their way toward it.

—A points system. We're still working on it. But it'll be transparent. So everyone knows how to reach that cozy endgoal.

—And so what role exactly will Mrdok play in all this?

—A similar to the one he plays right now, right here. He will be the democratically elected leader.

—…

—…

—…

—… How exactly is that the case, though, if I might ask?

—Well, let's just say, we'll call him the president to begin with. Because, I mean, come on, that's what he is—

—Yeah. It's me who's startin this fuckin thing up.

—Okay. I was only asking…

—Yeah? Well don't ask and I won't tell.

—So Mrdok will be the founding president, to begin with. It is difficult to have an election in the early stages—we'll just put it that way to anyone who questions it (though I doubt anyone will.) Then, when the time is judged right by all—all the senators, I mean—then we can have an election.

—If I may interject, just for a moment. Essentially, the political system on Settlers Landing, it will be by and large identical with that of the American democracy we have all come to understand and love—if not necessarily in that order. There will only be some minor tweaks and improvements—all of them for the greater good.

—Right. We're gonna fix all the fucked up shit. Make this an island that real shitballs will want to call home. Without all the trash and garbage clogging the streets.

—That's an elegant way of putting it, Mrdok.

—And the people who are there now—

—Well, they're not really people—I'm sorry, not really *citizens,* in the generally understood sense of the term. Even in Sagosia, now, what they call them is the quasinatives. And the, the, the whites, the British ruling class, they're known as the quasicolonials. See, nothing's real there. Everything's quasithis, quasithat. That's why we have an advantage. We're real.

—Now, I would like to turn the floor over to Abe. Most of you know Abe as our lead commodities broker. But, on Settlers Landing, Abe has a whole new responsibility: He is going to head the newly founded Ministry of the Environment. Abe.

—Well. As the Minister of the Environment, there's one thing I want to convey to all of you. The environment on Settlers Landing is *great.* It's a great environment for investing. Off-shore drilling starts next week. We've got loads of reserves of nucleite, ilmenite, and the Brits, the Pembrokians, the Sagosians, whatever the fuck they are— they're all blissfully unaware. The place is a goddamn driller's paradise.

—We've already gang-raped the competition.

—Hahahahahahahahaha.

—Rape is such an ugly word. Can't we call it an asymmetrical hatefuck?

—I have a feeling they're gonna be begging to be included in the list of first settlers.

—Oh fuck them.

—We have to be selective.

—They can fuck off back to Madagascar and rot.

—This isn't some, you know, a free-for-all…

—Definitely not.

—Right. Thanks for that fascinating presentation, Abe. That's an important point for us all to keep in mind. Don't shy away from exclusivity. Even as we're trying to attract people. We should at the same time be saying no.

—No to most.

—An environment where men can be men...

—And not have to put up with so much bullshit.

—When do we go?

—I'm very happy that you've all committed.

—Yeah. Thanks for not firing us, by the way.

—We only got rid of the ones who really had to go. The ones who were... extraneous to the organization in this new structure. And we do appreciate your discretion.

—And we appreciate your paying for our discretion.

—Gordo and I are in the process of making all the arrangements. Luckily, in the center of the island, there are many empty houses. The British populace has been leaving in droves in recent years, resulting in a sort of economic depression...

—Mrdok always knows where to find opportunity.

—That's right. It won't be easy, at first. Moving to a new land never is. But we will be sure that all the comforts of home will be transposed. We've budgeted more than two hundred ninety million alone in housing and infrastructure for employees. You, in a way, will be our first settlers. Ahead of the senators. We need you to keep the ball rolling.

—When does Manhattan cease operations?

—It already has. Officially at least. This meeting isn't even happening right now.

—Hahahahahahahaha.

—I'm sure you've all weighed this—

—The thing is, you are going to see a tremendous improvement in your family life as a result of this move. Just tremendous. There is already a well-regarded public school on the island. And we're going to bring in more schoolteachers, as well, so that it's not all British, the style of education there.—Fuck, I already sound like a politician, don't I?—Most of the infrastructure is already there. Part of what our budget will go toward is bringing it all up to date—

Speaking personally for a minute here. Me and Mrtol have been having lots of problems of late. She's been craving her own slice of paradise pie. My kid, too. Ever since he ate paint that last time, he's been a bit dull. I know I don't normally tell you guys about my personal life. There are reasons for that. Mainly, I like to keep it *personal.* But Settlers Landing, man. I just know for a fact, this is going to save my marriage. So I have to make it work. I have a lot invested, not just monetarily, in this, but on a personal level as well. And I want you all to have that personal level of investment.

–Excellent speech, boss.

–We want to stress to all of you that this move is *not* a running away. It has *nothing* to do with the current investigations. I mean, fuck the Feds. A few years from now, when this country has gone to shit, they're going to be begging to join us there.

–So what's next?

–We've got a big itinerary ahead of us in the coming days, me and Gordo. Tomorrow we'll leave for Cuba, try and get our plane back. Then it's on to Sagosia, check in with the office there that's already been set up. Then we head to Japan, where we have our first shitball, uh, *investor* meeting.

–Barbra Browneye?!

–Haha. You've got it, Rick.

–Ask her to show you her browneye!

–Hahahahahaha. I bet Rick's already seen it.

–Bahahaha. No comment.

–From Sagosia, it's gonna be Operation Chopsticks. Japan, then Taiwan, then Hong Kong, then back to Sagosia, where we're all gonna meet for our first on-site team meeting. That's three weeks from now. Rick and Marcia, the team here, they'll make sure you're all good and prepared. Of course, you're all welcome to take your spouses and families with you—though I think we mentioned that already?

–It was in the memo.

–Good.

–Another thing. We're gonna start talking to the media.

–Say what?

–Mrdok, are you sure that's a good idea?

–Isn't one of your golden rules—

–Yeah. It is. It *was*. But another one of my rules has always been: Necessity demands new circumstances. Or something like that.

–I believe the quote from the book is—

–Mrdok, I…

–Now me and Marcia have been practicing…

–Is that what they call it?

–He's getting quite good.

–Me and Gordo, too. As you all know, I've never given an interview before. But really, how hard can it be?

–We've come up with a few talking points here—

–That's quite correct. And all Mrdok needs to do is return to them, so as to always keep the conversation on the subject of Sagosia—sorry—Settlers Landing. Journalists these days, they are not very disciplined, poor dears. They quite often wander off topic. Which is why—

–Are there any of these scheduled yet?

–The first one will be next month, with the Factual News Network.

–FaNN? Are you sure those guys are friendly, on our side? Who's doing the interview?

–The homo. Sorry, Gordo. The, uh, salt-and-pepper queen.

–Well is he—she—it—whatever—on our side or what?

–We don't know.

–We're finding out.

–We want *friendly* journalists, okay? Guys we know. None of this fake news crap.

–FaNN aint fake. They're *factual.*

–Bahahaha.

–Do I own any shares in FaNN?

–I'm not sure.

–Find out. And if I don't, buy a bunch immediately. Like, a couple hundred thousand. At least.

–That should keep em on topic.

–Now, for the senators we're looking at. We've got Barbra Browneye. We've got the redneck Texan… Now, this Taiwanese shitball, he's new to me. What can you tell me about him?

–Do you want the raw facts or the key takeaways from the data set?

–I don't know. Give me a sweet mixture of both.

–Mister Ma is his name. Real estate.

–Real estate, real estate. So we got two real estate shitballs, if I'm counting correctly.

–Barb is kind of a half-real estate shitball, in my estimation.

–Is he a mo?

–A what?

–You know. A mo… *Ho*mo.

–I can't tell with these fuckin Asians. They're all a bit gayish seeming to me.

–He's a quality catch. Real nervous now about all the shit that's going on in China. In which he is embroiled, of course. You know the situation over there. All the Asian shitballs, they all have China in their portfolios now. Even if they want to scrub it clean, there's no way to. Thing is, his fellow Taiwanese don't even know the extent to which he's involved. Not that he tries much to hide it from them. But still, people would be shocked. That's why he's a good target. Settlers Landing'll be like a, like a distraction for him.

—Make it all less shittier.

—Yeah. That's the way forward.

—There's this other guy you're supposed to meet with in Hong Kong—

—Yeah, the Cuban deal. I already know about him.

—Once you get your plane back, are you really gonna deliver, Mrdok? I mean, what are they gonna do if you don't, hunt you down?

—Hahahahahaha.

—If I fuck them, then I can never go back there.

—Yeah? So?

—So I like it there. Cuba's a long-term thing for me. Let it go.

—Now here's an odd one. Lil Bigfoot.

—The rapper?

—Yeah.

—Good plan. We also need to think of the cultural life of the island. Architects, we need for sure. But also artists. Musicians. Poets…

—Poets! Great idea. Why yes. Settlers Landing will need a poet laureate!

—A poet laureate?

—What the fuck is that?

—Hey, I know! Let's get the guy who wrote *There Once Was a Man from Nantucket.*

—Can we go back to the rapper, please?

—Yeah. Lilbig. Why the fuck would he be interested?

—You know, the usual. Each time a fat check comes in, he has to spend it faster than last the last.

—That's racist.

—I'm not racist. I was just being… ironic.

—The '90s are over, Mrdok. There's no more irony left. It was all used up.

—What do you mean, all used up?

—I mean there was only a finite reserve of irony in the world. And it was all used up, by people like you, in the '90s. Now all we're left with, whether we like it or not, is total humorless sincerity.

—Gordo, I thought we fired all the millennials and zoomers?

—Anyway, doesn't sound like such an attractive target for us. If he spends his money so fast…

–Except…

–He is. The thing is, this kid is mad productive. He puts out a new track every five minutes.

–So we just need to get him focused.

–That's the idea.

–As focused on his finances as he is on his, uh, creativity.

–Yeah yeah. That's right.

–And. We have a little something here that we think can get him focused.

–What might that be?

–Rick? You got the file ready?

–Yeah.

–Marcia—you might want to bring in some Vaseline and Kleenex for this one.

–Hahahahahahaha.

–Oh Mrdok. What a wit!

–Holy fuckin shit.

–Right?

–That is… That's a cock, man.

–Holy fuck. She's, man…

–How *old* is that girl?

–Young. That's what she is.

–Ding ding ding. You hear that? It's the sound of money.

–Wait, can we even… Should we even be watching this right now?

–No. Of course not. That's the point. She's fourteen.

–Fuck.

–And that's not all… She's also his sister.

2.

—HE'S IN REHAB again.

–Bobby?

–I just got off the phone with Krstal out there. This time it's Europe. Greece or somewhere.

–You've got to be shitting me. I mean, what kind of mother?

–To her credit, she's actually paying for it this time.

–I'm surprised I hadn't heard anything.

–Well, you're not paying for it. And from what I understand, it's a miracle he's still alive.

–Let him dry out, get his fuckin face together.

–I think *dry out* is more of a term for alcoholics, Mrdok. He's a heroin addict.

–Maybe, you know what? Maybe the thing is we've gotta take him with us. Or—not to live—at least give him a place on the island. I mean, think of it. It could also be a solution for him. There aint gonna be any dope there, that much is for sure. They aint got any there now, they aint going to when I take it over.

–When are you leaving for Cuba?

–I told you. It's gonna be the day after tomorrow. Or tomorrow. I don't know. I've gotta ask Gordo.

–Can I come with you?

–Mrtol. Are you drunk?

–I know. I was only saying—

–How's Jaco doing?

–He misses his father.

–No he doesn't.

–You're right. How could he? He hardly knows you.

3.

–GET ME BEV on the line. She's gonna hate me for this.

–Hello?

–Bev. Baby.

–Hieee Merrd.

–Look. I'm really sorry to have to do this to you. But I'm gonna have to cancel tonight—

–No, Merrd, no.

–Look, I'm sorry. I have to leave early tomorrow for Tokyo. And my wife is about to fry my brains out. Jaco just got out of the hospital and—

–What the fuck, Merrd? I thought you were leaving this bitch.

–I am, Bev, I am. But it's not gonna happen *today*. Look, remember that island I told you about?

–Yeah. I think so.

–I wanna take you there. On a little retreat. A little getaway. Just you and me. It'll be fun.

–Oh Merrd. What do you think? I'm stupid? It's never *just you and me*.

–Well it will be this time. I swear on my mother's life.

–You never even knew your mother. Who knows if she's even still alive.

–Okay. On my father's, then.

–Your father's dead, Mrdok.

–Just you and me. I'm gonna—I can't fly there with you, I'm gonna be coming from Asia. But I'm gonna have Gordo book you a ticket. Okay? First class. Not even business. First. All the way.

–I thought you said there was no airport there.

–Well, there isn't. But you can fly to Pembroke, which is real close by, then take a boat there. You know what? I'm gonna have them pick you up in a yacht.

Mrdok makes a writing gesture; Gordo writes down YACHT in big letters on his notepad. Another thing to add to the purchase list.

–Do I need a bathing suit?

–How much do you need? I'll wire you the money right now.

–I don't want money, Mrdok. Jesus Christ. Every time I see you these days, I feel it's just for a quick fuck. Nothing else. Then you, then you shower money on me like I'm some kind of whore.

–Come on, Bev…

–No, really. Like what am I? When are you gonna *commit* to me? When are we gonna get married? Do right by me, baby. Be a fuckin man.

–Whoa. Bev. You're really going to make me lose my temper any minute now. Do you have *any idea* how much stress I am under. Do you? Because if you did, I don't think you would be talking to me this way.

–Talking to you how?

–Saying, whatever it is you just said. That I'm using you as my whore.

–Well isn't that what—

–No, it's not. Matter of fact, I think I treat you pretty effin nice. Matter of fact, if anybody's being *used* here, I think it's me.

–Mrdok…

–After all, I'm the one with the money, aint I? I'm the one who fuckin, who plucked you out of the dirt…

–Excuse me? I have never touched dirt at any time in my life.

–Yeah? Well you'd better get used to it, sweetheart. Cos that's exactly where I'm gonna leave you.

–Mrdok, what the fuck—

–You give me no choice. I've given you money, I've given you clothes. I've given you an apartment in the city—prime real estate! I've given you a tremendous amount of my time—which isn't easy, given my work commitments, never mind my family—and which you don't even seem to appreciate. None of it, matter of fact. Rather than appreciating it, it seems you're bent on just causing me more stress.

—You have been totally like *colonizing my life*, Mrdok, ever since we met. I've made plans. I mean, I thought we were going to have a future together. That's what you've told me. I thought we were in love.

—Yeah? Well guess what, sweetheart. Things change. Maybe better you learn this now, rather than have to figure it out later. It'll be much tougher then, once you've lost your looks, which is bound to happen in a few years.

—Fuck you, Mrdok.

—Yeah? Great, baby. Tell you what. Enjoy your last few days in the apartment. Cos it's gonna be gone soon.

—No fucking way.

—Yes way. I'm leaving Manhattan. It's over between us. There's no way I'm gonna continue onward with an ungrateful little bitch like you, who's just out to *fuck up* everything I've built. Have a nice time trying to hook your little cunt claws into someone half as important, as successful, as caring as I am. Someone who fucks even half as good. Goodbye, Bev.

Click.

4.

—STEVO REY. IT'S me.

—Dad? Uh, okay.

—How's it over there? You still like it?

—Yeah. I like it fine. Why?

—You okay livin side by side with all those Japs?

—Come on, dad. Just because they burned your ass in a business deal, that's no reason to be racist.

—Oh they didn't burn my ass. I burnt theirs. That's why they don't like me.

—Yeah. Whatever.

—Stevo. You can ask Murray. Ask Gordo. Ask anyone you want. It was the Japs who lost out on that deal. Not me.

—Yeah. Whatever, dad. I don't really care. Hey, when are you going to come visit?

—You know I don't like sushi.

–Come on, there's more here than just sushi. You know that, dad. Look, I know a place, I'll take you to have the best steak of your life. I swear to god.

–I can get a good enough steak on East 79th Street.

–Fine, dad. Suit yourself. Not to change the subject, but is the money on the way?

Click. (An instinct that kicks in automatically whenever anyone asks Mrdok for money. He can no longer control it. He's been programmed.)

He's going to Tokyo next week. He just can't bring himself to tell Stevo Rey. That's all. He'll have Gordo call and arrange everything.

5.

—DAD, IT'S ME. Bobby. Calling from rehab this time.

–Yeah, I heard. Mrtol told me about it.

–Yeah…

–I'm glad to hear you're at least making the effort, Bob.

–Well… I'm sorry, Dad.

–Hey, things could be worse. Like I said. You're making the effort, you're trying to get clean. I understand your mom is paying for your stay over there.

–Yes, she is. That's part of the reason why I'm calling, actually.

–Okay…

–Papa, can I have some more money?

–What is this?

–I need to get my teeth fixed.

–Teeth? What do you need teeth for?

–To bite shit. Food. Heroin fucked up my teeth. Well, not the heroin itself. The heroin made me forget to brush my teeth. For a couple years.

–I don't know, Bobby…

–Ten grand. That's all I need is ten grand.

–Ten grand?! What do you think, I'm made of money?

–Yes.

–You're right. I am. And that's precisely why I'm not gonna give it to you. To learn you a lesson.

–What lesson?

–… The power of money.

Click.

PART FIVE

CUBA

STILL, HE WANTED. His plane back, more than anything now. But a couple other things in addition. He wants the plane so that he can go back to wanting all those other things. The plane, he feels, will also help him attain those other things. Without it, those other things might very well slip out of his hands. If he is to go to Tokyo, then it has to be in his own damn plane.

Cuba in December. Well, it *is* the most bearable time to be on the island. We're going to get the plane back the easiest way we know how: we're going to buy it back.

We're on the patio of the Hotel Nacional waiting for the Renaldos to arrive. After berating me for my tardiness—I accepted Ricardo's invitation to visit a new gay club last night just off the Malecón that has opened since our last visit, and had a bit of difficulty rousing my bedside companion this morning—Mrdok launches into one of his caffeinated morning monologues.

–I tell you, before the Castro brothers took this shit over, this place used to be paradise on earth. I mean, everyone was down here—celebrities, mobsters, the president. Future presidents... Congressmen. That was back when shit was pure. When the world wasn't fucked up like what it is today. This quagmire it's become. Not this stinkhole it's turned into, desperation on every corner. I mean, why can't these people just get it together?

I put my fingers to my lips gently, a hush hush gesture. His voice gets louder the more impassioned he gets, and you never know who's listening in.

—Let em hear this. Fuck all I care. It's not cute anymore, Gordo. This goddamn shitshow. Something's got to give. I can just see this whole fuckin island crumbling into the sea, can't you?

I wonder how long this is going to go on until the Renaldos finally arrive. Intermittent flashes of last night come to me as I listen to Mrdok's monologue. The red lights of the dance floor, shirtless bodies, hips swaying to the music. I could never make my hips move fast enough, a young mulatto laughing at me beneath the swirling lights, swaying with me. He told me his name is Johnny as he pulled me up against his sweaty chest...

—Hey Gordo, fat fuck, are you even listening to me? Is there a Wi-Fi connection out here? How much am I worth?

We were dancing to the latest reggaeton hit, a song whose name translated into English, I was told, is roughly *I Don't Need No Wi-Fi, I Just Need Your Love.*

—No Wi-Fi, I tell him, hands raised in a what-to-do gesture.

I didn't want him to stay the night in my room. I thought it too risky. Even though the hotel had taken his ID, as is required in Cuba whenever you bring a guest back. Still, the chances of something disappearing in these environs is always uncomfortably high. But he insisted. Claimed it was too late for him to go all the way back home. And then he cuddled up next to me, with one of those looks that is just so hard to resist. So I gave in. This morning, not only was nothing missing from my suitcase; to my surprise, he hardly asked for anything on his way out the door. Just five dollars, so that he could take a taxi back home. He also left me his phone number, insisted that I call him. I took it, knowing full well I never will. Circumstance prevents me from forming such emotional attachments. After all, if this goes the way it's planned, we'll be out of here in less than a day... so long as the gods of bureaucracy turn out to be on our side. When it comes to Mrdok, they nearly always are.

Here comes the famous Hotel Nacional peacock, feathers you just want to pluck right off. At the table next to us, two midwestern tourists with Down syndrome stare out at the sea beyond the garden. Tuxedo'd waiters rush about, bringing everyone their morning espressos. A sweet waft of cigar smoke fills the air, as though to complete the cliché.

Suddenly, the Renaldos are standing before us.

To be honest, it's the first time I've slept in the same bed next to anyone for, well, for as long as I can remember. The last time, most certainly, was with my wife. But that's not a subject upon which I wish to dwell at the present moment. I did come out to her, in case you were wondering, and she was fine with it. I think she somehow suspected it, perhaps knew it before even I did. But as for our marriage—well, it won't be affected right now—though it's a subject that will have to be broached somewhere along the line.

—Oh my god! Look who it is! exclaims Renaldo 1 in a display of surprise that could only be classed as sardonic.

—Back in Cuba so soon! My man, how are you, hombre? Renaldo 2 picks up.

—Wow, such good actors. They must have pulled you two out of the theater academy. Am I right, Gordo?

—Haha, boss. Surely Renaldo and Renaldo aren't actors. There's nothing artificial about them!

The Renaldos signal over to the waiter, who sets two cups of espresso down on the table.

—Good news since we saw you last, hombre.

—And what might that be?

—Renaldo's wife is going to have a baby.

—Aww, that is wonderful news. Now which one of you is the father?

—Hahahaha. That's a good one, señor.

—Now about that plane…

—Before we get to the plane. Well. I want to let you know. I'm actually not here for vacation this time.

—Of course you're not, señor.

—You see, I have a new concern. A new business. And I think it could be of interest to you. To you people and… whoever it is you represent. You know what the problem with your country is? Your government doesn't have control over its own people. Not enough control. I've been here enough times to observe this with my naked eyes. You've got people wandering the streets, here in the capital, committing all kinds of lewd atrocities. Men exposing themselves, jerking off in front of school children. People robbing tourists in Old Havana. The cops come, they barely do anything about it. I mean, how can you expect them to? They're underfed, under-resourced, barely compensated. I bet what you guys earn… Well, I'll stop there.

—Yes, I think you stop there, hombre, before you take a step too far.

—Now listen. I don't mean anything insulting. We're amigos, right? I've been coming here for years now. We know each other well enough. I think we can speak frankly. Hell, Gordo here will tell you I only speak frankly to those I have the utmost respect for. I don't need to coat things in platitudes. You look at other countries—and

I don't care if they're communist or capitalist countries, whatever—the one thing they have that I don't see a lot of in Cuba is adequate surveillance. And when I say adequate surveillance, I don't mean the granny next door. I'm talking about the twenty-first century kind.

–I'm a little confused, hombre. I mean, the last I checked, surveillance is not your field of business.

–I don't know when was the last time you checked, but the fact is I don't have just one field of business, *hombre*. In fact, I have dozens. Hundreds, even.

–Indeed, as a twenty-first century entrepreneur, Mrdok need not limit himself to merely one or two fields, such as less intrepid, less enterprising businessmen might pursue. This isn't a mere street merchant you're dealing with, gentlemen.

The two Renaldos turn to look at me in silence.

–All this pristine sunshine here. What a shame to see it all go to waste.

–What exactly are you talking about?

–So much clarity. And yet you are able to see so little.

–I see just fine.

–We have our means, if what you're implying is—

–Political criminals, counter-revolutionaries. I assure you, señor, the people of Cuba know exactly who they are. Our administration…

–… is inefficient. Not up to par with other countries…

–If I might interject, Network Surveillance Associates, as a private company registered in Sagosia, a territory currently *not* participating in the sanctions against Cuba—

–Embargo.

–Embargo. Whatever you wanna call it. Our Network Surveillance Associates—NSA for short—is able to offer you top-notch internal security mechanisms without fear of reversal down the line by, let us say, some menacing external power on the world stage.

–Why should we trust you? You're still gringos. You still entered our country on American passports.

–The next time we're here, we won't be.

–Oh?

–We're issuing our own passports.

–Funny joke, señor.

–Look, we're not here to discuss passports with you. We come in a gesture of good will, to do a deal that will greatly benefit us both. You can ask anyone who knows me. It's the only kind of deal I do.

–What gives you the right, what makes you think you can meddle in our internal affairs? That the people of Cuba will sit back and accept—

–Spare me.

–or even *speculate* in that vein.

–I'm sorry. I have eyes.

–Like us Cubanos don't know how to keep our counterrevolutionaries, our CIA lackeys under control!

–What Mrdok means to say is, we don't particularly care *how* you deploy this technology. I mean, we would prefer to not know. Whether you use it to catch hardened criminals or people plotting against your little commie regime, we could care less. In that sense, we're not messing in your internal affairs at all.

–We're here to do bidniss. Sweet and sexy.

Renaldo 1 whistles a waiter over, whispers something. The waiter goes over to the couple sitting at the table next to ours, whom I hadn't even noticed before, and reseats them at a table at the opposite end of the patio.

–Okay, hombre. You want to talk business? Let's go. We understand exactly what you're trying to sell us. Backward as you may think we are, we're not dumb. Our Chinese comrades have made us the exact same offer. And it's a price tag we couldn't afford.

–Yeah? Sounds like your boss was talking to the wrong Chink.

–Watch it, señor. I might not look like it, but I have some Chino blood.

–Right. Cuba is an incredibly diverse place. A bit too diverse to maintain any credible social order…

–Enough, Gordo. Excuse my momentary bout of racism. It's just that I hate those bastards every bit as much as I know you and your leadership secretly do. I mean, look at them and look at you! They're filthy rich and you're stewing in the dirt. Now is that any way to treat a comrade?

–Yeah. And from what we understand, this software you're peddling *comes* from China. Is made there. So how in the hell are you going to get your hands on it without them finding out? It's not like you can just cut them out of the deal, the Chinese bastards. As soon as they detect the technology has hit our shores, the embassy here will be on the phone to Beijing—

–Relax, hombre, relax. We're not about to do anything that's going to jeopardize your delicate little situation with the Chinese.

—But from what I gather, your little NSA or whatever it's called— whatever you're trying to do with it—all you can be is middlemen, nothing more. You don't manufacture nada.

—Well, that's putting it a bit crudely, wouldn't you say, Gordo? I think we offer something far greater than just the product. We offer a couple extra layers of security. It's called motherfuckin *anonymity*. Get it?

—Who are you gonna fucking get it from, if not the Chinese?

—*Every single citizen,* I now sing-whisper in the background, so as to add some texture to the proceedings (as I sense the moment of closure is upon us.) *Tagged and monitored. Bring em online! Every single citizen…*

—Hush, Gordo. Where are we getting it from? You know, China might appear to have a monopoly on this stuff. But as with most of these appearances, they actually don't.

—So who if not the Chinese?

—There's a lovely little nation right next door—

—You mean North Korea?

The Renaldos look at one another and smirk.

—We have those bastards, too. I was just at a reception at their embassy in Vedado—

—Oh? How was the food? Look, I'm sure it's a fucking empty shell, their embassy, just like their country. And when it comes to offshore exchange, well, that's not the kind of info they enjoy sharing with their Chinese comrades.

—*Tagged and monitored, tagged and monitored… All artificial intelligence. Zero manpower necessary.*

—Enough, Gordo.

—This is getting more unbelievable by the minute. You're saying the operating system is built in Pyongyang?

—Not in Pyongyang. Some shitstall in the mountains. Where is not important. The military may or may not know. They may or may not be in on it with the government. It's complicated. We have our guy. He's reliable, he's nice enough. For what he is…

—There can be nothing on paper…

—Well, there will be a maintenance agreement. That's a key part of the package we're offering. We can word it however you'd like. I mean, I want this to be fair to you guys.

—You know our situation, señor. These pieces of paper. They do nothing for us. No international court—

—The gringos prevent everything.

—Let me ask you. Why the friendly gesture all of a sudden?

Renaldo 1 grimaces studiously. Mrdok leans in.

–Cos I wantz my fuckin plane back.

–Aha of course.

–We feel our price tag is quite reasonable. We realize, of course, that this decision isn't yours to make. We trust you'll take it to your comrades. It wouldn't be much of an exaggeration to characterize this as the deal of the century. We're offering you nothing less than the chance to bring Cuba up to speed.

–Yeah, Mrdok belches and smirks. What you need is to bring Cuba in line with the situation of total cynicism in which the rest of the world is currently enmeshed. Only then can your country truly evolve.

–Don't get left behind!

The Renaldos exchange glances. The first one gets up and walks away without bothering to shake hands as the second rises.

–You'll be hearing from us.

CHAPTER TWO

LIL BIGFOOT

LIL BIGFOOT OUT by the pool. One of those schemin nights, all lit up, party's hoppin. Lil Bigfoot all withdrawn, like a empty shell—seems he's there cos his physical person be, elsewise he be ghostin. Ghostin on this one and that. Like he got some vice he be coverin up through absence. Girls in string bikinis, girls topless, glowing pool vision and those soft red lights the steady beat the red sheen of midnight twerk. He be wastin without getting wasted, cigar in his mouth like he da man.

He da man. Lil Bigfoot know somethin bout forces you feel but can't hardly see. Lilbig the one to give voice to all these vision. He the craziest fool in this damn rap game—that's what his fans the critics like and, he give it to em, all and the same. Lil Bigfoot aint no smurf—he know the game is real. And when he aint winnin aint no one else be allowed to come out on top.

Step back into the crib, Lil Bigfoot. See the bruthas and sistas at the table cuttin lines out, gold chains and hundred dollar bills. Stacked and loaded, for rhymin bout gunshots and glory. No—that aint all—tryn to put a positive spin on shit. It extends from over here to over there. This room here. Bruthas be all alphabetin and shit. It's like naw, bro, never. This aint the only way to be. But it's what we got, cos they's kids and they don't know no other game.

Gold and platinum records on the wall, Rapper of the Year. Can't hardly read and write—it's a secret hardly no one knows—still, he a lyrical genius—this theys all knows. A oral tradition, Black blood gotz it. Don't be part of no pass dat say you don't. Bruthas be all measurin theyselves against the real length the Lil Bigfoot be gottin on. It's all part o' the heritage, bro to bro.

It's like he told that interviewer the other day. Growin up Black in the hood, you feel like you nothin. That's like the baseline, all what you got to work wit. White kid in the suburbs—they start out up there, we start out way down here. No wonder so many get good at runnin. You got all this distance to go, just to arrive at they's normal. Thing is this. You finally arrive, all the bruthas be strivin to tear you down. Like they can't stand you done won that race. Make a mutha-fucka paranoid. It's a race war, aight, and it *inside* the race. That's why we all be killin on each other for generations.

Growing up in da hood. Just to be somebody a dream. You feel like you nobody nothin till you is somebody. Just that elevation. This reality we in now somethin white folks they all take for granted. Most of em. Think they wants to know what it like to die on these city streets?

LaQueefah be comin over here, askin where LaRhonda at. Damn thong up the bitch's ass. Slap it. Bitch I thought I done told you to call me daddy when you address me. Bitch be right out on the street before she knows it. Shit, nigga. Back to where she damn comed from. Work the corner wif dem other common ho's.

Broke speech don't know no halo. Big fat lack spread on a cracker, jack, lick da sleaze off the government cheese. Motherfuckin Jemiah be interviewed in prison, older brother, be tryn to give our young lives da golden sheen. *But we aint never gone hungry,* he say. Yeah, that's cos we done cuffed the food. Police records tell the story better than he do. But MTV don't wanna hear that. They wanna get all in-spirational and shit. FaNN, *Wall Street Post,* don't none of them motherfuckers wanna hear the real troof, Ruth. Cos they do, they ears bleed. And Jemiah, he probly just don't wanna relive it again. Cos what would be the point. He already in jail, doin seventy-five. Got him all the best jew lawyers the money could buy, he still in there. A nigga is a nigga is a nigga, in da eyes of da law. Only when we get to the afterlife, we'll see whos king den. Who dun ruled the urf all along. Till that day, ya gotz to learn to slay. Get all dem mutha-fuckas outta my way.

> Numbers with which to explore your arid ass
> Throw you to the floor where I'll make a pass
> Suitcase blues for the man with a short fuse
> Bang-bang shoot ya up 'fore you even get a chance to lose
> Moby Dick—take a lick—big as a whale and twice as thick
> Flipflop off the scale and land in my sick
> Bitch in a wig made from real plas-tick

Aint good for the environment make you die real quick
Upside down, the bitch starts to crown
Didn't know she's preg it's too late to put it down

. . .

There that flow go. Aint none of these muthafuckas in the crib right now wants to go back to them days. Theys most of dem wasn't around, but we all the same hood ass muthafuckas. Nineteen years old, sleepin in my car on the southside. Fall asleep to a soundtrack of gunshots. Be coverin yo face up, just tryn not to see. Wake up all moist and sticky and frozen from the cold, that grime you could never get off, no matter how many showers you damn take once you hit the studio. The studio a motherfuckin refuge. I'd just stay all day, chillin, layin down the tracks one by one. Smokin weed. Slowlike. Aint got nowhere else to go. You go back out on them cold ass streets, you burn. Bulletproof vest a jerkoff fantasy life. Swingin dope nowadays not cos there aint no more option, but cos they simply kill you if you not slingin they dope and livin on theys territory. They gets you killed and along comes another muthafucka. And it go on. Shit. Dead if you do and dead if you don't. That's what it like to be a nigga in America. They shoot yo ass theyselves when the cops don't. Make a muthafucka paranoid n shit. That's what they want.

To provide. Know whose own family be. It aint right easy. Come from nothin and knowin nothin. A man loses perspective, it is true. The thing is not to lose yourself in the fame the fortune. You think I don't know that, shit, but then what we all out here celebratin.

In da eyes o da law. Can't be nothin more than half a man, at best.

Into da bedroom where we gotz da gatz. Gotta be keepin the crib on lockdown to its foundations, less some crude ass muthafuckas be bustin in, wartime meltdown. They take all yr shit away. Who da real enemy is. Not no white man no mo. Damn outtasight muthafuckas be fer realen, blowtorch dem bitches bikinis off out by da pool. Muthafuckas out there don't know what's real or not. Theys common niggas, all about the slingin, the gabbin, the fuckin. You get to be the king of the hood, all sorts of other parasite game be startin up. Be on the horn with the jew lawyer now. Be talkin bout some shit just drop. He a honorary nigga but still. Cant nothin good be in the works when he on the horn.

—Now Lilbig, he be sayin, I wanted you to hear it from me first. A bomb's about to drop, but I've already got a plan for us. It might get a little ugly, but I don't want—

–Cut to the chase, man, I don't gotz all day.

–A video got leaked. It's got you in it.

–Shit.

–Hello?

–Yeah. I's here.

–Do you have any idea which video I might be talking about, Lilbig?

–I gotz a clue.

–Yeah? Well, here's what we're gonna do. First of all, the girl. How old is she?

–Man, I don't know.

–Okay, good answer. Very good. This is a secure line, but just in case—

–Man, I made… Shit. I gotz to get my… How n the hell they got my shit, man?

–I don't know. Maybe you got hacked. Maybe it came from the girl directly.

–Shit. Who the fuck done leaked that shit? Where it goin out? *TMZ?*

–Right now, it's the Black entertainment media. It's going to leak on any number of channels, probably gonna be on some Twitter feeds… Okay, look, I'm not gonna sugar coat this for you, my man, this is about to go viral…

–Where the hell Shaneequah at?

–What?

–I aint talkin to you, man. I gotz my homie right here. Where Shaneequah at?

–I don't know. She at home, in Atlanta, for alls I know.

–Get her on the horn yo.

–Is this the girl? I wouldn't advise you to speak with her right now. Or ever again, for that matter. I would prefer you let me handle all communications with her and, ah, her family. In the meantime…

–What?

–Shit, man, I just—Her age and all that. I mean, if what they're saying is true… Look, my man, I'm gonna have to advise you to get on a plane and leave the country. Like A-Sap.

–… Say what?!

–You're in some hot water, my friend, and unless you want to face—

–Man, I gotz a tour that's startin up next week. Where the hell am I supposed to go?

–Well, maybe you should have thought of that before you recorded yourself having relations with an underage—

–Man, fuck you. You aint got no right to judge.

–You're right. I'm not a judge. But as your lawyer, at the moment,
I have to advise you—

–Man shut up.

Hang up the phone. What the fuck. Call that muthafucka in here.
Tell him to send all da other muthafuckas away. They bitches too.
We gotta get this shit on lockdown, yo. Streamline the process to
reach easy victory. Who knows what kinda shit they be pullin.

Phone rings again. Man what the fuck. Tell that jew ass lawyer he
be testin my patience. Aint no shit—

–Hold on, bro. That aint the jew.

–Who it be then?

–That be Mrdok.

–Say what?!

–That rich ass white motherfucker. You know. Rich ass Wall
Street nigga.

–Why the fuck he be callin?

–I don't know, yo. He axin for you.

–Hello?

–Lil Bigfoot. I mean, do you have a real name? Or is that what
you like to be called?

–Lilbig's aight.

–Lilbig it is then.

–Why you callin me, chief?

–Well, thing is, we have some friends in common. You know my
pal Rick? Rick Stewart. You know. Real estate. Does some numbers
deals on the side…

–Yeah, I know Rick. He work for you, don't he?

–Well, kind of… So I was just in Rick's office, he broke the news
to me. Oh my god, man. I don't know what to say.

–How the hell he know about it? If what we talkin bout the same
thang.

–The video. Shit, man. If that shit happened to me, I don't even
know what I'd do. As a longtime fan of yours—

–You listen to hip hop?

–You bet I do. Did you know I have a copy of *Outer Space Niggas*—I hope you don't mind me using that word (it is the title of your
album, after all)—I have a copy of it at home on vinyl. One of my
prized possessions. It just so happens that I'm down in Miami right
now—

–Thought you said you just met with Rick. He in New York.

–Oh, did I say that? What I meant was we just got off a Skype call. We conference every two or three days when I'm on the road. You know. Rick takes care of a lot of stuff for me.

–Yeah. Me too.

–So. I don't know if you heard. But I've got this plane with me here in Miami…

–You gotz a plane?

–Oh, it was a bitch to acquire. But yeah. Since I got it. She runs pretty good, I do have to say…

–Where you fly that shit?

–All over, man. Why I was just about to take a whirl over to Crete to visit my son.

–That outside the country?

–Crete? Yes. That's in Greece.

–And that's outside uh America.

–Uh, yeah. Last time I checked.

–Hold on a minute, man.

–… You still there?

–Yeah… Just hush a minute… Yo Wing. Where Wing at?

–Right here.

–Yo Wing man. Get these muthafuckas outta my crib. Clear the whole crib out.

–Whuddup, dawg, da party's just gettin hot.

–Get these muthafuckas the fuck *out*, yo. Da party's over.

CHAPTER THREE

COMING CLEAN

IT GOES LIKE this. Bobby's been through it so many times—seven, eight, nine?—he's lost count, that by now, it's become almost cliché, or at least limpid. The first month, naturally, is always the worst; that bending of time, prolongation of which, without junk, makes it seem infinite, unbearable. Mostly it's fatigue and constant endless lethargy—you want to sleep all the time, and, depending on the facility you've wound up at, you might even be allowed to. Mostly, they like to keep you on your feet and moving. Which feels like torture. There is the cramping and the sweating and the general flu-iness, yes. After three or four days of being dope free, taking your first shit in maybe two, three weeks. The pain of passing a large hardened elongated potato through your anus, oftentimes causing blood to flow—though this is the more pleasant of the pains, to get that giant festering turd finally out of your system—though immediately after, in the days to come, your bowels turn to liquid—quite the opposite effect kicks in. And you don't know where it's coming from, since you can hardly eat, there's no real appetite to speak of. Oddly, you don't want to do anything else, either—not even smoke. There's nothing that can be done other than to just sit there, once the writhing stops.

After six or so days, the cravings tend to subside. Within a matter of weeks, you have your life back, more or less, and if you can stay straight and not succumb to temptation—then you get back to your normal self, at least in a physical sense. For it is then that all the deep psychological shit starts drifting to the surface—all the reasons why you were using to begin with. Why, in many cases, you started using again. And thinking those thoughts, even though all physical cravings may have subsided and been all but eliminated, often makes people want to turn back to it—to get back to that scuzzy alleyway, on to that dirty mattress, and start smoking or snorting up that sweet brown sand or poking that sticky black muck, depending on which coast one happened to land on.

Another ride on the rollercoaster. The rollercoaster of sobriety… Great. But yeah: a thing needed. At least now. Rock bottom hit so many times, no longer worth counting. When you're that fucked up for so long you grow disgusted with yourself; the way the sweat smells. For, it is true, you sweat a lot when you're on heroin, especially at night, when you're sleeping. Especially when you're living on a small island off the coast of southern California and you didn't manage to pay the electricity bill and so there's no longer any air conditioning. Especially when you know you can no longer afford to get properly high and so you concentrate all your efforts on just dragging it out, rationing the dope: on *maintaining*. The grisly command. The sheer awfulness of day. Night somehow better, when you can at least pretend there's some mystical nothingness hovering out there, when the streetlights at least illuminate something, though by now, you've long learned to see in the dark…

Anyway, all that was over. Going straight and this time it would work. He didn't need a grand program. It was being offered to him anyway. Of course: the only kind of rehab he could get the Moms to splurge for. The medicine was always bittersweet, when not pukingly atrocious. All that higher power biz. Weeping in the intestinal folds of mercy. Something stronger than you, sure: why not the entire world? Why the need to name it with an upper-case G?

The truth is, mostly it is a giant D—Distraction, not Dick—that works. And that is no easy task when you have no real life to fall back on. No career, no job, no ambition, no higher goals. Getting high has been his life for as long as he can remember—which, owing to the memory-fogging side effect of heroin, isn't very far back. Or else gets coated in too many fine details to properly function as an archive. Forced to survey the landscape, as he now often is, he can retrieve some triggering events, see certain pictures from his youth flash before him, like a holiday slide show from back in the day when people still did such things. Driving up and down the length of Long Island on acid when he was sixteen, seventeen, his friends jammed into the back seat and the passenger side, giggling and jabbering their strychnine'd jaws off as their widened unblinking eyeballs dried out. Always the designated driver, for reasons he can no longer remember or fathom—maybe because he was so good at driving when tripping his balls off? Or was it just because it was always his car? It is a talent, of sorts, to be able to drive in that condition, though none he could list on any résumé, which is perhaps why he has never accomplished much in the job department—that and because his father is rich as hell, so there was never real need felt or genuine parental encouragement to do, well, much of anything. Like, what's the point when you can always invent some excuse for why you need more dosh—an excuse that'll never be believed, of course, which is further reason for not having to have a very good reason or having to elaborate or justify it all too much. The biggest threat is that sometimes the money was refused. But the point was, as both Bobby and Stevo Rey had learned, if you just repeat it and be annoying enough then eventually he'll give way and just give you the goddamn money to get you off his back. That's what happened in most cases. Though in recent years, since the Moms stopped talking to Bobby altogether, Mrdok would sic the new wife on his back. The new wife-slash-human shield.

Really, he was never paid much attention to. The only time they noticed him—or Stevo Rey, for that matter—is when one of them got into trouble. Either the school calling or Officer Friendly knocking at the doors of the crystal palace. And so Bobby started to do it more often, to his father's annoyance. Krstal didn't much care; which annoyed Mrdok further. And the more annoyed he got, the longer his business trips started to last. Till the sons only rarely saw their father, Krstal her husband. And that is how he eventually faded from the picture for good.

There's no underlying psychology. The past is a living nightmare from which everyone wishes to awake. Awake and escape. Into the, what. The forever beyond. But no, now there is nothing. Like a Paleolithic gazing into the roboticized future. Before there was AI. When one could scarcely fantasize beyond what outsized creature to hunt and kill next.

One thing for sure: he would have to get off that island. Not this one. Catalina. He couldn't go back there. Maybe it was the island, not heroin, that had been killing him all this time. Who knew. But he would never discover that deity with a capital D on such a place wholly bereft of it. Trouble is, he didn't know where to go next. Some options were put upon the mental table in front of him, discussed with his counselor, a tiny pensive Greek man with a bushy mustache that Bobby found alternately terrifying, endearing, intriguing, deplorable—usually depending on which phase of detox he was in. He could join Stevo Rey in Tokyo. He hadn't spoken to his brother in years; he had little reason to. They were continents apart—

and not just literally. And what would he do in Japan, really? He couldn't speak the language, knew next to nothing about the culture. What, play the tambourine in Stevo Rey's noise extravaganza? It seemed ridiculous. New York equally so. He'd tried the Big Apple, well, a semester at NYU at least. The city didn't hold much interest for him. Of course he'd spent most of his time getting high in the dorms. Some of his buddies from Long Island had followed similar post-high school paths and landed in the city at one institution of higher learning or another, many of them as ambitionless as he, more eager to kill brain cells than to elevate themselves to their parents' vaunted stature. Dropped out, or maybe gotten kicked out—the facts here, as in so many places, are hazy—then landed with a thud back on the left coast, where the Moms soon kicked his ass out of the house when she discovered him in his bedroom one day liquify-ing some brown powder with a lighter and tinfoil. (Thus finally solving the mystery as to where all her tinfoil had kept disappearing.)

The facts smelled bad, he didn't want them interfering. Called into dinner. Tonight's choice of steak tartar or eggplant parmigiana for the veggies, a labyrinthine bouquet of sides and starters at the buffet, ginger ale or soda water to wash it all down with. He ladles out a tremendous portion of Greek salad, gets a chair at a lone table in the back corner from where he can watch the passing parade of rich white kids of the Western world in competing states of detoxi-fication pass by and make a casual study of what each and every one has loaded on to their plates, and draw conclusions about them from that.

CHAPTER FOUR

LAST DAY

THE DAY NOTHING but clouds. Clouds all over the place, clouds to have a mistress by, nothing. Heads up in them, Aristophanes laughing, goddamn philosophers again. Leaving the royal city behind for a change, into the blank space of—what? Bev doesn't know. There she is, blanking. Clouds that don't move—those kind. That really just *blanket* everything. Till there are no more babys left to be bought. The world gets ridiculous at certain moments, moments we are never alone to hatch. Communal and voluminous. Mars is a baby, too. She looks like a waitress even though she isn't one. Soon she'll have to be. Mrdok's dumped her. Even if she wanted something, she wouldn't get, so it's useless to want. Just a middle-class girl from Staten Island. Sky breaks, some blue, a shape. That cloud looks like a little lamb—the kind you eat. Meaning: a nice slab. Not the cute-sifying effect. If you have time to do anything in the morning, then there's something wrong with you, guy at the next table says. A big fat wilted lollypop. That's what it looked like. Rhythm essential to the act. Lest even he wouldn't get off. Bev's head in the clouds, ten-der morning. All the wolves away; no more walking. Down the street, girlfriend takes out her pods to say hello. Grrl, you lookin good. Wish I could feel it. Grrl what happened to you. There aint no such thing as tenderness left in this world. Dreams be a-chasin. Do I really have to explain it? He dumped me, okay? Wait... *he* dumped *you*? I always figgered it be the opposite. So what's that mean? You saw it coming?

He's a man of certain appetites—that she always knew. Had she been naïve to conceive of herself as perhaps something a tiny bit more than a piece of ass on the side?

That's what she is now. What she finally realizes she is. Net worth zero. Not worth crying about. She'll clean out the apartment, move back in with her mother. A higher calling, nothing left to find. Back to suburban bedroom, her Manhattan adventure finished. Thought she'd have a baby and a life, TV marriage all her friends'd be jealous of. Mrdok not that kind of man. Thing is, she never did figure out what kind of man he is. Much as she thought she knew him. These bottoming-out moments when you finally see you don't know shit.

Here we are, scene of the crime. Doorman visibly stiffens at the sight of her.

—Hi Jake. Any mail for me?

Trying to play it all normal.

—I'm afraid not, ma'am.

—What's this ma'am stuff, Jake? I told you you could call me Bev.

—I'm afraid… There isn't any mail and I can't let you go upstairs, either.

—… Excuse me?

—You see, Mister Whiteman…

—Who the hell is Mister Whiteman?

—Uh, Gordon is I believe his first name—

—Gordo is not, Gordo is Mrdok's assistant. He doesn't own this apartment.

—Neither do you, ma'am. Now I'm afraid—

—Afraid what? What are you so frickin afraid of, Jake?

—… I don't know what to tell you. The apartment's been cleaned out. They told me not to let you up there.

—What do you mean it's been *cleaned out*? I just moved in two, three weeks ago. All my stuff is still up there. It's *my apartment*.

—Well, not anymore, apparently.

—I'm going up there.

—Miss. Look. I can't allow that. What I can do is—

—Out of my way, Jake. I need to get my stuff at least.

—Your stuff is not up there anymore, Bev. I'm sorry. I think the best thing would be for you to call Gordo yourself—

—What the fuck, Jake? Is this really how you treat—

—I'm just doing my job, Bev. Orders are orders. Look, I don't want to have to call the police—

—Call the police?! After everything I've done for you. All the tips I've given you, all the—

—I don't work for you, Bev. Never have. This is Gordo, this is Mrdok's apartment. I'm just following instructions they've given me.

She steps out on to the wintry avenue. Cold, even through the sun. Takes out her phone, finds Mrdok on her contact list. Thankfully she didn't yet delete him like she'd been considering.

What can you say when there are no words. Gordo picks up after the third ring.

–Gordo what the fuck?

–I presume this to be Bev?

–I want to talk to Mrdok.

–That is impossible, my dear.

–Why is that impossible? I'm outside the apartment now. Jake says I can't go in. That my stuff isn't there anymore. Can you tell me please what the fuck is going on?

–It's over, Bev. That is all I can say.

–Well thanks for the fair warning. What did you do with my stuff?

–It's not there anymore.

–What do you mean it's not there? Where is it?

–I… I had to throw it out.

–What?!

–Mrdok's instructions. He asked me to take it to the dumpster. So I did.

–That motherfucker.

–What can I say, Bev? I mean, I don't know what went on between you two, but maybe you should have given more thought to—

–To what, Gordo? What the *fuck* should I have given more thought to? How can a person do this to another person? To treat me like I'm not even a human being? Is this really the kind of guy Mrdok is, the guy you're working for? I'm going to sue the shit—

–Do you mind if I put you on hold, Bev? I have a call coming in from Hong Kong, it's quite important—

–The fuck you do. I'm going to sue the living shit out of him, do you hear me?

–I'm afraid that won't work, Bev.

–What do you mean, it won't work? He threw my shit, my personal property, out.

–Do you even know who it is you've been cohorting with for the past six months?

–It's been nearly eight months, Gordo.

–And who are you? Aha. Why, he has access to all the top legal expertise in the world. And what have you got?

–Gordo—

–And, I mean, legally speaking? Why I don't believe you even have a, uh, what is the crude expression? A pot to piss in?

–I am going to sue the living shit out of both of you.

–Do that, Bev. In the meantime—

–Put Mrdok on the phone right this instant.

–He's not even here, Bev. He's in Sagosia at this instant—

–Well where the hell is that? Somewhere in Long Island?

–Hahahahaha, you're hilarious. I can almost see now what Mrdok might have once seen in you. At least as a minor source of diversion in his, well, quite adventurous life…

–You shut the fuck up you little fruitcake. I'm going to—Is Sagosia the island he just bought?

–I mean, *somewhere in Long Island?* Classic. Hey Marcia, get this…

–You're making fun of me? I'll show you, you son of a bitch. You tell him—

Click.

Fuck.

She opens the door, starts to go back inside. Jake immediately rises from his desk and intercepts her before she gets to the elevators.

–It's not going to help you any if I wind up having to call the police here, Bev.

–When was it? When did they clean out the apartment?

Jake sighs. More exhaustion than exasperation. Honestly, he couldn't give less of a fuck.

Tears help. At first, he wouldn't even consider, but finally, when she genuinely couldn't stop crying, he agreed to let her in the back lot where the garbage was stored. He told her fifteen minutes, more just to say something; he wasn't going to hold a stopwatch. Mostly he didn't want to watch her go through it. He certainly didn't want to get dragged into it. He barely got paid enough as it is.

Even the furniture, brand new and most of it of luxury standard, had been stacked in a single narrow row culminating in the twin columns of dumpsters. What's most repugnant is how neat the arrangement looks. She can just picture Gordo directing the proceedings—it had his icy anal touch.

The dumpster, too, was some luxury specimen, the likes of which she hasn't before seen. It even had a door you could unlock with one of those round keys. Bev looked at Jake. He shrugged his shoulders and unhooked the keychain from his belt.

Inside, a series of tall plastic bags had been stacked neat.

–Get something sharp to open these with, Bev commanded, not in the mood now to feign friendly.

Jake came back with a boxcutter.

–Fifteen minutes, he repeated, then disappeared back into the building.

No illusion of plenty. There were actually only four bags. Very large ones, but still: just four. Bev hadn't lived there long enough to accumulate much. She'd recover what she could, whatever was important or valuable, and leave the rest to rot and shame.

The first bag she tried was organics. Old flowers he had given her when she moved in, alive and well just a week ago, now moldy and wilted thanks to this careless dank act of vengeful suffocation. They rotted upon some food containers tossed willy-nilly from the fridge and cupboards, jars of caviar and fine imported jams. She could tell Gordo had directed all this from a disinterested distance, or else surely he would have taken some if not all of these for himself. And as for the containers—obviously, no one in Mrdok's employ cared one wit about recycling.

Nothing there worth holding on to. The second bag a stack of papers and assorted flat objects, on top of which sat a photo of her bent backward. Like the person had begun to rip it in half, then changed their mind before completing the process. She looked at her likeness in a short floral dress and sun hat standing in front of a bistro in Soho where they'd rendezvous from time to time in the first couple months. Back then they'd been on fire. Those moments you always delude yourself into believing will last forever. She looked at herself and she felt discarded. It was the worst feeling ever, and so winded by it she was, she couldn't even bring herself to cry. She tried to smooth the bend out, then gave up, folded it back, and stashed it in her bag. At least her likeness wasn't going to the city dump.

Another bag just makeup and toiletries. She rescued three containers of her favorite shade of nail polish, some of the more expensive makeup, but left most of it. The final bag was all clothes, and it was here she was glad she'd brought the Fendi bag today, since it was big enough to hold a lot of them.

Then she goes back to the bag with all the papers. She lifts up a stack. Most of it is garbage, manuals for the refrigerator and TV, all the electronics he'd bought for the apartment. At the bottom, a white cardboard box. She wiggles it out from under the stack, all the other papers on top fly out of the plastic bag and coalesce on the floor of the dumpster around her. She opens the box to find a pile of shredded papers. She closes the box, without thinking, stuffs it in the Fendi bag. She doesn't bother shutting the dumpster door behind her.

She moves down the avenue in a state of post-stun. Bag hanging limply off her shoulder, wind dallying the hairs sprouting round her face in a half-circle from the Yankees cap she'd rescued from the clothes bag. Where to go. There's a coffee shop on the corner. She used to go in there every morning when she lived here—fuck, *when she lived here*—now she no longer does. In a short time, Rachel, the girl behind the counter, got to know her name and what she drank. Green chai latte this morning? she'd say at the sight of Bev's face. Never just *the usual?* Always the full drink name—no abbreviations necessary. That's how Bev knew Rachel wasn't from New York. She was a transplant. She was, in some sense, an outsider. And so was Bev, in her uncertain ways.

She goes inside. Rachel's not working. The wrong hour. She takes a seat without ordering anything. It's too busy now, she doesn't feel like standing in line. She just needs to rest. All her stuff. She goes through a mental inventory, tries to remember if she's forgotten anything back there. It's not like her perusal had been all that exhaustive. It occurs to her this is totally something Mrdok would do. Why should she be surprised? They had had fights, she had heard him on the phone with others, she knew how fierce and vulgar and everything else he could be. Just never toward her. Or at least never this, well, extreme.

To be well and truly left with nothing. The ultimate fuck. She's twenty-three and has to go back to Staten Island, live with her mom. This can't be happening. There has to be another way. She opens up her bag, looks at the box. She opens it. All these shredded papers, confetti. What is it all. She starts to pick out the pieces and put the puzzle together, now searching for any answer.

CHAPTER FIVE

THIRTY-FIVE THOUSAND FEET

—YOU KNOW WE aren't that much different, me and you.

–How much you pay for this plane?

–Well. I'm not gonna lie. It cost me a pretty penny.

–See. That's one way we different. I wouldna paid.

–How's that.

–I woulda got the record company to get it for me.

–Haha well. If I'm fully honest, Lilbig. I didn't pay much of any-thing either.

–How much dat?

–Ruby, can you bring Lilbig another glass of champagne? Thanks, doll.

–What we goin to Crete for?

–Well, we both needed to get out of the country at this particular moment, though for different reasons. Crete was just convenient for me. I have a son in rehab there.

–Why you send him all the way over there?

–Don't ask. It was his mother's decision.

Lilbig looks out the window. Cloud formations stare back at him.

–You know, I used to listen to a lot of hip-hop back when I was younger, Mrdok now offers. I was a big fan of the Wu Tang Clan. The Ol' Dirty Bastard. That's some dope shit, yo.

Lilbig ignores him, continues staring. He takes a cigar from his inner jacket pocket.

–You mind if I smoke this up in here?

–Go right ahead. You need a light?

–Lilbig flips open his Zippo.

–You got one of those for me?

He stares at Mrdok through his shades. Then he removes another from the same inner pocket. Mrdok lights his, then requests a refill of his bourbon on the rocks.

–So is it true? Mrdok suddenly asks.

–What?

–The girl. That she's your sister.

Lilbig sucks his cigar pensively.

–I mean, not that I really care. I was just curious. The fact that she's fourteen doesn't bother me too much. I mean, old enough to bleed, old enough to breed. Fourteen year old piece of ass splayed itself in my lap, I'm not sure I'd have the wherewithal to turn it away. But if it was my sister? I don't know, dude. I might have to give that one some more thought. I mean, of course I've fantasized. But that's because I never had a sister.

–It was you, wuddnt it.

–Excuse me?

–You know what the fuck it is I sayin.

–Was it me who filmed you? Was it me who—

–You da one who got the file. You da one who took it to the media.

–Oh, dude, come on. What are you talkin about?

–This some kinda blackmail thing you got goin? What is it you want, motherfucker? You got me here on this plane. You think I'm helpless and shit. I aint helpless. My muthafucka Fang back there. You see that muthafucka? All I hafta do is signal with my hand like this, put two motherfuckin fingers up in the air, he come right up here and toss yo ass right outta da plane.

–I find this hardly necessary. Hardly becoming of a gentleman like yourself. We each have our security detail here, okay? Do we really wanna watch them duke it out? Have a dick measuring contest? Cos, well… Okay, bad metaphor. I probably wouldn't win against a Black guy.

–That's some racist shit right there.

–What? It's a compliment, dude. I'm saying your cock is most likely bigger than mine. In fact, having seen that video—

–So it was you.

The airplane was meant as a thing. To both dilate his interests and sublate his pretenses. It was a setting. Its vehicular use was secondary. People don't own things to get to places anymore. That's a relic of bygone days. When going somewhere meant something. The past a place he rarely gives much thought to—but definitely a *place* for Mrdok. Not a *time*. A plane to show off to your rich friends.

Bullshit. Time in its constancy, he has needed this: for all of it, his entire journey, has been about extension. For none of these things separate from himself. The plane is Mrdok, the house in Miami is Mrdok, the house on Shelter Island, the tower in Midtown, the tower in the financial district, all the towers and homes and houses he has bought and forgotten about. The gadgets and devices Gordo keeps clean for him. None of them separate, but pieces of his soul extending into the stratosphere, into space. And now. Fat turkey on the fringe. With the plane comes a piece of sky. Restive votive warriors scream, the by-and-by. Clinking glasses at thirty-five thousand while a world he has left behind sleeps in permanency. Until, then, it awakens and takes cognizance of his absence. Then a new world will begin. But until then. The sky is his, and no other's.

—I just wanna playback what you're sayin right here. Cos it don't make no sense, my friend. If I were trying to blackmail you, don't you think I would've *kept* the video, rather than releasing it into the wild?

In the sky, the druglessness of time chases after you. The rapper stands up and stretches his arms, ignoring all that Mrdok has said. He looks around—Ruby the cocktail waitress in the corner, Gordo seated behind.

—You got a bafroom on this thang?

—Yeah, says Mrdok. At the front. You know what? We got two bedrooms, too. Mine's the master suite. But we also got a guest room, if you want to lay down.

—Lie down, says Lil Bigfoot.

—Pardon?

—It's lie down. Aint no *lay down* in the English language.

—I'll take note of that.

Lilbig disappears into the back of the plane. Gordo moves up into his vacated seat.

—Perhaps we should—

—Shut up, Gordo.

CHAPTER SIX

CRETE

1.

GIRL IN THE corner is here for coke. He thinks. Four main groups: the cokeheads, the alkies, the junkies, the everythings. Isn't anyone here for meth. Bobby supposes it's because meth heads can't afford a place like this. On a Greek island. Most of them European. Maybe meth isn't such a big thing in Europe. They have other problems here. Bobby can't pretend to understand the economics of it. Right now he's just tired of being who he is. He's in that phase.

Girl in another corner with the fragmented world view. Been shattered into shards by all the substances she's done. Italian, he's heard. But she's seen everything. Now she's been put here to glue the pieces together. See if they make a reality that coheres. Bobby somehow doubts it. Once a certain amount of damage. Well, completion takes its toll.

Dad's supposed to come visit today. Bobby doesn't know what to believe. The good thing is they don't make you do *duties* here. Chores. He's been to some rehabs where they make you. It's degrading. Like, the degradation is part of the process of getting sober. This is more of a Club Med scene. And if that's what it takes to get Bobby off the island, Krstal's only glad to comply. Bitch mother of the ages. Won't be seeing her happy ass here.

Bobby looks at the clock. Nearly 3 p.m. Lifts himself off the chair, makes his way down the hall through the voices achatter in foreign languages to the group therapy spectacle. Then down to the shore, the day's detritus washing up. Maybe a swim. A nap beneath the sun. Or just back to his room. Okay, being sober sucks. And now, the reality dawns: and so he announces it, for the benefit of those here for the first time. The truth is the cravings are really never going to subside. Not when junk was your poison. The euphoria leaves a permanent stain; a body memory. While you might train your mind to overcome it, the problem is the body never forgets how it once felt; how it's capable of feeling. Whenever the going gets bad, the body is gonna yearn for that comfort—for that feeling it knows is out there, somewhere. But we can't. We're stuck with that stain. And it can never be removed. Now. What to do with that.

And they look at him with an expression that borders on glow. It's the first time he's ever spoken in group. And what he says makes so much sense, some even begin to cry. And he wonders. Has he, like, found his calling or something. No. He still doesn't know where he will go next. But he has a voice. And it's a little stronger than it was maybe five minutes ago.

2.

THEY SIT AT an outdoor café beneath the lighthouse, watching the boats bounce around Chania harbor.

–So you've never been to Greece before?

–Naw. Yeah. We wuz in Athens once. When I wuz on tour.

–How did it go?

–What?

–The concert.

Lilbig smacks his lips.

–Man I don't know. You expect me to remember that shit?

The country is in the midst of a recession. In reaction to austerity measures, a clandestine group of anarchists had been blowing up ATM machines across the country—mainly in Athens, though the actions had recently spread to Crete. Another, competing legion embraced nationalism, calling for the expulsion of all foreigners—and, in particular, the dark-skinned ones. Mrdok and Lilbig's security detail had been beefed up accordingly—upon landing, they had been greeted by a fleet of gentlemen in white suits who now stood silent surrounding them as they sipped coffee.

–How many shows do you do a year?

–I don't know. Like two hundred. What is this, a bidnis meetin? A interview? You fixin to become my new manager?

Mrdok sips his coffee, stares out at the bay.

–Look, I don't want to make this awkward for you—

Damn cracker got some nerve, drawin out the hard sell n shit. Aint got but a wink o sleep on that damn plane, stressin on my phone the entire time. Fuckshit, yo, the press in the US be destroyin my Black ass, now it's in Britain too. Damn label aint said nothin, just waitin to get the call. Now this muthafucka over here be playin the best friend game n shit. Shit, he aint no honorary nigga. He aint even jew. He probably the one who damn fucked my shit up to begin wit. Course cant get no straight answer bout dat from his cracker ass.

–She aint even my real sister, man.

–Wait… She's not?

–Man… She's my sister from another mister.

–Yeah. But, I mean. Lilbig, man. That doesn't change it. You both still came out of the same vagina. Am I right?

–Man, you don't know what the hell you talkin bout.

–I don't? Okay.

Across the plaza, seated at another table, Gordo sits in awkward silence with Lilbig's bodyguard.

–So, says Gordo after a while, how did you get the name Big Fang?

Fang sits there like a rock. Nary a budge of recognition from behind those black shades.

–I must admit, I find it quite intriguing a moniker. Especially as, well… Your teeth appeared to me rather modest, I mean the brief glimpse of them I was afforded on the plane, when you were sampling the caviar… Did you find the meal sufficient, by the way? You're free to order anything you want from the menu. I mean, it's on us. I see here they have giouvetsi, probably my favorite Greek dish. Have you tried it before? Oh, it's simply divine. A bit high on the carbs, if you're following one of those diets that have become so trendy of late—it might not pass! But, well… I don't know about you, but whenever I travel, whether it's for work or vacation, I tend to let the diet go to bay. After all, who can resist that rarest of opportunities to sample new delicacies. I mean, certainly in New York, where I live—well, lived until recently, you might say—of course New York is known for its myriad, for its *smorgasbord* of international cuisines—why, you know New York, I'm sure… I'm sure Miami is even the same way. You can have a meal from a different country every night of the week for months on end! Well, okay, perhaps that is a *slight* exaggeration. But you know what I mean… Giouvetsi, anyway, is made with orzo pasta. Do you know it? It's a Greek specialty. A sort of halfway between rice and pasta. What they do with it is really marvelous… I mean, giouvetsi can be made with all sorts of meats, but here, I believe they do it with beef... Shredded pieces of beef, and then the orzo, and a tomato-based sauce that is a bit different from the Italian blend, coming as it does mixed with an array of spices that would be considered slightly exotic to an Italian palate, they add allspice (which, funnily enough, does not originate in Greece or even in the Mediterranean, but is native to the Caribbean, of all places... It must have ended up here as a result of the spice trade many centuries back...), sometimes even cloves and cinnamon and bay leaves... With, I suspect, a dash of red wine. Well, it's one of those things. I suspect each Greek mother has her own version of the recipe! Just talking about it makes me feel famished all of a sudden... Shall I order one for you, as well? Just that... You don't seem like much of a talker, I wouldn't want for you to go hungry... How long have you know the Little Big Foot anyway? I hope I'm saying his name right... I don't know much about rap, I must be honest. But I was a big fan of poetry when I was in college, read quite a lot of it. And from what I understand, rap is really part of the poetic tradition. Well, one can say that it expands or extends that tradition into the present day. Greatly enriches it, that much must be said... So, do you perform raps as well? Or is bodyguarding your sole art form? Hahahahaha... Well, it *could* be considered an art form. Just as what I do, well, it might as well! Not to unduly flatter ourselves, of course. But, coming as we do to the assistance of great men, we also should refrain from denigrating ourselves as mere servants... Wouldn't you agree?

At the other table, Lilbig and Mrdok have switched from espresso to ouzo.

–I mean, were you close with your sister? Sorry, maybe that's a bad way of putting it, considering the evidence...

–Half-sister, man. Stepsister. Man, why can't you shut the fuck up? You have no idea what it's like in the hood.

–So what? You were fucking her back then, too?

–Man, we barely knowed each other, aight? She comed up with another family. A whole other state. She was in Georgia, I was up in Chicago, then down in Miami. Two different whirls, man. Two different whirls. I barely knowed who she was when she came down. And I aint never grown up with a sister. I had a whole other idea what bitches was back then.

–Uh huh. I'll keep pretending I understand for as long as you wanna talk about this, man.

–So what you wanna talk about den? Man, what the hell we doin here anyway?

–I want to talk about solutions.

–Solutions.

–Yeah. Positive fixes to your, ah, situation.

–My situation?

–Yeah. You know. Like, how we might fix it. Together.

–How we gonna fix my situation?

–Yeah.

Lilbig lets out an audible smirk.

–What's in it for you? Man, I don't even know you.

–But you do. You know Rick. You know my lawyer, Marty.

–You got Marty?

–Yeah. Marty's done a lot for me. We're part of the same club, man.

–Da club?

–You know. The club.

–No. I don't. Man, what the hell you talkin bout?

–The club. The global elite. The ones who rule the culture. I know how much you're worth, man. You know how much I'm worth. We don't need to play around here. We don't have any secrets. We might look different. We might talk different. But deep down, there are some fundamental truths about who we are. Truths that unite us.

–You're makin my ears bleed, dawg.

–We both… rose up, in a sense.

There he go. Trynta front like he some common ground muthafucka. Like he know anything bout the game. Where I be and where he be, it's like two difrent planets cross from this here tiny ass table.

It's like the white kids who be listenin to my shit. Be paintin pictures for em so they get to thinkin they can understand what shit's really like. But what you can see you can't be. These muthafuckas can't see the limits. Or else they be refusin to see that those limits exist, what they is. Robs em of curiosity, once they think they knows somethin. Like it's my job to tell them what dat is.

–See, that's where you be trippin. You aint rose up from shit, I tell him. You think I don't know this? Yo rich ass daddy introduced you to that mafia lawyer who brought you up like he was yo daddy. Done taught you everything he knowed. I mighta been slingin dope in da hood. You was slingin somethin much worse, landin in the very same hood. Only you wasn't actually there. You didn't hafta see the repercussions of all that shit like I did. Live through it. Mamas losin theys babys. Peoples losin theys houses. Damn crackheads sellin theys asses so's to get mo crack and pay off yo crazy ass loans so they could get more loans to buy mo crack wit. You aint seen none o dat. But yous caused it. I was slingin dope, you was slingin hope. We both know that much is true. And what now. Now you up and trynta wreck anothuh nigga's life. Like you aint had enuf fun the first time. Wats up wit dat, jack? You jealous cos a Black ass muthafucka gotz more than you? Cos I earned it offa gift you aint never had, never will? You sad ass muthafucka.

—You keep calling me that. Motherfucker.

—Cos you got a face only a mother could fuck.

—I guess I could say the same about yours and a sister. A sister from another mister, was it. You even know the mister? Your own, for that matter?

—Naw. I don't come from a world of fathers.

—I come from a world of too many.

—See. That's how we difrent. Other planets.

—Maybe not that distant. We're at least from the same constellation. Different paths, maybe. But the same world, nonetheless. But hey. Speaking of the world. Well, I mean… Here we are. Funny, isn't it?

—Hard for me to laff at anyfing right about now.

—I've got you. But look, my man. I want to lay something on you.

—Yeah. What.

—I've been working on this project and I think there could be, well, advantages for both of us if you were to come in on it.

—This my escape route or some shit? What kind of projeck you talkin bout.

—See, there's this island.

—Here we go. Aint we on a island right now.

—Yeah. No. Not this one. A different one. It's called Sagosia.

—Sagosia. Where it at.

—The Brown Sea.

—Sounds far.

—It is. Well, not that far.

—So what you wanna do.

—Well. This island. I own it.

—Shit. It's all yours?

—Yeah. I just… acquired it.

—Yeah. I heard about shit like that. Brad Pitt, he got his own island. Jeff Epstein. Johnny Depp, too.

—A lot of celebrities and important people are doing it. Richard Branson. Marlon Brando had one, going way back. And, well. Now I do. But here's the thing…

—Wait: Marlon Brando had him a island?

—Yeah.

—That motherfucker was a bad ass. *The Godfather,* man. Dat's some shit right there.

—I agree. A great film.

Waning sunlight cascading off the water. Two fishermen unloading their silvery catch from a small motorboat on to the shore. A couple of tourists stop in front of their boat to take pictures.

—So what we want to do is transform the place. So it's not going to be, like, *my* island. Well. I mean. It is and it isn't, if you follow my drift...

—No.

—Well. What we're looking to do is build something entirely new that's never been done before. And we need pioneers. I'm talking more than just an island. I'm talking a new nation. A country. A place where... where people like us can start over. Get a fresh start. But still be part of the world out there. Only not proxy to its... well, to its less favorable conditions.

—When you say a country. You mean wit like passports and shit?

—Yeah. The whole nine yards. You married?

—Naw.

—Oh, I guess that sounds a bit right. I mean, what with the video and everything. That would be pretty bad news.

—Man, leave that shit, dawg.

—I'm leaving it. I'm, like I said. A chance to start over.

I'm startin to see where crackerface be goin wit this shit. That means I wouldn't never have to face no trial, no jail cell. No jew lawyers neither. Were I to be a citizen of another country. With no extradition to the US.

—So whut the hell's in it for you? Havin my Black ass be a part of this.

—Well. I would make you a senator, of course. Like all the senators, I mean... We're gonna be the makers of a world. So, you have to put a little something in in order to make this world the way you want it to be, if you get my drift... We're gonna be worldmakers.

Lilbig lookin out to sea.

—Man, I can't never go back there now, can I?

Mrdok shakes his head.

—No. You can't. I mean, her being your sister, that's one thing. Half-sister. Sorry. But, I mean... Fourteen years old, man. I think that's the main problem.

—What this island like?

–It's like… paradise. In a word. That's how I'd describe it.

–They got girls there, man?

–Oh yeah. And you can import anyone you want to bring in. As one of the founding senators, you have a right to give anyone you want a passport. Build a house. Build yourself a studio. Fuck, you can have it all, man. And be immune to prosecution. And extradition.

–Well. It's somethin to think about.

–You do all the thinking you need, my friend.

Lilbig looks at him. Curls inside at that *friend,* though. Tourists have gone away, Lilbig unnoticed. Now the fishermen are waddling toward the shore with their catch all wrapped up in giant sacks they have divided among their backs.

–Hey. You gonna go see my son with me?

–I don't know, man. I was thinkin of chillin, maybe hittin the beach.

–You've got beach in Miami. Come see my son with me. He'll be impressed. Me coming in with a big hip-hop star.

–I don't like hospitals, dawg.

–This isn't a hospital. It's a fancy rehab joint. You know. A Club Med scene. His mother, my ex-wife, she put him in there.

–Okay. I'll go. If it aint gonna take too long.

–Okay. Good.

They look out at the water some more. Waiter comes, pours some mineral water into their glasses.

–Just one last question, and then I swear I'll shut up about it.

–Go head.

–If you're gonna go do something like that; why film it?

3.

HE'S SWINGING FROM a rope over the ocean. Never felt more almost-alive than this before. Reality-at-large here. What could be better than opportunity regained, a chance to recalibrate?

Splash.

He's been sober—what—fifteen days now? He's supposed to keep count, but just at this moment, well—he's blanking on the number. Heroin does things to the memory. Even afterward—there are these patches of blankness you'll arrive at and are forced to traverse. He feels good about the fact that he's done this before, so he knows not to panic at these mental glitches. Knows that they are short-lasting. Proud of himself for surviving the detox. Proud for refusing (with Doctor Andrianakis's support) to go on Buprenorphine, which every junkie knows is not only a bit like cheating, but is actually far harder to get off than heroin itself. It's a par-for-the-course kind of treatment for junkies like him who have been in and out of rehab countless times, but uh-uh, he aint gonna do it. Cold turkey all the way, and he's already out of the most hellish part. Sure, he still has little energy, but even that's coming back.

He climbs out of the water, back on to the deck in line for the rope swing. Natural high. Drugs—who needs them? Losers—that's who. There is no such thing as a beautiful face on drugs. There is only nature, sweet nature, that can be of any rescue. Be of any rescue? What's he saying? He doesn't know. But he feels it. Feels something. For the first time in a long time. And now it's his turn to swing. To get that adrenaline rush going again—which is kind of almost better than getting high. Sort of.

—This is sheet-uh. Bullsheet-uh.

He hears the voice before he can locate the body it belongs to. Smells the cigarette smoke—a big violation of the rules. Finally, turns around. It's the weird girl from the cafeteria. Always sits alone, scowling at everyone. Now, in the sunlight, sees her in a different way. She's actually beautiful, gorgeous.

–Bullsheet-uh.

That raspy Latinate voice. What is that accent? He can't place it.

–Fucking sheet-uh.

He goes over to her.

–How long have you been here anyway?

She looks up at him. Skeptically, it seems, but it could also be because she has to squint and put her hand over her eyes to block out the sun.

–Seven days-uh. Thees sheet-uh. I tell them I want to leave, I had e-nuff-uh, they don't let me out of this hell hole.

–Yeah, he says. It's shit alright. I hate it. I want out too. My fucking, what is it, fifth time in one of these places? Seems like I can't get enough of them!

She looks at him. This time it's definitely skeptical.

–It was a joke, he clarifies. A weak one, I guess.

She sucks on her cigarette.

–Hey. You got another one of those?

She surrenders the pack.

–American Spirits, hey? They have these in Europe?

–I buy them imported-uh.

–Yeah? Where you from exactly?

–What do you mean, where I'm from-uh? You an idiot-uh? Everyone who hears this accent knows I come from Eetalee.

–Ah. Right. You see, I don't travel much. Never really had the time.

–Yesuh. Heroeen is full-time job-uh.

–How do you know I'm a heroin addict?

She gives him another one of those looks.

–Pleezuh. You think I am stupeed or whatuh?

–Well, I think we're all a little, uh, stupid… deep inside… Isn't that what Iggy Pop said?

Fuck. Did he just say that out loud? He waits. Now she won't even look at him. It's been a while since he's spoken to a woman at close distance. He's trying to be casual about it. Seems like it's not working. That, and not having dope in your body in the months following withdrawal does make you, well, stupid. Or if not stupid, then morose.

–So I'm guessing the sight of the Mediterranean doesn't enthrall you. If you're from Italy, you must have to look at it all the time… Well, not *have* to… But, like, do.

She lights another cigarette.

–We have the Pacific, where I'm from. The ocean. But it's not like this. Here, everything is so… Well, the water is much cleaner. Clearer… So what are you in here for? Wait… Let me guess… Uh, coke!

She looks at him. Bemused skepticism. Perhaps that's an overly polite or restrained way of putting it.

–No. Not coke-uh. Everything-uh.

–No way! I never would have taken you for one of the everythings.

Cocks his head.

–Now I can kind of see it… Well. Gotta say I admire the, uh, the *commitment* of you guys. It's like, why narrow yourself to just one thing, right?

Now he can see it. There's a wildness to her, a savage sophistication. She's so… What? Worldly? Worldly wasted? That's more like it.

–How much longer do you stay-eh?

–Where? Here?… I just got here. Well, three weeks ago. I'm booked for a six week stretch. We'll see. I'm starting to kind of like it. Maybe I'll stay longer. You?

–You just say you hate eet-uh.

–I did? Oh yeah… Well, uh, I mean, I do. But, it's, well…

–You don't-uh have a place to go-uh.

–Well. I do. There are a few places…

–But-eh no place-uh you *want*-eh to go-uh.

–No.

–You-eh have no one out there. No one is waiting for you-ah. Because you were alone-eh for too long time-uh. Shooting up alone in a room-uh, or maybe a house-eh. Yes, if you are here, eet was a house-eh. Maybe not a beeg house, but a house-eh. All alone, a pathetic leetle junkie. Chasing that nice feeling you get-eh when you steeck a needle in your arm-eh. Until you don't feel it no more. The feeling has gone away-uh. How you get it back-uh? You take more and more, nothing helps-uh. Maybe you O.D.-uh. You die a few times-uh. So what-uh? You might-uh come close, in your dying, but even ees not enough-uh. Your dealer, maybe. You stink of sweat and ceegarettes-eh, steel no one's there. What's worse is you never heet rock bottom-uh. Like everyone else-h. No rock bottom stories in theese rehab-eh. Every floor has a velvet surface. Whether eets your papa or your mama, someone is sending a check-uh every month-uh, supporting your habit-uh. You're an aristocratic junkie. You stay that way till you die-uh. Safe from care. Safe from worry. Your own. But also other people's-uh.

    –Wow. You seem to know a lot for a, uh… non-junkie.

    –I'm an everything-eh.

    –Right.

    –That means everything was my problem-uh. Not just drugs. Life. And I've been through my own eroween phase-uh. I know how eet goes-uh.

    –Sure.

    –Eroween. Cocaine-uh. Kaytameen-uh. Kreestal.

    –That's my mom's name.

    –… What?

    –Nothing.

She snorts through her damaged nostrils.

    –You know what ees the worst-uh?

    –No. What.

    –Thees. Right here. The boredom-eh. If we aren't high, what ees there to do-uh. Nothing. Niente.

    –Well. You can go ziplining over the water there. I was just at it. It's pretty fun.

She scowls at Bobby like he's pathetic for even suggesting it. Maybe he is. He's seriously all over the place recently. Mood bobbing up and down. His heart racing the more he talks to this girl, uncool though she makes him feel. Used to be, in the old days, the opposite: the longer they talked, the more confident he grew. But her. She's threatening to mow him down by the sheer force of her presence. A magic thing.

He asks her name.

—Coco. I like it. Like, uh, Coco Chanel, right? The fashion designer? I'm Bobby. Like Bobby Gillespie. My father's, he's a… he's a big Brit pop fan.

She says nothing to that.

—Say. Can I get another one of those cigarettes?

This is what it feels like to be on the other side of civilization. The morning dryness, nestled in a towel. Crete, where our great civilization began! With the rape of a goddess by a bull, being pulled out into the sea, the never-to-be-seen. Europa Europa, I am calling out to you; can you hear my wails?

As we arrive at the rehabilitation resort, the young clerkess behind the counter is snacking on her breakfast muesli. Being institutionalized must be fun, I flippantly elect to believe. Oh, a state of whimsy I have arrived in. Don't ask me why—the sun often does this to me. Perhaps it has something to do with the diabetes, my blood sugar. I'm not quite sure. I walk straight to the desk, as though I myself were Mrdok, I don't know why, but the words come right out of me: *I'm here to see my son.*

As though there were a son for me to have!

Mrdok looks at me, then pushes me out of the way.

—Fuck off, Gordo. *I'm* here to see *my* son.

The clerkess looks at us confused.

—So I don't understand. Which of you is here to see your son?

—Dey both is, says Lilbig, now stepping forward. And if you gotz a problem wit dat…

—Oh my effin fuck. Are you… Could it… You're… I mean, I don't mean to be racist… But you happen to look *a lot* like my favorite hip-hop artist.

—That's because he *is* your favorite hip-hop artist. And mine, too. This is Lilbig, the man himself.

—You want a autograf or sumfin?

—I was just listening to you this morning! *Spiced rum on ice / I don't eat no rice / Just turkey-fried turkey / with a bitch who got lice.*

—What is that, ebonics or something.

—Yo. That's some racist ass shit right there.

–It aint racist. It's the truth.

–Same thing.

–Wait. You're Greek. What the fuck do you know?

–Yeah.

He hates to say it, but Mrdok's right in this case. Or, if not right, then at least American.

–So what? Are we going to sit here all day and discuss this? I'm here to see my son. Robert Mrdok. I have an appointment.

–Oh. Right. You see this corridor here? It leads out back to the pool. Go past the swimming pool, down the staircase, through the botanical garden, the center pathway... It leads to a small white house, you know, Greek style. That is his lodging. He should be in there. If he's not, come back to the desk, I'll page him for you.

–Great. You've been most helpful. In a certain, abstract sense.

–Greek hospitality. It's what we're known for.

––Bobby. So good to see you. How long has it been? Your teeth look fine, by the way.

–Yeah. That's because mom paid for them in the end.

–She paid the rehab *and* the teeth?

–Yeah. Both.

–Well well well. That Krstal. My ex-wife. She's something. This is Lilbig, by the way. Maybe you've heard of him?

–The rapper?

–Yeah. That's me.

–No shit. Wow, dad. I guess you're a lot cooler than you used to be.

–Mrdok rolls with a rather diverse array of elites from the world over.

–Hi Gordo. Nice to see you too. So what brings you back into my life?

–Come on, Bobby. There's no need for any sarcasm here. This is a special moment. A reunion.

–... A reunion between father and son!

–Shut up, Gordo.

–How's the detox going?

–Well. Other than the fact that I'm not high right now, I'd say it's going okay.

–That's good to hear. One day at a time! Isn't that what they say?

–How the hell would you know? Who's the tough guy, anyway?

–Thass my bodyguard. He don't talk.

–How about a walk through the garden? Show us the place a little.

–How about I don't have much time? I have a meeting at seven o'clock. They don't like for us to be late.

–Skip the meeting. We'll go out for dinner!

–I'm not supposed to leave.

–You're not? You're paying for it, aint you? How come they get to make the rules?

–It's called rehab, dad. You pay them to make the rules for you. Maybe you should try it sometime.

–Watch it.

A rooster crows at the sun going down.

–They got roosters in Greece?

–I got a cock for ya right here…

–They're ours. We have our own organic sustainable farm at the center. We eat their eggs every morning.

–That would be hens, not roosters.

–Shut up, Gordo.

–Bet you get a lot of ass in here. Joints like this.

–Don't be disgusting.

–All that rehab pussy. Man. There's nothin like it.

–What does Lilbig think about rehab pussy?

–Any pussy is dope pussy yo.

–Yeah. Even your own sister's, from what I've heard.

–How he know? They got news up in here? Shit. Guess you aint so cut off from da whirl after all.

–She's not his sister, by the way. Half-sister. Stepsister.

–Whatever, man. It's fuckin gross.

–For your information, Bobby, my ungrateful little son. There's much bigger news going on in the world right now than that. News that also concerns Lilbig, even. Lilbig and me both, if I'm precise.

–What is that? Are you two fucking now as well?

–Very funny. We're not fuckin each other. But it looks like we're gonna be fuckin the world. Aint that right, my brother?

–I aint yo brutha, cracker.

–Or, rather: remaking the world. According to our own vision of it.

–Well. I'd hate to see that. What the fuck are you gonna do now, dad? Start a nuclear war with North Korea?

–Disruption. That's the way we do things in bidnis now. Hell, that's how they do it in the rap game, too. Aint that right, my brother?

–I'm gonna have Fang over here put a cap in yo ass if you call me that shit one mo time.

–Jesus, can someone shut that rooster up? It's getting on my nerves now.

–Why don't you just leave, then, dad.

–Not until we finish sharing this news with you.

–I don't want to hear your news. You can't even pay for me to get my motherfucking teeth fixed, now you march in here and want to pretend like you're my father again? After, what, fifteen years? How long has it been anyway? Heroin fucks with your memory.

–You need to shut yo ass up and listen, motherfucka. You wanna hear somethin? You lucky you is where you is today, and that yo damn father came to see yo sorry junkie ass. You aint seen yo father in fifteen years? Well guess what? I aint seen my daddy never. I don't even know who the hell he is.

–Great. A sob story. Maybe you should check in here, actually. This place is full of em. I have to listen to them every goddamn day. And you know what? I even tell a few myself.

–Okay, so what the hell do you want, kid? Is it an apology? Money? Some combination of the two? Cos let me tell you something. I've been giving you money for years now, Bobby. And every time I give you the money, well, what do you do with it? I don't know for sure. But I've got a pretty good idea. Because the next week, I get another phone call with you wantin even *more* money. And, for those of you who don't know me and might think any of this makes me a bad father, let me stipulate that this is *in addition to* the monthly amount he already gets from his trust fund.

–Shit.

–And lest anyone doubt these assertions, I have documentation here on my iPad to back it all up. A file containing a complete history of Mrdok's financial transactions with Bobby—

–Enough, Gordo. We get the point. And so what? You want me to feel guilty? You want me to apologize for having a rich father? You don't get to choose how you get born. That's something Lilbig can understand, I'm sure. If somebody here is gonna apologize, why don't you just apologize for being a bad parent? Cos that is something you *can* choose.

–Lil homie's got a point, yo.

–Bobby. You're not listening to me. You haven't even given me a chance to speak what I came here for. I'm not interested in dwelling on the past, okay? If you want to do that, then that's your business. I'm here to talk about the future. Your future, Bobby. Our future.

–There is no us. There never has been.
–Well, there is now. Potentially. If you want there to be.
Bobby looks at Gordo.
–What's he talking about?
–I'm talking about an island, Bobby.
–An island?
–More than an island. A new nation. An expansion of my empire into, well… the seas. Infinite. The land of dreams. Paradise. A place on earth that people dream about, but not many people realize actually exists. Well. That place is mine now. And, well, Lilbig here. He's a senator.

This ignites a spit-fueled laughter bomb.

–Wait, what are we talkin here? Did you finally buy that place in Hawaii you were always talking about?

–Son, that was years ago. Bought and sold. I know it's been a long time since we've really talked. But no. This place, this little island, it's in the Brown Sea. Sagosia, it's called.

–Sagosia? Doesn't that belong to Great Britain?

–Very… Well, almost true, almost good… How did you know that, by the way? Most people don't.

–I'm a mapgazer. Remember? I got it from you. One of the few things.

–Right. So…

–So the Brits are just gonna *sell* you part of their territory?

–It's more complicated than that, Bobby. Why don't you let me worry about the economics? What I'm asking is if you wanna join me. Join us. I mean… What I'm trying to say is, I'm offering you a new home. For when you get out of this joint.

–On Sagosia.

–Well. It's not gonna be called Sagosia anymore. But that's not the point…

–So what am I gonna do there? Are you saying… Are you saying you want me to be part of the business?

–Well. Let's not get ahead of ourselves here. You know how I like to work. Organically. Let things happen on their own. What I'm saying is… A fresh start, Bobby. Not just for you. For both of us. And for you and I together. As father and son.

–Son of a bitch.

–Is that any way to talk to your father?

–You act as though he were an actual human being.

–Bobby… Where is this coming from?

–Hmm, I don't know. Maybe the same place where you learned how to care? Place where the stars don't burn too bright, and neither do the bulbs.

–Bobby—

–I'm thinking about it, okay? I'm going to think about it and get back to you. Now. I have a meeting to go to.

–Can I just say one last thing?

–No.

–I know there's nothing easy about getting sober. Believe me, it's something I would never want to do…

–Your time's up, dad.

–Settlers Landing is gonna be, among very many other things, a dope-free isle. Okay? That means, even if you wanted to get high there, there'd be no way for it to happen.

–You sure talk pretty for a guy with no real class.

–What the hell's that supposed to mean?

–It means I know the talk, dad. I know how you do your deals. You've been doing it your entire life. You make all sorts of promises to lure people in, then when you get what you want, you abandon them.

–Now I must interject, Bobby. That is the furthest thing from the truth. Why, have you not read Mrdok's book? Are you at all familiar with his business philosophy?

–His philosophy, if you can call it that, can be summarized as follows: *fuck fuck fuck*. That's all he does. Fucks and destroys. Then moves on to the next deal, so-called. A giant fuck machine.

–Bobby, watch your mouth—

–Lilbig, man, I don't know what you're doing here, what it is worth for you to get involved with a man like my father. What you think you're gonna get out of this. But I want you to know, no matter what kind of win-win situation he's presented to you at the outset, in the end, you're not gonna win. Not against a bastard like that.

–I quote from memory here: *A good business deal is one that benefits* both *mutual partners in equal measure…*

–Shut up, Gordo. I tell you. You're putting a noose around your neck if you're gonna do anything with this guy. Sorry, dad. (Though I'm not, really.)

–That's fine, Bobby. You know what? I still love you.

–Fuck you.

–And I still want you to come live on Settlers Landing with me when you get out of here. Well, not, like, *with* me in the same house. With me on the island, I mean.

—*Settlers Landing?* What the fuck. Are you going to give me a, a *pilgrim's hat* to wear along with it?

—A new start, Bobby. A chance to reinvent yourself. In a dope-free zone. A place where the temptations will be zero. No drugs, no lowlifes. Just sophisticated people. *Famous* people. Like Lilbig here.

—You've gone this long without me being a part of your life. No need to start changing shit up at this late date. Just keep the checks coming, okay?

—I'm telling you, Bobby. This is a chance to be a part of something larger than all of us. A chance to help me make history.

—Go get stuffed.

Bobby disappears behind an azalea bush. The four men left behind exchange glances in a complex web.

—Well. That went well.

CHAPTER SEVEN

TOKYO NIGHTS

1.

BARB'S PLANE LANDED rather late. Narita Airport is half empty this time of year. No one wants to come to Tokyo when it's this cold. Too depressing. Southern hemisphere's the place to be, if you have the luxury to choose.

The VIP line is empty. Clears customs in five minutes. Her driver is waiting in the same place as always. He bows as she approaches, takes the Chanel valise out of her hand. She follows him out to the parking lot.

In her penthouse suite, the TV comes on automatically once she slides her card into the slot. A movie's playing on the plasma screen. A Hollywood courtroom drama. A famous Black actor—she always forgets their names—not just the Black ones—all actors' names—she's too busy to learn them, to occupy herself with minutiae like that—and who has time to watch movies these days anyway? There's a world to run, stuff to do in it. He's sitting in his lawyer's office with his adult daughter, the lawyer is begging him to take a deal, says he is fucked. The man protests that he's been framed—he doesn't even *have* any offshore accounts. *Don't do anything crazy,* his daughter begs him when they get out into the hallway. *Crazy is what crazy does,* he responds menacingly. Barb determines it's not a courtroom drama, but an action movie. Or maybe a hybrid between the two.

She calls the service desk, asks them to send the butler to turn the TV off—she doesn't know how to work these complicated controllers. *A-ri-ga-to.* She showers, emerges from the bathroom wrapped in a robe, opens her valise, unfolds a blue cocktail dress. Checks the time on the bedside display. Actually only 19:18.

—Okay, queers. This song is from our new album, *Full Metal Cockring*. It's called *Gay for Pay (Without the Pay)*.

The opening act is a gay hair metal band from the Bay Area called Urethra Franklin. They're *excited to be touring Asia for the first time*, according to an interview Gordo read in the local expat rag at the hotel. Mrdok and Gordo stand out in the small crowd of some two dozen spectators not by the mere fact of their whiteness, nor so much as their warring corpulences, but by their evasion of the cyberpunk dress code. Everyone else looks like either a space alien or an anime character or has otherwise adapted a studied retro punk look à la early 1980s Comme des Garçons or late 1970s Vivienne Westwood. In their coifed respectability, they're decidedly uncool by these Tokyo standards: Mrdok in his tailored Armani evening suit clutching an unlit Cuban cigar, Gordo adorned in some grayish shawl over a colorful collaged print the lights are currently too dim to allow for discernment, whether it might be an abstract pattern or else a jumble of masculine bodies color-tinted from black-and-white photos. His taste has gotten more outlandish—or has been evaporating into a light artiness—since his coming out, Mrdok has noticed.

The band launches into their awful tirade that sounds much like the mall punk that became popularized in the waning years of the century previous among the white suburban demographic. The crowd seeming mainly indifferent to it—more there to show off their outfits than to actually listen. Or, who knows? Maybe they're just waiting for the main act. Mrdok somehow doubts it.

He steps outside to light that cigar. One of Cuba's finest. A bouncer comes and pushes him back inside. He always forgets this crazy Japanese reversal—smoking outside is verboten, inside is okay. At most places. Thank god they got the plane back. Now they just have to add Hong Kong to this little Asia jaunt before circling back to Sagosia. Taiwan next on the list. He just isn't sure when. Who knows how long this Tokyo business will take.

She starts off with a drink at the hotel bar. Not the most original choice, but it will do. It might sound odd, but Tokyo is the one place she can actually unwind, finally feel herself to be. But for someone as innately cosmopolitan as Barb, well. She's at home in the world—put it that way. It's not like there are that many places left for her to see.

Business, sure. She wouldn't come here just to be here—that would be too much. But, truth be told, now it's really almost business in air quotes. She's just *checking up* on certain things. The economy has been shit in Japan for as long as she cares to remember at this point. She's holding on to the few bits she still has here, most of which were inherited from her father, and even that's not really enough to justify her coming. Not that she damn well needs to justify anything. But... Does she really want to sell? Not really. Rascally wiles of never-knowing-where-to-be. She sits alone sipping her martini: dirty, dry. She feels clean. A man comes up to her, not that old trick again. She says something that makes him immediately turn and go away. At least she hasn't lost her looks. Or her poison tongue. Can still pull one in now and then, when she wants to—though now, it is true, she hardly ever wants to. Barb wants to be alone. Later, she'll be surrounded. She knows how that feels, too.

The club is on the third floor of some decrepit former office building in Shinjuku. He gets a similar feeling in Tokyo that he always gets in London, too—that everything is somehow rotting here. There's no upkeep. The buildings, the infrastructure—it's all kind of wearing away, and nobody seems to notice or care.

The son comes out of the elevator with his girlfriend in tow just as Mrdok's about to stub out his cigar. Stevo Rey is a nihilist and has the nose ring to prove it.

–Dad! You actually made it?

As though he's really that surprised. This had been worked out a week ago by the home office.

–Yeah. I'm here. So when does the fun start? Where's the backstage? Where's the blow and the broads?

–Uh. This experience will include none of the above.

Mrdok smiles at the girlfriend, gives her his most charming hello. From her glazed response, he quickly garners that she doesn't speak any English. And Stevo Rey can't speak much Japanese. Apparently they've found other ways to communicate.

—All right, faggots and dykes...

They're blissfully unaware that no one in the audience—save for Gordo—appears to be of that persuasion.

–... thanks for making the first stop on our Asian tour so frickin fabulous. Good night!

Three people clap as the members of Urethra Franklin leave the stage. Mrdok and son stand at the back of the room in awkward silence while Gordo and Makiko fetch drinks from the bar.

–Bobby's back in rehab.

–I wasn't even aware that he'd left the last rehab.

–His mother's paying for this one.

–Well well. She's my mom too, you know.

–How could I forget.

–Sometimes it seems you can't remember.

–Anyway, we went to visit him. I took Lilbig to meet him.

–The rapper? How do you know him?

–He's an associate. What time do you go on?

–We're the final act. The headliners.

–It's just that I got this thing…

–Of course you do. What else could've actually brought you to Tokyo.

–I never asked you to move here, did I?

–Oh. So now it's my fault I've been excluded from your life? I'm so glad I finally understand.

–Enough, Stevo. Let's just have a fun night. While we can.

–How will you stay in Tokyo?

–Not long.

–Yeah. Well. The rest of the band's here. I've gotta go get ready.

A table overflowing with distortion boxes, mixers, voltage converters, guitar pedals, tape recorders, homemade metal boxes of wire and cables spooling out on to the stage. In addition to Stevo Rey, decked out in neon cyber goth matte brilliance, the rest of the so-called band consists of one noisician standing behind the table manning the unwieldy cables and controls, a slightly overweight middle-aged specimen wearing comparatively dumpy leather jacket and sunglasses, a desultory nod to rock 'n' roll semiotics; in daylight hours, he's a salaryman wearing the same cheaply made suit that clogs the streets and malls and office towers and subways of central Tokyo before the sun makes its daily disappearance.

–This next song is going to be called *Moist Towelette*.

Stevo Rey grabs the microphone and starts screaming into it until he runs out of breath, falls into a fit of coughing, and collapses on stage. The band, so-called, launches into an ear-assaulting shitstorm of fuzzed-out cringe. The larger crowd that has now gathered into the club ignores everything happening onstage in competing degrees of fashionable detachment.

Mrdok knows a little about the Japanese noise scene. In college, one of the art students he'd lived with had introduced him to the Boredoms, the legendary band from Osaka. Mrdok didn't really get it at the time. But now, watching his son flail around the stage and publicly humiliate himself, he begins to feel like it has all reached a tremendous dead end. Sure, now much of the feedback and distortion is digitally sourced, coming out of computers rather than the guitars and analog forms of amplification of eras past. But can you really call that progress?

Mrdok applauds loudly as his son collapses one more time. To his lard ass assistant standing next to him, he can be heard to shout:

–What a moron.

But Gordo doesn't hear a thing. His stubby fingers are plugged so deeply into his ears, the noise is a mile away; there they will remain throughout the following two songs, entitled *I Got Drunk With a Baby* and *An Old Person Stole Something From Me,* disrespectively.

As an encore, Stevo Rey announces they'll be doing the title track from their new album, *You Make Me Shit Like a Natural Woman.* As they launch into the song—if you can call it that—the only words Mrdok can make out being screamed over and over again are *You make me shit like a woman and your pussy is black.* A Japanese retro punk with a pink mohawk in a leather jacket pogos to the front of the stage, screaming *Brack purshy! Brack purshy!* Gordo leans over to ask Mrdok about their exit strategy, but finds he is too late. Mrdok is already halfway out the door.

She goes to all the ritzy cocktail places within walking distance of her hotel where the other rich foreigners go. Sometimes there are also rich Japanese there, but only rarely. Tokyo is still a very divided place. Segregated. That's how they like it. And the foreigners who live here or else come to do business, they have no choice but to accept it. Many of them even come to like it, viewing it as a reprieve from the hassle they have to put up with in their daily lives. At least this one, the form it takes, is expected. Barb knows what it's like. She's here often enough. Though she'd never consider herself an expat. She always stays at the same hotel, the penthouse suite when it's available. And it usually is. So, while it's not home, per se, it certainly feels enough like it.

This one has a particularly nice view over the surrounding neon sleaze. The sleaze that is nocturnal Tokyo. She's supposed to meet her local real estate broker here, but he's late. A voice from behind startles her.

–Barb! How are your tits doing?

Mrdok and his fat friend have manifested themselves in the seats next to her, as though they had been invited to do so. Moments like these, it would be great if the foreigners who came here would actually bother to follow local customs.

—Knock it off. I'm in Tokyo all the time now. Everyone who knows me knows. And even some who don't, apparently...

—But you live in Manhattan! *I* know you, Barb. We used to be neighbors, remember?

—But I sleep on my plane. Really, my new place in Manhattan doesn't even have a bed—there's no point.

—Well, sadly, we're both so busy, I have to come halfway across the world just to see you.

—What the hell are you talking about, Mrdok? Knock it off. What are you doing, chasing me down here? How did you even know I was in town?

—Oh, I just figured. This is where everyone goes in Tokyo, isn't it? The hot bar of the moment. Or is there a new place now that I'm not aware of? I might be a little out of the loop on this pocket of the world, I admit...

—We're actually in town visiting Mrdok's son Stevo Rey, Gordo proffers.

—Oh really? Barb seems vaguely interested. What kind of name is Stevo Rey anyway?

—What kind of name is Barbra Browneye?

—It's Brunnei. You asshole.

Mrdok shrugs. Jet lag settling in. End-of-the-world feeling. Thankfully he was able to perk up with some coke he scored before leaving Greece, from one of the dealers hanging out across the main entrance of Bobby's rehab. That took care of the post-flight Valium haze.

—What can I say? The kid was born in the '90s. At one point it was gonna be Stevo Reg...

—For Reginald?

—No. Just because it sounded cool. It's... ironic. You know. An ironic name.

—Hahahaha, that's hilarious. Are you telling me Mrdok was a, what, an indie rock geek? Did you dye your hair blue and wear black-framed yellow-tinted glasses too? Ironic t-shirts? Ha! From indie rock hipster to corporate thug!

—That's corporate thug *trillionaire* to you, Barb. In case you were wondering...

—I actually wasn't. But while we're on the topic: What kind of name is Mrdok?

—Slavic.

–Slavic?

–Yeah.

–Sounds vague.

–How do you mean.

–I mean, Slavic. That could be anywhere in Eastern Europe. Not just Russia. Lots of countries.

–Slavic. Russian. Czech. I don't know.

–You don't know your own background?

–Who's interested in that shit? I'm white. That's all that matters, isn't it?

–Well, there was a time when people weren't just *white*, Mrdok. They actually came from places. Physical places. On a map.

–I like maps. But I'm not fixated on the past. I like to look to the future. I know my background aint as colorful as yours, babe. But I know enough of mine. Enough to get through life.

–Mrdok the Slav.

–What about you? You speak Greek?

–I do. I even learned ancient Greek in school.

–You can translate the oracles?

–Hmm. Maybe not. But I do know something about tragedy.

Barb gives them both the evil eye. Gordo excuses himself to go to the restroom. By the time he returns, his man has already cut to the chase.

–That's the most ridiculous thing I've ever heard. Why *an island?* Barb is saying. And, more importantly: why a country? You could have your own estate with all the land you want, as far as the eye can see, in any country in the world. Call it Mrdokland. When you're at our level, it doesn't matter what the local laws are. You can pretty much write your own. You don't have to call it a *country*. If you're lonely, just bring all your friends there to live with you. Why does it have to be a fucking *country*, for chrissake?

–You don't know anything about thinking big, Barb, he retorts. It's fine, you don't have to. With your silver spoon existence, I guess daddy did all the big thinking for you, didn't he? And grandpappy too. You're content to just sit back and watch the world get built up all around you, taking for granted who the builders are—their ambitions. Your five-star hotel existence, going from airport to airport, watching all your projects, so-called, get under way. What do you *burn* for, Barb? That's my question. Surely there must be some seaport you landed at once or twice, thought, *Hmm, maybe I could lay some tracks down here?* You know, actually *build* something from the ground up. Rather than delegating the task to your little minions.

–I think you're being a little desultory in your descriptions of me, Mrdok. I might have had a comfort or two that others didn't have when I was growing up. But you're also forgetting that I built a real estate empire *by myself*. My father didn't do that for me. I laid all the groundwork, fuck you very much. That's why it has my name on it— not my father's. Christ, why am I even arguing with you?

–Right. So your born wealth was a major impediment to your future fortune?

–I don't need your insults or condescension. I don't buy into that sort of tough guy seduction that you're used to laying on your cronies.

–Barbra. I respect women. That means I don't treat you any different than I treat the dudes I deal with.

–Maybe you need to treat everyone you deal with differently. Nobody wants to deal with an asshole, Mrdok. Funny you still haven't figured that one out on your own.

Her phone lights up on the table in front of her. She picks it up, reads the message. Real estate guy canceling, asking if they can reschedule for tomorrow night. Shit. Why hasn't she gotten around to firing this flaky bastard.

It is true, at least, that Barb came from old money. Father Japanese, though he never spoke it with her Greek mother. Ancient money, some might say. Her parents' marriage, though not arranged in the traditional sense, certainly had all the hallmarks of an imperial arrangement. And thus it is hard for her to mask her disdain for *arrivistes* like Mrdok and his diseased harem. The world they come from is not normal to her. Barb has never been one to rest on the laurels of her moneyed background, however; rather, she's used it as leverage. When she moved to New York, she had gone undercover, for a six-month period, working as a cocktail waitress at a Wall Street bar where stockbrokers took their boozy and cokey lunches. This is where she learned the trade and its secrets. When she herself began to trade stocks, her broker worked for her and her alone. Fortunes were piled upon her fortune. Ultimately, after making enough of a pile, she got out of the game—more out of boredom by that point than anything else—and decided to settle in to real estate—namely, the gentrification of Manhattan. Even sold Mrdok a building once, through an intermediary, long ago—which of course he flipped. If she had any respect whatsoever for Mrdok, it resided in the fact that he didn't go in for clichéd notions of glamour so often coveted by the nouveau riche—as far as she knew. And yet here he is now, setting before her this harebrained island deal. It revealed a weakness in thinking on his part. Little more than an extreme version of the dick-enlargement fantasy that leads so many middle-aged men into the purchase of Italian sports cars—or planes, for those who could afford them—she had seen it herself in three of her ex-husbands. That is to say if it wasn't concealing a more nefarious plot, which she felt fairly certain it was, and now had a vague curiosity to get to the bottom of... No, sleaze like Mrdok is far beneath her. He should feel lucky she hasn't left the bar and moved on by now. Perhaps now is the best time to let him know.

–Barb, can I ask you when was the last time you got some?

–Ask away. You won't find out.

–Is that because you can't remember?

–Why don't you go chop it off, Mrdok?

–Aww, come on, Barb. For a doll of your age, well... Not a bad piece at all.

–Is that so, Mrdok? I'm happy to learn I've landed so high on your rating scale. My self-esteem just shot through the roof.

–You wanna know something about me? In college, my frat brothers used to call me Big Floppy. You wanna know why?

–Oh Mrdok. You didn't go to college.

–How do you know that?

–Everybody knows.

–Bullshit. Who told you that? I wanna know.

–I read that profile they did on you.

–Who?

–*The Post.*

–Lies, lies, Liza Minnelli! Gordo spits back. It's a freakin tabloid, my darling, and we didn't even give them the time of day. You should know better than to believe such sultry insinuations. They just made it all up! Why, it's the modus operandi of the yellow media: the fake news industry. You of all people should know that, Barb.

–Mrdok. I don't care what your homo-in-arms over here says.

–He is acting a little gayer than usual, I've noticed.

–A little? If he gets any more flaming, we're gonna have to get the bartender to pour a bucket of seltzer over him.

Gordo pouts; solitude's best friend.

–It's *the Post*, Barb resumes the subject. My father owns the paper. Or he did before he sold it, at least.

–To that Australian scuzz bucket...

–Well.

–Fuckin Australians...

At a loss. There must be a racist term somewhere for Australians. Kangaroo-humpers? Mrdok makes a mental note to have Gordo research one for him later.

A few drinks pass, Gordo's increasing laughter at each of Mrdok's cracks, Barb eyeing the situation skeptically and mentally plotting her escape route, until she is too drunk to care.

–Oh Barb, Mrdok is such a wit, isn't he?

–Definitely something that rhymes with wit.

Mrdok snorts.

–Don't kiss my ass, Barb.

–Oh, I'd never dream of it. I wouldn't want to risk catching AIDS.

Gordo breaks a laughter bomb. Mrdok grimaces. Noticing, Gordo clams.

–It was a joke, dear Mrd. Don't you get it?... It *was* meant as a joke, wasn't it, Barb?

Barb not willing to help out her fat friend in this particular instance. The taste of victory too fruitful and frothy fresh. Like the aftertaste of a vomited skinny latte—worth savoring for curiosity value, if nothing more.

–I'm gonna get you to come in on this deal if it's the last thing I—

–What deal, Mrdok? I mean, really, what deal? It's ridiculous. You think I'm going to upend my entire life, put a big chunk of my holdings into your pathetic little shitstorm island fantasy?

–You can say what you want about me, but I have never—

–You're reckless, Mrdok. I'm a disciplined investor. You're the opposite of me.

–Honey, Barbra, please. Is the sun shining out of my asshole at this moment? I mean, I have people, right? They tell me things. I don't research these things myself. I've been way too busy. But from what I hear— not just from my people, either— the word out on the street— things are stagnating for you, baby. Have been for quite some time.

Barb is careful not to respond to this or show any reaction. People who put up a lot of defenses generally don't have a lot to hide. It's one of the first lessons she learned in business, one she had internalized over the years dealing with all sorts of egomaniacal men with too much money and all the arrogance that typically accompanies it. Let him think what he's saying is true. Strength lies in letting your adversary stew in his delusion sludge.

—We have a fundamental difference in philosophies, honey. That's all, she says coolly.

—Cos I like to multiply and you only subtract? Come on, Barb. We both like the high life. We both can see there's a big difference between the sky and the ground. We're on our planes all the time, lookin at the earth from above. That's our perspective. It's a thing we share… Now I'm offering you more than just an opportunity. I'm offering something that, well… A legacy, Barb.

—Get your paw off my leg, Mrdok. You know what? Your breath stinks and you stink. Who the hell do you think you are, tracking me down here—*stalking* me in Tokyo—like, you know how to get in touch with me through normal—

—Do I look like a guy who ever goes the easy route, Barb? Come on. You know me better than you're pretending right now.

—I'm saying I don't like your style.

—What style?

—Exactly.

Noise in the moonburnt night. The Nightingale, Tokyo's premier noise hole, on the second floor of one of the ramshacks comprising the Golden Gai bar district. Merzbow's *Pulse Demon* screeches through the speakers. The place is empty, save for Makiko and Stevo Rey, the rest of the band, so-called, having gone home. Sipping their whisky, both heads slumped in cerebral appreciation for the flood of sound warping what little's left of their sobriety. Place is really an art installation slash old-fashioned listening room, record player a holy instrument tended to by the omnipresent barman slash proprietor Masaru Hantaka, himself one of Japan's most respected and coveted noise connoisseurs (Stevo Rey drinks for free here.) Suddenly his head rises and he starts shouting—to Makiko maybe?—over the noise.

—I mean, what the fuck, right? He comes all the way fuckin here, I haven't even seen the fucker in, what, I don't know how long, five frickin years at least, he can't even manage to stay till the end of the set? Off to—what—probably suck a dog's dick, for all I care. Do some deal that'll involve the murder of a bunch of Third World African children while he snorts coke off a gold plate. Fuck. I don't know, man. The only thing I ever asked of him was the tiniest amount of respect. Even that he couldn't provide. Nevermind *understanding*. I mean, he gets it, I know he does. He was a child of the '90s. He was in London back when it was still cool, when interesting shit was happening. He's at least heard of the Boredoms. He treats his kids like he treats everyone else he deals with—that's his problem. That's why me and Bobby, neither of us'll ever measure up. Probably Jaco too, that poor little bastard. Did you know I still haven't even met that little shit? And probably I'm not going to, either. And he's supposed to be my little brother! Stepbrother... Half-brother... Whatever the fuck. Mrdok's the real reason we've all turned out the way we have. Bobby's probably gonna OD, if he hasn't already. At least I'm a successful artist. Not that I consider what I do art. It's too important for that. Fuck man. Just wait till he reads my latest blog post. If he even reads it. Probably just has Gordo read it and summarize for him. Sugar coats everything. That disgusting yes-man... That's all he is. The type of fucks my father surrounds himself by. Hey, do you think Kenji was serious about turning my blog into a book?

But Makiko doesn't answer. Her eyes are on the screen of her phone. She's playing some game that involves placing ants on a stalk of celery. Truth is, she hasn't understood a single word and, like the barman sloped in a noise doze in the back corner, can't be bothered to feign caring.

2.

THE NIGHT BELONGS to Gordo. Released from the bonds of servitude, in a state of jet lagged sleeplessness, he wanders his way through the neon twilit haze of Shinjuku Ni-chome, bars stacked upon bars, many of them closet-sized, with rooms for five six customers max, catering to increasingly specific tastes and combinations of tastes, some of which get so specific, it is questionable as to whether they are still even gay or queer. This one is a bar for expat Taiwanese bears, that one exclusively for guys with a transman latex fetish. Still others for twinks, rent boys, drag mothers, pre-op trans ladies, post-op M to F lesbians, transgender and non-gender, binary and trinary, serial monogamists and transparent polyamorists. Fishhead fetishists, nylon dope sniffers. Those who want to be beaten, those who want to beatbox while they get fisted, those who want money for sex and those who can only get off by paying and don't even need or want to be touched. Those who want real love and those who are repulsed by the very concept. Those who fuck to fantasies of murder playing out in their heads; those whose cravings extend to the injured, the temporarily or terminally sick, the diseased and insane and the dying. Those who only come out under cover of night; salarymen who have difficulty keeping their eyes open but still want to play. Those who are desperate and in denial, those who go out in defiance of their shyness when it would be so much easier to turn on some app and get it delivered at home conversation-free with a side of sobu noodles. Those who keep others' secrets and have none of their own to share. Ladyboys and piercing fanatics, vinyl gropers and saline shooters. The pube shavers, the refugees, the refusés, the fervent nationalists and gender nonconforming daughters of fascists. The nudists, the prudists, and the suitists. The mean, the green; the shit machines. The piss drinkers and abstainers, the alcoholics and the activists, the incorruptible and the in-crowd hangers-on, the putrid sadists. Those with desires they themselves don't fully understand or else can't properly articulate but need nonetheless to fulfill at any cost, those who have done absolutely everything there is to do sexually and still feel like they need to experience more. Serial onanists, sock and underwear sniffers, pathologically asexual amyl nitrate addicts. Those who can only get off to the sound of fingernails screeching their way down a chalkboard, those who can only get off in total silence, for whom the slightest noise results in impotent blueball frustration; those who can't get off at all, but like to watch nonetheless. Tranny chasers and bandanna wearers, old-fashioned handkerchief displayers and Harley-riding hogchasers. Lesbians who think they're men, men who think they're lesbians, men who don't care what they are, who never saw any sense in labeling it. The terminally unfashionable; the terminally ill. Soot-breathed mental wrecks, charming geniuses with an ill-concealed streak of perversion, utterly confused people with runway model looks and the sense of fashion to go with it but who don't know what they are, who they are. Men with a history of all kinds of inanimate objects inserted up their rectums, baseball bats and incense sticks and billiard balls, con artists and former encyclopedia salesmen and unrehabilitated convicts and CEOs on the down-low... These streets belong to Gordo and all his fellow nocturne infatués, seeking solace in the seething proliferation of invented categories and the desperate effort to correctly mold themselves into one.

He doesn't know which one to choose and as he is reeling in the confusion of it all, he manages to step in a pile of dog shit—highly unusual for the pristine streets of Tokyo, even if this is one of its seedier hoods. Scraping his shoe on the pavement, he figures he might as well take this as a cue of arrival and enter the bar whose sidewalk he's just wiped his shoe upon. Entering, he immediately feels odd. The reason why is apparent—at five foot five, he's towering above all the patrons and the bartender alike. After casting their attention his way, the gay dwarves return to their prior activity of drinking and quietly conversing. Standing there, Gordo is uncertain of his next move. The bartender gestures at an empty stool at the end of the bar. Gordo, in a display of smooth calm, inches his way (with no pun intended) toward the seat.

He orders a Tom Collins—not that he's ever had one before. He just likes the sound of the name. The bartender places it before him with a bit too much ice and minus the Maraschino cherry, which Gordo knows is scarcely to be found outside the U S of A.

He cannot determine what the dwarf next to him is looking at, not being at eye level. Even when he turns to address Gordo, he seems to be looking in the wrong direction, the result of a lazy eye. Actually, maybe both eyes lazy. When he speaks, it takes Gordo a minute to understand—almost like he has entered into some odd phase of reality in which there is a permanent delay.

–Big red circles under your eyes.

Is what he thought the dwarf just uttered. Gordo's expression a razor indication he could not comprehend that combination of words.

–I said your head looks medium-sized. Don't worry. It's just a joke we tend to put to the rare towering verticals that make their way in here.

–I see, says Gordo, feeling slightly disturbed as he remembers his Tom Collins and leans in for another sip. I hope I am not disturbing the, uh, natural order of things.

–Not at all. I myself tend to like normals. Most of the guys in here, though—well, in the event that you're a chaser, I have to say, you might be S.O.L. when it comes to choice and variety on this particular night.

–Your English is quite good, Gordo says, feeling quite confused.

–I was born in the USA, says the dwarf, who Gordo now guesstimates to be around fifty-four years of age and is adorned in a stylish medley of purple scarf, jeans, cowboy boots. Though my parents were from here originally. I came over after college, and, what can I say? Took to it. Never left.

He leans in.

–Tokyo has the best nightlife in the world, you know. Better than Berlin, even.

Suddenly one of the younger-looking dwarves—this one probably mid- to late-twenties, with a gay fashionista faux-hawk, wearing tapered black slacks and a t-shirt reading BORN TO BE MILD—

falls off the bar stool and begins to shake and froth. His boyfriend hops off the neighboring stool and bends down next to him, yelling in Japanese at everyone over the music.

–What's happening? Gordo turns to his new acquaintance for a translation.

–Oh, that's just Taco. He's having another seizure. Don't worry. He does this all the time. Every Friday. Almost like clockwork.

The boyfriend removes his belt and whips the seizuring punk dwarf across the mouth a good lucky three times. This seems to function as the miracle cure, as the fashionista suddenly awakens and hops to his feet. He blinks his eyes pointedly, as though adjusting them to what little there is of the light. Then he climbs back on to his stool and grabs up his beer, as though nothing's happened.

–Say, says the dwarf, now nestling up to Gordo. You look like the kinky type. Am I right?

Gordo chokes.

–Well, it depends on what exactly you mean by *kink*...

–How well do you know Tokyo? The nightlife here, I mean.

–Not very well, I must confess.

The dwarf extends his hand delicately.

–Call me Miki.

Gordo reaches down. The hand feels warm fat and quavering in his. It is, he now realizes, the first time he has touched anyone since leaving Crete, the first time anyone has touched him, since touching down in Tokyo. And, for whatever reason, Gordo doesn't want to let go.

These Tokyo nights. Fading flowers in human guise cloaking the streets. Sour awareness of light cast down upon the shapes hurriedly moving through the accumulated signage of yesterday's fading progress: sex shops and sushi stands and hostess bars and robot restaurants and arcades and vending machine extravaganzas and who knows what that one is. Certainly not Gordo, synapses abuzz and floating weightfully among the carnal drift. Following two steps behind so as to not step on Miki. That dragon gait with faint whiff of promise floating upward in the direction of Gordo's nostrils. Gordo hardly knows what he's doing, what he wants anymore, if he ever really did. Immune to all the puritanical inhibitions that once saddled his jeunesse, he's ready to be seduced by the shadows, no matter how contorted their forms. His own shapeliness now a fetish item for certain pairs of binoculars worn by eyes maladjusted to the home-grown and -hued perversion, the lustliness of the all-seeing, all-perceiving; the sweet rotten fruit of the fallen empire. The froth of the eternal night. The inability to escape the perceived promise, however its true nature might congeal.

He is led down a dark alley off one of the pedestrian streets. The stink of oil and urine, lust served up as a side dish. Tranny hooker giving salaryman a handjob behind a dumpster, screeching car startles her hand away, the pair laugh and she slides it back down into the greased hair warmth of belonging. Doesn't even matter if you are here—this is hardly a place, the rice paper walls're all see-through. Half-sober and alone, he would've gone back to the hotel. Now immersed in the violence of the scenography, he'll never feel fully at home again wherever he may land. Such is the cryptic curse this place casts on you: full ontology of perennial outsiderdom. The world is melting through your fears.

Miki leads him past the crowded magazine racks peddling every shade and variety of flesh, the dusty DVD boxes, the used panties on display in the glass vending machines, the dildos and gumjob granny sex dolls and maid uniforms and leather harnesses and anal beads, into a backroom where staid jerkoffs wait in silence for the next bit of hot action that might come their way. Some raise their glances from the porn they're watching in their palmed smartphones, stiffen at the sight of a foreigner, some at the sight of the dwarf leading him; everyone stares. There's not much else to look at.

Miki leads him into one of the booths, locks the door behind. Tiny TV screen in the corner plays hardcore S&M porn; in this one, a leather jock has his entire left foot up the rectum of a Japanese twink that must be of legal age, but could also be twelve. The twink is whimpering wildly, womanishly; all of a sudden, a giant vat of green slime is overturned on him. The twink screams in terror and sickened disgust as the leather jack moves all the way in up to his kneecap…

Gordo looks on in stunned fascination. Below him, Miki begins unfastening his belt buckle. It's all too much for Gordo.

—Look, Miki, I apologize. This isn't what I had in mind when I accepted… This booth, it's… Well, it is rather narrow…

—This is the biggest one they have here. But yeah, now I see. You are a big boy.

—I just feel… Miki. Look. Someone's watching us.

—What?

—Look. Over there.

—Oh. That's just the glory hole.

—The what?

–The hole of glory? Never heard of it?

–I...

–Okay. Come on. Let's go.

Miki leads him back out into the night. On the screen left behind, the teenager farts out the leather queen's final ensheathed toe.

Miki leads Gordo through the stainless steel doors of Ratzinger, the notorious leather bar owned by an ancient German queen who'd been resident in Japan for more decades than there are numbers to count. As for the name, local lore had it that Herr Fräulein had been a close associate of the once-pope during their golden years in Munich, where their mutual love for rough sex had greased them into the same social circle. Herr Fräulein had then watched in disbelief as Ratzinger worked his way up the rungs of the Catholic Church, eventually becoming its leading lady. Still, as Herr Fräulein was prone to reason to whoever was drunk and bored enough at the bar to listen to him ramble on, it made some sense, given that the men who had elevated the reptilian pope into that position needed one thing more than any other: protection. Who better to protect than someone with his own secret to hide. For they were all pedophiles and/or homos, the lot of them. If one man could be counted on to protect the guilty, surely it was this wretched looking creature who was guilty of engaging in far more heinous perversions than all of them. Ratzinger had kept it up until it all became too much; in this world, you can only protect pedophiles for so long––the public just won't stand for it. His cover had begun to fade, there were whispers throughout Rome that had managed to leak outside the Vatican, and the threat that reports of his youthful indulgences in safe-wordless extremities might hit the media any day forced him to do what any reasonable hypocritical patriarch would in the same situation: gracefully ease himself out of it.

Anyway, Gordo's now in a cage. Miki outside. Having adorned Gordo's neck with a collar attached to a leash, he gives it a yank, pulling Gordo's head against the bars. The sound of whips cracking and screams to a dark techno beat. Face to face with a meaty slice of Gordo's stomach, Miki cruelly begins to tickle it with three small fingers. Gordo, up against the cage, can hardly do anything but snort and struggle. Stop! Stop! he cries, and yet the dwarf continues. Finally Gordo is able to free his foot from under him. He kicks it through the bars of the cage, almost as a reflex, sending Miki flying across the darkroom, only to land in a gigantic tub of fisting lube.

Of course it was tough going, getting Miki out of it. Gordo couldn't assist; he, after all was trapped. Three different clientele of the club and one of the barmen kept taking turns reaching into the tub, but Miki's hand would inevitably slip right out of theirs, and after repeated attempts, one by one each of them went sliding, until they were a writhing mass of human worms inside the lube pool, Herr Fräulein drunkenly swaying over them shouting incomprehensible instructions in a German inflected with Hitlerish tonalities.

As Gordo stood helplessly watching it all, an odd flash of spiritual meditation came upon him. The world is fucked in so many ways. A schoolteacher asks her students if they might name some of the ways in which the world is fucked. They compile a list upon the chalkboard of some seventy thousand entries. The solution for all this might be the entry of some Godish figure upon the scene; but, as Gordo well knows, there is none to be had. We live in a gulf, and call that gulf freedom. Those who find the void of their lives unbearable often turn to gods that others have invented for them. It is a comfort, not having to seek explanation for themselves. But within these divine scenarios, there is the fartless culpability of countless shadows moving beyond the will of grace and all deitous exteriority, spurned by impulse and all its deep dark mystery meat. Truth gets pregnant by fornicating freely with found fortune. In the descent to Hades, pruned with ribbons bearing gifts like hairs afflicted with lice, one need only reach out one's hand to be received by a dog-faced creator. A man with a leather dog mask now peers into Gordo's cage; is that you, Cerebus?

Eventually, with the help of several pairs of latex gloves, Miki was released from the mess and slid across the club to the showers.

Gordo's imprisoner was now his rescuer. As soon as the door was unlocked and Gordo found himself liberated, he knelt down to beg for freedom of a different sort.

—I think it's not... Look, I... Could we perhaps find another place? I don't feel fully comfortable here.

Miki looks up at him with his lazy-eyed smirk.

—Sure, baby. I know some place a bit less intense. More, uh, relaxing... You like spas?

—Oh, that sounds divine. Simply wonderful. After yesterday's flight, I could really use—

—Sure. I've had my bath, now you have yours. I know just the place.

In the steamroom, Miki unwraps his towel to reveal the longest and fattest appendage Gordo has ever seen on any man beast or computer screen. His gasp resonates throughout the damply lit space, adding another note to the chorus of grunts and whinnies of passion resounding, rebounding. Miki's nude body is covered in tattoos. This sauna, he'd explained to Gordo earlier, is the only one in Japan that lets in men with tattoos. In that sense, it's sort of special. And given this unique privilege of access, it is also favored by certain members of the yakuza—gay, straight, and in-between—unable to conceal the art polluting the hidden parts of their skin and the sin polluting the hidden parts of their lives.

Before he's even aware of what's happening, Miki is rubbing his face in the blubber of Gordo's stomach, groaning. Here, surrounding, a very precious kind of hell, one unique for its pretense of hygiene and hygiene's pretense to moral rectitude. Nothing but moans and cries of comfort to distract them from their act, which is also on offer for others to watch and even partake in. Now, a dragon stands in the corner watching. Tongue aflame, his thirteen eyes take in every angle of the dwarf and the fat man and their gyrations, and his height rises with ebullition, as he slithers toward this late evening buffet.

3.

MORNING. SCARRED MORNING. Where the dread deeds of night having manifested themselves through the screeching crags, a calm feels itself justified in having been attained. Morning, when light is nothing more than an artificial sick gold cast upon your borrowed pillow, the window still unopened for fear of what it might bring in. Waiting, almost, for the sky to pry it open. What feeling left behind is now all washed up, an unsettling quietude here to evaporate into the coming-forth that is about to expend.

–That's a beautiful ring, by the way.

–You like it? It doesn't mean what you're thinking. Been divorced for years.

–I know, Barb.

–You know everything, don't you?

–I know… enough.

A mild restraint. Who needs more at hours like this?

–I keep thinking—

–It doesn't mean…

—… What?

—I said it doesn't… necessarily mean what you want it to mean.

—What? The ring?

—No. This. All of it.

—Oh.

Mrdok furrows his brow. Quick to not react. No telltale signs when both facing forward. (When forward happens to be the ceiling.)

—You ever been to Easter Island?

—No.

—Me neither. Funny.

—What.

—It's just… All this time we spend traveling. Our minds're always on other places. The next destination. It's like, we can never stop to appreciate the place we're at. What's driving us inside won't allow it.

—Speak for yourself, Mrdok. I travel a lot, but I don't go to that many places. I mean, I have my territory. And no real desire to expand it. If someone were to tell me today, tomorrow, you can't ever leave Tokyo ever again, I'd probably be fine with it.

—Really?

—Yes. Really.

An alarm sounded down the hallway. The hotel fire alarm. In their silent unmoving, both agreed to ignore it.

—What did you think I wanted it to mean?

—Huh?

—You said before, just now, it doesn't necessarily mean what I want it to mean.

—That I'm… Me spending the night with you is completely separate from last night's discussion.

—You mean the deal.

—Yes.

—Of course. I never thought this would be a part of it. What kind of man do you think I am?

—I think I know what kind of man you are.

—What.

—The kind who doesn't mind seeing a woman cry. Or making a woman cry.

—No…, he says. Men and women. Make each other cry.

—Well. Not in my experience, she says. Anyway, I don't want to talk about islands right now.

She rises into the half-light.

—What do you want to talk about?

–Breakfast.

–Call room service. Order it for two. Let's do it Tokyo style, with fresh sushi from, what's that famous fish market?

–I'm afraid I won't have time for that. I've got a full schedule today. I'll get it on the go.

–Come on, Barb. Are you really so eager to do the walk of shame? How about another round? I'm good to go…

He lifts the blanket to show her.

–… then we can *both* have dessert for breakfast.

–As charming as that sounds…

–Oh, so now you're putting your airs back on along with your dress.

–What airs?

–The Barbra Brunnei I'm-too-stinkin-good-for-the-likes-of-you airs.

–I told you I have a schedule.

–You know what it is? I think you're scared.

–Scared? Of what?

–Of your own feelings.

–Ha. Scared of boredom, maybe.

Of losing everything, she doesn't bother to say.

–You'll never be bored with this.

–Look. This was a mistake. I'm going soon.

First she goes into the bathroom. Runs water, washes her face. How many of those fucking dirty martinis. If she could just wash last night in its entirety off her. Does she even bother with a shower? Fuck it, it's a fifteen-minute cab ride to her hotel. Better shower there anyway.

–You know, Barb, a crowd can be mistaken. Often is. A single individual, be it man or woman, acting alone or in concert with other forces, almost never is. I don't know what you'd call it—one of the hidden laws of the universe or whatever—but it's something I've found to be true. Through all my misadventures—failures and successes alike. You can't just go up against gut instinct. Fight it all you like. But in the end, whatever you're leaning toward, it will swallow you whole. Resistance is fine maybe for the beginning. But… Well. Prepare yourself, is all.

These are the last words he says to her as she's walking out the door.

4.

THE NEXT NIGHT, the middle of it. Too many drinks later. For a bald-headed whore, she was as sophisticated as they come. Mrdok couldn't believe his luck. Then again, he was paying the price. The price to get in the door. And the drinks. And they hadn't even begun negotiating yet.

–What brings you to Tokyo?

–I'm looking for… interesting new experiences.

–Well, Mrdok. Would you like to have an interesting new experience in my mouth?

–Haha. You're an ironical slut. I like that. And your English is very good.

–Ivy League.

–No shit.

–Yes shit.

–And you came all the way to Tokyo… to be a whore? With that kind of education?

–Well. The truth is, I'm working on a book.

–Ouch. You kind of just ruined the whole experience for me.

–Why is that?

–I have… a certain profile. I can't let people—

–Oh you don't have to worry about that. I'm not planning on using any real names.

–Well that's reassuring. Now can I get that in writing?

–Haha, you're funny. Where are you coming from anyway?

–New York. By way of Sagosia. By way of Venice. By way of Crete. By way of—

–Wow. Your carbon footprint is sooooo big.

–Well, you know what they say…

–And your cute, tiny little hands—

–Hey. Easy with the hands.

–Here. Let me put mine right there.

–Mm. Now you've got my attention. Too bad I can't feel anything.

–Why is that?

–I have no feeling in my right hand. Long story… So you just, what? Said fuck it, left the good ol' USA behind, said, hey, I'll come over to Japan, other side of the world, take up the game…

–It's a little more complicated than that. Japan had been on my radar for some time. I wrote my master's thesis on Yukio Mishima.

–Who's that?

–Don't worry about it.

—I am worried. Worried I'm gonna have to pull out my cock and fuck you right here if you keep up with that.

—Aha. Wouldn't be the first time.

—For you or for me?

—Ahahaha. For either of us?

—Are you telling me you've fucked a guy in the bar here? Right in front of everyone?

—Well, we were kind of discreet about it... Though not *that* discreet.

—Tell me more.

—I'd love to, but my drink is empty.

—So tell them to refill it.

—If you want to hear more, you're gonna have to tell me a little something about you. What is it you do, you said?

—Well, lots of things. I'm starting a new country, for one.

—Aha? Great. Haven't heard that one before. You're an original, aren't you, big guy?

—Yes, I am. Big, that is.

—And (pretending that I believe you for a minute) where exactly is this country going to be located?

—It's an island. In the Brown Sea. You ever heard of Sagosia?

—No, but you mentioned it earlier. Sounds exotic.

—Oh, it is. It used to form part of an archipelago. But now most of the surrounding islands are underwater. So it's relatively isolated.

—I see. You into isolation?

—Sexually? I'm into lots of scenes, sweetheart.

—Tell me about that. What is your number one Tokyo fantasy? I mean, you know what this city is like, right? You can have anything you want here. Anything.

—And you're gonna, you're gonna arrange it for me? And go along with it, if I so wish?

—Hey. Isn't it my job to make your dreams come true?

What a whore.

None of the men I go with ever admit it, but they all like me because I shave my head. It makes me look like a boy. That's why they won't say. I know the reason. Because all men are at least part gay and don't want to admit it to themselves. And so women who look like me wind up being quite popular. Some compliment me on what they call my punk look. And anyway, punk is so passé, why would I bother moving all the way to Tokyo to take it on?

This one is typical, another fat rich jerk. My novel is going to be full of them. I need to find some way to vary it or else it'll get really boring. Of course most people will read it just for the sex. I can't say I blame them—that's just how human beings work. Hell, it makes the job sort of easy for me. And, let's face it—much more fun than going into boring ass academia.

A curly-haired rich creep from America. Likes it that I'm from there too, that we speak the same language. Honestly I didn't come halfway across the world to service American guys. But it's late, and what the fuck. It's about the money, sure. But it's also about the material. See what he has to say and whether it'll be useful. Make it into something useful, if it's not.

He buys me drinks, we shoot the shit. I do the flirty birdy thing. Get him all hot and excited. Even rest my hands on his hand, which turns out to be fake. Then move down to his inner thigh. Move them up toward the source of all that spending, feel it harden through the fabric. Offer him a Viagra. He says he doesn't need it.

This one's as extravagant as they come. Says he's had a stressful day, that it's just the beginning of what is bound to be a really long trip. He wants to party all the way. Go to the limit. I ask what his fantasy is. We go back and forth like that, a bunch of bullshit, till I get him to spill something coherent. He wants to flirt some more, it takes a long time to pull it out of him. When I finally do, it's like, okay. It's nothing I haven't done before, and it certainly doesn't come as a big surprise—a lot of these big spenders who come to Japan want it. Hell, some of them come here for that very reason. Blame porn, I guess—if *blame* is really the right word to use for, well… our industry. It *is* a promotional tactic, after all. It's very little actual work for me. I mean, the build-up is so much more. This right here. It's just sort of a bitch to arrange. Especially at this hour. But not impossible. Just have to put in a call to the asshole hotline, which runs twenty-four hours.

I cater to a particular taste, it is true. A far cry from the geisha fantasy so many still entertain. Usually it's Japanese guys, salarymen eager to indulge their own racist fantasy. A lesson in degradation: that's in many ways what my novel is going to be.

There's nothing more transparent in this world than what men want. That can't be what the novel's all about. If it's just that, then it would be a pretty thin book. It would mean I'm wasting my time— not to mention my youth. Not to mention putting everything at risk—my health, my well-being. *Diary of a Tokyo Call Girl.* I thought of that as a title once, but now I don't know, it sort of sounds too obvious. Maybe something more poetic rather than something to-tally commercial. But if I get all artsy and abstract, then will the thing sell? I guess it's one of those things about being an artist. It's so hard to tell sometimes.

By the time we get back to his hotel, there's already a couple of slobs waiting for us in the lobby. One of them, wearing this maroon leather jacket, I know from work. Meaning I've worked with him before. I haven't done a ton of porn—I don't want to risk that kind of exposure, it won't be good for my later writing career—but there's this one company here where they blur everything—including the faces of the models, if you ask them to do it. Once part of the cen-sorship laws in Japan, but it's been going on for so long now that most Japanese guys actually get off on the censorship—if it's not blurred they can't even get aroused. Something about memories from their teenage years when they were first starting to jack off and look at porn, back when the censorship laws were way more strict, having to use their imaginations to (no pun intended) fill in the gaps. Like being confronted by the actual thing now robs them of the mys-tery that must have so titillated them back then.

We didn't fuck or anything. It was just a tickle fetish video. He's a Shinjuku dick for hire. Probably hasn't left the neighborhood in years. Decades, even. He's been in a lot of stuff. Everything from fetish to hardcore. Mostly fetish, I guess, which usually means no fucking. Anything from smearing goo all over a woman's expensive clothing (yes, guys actually pay money to watch this and masturbate to it, don't ask me why) to getting tied up and mock tortured. It's hard to know whether guys like that actually still enjoy doing what they do. Whether they even once did. My guess is not. Not anymore, at least. The terminally unemployable sort that turns low lifery, base instincts into a fine art form. If that's not putting too flowery a spin on it.

The other creep I don't really know. Just another sad sack whose perversions have thrown him into this gutterish existence. God, lis-ten to me... He looks middle-aged, actually not half bad, and is wearing beneath his coat an old worn suit, giving him the air of a former salaryman fallen on hard times. Like his wife kicked him out and he's just living out of different capsule hotels. Maybe that's ex-actly what happened. I've seen enough of it to know. It's not like I'm going to bother to ask anyway.

Up in the suite, I start to prepare the room. I tell the client to call down to reception, request extra sheets and towels. He asks me how many. I tell him, I don't know, use your head. The one on your shoulders this time. That gets a smirk out of him. There's no longer any point in being polite right now. The jerk is clearly so excited by what's about to transpire, he can barely keep it in his bathrobe. It's not like he's going to suddenly pull the brakes. He's already paid me half the money as a deposit. So I've entered full in on the mode of getting this over ASAP so I can get the rest of it and just go the fuck home. It's late.

The doorbell rings and I go to open it, thinking it's the sheets and towels. Instead it's three more guys, including Kazumi, a yakuza guy I used to date with. I purposefully called him in to participate, more for protection than anything else. You need someone you can trust on your side in these scenarios.

The doorbell again, and this time it is the sheets and towels, followed by a room service tray with champagne, whiskey, beer, and a bunch of glasses. I tell them to put it up against the wall next to the wardrobe. The sad sack goes immediately up to the makeshift bar and pours himself a whiskey. The other guys ignore the booze for the moment. All the furniture's been pushed against the wall and I spread one of the bedsheets out on the floor. Phone rings again and two more guys come up.

Kazumi takes his shirt off. His entire torso is covered in a tattoo that's expanded since the last time I saw it. Yakuza guys have some of the loveliest art work on their bodies. This is why I never mind going with them. I always make a mental note, write down a description of the tattoos after. (I mean, it could be really poetic to have an entire chapter of the novel just be descriptions of yakuza guys' tattoos?) In Kazumi's case, it's like full body armor against a black background. Only the armor is dragon skin. He's a man until he takes his clothes off, then he transforms into something reptilian. In the middle of his stomach, a bright red koi fish. In the middle of his back, the smiling dragon's head.

The other guys follow his lead and start to disrobe. Their bodies are less attractive, more dumpy, unsculpted. It's late, it's all we could get at this hour. The American client goes into the bathroom to take a piss, re-emerges in his white terrycloth robe, swigging from a bottle of champagne he can't be bothered to pour into a glass.

Tattoos in Japan aren't meant to be shown; they're meant to be hidden away. Moments like this, when they're revealed, like the genitals, it's like the sun rising in the middle of darkest night. I ask the client how he wants me—in what state of disrobement. It varies, and something like that, you can never make assumptions. First he offers me a swig from the champagne bottle. To drink after him would be to create an illusion of intimacy that's not included in the package. He tells me to take my top off. He wants my tits out, the panties he says I can leave on.

Is it Wednesday night or Thursday? Hours like this, you never know anymore.

The Japanese guys are all in their underwear now. Nobody has to instruct them, they know exactly what they're doing. They're professionals—if you can really ascribe any degree of expertise to what they variously do for a living.

It's not that many men, anyway. If it were any more, it would be close to unbearable. As it is now, this is something I can handle. I've had worse. Entire yakuza gangs—several dozen guys at a time. But that would be too interesting to describe here. I'm saving it.

I tell the American to bring me a couple pillows. He gives me two. I throw them in the middle of the sheet on the floor, then tell him to bring me a third. I sit on the ground. Kazumi bends down, asks me in his broken English if I'm doing okay. I tell him in Japanese I'm fine, that I just want to get this over with. He stands up and makes a formal announcement in Japanese, too fast and ceremonial for me to understand. The Japanese men in the room all applaud politely, then go back to fingering their cocks outside of their underwear. The American looks on in mild bemusement, taking swigs from the champagne bottle.

To get the guys excited, Kazumi lifts me up from behind, holding me on either side under the knees, shows my panty cameltoe off to the guys standing in a circle around me. The only one who makes much of an expression is the one fat guy who came in toward the end. The others just stare blankly and continue to play with themselves nervously. No one's taken their cocks out yet. One of those peer pressure situations where each one is waiting for the others to go first.

Kazumi splays me flat on my back, plays with my tits. They're much bigger than what Japanese men are used to, though not enormous. The combination of big tits and bald head turns a lot of them on. (Again, a gay thing.) Kazumi starts sucking on my nipples. It feels really good, I like Kazumi, I don't have to pretend that I'm enjoying it like I normally do. By the time he moves to my lips, I'm actually turned on. The men in the room all staring.

The guys are all wearing different underwear. I make a quick study. For Japanese men, black briefs are the standard for some reason. The minimal aesthetic, I guess. A couple wear boxers. The

American Paymaster, I think, probably isn't wearing any at all. He still has his robe on.

My mom was someone who made t-shirts for a living. Her specialty was natural disasters. When I was growing up, whenever something catastrophic happened anywhere in the country—hurricanes, tornados, tropical storms, droughts, floods, nor'easters, you name it—whenever there was a natural disaster that did significant damage and made all the national headlines, my mother would pack me and my little sister up in her car and off we'd go. That's how I saw and learned about America: touring through its natural disasters. Well, the aftermath. It ensured that I saw every place at its worst, its people at their most downtrodden. It was a good business, but maybe not the best for our education, my sister and I—we had to miss a lot of school. Thankfully, we both had enough brains to study on our own and ace it. So the school didn't even say anything to my mother about all our absences. All they care about is test scores, anyway.

Disasters and profitability. People, after all, like to have a memento whenever they manage to survive something on a national newsworthy scale. They always give these catastrophes human names, so as to anthropomorphize them, I guess. Hurricane David. Tropical Storm Larry. Tsunami Margot. Desert Drought Dinah. Forest Fire Bettina. Making it real easy to create a t-shirt out of them. You really need a good name in order to make it a memorable t-shirt. One that will sell. Mom used to clean up. She didn't even need a storefront. Just sold them out of the trunk of our Volkswagen. It was a cash business, like the one I'm in now. The key is to have just a simple design, one that will *go viral,* in today's language, though we didn't have terms like that back then. We didn't even have the internet to rely on, the web was just in its infancy. It was all word of mouth. You have one design, but you screenprint it in many different colors. So as to individualize. People like to feel as though something special has happened to them. And that they can advertise it on their chests in the aftermath. Wearing it like that brings a form of pride.

Tattoos not meant to be seen. Natural disasters meant to be worn. Underwear all black except for a single pair of unfashionable white briefs—salaryman, of course. Kazumi rubbing my clit through the underwear. Turned on and yet simultaneously numb to the arousal. I can barely feel a thing.

Whoring makes you frigid, someone warned me back when I was first starting out, a girlfriend I went to grad school with. She'd done it her first year at Barnard, then got bored with it, or else busy, I forget which. Didn't like what it was doing to her head. One of the reasons she'd started doing it is because she'd always loved sex, figured this was a way she could get more of it and paid on top, what couldn't be good about it. Now she found it difficult to attain orgasm even when she was alone masturbating. She and I are different. I never liked sex all that much to begin with. Not that I ever hated it. It was always just more of an intellectual than a bodily thing for me. I don't have a man's appetite for it, like certain women do. Those girls who like to fuck all night long and never get bored with it. I'd just as rather roll over and go to sleep after thirty, forty-five minutes max—even if I don't attain climax. I have the ability to detach. Some women don't. My whore friend, she also didn't like it when the guys stuck around after, and being a whore made it worse. I kind of don't mind being in a relationship every now and again, as long as the guy knows his boundaries and knows when to shut the fuck up. But not many guys want a long-term thing with a whore. And the ones who do are usually whores themselves—even if they don't do it for money.

Kazumi takes charge. As he takes out his prick, I hear my phone ringing in my handbag across the room. I forgot to put it on silent. Who could be calling this late. Must be past two, three in the morning. Maybe mom. She always forgets about the time zone difference. Kazumi's prick is hard when he takes it out. The other guys soon follow suit: monkey see, monkey do.

Mom always said I should be a lawyer. I would have been good at it. Instead, I turned out to be a humanities girl. Which is like a half-assed lawyer, in essence. A sophisticated argumentative bitch with no money. What would I be if I wasn't here right now, fingering my pussy. Boxer shorts go down, hit the floor. I wonder which one of these jerks will be the first. Raise my glance above crotch level to get a good look at their faces. I have to bite my inner cheek to stop from laughing. I don't know. It's not any one of them in particular. I guess it's just all men.

My laughter must spurn something in the fat one, he's the first to step forward. I inch my face next to his stubby cock because I have the intuition he's not going to be much of a squirter. It's kind of a letdown for the client if the first load doesn't hit. My prediction turns out to be right. Thankfully there's not much to be said for the volume, either; just a dab on the left cheek that can be readily wiped away with a smile-grimace. I have no dimples for it to get stuck in.

What does he expect anyway, some honey-sucking gobbler. You get what you pay for at three a.m. Actually I'm selling myself short here. He's getting quite a lot; Tokyo's big and you can get pretty much whatever you want here, but a bald white girl with tits for a bukkake scene at this hour—well, I should probably be charging more. Moments like this, when awarenesses like that start creeping in, I have to remind myself that it's also research. That I'm actually getting more from them than they are from me. Anyway. A rich bastard like this. I will likely get a huge tip.

Then Kazumi splatters. Droplets rain down, about half of them miss me entirely, a couple splatter just above my tits, one big gob on the forehead. Wow Kazumi. Either you're real turned on or else it's been a real long time.

It usually goes like clockwork in these scenarios. Monkey see, monkey do—or am I repeating myself now? As soon as they see another guy cumming, it sets them off. Closet cases. The boy-lookalike girl is just here as an excuse for them to look at each other's squirting dicks. Make whatever comparisons they need to. An elaborate ruse, and it works every time. At least one can hope. The worst is when there are two or three who can't cum, who take forever to blast it. Because you really have to wait for them till the sun rises with the other guys' stuff crusting on you.

Looking over at the client, what's his name. He still has his robe on, hasn't bothered to take out his wand. Clearly playing with it under the fabric, bouncity bounce. But I get it. He wants to watch all the action, be the last to blow. Who wouldn't? It's his hotel room. Not like he wants to shoot and then sit around waiting for all these other slobs to blow. He paid for a show, now he's getting one.

We were on the road a lot. I remember this one town in North Carolina, near the coast, it must have been after a hurricane. This boy my age comes walking toward me, his face was all fucked up. I must have been fifteen, he was twelve. We found out later he'd been helping his dad clear trees in the yard after the storm, he was walking over an overturned trunk when he slipped and fell, fucked up his face. It was actually just heavily bruised. I thought that bruised face was the most beautiful I'd ever seen. Been a bruise enthusiast ever since. I wouldn't call it a fetish. Not like I have to have it around me constantly. But I can appreciate rare beauty when I find it. It's just that there's nothing like a fucked-up face. Even when it's deliberately fucked with. My first boyfriend over here, his face was full of piercings. Couldn't even make out properly, he'd always give me a mouth full of metal. But I loved it. Face tattoos, also. The Marquesan islands, the Maori of New Zealand… That's something that yakuzas never do. Never any tattoos above the neck. But a fucked-up face. Give me that any day over conventional good looks.

I thought about that little boy's fucked-up face, that image that has been burned into my mind, some more while someone else came on me. Then another, right after that. I'm no longer looking up at their faces. Just thinking of the little boy's instead. I lose count pretty soon, go into a sort of daze. That always happens. Once I had to do a bukkake with like forty guys. After three or four of them blow, you sort of stop paying attention. You just have to separate from your body. So as not to notice the disgust you're enduring. You've become an object by this point anyway. Might as well imitate one.

It's the middle of the afternoon over there. That's why mom's calling. She's so absentminded. I occupy a sort of middle zone, living between the extremes of the two, east and west. As good as any description of Tokyo. This place is blasted. It's not what it was, the golden era was like what, the '80s. Or the '60s or something. Now, it's all aging infrastructure. Guys like these standing around me who've all seen and done way too much. Who have been corrupted both by the lack and the torments that have been inflicted upon tradition. A tradition whose lineage they all know, though they cannot begin to comprehend the ways in which it determines their everyday behavior, their impulses.

After this, I'll go out into the streets brushed by morning's first rays, maybe pass by a face or two that I used to know. Where does all the money come from? That's a question she seldom asks me anymore. She just knows I have something going over here. Something that's not a t-shirt business. And so she'll tell me about shit at home. She doesn't bother asking too many questions anymore. Never once has dared to visit. She somehow senses the value inherent in staying away.

Another of these closet gays cums on me. There was a time I was innocent, I reflected, a time when I didn't even know what being a whore is. On the highways of rural America, mom and my sister in the backseat with all those boxes of shirts. Staying at chain motels, eating at highway diners. We'd go to truck stops sometimes. They'd flirt with my mom, always in an innocent way. No man ever tried to touch me until I got to college. By then, I wasn't so innocent anymore. It didn't take me long to figure out what I wanted.

By now, I'm covered in jizz and feeling numb, dead inside. I'm beyond wanting this all to be over. More that I'm in a place where time has stopped. All this wasted sperm on my body. Think things like: All substance is ultimately waste. Sperm not different from shit or piss or blood, marrow. In this respect, I am waiting.

Do any of these guys have girlfriends. People stumble about in a state of confusion, going from one person to another, never sure of their emotions—it's the Japanese way. It didn't take long to figure that out after moving here. Any guy I wanted, I could have my way with him. Not like it wasn't the same in America. But here, there's a sort of brazenness in the endeavor. I can't call it sexism. I never went in much for the cavalier bullshit—it's always fake, even when done well.

The client is last to bust. Exactly how it was planned. By now some of the jizz has hardened into a sort of glaze. It's supposed to be good for the skin, I don't mind. All this protein leaking into my pores. I have my eyes closed because I don't want to get any stuff in it, I squint the left one open to see him breathlessly going at it, the hog. Finally he exhales strongly and shoots a thick spatter right across my nose and lips. Just as he does so, the room key sounds, the door opens, in walks a middle-aged white woman. I wipe the stuff off my face to reveal an oh-shit expression written across his.

–Oh, Mrtol!... What the hell? What the hell are you *doing* here???... Um... I would like to introduce you, this is my good friend Tanya.

5.

THAT MUST HURT, she thought to herself as the fat person splattered on the pavement in front of her. She walked past with that flawless ease that can be so readily mistaken as grace by the lazy eye, but in reality is just confidence unmarred by any inkling of self-doubt; it's just how Barb was raised. She doesn't help people up. Nobody helped her. Certainly no one with a third leg.

She moves past the crowds, the crowds move past her. She is indifferent to them. Another petite middle-aged foreign lady, alone in the land of the rising sun. Soundtrack of this season's menu of pop music hits clouds her head. The songs you hear everywhere when traveling, the international, the transnational, certified sugary pop hits. The ones that blare at you from open storefronts, fast food restaurants. The soundtrack to global capitalism, the sounds that keep the world moving.

Nights like this she gets to thinking about her son. It all gets to be too much and so all she can do to keep these thoughts at bay is to keep going deeper into it. The night. Keep drinking. Some company, some anything. She doesn't really want a man. She doesn't want to be alone, either. There are places you can go in Tokyo, but it's all so regimented. Nights like this it annoys her, this regimentation. But it also provides damningly simple answers. Perhaps that's what frustrates her most. Barb herself doesn't know. Well. Most of all, she doesn't want to go anywhere where she might be seen, where someone she knows might recognize her and, god forbid, strike up a conversation. Not like last night's disaster. No. Better to immerse oneself in the shadow world of sunken strangers than to risk too much familiarity.

What is satisfaction but the hollowed prospect of a better day? A day better than this one, at least. That ever-desirable precipice, how can it ever be reached? What do we attain by losing ourselves in the nocturnal foreignness of a place, a place that by its very nature can never receive us and our inner inherent strangeness with the remotest degree of warmth? Barb in her furs on the streets of Shinjuku. Gracefully ignored by each passerby, each deeply ensconced in their own quest for nightly inhibition loss.

She was thirty-nine when it happened. Which is too young to lose a son and too old to have another one. Where was she at the time. It must have been Manhattan. Yes. Still the New York years. She was watching the maid clean the kitchen floor when the phone rang. You're perfectly fine, in a humdrum sort of way, one minute. The next, the depths of despair. This is what it's like.

She can't even recall the exact wording, the person on the other end of the line. But it was from somewhere out west. Not San Francisco—further up. Paulos had been living out there not long, maybe half a year. It was an understated thing, his sexuality. By his choice. She would've been fine talking about it. He didn't want to, for whatever reason. Humboldt County? Where they grow all the marijuana, Barb thinks. Or somewhere like that. One of those. Mendocino? Strange she can't remember the exact place right now. The protections of memory. It'll come to her.

She had fought it ever since she found out. But he was bipolar, and as much money as you can throw on that problem, there's not a lot that can be done about it. It all comes down to the medication. Which he took sometimes, but which he didn't like to take—as is common, Barb came to understand.

He was living out there with his boyfriend, a chef in some vegetarian restaurant. Very much the hippie lifestyle—which Paulos could relate to, having grown up in the islands. They'd had a fight about something, Barb never found out what. Somehow she knew not to ask, she felt it would have been too intrusive to even know. They had a fight. While the boyfriend was asleep later, Paulos came with a kitchen knife. The boyfriend woke up covered in blood. It took him a minute to realize the blood was coming from him. Paulos standing over him, watching.

Most of this she got from the police report. She actually never heard anything from the boyfriend. To his credit, he could have tried to take her for all she was worth. Or a lot of it, at least. But he never made the slightest effort. Didn't want anything.

Perhaps in the end he was just happy to have survived.

He awoke and he saw the state he was in and he begged Paulos to take him to the hospital. To do *something.* Paulos just stood there. And then he ran out the door.

By the time they found the body, the boyfriend was in the hospital. The way he'd curled up in the bed after the stabbing, it must have stopped the hemorrhaging. That's the only way the doctors could guess he was still alive.

They found Paulos's body at the bottom of a cliff some twelve miles away from their home. He must have thought that was it. That the boyfriend was dead. That he would spend the rest of his life rotting in some prison, and who would want to face that.

Since Paulos died, it was all business. She was already divorced. She couldn't bring herself to get close to another person. Certainly not any man. Certainly not romantically. There had been flings, sure. But nothing sustained. She has to admit to herself now that there is something vaguely attractive about Mrdok, else she wouldn't have done what she did. Much as she was also repelled by him; that part of her had obviously been burnt off by the booze. But the repulsion: could that also be the source of the lust; this perverse feeling of disgust and fascination congealed? His very presence. A lot of it, upon reflection, has to go back to childhood. *The dirty people.* That's the name Barb's mother gave to the nouveau riche whose daughters went to the same boarding school in England when she was growing up. She wasn't meant to socialize with them, but of course she did. She couldn't really see the difference her mother was always going on about. Anyway, she wasn't one to talk—Barb's mother had been cut from the same cloth, more or less. Still, as tends to happen as a matter of insecure convenience, she had managed to evade thinking of herself in those terms. The dirty people—they were always someone else. Not her or her family. As soon as she married Barb's father, the esteemed German-Japanese yacht manufacturer Yawazaka

Brunnei, she did everything she could at every opportunity to minimize her own arriviste background in elevation to what she perceived to be her god-given regality.

When she wasn't away at boarding school, Barb had spent a lot of her life growing up on boats. Her grandfather had been a Greek shipping magnate—a mere self-made millionaire, which paled next to Brunnei's billions—but with the two families now imperially linked, it made sense that much of her early biography would play itself out next to or on the sea. The family spent most of their summers on the island of Mykonos, which Barb still considered a second home—wherever the first happened to be.

Isn't that where all the homos go? Mrdok had asked her the other night. Why don't you ask your friend over there, she spat back. She'd long ago mastered the art of out-tough-talking the tough guys. Though it made her sick to her stomach, having to do so. The type of man who likes to see a woman cry. She hadn't chosen this phrase arbitrarily. So many had done it to her, it was almost like a contest for them: for a certain kind of man. The exact sort you have to deal with all the time, the higher up the ladder you go. Paulos's suicide the symbolic crown.

Her family had owned a home there since well before the Jackie O days. That is, the actual Jackie O, not the Jackie O seaside bar where all the glitterati—gay and straight alike—go to primp and preen in their designer bathing suits. Jackie had *discovered* the island, in air quotes; the gays followed. Now they summer there every year, from all over Europe. The glamour gays and the dirty people; negative reminders, Paulos and her mother, both dead. The *arrivistes* who arrive to spoil all her childhood memories. A paradise that can never be regained.

A certain type of man who really isn't a man. A certain type of man who has to amp it up, weaponize his manliness because deep inside, he's just a squealing pipsqueak. Dread nature of all these sordid walking wounds. The pictures they draw in their minds of the worlds they occupy, so pitifully distorted, you would laugh were you able to see.

She doesn't want to think anymore. Not this night. But how do you make thoughts shut up? Not like there's a button you can push, a way to eject them from your skull. Well, there are a couple of ways.

She has a place she likes to go on nights like these. Nights when there's no other way to get around it.

The two young men opening the doors for her look like they could be twin brothers. They have the same bleached blonde dye job at least.

The boys line up in front of her. The maître d', who looks like a slightly older slightly weathered version of them, comes over and asks what she's in the mood for. Honestly she just wants someone to talk to quietly. Someone to hold hands with. She knows Tokyo well enough, she doesn't have to feel embarrassed to say it. Say what you want about this city. Whatever you want, you're paying for it, there's no reason to feel any shame or embarrassment.

The boys—young men, really—are all coifed and manicured to look like the latest J-pop boy bands. Gay-looking, for sure, but it's the style here. Even grown women, women Barb's age, crave this somehow. Not sex, necessarily. Just the attention from a being that looks like this. Barb is confused. She never knows which one to pick. She knows better than to show her confusion. Always attack every single decision with full-on certainty—the appearance thereof. That way no one can perceive any indication of the anguish inside.

What do these men do when they're no longer of an age considered to be desirable? Barb selects one at random. He looks to be about nineteen. She asks him his age, he tells her twenty-three— which means at least twenty-seven. They sit at the bar. He asks if she's thirsty. They get paid to order as many bottles as possible. If you don't order enough, they show no compunction about getting up and moving to another table. They have contests each week, the one with the most bottles to his name is host of the week and gets a huge bonus. Is even showcased on the wall, so that even more customers want to go with him. In effect, they all become alcoholics, adding a further dent to their shelf life.

Barb takes care of this by ordering the most expensive bottle of champagne on the menu. Her host nods satisfied, impressed. He tells her how happy he is, how happy she is making him. A beautiful woman like her, treating a man like him so well. Barb knows it's all bullshit but allows herself to succumb to the charm.

—When I was young… child… I has Engrish teacher. She… just like you.

—Was she? Well, she did a fantastic job, Kenji. Your English is marvelous.

She says it in the least condescending tone she can manage to cough up. The bottle arrives, two glasses are placed in front of them. Kenji picks up the bottle and delicately pours champagne into the two flutes. Barb slides her hand across the table into his, envelops his knuckles. His hand is soft and warm.

—Can I say you something? Kenji leans in for a whisper. I… never has a sex… wif foreign girls… before.

—Well— now it's getting awkward— you're not missing much, I'm sure.

He leans in further.

—You want a sex? he whispers under his breath, eyes darting away for a cool nervous second.

—No. I don't.

—You want me sing you song?

—No song. No sex. Hand, she says, gripping his tighter now. Hand.

CHAPTER EIGHT

A TASTE OF FORMOSA

AFTER THE FRIGID temperatures in Tokyo, Taipei's a lush tropical paradise. Mrdok's here to meet Mister Ma. Mister Ma's millions were made out of real estate deals, so that gives the two of them something to talk about over lunch, roast duck at Yen inside the W Hotel. Ma keeps a low profile— something Mrdok finds admirable— but is known in certain circles to be philanthropically inclined in directions that others tend to regard as restlessly— or recklessly— earnest. This tidbit was handed over to Mrdok from the home office-in-exile as the golden nugget to pounce upon, to *capitalize* on, as it were. Still, Mrdok knows in advance that this one will be slow going. One of the things he despises about doing business in these Asian countries is the endless layers of etiquette that turn every deal into a long needlessly drawn-out feast of intrigue, an epic battle of endurance. He knows not to bring up the chief reason of his visit too abruptly. Definitely not now, while they're eating. Ma is rambling on about his family, his daughter studying at Harvard. Mrdok politely nods, Gordo enthuses that practically all their interns came out of Harvard. Mrdok's role is to be deferential towards Ma, who is older, but also restrained in his displays of interest; Gordo's role essentially is to lick ass. Neither of them is surprised when Ma concludes lunch without bringing up the subject of business. As they are taking their final sips of tea, Ma suggests they visit his favorite place in the city— a place Mrdok has surely never seen. Mrdok knows better than to decline the invitation.

Minutes later, they stand at the lip of the February 28th Memorial Park regarding the palatial Western-style structure. It's a clear relic of the Japanese colonial era, when this sort of pompous riff on imposed power forswore any attempt at subtlety. The heavy columns supporting it seem to stab their way into the concrete as though demanding this and all further territory, while the brutalist monolith they support, with its repetitive grandeur, serves as a sterile shield of victory.

–What is this place? Mrdok asks in bored earnesty.

–The Land Bank Exhibition Hall, Ma answers, a hint of civic pride in the back of his throat. Shall we go inside?

–Lead the way! chirps Gordo.

Slipping between two of the neo-classical columns, sliding glass doors open on to the skeletal feet of a massive sauropod digging into a plot of artificial earth.

–Whoa! says Mrdok. Didn't see that coming.

–In terms of museums, historical sites, there is really no place like this in the world, says Mister Ma.

He nods at the guards at the main entrance whom they brush past unticketed.

–It is at once an exhibition of natural history, as you can see…

He gestures at the wall to his right, whence commences an illustrated display on the origins of life on our blighted planet.

–… as well as an exhibition dedicated, as the name suggests, to a more local and man-made phenomenon: the origins and evolution of our own Land Bank, which has been a Taiwanese institution since the founding of our republic.

Behind an old-fashioned clerk's desk, the entrance to an ancient vault they now step into. Its formerly locked shelves have been hollowed with the exhibition contents dedicated to the bank's hallowed history.

–Pretty fuckin awesome, utters Mrdok.

Mister Ma nods his agreement.

They move through the exhibition now to Ma's chattery summary. A longing for origins, the establishment thereof: the vault exhibition commences with a brief history of banking. Mrdok stands before a glass display case regarding a collection of Song Dynasty coins, replete with square holes piercing the center. Gordo reads the accompanying texts avidly and with great interest. The evolution of banking in the East versus the West. The West, the history known well enough; the finance industry, as we have come to understand it, has its origins in the late medieval period, the thirteenth and fourteenth centuries to be precise. Among the most important early locations for the practice's development into a full-scale industry: Venice and Genoa. Both port cities on important trade routes. As trade flourishes, new needs arise. All those conflicting currencies:

how to know what is genuine and what not? How to conduct a fair exchange? A new profession was the sure thing to arise from all this confusion: the money-changer. They not only invented and mastered the specialty of overseeing these new needs; they also became storage houses for the silver and gold belonging to the wealthy—in turn, amassing significant fortunes of their own, since they were in a position to lend those treasures to other merchants. Hence the evolution of the modern notion of credit, which has so influenced the American economic system and, well, global capital more broadly. In Britain, these money-changers would come to be known as goldsmiths, performing a similar duty, yet further elaborating the modern system of finance by issuing bills when loans were made to merchants, effectively giving rise to the first checks and bank notes. Gordo, fascinated to see how similar needs arose here in the Far East. Though there is no reliable record to determine how the banking system arose in China, by the reign of the Qianlong Emperor in the Qing Dynasty of the 1700s, two sorts of banks had come into existence: private banks and draft banks. The former were largely centered around the flourishing business center of Shanghai in the south, while draft banks, run as traditional finance businesses largely in Shanxi province in the north, developed as a result of the dangers and difficulties of transporting silver ingots. In Japan, on the other hand, the money-changer system reigned supreme well into the nineteenth century, with the lenders being rich merchants, the borrowers comprised largely of feudal lords and less successful merchants. Financing in Taiwan during the years of the Qing Dynasty revolved largely around land ownership, the landlord and tenant farming system, and commerce and trade. Financial institutions were rather limited in their activities, serving as a mere high interest subsidiary between landowner and merchant, providing a means of securing land profit while simultaneously guaranteeing smooth business transactions. So in practice, the evolution of finance was rather slow in Taiwan; rather than deal with such dubious institutions, the wealthy preferred to invest their money in land or—well, do the same thing but in a far more literal sense—hoard their capital by burying it in earthenware jars in the ground. By the latter years of the Qing Dynasty, however, Taiwan had emerged as an important port in the bustling tea trade. New solutions were needed. Thus, the rise of institutions such as merchant houses and remittance houses further accelerated the development of a mature banking system. This process reached its apotheosis with the emergence of the very first bank in Taiwan at the tail end of the nineteenth century, when the island was under the colonial rule of Japan.

Fast forward to 1945. The Second World War is coming to an end. Japan has lost all its colonies, and a civil war in China will end four years later with Chiang Kai-shek and the Nationalists fleeing the mainland and setting up their provisional Republic of China, the official name of Taiwan, while Mao and the Communists would announce the foundation of the People's Republic of China. For the new ROC government, land reappropriation became one of the dominant concerns, as would be made clear by policies like land rights equalization and the land-to-the-tiller program. The government appropriated sixty million dollars from the national treasury and took over several branches of a former Japanese bank. Hence, the formation of the Land Bank of Taiwan.

–The bank's history, of course, is really Taiwan's history. Here, you can see our republic's evolution since its founding, from an agricultural post-colonial backwater, to industrial powerhouse, to… Well, perhaps there is a justified resistance in the displays to the melancholia of the present moment in which our economy finds itself.

Mister Ma emphasizes this irony with a gentle smile.

As Chiang Kai-shek's brutal military dictatorship squashed dissent, it simultaneously oversaw a series of economic reforms that would lead to Taiwan becoming one of the richest countries in Asia. Many of these land reforms, Mister Ma points out to his American guest, were initiated by the United States. This resulted in a reduction of rent, the extension of leases, government land being sold off for cheap. As a result, by 1960, only ten percent of the Taiwanese population occupied the role of tenant-farmer—compared to nearly half the population in 1949. As agricultural productivity rose, there was an increasing demand for more industrial goods; by 1960, then, industry had replaced agriculture as Taiwan's largest share of GDP.

–And so this is the bank's original building? Mrdok interrupts Ma's discourse now to inquire.

Ma appears startled by his guest's obliviousness to this obvious naked fact.

–Why yes. Yes it is.

–Ahh! I get it…

The bones of the building also on display—every nook and crook of its anatomy seemingly sacred. Gas meter behind glass-encased door dating from the colonial period, made in Osaka. The coat rack for the chief manager, a sign announcing it has been reinstalled in the exact location where it originally stood. Glass protecting everything.

—And the dinosaurs and shit? What's that all about?

—Yes. The dinosaurs. Let's move to the main hall and take a look at them, shall we?

Gordo following close behind in obedient silence.

The origin of life, its source being a *warm little pond,* explains the display. Yes, Mrdok recalls having heard or read about that somewhere. Something about all life having originated in water. Darwin, he supposes.

But before that, there was just this watery ball with a bunch of rocks stuck to it. The blistering thunder of asteroids, meteorites crashing some four thousand six hundred million years ago—the rain in that perpetual night. Then, embedded in the crags of those scattered rocks, very gradually things began to curl, to curve… The babies of history, microorganisms, their fossilized remains now three thousand five hundred million years young.

The exhibition takes them through it all, Mister Ma narrating the subtleties, in that Chinese sage way of smiling implication and understatement facilitated through the graceful ease of simplicity that connotes wisdom and is at the same time such a far cry from the American style of bluntness with which Mrdok is more intimately accustomed—though he plays along here by nodding.

—… and a new theory emerged: continental drift. It turns out that these solid land masses with which we are all so familiar perhaps aren't as solid as we might like to think. Well, it's one theory that I think certain men in China are not so fond of!

Behind them, Gordo coughs twice, which is the prearranged signal for Mrdok to not take the conversational bait. Though they both know that Ma had made his dosh locally, before Taiwan's economy sank and China took on the role of the West's sweatshop, this sinking eventually forced its intrepid entrepreneurs to turn toward the Great Red Frenemy in order to anchor their rise into the ranks of the nouveau riche or at the very least sustain the level of prominence to which they had already risen. Although they couldn't be sure to what extent Ma had been pushed, the reality is that exactly nobody in the entire Asia Pacific region doing business can do it anymore without at least some dealings in China. Being an outsider, Mrdok isn't one to comment, interfere, or even inquire. This is no place for a foreigner's opinions. And anyway, he's not here to talk politics. He's here for an investment. He must stay quiet and endure.

They stand before a display elucidating the geological strata of Taiwan. After a moment of silence, Mister Ma suddenly turns to Mrdok.

–Your Sagosia… Was it formerly attached to a continent?

Mrdok looks across the hall for assistance. Gordo is standing on a raised platform, gazing into the enormous butthole of a skeletal psittacosaurus.

–No, he replies. It's purely volcanic.

–Ah, Mister Ma perks up. Like Taiwan!

–Yes, Gordo finally having removed his head from the dinosaur's ass. The geological foundations are much the same. I mean… Some say that the island was originally continental. But well, *our* scientists *hardly* buy into that theory.

Mister Ma nods his head with approval.

–Here in Taiwan, we suffer quite often from typhoons, tropical storms. As you might know by your location on the Brown Sea…

–Yes, such storms are an inevitability, we are well aware. A fact that has motivated much of our conceptualization of infrastructure development, Gordo asserts with trilling bravado.

–Everything is being built to last, Mrdok underlines.

–Built to weather the fiercest storm, to employ an age-old, but here, rather fitting cliché, Gordo rebounds.

–I won't lie to you, Ma responds. I have had some investor colleagues of mine visit the island—a fact to which you are likely attuned. They found most of the native population living in dingy trailers… Trailers that get knocked down and then rebuilt with each passing storm. This is not the kind of…

–Exactly, it is a disgrace! Gordo proclaims loudly. *Not* the model of Sagosia we have in mind. As a matter of fact, the current citizens of Sagosia are to live under much higher standards when a builder of Mrdok's experience and expertise is allowed to develop the island. We have an entire quarter planned with houses made of concrete in which the current inhabitants will be allowed to dwell, rent-free, for a period of ten years.

–And after that?

–Well, by then, the economy will be so well developed, they will naturally be able to pay rent. Heck, it wouldn't surprise me if some of them were even wealthier than the new settlers on the island.

–So you are looking for developmental assistance.

–Yes!

–Not exactly.

–… Well, which is it?

Ma watches closely as Mrdok and Gordo exchange glances to determine who will speak next; Mrdok.

—Mister Ma, the opportunity presented by Sagosia is that it is both a charitable endeavor *and* a golden investment. I know that may sound unusual and contradictory. But it's the kind of project I've been involved with my whole career. You see, merely making money has never been good enough for me. If I'm not somehow benefiting the local community with my actions, well… I want no part in it.

—Naturally, Mrdok can't do this alone, Gordo butts in.

—Well. I could. But it's *no fun* to do it alone—

Now they are sitting at a table in the coffee shop on the top floor overlooking the dinosaur exhibition. Gordo and Mrdok watch Ma sip his tea calmly.

—Do you see the natural progression? Ma asks.

—What do you mean? says Mrdok.

—The entire world is an island. Look at all these extinct creatures surrounding us. The skeletons, those structures we all bear that never perish (unless we incinerate them, it is true.) Creatures that, we can guess pretty well, knew nothing other than to follow their own savage instincts, to prey on those lesser than them while avoiding being trod over or worse—by all those greater. Creatures that were well on their way up the evolutionary ladder, when something—no one is quite sure what—got in their way in the most violent fashion. Stamped them out.

Ma brushes his hands together as though he were washing them.

—Now along came us humans. Well, badly put. We didn't just *come along*. We evolved beside them, or after them. Out of synch with, never in harmony. But we evolved. Again, no one knows how and when. What science has best is estimates. There is a whole prehistory of being that, we must accept, we will likely never be able to access. But one thing is certain. We have our achievements. Here they are, all around us. The growth—of an entire industry. The implementation of tools, to mark our growth, to demonstrate our progress. To show, not the world, but ourselves—for we *are* the world—what we are capable of, and to celebrate that fact. To celebrate it by *rewarding* ourselves.

… The dinosaurs are dead. Extinct. We are alive. What's more remarkable, the institutions we have developed are alive. Are, in a sense, thriving. All around us. We take pleasure in being justly rewarded for our efforts. For taking the rigid primitive gifts this land has given us and turning them into a force of luxury. Divinity—one of our finest intellectual creations—was invented as a sort of mirror for those of us who have attained its heights on our lowly positions here at ground level. The Greeks, of course, had their own system for this; we had ours, too, here in Asia.

The dinosaurs gave rise to all this, what we're surrounded by. A global system. That helps everyone, and rewards the merits of, well, an enlightened few— those of us who have won the evolution game. Those of us whose destiny it is to shape the future.

The story of this museum is the story of our future, gentlemen. The Golgothian motherlode of everlasting salvation. Capitalism the apotheosis of what human civilization has attained, the very thing that raises us high above all these creatures that we stand before now. Powerful though they might have been in their time—today, we have overtaken them by the sheer force of will and the power of organization. The power of intellect. Of powerful intellects working in cohesion: for that, in a word, is what an institution is.

Gordo looks at Mrdok, wondering how much of this he is getting. Mrdok looks at Gordo, wondering where and how he should jump in.

Ma resumes.

—The question is where we will go next—if there is any place for us to go. And so now you come to me with this, I have to say, somewhat odd proposal: to form our own institution. Well, you came to the right man. Because that is precisely what I do. I have been building institutions for almost fifty years, gentlemen. And I know exactly how to contribute to the underlying structure of this one.

—We're not asking—

—I know you're not asking me to be the source. I understand there are limits. But, working within those limits, there is much I can contribute.

Gordo and Mrdok look at each other. Is it really going to be this easy?! All they had to do was endure all this?! Just then, Ma's phone buzzes. He excuses himself, picks it up, listens, and says some words in Chinese. He puts the phone down, stands up as though to go. Mrdok and Gordo rise, confused as to what is now happening. That is when Ma suddenly notices they are still there, at the table, in front of him.

—Gentlemen. I must leave you. For now, I'm very sorry, he says. My daughter... My daughter is dead.

Gordo and Mrdok look at him, then look at each other. Dumbfounded. Neither can find the words. Ashen Ma nods his head and starts to walk toward the escalator. Mrdok calls after him.

—Hey!... Sorry for your loss. But… Hey, don't worry! Everything will be better in Sagosia!

NO AND YEH

1.

THE PORN STAR stands before the Saudi sheikh.

–Hi there. My name is Manmeat Entertainment Exclusive Kingsley Lane, and I'm here to commit a sin against God… Wanna help?

He grabs his crotch and winks.

Gordo's in his hotel room watching the latest episode of *Cruisin' for a Bruisin'*, the crossover reality porn series on FaNN in which the so-called renegade porn director Harlen Oates takes a select group of gay adult film professionals to countries in which homosexual acts are either illegal or officially frowned upon, in order to initiate encounters and film them. (*If I can't turn the Global South gay*, Oates asserts in the opening credits sequence, *no one can.*) After last week's episode, which climaxed in a full-blown riot in downtown Kingston, Jamaica, Gordo is hooked. He barely registers his phone going off, but finally picks it up after the third ring.

–Hey, you fat fuck. Where the fuck are you?

–Oh, Mrdok, I'm sorry. I must have overslept or something. Why… What time is it?

–10:38, Gordo.

Shit. The 10:30 breakfast meeting with No. Why hadn't the alert on his phone gone off? He throws off his robe, wraps some clothes around him, then darts out of his room to the row of elevators that will transport him to the lobby.

Mrdok and No sitting at an awkward distance from one another. Through no fault of No's, it must be said: the table is far too large. By Mrdok's logic, this is quite fine; it is, in fact, a tactic straight out of his arsenal. When facing an uncertain opponent, an overly large table positions him at a significant emotional disadvantage, for one simple reason: while you are fully aware in advance of the distance that the table will put between you, he is not. On being sat across from you, he is the one to confront the intimidating grandeur of all that open space in between, while you have mentally prepared for it in advance. Mrdok had deployed this tactic on a number of instances in the past when victory was not at all certain upon going in to the situation, but immediately became a clear certainty once his opponent was confronted by this cruel and clever tactic of spatialization. Once, it was in London I believe, a man came in for a real estate deal. The minute the man entered the room, you could tell by the look on his face he no longer had any idea who he was. He had lost that sense of self that was needed to make such deals. One could hardly call it a trick, on Mrdok's part; what it was, indeed, was a tactic. As soon as I saw that he was using it with No—for I had seen the meeting room myself the night before, I had checked it out just to make sure it met our specifications, but there had been a completely different, smaller table in the room at the time—as soon as I saw it, I also realized Mrdok's intentions, and I knew the ageless North Korean didn't stand a chance in the events that were about to transpire.

No shifts uncomfortably in his seat, then starts speaking rapidly.

—My associates tell me you are interested in our product, and wish to bring it with you to a certain Caribbean territory that is—

—Wait.

Mrdok raises his hand.

—Who gave you those details?

—Well, don't look at me, I protest.

—I can look at whoever the fuck I want. Last I checked I'm the one in charge here.

—Sorry, boss, I didn't mean—

—*Who* gave you those details? I really want to know.

—Mister Mrdok…

—No mister. Just Mrdok.

—Mrdok. You must understand the delicate situation I am in here.

—Yeah? I think we can dispense with formalities. Go bitch about it with your dear leader.

—I can assure you, the government knows nothing of this—

—But you *are* the government. Are you not? Otherwise, how in the hell could you be sitting across from me right now? I'll have you know I have the services of the foremost North Korean intelligence expert—

—Mrdok. I am in Hong Kong as an *independent entity*. On this deal, at least. What I do outside this conference room, you need not worry too much about.

—Oh yeah? It may surprise you to learn this, but I've heard that one before. Can you answer me just one thing?

—I'm sure we are *both* going to leave here very happy…

—Just one thing.

—… What?

—Did you come here to *fuck* me?

With that *fuck,* Mrdok slams his fist down on the table. No stiffens.

—I beg your pardon.

—You heard what I said. What? You want to get someone in here to translate it into Korean for you?

—Mrdok, the fact that this is essentially a sale to Cuba being filtered through your enterprise—

—No. No. Not *filtered.* And not *my enterprise.* You don't understand anything, do you?

—I understand business very well, sir. I am *business graduate* in DPRK. I have spent lots of time aboard—

—*Abroad,* you mean, I correct him.

—… *abro-ad,* doing all sorts of business. And when you come from my country, sir, I do not think I need tell you: you have to become expert in loopholes.

No snorts. His eye twitches. I'm rather sure he's high.

—The challenge here is not so much from my *government,* per se, but a third party government's intelligence intercepting and—

—This room been checked? Mrdok interrupts. He looks at me.

—Why, yes, I—

—*Did. You. Check. The. Room.* Gordo. It's not a fucking trick question.

—I had our security detail go through it this morning, yes.

I pick up my phone to text our security guy and make sure he had, in fact, checked for any bugs.

—Maybe we should take a walk.

Mrdok stands up and walks around the room furtively. He gets up on a chair, looks in the curtains. No stands up, as well.

—Sir. Allow me. This happens to be my area of expertise.

—I'm sure it is.

No combs through the room, even removing the coffee and tea mugs and leaving them on a tray at the other end of the hallway.

—There, he says upon returning. We should be fine.

–There can be no paper trail on any of this, Mrdok says. If I'm not stating the obvious here.

–I don't think I've ever done any deal involving paperwork, sir. This is not how it works.

–Good. It sounds like we have the same concerns and interests. The same methods, too. You don't talk to any Cubans, do you?

–It's not in my domain, sir.

–Good. And you are based here in Hong Kong?

–Sir, I would rather not reveal too much. It is in your interest to know less about me.

–Yeah yeah. Just wondering.

–So. Here is the briefcase. I will pop it open here and show you. The code, you see, I have written it down for you here, 209309.

–Easy enough to remember. You got that, Gordo?

–I said I have it written down here for you…

–I thought nothing in writing.

–You can throw it out after. It's a bunch of numbers, sir. I don't think—

–I'm fuckin with you, No. What kind of name is No, anyway? That a Korean name?

–It is a Korean name. And I—

–I'm fuckin with you again. I know that's not your real name.

–So the briefcase, as you can see, there are these straps here. The stacks of money should fit nicely under the straps— we already tested it out for you. You just deliver the case to the address in Macao, I have already given it to your assistant here, he knows where the place is.

–I actually ate there last fall! Delicious Portuguese food!

–You have Portuguese food in North Korea, No? Do you have food at all, actually?

–We have many restaurants in Pyongyang.

–I bet. All of them sprinkled with Michelin stars.

–I would like to get down to the details of the sale. Of the transaction, I mean. Are you with me on this, all of this, sir?

–Yeah I'm with you. We're both with you. You see my man Gordo over there? He's the one who's gonna be taking care of the particulars. I'm just here to oversee. To put my stamp of approval. Without actually using a stamp, of course.

–The money will be delivered in this exact briefcase. This is important, because it is this briefcase that the contact will be looking for. If you try to give it to him in another case—

–The whole plan goes to bust. I got you.

—And, in return, he will give you a bag that looks exactly like this one. Again, the same thing: If he tries to give you a different kind of bag, don't accept it, take your briefcase back here and leave.

—Funny.

—What?

—This bag.

—What about it?

—It has a Samsung logo on it.

—And?

—It's a South Korean company.

—Ah. Yes. Well, what can I say? We do a lot of business with them.

—With Samsung?

—Yes.

—Isn't that illegal?

—Haha. You're very funny, sir.

—It wasn't a joke.

—He was just curious, Gordo clarifies.

—Politically, it is true, we do not get along. But, eh… What is the saying in English? Business is business?

—Yep.

—A saying dear to Mrdok's own heart!

—Glad to hear. Now. You have the particulars? The address? Tomorrow at 3 p.m.?

—We'll be ready for it. You just be ready with all the hardware and software.

—Now. I know our time is limited here. I feel rude to be so forward. But I know you are only in Hong Kong for a small number of days, and, well, I have an *associate* I'd like you to meet.

—… An associate?

—Well, yes. A business interest of mine. One that I think could be of interest for you, as well.

—If it's anything blatantly illegal, then no… I'm not doing meth, I'm not doing counterfeit currency. I know you people. Whatever you've got cooking up—

—Oh no no, nothing like that. I assure you. This is something— how do you say it? Above bo-ard. This man… A very impressive man. A doctor. He works in pharmaceutical business, No whispers.

—Like I said, I don't want your crystal meth.

—No no, he don't do ice. No drugs. Legal medicine only. We meet tomorrow, after the deal is made. We have a drink together. Not in

Macao, here in Hong Kong. On Kowloon side of harbor. I know good place. We meet the honorable doctor there.

–The honorable doctor.

–I think you will like him. He has made very important medical discovery.

–He's a North Korean?

–No no. He Chinese. He was in Korea last year. But he live here. In Hong Kong.

Mrdok looks at Gordo.

–You know, we don't have a lot of spare time in Hong Kong. I have an agenda, you get it?

–What Mrdok is trying to say is, we cannot actually make any changes to his schedule at present. However, if you'd like to phone our temporary headquarters— under a different name, of course— perhaps choose something catchier than No next time…

–You do not understand, sir. It is something I cannot put right into words. This is *going to change entire world*. This is opportunity not like every day.

–Now he's sweet talkin me.

–Mrdok really dislikes being sweet talked, No. You're going to have to fill in a few more blanks if you want us to show up at your little meeting tomorrow.

No snorts and raises his shoulders to begin his pitch.

–America has big problem.

–Oh yeah? Besides your country, what would that be?

–Pain.

–I don't follow.

–It is true, I never been to America. But I know things. The whole world knows. It's no big secret.

Just then, a window cleaner suddenly appeared on a ledge made of bamboo. They weren't that high up, for Hong Kong standards— only the twenty-second floor. Still, with all the talk about the room being bugged, Mrdok and No both appear unnerved by this development.

–Gordo, call someone. Make this guy disappear.

I have a much faster solution. I bang on the window and motion in the direction the cleaner came from. The cleaner shrugs, presses a button, and his bamboo ledge slides out of sight.

–Pain is biggest problem in America today, No continues.

–No, you're starting to cause *me* a great deal of pain in a certain region…

–Sorry!

No takes out his phone and enters something into his translation app. His face lights up.

–Sorry… Not pain. Exact term is: *pain management*.

Mrdok looks at me.

–You know what he's after?

I look at my watch. It's a Breguet, the kind with all its inner workings exposed in the display. If we time this right, I can get in another episode of *Cruisin' for a Bruisin'* before I catch the ferry to Macao.

–My guess is that, what do they call it, the medication they give those suffering from incurable illnesses. Oxy…

– … moron?

–Oh no. It is something better than that, sir. Something that has just been invented. Something the world has yet to see. But you. With your help, we can introduce it to the world. We need… a miracle investor.

–A miracle investor, huh?

I can gauge a certain inner arousal taking place as Mrdok's imagination dances through the possibilities.

–And this person we're meeting with is? What?

–He is the inventor, actually. A doctor and biochemist. He has three degrees. Very highly respected. Though also very discreet.

–And he's Chinese? Why hasn't he sold them this magic potion? No leans in.

–Well, it is complicated, sir. He was working on a project, kind of secret, with us in Korea.

–North Korea, you mean.

–Yes. North Korea, as you Americans call it. There is, however, only one Korea.

–Enough of the diatribe. So this doctor…

–He has little bit of problem in China. The mainland, that is. Here, he safe. He do not want to go back China at this moment. Probably not again.

Mrdok taps his fingers on the table. Shoots a look at Gordo that Gordo translates as *what am I supposed to do with all this?*

Gordo advances.

–Your associate, as you put it, can have forty-five minutes of our time tomorrow evening at 6 p.m. No more, I'm afraid. It's already quite a sacrifice we're making, as Mrdok's schedule is—

–I understand. I think you will not be sorry.

No rises quickly to leave.

–Bar Nun in Kowloon. N-U-N Nun. 6 p.m. tomorrow night. And do not forget the exchange in Macao.

–Obviously.

–How could we?

–All right then.

No is out the door. Mrdok and I look at each other.

–Pharmaceuticals? I ask quizzically.

Mrdok shrugs.

–I've had weirder shit come my way from these people. Who knows. Could be a winner.

–It could indeed.

–I doubt it, though.

Mrdok makes his way toward the exit.

–Remember, Gordo: Never trust a North Korean meth head.

2.

IN HIS ROOM, Mrdok is startled by a ring at his doorbell. Wrapping himself in his regal robe, he opens the door to a large bouquet—though instead of flowers, an arrangement of multi-colored multi-shaped sex toys—dildos and vibrators and cockrings and anal beads of every shade stand erect and glowing under the soft hall lighting. The miniscule snail woman who presents it to him looks down to avoid eye contact. As soon as he relieves the weight of it from her arms, she does a small bow before scattering off down the hallway.

Mrdok drags the thing into his room and swiftly shuts the door before anyone sees. Elevating the basket on his nightstand for closer inspection, he zeroes in on the envelope the same color as sand. He opens it to find a card with a photograph of two elephants caressing one another's nipples with their trunks and a handwritten note inside. He feels something else. A folded-up looseleaf of lined paper.

The card first. *Dear Mrdok, Greetings from Koh Samui. Today I visited an elephant sanctuary, where I got this card and envelope. The envelope is made from recycled elephant shit. Who knew? I thought you'd like it, hahaha. Something else cool—elephants communicate by touching each other's nipples. If only we could get away with that with some of the babes from the home office, it might actually make coming to work fun. Anyway, hope you're enjoying yourself in HK. I know how much you hate China, but the nice thing about HK is… it's kind of not, I guess? Enclosed, you'll find a list of everyone HOT who happens to be in town right this moment. Including their mobile numbers, hotel rooms and extensions. Consider it our little gift. Maybe you can use these toys on some of them, hahaha. Best of luck, Rick from the home office (which I hope Gordo hasn't already renamed the homo office.)*

The information economy. Mrdok unfolds the list. A quick scan. His eyes fall on one name that almost causes him to drop the damn thing.

Holy shit.

As he reaches for the phone, the basket of sex toys crashes to the floor. A purple hot mess of lube explodes, spitting up at him like a slithering swamp, a chorus of vibrators dances in the newly released mud, and a double donger bounces up and bangs the flatscreen. Mrdok bends down and unearths the fallen remote control, mutes FaNN as Gordo picks up.

—Gordo! You're never gonna guess who's in town.

—Weyuhl, bah gosh, lets jest call it serendipity. Aint it?

Lallyburt's already good and liquored up by the time Mrdok makes it to the hotel bar.

—Could it also be that the Lawed wanted us tuh meet raht here on thuh othuh sahd uh His green urth.

He grabs his companion's ass and gives it a good squeeze. She squeals and returns his gesture with a playful slap.

—It's been a long time, Lallyburt, says Gordo.

—It aint been that lawng.

—What might you be drinking?

—Hahh bawl, drawls Lallyburt.

—Well. I'll get the drinks and leave you gentlemen to get *right down to it.*

Gordo performs a swish of the hips to those last four words. Mrdok registers the reactionary distaste across Lallyburt's visage.

—We're all being *very supportive* of Gordo these days. You know.

Before giving Lallyburt a chance to answer, no doubt with some wise words from the New Testament, Mrdok holds his hand out to the lady.

—And who might you be, Miss?

—You can call me Vanessa.

—Vanessa? I love how they all have English names over here. Don't you?

—Ah dam arpreciate it. Ah lahk a woman whose damn nayme ah ken say.

The drunker he gets, the more the Texas seems to leak out of him like some kind of toxic pus.

Mrdok mumbles something about how he can't keep up with half of them anyway.

–You know, Lallyburt. I'm real glad we had the opportunity to meet this way. Cos for a long time, you know what? I've been wanting to thank you.

–Tuh thank me?

–Yeah.

–Fer wuht? Fer not lettin you tayke a biyig stinkin dump on mah layund? Har har. Vaness, this here dam fool thought he wuza gonna triyick me raht outta mah own propety. Now whuhhuya maykuh thayut, you sweet yung thang?

Vanessa laughs hysterically and takes another sip of her cocktail. It's apparent to Mrdok that she has no idea what Lallyburt just said. Hell, he barely does either.

Mrdok presses on.

–You know, I am usually not not-right about stuff like this. But I somehow managed to get my instincts all twisted up on that one. And man. You. You really saved me!

–Through mah refyusal.

–Yeah. That's right. Through your refusal.

–Weyuhl. Ah do deklare. Big shark Mrdok comin round with his tayel between his legs.

–I think fin would be a more appropriate appendage, Gordo announces with a tray of drinks in his hands. Lest we mix our metaphors.

–Skyuuze me?

Mrdok kicks Gordo's leg under the table. The preordained signal for *shut the fuck up you fat fuck.*

–I'm grateful, is what I'm trying to say, Mrdok continues. Let's have some champagne, shall we? For the table. For all of us here. I'm in celebrating mood tonight, that's for sure.

–Ahum always in a celebratin mood when I cum to this towwn.

Lallyburt leans in to slobber over his lady of the night.

–Y'know, Mrdok continues, I'm more sensitive than I look. People around me were starting to imply things. Things about my mind that didn't sound right. That didn't make me feel good about myself. The decisions I was making. The directions I was going in. Meeting you, that whole city project... I mean, damn. That was a wake-up call, man. I nearly reached the edge there. And the thing about the edge is... Once you go over, you don't come back.

–*Cham-pagne! No pain! Aint no pain when theres cham-pagne!*

–But then I got to thinking, Mrdok continues. Me and Gordo were talkin about it one night, matter of fact, not long after the whole deal collapsed. Y'know, I have to confess. For half a minute, I thought I might've lost my magic touch. Not sure if you've ever been there, too, Lallyburt...

–Ah want me sum ass cream!

–Some ass cream? Turn around, Gordo.

–No, you dam queeuh. Ah sed ah want sum *ass* cream! Caint you tawk Amehrikun? Vanilla and raspberry with fuckin chocolate sprankles.

–Coming right up! Gordo sprints to the bar.

–So I got to thinkin. To kiss the ass of disaster—that's a scenario we all want to avoid. To come close, okay. But to go all the way? With no signboard? Nothing to, uh, preannounce our good intentions?

–Whut the samheyl you tawkin bout?

–Lallyburt, I'm gonna let you in on a little secret. You won't remember it, in your condition, but I'm gonna go ahead and tell you it anyway. I always do two things at once. Always. Whenever I make one move, I'm always making another, opposite move right behind the scene of the first one. You see where I'm getting at? That's how risk gets mitigated. You bet on success. But you bet on failure at the very same time. You bet against yourself, in other words. You know, everything you do, any gesture you might make, there's always gonna be one of two outcomes. So why not make sure you get the benefit of each? Cos none of us, I mean—in spite of all our good fortune—none of us really has access to a crystal ball. Am I right?

–Ah still don't know the damdest thang yer sayin raht now.

–Haha. Good. I'm glad. Gordo, could you go get Lallyburt another drink? He's gonna need something to wash that ass cream down with.

–Goshdarn crystal bawl. Whut the hell you tawkin. That there's witchcrayaft, devul's tawk. Crystal bawls're instruments of thuh devuhl. N where the samheyl re mah goddam sprankles. Did ah not say ah want me some choclate sprankles?

–Go ask for some sprinkles, Gordo. And let's not get our panties in a bundle. Especially you, sweetheart...

Mrdok winks at the whore.

–Let's not act like we're offended when we're really not. You like to pretend we're different, Lallyburt. But I know we're not. You know the thing that unites us?

–No.

–Besides our love of pussy, of course. We're dreamers, you and I. Dreamers of the big dream. The dream so big, it's beyond most people's grasp. Most people—it's not that they can't see it. They can't even *fathom* it, is the thing. It's *that* big. But what further separates us from them. We know how to attain it. Don't we, sweetheart?

—Oh yeah, says Vanessa, now rubbing up against Mrdok in her state of drunken confusion. I like *big dreams*. Big things in general. You wanna show me your *big dream*, baby?

Lallyburt violently yanks the whore in his direction.

—Ow! My shoulder!

—Wuhl that'll teach ya to stay away from this dam yankee sinnuh.

She play-slaps Lallyburt's face. He pushes the half-eaten dish of ice cream off the table. It crashes into a pile of glass upon the floor.

—Come on, cowboy, says Vanessa. No need to play rough with me. We already have our plan for the night, don't we?

She rests her index finger on Lallyburt's sticky lips.

—Ah don't need all yer fancy tawk, Lallyburt now shouts in Mrdok's direction. Yer hahfalutin yankee birdsquawk. Yer nothin. You aint got nuthin on me. This towen, you wanna know somethin bout this town? If I were to dam take my muney outta the banks here, this whole dam town would collapse around us. I'm tawkin, I'm the one here holdin mutherfuckin Hong Kong afloat. *That's* somethin bet *you* dint know bout *me*.

—Oh, we've all got money in the game here, dear Lallyburt. No need to blow your trumpet in my face. I'm blowin right back at you, baby.

—Ah don't think so. How much bacon you got in this heyer frahn pan? I bet you don't even know. Get yer faggity accountant ovuh heuh, tell him to tell us. Lets mayke us sum fuckin notes. Sum cum*pari*sun. I dam want to know raht now.

—I don't think the moment's right for a dick-measuring contest. Be a gentleman, Lallyburt. You don't discuss business in front of ladies… Unless, of course, they're the object of the business.

He pinches her lightly. She squeals.

—Ah dam told you. This here's *mah* woman. Now ah aint got no choice but to, but to *defeyend* heh honuh. To, to, to…

Lallyburt falls down. Vanessa shrieks with shock and laughter, but doesn't bother to bend down and help her date back on to his feet. Gordo leans down instead.

—Get yo hand offa me! Ah aint no faggit!

—We never said you were. But oh, how we're enjoying your company tonight.

The three of them watch as Lallyburt rouses himself, then stumbles across the bar in the direction of the men's room. He manages to trip over his own foot and crash through the giant fishtank, containing some thirty-seven exotic tropical species, which spill out and shatter on to the floor as the waiters and bartenders and maître d' all issue a collective gasp.

A decision is reached to leave Lallyburt to wrangle with the bar staff. Gordo leads, Mrdok grabs Vanessa, they make their escape to another bar down the road. This one's a real after-hours type joint, empty save for a lone elderly Brit, one of the bitter leftovers of the colonial period, who makes some flaccid attempt at conversation before ignoring the new arrivals.

–Gordo. Drinks.

Although Mrdok's had nearly as much as Lallyburt, he's not showing it, or at least manages to hold it together, and is getting off on demonstrating this. Vanessa seems to be enjoying her newfound role in the symbolic castration of Lallyburt.

Gordo returns with a tray of cocktail glasses, their rims frosted with a rainbow'd glaze.

–What the hell is this? Mrdok asks with a pointed tone of disgust.

–My treat! Gordo announces all gleeful. It's the house specialty here, it turns out. It's called Lavender Surprise!

–Get it the fuck out of my face.

The whore roars.

–Oh Mrdok.

–I mean it. Take it away. Get us some real drinks. Not this fruity crap.

–Raaaaa ha ha ha haaaaa haaaaaaa…

–I'm so sorry. I thought you might wish to sample some local flavor.

–I'm about to sample the local flavor right here.

He grabs Vanessa and pulls her close.

–I don't need to drink some fruit bartender's piss to get it.

Vanessa roars anew. Oh Mrdok: what a wit!

–I've got it, Gordo concurs. Two old-fashioneds then. Coming right up!

–And something for yourself, of course.

–… I'll sample the Lavender Surprise.

–I bet you will.

–Raaaaaaa ha ha haaaaaaaa haaaaaaaa…

–Well, aren't you a little bundle of riots tonight.

–Aha am I? We *do* like to riot in Hong Kong.

–So I've heard.

–What have you heard?

–That you've had a couple problems with your neighbor next door?

–A couple? Raaaaaaaa ha ha ha haaaaaaaaa haaaaaaaaaaaaaa…

–You ever go with Chinese businessmen?

–You mean mainlanders?

–Yeah.

–Of course I do. They're my main clientele.

–I guess you don't have much of a choice.

–You take what you can get.

Vanessa opens her phone cam app, puts it in selfie mode to check her appearance.

–So how long have you known Lallyburt?

–That guy? The one we just left behind?

–Yeah. Him.

–He's a newbie for me.

–Yeah? He's in Hong Kong a lot.

–So? Doesn't mean I know him.

–You didn't hesitate much to leave him behind.

–Drunks are always a hassle. And the condition he was in… I mean, it would be a struggle to get paid. First I'd have to drag him back to wherever he's staying. Then, they probably wouldn't even let me up in the room, figuring I'm some hooker out to rob a guy—

–Well aren't you?

–Haha very funny. And even if they do let me in his room, okay, he's too drunk to do it. We'd end up just crashing out, going to sleep. And in the morning, he'd probably—I know for a fact that he would have a hangover and not want to do it then, either. That might lead to an argument over payment.

–Because, yeah, why should he pay you when you haven't done anything?

–Exactly.

–I can see his viewpoint. Or his potential one.

–I wish I couldn't.

–Ha. You've got a mouth on you. I like that in a woman.

–A woman who doesn't know when to shut up?

–Well, I wouldn't put it in precisely those terms…

Gordo brings the fresh drinks over.

–I am so sorry. I just got into a conversation with that gentleman at the bar over there. Apparently he has lived in Hong Kong for more than fifty years! Can you imagine?

–So go fuck him. We were in the middle of a conversation you're now interrupting, Gordo.

–Oh mercy me. Well I'll just fade *right* into the background!

–Do that.

–Woo-hoo! exclaims Vanessa. This drink is *strong.*

–I'm gonna ask you to use your imagination for a minute.

–My *what?*

–Don't worry. I'll pay you for it.

–Okay!

–I want you to imagine that you never met that guy. That bastard we just left behind.

–… That's all I have to do?

–Pretend you don't know who he is. Pretend you know who I am. I know it's tough, me being a stranger. Hell, we're strangers to each other right now, aren't we? But I want to pretend that it's all different. That, uh… That my wife isn't leaving me. That I can be attractive. Attractive to a woman like you. Were she not, uh—

–A whore?

–A professional, I was going to say. But mostly, that we live in a world that that motherfucker never arrived in.

–You can't even bring yourself to say his name right now, can you.

–I can't even remember his name right now.

–You and me both, sugar. Raaaaaaa ha ha ha ha ha haaaaaaaa haaaaaaa…

Meanwhile, Gordo makes his presence felt before the Englishman left behind at the bar.

–You know, I think of myself in some ways as an honorary Brit, having studied there for a time…

–Do you live there now then?

–I don't, I must confess.

–Then who exactly has bestowed this honor upon you?

–… Oh, but of course…

–No one, then, I presume.

–Perhaps *honorary* was rather the wrong term to use in that sentence. I do, however, feel a certain *affinity*—

–Well I bloody well don't.

The grayed-out recluse taps the bar. His drink is refilled a beat later.

–Have you been back to the, uh, motherland?

–By which you mean… ?

–Great Britain.

–Dear boy. I must get you to understand. Great Britain is not my home. I was born here, in Hong Kong. At the time, it was a part of Great Britain…

–Perhaps I chose my words wrongly once again. Have you ever visited Great Britain?

–Only once. Years before the handover.

–And?

He looks at Gordo quizzically.

–Well what? I found the food bloody well reprehensible.

–Yes, well. Food and weather. Neither of them particularly British specialties…

–Oh bugger it all. My home is this place. Which is to say no place. Not-belonging, that's my home. Not belonging to any of it, anywhere.

–Do you speak Cantonese then?

Another glacial glare.

–Go ahead. Try and find one single white man on any of these islands who can speak a word of it. I bloody well dare you.

–Oh, I believe you, says Gordo, meekly.

He hunches his shoulders and faces straightforward, away from his drinking companion's disapproving glances. Then he gets up and reseats himself equidistant from the disgruntled Brit and the following scene he is just close enough to monitor.

–Why are you so, so… graceful, Mrdok inquires.

–In my past life, Vanessa whispers, I used to be a dragontail butterfly.

She leans her head back and opens her mouth in the widest dentist office ahhhh, then stumbles forward in a fit of silly laughter. Mrdok grabs her by the back of the head.

–In my past life, he leans in, I used to be a professional fuck machine.

She opens her mouth as though to croak or laugh or scream. But this time, not a sound comes out.

3.

MRDOK'S IN THE mood for walking, and anyway, the bar's right around the corner from the hotel, or at most a ten-minute saunter, so they make their way through the musty streets of Kowloon. The humidity is almost too much to take for Gordo— same humidity as in Taipei, actually, but here, the city seems so much filthier, the streets narrower, so many bodies and smells to move past. He wonders if he can persuade Mrdok to take a taxi back to the hotel after, but puts that in the back of his mind for now. Best not to bring these things up when anxiety's the dominant mood.

They arrive at Bar Nun ahead of schedule. The bar's logo features a cartoonlike illustration of Bruce Lee cloaked in titular habit. Inside, no sign of No or his fabled doctor. The two choose a discreet table in the corner. The waiter immediately comes over and takes their order. Bourbon on the rocks for Mrdok; a mai tai for Gordo. Hair of the dog for both of them.

Mrdok looks at Gordo skeptically.

—Mai tai?

—All these tropical islands. I've rather developed an affection for them!

Mrdok shrugs. Whatever.

—I take it no problems with the pickup? Macao?

—Everything went swimmingly.

—Good.

—Oh, but Ma called.

—Taiwan Ma?

—Precisely.

—How's he doing? They have his daughter's funeral yet?

—She was buried yesterday.

—They do things fast in Taiwan. Especially when… when the death is said to be… tragic.

—It's a shame. How old was she?

—Twenty-three.

—A tragedy. A real tragedy… So any word? Is he in?

—Well, that's the news. That was the main subject of the morning's call, in fact. You know, he already sent his people to visit the island. Vincent showed them around. He understands the deal with the bank. What he's hoping to do is to go in with you as a partner.

—What do you mean?

—On the bank.

—Ha. Fuck no.

—Well, these are the conditions.

—Oh Gordo. You should have let me handle this. You didn't try to *negotiate*, did you?

—No no no. I am only the messenger.

—Yeah. Only you have a tendency to forget that at times.

—I only want what is best for us. For the organization… For Settlers Landing.

—So he wants part of the fucking bank? Is this guy nuts?

—It does make a bit of sense, now, in retrospect. Taking us to that bank museum.

—Yeah. Real subtle. Sucking me off while shaving my balls. I'll call him back after this. The fuck.

—Better you wait till tomorrow. Who knows how long *this* is going to take. And remember: we're in the same time zone now.

—Right. Taiwan.

Just then, No enters the bar with a middle-aged man in gold-rimmed spectacles following close behind. The man wears a red flannel shirt and a blue blazer jacket over it, khaki pants—definitely not summer wear, and mismatched, but it somehow works. Gordo waves them over from the corner. As the two men reach the table, Gordo and Mrdok rise ceremoniously.

—I'd like you to meet Doctor Yeh, says No.

—Doctor Yeah?

—*Yeh. Yeh,* corrects No.

—Have a seat, directs Mrdok following the requisite half-bow handshake.

—Shall we have drinks, or… ? We've already gotten started here. What will it be?

—The honorable doctor doesn't drink. I'll have a whisky. A Japanese kind, if they have it.

So far, the honorable doctor hasn't spoken a word. Since Mrdok doesn't really know why he's here, he decides to dispense with formalities.

—Well, gentlemen. Much as I would love to shoot the shit until the bulls return home to rape the cows, my time here is limited. So why don't you tell me all about your little magic potion and, most importantly, what it is you want me to do with it.

No glances at Yeh nervously. Yeh says nothing.

—Sir. The drinks have not yet arrived.

—So what? We're supposed to have a staring contest until the drinks get here?

The bartender then appears and sets the drinks down on the table before the men.

—I solve problems.

The sentence came out in a robotic croak. Mrdok looks at Gordo, then back at Yeh.

—Did you just say something? Or was that my phone?

—I solve problems, he repeats.

—Well, isn't that… weird.

–What is weird?

Mrdok leans over and whispers into No's ear.

–Is this guy like on the spectrum or something?

–I solve problems. It is what I do. It is a thing to make clear.

–Okay… Doctor Yeh the problem solver. Hi, I'm Mrdok the marketeer. Nice to meet you.

Doctor Yeh rises from his chair as though making to leave. Then, just as sudden, he sits back down again.

–I need to know you are serious.

–You… need… to know? To know what? I'm sorry, I'm totally fucking confused right about now. I thought you were supposed to be making a pitch to me. Not the other way around.

–Perhaps some parameters would help, Gordo diplomatically offers. I always like a good prompt, don't you? Doctor, perhaps you could state in, say, one sentence or less why it is that you have come here today.

–I solve—

Mrdok stands.

–Now I'm the one who's gonna fuckin leave.

–Please! Sir! Sit down!

No rises in a panic and holds Mrdok's seat out for him. For reasons unknown even to himself, Mrdok retakes it.

The doctor begins to speak calmly.

–We all have problems. We all have pain. There are gradients. How can they be measured? This pain, these gradients. In a word, they cannot be. Because they are bound to relativity. To human experience. One example. A child goes to the doctor, complaining of stomach ache. The doctor looks, finds nothing. There is no underlying disorder. Nothing visible to science, to the scientist's eye, can be discerned as a cause of this pain. Two options, then. Either the child is lying or the pain is real, the cause unknowable. What to do, in such a situation? You ask questions, of course. A task that doctors are very accustomed to. We ask. And still, the information forthcoming is very often not good enough. The details lacking. Or else, just as often, they flatly contradict each other. Making a diagnosis all but impossible. The doctor becomes a medium. Guesswork sets in. Very often, we are right. Our instincts sharpen as a result of these daily transactions. What if, however, there were a solution that was more permanent in nature? A one-fits-all solution. Not that everyone who endures pain—whether it be mild or severe or exaggerated, mental physical emotional whatnot. Not that everyone would *need* this solution. But some, indeed, will *want* it. And the doctor's role, of course, being to determine whose want must be fulfilled, given each particular set of circumstances. Are you starting to get a picture now?

There is something mesmerizing about the way the doctor speaks. Those short clipped phrases, as though adapted to an oversize intelligence, capped with modesty and captured in breath. Gordo looks over at Mrdok and is alarmed to see the extent to which he is being seduced. He feels compelled to speak, to say something, to break the spell.

—We do get the picture, Doctor Yeh. We understand very well what you're trying to say. What we don't understand is what you're trying to sell. What is the miracle product? Because, quite frankly, we've seen quite a lot of miracles come and go over the years.

Gordo lets out a loud sardonic laugh that he expects to catch on. But Mrdok's not laughing.

—You've got my interest, he says. Now. What are you going to do with it?

Yeh leans in.

—Cancer patients. The terminally ill. The suicidal. The neurotically inclined.

He leans in even further and slows his speech to a whisper.

—The addicts.

Mrdok winces.

—What are we gonna do with them?

Yeh leans in even more.

—We're going… to take care of them.

Now Mrdok pushes back.

—Are we? How?

He appears to snap out of it altogether, turns to No.

—You didn't whisper a word to him about… our other deal. Did you?

No widens his eyes at the very utterance of this taboo.

—Then what are we—

—Like I said, Mrdok. I am here to solve problems. I am only interested in solutions. Solutions with brave repercussions. I am interested in… healing humanity, as it were.

—Healing humanity?

—You heard me very well.

—So this… this… *miracle* you're about to pitch me… He is going to pitch me something today, am I right? Or is this just a, just a… what is this? A voodoo session?

Gordo laughs to encourage this welcome return of Mrdok's sense of irony.

Yeh goes on, undaunted.

–You have heard claims. The new pain wonder drugs you have now in America. All over the world, really. But coming from America. What if I told you, the newest, the most potent—the most lasting… the most revolutionary of these drugs, was not going to come from America.

–I'd say, firstly, I don't give a shit, and secondly, you're absolutely right if you're planning on me being involved somehow. Because I've left America, doctor. It aint my domain no more.

–So we've heard.

–You've heard?

Mrdok looks at No.

–We've both heard. This is an island, as well, Mrdok. You happen to know islands pretty well. One thing about them is that words travel very fast.

–Yeah, well. There's a yes and a no to that. Hong Kong is a very different island than the one we're building. Hong Kong's more like Manhattan. In a way, it *is* Manhattan, only…

–Only what?

–Only different. Look. I don't have anything with pharmaceuticals in my portfolio. Which isn't to say I'm *against* it. It just hasn't been my thing… Yet.

–The island as a domain. This is something that interests us a great deal.

–I'm interested in why you're interested.

Doctor Yeh looks down as though gathering his breath after a strenuous mountain hike.

–Introducing… Viutex.

Mrdok looks at Gordo.

–What is this? A fuckin infomercial?

–Sorry, says Gordo. It seems… we don't quite follow…

–Viutex. It is more than a drug. It is a solution, you see.

–It… What?

–To date, science has only managed to produce an opioid with immediate release and controlled release formulations. For the latter category, the duration lasts only ten to twelve hours.

–Only?

–What if I were to tell you, Mrdok, that there are forms of pain in this world far greater than that. Pain, a horrible thing to endure. Some live their entire lives cloaked in it, unable to escape. They know no other existence but one wrought with pain. Imagine. What if we were to show those people that there was another way? What if we were, in a sense, to solve their greatest problem?

–Turn them all into junkies. Keep talking.

–That is crude. I do not hurt people. You have a misconception about me if you think that.

–When was the last time you had sex, Doctor?

–Pardon me?

–You heard me. The last time you got laid. I wanna know.

–Sir, this is not the way we do business in Asia, No gesticulates nervously.

Mrdok pounds his fist on the table.

–Answer the fuckin question.

–I engaged in relations two nights ago.

–With who? Your wife?

–I feel I have answered enough of your inquiry.

–Who was it? Your wife? Your mistress? A pro?

–The latter.

–Huh?

–It was… a professional woman.

–A hooker.

–If you wish. Why do you want to know this?

–I'm just curious.

–Curious?

–I'm a man of certain appetites. I like to know the men I do business with. To see if they have the same kind of appetite I do. You follow me?

–You wish to confirm… my manhood?

–Ha. No. I don't want to see *that*.

–I mean… My level of manliness.

–What I want to know is… whether you're *on* the level.

–On the level?

–Yeah. You know. Like, face to face.

–What Mrdok means is, Gordo interrupts, he wants to confirm that you're a gentleman of honor. One who is going to fulfill any promises, any obligations agreed upon, in the event that paperwork is not deemed fitting for this… transaction, whatever it may be.

–Yeah. What he said.

–And my sexual life is… ?

–It's not important. Not anymore. Let's get on with it, shall we?

–Viutex.

–Viutex. Definitely sounds medical. What does it do?

—Normal extended release Oxycodone only works for ten to twelve hours. You get the concept, how it works, right?

—Yeah. Extended release. It keeps… extending.

—Yes. Within a limited frame of time. Viutex, however, removes that frame.

—What do you mean?

—Precisely that. Viutex is infinite-release. An infinite-release opioid.

Mrdok drops his napkin.

—Holy shit.

He looks at Gordo.

—Is such a thing possible?

Gordo responds with a *why are you asking me?* look.

—It certainly sounds… intriguing, he manages.

—Doctor Yeh has the formula, says No. He invented it, in fact.

—So what, this is for people suffering from… chronic pain?

—Or just want to get high. And stay high.

Mrdok kicks Gordo under the table.

—How does this thing work, exactly? It just comes… like… a pill you take and you stay high forever?

—Relief—

—Oh I'm sorry. Not high. *Relieved*…

—You are *permanently relieved* of all pain. Yes. It is a cure. A—how you say—miracle cure.

—And how… The medicine… just keeps regenerating?

—I am sorry to interrupt, but I can't help but think…

—Yes, Gordo?

—What if one wants it to stop?

—It's a fair enough question. And it helps me answer another posed earlier, that I still haven't gotten to, because you won't allow me to talk.

—You need to be more assertive, Doctor.

—Yes. Now I see. It is not a pill you can take, no. You can think of it as a piece of hardware. Like a computer chip. Only it is comprised of a chemical compound for which only I have the formula. It can be surgically inserted into the body, through a procedure that I have already perfected. Alternately, it can be injected—though this must be done under medical supervision. Patients who attempt to inject it on their own—

—Is there any risk?

—There is no risk. Except that it might not be successful.

—The high might wear off, in other words.

–I have not said anything about a high.

–Maybe you should at least consider it. The opioid crisis?

–This would put an end to that.

–What?

–How's that?

–This would accomplish two things, on the macro level. It would eradicate pain. But it would also eradicate addiction.

–I think I almost see your logic.

–It would end all opiate-related overdoses. All dependencies. It is a solution that is so obvious, that the people in charge, who run things—regulators, politicians, judges, lawyers, pharmaceutical industry executives—cannot even see it.

–I'm sorry, you're saying… If you stay high forever, then that means you're not really high?

–This is a mangled version of what I am saying. I'm saying that the chronic pain patient no longer has options limited to bad and worse. Which are the current two options. Bad being the risk of addiction. Worse is forgoing the medication because of the risk of addiction… Or vice versa, depending on one's perspective.

–You insert this chiplike thing in your body, and it just continues to extend its release of the medication… Until when? Until you die?

–Until the body ceases all functions. Yes.

–Can we just have a word?

–By all means.

Mrdok and Gordo get up, move to a table at the other end of the bar.

–Gordo. Moments like these…

–Yes.

–I mean, if what he's saying is real, and not…

–Yes.

–I mean, *huge*. Like, once in a lifetime…

–Yes.

–Will you quit fucking saying yes for a minute and fucking listen to what it is I'm *trying* to get out? Because, the thing is, we can't let on how astounded we are by what it is we're hearing right now. We have to keep this *absolutely* fucking cool. Like, under the radar. Which means, really, being skeptical. Because, in a way, I *am* skeptical of everything I just now heard. And, I mean, how are we going to get the proof? What I'm thinking now is, we've gotta test it out on one of our own people. We can't rely on *their* lab tests. Whether that someone be—

Gordo's eyes light up.

—Bobby.

—…What the fuck did you just say?

—Well, consider it in more detail, Mrdok. For what the doctor is not saying, but, I believe, is implicitly implying, is that this could also be a *cure for addiction*. No? You just, just, *give* it to addicts, and voilà. You put all the rehab centers out of business, no longer any need for, for the substitute drugs, for Subutex and Methadone and all the other substances that are in many ways *much worse* or at least more *addictive* in their own right than the very drugs they are used to get off of—

—I mean, I see your reasoning, Gordo. But this is my son we're talking about.

—Well, of course we would never do it without his *consent*. Or, at the very least, taking his consent into consideration.

—Yeah… His *consent*. That sounds good. I like it. Honestly, where do you come up with this shit, Gordo?

—Just doing my job, boss. And what about No?

—He's out of the picture. We'll pay him a commission, he goes.

—I'm sure he wants more than that.

—He's not stupid. He knows that's all he's gonna get. Whatever fucking front company he's got going here, ninety-nine percent chance the UN already knows all about it. That's the last thing we need right now, to stir up some international shit for violating North Korean sanctions.

—We give him another suitcase, he disappears.

—Yeah. But we're getting ahead of ourselves. What we wanna do now is, we wanna go back to that table and not look too eager. Say we need to test this shit out for ourselves, and with our *own* doctor, our own lab conditions. That's important. Cos who knows what the hell—

—Right. He gives us the chip, the substance, whatever it may be, we use our doctor to implant it in our human subject—

—And we monitor the results.

—It's important to get an *independent opinion* on this, as well. I will contact some labs, get some quotes—

—Yeah. Absolutely. We have to test it ourselves. And then, if this shit is what the guy is saying it is, well. The sky's the motherfuckin—

—We just have to… Well, we must also consider why he is bringing it to *us*. What I'm curious is how many others—

—I don't think he did. I get the sense we're the first choice. At least that's what No seemed to imply.

—And? You said yesterday that you can't trust a North Korean meth head. He's not going to give us—

–You let me worry about the *deal* aspect of it when the time comes. I'm gonna market the fuck out of this shit. This deal alone could pay for the entire fucking island. You hear me, Gordo? This means we won't even *need* the other shitballs.

–Yes, but surely, there are other advantages to having the shitballs on board besides merely *money*…

–Oh yeah? Like what?

–Insurance, for instance.

–I mean, yeah, you're right. We need shitball money to fall back on.

–In case of any number of scenarios!

–Well. We've got to study that, too, to make sure—

–But for now, we should just focus on the task ahead of us.

–Yes. Seeing the future.

–*Being* the future.

Back at the table, No's the first to speak.

–Doctor Yeh was just expressing his grievance to me. He was saying he feels you are focusing exclusively on the negative aspects of his miraculous invention, while ignoring all the benefits it will bring to humanity, not to mention investors.

–Oh, we see those benefits, Doctor. Don't get me wrong. You're a man of science, but I'm a businessman. You have your tactics, I have mine. And part of what a successful businessman does is not act too eager when someone puts the deal of the century in front of him. Which, I feel, is exactly what you've just done.

Yeh and No look at each other with relief, victory. Gordo looks at Mrdok in disbelief.

–Now. I don't want to go overboard. We do want to test this thing with our people, make sure it is what you're telling us it is. In the meantime, I'm going to have my lawyers draw up a confidentiality agreement and a preliminary contract. I'm gonna have em send it to you *tonight*. In a couple hours. And I want you to send it back to me tonight, too.

Yeh and No exchange glances.

–But…

–No buts. I want this thing to be exclusive, between you and I. And I'm gonna tell you why. When I enter into a party, Doctor, I like to be the first one there and the last to leave. That's just the kind of guy I am. You might not appreciate it now, but you'll come to appreciate what it means having a guy like me on your side. It means I'll never leave it. You and I, my friend, are about to do something really incredible together. The minute we join hands, well… It's gonna be a beautiful, beautiful thing. Because we're gonna be dependent on one another. I could never do what you're able to do. And, well, I believe the reason why you invited me here today is because you realize you can't do what I can do. We really need each other. I really and truly believe that. And you wanna know something else? The world needs us, too.

Mrdok leans in to deliver the final deal-clincher.

–And such needs don't come cheap.

After No and Yeh leave, Gordo stares at Mrdok, aghast.

–… What just happened? he asks timidly.

–In between our private conversation and our way back to the table, I got one of those flashes. You know… the thing I get from time to time… What's it called again?

–An epiphany.

–Yeah. That. Y'know, if this thing is the thing he says it is, then it's not just a single product. A whole line of products—an entire *ecosystem*—is gonna have to eventually grow around it, in order to treat all the things that go wrong because of it. Purdue Pharma: you know what they're doing now? Rehab medicine. To get people *off* the drugs they got them addicted to in the first place. And they're making a *killing* once again. All the negatives in this can be turned into a highly profitable positive. I mean, think about it. You're gonna have people on this thing who are terminally constipated because of it, need relief: a new line of stool softeners. People all itchy, can't stop scratching: something to fix that. Something to keep people awake, the ones who keep nodding off. People who don't take to it, who want to get it removed…

–This could actually be an *ideal* job for Bobby. He knows precisely the ordeals that afflict the common addict!

–It could be a nice little position for him on Sagosia. A way to keep his nose clean. Enter into the family business. While also helping… you know, people like him.

–Yes. And finally showing that kid, once and for all, that there is an *honest* way to make a living in this world!

CHAPTER TEN

PRIVATE ISLANDS

1.

ELIAS BRYNN MRDOK is the type of entrepreneur who was seemingly designed for the twenty-first century. From real estate mogul to philanthropist to Wall Street trader, Mrdok has worn so many hats that he can be tough to recognize. Now, he has added private island owner to his résumé. This autumn, Mrdok purchased Sagosia, an island measuring in at just over fifty square miles in the Brown Sea. What's more, in an unusual move for purveyors of private islands—and certainly a first for this magazine—Mrdok has been negotiating with the authorities to declare sovereignty over his new property, which he has given the name Settlers Landing.

Recently, *Private Islands* was privileged to catch up with the media-shy Mrdok for an exclusive interview in which he revealed plans for his new Brown Sea micronation.

PRIVATE ISLANDS: Congratulations on your recent acquisition, Mr. Mrdok. Can you tell us your current plans for the island?

MRDOK: First off, you can drop the Mister. I just go by Mrdok. As for my plans, well, it's been an interesting process. They've evolved quite a bit from the beginning, you see. At first, it was just intended to be a private retreat. It was sort of my wife's idea, actually. She apparently wasn't satisfied with any of our current homes!

PI: But you are getting a divorce, are you not? At least this is what the story on FaNN, detailing a rather sordid incident in Tokyo—

MRDOK: I actually don't want to comment on my personal life.

PI: … But you just did. You said the purchase of the island was your wife's idea, and went on to say—

MRDOK: Like a lot of married couples, we've had our ups and downs over the years. But I'm not here today to talk about that. I'm here to talk about Settlers Landing.

PI: Right. We're getting there. But to help our readers understand… You are known for being one of the world's wealthiest men, of course, but also one of the more hermetic. At least you don't actively court the media like some of the more flamboyant billionaires who have become household names. Is it that you have purposefully avoided fame? Or do you have something to hide?

MRDOK: It's true that I've never been much of a publicity whore. I'm a private citizen, and as such, I prefer to conduct my affairs outside of the limelight. In fact, this is the first interview I've ever given. How am I doing? As for my income, I can assure you that all of my business is conducted in a manner acceptable both to the laws of the United States government and those governments in whose countries I do business. International real estate is a very complex industry, and I've been very fortunate in that I've been able to work with some of the best and brightest in the field. And, for your information, nearly all the work I've done over the years is centered on philanthropy. That's going to continue with Settlers Landing.

PI: How, exactly?

MRDOK: For one thing, we're planning on building an orphanage. It's the kind of project I do well: helping other people by helping myself. A motto to live by.

PI: Generally, when investors purchase islands, it is either for one of two reasons: as a personal residence or vacation spot, or to develop it for the purposes of tourism. Your plans, however, include neither, from what I understand. You want to do something wholly different, that I believe has never been done before. You are purchasing the island in order to start a new country. So I have to ask: why the need to declare sovereignty over the territory? Isn't ownership sufficient?

MRDOK: Of course part of me just wants the whole goddamn thing to myself. But then, what good is that? Movie stars do that kind of shit all the time. So what, so I can *be alone? On an island?* It's unthinkable to me. I'm a social creature. I don't know. If I want one for myself, I can also get one of those… Actually, cut that out, don't use any of that. Let me go again… Look, it's way too early in the process for me to go into great detail on this one. But if you think I'm merely trying to set up a renegade nation-state as a tax haven for the rich, think again.

PI: Could we go into more detail about how you acquired Sagosia? An inside source tells me that you went about it in a rather roundabout manner. That you, in fact, did a forceful takeover of the island's bank—

MRDOK: The island was acquired in a legal manner.

PI: Mr. Mrdok—

MRDOK: Just Mrdok.

PI: You are said to be worth two or three developing nations' GDP combined. Why the need to assume *leadership* over your own?

MRDOK: Must be because I'm a power-hungry shark! Or a deep dissatisfaction with existing social and governmental conditions might have something to do with it. Ever watch the evening news? A lot of people are real unhappy right now. Lots of folks are hurting out there. I'm here to provide a refuge.

PI: Now you sound like a politician.

MRDOK: If they had the means of doing what I intend to do, I'm sure more people would.

PI: Now do you intend to be the chief inhabitant of the island?

MRDOK: No no no. There are already people living there, you know.

PI: Who, I suppose, will be granted citizenship? How will this work?

MRDOK: Life is about to become much better for all of them. Much, much better.

PI: Okay… What type of settlers do you intend to attract and how will you attract them?

MRDOK: My staff and I have been going through a lot of different propositions and I'd be lying if I said at this point that we have a definite answer to that question. All I can tell you right now is that, yes, we want to attract other settlers to fulfill a myriad of different roles. We're not talking about just a home here, but an entire infrastructure that's being built. A national infrastructure. An economy. Of course it will be much smaller than most nations. In this case, smaller is better. Small, but not unpowerful, and not without influence. There will certainly be a place there for some of the natives of surrounding islands who, for whatever reason, may be unhappy where they are.

PI: Which islands are those?

MRDOK: Oh, there are several. The closest archipelago is the Seashell Islands, of course. For instance, we've established strong relations with Tinique. I personally have spent some time on that island, and can tell you that the people there are wonderful, just wonderful. They've given us a lot of useful advice, and just generally warmed us up to the idea of life in the Pseudotropics. No pun intended! One fun fact: Sagosia itself was once part of an archipelago, but most of those islands are now underwater.

PI: How do the Sagosians feel about your intention to declare sovereignty and change the name of the island?

MRDOK: Well, we haven't been in contact with all of them yet. It's simply too early in the process. There have been some preliminary talks with some of the island's authorities.

PI: This seems like a risky endeavor.

MRDOK: You know, I get to feel more alive when I'm taking risks. When I'm doing things the safe way, well… Do you know of any billionaires, self-made, who got there by playing it safe?

PI: Let me ask this another way—because I'm not getting a firm sense of how you intend to govern. Could you describe for me some of your political beliefs?

MRDOK: (*sighs heavily*)

PI: I don't mean to be rude. But I don't see how the desire to attain sovereignty can be totally detached from the issue of your wealth. I don't hear you spouting Randian libertarian doctrine, but also somehow doubt that you intend this place to be some kind of socialist utopia. So what is it, then? Starting your own country will allow you to practice whatever form of governance you want, or even formulate a new one. Are you to be a monarch? A president? An ordinary citizen? What, exactly?

MRDOK: Those all sound like equally intriguing ideas to me. But look, seriously, the question of government is a tough one. We don't even know at this stage whether our negotiations for sovereignty will be successful or not. My political views, well, they are very much rooted in how I grew up and how I choose to live my life today. I'm not a fan of big government, it is true. But I don't subscribe to any one political party's philosophy. I tend to vote for the guy who supports my view of getting rich while helping others. Other than that, I prefer not to go too much into politics right now. Certainly Settlers Landing will be a place where a lot of the political B.S. that goes on in Washington, you won't have that here. I will tell you this much: I am hoping that the settlers we attract will be largely capable of governing themselves. Do I intend to be a monarch? No, not really. The people who will come to live on my island aren't the type who will need to be told what to do, how to live their lives. They will, in all likelihood, be inspired by my vision, though. Having said that, I hope that we will at least be able to count on their loyalty. Loyalty is what I treasure most, by the way. It's at the bedrock of every nation, I think. So I imagine that the application process that determines who gets to come and live on my island will involve a test of loyalty of some sort. I just can't tell you at this point what all that will entail.

PI: With all your talk about infrastructure, surely you must have devised at least a tentative plan of how the nation will function. It is extremely difficult for an island to remain self-sufficient if its dealings with the outside world are to be limited. Look at the economic problems that Cuba has been experiencing over the years.

MRDOK: Well, hopefully our dealings won't be *that* limited. We're certainly not looking to become another Cuba. One model that's been suggested is that settlers have to earn their way toward non-taxation, at which point a title will be bestowed on them.

PI: Sounds a little like serfdom. Or slavery.

MRDOK: I don't know why you are going to such great lengths to find something sinister in all this. What are you, some kind of a *Marxist*?

PI: From what I have found in my research, it seems that you have largely concentrated your real estate enterprise on countries where building regulations are much more lax than in the United States. Countries where local officials are noted for accepting bribes in exchange for permits and where it is quite normal for people to live in squalor. Care to comment?

MRDOK: Now you're going too far, young lady. I'll have you know that we run projects all over the world, including Europe, where the laws and restrictions tend to be even stricter than they are in the United States.

PI: Ah yes, Europe. In the *Süddeutsche Zeitung* recently—I happen to read German—there was an article on one of your apartment buildings, or rather, your tenants' struggle with the local management company. Apparently the building is rather run-down and the landlord refuses to do anything about it. In the photo accompanying the article, someone has graffiti'd the words *THIS PLACE IS A DUMP* in block letters across the façade.

MRDOK: I'm glad you brought that up. Proves my point exactly. Have you been to Berlin before?

PI: I have not.

MRDOK: The building is located in a neighborhood that has historically been known as a not-so-safe area.

PI: They have such neighborhoods in Berlin?

MRDOK: Drug dealers, immi—*extremists,* it's terrible, terrible. Lately, a bunch of bratty artists have moved in, attracted by the cheap rents—your classic gentrification story, right? Now, if we wanted to be greedy, we could have easily raised the rent three or four times what we were asking a few years ago. Did we do that? No. We happen to like the artists. They do good things for the building, the community—we want them in there. (My wife is a major collector of contemporary art. I'll bet you didn't know that before. Our latest acquisition is a sculpture by the Swedish homosexual artist Olov Blom. It's a very controversial work, because it's actually an enormous, eight foot long butt plug made entirely out of crystal meth. The work is a profound commentary on the current gay condition. They can't even show it in most countries, because it's made from an illegal substance. But you'll be able to see it in the museum of contemporary art we're planning on opening on Settlers Landing.) So anyway, these ungrateful bastards—most of whom grew up in conditions much more nicer than what I grew up in—they throw a fit the minute something breaks down or if it takes the super an extra minute to fix the furnace. Instead of whining to mama about it, they immediately go on social media.

PI: I wouldn't be doing my job if I weren't at least a bit suspicious. Nations have traditionally been formed by people, Mr. Mrdok, not individuals.

MRDOK: Quit calling me *Mister* Mrdok, okay? I'm perfectly well aware of that. But we're living in a new era now. An era of global capital, where the horizons have extended to a height our forefathers would never have even fathomed. What's so wrong with that? Are you an *enemy of progress?*

PI: There are many versions of progress. It seems to me that we will have to wait until your country comes into being to see which version it is meant to represent. One final question for the copy editors: where do I put the apostrophe in Settlers Landing?

MRDOK: There is none. Go figure.

2.

BUZZ BUZZ. IT'S the private line: Mrdok. Marcia picks up.

—Hey, boss. How did the interview go?

—Horrid.

—What… ?

—Tell them to can it.

—Who?

—The magazine, you idiot.

—How do I do that?

—Call her editor!

—Mrdok, I'm sure you're overreacting. It was the first time you've done an interview, I know, but you're so articulate! I'm sure it was wonderful!

—It wasn't me, you idiot. It's that cynical cunt journalist. She's gonna try to make us look like villains, slumlords. I could tell by the questions she was asking. She even brought up *Berlin*.

—… I don't know that we can make them not print it now that you've already given the interview.

—Oh yes you fuckin can. Call Gordo. Nonononono, don't call Gordo. Call Rick. He'll be able to figure out a way.

Click.

—Rick. It's Marcia.

—I know, babe. Your name shows up on the display each time you call.

—Oh yeah? How come my office doesn't have that yet? I guess it's not connected…

—This weather, though. The humidity!

—I'm starting to get used to it.

—Hm. So what can I do for you, Marcia?

—It's Mrdok.

—It always is.

—Apparently the interview didn't work out the way he wanted. He has a bad feeling about their intentions. He's looking for a way to halt publication.

—Jesus fuck. What happened exactly?

—You'll have to ask him. Actually don't. He said her questions were slanted, that it's gonna make him look bad. She brought up the German article. Could seriously jinx the whole project. That's what he fears.

—Tell him not to worry. I've got it taken care of.

–How are you going to do that? I'm curious. He *agreed* to do the thing. They're not gonna let us pull the plug *after* the fact.

–I'm not gonna do it. The lawyers are. Thanks, Marcia.

Click.

–You have reached the law offices of Heimach, Hynek, and Silverding. How may I direct your call?

–It's Rick, calling from Mrdok's office. Give me Marty.

–Connecting.

–Marty, it's Rick.

–Didn't you fire me?

–Not at all. That was Gordo.

–Who works for Mrdok.

–You're not fired, Marty. Look, I need your advice on something. How do you stop an interview from going to press after you've already agreed to it and done it?

–Technically, you don't. Ever heard of the First Amendment?

–Sure as shit, but I'm talking muscle here, Marty.

–Why the fuck did he agree to an interview in the first place? It's on the Sagosia project, am I right? I thought there was a no press rule. Why is he breaking it now? You tell him that was a good idea?

–Yes. For the island. He thought it'd do him some good from the authorities on Pembroke if he got some positive publicity flowing, so he chose the most harmless vehicle he could find—*Private Islands* magazine—y'know, the type of place that specializes in giving guys like Mrdok blowjobs in print. Instead, they laid a beartrap, sent along some Seven Sisters cunt with teeth.

–Classic. What do we got on paper? He grab her tits or something?

–Worse. She went for his balls. So far, looks like… a bunch of emails fleshing out the particulars? The interview took place this morning in South Beach.

–Did you get a copy of the transcript? Or, better yet, the recording?

–Not yet. I thought it was too soon.

–Maybe we don't even need to go that far. Look, Rick, you're a clever guy, and I know Mrdok pays you a pretty penny to clean up his shit after him.

–Actually, that's Gordo.

–What?

–Gordo. He's the shit cleaner-upper. My new title is CVO.

–CVO?

–Chief Vibes Officer.

—Whatever. What kind of tie-up do you have with this magazine?

—Uhh… I think I know what you mean.

—Of course you do. Need me to spell it out? There's a goddamn knot there, isn't there? Untie it. If there's not a knot, you'd better go and make one.

—Always nice talking to you, Marty.

—You too, kid.

Click.

—*Private Islands* magazine, how may I direct your call?

—Editor's desk.

—Doctor Boyle is out to lunch. Would you like to speak to his assistant?

—Even better.

—Editorial.

—Hell there. This is Richard Stewart calling from Mrdok's office.

—Oh hello.

—You guys are out in California, am I right? What's the weather like out there today?

—Oh, you know, bright and sunny as always.

—Good. Glad to hear it. Same out here in Sagosia.

—You're calling from… ?

—That's right, I am. Sagosia. My lady friend, by the way, she just *adores* Santa Monica.

—Uh, is there something I can help you with, Mister, uh… ?

—Oh, sorry, you must be really busy. Well, as you know, Mrdok had an interview this morning with one of your journalists down in Miami. Apparently the thing went down so well that now, the boss-man wants to buy an ad to promote Sagosia in the same issue.

—Well, that's good to hear. But I'm afraid I'm the wrong person to talk to about that. Here, let me connect you to advertising.

—Wait-wait-wait. I think you don't understand… I mean… Sorry, a bit overworked here, not used to all this sunshine, it's starting to fry my Manhattan brain!… You do understand, of course, but, um… Look, there's something I wanted to ask you. An editorial matter. Concerning the article.

—And what would that be?

—We were wondering if we might get a transcript or, even better, a recording of the interview sent to our office. I was just on the phone with the lawyers and… there's some concern that Mrdok might have let slip a detail or two that we're not yet at liberty to reveal to the public. If you catch my drift.

–I'm… sure that's doable. I'll have to talk to Miz Reiss, the journalist, first, though. I haven't heard from her yet today.

–That's fine. What was your name again?

–Herb. Herbert Schneider. I'm Doctor Boyle's assistant.

–Doctor, hey?

–Yes. Doctor Boyle gave up his surgical practice to start this magazine. Private islands are his passion.

–Well well well. How poignant. And serendipitous! Do you think Doctor Boyle could give me a call when he's back in the office?

–I think so. Meanwhile, I'll redirect you to Advertising.

–Thanks, Herb. Do tell Doctor Boyle I'm looking forward to that call.

–… Yes.

Click.

–You've reached the *Private Islands* magazine advertising office. This is Marie! How can I help you today?

–Wow, so cheery! I love it. Must be that California sunshine, haha. Marie, this is Rick Stewart calling from Mrdok's office. Do you know who that is?

–Mister Mrdok? Why yes indeed! I heard through the grapevine that we are going to be running a very big feature on him in the next issue!

–Well, you really have your ear to the pulse, Marie. I can already tell that you all are a bright bunch over there.

–Would you be interested in speaking with one of our ad executives? I'm kind of surprised they haven't reached out to you already.

–I'll level with you, Marie. I'm about to make the day of everyone working in your office. I'm talking like, news flash! Bu-bu-bump! Put me through to your most senior ad exec. I mean, the guy (or gal) who handles the big kahunas. I need someone with lots of experience, Marie. Cos this is Big Business we're talking about here. Put me through to the Boss Man!

–That would be Doctor Finkelstein! Connecting!!!

–Finkelstein here.

–Tell me, do you have to be a doctor to work at *Private Islands* these days?

–Uhm, who is this?

–How rude of me. This is Richard Stewart. You might know me better as Mrdok's personal assistant. Well, one of them, at least!

–Ah, Mister Stewart. But of course. How are you this afternoon.

–I'm great. But really, what's with the doctor thing?

–Oh, there's just two of us, I assure you. Doctor Boyle and myself. We pooled our savings together and retired early from the medical profession a few years back…

–… and succeeded in creating the world's most illustrious publication dedicated to the pursuit and cultivation of the private island.

–Couldn't have said it better myself.

–Well, you don't need to, because that's what I'm here for. It's a fine art, Doctor Finkelstein, a fine art. And a fine magazine, I might add. I mean, what an accomplishment! Everyone here in the office subscribes and reads each issue *religiously*. I can't tell you how much of a thrill it was when we heard Sagosia was going to be featured in the next issue.

–Well, I'm sure—

–No, wait, I take that back. I *can* tell you how much of a thrill it is. Are you ready?

–…

–It is such a thrill for us that we want to be featured not once, but twice. Do you see what I'm saying, Doctor Finkelstein?

–You want to buy an ad?

–Haha. Really, what Mrdok wants more than anything, is to offer you guys a hand. You know, he *really* believes in what you're doing. He doesn't just view you guys as another media outlet. You know, all the big ones have been clamoring for an interview, not just for the past months when word about the Sagosia project came out, but really for a number of years. Mrdok has always said no, to all of them. Why is that? He just doesn't believe. Doesn't believe in what they're doing, what they stand for. But you guys, on the other hand. He can almost envision you out here on Sagosia with us.

–Are you saying… ? Well, what *are* you saying, Mister Stewart? If I recall from my conversation with Doctor Boyle, we did try to get out to Sagosia for the purposes of the interview. Your people insisted it wasn't ready yet, that's why we ended up doing it at South Beach. We would have much rather—

–Oh, I know, I know. Between you and me, Doc, I was personally really annoyed by that, as well. But the thing is, it's not Mrdok. He really wanted to bring you guys out there. It's the frickin lawyers. You know how that is. There are a couple of conflicts right now with the local municipal government that we haven't yet managed to get ironed out—

–You mean the whole sovereignty thing? Mister Stewart, it all does seem rather… questionable, from our vantage point.

–That's only because it's never been done before. But Mrdok does have a vision, you know. And that's what I want to talk about with you. We've done the interview— and I'm hoping it will be the first of many conversations between you guys and Mrdok in the coming months— now, we're looking for another way, a, uh, *visual* way of presenting that... well, *vision*... in your pages, if that makes sense?

–Right. A visual vision. Makes sense to me! So I can email you the ad specs—

–What is the most prestigious place in the magazine for an ad? The back cover, I'm guessing.

–Well, yes, that would be the most prestigious, certainly, in terms of visibility... But we have a long-standing agreement with Luxia, you might know them? The real estate company, they specialize in private islands, lakes, mountains, that type of investment property. And the inside back cover, I'm afraid is reserved for our sister publication, *Private Yachts*.

–We want to buy the *front* cover.

–Ahahahahaha. That's a good one, Mister Stewart. You almost had me there for a minute.

–No, I'm serious.

–Uhm, Mister Stewart, the front cover is not for sale, I'm afraid. It's a magazine, not a catalog.

–You know, the decline of print media and all. Such a sad state of affairs. A lot of magazines have taken to doing it. You just staple our ad on to your cover. It's like an added bonus for the reader. Another little piece of content they get for free. It certainly doesn't detract anything from, from your *own* cover, the cover of the magazine, that will go beneath it. What we want—

–We're a luxury high-end publication, Mister Stewart. That kind of advertisement is not necessary for us. Or for our readers, for that matter.

–How much do, uh, Luxuria? Luxury Diarrhea? What are they called again?

–Luxia.

–How much do they pay for the back cover? If I may ask.

–The price for the back cover is sixty grand, Mister Stewart.

–Okay. Sixty k. I'm writing this down here in my notes. Well, I have to say, to us, that's really not a whole lot of money, Doc. I mean, I don't know how much Mrdok told your journalist the scope of this project— I haven't gotten a chance to read the interview yet— we're all here in the office really looking forward to seeing it— but what

Luxia gives you guys really pales in comparison to what we're ready to—

—What is your ultimate aim?

—Excuse me?

—Why do you want to buy an ad? You're already getting free publicity, in the form of an article. Why do you also have to—

—We see this as more than, than an article. More than just publicity. We're really trying to build a *relationship* here with you guys.

—A relationship.

—We want to be partners. Going into this. Which is why we're willing to offer—

—It didn't go well, did it.

—… What didn't go well?

—The interview today.

—Well, uh, look, Doctor, we all have—

—I'll have you know Miz Reiss went to Berkeley, one of the finest journalism schools in the country. She just graduated, she's a little feisty—

—Berkeley, you say. So it all makes sense now.

—We need people like her to, to. Well, I can't speak on behalf of the editors, though this is my magazine too, damn it. We need people like her, with different voices, *critical* voices, to give the magazine texture. Otherwise we stand accused—

—Look, I've got nothing against a person doing her job. Who exactly does the fact-checking at your magazine? Might we expect a call—

—Our editorial department isn't huge. We have a small team. A small, but able team, I might add.

—I get that. Which is why I think you will probably need my help in the fact-checking process. Which is why I really need to get a complete transcript—

—I can transfer you back to editorial.

—But it is your magazine, as you just said. I really prefer to communicate with people at the top. Especially, as I said, if we're contemplating entering into a partnership—

—What kind of partnership did you have in mind, Mister Stewart?

—Drop the mister. Just call me Rick. I can call you doctor, I don't mind.

—I'll ask again: What kind of—

—One hundred grand.

—Pardon me?

–You give us the back cover, the rights to review the transcript prior to publication, just to make sure—

–Mister Stewart, first of all, we don't sell our ads at auction. Secondly, we need to ensure the editorial integrity—

–We want to ensure the editorial integrity of the interview, as well. But from our side. You see what I'm saying?

–Mister Stewart, *Private Islands* is a small publication. We don't even have much of an online presence at the moment (though we are hoping to improve that in the near future.) Why are you taking such an interest in our—

–A small, *targeted* publication, I'd call it. And our target audience happens to align very well, Doc. Which is why I'm proposing we make the most out of this mutual interest. We can't do that, however, if there is someone between us who doesn't have our mutual interest deep in their hearts. If you follow my drift…

–Was the interview really that bad? I mean, I know she can be feisty, but—

–She did ask some questions that, from Mrdok's perspective, were rather surprising. Given that—not that *he* felt insulted by them—he just felt that they, they reflected *badly* on the part of *Private Islands* magazine. I mean, from what I hear, your subscribers' list includes a number of very influential people. I would hate… I mean, a lot of these people, Mrdok is *very close* with. Wouldn't it be a shame, if you were to *alienate* a large segment of your readership? Since the, like you said, you *are* a small, exclusive magazine—

–And so what you propose is—

–Don't get me wrong. We respect your editorial integrity. We want that, too. We absolutely want the interview to run. But, to protect our interests, we will need to collaborate to make sure the correct version of the information is going out, and not a skewed version, filled with inaccuracies, you know, fake news is I think what they call it—Surely, you don't want *Private Islands* to become associated with fake news. It's such a problem these days, in today's media environment—

–Well, if you can help us on that level, then I think an argument might be made… But, um, strictly speaking, I only sell ads. So you were saying, one hundred grand for the back cover? Now would you like our in-house designer—

–Oh we have our own designer. Our media team is very strong, very strong. We're like you guys, you know, we have our own editors and fact-checkers and everything. So think of the ways we can help. Just think. So many ways! So many, many ways…

CHAPTER ELEVEN

ISLANDS IN THE STREAM

A SECRETARY BURNS papers. A pilot glides a plane. World commences its descent into underworld; the blockage of a toilet is suddenly relieved. The blockage of a man is complete, allowing a double flow. There is such a thing as night here on planet Earth, but you have to be in the right spot in order to experience it. Hard to accomplish when you're never still. There are places to be, people to thrill. Others you wish to kill. Some you will be surrounded by by want of luckless opportunity, the pursuit. Like the porn star who risks his life for a brief glimmer of notoriety. You are already here, might as well make yourself useless.

An S in the landscape. See that car, driving real fast through the curve. Should be *around* the curve—but this one goes right *through* it, across the foliage to the other stretch of road. Violating the curve. Oblivious to all threat of danger. It is a red Chevrolet Corvette and it is being driven by a billionaire—which makes it all the sexier. Fast car fast car, drive into a star. Keep going until you don't know where you are. Where is he anyway—this scape, it must be somewhere in the south of Europe. He can never get fast enough, no matter how far he goes, and that is a shame. Even when he's alone, there is someone right behind. A wolf at every door.

***

CRETE: High on life. The days pass this way. They are endless, which is exactly how we like them to be in these summer climes. Slide down Coco's breasts and into her mouth. A cherry—plop—the sweetness and some laughter. Because every time they see each other—whether it's in the dining hall, outside by the pier, sneaking off somewhere to smoke or recreate, a chance meeting coming out of the locker room on the way to the pool—smiling their faces off. Holding each other tightly every chance they can get. Time has no structure to it, now is when you feel that formlessness the most. The picture of her; the sound of her laughter the rattle in your soul.

SAGOSIA: At the end of the dirt lane where Maria and her family's lot is situated, the neighbors like to take turns blasting music from their trailers each day. There's one system to go around, and it rotates each morning. Today's Tuesday, so it's Maria's turn. She doesn't have to work today, her husband and the boys're all out of the house, so she lazily slides Creedence Clearwater Revival's greatest hits into the disc player, cranks up the volume to max, then heads outside with the laundry basket.

SHELTER ISLAND: Jaco walks into the room, announces to all present:
    —I farted.
    The t is repeated somehow: *I fart-ted.* As though the kid had a stutter— which he never had before the last paint-eating incident. Mrtol too distraught to feel concern or otherwise admonish this vulgarity, just shakes her head.
    Jaco leans against the doorway shyly.
    —Jaco! she now says. Get your fingers out of your mouth!
    Roused from her pity stupor, almost ready to go back to being a mom again.
    —He's at that age, she explains to her own. You know. Obsessed with their own farts.
    —Well, says grandma. We both know which parent he got *that* from.

SVALBARD: It's the middle of winter, the arctic night that lasts twenty-four-seven, and a family of three polar bears is on its way in to the Svalbard Museum to see the new Olov Blom exhibition.
    —What is AIDS? the daughter asks her father.
    —A disease that humans get, he replies.
    —*Used* to get, the mother corrects.
    —I don't get it, says the daughter. He's written across this canvas, *Thanks for giving me your AIDS.* Why would someone be thankful for getting a disease?
    —He is just trying to be provocative, the mother says.

—Well, I think it's more than that, says the father. The artist is a homosexual. For humans, this is regarded as an unnatural practice. He is therefore making an ironic commentary on the self-nature that is instilled in those who engage in that kind of pleasure.

—Can we polar bears get AIDS? asks the daughter.

—Oh no! says the mother. Thank goodness not.

—We are free to engage in whatever unnatural practices we wish! says the father.

—Some say that looking at art would constitute an unnatural practice.

—But the Norwegians built this just for us! What could be unnatural about it?

—The human world is doomed, says the mother. That's why we shouldn't feel guilty about eating them.

—Indeed, affirms the father. Because if we don't eat them, they will take our skin off. They like to put it in front of expensive fireplaces.

—Humans are indeed strange creatures.

—I hope I get the chance to taste one some day, says the daughter. The parents embrace her.

—You will, my darling. You will.

STATEN ISLAND: Numbers. That's what she gets when she glues the pieces together. Just a bunch of numbers. But what could it actually mean? And what is Belle Encoding, with the mermaid logo she keeps seeing at the top of each sheet, in that strange green font? It's like a super complex puzzle, and she's hooked. And so she sits there for hours on end moving the little shreds around and gluing them together. What else is there to do anyway.

MANHATTAN: Mrdok's favorite book, the only one he ever finished reading: *Moby Dick*. His favorite band: Belle and Sebastian. His favorite all-time song: *Respect* by Aretha Franklin. There was even a water cooler rumor at the home office in Manhattan, when the home office still existed, that he employed a harem of gospel singers to serenade it to him as he took his morning dump. I know it's not true. I also know that this is the sort of rumor that Mrdok doesn't mind circulating.

JAPAN: After they fucked, before they fell asleep, she told him all about her childhood. He told her nothing, it just now occurs to her.

There she was, making an ass of herself waxing drunkenly poetic about the taste of the Mediterranean on her lips in the summertime, swimming in the warm clear waters off her father's yacht, the tzatziki and hummus and olives, how much she still loves her little Greek island even though it's been ruined, she just can't divorce herself from it and how that is most certainly rooted in those idyllic summers of her childhood she can somehow never leave behind… How he *got something* out of her. Something with which to leverage. Goddamnit. Now she has no choice but to destroy him.

MADAGASCAR: The lemur surveils the naked field. Empty of all machinery, empty of all human inhabitance. Empty of ground, even. Where has it all, everything, gone? Where does the forest begin? Or if the forest has ended, how will it then regrow? What must one do now to find something to climb upon, to chew on? How long to travel before one discovers a friend that can be recognized as such— as oneself?

MANHATTAN:
—How long is this going to take? she asks.
Marty looks at her.
–Well, pending Mrdok's cooperation—
–Fuck. So you're telling me—
–Mrtol. I know you want him out of your life.
–No, Marty. I don't want it to be that easy for him. I want it to be easy for me. Not for him. I want that bastard to suffer.
–Well. I can't *guarantee* that.
–Yeah? Then maybe I need to find a lawyer who can. Why do you think I came to you, Marty? I would think you would have an interest in this too, after the way he treated you.
–Divorce is *never* easy, Mrtol.
–Oh yeah? Did I forget to mention? I have proof.
–Proof? Proof of what?
–Proof of adultery.
Marty sits up in his swivel chair now, interested.
–If this isn't enough to nullify the pre-nup…
She slides her phone across the table.
Marty's mouth agog.
–Where was *this* taken?
–Tokyo. I'd decided to pay him a surprise visit. I walked in on this delightful little scene in his hotel suite.

Marty studies the image on the iPhone, then picks up the landline on his desk. –Maureen? Get Markowitz on the line.

SARDINIA: Now he's on a motorcycle, a Ducati 916. The traction on these beauties is such to send celebrity millionaire poet Frederick Seidel into reams of versal spillage and self-ironic epiphany. Mrdok's not so verbose about it. Nor as enthusiastic. But he can appreciate a good well-made ride, and he doesn't so mind the fast-going. Speed on the ground is fine. It's when he's up in the air so high that it bothers him. Bev used to say it had something to do with how he was an earth sign. It makes a kind of sense. In an airplane, he's okay if he's real high up. But if he is able to see the ground, that's when he panics. And no amount of Valium will help. But Mrdok never bothered to learn anything about astrology. It's just not his thing.

SHELTER ISLAND:
    —Do *you* fart, grandma?
    The kid had been an accident, arriving late in the marriage, but as good a reason as any not to split up. Not that Mrdok was ever around. He had gone into himself, further and further. Kid had grasped the domain of play so hard, he could do whatever he wanted with it. He didn't need this world, he was ceaselessly creating his own. Which is why, as she stares at him now, she thinks in her mind just how very unstressful the divorce will be on him. She could go further. The kid will have a better life with that asshole of a non-father out of the picture altogether, or as far outside the picture as the judge will ultimately allow.
    –No, Jaco. Grandma never farts. Never, ever.

SAGOSIA: He's in the back of a Benz truck, tinted windows, bullet-proof, being driven. It's been specially imported, just for him—he's the first on the island ever to ride in one. The island's exotica opens up to him—he doesn't know the names of plants or trees, but he can tell when a tree is old, and these are ancient—their trunks're like elephant trunks, twisting confusedly yet firmly into the birch-colored soil they speed past down the main paved road, into the center where the grands maisons are said to occupy the terrain. He looks away to scroll down his social media feed, take stock of all the damage that's been done. Until it all gets to be too much—he's already growing numb to the repercussions—and looks outside at the foliage, the houses with the weird squiggles, and begins to accept all this as his new reality.

CRETE: He's getting stronger, he's swimming every day. Swimming and fucking—until it all congeals into a swirly happiness. Definitely never this happy before. He wants to do things now, go places he hasn't—he never really traveled, never anywhere that far away or interesting. Through her, the world's grandeur opens up to him. The meetings, sessions are almost incidental. He knows he's nearing the end of his time here. But where will she go. What will she do. He can't bring himself to bring it up with her. Not quite yet.

SAGOSIA: He runs through the night, torch in his hand, friends screaming drunk running close behind. This feeling of freedom like no other, it is the ghost in the machine's lower intestine. Running through the abandoned trailer park, setting everything man-made alight. Trailers aren't easy to burn. Certainly not from the outside. You really have to go inside them, do it in a way you can escape. The goal, always, is to get a circle of fire burning around you. Watch as the night sky sucks the smoke right up into the stratosphere.

CUBA: *The Mark of Linear Motion.* That's what's written on the sign that is the first thing Gordo sees when he clears customs at José Marti International Airport. It's being held by a blonde woman in horn-rimmed glasses who doesn't look at all Cuban. Before he has a chance to contemplate the possible meaning of this, a hand startles him by clamping itself on his shoulder. He turns around to the Renaldos.

–So nice to have you back in Havana!

While the other one unburdens him of the briefcase containing their prize.

SAGOSIA:

—It's untranslatable. There is no word for *goodbye* in the quasinatives' language. The island is too small to contain such notions.

EARTH: Scattered, the lives threaten to spend themselves sideways. Across this granite planet, dues being paid and debts renegotiated, drones buzzing over the plastic soldiers crawling into plastic surgery clinics where morticians paw at decapitated Barbies under general anesthesia. Milky rabbits produced in sweatshops in yesterday's Third World are collected in aluminum wire baskets to be shipped to today's First World accompanied by fantasies of increased returns, only to be dashed on that road to discovery we ride down so fast there is no hope of imprinting one iota of landscape data upon our digitalized membranes.

Shards of cognition, cognites, viewed from behind rain-stained spectacles worn with a strap. Loose-jawed mothers teaching their daughters the pull-out method of birth control because nothing else is available. Malarial mosquitos bite the hanging giant willises of the leaders of the tribe as they wonder which big animal they will kill next or whether a big animal will come and eat them first.

Moon-sized drill is inserted into the earth to extract from the layers meant to bury us all the precious treasures geological rot endeavors to foment when the centuries are on its side, disturbing the tectonic plates and readying the earth for its next great extinction miracle.

The earth generates its own mathematics, scientists and scholars scramble to understand.

On a volcanic island in the sea of Japan, a son of Mrdok stands on a hilltop with microphone in hand, recording silence's tricky engulfment proceedings.

***

The chopper cuts through a cloud, making a steady cautious descent above the shimmering glass. Vincent stands upon the wettened shores, smoking a hand-rolled cigarette, silently appraising the wind's mild midday violence being whipped up from above. Stares up at the fucking sky machine coming down toward him, his island. Snorts.

Here are some rich white people. They've paid an absurd fee to be taken around the island. Used to be you'd see them once or twice a year. Now suddenly they're coming in droves. Some are tourists, but many are coming for other reasons still not too clear to Vincent. He's just paid to take them where they're meant to go. If more keep coming, he will eventually have to enlist others to help him. Teach them what to do. Where to move them. How to talk to them. Vincent himself hardly knows. But he knows his island; that he knows well. Humdrum things to him fascinate them. The names of the plants, the trees; the marks on the sides of the buildings. All he has to do is show them and explain. Drives them to their destination in the center. They give him money in return. Eagles squawking overhead, the helicopter lands in the middle of a momentary sandstorm. Vincent stands idly by, smoking.

A man and a woman, a married couple, they're all smiles and eager to know you. Americans, he supposes. The last couple, they were

Swiss, or maybe German. Hard to remember. Spoke in a language he couldn't understand. That much he remembers. What block of land they belong to, it's all abstract. Vincent's never been anywhere outside of Sagosia except for Pembroke one time.

–Sorry, calls out the lady, the furious chopper slapping her hair all over. We're looking for someone named Vincent. Is that you?

Rich people are bored, he supposes. They want to see things they have never seen before. An island is an exotic thing to them. The clarity of the water, the weird formations of the exotic trees. Tropicalia of a sudden breeze. Next thing he knows he is about to sneeze. At times he imagines it all from their perspective. It's fun to try. To put yourself in that foreign frame of mind.

The day will come he is no longer a fisherman. He will earn his keep from these other activities. He'll become a customer of the men he once fished with. There might even be money left over. Then he'll have to figure out what to do with it, what to spend it on.

Vincent snaps out of it, stubs out his cigarette.

–Yes, Vincent, that's me. Welcome to Sagosia. This is my home.

BOOK II

PART ONE

MIDDLEMEN

1.

HARRY HULL STANDS naked against the morning sun. It has been his morning routine these past few weeks, since shortly after arriving. He is sure to be here early enough so that everyone can see him as they arrive at the office to begin the day's shift. A silent protest, vulgar and placid in the same gesture. A naked standing. The Presidential Palace, the headquarters—for everything, really—a newish building, construction having begun five years ago, shortly after the quasi-elites' arrival. The architect brought out here from Los Angeles, a mutual acquaintance having introduced he and Mrdok—well, they had the same coke dealer, according to local lore. The resulting morass looks like an old-fashioned ocean liner given the robotic futuristic spin. Concrete and chrome, a style that Harry had heard the asshole architect deem Streamline Po-Moderne—even pronouncing the E at the end like the letter from the alphabet—one night at the Wet Nasty, the bar in Olde Colonia where all the quasi-elites congregate after their shifts at the headquarters to spew their gossipy bullshit, trade bitchy jibes, and plot against one another in a maze of faux cork-lined VIP rooms. Harry sitting at the bar, ignored, watching them all in a state most would ascribe to mere envy at the fact of his exclusion.

Sun pours down like rain, turning his skin from gold to brown. Today it's not so bad, his flesh has grown accustomed to the rays. The worst was a couple weeks before, when he'd had the herpes outbreak. Sunshine and herpes don't complement one another. Harry learned this the hard way. Talk about a sight to shield your eyes from. What's the saying—a sight for sore eyes? This was a sore sight for, well, unsore eyes. But it had made that week's protest all the more punishing, in a way. All that harder to ignore—if the sight of a naked man standing beneath the harsh punishing sun before a slab of gray concrete Brutalist monoliths that someone had had the sardonic gall to deem a palace wasn't hard enough to block out on its own.

2.

THE SEA'S GRAYNESS a wasping, a shunted avery.

Oh no. That's not it. What would be the best way to describe the sea. Not describe; evoke. The sense of. Seaness of. Comparison with some kind of animal, for sure; has to be. Not an obvious one, either. Hence, *avery* instead of just plain jane *bird*… But wait, avery isn't an animal… Was it avery or aviary he meant to write? Shunted or stunted? Aviary is the, where the birds live. Shunt is like, uh, to sidetrack. How is the sea, its grayness, like a, like a place where birds live that's been sidetracked? Fuck. The point is, always has been, to shock the reader. Not shock necessarily, but awaken, *startle*—with an unsettling, or at least unexpected metaphor. Else it isn't much of a poem. Isn't that what old Forrest Barre taught us in his MFA workshop all those years back? Those years of certainty. Lacking, perhaps, the alcoholic wisdom of the middle years. Now losing the thread. The point is the sea and how to, not *describe* it, but evoke the damn thing. Poets don't *describe*. Poets going back to Homer, with his, what was it, wine-red? A glass of wine would be fine right about now. Not red, though. Red is for evening. The evening-dark wine. The poet looks at his watch. Just past 10 a.m. Sometimes a poem emerges from the stuff of morning. One must be, what is it, vigilant, on guard, constant, lest it get away. A sunrise, for instance—prime material for capturing something. Mostly, it's a fettering-away at an absence, a present absence—or else vice versa. He drops his pen in his notebook. What matters most, perhaps, is the *evening* sky. A change of scenery, then. A suspension until then.

How had it all come to this? Well, he knows. After being denied tenure, he'd retreated upstate, where his family still had their vacation cottage in the mountains. There, he'd settle himself before the laptop each morning with a mug of steaming herbal tea with just a splash of bourbon to embark on that crucial activity well known to all North American non-tenured poets: filling out fellowship applications and writing grant proposals. More time on this than on the actual writing of poetry, of course. But that's the life that chose us, as a tear forms in the eye…

–Well, if it isn't our great bard!

The pinched nasal voice startles him every time and has a habit of nearly always originating somewhere behind his stiffened back.

–Oh, but don't let me disturb you. I can see that you are composing *in situ*. I wouldn't want to interrupt that permutation of genius that is no doubt emanating from somewhere deep within your cerebellum and then radiating outward to the very tips of your manly fingers. I was just driving past, on my way to another day of earnest endeavor at the Presidential *Palais*, when I happened to see you and thought this might be an opportune moment to finally hand you a copy of my own modest tome, an extra one I just happened to have with me here in the car.

Nailpolished—wine-red!—fingers, manly, then held out to him a hardback wrapped in glimmering dust jacket boasting an extreme close-up of its author's heavily botoxed heavily made-up visage, its title rendered beneath in cursive hot pink lipstick lettering that somehow clashed with the overall aesthetic, giving it an '80s hair metal vibe: *Man Enough to be a Woman, Woman Enough to be Gordina.*

–Thanks, offers the poet in a rather thankless tone. I was just getting ready—

–Absolutely no thanks is necessary. I have taken the liberties to inscribe the tome, if you'd like to take a look.

Birchfield opens to the scrawl on the title page: *With burning admiration to our premiere Poet Laureate…*

–Will we be so fortunate as to have your presence grace us this night at the Wet Nasty? I'm sure I speak on behalf of the entire Settlers Landing artistic community when I assert that we'd love to hear some of your recent verses read aloud, even if they are still currently confined to the format of work-in-progress.

–I, uhh… I'm not *quite there* at the point where I'm prepared to read anything new. You must understand, my process… I rewrite *a lot* before I get to where I'm ready uh… I guess I could read from one of my older books?

–*That.* Would be splendid.

Gordina shimmers her shoulders and offers what the poet interprets to be either a half-wink or a reflexive twitch. Whatever it was, it is hard not to interpret it as clumsily invitational. Such gratings making it even harder to write around here.

–Well, I'm ready whenever you are, Mister Birchfield.

The last thing she says to him before she winks and speeds off toward Olde Colonia in a Pagani Huayra the same shade of maroon that lines her eyeballs.

3.

THESE PAST FIVE years have flown past us with the chirping velocity of some gay songbird. Matters of state have proven to be even more stimulating than matters of business, I am pleased to report, never having suspected that such a thing might even be possible. And if Mrdok's case is any example by which to set a lasting precedent, we might without hesitation confirm the never-before-tested hypothesis that a great businessman doth a great leader make!

Which is not to assert that this half-decade has been completely free of trials. Certain traitors manifested themselves out of the mist who had to be expelled from the inner circle. Rabble rousers with a minoritarian viewpoint may have attempted to sow the seeds of discord on our idyllic isle. There was the messy matter of the removal of Mrdok's former wife from the life narrative—whom we would indeed bother to feel sorry for had she ever been truly deserving of Mrdok's love. But why dwell on such unfortunate creatures, when they will no doubt emerge in their rightful place in the overall historical flow, which like a river is naturally cognizant of its own rightful direction. And, secondly, why dwell on the negative when there is so much bordering on the utopian to wake up to and bask in and celebrate each and every morning?

In short, I have also undergone my own struggles, including a recent bout of sleeplessness that perhaps unintentionally lends my narrative a certain hallucinatory intensity, for which I must apologize. But I have reached the point of enlightenment in my own life in which I fear not my own struggles, and will make no attempt to conceal them from my readers.

After giving it a good honest attempt for a number of years, I came to comprehend that the male homosexualist lifestyle just wasn't for me. I had reached a state of confusion regarding my own identity, and had very little time available to address the issue in any detailed way. I was, after all, in the process of establishing a new country by Mrdok's side, which involved everything from diplomacy to lawmaking to military and cultural affairs and beyond. What is more, I had already announced my intentions to divorce Joanne by then—coincidentally around the same time that Mrdok was engaged in his own legal separation from Mrtol (for it turned out, in a stunning revelation of Mrdok's cunning foresight, that they had never actually been legally married; the wedding event had been, unbeknownst to Mrtol, engineered as a staged event, replete with an actor playing the priest, by Tony Fatballs in order to protect Mrdok's future financial interests against any matrimonial claims.) Little more to say on that subject, other than that the tensions between Joanne and myself had risen steadily as the permanency of my move to Settlers Landing became increasingly apparent. Our chief mode of communication became the scream call. I had, of course, been very open to her about what I believed at the time to be my authentic condition of homosexuality, and she had accepted this without reservation, since the romantic aspect of our relationship had not been so pronounced for some time. Then, in the course of one of our many arguments, certain salacious revelations about Joanne's relationship with Dot the mail lady came to the fore. I cannot say I was all that shocked by the news. Though its debut in the open air did in simultaneity unveil the naked statue of a truth we had both long been wrestling with and had been ineffectually arguing our way around: namely, that we had been in a marriage of convenience all along without fully realizing it. And the only remedy for this sad state of affairs would be to disentangle ourselves from the legal union, the last ribbon that was binding us. Once free of that weighted piece of symbolism, we would both be free to traverse the respective pathways that life had destined for us, free of any burdens upon the conscience.

Yes, the time had come for each to forget who we once were and to become ourselves anew. My self regained: a daunting prospect, for I knew not what I really was. And yet the world, every aspect of my life, had been shouting it at me for so long. All those times I had answered Mrdok's phone and the other party had asked if I were Mrtol, or Bev, or whomever his mistress of the moment happened to be. Those nights lying awake in bed, staring down at my bralessness once the book was set aside and sleep refused to take me by the hand. Where was it I so longed to go? It was more than a bra that was missing. I was inside a person I had never really wanted to be; a lifetime lacking fulfillment. What uncovered gap need I traverse in order to arrive at that revelatory precipice wherein I might finally feel what others mean when they utter the word *nature*? The me that is not; the me that never was, but might one day become… the me-to-be?

Hormone therapy being the most direct route to this destination. Thankfully, one of our first tasks upon the island had been the establishment of the Settlers Landing International Hospital, its medical staff recruited from the topmost of notches. Without all the pesky regulations that individuals in my position are regularly prone to face in America and the so-called developed world, I was able to embark upon my journey of transitioning almost immediately, within hours of the idea's initial manifestation within the corridors of my brain.

Gordon Abu Lary Whiteman was no more. Gordina Orlanda is now five years old.

4.

—WHAT WE WANT is something along the lines of what Shakespeare did for England with *Hamlet*, Goethe did for Germany with his *Faust*, what Cho Ki-chon did for North Korea with *Mount Paektu*. What *Don Quixote* did for Spain, *The Odyssey* for Greece, *The Kalevala* for Finland...

–You want a national epic, the poet interpreted.

–Why yes, you took the words right out of my mouth!

Ignoring for the moment that national epics were usually composed spontaneously rather than commissioned in this manner, the poet covered the receiver to snort. He was having tremendous difficulty remembering which program he'd applied to so that he couldn't be sure what this lady (?) was offering. Once he finished the applications and hit send, he habitually gave little thought to them until the rejection letter arrived. This thoughtlessness being the method by which he constructed his defenses against what he came to think of, for good reason, as the inevitability of rejection. But here he was actually being offered something, by someone who knew who he was and had even read his work before... Or so it seemed. The mysterious caller's breathlessness only adding to the confusion.

–Can you, uh, clarify what the residency entails? What is covered and all that? I'm away from my desk, you see, I don't have my notes with me...

–Oh, this isn't a *residency*, Mister Birchfield. Well, not in your conventional sense. You see, we are going to make history. Well, we already have... But now we are asking for *your* contribution to it.

–Gee, I, uh...

–I'm assuming you have heard of Settlers Landing.

–... Oh. You mean the island guy?

–The world's newest and—some would say—greatest country. Floating in the warm placid waters of the Brown Sea...

–Yes, I do recall reading something about it. But, forgive me, I'm going through my logbook now, I can't—When exactly did I apply for this?

–Oh, you haven't applied, Mister Birchfield. There was no *open call*, haha. This is a direct commission. I'm sorry. I just thought— with all the press coverage we've been receiving of late—and the recent publication of my own best-selling tome documenting my four-year journey of transitional self-discovery—I thought the name Gordina Orlanda might mean something to you.

Here he had to pause (again.) How might he convey, delicately, that it had been years since he'd read a book, even longer since he'd

bothered looking at the Books section—if they even still had them—
of any major newspaper?

Thankfully, the breathlessness on the other end of the line continued to gather wind.

–Though I do respect that poets—great poets such as yourself, I
might add—often occupy their own private sphere of the cosmos.
You see, it may surprise you to learn that I am a great lover of poetry,
from the Metaphysicals on down. Well, a great lover of the literary
arts in general! I remember reading your first book, *Autumn's Cre-
scendo,* the year it was awarded the Yale Younger Poets prize, and I've
been a devotee ever since. I even have a signed copy of *Yes and No*
in my home library here.

–Wow, that's impressive.

He decided to withhold that both books were long out of print—
something that the caller was likely cognizant of all the same.

–Think of it as an all expenses paid open invitation. From a devoted fan, who is, well, now in a position to become something like
a patron. You see, of my many duties here on Settlers Landing—the
most famous one being, of course, right-hand woman of President
Mrdok—the one I really hold most dear is that of Ministress of Culture. From arranging exhibitions of the indigenous Sagosian
markmakers abroad to fostering our arts scene here at home, my
passion really is for the arts. Always has been. But, besides myself—
and I really can't even call myself a writer; not even in air quotes;
especially not in front of such a master of the written word as yourself—there really aren't any writers of note upon the isle. Poets, even
less. And, in my delicate estimation, well: What *is* an island without
a poet? Hardly an island at all. An island, perhaps, in a physical, geographical sense. Perhaps…

As the caller's voice rattled on, Birchfield began to suspect he was
speaking to a deranged person. While the caller referred to themselves using a feminine pronoun, there was an unmistakable
huskiness there, some buried remnant of a nasal baritone not yet
quite deceased. (While the transitioning had indeed heightened its
pitch, the hormone therapy had adversely deepened the previously
near-nonexistent timber of G's voice—a rather unexpected side effect, but not an unheard of one, according to Doctor Soukowski,
who, prior to his appointment in Settlers Landing, was Eastern Siberia's foremost reconstructive genital and transsexual specialist.)

–So let me get this straight, the poet now interrupted. You're going to fly me there, give me a house in the city center—

–In the artists' quarter, Gordina interrupted. Just to be precise.

–Yeah. Okay. And… What was it? Pay me a monthly stipend—

–Insurance and all benefits covered—

–Just to write poetry?

–To be our Poet Laureate. We are even planning on establishing a publishing house with international distribution with the sole intent of bringing *all* of your books back into print. Our only stipulation, of course, is that you produce our national epic. Our *Kalevala.* For you, in a sense, to use your poetic gifts to forge our national conscience.

–… What's the catch?

–Mister Birchfield. I assure you, there is no catch. It is you, your vision alone, that I—that we want. This is coming straight from the highest office in our land, that of our president himself. I am merely the messengerette.

Birchfield looked around his kitchen. Dirty dishes stacked up in the sink. Empty boxes of supermarket wine surrounded by piles of unopened bills and unread newspapers on the dining table. Three day old milkstain on the floor that still hadn't been mopped up. Birchfield had long forgotten which closet the mop was in, hadn't even bothered to go rummaging around looking for it.

Into the receiver:

–When can I leave?

5.

Excerpted from www.settlerslanding.sl/newsettlers/recruit-mentapp.html

OUR NEW CITIZENS have already begun to speak of the Settlers Dream in the same reverential tones with which many once spoke when evoking the American Dream. That is why now, some five years after our establishment, is such a timely moment for our doors to finally creak their way open.

President Mrdok, our beloved founder and dear leader, is often asked what made him decide to found the world's newest and most glamorous country. His answer can be summed up in some simple word: Hunger.

Hunger has been man's driving force since the dawn of evolution. Humanity, of course, represents the topmost layer of evolution, but within the human race, there are numerous different levels of intelligence, cognitive ability, and overall quality. But the world's leading scientists all agree: the most developed minds among us have always contained a gene that impels the desire to break away from the group in search of new territories. This is the same gene that, on a fundamental level, makes us desire new life experience, explore new tastes, new ways of seeking and belonging to the world. Since the very first caveman, so many millennia ago, arrived at the brilliant idea to leave the clan behind, taking with him only a select few, in search of more fertile hunting grounds, a precedent was set that would come to define human civilization as we now know it. History is rife with examples of such individuals, from Jesus Christ to Christopher Columbus on down to our very own intrepid President Mrdok.

Upon landing in Sagosia, as the island was formerly known, for the very first time, Mrdok sensed that he had arrived at the last undiscovered pristine slice of paradise that our planet has left to offer, and instantly began dreaming of the ways in which it might be improved. Mrdok, as a seasoned global entrepreneur, had seen much of the world by that point, and was convinced that he had seen it all. At the same time, he felt increasingly crushed by the weight of political systems in both his own country and many of the countries where he operated as a highly successful businessman. In so much of the so-called developed world, development has come to be defined by disorder, dishonesty, and petty forms of legal bickering. Wouldn't it be great, Mrdok often wondered, to be somehow liberated from this sad status quo? What if there were some sun-drenched land set far away from such dismal conditions, a paradisiacal land where a new brand of brave elites and their conjoined business ventures might take charge beneath the welcoming sun umbrella of a shared vision? A land where privacy would be protected by law, where the elite new settlers might mingle freely among the friendly welcoming populace, free of the intervening hand of overreaching governance, where the global elite could come and dwell and feel themselves to be part of a veritable brave new world where their wealth, aspirations for the future, and opinions on life might be both respected and nourished?

It is one thing to dream such dreams—so many of us have. But it takes the leadership abilities of a true visionary pioneer to actually make them come true.

Settlers Landing is the world's first patent-pending utopia. A surveillance-free, tax-free state governed by and with a majority population of global elites. An island measuring at just over fifty square miles, with golden coastlines and a shimmering lagoon surrounding much of the land. Beyond its attractive coastlines, the island's topography is marked by lush tropical plants and the entrancing interlocking branches of ancient banyan trees; Baldheaded Mountain, the island's highest peak, so named for the enormous bald head cresting its top which is upheld by a slender narrow fully scalable base, with two large boulders nestled below its southern shadow and a massive forest surrounding its northern approach; and an interweaving network of roads leading to the capital, Olde Colonia, which is minute enough to provide its residents with the safety and comfort of a small town atmosphere, but with a sophisticated up-market populace stemming from all corners of the globe that endow the town with a highly enviable cosmopolitan air. Rich natural reserves of nucleite have been discovered in the waters just off the coast, and are mined in a sustainable way that greatly benefits the local populace, without harming the abundant marine life that has long characterized the waters of the Brown Sea.

Like an expertly run Fortune 500 company, President Mrdok's government consists of some of the world's most impressive entrepreneurs, entertainers, and philanthropists, who have each done their part in helping to shape and mold the country's unique addition to the world stage. Some of our distinguished senators were famous even before embedding their prints in the sand at Settlers Landing, while others were lesser known, though highly respected in their fields, and have since emerged as household names.

Lil Bigfoot, perhaps our most famous senator, is a global hip-hop phenomenon. With the release of his debut album, *Outer Space N*ggas,* which set a world record by going triple platinum within three-and-a-half seconds of its release, Lil Bigfoot instantly emerged as a voice of his generation. In the words of *Rolling Stone* magazine, Lilbig's footprint on the hip-hop scene is so big, it makes the knees of lesser rappers quaver. In Settlers Landing, he is continuing to break musical new ground with his innovative melding of gangsta and corporate stylistics.

Barbra Brunnei, formerly known as Manhattan's leading real estate magnate and the queen of Tokyo office tower and love hotel acquisition, she is now overseeing, building, and remodeling luxury living and working quarters throughout the greater Olde Colonia region.

Ma Lin is famously known as Taiwan's third-and-a-half richest man. According to Forbes magazine, he is probably also Asia's second most generous philanthropist. Serving as both senator and as head of the National Bank of Settlers Landing, Ma has overseen the country's rapid financial development since its inception, while also helping to conceptualize a number of key infrastructure projects.

Lallyburt Edison Dryer III, who built a paper towel and toilet paper empire singlehandedly, with almost no assistance from his oil billionaire family, has had his large Texan hands (hands that might perhaps better be described as tentacles, both for their quantity and the length of their reach) in any number of industries over the years, from real estate to tech to securities to his latest venture in what he has deemed human engineering, an exciting new field that merges current fads in AI, genomic research, robotics, and social media. His cutting-edge entrepreneurial profile might clash with his classic southern gentlemanly demeanor, but it also adds an extra layer of intrigue and integrity to the Settlers Landing family of founding senators.

Now that our foundations have been laid, we are finally preparing to open our doors for the second wave of settlers. Given our land's precious size, we must pursue this task through a highly competitive process. If you think you have what it takes—not just to relocate to one of the world's most beautiful islands, but to make a real and lasting contribution to the legacy of our sovereign nation—all you have to do is fill out the following electronic questionnaire and submit it, along with the application fee, payable in our national currency of SL Lira.

Note: Leaving any questions unanswered will undoubtedly disqualify your application. Note as well that each question may or may not have more than one correct answer.

1. What best describes your current financial situation?
    a. Struggling to locate new offshore targets to safely preserve my assets for future investment projects;
    b. Mulling innovative and dynamic options for shuffling my investment portfolio with a wide open mind toward diversification and, naturally, profit maximization;
    c. The overwhelming majority of my assets are currently being held in the form of cryptocurrency and/or precious metals and/or other investments and I am currently seeking means through which I might enjoy them without the traditional burdens that liquidity often brings (i.e. excessive taxation);
    d. It's mostly about real estate and futures these days;

  e. Saddled with doubts about the current state of the global economy and occasionally frozen into states of near-paralysis that are only upended by frequent forays into high risk investments which give me an adrenaline rush comparable to a narcotic-based high, particularly when finding new ways to explain to concerned friends, family, and colleagues that such an investment is in actuality risk-free;

  f. All of the above;

  g. None of the above.

2. The prospect of having to earn my way toward non-taxation (through a series of infrastructural development and/or philanthropical endeavors, as defined by the Settlers Landing constitution) leaves me feeling ______________.

  a. titillated

  b. exasperated

  c. frustrated

  d. strenuated

  e. concentrated

  f. pupils dilated

3. My attitude toward long-term wealth acquisition can best be described as follows.

  a. In a neo-Randian world order, all marbles should naturally roll into precisely fitting slots.

  b. The hardest labor in the twenty-first century is ultimately performed behind a portable screen with cool drink close at hand.

  c. I should be able to earn money without leaving the comfort of my bathrobe.

4. Rate your level of daily alcohol consumption.

  a. I generally abstain from alcohol, save for those moments when to do so would ultimately be detrimental to the well-being of myself and those around me.

  b. A fine scotch throughout the day, with a splash of water and lots of ice, keeps the fire burning.

  c. A glass of wine at dinner each night, to help with digestion. Preceded by an aperitif and followed with a digestif to help even more.

    d.   Whisky and fine wines both feature prominently in my investment portfolio.

    e.   Alcohol, alongside religion, should be used sparingly, when at all.

5.   Your thoughts on the subject of surveillance might best be summed up as follows.

    a.   A nation of the naturally eximious has no need for surveillance.

    b.   I don't mind if they're watching, as long as I can see it as well.

    c.   I am largely indifferent to those mechanisms tracking and recording my every move as I go about my daily peregrinations.

    d.   Surveillance is the fine art form of the twenty-first century.

6.   How much do you consume at dinner each night?

    a.   My appetite for food rivals my appetite for making money.

    b.   *Banqueting* is a scowlish term employed by unprivileged people who can't afford to do it nightly.

    c.   With food as with fine wine, it is quality, not quantity, that counts.

    d.   Eating is for lesser creatures.

7.   When I hear the term *island communism,* I think ___________.

    a.   of a commune of the global elite, many of whom have pre-existing business relations to begin with, pooling their wealth from a centralized paradisiacal power base, and using that shared collective wealth not only for personal projects but for the ultimate philanthropical concern of global domination, in order that a fairer, more just world might be built that will topple all existing government structures that have endeavored to enslave and/or variously restrict our good initiatives over the years through overreaching aims such as taxation, regulation, legislation, litigation—essentially any word ending in -ation.

    b.   such a lofty pursuit is impossible on this planet.

8. Trickle-down economics ________________.
   a. naturally benefits all parties, and in particular, those clever enough to have come up with the concept in the first place.
   b. is a historical concept that could have worked quite well, had it been practiced in a more efficient manner.
   c. was a grand project, ultimately hindered by the tangled imposition of -ations described in #7a.
   d. is a worthwhile endeavor, particularly if employed within such a structure as implied in #7a.

9. When embarking upon the grand project of launching a new country, which of the following is needed?
   a. A coherent vision
   b. Recognition of sovereignty by other sovereign nations
   c. Capital
   d. A military
   e. All of the above, but in reverse order of importance.

10. Based on your understanding of Settlers Landing, our socio-economic system might best be described as follows.
    a. Capitalism with a nonhuman face.
    b. Island communism.
    c. Corporate anarcho-libertarian paternalist commune.

11. The role of children is ________________.
    a. to be taken care of by nannies and inherit wealth and property.
    b. to be quietly nurtured and left to their own devices.
    c. to make as much advantageous use of their docility as it lasts, hopefully forging an impression that will last well into adulthood.
    d. to force us to acknowledge that we ourselves once occupied this precarious state, and were able to overcome it, though we can hardly expect that our own progeny will necessarily share all of our unique traits, thus the need to put certain measures into place to preserve their precarity and to

potentially prolong their docility for as long as fate will allow.

    e.   to serve as the great beneficiaries of trickle-down economics.

12. Nuclear power _________________.

    a.   implies possession of adequate nuclear warfare, an effective means of confirming a nation's sovereignty to other nations throughout the world.

    b.   is a great thing for the developing world, particularly since nuclear reactors require nucleite, which is either already in my investment portfolio or I intend to get involved with it very shortly—though I would never want to live on an island that uses nuclear power—not in the twenty-first century, having learned my lessons well from history—though, from an economic standpoint, of course it makes a great deal of pragmatic sense for less financially empowered nations, so long as the correct safety precautions are put in place by the authorities.

    c.   is increasingly less investable than wind or solar, though to be safe, my investments cover all of the above—for one never knows for certain when the wind will stop blowing or the sun shall cease shining.

6.

MIDNIGHT AT THE Wet Nasty. Pastel ties loosened over tropical colored fabrics, what was once sort of offensively referred to as Hawaiian shirts though done in Sagosian style with thick dark twisting Banyan trunks and poisonous looking meat-eating plants showcased in place of leaves and flowers. A couple of the younger clientele adorn t-shirts bearing the black squiggles and scrawls of some of the better known Sagosian markmakers—nod to locality by the hipster neo-colonialist who makes a pretense of belonging that masks a certain insecure yearning for an authenticity never known and thus poorly understood. Senatorial glances shoot across the room. Scenes with no inner logic play out in this bluely lit cavity—busted vestibules and no clear corollaries. Vines of transmitted dialogue severed mid-sentence with lukewarm liquids poured over them. Clinking glasses, an accordion orchestra's instrumental rendition of Dire Straits' greatest hits played at humalong volume.

    —Yeah, I smoked crack wit Whitney. It wuz just one rock tho.

On a couch imported by Lallyburt rendered entirely from rattlesnake skin and dyed a dead ivory cream, Lilbig is regaling a twelve-year-old visiting fan with tales of his former rock star excesses Out There, which has become local patois for a distant world no longer relevant and shaded with a thin coating of nostalgia. Which for Lilbig, was back before the scandal. Before he either retreated or else became a bona fide founding senator, depending on which narrative one prefers.

    —That is like sooo…

She blinks for the right word, nods her head, then nods out. It's been a week since she's had the Viutex treatment and she's still getting used to the endless state of regenerating pain-free… Thankfully Lilbig is there to slip a comforting paternal arm around her shoulder.

Krstal saunters glasslessly across the bar and into the ladies' room. Coco is cutting lines with her gold SL Express card on the silver-encrusted mirror surface accompanying the row of sinks.

    —You want a line-uh?

Krstal shakes her head.

    —Sorry, honey, but I stopped doing blow at the end of the aughts, after I had my last invasive procedure—well, the last one on the face, I mean. My snorter don't work too good since then. Though if you have one of them extra long straws, you can do me Stevie Nicks style, blow some up my poop shoot. Or if that husband of yours happens to have an extra long one hanging between his thighs, he can tap out a line and shove it up me bareback.

—He ees your sun-uh.

—Oh right. I keep forgetting.

Coco grimaces disgusted as she bends down to insulfate.

—Though that's our family secret, Coco. I love Bobby and Stevo Rey, I do, but I'm only their mother Out There. On Settlers Landing, I'm too young to have had any children. It's a career decision. I'm sure you can understand.

—Yes-uh. Eef you keep telling eet to yourself-uh, maybe one day someone else will believe eet-uh.

Snort.

—Sorry, says twelve-year-old Shelley Silverding of Long Island City, New York, as she jolts back awake. I like, I mean, I think I just went into the fucking whateverness of time…

—It's aight, says Lilbig, pawing her crown of straightened curls. I know I got sumfin it'll make you feel better. Let's go back to my crib and burn us a blunt.

At the bar, Gordina is blabbering to a visiting journalist as they await Mrdok's arrival.

—We have become the world's premiere destination for medical tourism. And it's not just our trademark Viutex treatments, such as young Shelley over there—

—Is that Lil Bigfoot? With his arm around her?

—Well. She's not *that* young, actually…

At the other end of the bar, Stevo Rey and Bobby are having one of their under-the-breath arguments everyone has learned to studiously ignore; there's no benefit to be excavated in publicly gossiping about royalty.

—I think Makiko's right.

—You can't even understand her when she's wrong.

—Oh, we understand each other very well. We have an understanding that goes *beyond* language—

—Whatever. There's no way dad's just gonna say yes to it. He's on *my* side.

—The fuck he is. He gave up on your junkie ass a decade ago—

—Who the fuck are *you* calling a junkie? You fucking meth-fried—

—Who was the one who got the idea to supply Pembroke with the supply-side—

—Oh I believe that was *my* wife, *my* initiative—

–It was me and Lilbig who had the contacts over there. Who actually *went* there, from his *heliport,* the *only private one* so far on the island, and *fuck you* and your golden egg-laying Italian whore.

–I will make sure she knows you said that the next time you come sniffing around for a line.

–Give me a fucking break. Your weak shit? I've got my own fucking dealer, Lilbig's guy—

–Oh yeah, your gangsta friend you keep mentioning. What about when he finds out what you've been up to on the side? Oh, and how's the new album coming along, by the way? Shit sounds so horrendous—oh wait, I forgot—it's *experimental,* how unsophisticated of me—

–Since when do you know a goddamn thing about music, Bobby? Or about anything, for that matter?

–Since mom—I mean, *Krstal*—she gave *me* the piano and guitar lessons when we were growing up. It was me, she always insisted, that *I'm* the one with the musical talent. And I heard that straight from *both* Rosalitas, which is pretty much confirmation that mom—Krstal—actually said it. You were supposed to be the jock and the model. Obviously you failed on both fronts. You're just jealous, that's all. They neglected you. Just like dad's neglecting you now.

–... why, I myself have been privy to the veritable *medical miracles* for which Settlers Landing has become known. As you are well aware, I was once upon a time known to the world as a rather bloated, intrinsically frustrated figure trapped in the confines of a cis-gendered male body. Well, I don't have to tell you all the details; of course you've read my best-selling tome. Suffice to say that it was only here, once we had established the Settlers Landing International Hospital and I felt truly confident about the level of assembled medical expertise, that I allowed myself to undergo the transitional procedure that has put me into my rightful body. And quite an incredible thing happened in the process, for which the professionals have no explanation, but for me is proof of their inestimable talents: after running some routine blood tests once the surgery was complete, they discovered that the sex change had simultaneously cured me of my diabetes!

Coco snorts the last of the four lines she needs to get her through the next forty-five minutes. She smooths her hair in front of the mirror, applies another layer of Nighttime Magenta to her lips. Back in the bar, Stevo Rey and Bobby are at it again. Fuck. Does she go and interrupt it or slink back into the bathroom, maybe do one more line?

It had taken her some time to get used to it. *Your father is who-uh?!* She recalls screaming so loud it nearly startled Bobby off the autobahn. She herself was nearly coronaried by the news, though in retrospect, it probably should have been a bit less unexpected, considering the smallness of the world they all traversed. Bobby had just let it drop like it was nothing—as to him it was, given the mutually neglectful nature of father-son relations. They were driving her cousin's restored antique Alfa Romero somewhere between Munich and Switzerland, on their way to a distant relation's weekend mansion, and Bobby was wobbly behind the wheel. It must have been a week since they'd left the rehab resort together and Bobby barely knew how to drive a stick, though he kept telling himself he could. Fuck, he'd told her, you really have to be careful with the high-pitched noises, I'm not used to driving in Europe. Driving at all, was more like it. And yes, he's my father; but so what? I mean, is there a problem?

She explained that they knew each other from Venice. That, matter of fact, every time Mrdok was in Venice, he had spent nearly all his time there with Coco. Then you must know the guy better than I do, Bobby had said, a twinge of envy in his voice, though disguised deep enough for her to miss it. She had nearly said *getting high in Venice,* but she had felt compelled to leave out that part. Them being freshly certified sober and all. She didn't really need to say it—to Bobby it was obvious. Not that his father did drugs, but more because it was with Coco—what else would she be doing hanging out with some guy twice her age if not getting high with him? It was only a couple months later, when they were both high themselves, stumbling around some castle somewhere in Corsica having snorted up a fresh round of speedballs (one of Bobby's rare lapses back into the brown stuff since that last rehab stint) that Coco let it slip: You know your father fucked me, right-uh?

It was a blessing from whatever god or goddess currently reigns over the Earth that they were both high at the time, since it saved Bobby from having to feel bad about it until much later. Bobby has since learned to quietly forgive his father—which is a mild way of saying that he has never brought it up. Best to bury it in some Freudian graveyard—along with all the unpleasant mental images accompanying—and hope that the dead don't rise. Thankfully, with the addict's unique talent of compartmentalization, Bobby has largely been successful in this endeavor to date.

—… it is almost as though the excess glucose had been removed in simultaneity with the excess genitals. At least this is how I have come to think of it. Two life-improving surgeries for the price of one—and you can quote me on that!

She's a tough journalist of the investigative bent (though, it is true, she is of late normally dispatched on these rather fluff assignments, which she has come to deeply resent) and is clearly not impressed with much of what Gordina has been volcanically spewing for the half hour that has just swept its way past them. She is used to getting her own way, used to navigating her path around professional liars, politicians, PR agents, as well as seemingly every other person who has discovered a profitable mechanism for clinging on to those occupying the highest rungs. Now, she nods at the figure of Barbra Brunnei, having just walked in and given her wave signal to the bartender before disappearing into one of the VIP rooms.

—Her and Mrdok. What can you tell me about them? My sources tell me a spot of fuckery went down.

—Well, I'm assuming you're somehow referring to her senatorial role here in Settlers Landing? In addition to her lawmaking duties, Miz Brunnei currently heads up the Ministry of Real Estate. She—

—I don't mean that. I mean, are the rumors true? Are she and Mrdok an item?

—Why, that's simply outlandish. Mrdok is happily married—well, happily remarried, to be precise, having become acquainted anew with his first wife, Krstal Mrdok, our first lady. He prefers not to speak to the media about his more intimate affairs, by which I mean *matters,* not affairs as in love affairs, because he simply does not have the time or inclination to indulge in such sordid activities. And even if he did, I must say that it would be highly inappropriate for a journalist of your stature to inquire into such unsalient interests. (I mean, really, we invited you here because you represent the *respectable* media.) Rather, what we might say is that this regeneration of President Mrdok's relationship with the First Lady has allowed them to come full circle in—

—But are they fucking? He and Barb? Come on. Off the record.

She plops an olive from the snack tray into the olive-shaped opening of her skeptical scowl.

—I have to say, I take issue with your tone. Why, President Mrdok is a dignified world leader. Would you talk about the president of your own country utilizing such colorful terms, Miz Ambrosia?

—Matter of fact, yes, I would. Flattery isn't a part of my job description. I guess that's where you and I are different. Well, one of the ways, at least…

–I just want to say that I regret the transphobic implications of your most recent comment.

–Then you're reading way more into it than I ever intended. That whole neverending story about your miraculous sex change operation slash diabetes cure? Let's just say I was in a state of, well, how shall I put it? Internal exile. Now how about you give me something I can use, so that I can leave here with more than just another fluff piece for your fantasy fugue? It's been five years now since you've launched this whole mess. I've got news for you, honey: the world is sick and tired of hearing about how wonderful it all is. If you want to sustain interest, you can start by showing me how it's not all one gigantic shit show.

–Well, my dear, if you are sniffing out the proverbial dirt, I am afraid there will be very little for you to discover here. They don't call our island pristine for no reason.

–You're the only one I've heard calling it pristine—

–People have already begun to speak of the Settlers Landing Dream in the same reverential tones they once reserved for the American—

–Jesus H. Christ, you really are a brochure in high heels. Tell me more about Brunnei's investment, then. That's a matter of public knowledge. Seems she alienated a great deal of her paternal family with that move. I know from her former real estate broker in To-kyo—he showed me all the papers—that she completely rid herself of all those properties in Japan, effectively transferring the entirety of her wealth to Sagosia. I mean, if it sounds insane, it was also ugly. She fired a lot of people, nearly crashed a huge sector of the Tokyo real estate market. In my experience, people usually don't behave so recklessly unless they're either impaired or else romantically—

–Let me stop you right there. First of all, it's Settlers Landing. Not Sagosia. (We have filed lawsuits against publications for using the island's former name, so bear that in mind.) And, from what I understand of the matter, Barb had actually been contemplating a move out of the Japanese market for some time. After all, it's stag-nating. Here, on Settlers Landing—*not* Sagosia—it's blooming. Like a disciplined investor, we might fathom that Barb spotted an oppor-tunity that was too good—

–The name. Right. That's another matter, isn't it? You haven't been very successful in any of those lawsuits. You also haven't had much luck in getting the locals—the quasi-natives, as I've gathered they're called—to adapt it, have you? They're still sticking with Sa-gosia. Reveals a bit of simmering discontent beneath the surface of the way things are going, the way things have been done. Wouldn't you say? You can't just impose a new national conscience upon a people and expect them to—

—By golly, what locals are you talking about? We are now faced with a room full of them! Why don't you ask some of *these* locals how they feel about the name?

—Don't make me laugh. We're in a room full of government employees, of elites. I don't see a single quasi-native in here. There are hardly any on the streets of Olde Colonia, where you try to keep the press cordoned off from the rest of the island. Most of the ones who are here are employed in low-level positions—hardly the kind of empowerment your government, so-called, has claimed to bring them. But let's get back to Barbra. Why is it you won't allow me to talk directly with her?

—In point of fact, I have not made the slightest effort to impede your access. But this is *government business,* Miz Ambrosia. You have to make an appointment with *her* office, not mine. When you are in Washington, DC, it is not as though you can march right into the Pentagon—

—Actually, I can. And this is about the furthest you can get from DC. I mean that literally *and* figuratively. Secondly, you've blatantly steered me away from her on at least two occasions when she's entered the room and I attempted to introduce myself. Now what do you call that?

Given the flat monotone of singer Mark Knopfler's voice on popular tunes like *Money for Nothing,* recreating it via the medium of the accordion requires a nervous percussive tonal indulgence that induces a near catatonia in those Viutex tourists who have crouched themselves throughout the bowels of the Wet Nasty; amidst the varying edges of chattering—from merriment to nastiness wet and dry and all colors in between—they form a somnambulant orchestra of exploded neuronal feeling akin to a fur-coated murmur that jettisons them cushionishly into the scene's subtly air-conditioned and dehumidified primordial clay.

Harry Hull walks into the bar like he expects a punchline. Or else just to be punched.

—Hey, look who decided to put some clothes on! someone shouts and a few snorts of derisive laughter ensue.

—Isn't that the naked guy from this morning? Outside the presidential palace? the journalist now asks. What's *his* story?

–Him?! Gordina visibly holds back her laughter. Or else, like with most things, it's just an act. He is *definitely* not worth a moment of your attention.

Miz Ambrosia now suspects this is something more than just a line, since Harry Hull has seated himself at the very end of the bar and appears to be ignored by all of the patrons, as well as the bartender, who turns his back to the noise as Harry motions for a drink.

–Can you do me a favor and call the hotel for me? the journalist now turns to Gordina. I think I want to prolong my stay.

On her way out, she slips Harry her card.

7.

GODDAMN MOSQUITO BITING my knuckle. It's because the window rolled down, I know. When there are no passengers—like now. It's cos—what else? Saving money on the A.C. These batteries don't run themselves. When the diesel runs out, no more vehicle. A ding on the device. Well hell. Already well on the way down Yarmouth toward Cove Beach, have to turn back again to Olde Colonia. Some elites want to go to Cove. Knuckle still itch.

Ding di-ding of course I accept the ride. For what else is there? Father, god rest his soul, never wanted me to be here. Lost on, what, these three main roads, forever circling. And whoopee-dee. Riders gone from A to B. He wanted me at sea. Place the real men went to, where there are no roads. What it means to be Sagosian. You'll never know. A car driver? How the hell one make a living doing that?

Well, when the quasi-colonials was here, fore they got chased off, twas a business. Not so many years past. No one else thought it up. Just Robinson thought it. There was a fleet of three, Robinson the master of it all. Those the days when the only road going outside Olde Colonia *was* Yarmouth. They had money to spend, the colonials. Gave freely—well, relative. Let's not go romancing. But Robinson, he told his other two drivers, we stick to honesty. That there's the only way to be. Year in, even installed meters—made em like proper cabs. Like they got in larger places like England, where all the quasi-colonials comed from.

No more of that now. That all changed when the torch got passed. But one paved road before. Now there's a couple. Three even. But they's building all the time. Who knows. Olde Colonia aint gonna look the same. The new regime. Juan and Horse, they done left it behind. Say the economics of it don't make no sense to them.

Used to be with the colonials, we get tips all the time. The new ones come in, the quasi-elites, they most of em hardly even know what a taxi is. The concept. They want Uber. Thing they got on all they phones, fore they even puts their feet in the amber. And so Uber's what they get. What we got. What I got, seeing Juan and Horse is now back out to sea. Least they's got their freedom from this. I got my freedom from the sea. Afraid of it. I don't know nothing but the roads. No tips and diminishing returns. Gets to be, when you're used to a thing, you don't got the imagination to see it change. To let it change in the actual. So you return to what's comforting. Sea's in our blood here. We're all pirates deep inside, even if we don't speak the language no more. One of my ancestors must've drowned.

Not that it didn't take a while. Used to be carsick. Not anymore. Now, in a way, it's like no more thinking. You turn on the app, machine does all the thinking for you. Father said there are three ways of being on this island, only three, but only one of em that matters. There's the inherited way, the quasi-colonials—and not cos they inherited it for real as a gift of Yang Zhu, but inherited more like sarcastic like, like they done took it and so walk with that air that they're entitled to it all, our Sagosia. That don't apply to us, never did. There's the middling path, where you get some return for your efforts, but never enough. A life of compromise is all it's about, where you soak your troubles in rum at the end of it and submit them to the feet of Yang Zhu. Then there's the real quasi way. By which he means the quasi-native way, of course. You live right next to the water because you spend most of your life on top of it, inside it. No real escape cos the answers're what you'll find once you submerge yourself deep enough.

Then when you get into Olde Colonia, there's the island's sole traffic light. Reason so many of em stopped taking cabs is cos the quasi-elites bringed all they's cars and drivers with them. So little demand, only one for-hire needed. That's how's old Robinson here got to be the first and only Uber driver on the isle.

Stopped at the light dumb Prince he come right up to my window. I ask him what the hell he's doing here in the town. He answers me in Sagosian, language he knows damn well I can't speak. Family all mixed up to ever get that language passed straight down. No one shit on me bout that till lately when Prince start up with all his business. How can you be a real quasi when you don't even talk the language? Prince's younger than me too. A lot younger. Makes it all the more. But then, he crazy, I'm not.

You no be disrespecting Robinson, you motherfucker, I tells him. I'm your elder. You want to talk to me, you talk in English. Elsewise I don't want nothing to do.

You can't talk Sagosian, he says, you might as well drive your shabby old vehicle on into the water. Go off the docks, where your old man died. You just a mule for the elites, you aint nothin, old man. Tonight I set your trailer on fire.

Don't you make me get out of this vehicle. I got surge pricing going on.

You got surge pricing going on every goddamn day at every hour. You the only one out here. What you don't got is a lot of sense, old man. If you did, you'd wake up to the fact that all this aint got no future. Not with these quasi-elites messin with our ecostructure. They're out there right now, drillin holes in your father's seagrave. What you think of that, old man? You gonna go chauffer em all around, till they runs out of things to drill, then they starts drillin you?

Light turns to green, time to accelerate. Raise two fingers behind to Prince as I leave him behind in the dust, Sagosian signal expressin violation to the person's ancestors—worse curse. Not that my signal means nothing to him coming from me. Just like his words don't mean nothing to mine ears or my ancestors' either for that matter.

8.

PRINCE AT THE temple, regarding the restoration work. It's a project of his gang—not his idea, per se, but he feels no guilt taking credit for it. At least his mom is proud, yelling at him now a lot less. No more yelling. A sense of rediscovery.

He can feel himself changing, Prince. Maybe it was the quasi-elites' arrival that catalyzed these changes. Maybe that arrival was just a scapegoat, a way to explain something deeper happening within. Something both spiritual and psychogenetic at the same time. Something about the bloodflow. Both who he is and what he is meant to be. How he's been off track for some time. But not in the way the others've perceived it.

They've given the interior a fresh coat of paint. Prince's not sure of the color—a sort of welcoming peach. Is it too fleshlike. Too corporeal to pass as truly spiritual. Not that the body has ever been fully negated in any of the doctrine. Not that Prince has been able to find, in all those scattered references to Yang Zhu that remain. But we're trying to build something here. And we got to compete with so much filth, so many other visions. All the imported religions, spiritualities. He's only recently gone back to the holy texts. He's on a path of rediscovery, or more like recovery. It is a mission and a journey. A path to awareness, a journeying into focus, an excision toward precision.

—These torch holders too damn high, he screams out at his soldiering minions. Move em closer to the ground. The idea bein, when the peoples they come into the temple, they can feel the flames—the heat, the warmth. That is when they can know they is in the presence of Yang Zhu. They need to *feel* it. Not just know it. That is what a temple is meant to be about, man. *Feeling.*

Temwen shrugs. He has a wig on backward.

—We put it too close to the ground, man, the peoples they gonna get all burnt up when they get in here. Safety first, man. We already done secured the walls the best we could do...

—These walls are concrete. Why they need securin?

—Nothing holds forever. This building old as Sagosia herself.

—That's what I'm sayin. And you know why? How it been protected all these years, all these storms that done knocked down everything else? It's cos of that.

Prince nods at the figure of Yang Zhu grinning wizenedly from the center of the pulpit.

—Aint no concrete. It's our sacred ancestor. The one that got brought here all those years back. The one that *guided* them. The same spirit that makes this place blessed. And like no other. That make us *unique.*

—I got it, man. Not like I the one that needs to get converted. You don't need to tell it to me, man, I'm on your side.

And Prince knows this is true. Temwen has been setting fires with him since they was old enough to run off on they own. Not like the young children now. They barely twenty, but there already a generational divide. That's cos the quasi-elites tryin to ruin history even. Teaching the kids in school the old history don't matter, that what they call Settlers Landing is the real history. Just five years old, still like it some event in mankind's evolution. Bullshit.

—Why does fools fall in love with gods that aint got no faces?

He's lookin at the statue of Yang Zhu. He know he talkin bout his own father now. But he don't care, Prince don't. Moments like these, it's the holy spirit talking through him.

—It's cos they don't live in a place where they gets blessed automatically, in the birth process, he continues. Or else they do and not aware. That's where we at. We Sagosians. It aint that our ancestors discovered this land. Naw. They were *directed* toward it. Yang Zhu, he was searchin for a home. Home he couldn't find nowhere else. All those years, out at sea. Searchin. A man comes into yearning cos it's the only place he knows. Don't even imagine there can be a recuse from it, place where there might be some solace. But he done found it, didn't he?

Prince opens his eyes again to the rays of day emanating from without.

—Okay, we move down the torch poles then, says Temwen. I tell the others. We do it tonight. Before the night's fire ceremony.

Since Prince got spiritual, nothing Temwen can say will shut him up. Gets damn exhausting.

—You can choose to listen to me, you can choose to ignore it. All I is is the middleman, Temwen. The vessel. The important thing tho is that you choose. If you don't choose, then you lost. Then you might as well go live among the quasi-elites, be they servant. Plenty have. But then don't ever think you can just come and be a Sagosian again.

Temwen turns to face the shadow darkening the doorway.

—Who the hell—?

Now Prince turns in response. Some bumbling old white fool tryin hard to hide his bald head with a combover, collared shirt all stinkin and stained with sweat cos the humidity's a foreign entity to his blood, glasses hangin midway down his half-buttoned shirt.

—Oh, hello, I, uh—I wasn't expecting—I'm just here to tour the temple… Do I need to pay an entrance fee? Maybe, you know… I'm Collins Birchfield? Poet Laureate of Settlers Landing?

—What you doin here, man? Who sent you?

—Why, uh, I'm just, exploring the island, doing some research. I actually found this temple in the Lonely Planet guide—

—What the *fuck* is that?

—I, uh…

—Man, this here a sacred site. Like Holy Mecca. You got that? It's only for the islanders. I mean, the *real* islanders. The Sagosians. The quasis. You get your ass back to Olde Colonia right now. You tell all them quasi-elites to take this temple outta they book. That this aint no place for them. That if they come back here again, aint no guarantee it's gonna turn out right for them. You hear me?!

Birchfield disappears real quick.

9.

–GOOD MORNING, MISTER President.

Mrdok strolls past Merrill, the bespectacled former porn star cast as secretary, on his way into the Diamond Office.

–Any calls?

–A Mister de Broqueville. Or *Monsieur,* I guess I should say?

–Who?

–He was put through. Says he was from Oostern Nucleite?

–… the fuck? We buried those fuckers ages ago.

–He said… Oh, I have it here. He says *give me a callback, I have a very funny joke whose punchline your president is sure to appreciate.*

–Uh. Okay. Connect me in my office.

Mrdok doesn't remember any of those clowns as having had much of a sense of humor, but whatever. He closes the door on the Diamond. Inside, all the furniture and fixings rendered in silver. Silver things everywhere—no gold. Gold being strictly outside the Mrdokian register. Here, everything runs according to the silver standard. Written into the economic policy.

–Mister Mrdok. Oh wait… I'm sorry, *President* Mrdok.

Sardonic chuckle. Knowing that he hates mister. Mrdok allows it to wash over him like a cool spring.

–You might recall. We spent a lovely tropical evening together watching the lemurs in Madagascar a few years ago. You regaled us with one of your typical American vulgar jokes.

–And then I sank your company. You don't need to remind me. My memory is one of my strongest assets, Mister—whatever it was you said your name was. I can't speak Belgian.

–Aha. Very good, Mister President.

–Anyway, you should be grateful. I did you a big favor. There's no way your shareholders—

–Oh, I must admit, things were very rough for me. For a number of years. Very, very difficult. How clever of you, the way you went about it. All those offshore shell companies of yours. Buying stocks, dumping them, short selling… And your futures trading—ha. You got us in a, what is it called in your wrestling? A headlock? Very, very difficult. But you know what, Monsieur uh Président? I've uh landed on my feet. In a very nice building, actually. Back here in Brussels. Feels so nice to be home.

–So good to hear. I'm sure the frogs they got over there taste much better than the African kind.

–The European Commission for Natural Resources. Can you imagine? A man of my experience? Well. I can. It is a perfect fit, actually.

Mrdok opts for silence now as he examines the gleam on his ring.

–But anyway. I'm not calling you to gloat over my good fortune. I just heard a joke that made me think of you. Are you ready? Here it is: A beautiful woman who has no happiness decides she has had enough with this life, that she is going to end it all. So she goes to a bridge and is about to throw herself off when she is approached by a stinking homeless man. Please, he tells her, if you are going to do this drastic action, at least make love with me at first. The beautiful woman recoils. Get away from me, you stinking bastard, she tells him with disgust. Fine, he says with a little laughter in his voice, go ahead and jump; I can just wait for you down there.

Click.

10.

THE MOIST ARMPIT is the name of the VIP lounge inside the Wet Nasty. A most unfortunate name that must be said with a pained wince every time, but what can be done, Mrdok got to it before Barb did and it stuck. (Stunk.)

Speaking of Mrdok, he's late again. Leaving Barb to sit here and feign awkward small talk with the Texan cowboy. Great.

–… Whut we don't want is sum goshdarn hippies comin on up in heyuh throwin up on the carpetin, he drones on.

Of course the place is bugged, or at least Barb suspects it is, as do all the other senators, and so despite the lounge's VIPness, one can never be fully certain whether what is said is truly meant by the person saying it or just being said to throw off the recording devices. So some fine reading-between-the-lines goes down in the room each night.

By hippies, Barb garners, Lallyburt means something like radical left-wing environmental activists—who often are, it is true, hippie-ish. The press has been hot of late, and not in a good way. The nucleite operation has been a massive success—until now. But there's no real way to take an inconspicuous shower in gold, or in their case, silver. The glitter draws attention—followed by chasers, followed by dissenters, always in that order. But it is a process that can be managed, and really has to be. It has to be done properly. Hence, the current ongoing convening.

Now Gordina enters the lounge in some slutful get-up, clutching her sequined iPhone case in one paw and Fendi handbag in the other.

–I just got off the phone with Mrdok, she pants. He's on his way. He had some last minute papers to sign in the Diamond Office.

–Whut paypuhs?

–Oh I don't know. Something regarding the land lease deal on Cove Beach it would appear—

–That deal is supposed to go exclusively through my office, Barb now speaks up.

–Why yes, of course, Barb. You've done a fine job managing all the particulars. But the president still has to sign off on it. According to our regulatory measures—

–Is Ma in on this? Is that what this is all about?

–What?

–You heard what I just said. What kind of cut is he giving to Ma?

–Oh Barb. Mister Ma is just head of the national bank. *Nominal* head, I should say. We all know that Mrdok oversees international investor transactions—

–Well, Ma's not here to answer for himself, but I know he's coming in next week. Should I just ask him then? Or do you want to go ahead and tell me yourself, Gordo, I mean *Gordina*—

–I think you're being awfully petty, Barb, deadnaming me like that.

–Well I know better than to think I'm gonna get a straight answer out of Mrdok—

–I think you need to have more respect for our dear esteemed president. Transparency and security have always been our topmost—

–Weyuhl ah hafta piss lahk uh rattlesnake. Scyooze me, mayuhm.

Lallyburt giving Barb a subtle conspiratorial nod on his way out the door.

–Now that the redneck's gone, why don't you cough up the truth?

–Oh Barb, I can tell you this woman-to-woman, because we actually like each other. The truth is, the deal isn't actually going to go through. We never had any intention of it going through. We're doing this as a favor to Lallyburt. His family has some connection with the Saudis, who so oil-burningly want a piece of Settlers Landing, they would practically execute half of the royal family—even the men!—to get it. Mrdok wants their money, but he doesn't want them. So the protocol seems to be: make a gesture of acceptance, get some of their coin as payment for that gesture, then throw the Saudis out, without actually letting them in to begin with…

—And so you *railroaded* me on this?

—We're going to give them the illusion that the deal is going through, then invent some regulatory thing that will prevent it, return them the investment, minus, of course, some banking fees, hence Ma's quote-unquote involvement, which I'm sure he doesn't even know about—Look, Barb, this is all part of the fun of being in at the beginning. We get to make it up as we go along!

—What the fuck are you telling me? I've put a lot into this. We did an entire *media campaign,* for the local populace. All the *jobs* the resort is supposed to bring—

—Come on, Barb. Are you really that naïve? That can all be corrected with *another* media campaign. We just have to highlight the Islam aspect, the human rights abuses, the threat of terrorism on the island, homeland security… Why, I could think of a thousand things. Just show them some photos of explosive devices, a bomb hidden beneath a burqa, that'll get the message across real quick. Our people are smart like that.

Gordina waves the ringed fingers of her right hand around in an abstract way, as though pawing the dilemma's answer out of the ether.

Barb knows better than to go much further. Not now. Definitely not here.

—It's ugly, honey. Real women don't wear that many rings. Just to let you know… I've got some calls to make. Text me when Mrdok decides to show up.

—Barb…

But she is through the Moist entrance before Gordina has a chance to spew any further verbal diarrhea her way.

She walks into the men's room, where Lallyburt is inspecting his teeth in front of the mirror. None of the three gentlemen pissing at the urinals say a thing. She is a senator, after all. She can go pretty much wherever she wants.

—It's what we suspected, she murmurs. Ma's doing behind-the-scenes acrobatics with the Saudis.

—Goshdawn, ah knew it. Ah almost wanna tayke thuh Lawed's nayme in vain raht now.

—Look, what with the Saudis…

—Well hunny, I caint screw them thar bois. Wah the crown priyince has been a close personal fraynd uf mah fathuh—

–Can you wait till these jerks finish pissing? Barb says it under her breath, though, upon pronunciation, said jerks briskly zip up and exit without bothering to wash their hands.

–I agree, Barb now continues, the last thing we want or need is some pissed-off Saudis on our hands...

–We all saw whut they done did in New Yawk Citee when they dun fell out with thuh Bushes. Even though it *is* the capital of *sin*, so it *wuz* somewhut justifahd. Stiyil, ah wuz un *Ameri*kun at that tahm. Seein that wudunt easy to watch, oh no mayuhm...

Barb has to grimace her way through at least ninety percent of her interactions with the cowboy hat, but what can she do? Mrdok created this situation and, in a sense, she had willingly walked into it—a move she is increasingly coming to regret. Lallyburt—what would mother have made of him? Not quite one of the Dirty People—her classification system didn't quite take into account the complexities of the American rich—because most of the time, he certainly acted as if. It's the Texas thing, of course—having all that money and power and influence but not having the culture to back it up, so it manifests itself as sports teams, Jesus fanaticism, immature schoolboy pranks, idiot politicians with transparent motives, racial slurs, latent alcoholism—just general crudity. So overbearing but you have no real option but to roll around in the hog droppings alongside it. The threat being the omnipotentiality of getting smothered.

–Lallyburt, silence. Do I need to spell this out for you? He's not screwing over the Saudis. He wants to make *us* think he's screwing them over. But if what I suspect is true, if Ma and Mrdok are in on this together, they're actually working together with the Saudis. So actually, it's the Saudis and Mrdok and Ma all screwing *us* out of the deal. It's clear *why* they're doing it. We just need to figure out the *how*.

How to make the cowboy understand the subtleties of symbolism?

–Look, we've both been watching him for a long time. Well, long enough. Long enough to know that when he pulls shit like this, it's always with a certain amount of recklessness. In other words...

–There somethin thar he aint seen.

–Maybe not even a blind*spot*, per se. I'm convinced that, in a lot of these scenarios, it's the overall shape of the thing he can't see. Its architecture.

When Barb was a teenager, her parents one summer had insisted she gain work experience, so-called, rather than the experience gained by working on her tan while further degenerating alongside her friends—in truth, she realized in retrospect, they probably just wanted to see much less of her around the house and redirect the policing hours of the staff toward more profitable and/or personally satisfying ends—and so she attained part-time employment at the Prada store in Chora. It was fairly banal retail work, folding clothes, standing on the floor with insincere half-smile, responding to consumer impulses manifested by those few who brushed past the security gates and actually leaned toward buying something (as most of those who came in merely wanted to sop up the A.C., perhaps kill a few minutes between the beach and dinner, the whole shopping-as-a-means-of-generating-hunger routine.) Nothing you could call particularly memorable or with even a thread of the educative momentum her parents—themselves perhaps the most detached from the workaday world of all the island dwellers—had allegedly hoped for. Except for one mildly stimulating episode involving the granddaughter of the ruler of one tiny-but-influential middle European country-slash-municipality—let's just call it Liechtenstein. This princess suffered from a malaise that so often afflicts a certain contingent of the gilded youth, the syndrome of sticky fingers. It is an affliction, of course, that is rooted in a boredom more profound than that experienced by any mere mortal, for privilege can afflict very unusual and site-specific forms of suffering upon the beknighted soul for which the modern discipline of psychology has manufactured very few, if any, effective cures.

Like many the sister of an A-lister, the princess's game was as deft as such games were wont to get played. As was customary in her clan, she was spending the entire summer cloistered in her manor in the hills, but would frequently have her driver drop her in the town center in those hours when the throngs were at their height and store security and personnel were at their most distracted. Prada wasn't the only luxury outlet she'd hit, but it definitely featured on the list. Everyone in the shop's employ knew; catching her in the act, however, was another matter entirely. The problem, as Barb understood it, was related to the shop's tubular architecture, which made it difficult for that era's rather rudimentary surveillance cameras to capture certain corners. What's more, all the cameras were clearly visible, and the shop had been well scoped by the princess, who by then had attained the equivalent of a master's degree in shoplifting.

Store detectives and regular employees alike had simultaneously attempted to track the princess's movements from a subtle distance, all to no avail. Certainly, the shop's inventory-accounting ability outmatched its security, an oversight that ceaselessly worked in the thief's favor.

Barb made it her mission, not to catch the princess in the act—for that would be too vulgar, like betraying a code of honor, to inflict this form of embarrassment upon a fellow blueblood, not to mention the repercussions it could have on their respective families' business interests, complex as they might be—but to find an equitable solution to this form of stress radiating from the management, who feared imminent involvement from the corporate head sales office, and who knew what fresh hell that would bring. The solution did involve a certain amount of detective work on Barb's part. She worked overtime, so that she could be in the store virtually whenever it was open—something that is technically illegal under Greek law, but 1.) given their desperation and Barb's avid assertion that a solution was close at hand, her managers were willing to scramble the books on this one and pay her in cash that she did not really need but accepted nonetheless for her extra hours and the efforts that came with them, much of which were filled with interminable waiting, because 2.) the princess would come in at random hours every time, morning afternoon evening, so there was no real way of guestimating when she'd show to do her dirty deed.

All this to prove, finally, that her hunch had been correct. After following her around the shop for more than three weeks, and doing some highly intricate side-glance work, then checking her accumulated data against the security camera footage in the back room, Barb had come to determine that the princess was cleverly stealing only from those corners of the store that the cameras were not able to capture—which were, incidentally, where some of the shop's most expensive merchandise was dumbly put out on display. All they had to do was change around the store display so that all those wares geared toward the poorer customers—t-shirts, tote bags, basically anything with the Prada logo emblazoned loudly across it—were positioned. In this way, Barb asserted in her final PowerPoint presentation to upper management, the likelihood that anything further would be stolen was essentially nil, since no princess would steal outside her taste range, and even if she did, these items were essentially worthless, sent in by home inventory as shop filler, and could be easily written off.

Riveted by her detective work and the intrigue of the subsequent cost benefit analysis, the sixteen-year-old prodigy was rewarded with the offer of a promotion. She then received a rival reward offer from her parents, permission to quit the Prada job altogether, lesson so-called having been learned, to spend what remained of the summer break on her family's private stretch off the Mediterranean with her girlfriends—an offer she promptly accepted.

—Wait a minute, says Barb now as the thought crystallizes. Is your family still selling the Saudis bazookas?

—Last ah dun tawked with mah sistuh, yeahyuh.

—Call your sister. Tell her to hold off on any further deals, any communication whatsoever for the time being.

—Wah in thuh sayuhm heyul would ah wanna do that?

—Because trust me. Do you want to see this resort get built or not?

—Wayuhl, ah do deklayuh, ah don't care so much for the resow-uht, ah jest wanna sayve mah family's relaytionshiyip with them Saudi bois…

—You will. We will. You're gonna leave it to me. I'll get my resort, you'll get your Saudis. Just do what I say, cowboy.

She doesn't want to wait for him to drawl out some response to that, and she also doesn't want to be in the piss-stinking mirror-stained men's room any longer, so she lets the door slam behind her as a full stop to that last sentence.

11.

A FAINT BUZZING prepares him for. For what? The sentience long lost. He thinks about whether to report it to Gordina, the incident just now at the temple. Truth is, he'd be a little embarrassed to do it. Like he was taking sides in some debate he can't fully fathom. Or she might tell him that he should have known better than to go there. Would feel stupid after hearing those words. Even dumber than he feels now, post-confrontation. Nothing in Frost's poetry prepared him for moments like this. Maybe he should, who's the one, somewhere in the Caribbean, an island poet? Walcott. That's the one. Yes. Maybe he should read Walcott. What he can do he can head back to Olde Colonia see if they have any of his in the bookstore. Library might be a better choice. Can check both: good way to kill time. Now that the afternoon's shot to shit. Gordina's made sure poetry sections in both library and bookstore are well stocked. Even though just for the two of them it seems. Thing is. Words he keeps forgetting. Maybe it's for good, for the poetry, to be liberated from meaning like this. Yeah. The doctor said minor aphasia, likely brought on by the drinking. Emphasis on minor. Can't interfere with the work. And if he can stop the drinking. Clear up on its own. Does

Walcott even count? He's a Caribbean poet, this is the Pseudotropics. Entirely different thing. Doesn't know of any poets from this part of the world. Didn't think to research till now. The bleating sun, feel the sweat lacing your back even beneath the shade of the banyan tree, far-reaching. Uber driver will be here in ten minutes. At a sufficient distance from the mosque, scary guys. Not mosque. What is the thing? Theme. Thing-theme. Place where people worship it is not a church. Or, the Jewish thing. A *temple*. Right. So much thirst, maybe have a drink as soon as Olde Colonia. There's that bar across from the book place, where he's designated the Uber driver to drop him. Could go in there first, not to get loaded, just to quench thirst. Place with a faintly bohemian atmosphere. As bohemian as it gets here, this island. That's because of the Viutex people all hanging out there. Viutex tourists. Takes them a while to go home once they're on the island. Eventually they get the message. Suitcases are packed for them. Told they can't stay. Medical tourist visa limited to ninety days. If they want to extend it, they have to get more procedures. Some of them plastic surgery, facelifts, botox, tummy tucks, breast implants, penis implants, neck enlargements, backroll reductions... What someone told him—Gordina?

Like having a hole deep inside your mind, where the words are supposed to go. Your brain works fine but the words. The words become the problem. Embarrassing for a poet. Like a driver who forgot his atlas. This must be the Uber. Old silver Volkswagen, not like the kind they got in the US. Must be for another market. Uber pulls up, the poet opens the door and gets inside. Olde Colonia Books? says the driver. Poet asks the driver his name. Seeing as how we keep meeting. Uber driver laughs and says isn't it on the app. It's cos he's the only Uber driver on the island. Where the words have no meaning. What do you mean *only* Uber driver, poet says. I mean just that, driver, name is Robinson, says. I mean it's me and they aint got no others. Least at present. Maybe if the settlement grows... Poet looks out the window, the landscape trespassing. Red ruby-colored mud and the sparkling trees and the new houses still under construction after five years said to be for the quasi-natives otherwise still living in trailers and shacks. I was just at the temple. Now testing the waters. Driver a quasi-native. See what he has to say. The temple, says the driver. An indifferent tone. Robinson turns on the radio. Ignoring the question like. Middle of a song. Birchfield still getting used to the indigenous sound. A sort of reggae blues. Something you can barely move your hips to. Lazy island sway. (The only music from the outside world that has caught on among the quasi-natives, for reasons never sufficiently explained to Birchfield, is that of Creedence Clearwater Revival.) Seems like the guys in the temple didn't want me there. Birchfield trying again. Disrupting sacred space. Something like that. But, you know, I'm a poet. Sacred spaces are kind of my bag. Do you think, maybe… His voice trails off. Robinson's been humming along, seeming to ignore him. Can't sing the words cos he doesn't know Sagosian. It's cos they scared, he then says. Who? Those guys in the temple. Scared of what? Robinson sighs. They scared of the future.

And then the song is over and the disc jockey's voice comes on just as they are pulling into the town. Tuesday night the most singular sage of Sagosia, Silence, will speak. Down at the John Bowen Amphitheater (so-named for the esteemed pirate king [whom historians have proven actually never stepped foot on Sagosian soil, but still.]) Excuse me, poet says to friendly but disinterested driver as *Run Through the Jungle* comes on, what is he talking about? Robinson eyes him with a smile in the rearview. You mean you don't know? It's Silence, man. The talking dog. He talks in rhyme. The damndest thing. You won't see anything else like it in all the world. Only here. In Sagosia. It's on Tuesday? poet says. Yeah, man. Tuesday night. And is it possible to book your Uber in advance. I'm not used to this app thing. Robinson pulls up in front of the bookstore. What time you want to go? Don't use the app, man. I give you my number and a special price.

12.

FREEDOM FROM REBIRTH, the naked man. The holyman passes the protester at breakfast hours as the streets of Olde Colonia are just rustling with morning routines colliding. Hull on his way to protest, Taggerston to preach. So the same activity, two different men. Taggerston having landed way before Hull ever did. Before Mrdok, even. Taggerston, former resident of Pembroke, island drifter launched via his US exile. First the Caribbean, then the Mediterranean, the South Pacific, finally the Pseudotropics; archipelago-bouncer of the twenty-first, sailor of seas not-so-open, still knew very little but how to drift, lost in some primordial impulse faith could no longer heal. New administration of Settlers Landing quite unsure what to do with these few stragglers of the Ancien Régime, Taggerston being the most prominent, having relaunched his televangelist endeavor anew here and garnered a certain base among an aged demographic of quasi-native, and so Mrdok decided to embrace the irony, allowing the scene to play itself out, for his *own* entertainment purpose. (Harry Hull a different matter altogether. Best to save that one for later.)

In these farthest reaches, morphings, reinvention inevitable. Here, Taggerston no longer the savior incarnate, the descendant, the messenger of the Lord. New locale, new era demand new concept. Here, Taggerston won points right away from the quasi-natives for his inherent display of modesty and assertion of a corporate vernacular never before heard on the island, describing himself as Jesus Christ's administrative assistant. A title ringing with some unknowable bureaucratese, sounding official-like enough to ring with a faint intimidatory hollow, faith requiring fear always. Start low, then you can ride so high on the self-esteem rollercoaster, come crashing down into the splash of a waterfall, new flock all around.

He makes money and Mrdok likes that. Now it's about power; maintaining the balance thereof. He goes on the air and preaches his persuasive holy pitch, clears the quasi-natives' households of bothersome surplus, maintaining intact the abject poverty line that yields status quo preservation. Taggerston, of course, sure to pay his taxes until he earns the requisite ten points needed to attain tax-free bliss. He's at three as of this writing—a long road ahead—but he's in the driver's seat. Unlike some. Many. Especially Out There, perhaps.

Not to say that once the cameras are clicked on and the lights shining in front of him, the message has changed all that much. The messenger has shifted his position, that's all, peppered with crustations from the corporate world, a world as foreign to most Sagosians as the very kingdom of heaven from whence he came.

—What I'm telling you right now are words you aren't likely to hear from any other source, whether that source be human, an app, or belonging to our AI brethren—who are, in fact, remote controlled by Christ, and so equal to us. And you wanna know why that is? That's because we're on the verge of a holy war. A war that is, well, inevitably going to be lost, to the forces of power and evil. You might like to think you are safe from all that. Because of distance, and what else. That it's only places Out There, those places you read about in books, see in the movies, but have never visited before—America and all the other global multinationals. I know this line of thinking. Before Jesus dispatched me here to do His administrative work, I happened to live in America myself. Then, zippity-zap a-rip flap, doo-werp dippity-dap.

He can lapse into these linguistic abstractions here, his own brand of tongue-speaking, the people all seem to appreciate it—or so the viewer survey recently conducted seemed to imply. These liquefied transmissions of the holy brain.

—I was sent here, from the Biblical province of Corporate America, I *materialized* here, with my little Bible in one hand, my iPad in the other. Here to do the Lord's accounting. Not that this was a place that *needed* saving. Oh no. All of us living here, here on this, this Settlers Landing, as uh our, our holy ambassador here on Earth has deemed it—

In the beginning, Taggerston had slipped once or twice and used the old name of the island in his broadcasts, which is illegal, and had to pay a fine. Such slips were, naturally, in deference to his audience, the majority of whom had no inkling to recognize the island's new official name. Of late, he has masterfully figured a way to integrate Mrdok into his master narrative, which no doubt went a long way in earning him his latest tax point.

—We have been blessed just by the nature of our very occupancy. Because, when our CEO comes back—and He is coming back, and very, very soon—this little island is the place where He shall manifest Himself. I have it on good authority. Namely, my own.

On the nature of this imminent manifesting: It's not that Taggerston actually believes it is imminent. But it is not as though he *disbelieves* it either. Being a televangelist is tough at times. You have to talk a lot and make sure no new meanings accidentally slip out at the same time. Nothing that will change, too much, the old assumptions, the conventional order of things. Rather, you are just adding a little touch of baroque finesse to the existing order. Once you start losing control of the words coming out of your mouth—easy to do when you have to speak at these often marathonlike lengths—hell might quite literally break loose. There is a certain order that must be maintained in what we might call the spiritual universe. Or the spiritual universe as deigned by one's subscribers, to be yet more precise. For they are the ones, ultimately, who comprise and compose it. You are selling to them the Jesus that they want to hear, that they want to be a part of. Not some other Jesus, the one vended by the Pope, for instance, the Holy Roman Church. Or the Orthodox Jesus, with the rather pointy beard and all the stinky incense. This is the new Jesus. The Sagosian Jesus might have been different. Jesus of the parrots, the mixed race Jesus descended from the pirate clan. Jesus seen in the telescope out floating upon the holy waters surrounding, mast beneath him smashing through the coral reef. The Jesus that might manifest himself in the ruby sands along the sun-fried beach by a fisherman returning to shore. Jesus needs context in order to survive. This is a new Jesus for a new era in the island's history. The Jesus of new technologies; the Jesus who earns billions and personally downplays it while simultaneously marketing it. Christ, who has sent me here to teach you the secrets on how to get as rich as I have. Keep this in mind. Jesus only saves those who might recognize his likeness.

–How do I know that Jesus has chosen this, our homely little isle, for His imminent return? It is because of our very distance from all the evils of the world that this place gives us hope for salvation. In a world bereft of goodness, a world that has been shattered and ripped apart by human greed, Christ needs a safe space whence he might begin to build His new home office so that he can enrich us all with His love and guidance. And all He needs to begin building it is three hundred fifty thousand SL Lira. Which is why Christ's imminent return begins with you.

13.

LILBIG REPOSING ON the almond-colored settee beneath the massive yellow-backgrounded painting of the gleaming Colt .38 in his home Chitlin Studio. His palatial crib is situated on the far outskirts of Olde Colonia, in the island's relatively undisturbed northerly sphere. He prefers this relative isolation to that of the hills around Baldheaded Mountain to the south of the capital, where Mrdok and the rest of the senators have moved into the mansions formerly inhabited by the quasi-colonials. It's about business; about security, also. The northern tip of the island being the location of the wharf, and Lilbig has involved himself with the import-export trade, and also likes the idea of being a fifteen-minute drive away in case the helicopter can't get off or on to his rooftop heliport and he needs to get off the island real quick. Lilbig the first to import armed guards from the US, leftover soldiers from that nation's ill-fought wars, many of them dishonorably discharged or else retired with symptoms in varying degrees of post-traumatic stress disorder—hence the reduced rate at which they have been bought.

Stevo Rey seated across at the ivory desk, headphones on behind a swarm of gadgetry. Lilbig smoking a blunt, checking his phone.

Stevo Rey removes his headphones.

–Yo, listen to this shit.

Zigzagging rhythm comes blaring from the SurroundSound, kinda outer space cos of the reverb. Then a lazy mangled tropical guitar strum, strung on a delay, slightly off-kilter with the beat of the distorted drum kick. Extra thick.

Lilbig hops up and grabs the wireless mic.

> *Y'all bitches can't wait*
> *Gotta 'nihilate*
> *All dem greasy mothafuckas done pollutin dis state*
> *Y'alls bitches stay up late*
> *On da Pornhub masterbate*
> *With a gat in yo pussy gonna seal yer fate*
> *Blown away by the every day*
> *You can't fuckin stay*
> *On my capital A—*

—Yo what the fuck you doin? Dat beat was dope yo. You just went and changed it.

—What?! Stevo Rey screams over the avalanche of noise. No, wait, this is like the *harsh* part. The interlude! Listen to this shit.

There he go again, tryna bust someone's goddamn eardrum wide open. He don't know what riddim is, its function. Makiko come in with the sushi.

—Makiko, tell him to loop this shit, man. He cant be bustin soma that noise shit in da middluh my flow. Likin to ruin the whole goddamn track. That aint how it work in hip-hop yo. You need to get on da game, son.

—This is how it works in *noise*, bro. That's what we're trying to do here, I thought. A crossover. Hip noise. No: noise hop. Sounds better.

Lilbig bristles at the sound of both those word combinations slung together.

—Listen to this.

Now this crazy ass motherfucker done throw in some Middle East soundin violin playin in da mix and da sound of a vacuum on top of it. Like what the fuck he do? Lilbig coverin his ears, Makiko standing there all blank eyed, like she in a daze. Like she still don't know what the fuck it is she doin on this here island. Cos she probly don't.

—Man just turn that fuckin shit off right now. I need time to think yo.

Radio silence. Lilbig loads up his think machine, a neon pink bong.

–Makiko, you can leave now, says Stevo Rey.

She walks back toward the kitchen.

–Thanks for the sushi! Lilbig yells after her. This sushi is dope, yo.

–She makes it herself, you know.

–Yeah. I do know. Enuf music for now, man. We need to talk bidnis.

–Alright. Let's talk.

–Your brother.

–Yeah? What about him?

–Like is we workin together on dis shit or not? Cos I don't even know no mo.

Stevo Rey sighs. Bobby again.

–You got him makin the runs, right?

–Technically they're flights.

–What?

–They're flights. Not runs. The flights to Pembroke. Once a week. To distribute the product…

–In exchange for *our* produck. I got you. Cept for one thing.

–What's that?

–He be mingin off the top.

–Minging?

–You know what I'm sayin.

–Not really.

–I think he got a little side hustle goin on. He and dat mafioso bitch o his.

–Bro. He brings in the weed for us. That's all that matters, right?

–I want him out. He be mingin.

–I'll talk to him. But before I do that, you need to arm me with some more specifics.

–Let me ass you a question. Cos I aint never had no brother. How well you know him?

–Who? Bobby?

–Naw. Santa Claus.

–It's complicated. We didn't really grow up together. Well… We did and we didn't. See, I was pretty young when they got the bright idea to send me away. Boarding school. What was I, eight years old. Before that, it was pretty normal. Well, whatever normal is. Dad working all the time. Mom at home, but inaccessible. We had these two nannies, both named Rosalita, who took care of us. I learned Spanish that way, but forgot most of it.

—These the same Rosalitas that be lookin after Jaco?

—Yeah. Dad brought them both over when he divorced Mrtol.

—What I hear…

—Yeah, well. What's she gonna do about it? Sue him? Start an international incident? From what I hear, she's buried pretty deep in the bottle anyway. (We can't let Jaco know that.)

—So dey sent yo ass away? Bobby too?

—Bobby got to stay. I remember it made sense at the time. Somehow. Not that I wasn't scared. Scared and angry. Any disruption to normalcy at that age, your instinct is to fight against it. Mom had an entire wing to herself. It wasn't enough. She wanted more. Each room has to have its own single purpose. I've gotten over it. That's just Mom. Krstal. It's who she is. We're cool now…

—But deep inside you resent it. Cos Bobby got to stay. Least a little while longer…

—A little while? Fuck. He got to grow up there, man. I mean, the school I got used to as well. California sunshine. No freezing winters. Though I started to miss those, as well. Which I guess is why I dig Japan so much… The order, the daily routine. It was no rat trap. I had my own room, a butler…

—Why you and not Bobby?

Stevo Rey lets out a deep sigh.

—It was a real estate decision.

—Real estate?

—The location of my room? In the house. Also, my room had a slightly bigger walk-in closet where Mom could store her cosmetics. Seeing as how I was a year and a half older. Mom already had a dressing room. She needed a separate room to do her makeup. So one of us had to go. It was inevitable.

—So you older than him? I aint never knew. I thought you was—

—That's because he *looks* older. It's the drugs, I think. Though I read somewhere that heroin actually acts as a preservative. That as long as you don't OD, it can keep you alive longer. Junkies actually have really good skin. It's going *off* the heroin that's the problem. That's what ages you really fast.

—All them Viutex motherfuckas walkin round out there gon live forever.

—Haha maybe. Fire that up, man. Give me a hit of that.

—So anyways, this like I thought it was. You and Bobby. You barely know one another.

–So? Lots of brothers—

–Aint no lotsa bruthas, man. Most bruthas, they be close n shit. Close enough to know what loyalty is. You and Bobby, man, how you even gonna know? You know that phrase, divide and conquer? Your parents, son, they divided you two early on. Divided and conquered yo ass in a way you don't even know. See what it is? They done saw you two for what you is, what you was to them. A threat. A potential one, at least.

Stevo Rey exhales a purple cloud.

–Even if that was the case, bro, we're like adults now. Me and Bobby, I know we fight all the time. I know how it must look. But this is the closest we've ever been, man. And it's like, we're doing something new now. Like, together. We're in business together. I just can't… Like, neither one of us is gonna do something to screw that all up.

–Then it's the gurlfrien, yo.

–How are you so sure they're skimming off the top?

–Import-export. The rulez is real simple. Our produck go out, theys come in. We send em our Viutex, they send us dey weed. Dey sell our produck, we sells deys, everyone happy wit da arrangement, go on back and trade some mo…

–I know how it works, bro, you don't need to summarize the process. Why do you think—

–Cos I done the calculations, son. How come our profits be fallin? Man, this a small ass island. We aint got much in da way of captns n shit. Our crew be real small.

–The Uber driver? You ask him about it?

–I done talk wit da Uber driver, man. He dint want to name no names. We need his ass, yo—I wuddnt about to give him no shake-down. But what he said—I don't know, man. Point is, you gotz to talk wit yo brutha.

–It's probably not him. Though, okay. It *could* be Coco. I never trusted that chick. Not completely.

–Where are you, baby?! I need my medicine!

Shelley Silverding's voice from the bedroom echoes throughout the corridor into the Chitlin Studio. Lilbig ignores the sound.

–Look. Stevo. Lemme just tell you somethin, man. You wanna know why us Black folk don't like dat noise shit you do? It's cos the noise is what we gotz to live with every goddamn day. We didn't grow up in no sunny ass boarding school, wakin up to pristine silence in the mornin. We grew up wit real noize, son. The noize of sirens and gunshots. We put dem headphones on, we want to *cancel* da noize. Only a crazy ass Black muthafucka gonna wanna *embrace* it.

–Dude, I thought we talked about this, like, five times already. It's about artistic innovation, man. We're, we're like *both* taking things to the next level by teaming up here. Nobody in the history of hip-hop has done what you're about to do. Once those tracks drop, man, they're gonna forget all about the past. They're gonna recognize you again for the pioneer you always were. And when my label in Japan gets wind of this, yo, we're gonna, like, *own* Tokyo…

Lilbig rises.

–Get me my missin produck, yo. I don't care about da music no mo. But aint no one on this isle gonna be eatin into my profit. And I don't care who *da fuck* you is.

Lilbig dematerializes into the bedroom, leaving Stevo Rey to stare at that painting of the gat on the wall above the settee.

14.

THE YAPPING DOG is a retard. Mrdok kicks it as he corner-eyes Harry Hull on his way into the office.

He has rather grown used to the despicable sight by now. Still, it is a discomfort, and he has been too preoccupied of late to move much in the path toward resolution, since he typically tries to erase the visual memory of the naked man as soon as the air conditioning hits. Everything has its deadline. Now, for whatever mysterious reason, this morning, his patience has boiled over.

–How the hell did he get here? Mrdok screams in my direction as I enter the Diamond Office with a sheath of papers awaiting the president's signature. Who let him in?!

I immediately garner that the *he* to which he refers is Hull. I assure the boss that I will launch an immediate investigatory inquiry, and will put aside all cultural affairs to make it my morning's priority.

It is a turbulent time, I must admit, what with the stalled publication of what would presumably eventually become the Settlers Landing Constitution. Getting to this stage has been no easy burden. It has been an amalgamation of mornings sitting in a room at a very long table with each of the senators present, listening to their often vapid or else merely selfish ideas and complaints. Very often, the pressing realities of statehood were the furthest thing from the imaginative fancies that had set up residence within the plaited hallways of their inner shitball faculties. It was up to myself and Mrdok to interrupt these fantastic ramblings with interjections of silvery pragmatism, until one day Mrdok ran out of tolerance and abruptly put an end to the meeting by informing his senatorial council that enough had been heard, and that a draft of the constitution would be imminently appearing in their inboxes for approval.

As soon as he uttered these words, I interpreted that the imminence so emphasized might be more accurately left in air quotes. Of the members comprising the senate, one could barely write his own name; one so openly resented our president that he would inevitably reject any draft submitted without even deigning to read it; another was content enough in his symbolic role as head of our national bank (a role he had been deluded into believing was real) and still so steeped in mourning over his lesbian daughter's suicide that he cared for little else and was rarely on the island anyway; while our sole lady was far more preoccupied with real estate schemes and, rightly or wrongly, considered the matter of law to be the domain of those dwelling in some nether region far beneath her. The constitution became yet another small formality to be dispensed with as far more pressing matters of state coalesced into the formation of a foreground.

–Might I ask what this… obscene gesture is all about?

I masked my direct gaze behind a pair of dark shades. I did not want to appear prudent, of course, since this was all clearly being done to test local laws of tolerance. Given the slightly remote locale of the presidential palace in the easterly suburb of Olde Colonia, only those in the immediate employ of the state were privy to this daily display of cis-male genitalia. A rumor had been floated about that I was even behind it—since, as Ministress of Culture, it was well known that I had begun to launch a series of artistic initiatives upon the isle. Perhaps, the reasoning went, this was some endeavor in the field of performance art meant to enlighten the quasi-natives. (As though I were afflicted with such vulgar taste!)

–Gordo… Is that… *you?*

–It's Gordina now, Harry. Now tell me what in the hell—

–I just want my job back.

–Your job?

For what else could I do at such an absurd declaration other than mimic his response and stand back in surprise?

–Or *a* job. Any job.

–There is no job for you here, Harry. There is no place for you here.

–Then I will stand out here, I will do this every day, until I am recognized.

–Until you are… What are you even talking about, Harry?

–Until my contributions to this organization have been recognized and I am rewarded.

–Have you gone mad?

–I did my part. I did my job, to the best of my ability—it was my efforts that brought Mrdok to where he is today.

–What nonsense.

–If it hadn't been for *my encoding skills*—

–You were a hired hand. We could've easily found someone else.

–It's not so easy to find someone with morals as loose as mine. I enabled you to essentially defraud the entire one percent—

–I advise you to be silent immediately, Harry. You're not on US soil anymore. We can do what we want with you.

–Not with all the international media you've got poking around. Your cute little PR blitz. It's so you, Gordo. I know you've always secretly craved the spotlight. I could tell just from our few little interactions in New York. Olde Colonia Residential Inn? They're all staying there, all the reporters you bring in. There aren't *that* many accommodation options, makes sense. So guess what? I'm staying there, too. Every morning at breakfast, we chitter chatter. Buddy-buddy. I'm sure to get close with all of them, real quick. I'm surprised none of them have started asking you questions about me.

–They probably think you're mentally unbalanced, standing out here in your birthday suit. A conclusion not so unique now, I'm sure.

–You owe it to me, Gordo.

–It's Gordina.

–*Mrdok* owes it to me. I took the fall for him. If it wasn't for me, he never would have been able to get out of the US.

–How *did* you get away from our friends in the FBI?

–Ha. A doorway appeared. I walked through it.

–What did you give them?

–What they already had. Look, I'm not going into any more details until I'm let into that building.

–Then we're at a standstill, my darling. Because I'm not about to present you to Mrdok until you give me something I can use. You'd do best to put some clothes on and come back when you can make something of substance manifest. How did you get on the island, anyway?

–I arrived by boat. From Pembroke.

–Who the hell let you on? Show me your visa.

–Oh, you're hilarious. Did you not know? How… how *diuretic* your little visa scheme is?

–What are you talking—

–On Pembroke. The only place in the world one might currently obtain a Settlers Landing visa. Am I right? Well, guess what. You remember Nelson Rodgers? Guy you exiled? He's infiltrated, he's taken over the *entire* racket with his people.

–… I beg your pardon.

I'm trying to mask my panic at this pronouncement, but have found, as a woman, that my emotions rush out much more fluidly, uncontrollably, than they did in my previous guise—a hormonal thing, to be sure. Has our Pembroke visa office in fact been infiltrated? If what he is saying is accurate, then our safety, our security, is, well… I hate to even think the word, let alone write it. I hate, even more, to try and imagine what Mrdok's reaction would be to this news. For sure he must not find out until I am able to confirm it… The odd thing being, in retrospect, the ease with which Nelson Rodgers and the few straggler quasi-colonials left—couldn't have been more than four or five dozen, though I was never asked to confirm their number. I had worked with Mrdok for long enough by that point to be used to a certain amount of drama that arose among the shitballs or else those just sour or jealous of his cunning fabulosity and the ease with which he manages to glide near-noiselessly through most interactions and always come out on top. And, naturally, so wrapped up was I in all the excitement of transposing our base of operations that it seems I hardly noticed the sullen pragmatism with which Rodgers effectively vacated the premises. He had made some halfway valiant efforts at preserving the quasi-colony, but once we took over the national bank, well. History does tend to write itself under such auspicious circumstances, and a man of Nelson Rodgers's education would be well aware of this indefatigable truism.

Odd, too, I have suddenly come to realize, that nary a peep (nor a squeak, nor a thud, nor even a cadoodle) has been heard from Nelson since his retreat to Pembroke. I suppose in my mind I might have hastily chalked this display of silence up to the academic, professorial side of the man's character—the only side we really experienced of him directly, you might recall. What's more, it is not as though Pembroke were the worst place for a man in Nelson's position to land. It isn't far from his native Sagosia, it is similarly an island in the Pseudotropics, comparatively overdeveloped, saturated with resorts that, it is true, have lately begun to die since we built the airport and have gradually succeeded in transforming our own island, left so abandoned by the quasi-colonials, into an international hub of intrigue. But we also knew that Nelson has plenty of buried wealth with which to sustain him from here on out, and that he is not a man of Mrdok's ambitions. It seemed likely he would simply fade beneath Pembroke's own strain of the banyan tree with its elliptical leaves, sipping his English tea—a comfortable, perhaps slightly boring exile that, he likely would conclude, would have happened sooner or later, for one bad reason or another. Now, at least if there is even a thimbleful of truth dissolved within any of Harry Hull's brewed assertions, I am forced to consider whether this represents an oversight on our part or at the very least an underestimation of Nelson's true person.

Well, there is only one way to find out.

—Okay, Harry. Put some clothes on. I've found a job for you.

15.

—I'M IN PAIN.

The M.D. removes his glasses, squeezes his eyes, rubbing them with his fingers. Then:

—You're going to have to give me something better than that. What kind of pain?

She fidgets in her chair.

—All over.

The doctor winces again. Gets up like he's about to leave the room, then sits back down again.

—Look, I don't know what kind of research you've done, how well you understand this. This isn't some, some backwoods Appalachian pain clinic dispensing prescriptions for hillbilly heroin, okay? Viutex is a sophisticated medical product…

—Product?

—What it is, really, is a solution. A final solution. For pain management. It's designed for patients who have really tried everything else, and are still suffering.

—Where are *you* from, Doctor?

—Me?

—Yes.

—I'm from the Upper East Side. Of Manhattan.

—I see. They must be paying you a pretty penny.

The doctor winces a third time.

—Look. Miz, Wilkinson, is it?

–I just resent the implication that, because I have a slight Southern accent, I'm some sort of backwoods hillbilly.

–It has nothing to do with you personally. I'm just trying to be crystal clear on this. It's a life-altering decision you're about to make. I cannot allow you to do this unless I feel you fit the category of patients currently on the treatment—

–I was given a *visa* to come here. A medical visa. To get this specific procedure done. You know how much that cost me?

–Miz Wilkinson, just because you were granted a medical visa to come here for a consultation doesn't mean you automatically qualify for Viutex treatment. There is a protocol that must be followed—

–You just wanna get more money out of me. Isn't that what it is?

–Miz Wilkinson. I assure you that both our medical ethics and the level of our medical practice meet, if not exceed, international standards—

–And is that why this drug has been approved exactly nowhere else in the world? Why many governments have put forth motions to actively suppress it—

–I think you knew before you came here that Viutex has been subject to a certain amount of controversy. Many new therapies are when they first come on the market, Miz Wilkinson—it is the nature of progress in the medical industry. And, just for your information, we do not refer to Viutex as a drug. It is really a treatment or a therapy—

–Yes, I know that. One that permanently relieves you of all pain. Through its infinite release system. I've done my research, Doctor. And I am ready for it. I can assure you. Now, when can I get it?

–It's not that simple. According to Settlers Landing law, the patient must have a minimum of three consultations before she or he is approved—

–Are you shittin me?

–This is the law here, Miz Wilkinson. I do not make. I just obey it.

–And how much does each of these consultations cost me?

–It's three thousand SL lira per consultation.

–… You've got to be kidding.

–Look, surely you must know that one of the things that is unique about this country is the extremely high quality of its medical care. The founders really sought out the finest team of doctors and medical experts from around the world. I mean, they properly *scouted* us. It was a long, intricate vetting process that landed me—and my colleagues—here. You have to *pay* for that kind of quality, Miz Wilkinson. It doesn't come cheap.

—It's just that my insurance won't cover—

—Nobody's insurance covers this procedure. It's too new. Moreover, there is no insurance on Settlers Landing. We have no need for such a system. If you read the information given to you when you applied for the visa, you would know there are significant expenses involved. Now if you're not prepared to go through with this, you can do what a lot of our patients do when they change their minds, which is sit back and relax, enjoy the beach, treat yourself to a nice vacation—

—So after three consultations, then what? I'm then *allowed* to go through with the procedure? I know how much *that* costs. I was under the impression that that's all I'd have to pay. The literature didn't mention anything about the additional consultations. Which is why—

—It's in there. It's in the fine print. A lot of people scroll right past it, just click the box at the end. We don't encourage that. We actively discourage scrolling. It's our stance.

—Your stance.

—Our anti-scrolling stance. There's also a section of the fine print where you can read about that. It's all part of our medical ethics. We always ask our patients, implicitly, to never scroll.

—You might understand, Doctor, that if a patient is in a lot of pain—which all of your patients presumably are—the idea of sitting still for five hours or however long it takes, decoding all of that legalese—

—You know, you still haven't told me what kind of pain it is you're allegedly suffering.

—What do you mean *allegedly*?

—What kind of pain? Is it physical pain? Psychic, emotional anguish… There are all kinds of pain that we treat here, Miz Wilkinson. But there's no such thing as allover pain. No *real* thing. Not even quadriplegics experience allover pain. And we treat a lot of them, trust me on that one.

—I get headaches, for one thing.

—Headaches?

—Yeah. Migraines. They come on strong, unexpected-like. Other people get them, they might be out a few hours. Mine last for days.

—Days?

—Days. Three, four days at a time. I can't do anything. Can't even eat. See how thin I am? That's one of the reasons.

–Do you have a history of taking pain medication?

–You mean like…

–Oxycontin. Codeine. Vicodin. Percocet. Any of the opioid medications.

–You wanna know if I'm a junkie, right?

–I would never use that word.

–I've… tried a number of different medicaments over the years. Narcotic and non-narcotic. Nothing really solves the issue. The pain always comes back.

–How many a day are you taking?

–You mean like now?

–Yes. Now.

–It varies. According to the degree of the pain.

–Miz Wilkinson. You can be as direct or indirect as you want with me. We could also just bloodtest you. That would give us a crystal clear idea—

–Why are you doing this to me?

–… I'm sorry. What is it I am doing? Other than the obvious. (My job.)

She lets out a profound sorrowful sigh with a slight whistle in the background that sounds like a baby gasping for air, the doctor observes.

–It starts out, well, as a certain… sensitivity to light. Not so pronounced. Not the kind of sharpness that I'd initially define as pain. You know, pain-pain. But it's there. The body sending a message. Describing it this way, I can almost bring it on. That's why I don't like describing, talking about it. Makes me afraid.

–You don't have to be ashamed, you know. It's a major problem right now, especially in your country. Has been for many years. There are a lot of people in the same exact position as you are right now.

–The light eventually starts to take over. It's like you're in this long tunnel. But the light coming through at the end… How do I describe this? It intensifies. Until eventually it's no longer about the tunnel. There's just the light. And you can't evade it, can't escape it…

–Though you want to, of course.

–One has ways and means.

–So many resources at your disposal.

–Well. What do you expect? It was one of you who made me this way.

–I beg your pardon.

–Don't get offended. It's not a Jewish thing. I'm talking about doctors in general.

–I wasn't—

–Did it stop working eventually? The dose they were giving me? Yes. It did. I did my part. Played my patient role. When he asked, I told him. The solution was to give me another prescription. For something stronger. His idea, not mine. I just went along with it, in my state of not-knowing, trusting the white coat and what it said I needed to take.

–Indeed. I can understand your anger. We failed you. In a sense. Well, *they* did. I personally cannot be held liable—

–Oh please. Are you gonna sit there and tell me you never once wrote a script.

–I was… I was never put in that situation, Miz Wilkinson. I was a cardiologist before I came out here, took this job.

–So much of my time has been lost, I feel. I just don't want to lose anymore time.

–Well. I'm not saying you *won't* be eligible for the treatment. Eventually. But it's going to be a process. It's got to be a process.

–Okay, so fine, I'll do it. Sign me up for the next two sessions. What did I get this new credit card for, anyway, other than to max it out?

–I'm afraid our payment system is cash only at the moment.

–Why am I unsurprised by that revelation? Can you tell me what the other two sessions are gonna be like? More of this? I mean, what would you call this that we're doing right now? Therapy?

–I'm afraid in your case, it's going to be a little more than just two more sessions.

–What are you saying now?

–We're going to have to detox you first. Rehab.

–No.

–This is what we have to do with all the addicts who land here, hoping to go on Viutex. The pills that you're on now. Did you bring them with you to the appointment today? Show them to me, please.

–What are you saying? No. There's no way.

–This is your only option. It's for your safety.

–My safety?

–When you're already taking—When you body is addicted to strong opiates, we have to get you off of them first. To put someone in your vulnerable condition on Viutex is extremely risky.

–I'm willing to take that risk. Give me a waiver to sign.

–Well, there are no waivers. And we're not willing. The liability issues effect everyone, patients and doctors alike… That includes the patients that are already on the treatment and those like you who want to be on it.

–I'm sure you can make one exception, Doc.

–And possibly kill a patient? I think not. Look, what are you taking? I'm not blind, you know. I can see your miotic eyes. Is it heroin? Because you've nothing to be ashamed of, Miz—

–How do I even know that you're legit? That any of this is?

–I'm sure you've read the studies online. When did you arrive? Have you had the chance to meet any of our Viutex patients yet?

–Two days ago. No, not really.

–Stick around long enough and you will. They're all over the island now. They're pretty easy to spot.

–So I hear. The island of zombies. Even more fucked-up than the worst junkie.

–And yet they're not. It might appear so, because they are in the early stages of the treatment. They are people who, like yourself, were once in immense pain, and now no longer are. Who never have to worry about that problem occurring ever again.

–Who can't feel anything. Except an endless chain of euphoric bliss.

–Now…

–Who chain smoke cigarettes. Forget to bathe most days. Probably don't smell too nice. Nod out at the dinner table now and then.

–Well at least you are aware of the *potential* side effects. Not everyone gets them, by the way. Some acclimate right away. You also have the potential—

–Or I can just keep manually doing this to myself. Seems like that might be the simplest solution.

–Until you eventually overdose. It is the safety of permanence you are craving. Which is what has brought you here. I tell my patients, it is useful to think of Viutex as plastic surgery for the soul.

–There are entire days where I already feel like a piece of plastic. Sweaty plastic.

–I can only save you if you'll allow me to. But first, you have to allow yourself. Allow yourself to save yourself. That's the first step.

–There has to be some other way. Some black market where I can get this stuff.

–You can't. It's sealed tight. It's not like a pill or something you can readily inject. Only the doctors trained at this clinic know how to perform the procedure. You can look around all you want, comb the streets. Scour the dark web, even. You won't be able to find Viutex. Or even any knock-offs, for that matter. No one knows the formulation. It's been blocked from getting out there into the world. It goes from our pharmacy directly into the patients' bodies.

–Why all the secrecy, Doctor?

The patient smirks. A yellow glint to her skin. Probably a smoking habit, the doctor concludes.

–There are patents pending. Tests still being done, in other countries. There's a chance it might become a bigger thing than it is now. But we're talking years, decades down the road. You won't want to wait for that to happen.

–So right now it's just in Sagosia.

–Yes. Settlers Landing. Which, speaking of. I might also warn you that you won't find any opiates—any narcotics at all on the island. Medical or otherwise. So, I'm just saying this to warn you, once your current supply runs out…

–So I've heard. Part of the plan of the founders. The world's first drug-free country.

–And surveillance-free. Goes hand-in-hand.

–And yet. I can smell marijuana burning everywhere.

–In our constitution, that is technically not a drug. It's regarded as a plant or a vegetable.

–… And the cost of the rehab?

–I'll have to check. But it's around ten K in the local currency.

–What?

–The good news is that it only takes a week usually. Depending, of course, on individual circumstances. Detox is often the easy part. It's the psychiatric treatment that can take up a lot of the time, considering… But we have come up with innovative ways of expediting the process of drug rehabilitation. It actually winds up saving our clients a lot of time and money, considering how long and drawn out they can make the process in the US and other countries. A lot of medical tourists actually come here just for our expedited rehab service.

–Well, I won't need that. The psychological counseling and all. So you can expedite it even further for me. And the price along with it.

–The fact that you're protesting, Miz Wilkinson, gives me the impression that you are in fact very much in need of it.

She doesn't want to scratch in front of him, but she forgets momentarily, goes for the back of her neck. The doctor half-grins, knowingly.

–You can't win, can you, she sighs.

–No. Not when you're a junkie.

–Hey. You said you weren't going to use that word.
–Do you want me to help you or don't you?
–Can I have a few days to think on this?
–When exactly does your visa run out?
–Next month. The thirtieth.
–Then there's still time.

16.

WHEN ROSALITA, THE young one, gets bored, she lets me out to play. Lets me out and doesn't even watch me, which is good. Most of the times I have to play indoors. I tell her I'm too old to play indoors, but that doesn't matter much to her. She just wants to take it easy. Says it's dangerous out there, that I'm only nine, that we're in a new country now, it's not like it was before, back home. But when she gets tired, all those dangers somehow disappear. Then I can go outside and do whatever I want.

Dad got me a drone for my birthday last year. It immediately got the attention of some of the local kids. They're always around when Rosalita lets me out and so we play. Usually I'll take the drone out, it's the thing they're most impressed by.

You spin it three times on the ground in each direction to calibrate it. Then you do a gyro calibration with your joysticks on the controller. You get GPS really quick, especially on our property, where the connectivity is ace. Once you leave our property, the connectivity is not as good, I don't know why. This mainly matters for calibration, take-off. You hold it at altitude for a second. I was doing this for the quasi-native kids for the first time, they were all so amazed. I think some of them hadn't even heard of drones. There weren't any on this island before. It lifted off the ground, and of course mine is the silent kind, you can't hear a thing. Maybe the slight hum of a dragonfly. But that is all.

–How come it don't make a sound, says Alexander. He's thirteen and wears thick glasses and has the blackest hair I've ever seen on a person. Even though he's older, I'm still taller than him.

I like it when older kids ask me important questions like this. I don't get to go to school yet, because Dad and Krstal and Rosalita all say the schools here aren't quite good enough. They're building one that will be good enough for me. In the meantime, Mister Wildersen comes every day. He has an English accent, even though he comes from Sweden.

–It's because of technology, I tell him. And look—it has a camera, too.

–What do you mean a camera.

Alexander's sister's name is Wessel. I always thought that was a funny name for a girl. A lot of them have funny names here. This is the island of funny names. It's because they're all descended from pirates Mister Wildersen says. They're all named after different islands their ancestors landed on and raided. Says it in a funny way, like he wants to warn me. Maybe that's why I'm technically not allowed to play with these kids.

–See here on the remote.

I show him.

––It's making a video of us right now as we fly it.

Alexander and Wessel look at themselves on the screen.

–Holy shit, says Wessel. Look, that's us.

–Watch this.

I switch it to GPS Follow mode, then start walking away. At first they stay behind, puzzled, looking at me and the drone. I motion for them to follow me, and then they follow.

–Look! Here on the monitor.

–Alexander look! It's following us! shrieks Wessel.

–How do you make it do that?

–Magic, I say. I've got magic abilities.

–Is that why you're not allowed to come and play?

–Look! It's going sideways now!

I have no control over that. When it's in GPS Follow mode, it flies all sorts of weird ways in order to trail you. But I won't let on. I don't want them to think I'm not controlling it all.

–What do you call this thing?

–It's a drone, I say. The military has them too. You can use it to spy on things, people.

–How come you got one?

–Because my dad is the president.

–That's not what our mom says, Alexander speaks up. He says your country is fake. That Sagosia is the only real country here.

–Why would she say something like that?

I don't get what these pirate kids are talking about now. But I don't really care. I've still got more drone tricks to show them. I enter the number five into the radius and the drone starts to go, I run around to try to get into the center of the field surrounding our property, but I run in the wrong direction and the drone goes crashing into the grass.

–Holy shit, says Wessel.

–Is it broke? her brother shouts.

–It's not broken! I assure them running over to get it, though I'm not so sure. It would be embarrassing if that happened, like they would think I don't really know how to operate it. When I'm really an expert.

–Look! Nothing's broken on it.

The one thing I had to check was the gimbol which gets broken all the time in these crashes. But the gimbol works fine. I have to calibrate it again, but once I do that, I send it right off. I know I have to do some tricks soon, or else they'll get bored and stop playing here.

It's up in the air again, circling around us.

–See, it can take photos, too. Not just video. You guys have phones? I can share with you the password, you can also get the photos on your phones.

Wessel and Alexander look at each other in a way that lets me know they don't have phones.

–It's okay, I quickly add, I'll show you how to do it on my phone.

I take a photo of us from a long ways away, the drone way up in the sky in the direction of Cove Beach.

–Look. It's us.

I zoom in so they can get a better look. There's me holding the remote, Alexander wide-eyed with his mouth hanging open, Wessel in her white dress looking doubtful.

–I've never seen Sagosia from up above before, says Wessel.

–What's that over there? Behind us?

–That's Miz Brunnei's house, I tell them.

–And that one? Over there?

–I don't know that man who lives there. I think he works for either Miz Brunnei or Mister Ma. He's never home.

–And that one?

–I don't know. They're never home either.

–So all these big houses are empty?

–They're not empty. People live in them. They go away and come back. Aren't you guys from here?

–Of course, says Wessel. But we're not allowed to play over there. We're not even supposed to come this close. We do sometimes. To play in the empty houses.

There are some abandoned ones on the edges of the field where no one lives. They've been empty since the quasi-colonials left. More of the people moving to Settlers Landing for jobs have been moving into apartments in the city. There are a lot of new apartment build-ings the old Rosalita says look much nicer than the ones they've got in Manhattan. They brought in an architect from England to design them for the people.

—Your nanny lets you do that? I say. Mine won't let me go over there. She says the abandoned houses are dangerous. That the ceiling can come down and crush you. I mean, she says it to me in Spanish, but I can understand now. Does your nanny speak Spanish too?

Wessel and her brother look at each other again. Then they look back at me.

—We don't know what you're talking about, Wessel says. What does a nanny do?

—Nanny is what he calls his mom, says Alexander.

—No! A nanny is a person who takes care of you. She works for you though so she's not really your boss. Your dad and mom or step-mom are the real bosses, they're the ones who tell the nanny what to do. But she takes care of you so that they can work or get their nails done.

The two kids look at each other again. I wonder if I'm saying the words wrong. Maybe they don't understand English that well. But they seem to speak it fine. Mister Wildersen says they have another language here, Sagosian, but that younger people don't really speak it.

—Okay. If you guys don't have a nanny, then I don't get it. Who takes care of you?

—Our mom.

I'm getting impatient. I don't understand what they're doing, maybe playing some kind of joke on me.

—Haha, funny. But who does your mom get to take care of you when she's not around.

—Nobody, says Alexander.

—When she's working, that means we take care of ourselves, says Wessel. Like right now.

I still don't really get it, so I try to direct their attention back to the drone.

—See, it can do circles. Even fly upside down like that. But you don't want to do it upside down for too long, because then it gets hard to control.

—Let me try! I want to fly it!

—No, Wessel says to her brother. You can't.

—Why not?

Wessel whispers in her brother's ear that this shit's expensive. If it gets broke, we'll have to pay for it, and mama will whip your ass.

—I'm not gonna break it! Alexander screams, oblivious to his sister's whispering.

—You can fly it for a second, I tell him. Here, I'll show you how to do it with the remote controls. It's easy. You just have to look into the monitor here. Don't look up at the sky. That's the hard part. Because you want to look up at it, but you have to fight that impulse. Just look down here at the monitor.

—What's impulse? Alexander says. Never mind. I'm flying it! Look!

Wessel doesn't look impressed. Girls don't always like this type of thing.

—Look at the picture! Look, you can see the water. That's Cove Beach!

We look at the screen. Two fishermen are pulling their boat in with the day's catch. When they reach the shore, they remove a big net full of all kinds of silver fish, thrust it down in the sand, then start to unfurl all their equipment from the little boat.

—Go over to the right.

I make a right and fly along the coast. I am showing them their island.

—Wow, the beach looks so pretty from up high, Wessel now has to admit.

—That's how it looks all the time, Alexander corrects her. It's just you can't see it from this high. Not unless you're up in an airplane.

—I've been in an airplane before, I tell them, thinking they'll be impressed by it. They just look up at me, then look back down at the monitor. Like it's nothing.

—Make it come back now!

The easiest way to do that is to switch it back into GPS mode, so that's what I do.

—Look, it's going over—Look, that's Baldheaded Mountain!

—I can make it go past the mountain, but we have to be careful. If it bumps into the mountain and then falls, then it's hard to get it back. Like if the battery gets knocked off, we'll have to send someone to climb the mountain to get the pieces back.

Wessel and Alexander look at me.

—Who are you going to send? Your nanny?

—Don't worry, we won't have to. Look, it's coming back now.

—There it is! says Alexander, pointing up at it. You can make it land?

–Sure I can. Right here in the field.

I'm bad at making it land, so it tumbles a little. We all run to go get it. None of the pieces have fallen off.

–Like magic, huh? I ask them.

–Yeah, says Alexander.

–We have to go home now, Wessel tells me.

–Where do you live?

–Over by the temple?

–I don't know where that is.

–It's that way! says Alexander. He's pointing to the place between the hills and Cove Beach, but I can't see much of anything except for grass and trees and a narrow dirt road. No houses over there.

–You can come over, says Wessel.

–Yeah! Bring your drone with you.

I want to, but I'm not allowed to follow them. But that's okay. I tell them another time. As they go along, I follow them with my drone, so it's almost like I'm walking with them. I do that for a while, until they get too far, and I'm afraid of losing it, so I put it back on GPS and fly home.

17.

AS TAGGERSTON'S MORNING televised administrative work is winding down, the cast and crew of *Lives of the Innocents* accumulate at the studio and commence setting up for the afternoon shoot. There's only one television studio on the island, so they have to share. A scene of film set banality ensues—crew setting up, large metallic objects and green screens on stilts moved to and fro, thick cables tripped over, groggy men cursing loudly into walkie-talkies and mobile phones, the bearded fox in the director's seat making regal gestures next to the iPad-bearing female assistant, the scent of coffee and electricity, the whir of electric fans beneath the thin murmur of voices. Lucia always arrives early to pick up the script, a sense of demonstrative duty. The actors only have an hour to learn their lines before shooting starts. Time to find out where Hornby is going today. Krstal Mrdok brushes past her toward the coffeemaker.

–Why Lucia, I have to say, that is the loveliest dress I ever saw you wear. Did you get that around here? Or did you have someone make it for you?

It's been around three years now since Krstal Mrdok was written into the show. Actually she's the first non-Sagosian, quasi-elite actress ever to appear on *Lives of the Innocents* since the show started some twenty-three years ago. Her character arrived rather mysteriously, as *Lives of the Innocents* typically evades referring to real life events on the island, opting instead for a sort of idealized or fantasy version of Sagosian life. It's not even really Sagosia, more a fictionalized version of what used to be called Sagosia, named Port Matthews on the show—though the quasi-native audience can clearly recognize all the local referents, from the typical Sagosian accent to locales (on those occasions when they venture outside the studio to do outdoor shoots—something the producers generally frown upon since it requires extra expenditures, particularly given the unpredictability of the weather in the wet season.)

One of those awkward moments—innumerable since Krstal first came on the set. Can't skate away from this one—Lucia takes her blades off outside the studio door, to avoid being bitched at by the crew. What it is is that Krstal is fishing for friends. She's zeroed in on Lucia for whatever reason and Lucia is largely indifferent to these efforts. Not indifferent in a cruel sense—more just busy with the patter of her preestablished life and seeing no real need to alter it.

–Better go learn my lines, says Lucia and she starts to walk away.

–Honey, I already checked. You only got three lines in this episode! Let's go have us a little chat, what do you say? I'm dying for a cigarette!

Shit. Not that she dreaded having to talk to Krstal so much as she felt a premonition bad things were in store for her character on the show. In terms of screen time, she was on a noticeably downward slope the past few weeks. A sure sign that the writers are running out of ideas for what to do with her. Or, worse, that they are just responding to a command coming from above.

It has finally stopped raining and so they step outside to taste some of that pseudotropical post-rain breeze still so exotic to Krstal and, well, unnoticeable to Lucia.

–Twenty-three years on the show. Why, you must be one of the longest running characters in all of soap opera history, girl!

She must mean it as a compliment, but to Lucia's ears, it sounds like she's just being called old. Lucia studies the mangy white van pulled on to the curb in front of them. Out of the back, all sorts of wire and cable spillage. Three of the D.P.'s assistants are there disentangling, joking with each other in Sagosian.

How many more manifestations *could* Hornby weather? That's the question of the hour, the minute. Krstal plays Lynette Merriwether, astute businesswoman, what kind of business so-called she's engaged in never really mentioned, at least not so far, having relocated to Port Matthews for equally murky reasons. What is unknown, at first, but has now surfaced (to the viewers) is that this rich white lady is actually the reincarnation of Hornby's long dead sister Anesthia, who has risen from the dead not only to wreak havoc in the islanders' otherwise (not really) drama-free (somewhat) idyllic lives, but to send a resounding message to Hornby that her powers are, in fact, limited. The ostensible fact being that white magic can turn gradations of gray or even a mulchy black when the practitioner is not in full control of her powers. Yet another indication to Lucia that she is on her way out.

Life expectorates you, slaps you across the face. No one completely sure where Lynette came from. This deliberate openness, masking indecision in the writers' room, also a foil for future invention. It gets wild, sure. Anesthia was on the show so long ago, those episodes haven't even been digitized yet. The actress who played her, Tupai, now long dead. Lucia remembers her. Tupai always wore her hair wrapped in a shawl the colors of Christmas. Like she was celebrating it on her head year-round. Always lit the cigars she smoked with wooden matches—never with a lighter. As dementia got her— some said it was brought on by indulging in one too many nocturnal markmaking sessions—she kept flubbing her lines. This was back when they shot on tape, so the mistakes started to add up, cost-wise. Lucia did what she could to try and save her. Would go over her lines together with Tupai in the makeup trailer each day, arriving two full hours before shooting began—they never got their scripts much earlier than that—but it turned out to be one of those situations that just couldn't be salvaged. Tupai died not long after her character Anesthia bit it on the show. The writers at least gave her a bang, big spectacle to go out by. It hadn't been their decision, of course, but the producers', to write her off the show. The writers had actually enjoyed writing her every week—she was one of those madcap characters they could keep inventing, pretty much do whatever they wanted with. An easy write, in other words. When the dementia started to show itself, they even managed to write that in in a way; they'd had her start to go mad, some spell Hornby had put on her sister to help her gain the trust of a corrupt tax collector who had set out to bankrupt Rae, Hornby's daughter on the show and the recurring protagonist (by wont of looks alone, some of the more cynical cast members would privately aver, as she never seemed to age— and, in fact, was one of the cast members frequently replaced whenever the producers decided new eye candy was needed, and all the other cast members would have to pretend as though the new Rae were the same Rae as the one before [and the one before that, ad infinitum.] Another disconcerting coincidence being that the actresses that played her were somehow always named Maria, spurning certain difficult-to-explain supernatural fears among some of the older Sagosian cast members.) Anesthia was supposed to enter the tax man's office with a glaze of unmistakable charisma and, well, not exactly seduce the tax collector, but, using her newfound prowess (as Anesthia's personality was otherwise considered by those outside her immediate family, who knew intimately her tendencies toward craziness, to be anodyne to a fault) to stir him into a sort of daze of intrigue, whereupon she would unfurl a certain Yangist scroll brought to the island by the sacred ancestors and, while written in an ancient Chinese very few could still read, Anesthia still rather secretly had the capability and, upon reading such a scroll, Hornby assured her, Rae and the rest of the family would eternally be protected by Yang Zhu from any further interference by corrupt financial authorities and be free to pursue their own modest wealth-seeking initiatives that virtually everyone watching the show could relate to (with the corrupt tax man clearly being a foil for the quasi-colonials then ruling Sagosia.) However, only hours after ingesting, the spell turned sour as a result of Hornby mistakenly using salt water instead of tonic when concocting the potion, a mistake owing to a grease smear on the page of the recipe in the ancient witch doctor handbook that had been handed down to her from her great-great grandmother so many decades prior... So, long story spayed and neutered, that is how Anesthia ended up high in a banyan tree by the shore just as a pseudotropical storm was in the midst of whipping up its fury, frothing at the mouth and barking at the gods, who responded in kind by issuing a bolt of lightning that split her in two.

Now Krstal wants to get some acting advice from Lucia. Apparently.

—You remember that scene we shot yesterday? The one with the jade dog?

Krstal lights another one of her extra long skinny ass cigarettes and puffs out a thin plume. In the scene in question, Hornby, now employed as Lynette's herb gardener-slash-masseuse, arrives at the mansion to find Lynette's beloved living room set piece, a Ming Dynasty antique acquired in Macao, shattered in pieces on the Turkish carpeting before the olive green late Austro-Hungarian Empire settee. (The hodgepodge of interior design elements here not a direct inheritance of nouveau riche [anti-]aesthetics from the Far West, but more a reflection of Sagosia's unique neo-colonial islandological inheritance.) Hornby climbs down to the floor and commences dutifully assembling the broken pieces when Lynette enters the room and stands behind her menacingly. She then slowly begins to lift a Greek statuette of Apollo off the table, but just as she's about to make it come crashing down on Hornby's skull, she suddenly snaps out of it—Anesthia's spirit vacates her, Lynette regains possession of herself. A second later, Hornby turns around and is startled to find Lynette hovering over her zombie-like, just as Lynette herself is started to find herself hovering over Hornby, having no recollection of how she arrived there.

—When we played that scene yesterday, I didn't get a chance to tell you, but I was just so impressed by that look of shock that washed over your face when you saw me standing there. What are the words I'm looking for to describe it?

Lucia just stares at her. She's not consciously trying to unnerve Krstal, but she also doesn't want to come across as insulting her by stating the obvious, which is, well, all that can really be stated in this situation.

—Anyway, I had this idea I wanted to run past you, goes Krstal, oblivious to all nuance. I'm thinking of organizing a scene study group—just for us girls. Cos I think we can really learn from each other! I was thinking me, you, Maria of course, Bora, Phi Phi, and Vis. Because, you know, even though we're all professionals here, I don't know about you but I'm the kinda bitch that likes to sharpen my craft, mmmkay? Ha ha ha!

Lucia's not laughing. Krstal doesn't seem to be bothered by this.

—I'm thinking we can just work on the classics. Shakespeare, Tennessee Williams, and, um, who was that Norwegian guy who wrote all those classic roles for women? Because I'm all about empowerment. I want you to know that. Even though I am the president's wife, I just want you to know that I really stand for the empowerment of *all* women on our island, whether you identify as a Sagosian or a quasi-native or quasi-elite or whatever. One thing I am really *not* into is division of any kind—and *especially* among women. And, I mean, among us actresses, come on. You know about my film production company I'm starting, right? I mean, even though you're of a certain age—well, we all are, some just more so than others—but that doesn't mean, like, you always have to play the help, I'm always the savvy businesswoman or else the rich, powerful wife—I mean, who *writes* these ridiculous roles, anyway? Am I right? We've got some really great projects in the works that I think you'd be excellent for,

Lucia. I really want to bring you on board. I mean, your voice needs to be heard.

How is Lucia meant to reply to this, what, what she doesn't even really recognize as an offer, if that is actually what it is meant to be. Yes, she's the president's wife. But that doesn't hold much sway for Lucia, who identifies more as Sagosian and less as opportunist, though she's of that generation, being well into her fifties now, that can't be said to attribute their inclinations in these matters to one articulable political persuasion or another. Her essential quotidianism is about the furthest thing from a southern Californian social climber that might be conjured by a rational mind; now Lucia wonders whether Krstal is even in possession of one.

Lucia looks down at the script in her hands, opens it and starts rustling through the pages, until she finally arrives at one with Hornby's name on it. She looks up at Krstal.

—It says here, on page seven, I confront you. I mean, Hornby is going to confront Lynette... I'm supposed to slap you.

—Ha! I know! Isn't that going to be fun? Why, I haven't done a slap scene since, I think it was in the late '80s, I was doing one of those bikini teen movies, you know, back when that was a thing, I forget the name now, it might have been *Perky's Resort Part III: The Morning After the Morning After,* me and Rosa Fernandez, if you remember her from the *Wild Cherries in the Snow* franchise, she had to whop me one after the wienie fell off the barbeque skewer I was holding and I sort of waved it around screaming drunkenly and accidentally unhooked her bikini top with it, exposing those big titties of hers to all the horny spring break boys on the beach. God, now that I think of it, I really miss my Florida years sometimes. I did some of my best work then. But, you know, the industry has changed so much since then, don't you think? I mean, I know the industry is different here in the Pseudotropics, but still—

—I think we can start the scene study right now. But we should just focus on this afternoon's scene. I can show you some of the techniques I have learned. To make the slap look real. Very real.

Krstal now stares at Lucia, as though something new has just occurred to her. Something she hadn't clearly seen before.

—I been acting a long time too, continues Lucia. Maybe not as long as you. Maybe I aint been in any Hollywood titty films. But I had to learn to do a lot on this show. Maybe it don't seem so. But you know. It's a hard job, having to work here in Sagosia with no fancy stuntmen to do the hard work for you. So an actor learns to do some tricks on her own. I could show, if you want.

–But… Ought we not to rehearse it with the director?

–Oh no. You know how Jersey works. He don't like to rehearse so much. He just want us to *do* it.

It is true. Jersey, the show's ninth and current director, tends to treasure a certain amount of spontaneity on the set with regard to the actors' interpretation of the script. Which doesn't mean he won't suffer them all kinds of vile eruptions when their interpretation clashes in an offensive manner with the one in his mind. But he more often unleashes his bad temper on the crew members, as he likes to pretend he has a special understanding of and hence relationship with actors—not just the actors on the show, but all actors in general.

–Well. I suppose we could give it a try…

–I think so. You want to do it here? Too crowded, I think. Let's go back behind the makeup trailer.

–Over there? Well. Why not here?

–Too many people watching. I get nervous in front of crowds. I like to hone in my focus. My focus on the action. That's the most important part of being an actor. Wouldn't you say?

–Hmm. I… Well, yes! Yes it is, Lucia. You are right about that.

–So go get your script. I'll meet you back there.

–Lucia…

–What.

–You're not… going to actually *hit* me are you? Because, the thing is, you know… I've had some rather expensive procedures done on my face. I just wouldn't want to—

–We've got to make it *look* real.

–Well, of course. We want it to *look* real. But that's different from—

–Don't worry, says Lucia. I won't hit you any harder than it takes to get the shot. I won't cause you no pain, Missus First Lady. You can trust my instincts. I an actress too, you know.

18.

VINCENT ON HIS motorcycle that looks as though it was ridden on to the island from somewhere in the future. Gliding along the newly paved roads in electric silence. It is the first of its kind on the island and he is never going to let it go now. Given to him by the big boss, leader of the security apparatus; he needs a fast and easy way to get around. Past the trees with their enormous trunks, up ahead's the main street with the abandoned town hall, where Nelson Rodgers once conducted his business in days past, a moment that's been consigned to the dusty archives, soon to be incinerated. Vincent carrying some feathers of this past like a disease inside of him. He knows the weather is fake on this day—it always is, this duplicity right before a storm's arrival. Where everything is so calm and radiating this inner glow, that is when you know. Not even a faint wind to ruffle the leaves. He can read this island in its entirety with a single sullen glance at any minute aspect, and so he need not bother—especially when it is all going past him at this velocity.

There are maggots eating their way through a hole in the ground. Making the hole, with their maggoty munchings. Waiting for the breath of a savior to come destroy them, they won't stop if this doesn't happen. If they can reach their destination, down in the Earth's furthest reaches.

There is a building that people go into and come out of. Soldiers, mostly, men, mostly men, occasionally women. But its facility is a mystery—no signs announcing what purpose it is meant to serve. You can stand there and watch all you want, you won't be able to figure out who they are, what they're doing. What the building is for. Behind a gate, with a guard to lift the barrier and let you in if you present the proper documentation. Some buildings are just designed that way. Naked in their bureaucratic grayness, tricking the eye constant to devoid. Actually, the uniforms, nothing the people are wearing, give it away. You can't call them uniforms, not even really suits—not even business casual—it was as though they have been instructed to be transcendentally drab in appearance before they can go in or come out. A caring glance might presuppose purpose. A small office molded by fluorescence, place where papers might be stamped? There are places where transparency goes to get a back massage. Hidden middling sullenities that mask their ultimate purpose behind the piped-in flutesong embedded in hidden speakers in the potted flowers surrounding. In a world without justice, we tend to devise our own. In a world without justice, we tend to worship it all the more.

Like most gods—absent.

Vincent makes his way past the gate—he doesn't need to show ID, the guard knows his appearance well by now—and parks his motorcycle in the near empty lot and becomes one of the people entering the building with no name and no apparent purpose.

19.

–IT'S THE *PRESIDENT*. On the line.

–What do you mean, it's the president, you fuckwit? *I'm* the fucking president.

–*No*. I mean the *other* president. The President of the United States.

–… Wha? Are you shittin me? How'd he get my number?

–I don't know. He's the President of the United States. He can get anything he wants.

–… Connect me in my office.

–Mister President?

–Now, to begin with, this conversation never took place.

–… Okay. Fine.

–Glad we're in agreement. Now, I want you to know, we know everything, Mrdok. Every fine little detail. And, I just want to say… There is a certain amount to be *admired* in what you have done. Or… Okay. If not to be *admired*, per se… Then grudgingly acknowledged, might be a better way of putting it…

–So you're saying, you're *acknowledging*—

–Oh I'm not officially acknowledging anything. Nor will I ever, truth be told. Like I said, this call never took place. What I'm doing here, Mrdok, is offering you an opportunity. Now I could have back-channeled this. That is what my advisors unanimously begged me to do. But that's not my style. I had a hunch.

–A hunch?

–That you and I are alike. Even though we've never met before. Probably more alike than any other two men on this planet. Well, we're both Americans, after all.

–I'm not. Not anymore.

–I mean American in a very quintessential sense. We wouldn't be where we both are if we weren't. We don't go chasing after dreams. We create them. We manage them. We make dreams for others. Tell them what their dreams are, what they could be. What they *should* be. Surely what you've done out there on that island—

–If you're not going to recognize us, then why the fuck are you calling?

–I'm calling because I want to give you a chance. An opportunity.

–You're calling to sell me a dream? Figures.

–Like I just said, Mrdok. I don't deal in dreams. I can only offer you a reality that, okay, it might taste bitter at first, but once you allow it to sit in your mouth for a while, you're going to find it's the best-tasting decision you ever—

–Enough with the sales pitch, Prez. I don't care how official or unofficial this call is. I don't even care whether you're going to recognize us or not. What I demand is that, if you're going to talk to me, you address me as a fellow head of state. Or else this call is gonna come to an end real quick.

–Total immunity. That's what I can offer you. You come back to the US—

–I'm never going back there. Never.

–We'll return your passport to you. You'll be a red-blooded American. Just like you always were.

–You're boring the shit out of me. I've got about a dozen passports. There's only one that means anything to me.

–Which is essentially worthless, Mrdok. I mean, let's be frank. You can't go anywhere on it. No other country in the world has recognized your sovereignty.

–You know why it is I think you're callin?

–Mrdok! There's no one reason. There is, if I may be blunt, an entire clusterfuck you've cobbled together that we can no longer just ignore. Forget about all the blatantly criminal shit, all the fraud you pulled back here—

–Nothing I have ever done has fallen outside the law. It's not my fault that the laws are so ambiguously worded.

–I don't even care about the past. Like I said, total immunity. But, the island, man… You're violating international sanctions, turning people into, into zombie drug addicts with your dubious medical practices. Your offshore drilling is—

–I've cornered the nucleite market, is what you're worried about. That's the thing that keeps you up at night. Am I right?

–Mrdok, you've put together an armed militia, for Christ's sake. There's nothing in the Geneva Convention—

–It's not an armed militia, Prez. Can I call you that? I'm going to anyway… It's not a militia. It's an army. Which we are entitled to, as a sovereign nation, whether you're prepared to acknowledge us as such or not.

–And where, pray tell, did this army come from, Mrdok? I don't need to tell you from where. We both know. Our intelligence knows.

–Yeah, that's right. They're veterans. All of em. From your sordid, stinking wars.

–So what are you now suddenly? A peacenik? You can insult me, the American people, all you want—

—I find it sad. I find it—what's the word? Reprehensible. A lot of these guys, they came over here with PTSD. Untreated. That we, with our vastly superior health care system, now have to take care of. Which we're doing fine, by the way. Welcomed them with open arms. They've been more than just left behind. They're angry. Confused. But you know the one thing is that they've still got? They've got fire in them, Prez. That fighting spirit, that you, your government, instilled in them. They still *want* to fight. They're just looking for the right opportunity.

—These men have been decommissioned for a reason, Mrdok. These are dangerous individuals we're talking about.

—Now look here. I will not have my men insulted.

—Your men.

—Who contacted you? Is it the EU? That fuck in Belgium?

—This is not what it's about, Mrdok. I'm looking out for your best interests. As a fellow—

—I don't doubt you know me as well as you think you do. I imagine you've got it all in a neat little file on the desk right there in front of you. Where are you calling from, by the way? Is it the Oval Office?

—If it makes any real difference: yes.

—Interesting. You wanna know where I am? What we call ours? The Diamond Office. You wanna know why that is?

—Because it's shaped like a diamond?

—It's not, actually. Guess that's one place where your intelligence falters.

—I'll update our files accordingly.

—It's because the diamond is a symbol for strength, potency. For flint peckers. Which we got plenty of, here in Settlers Landing.

—You're playing with fire, Mrdok. To put it mildly. You're not just pissing us off, Europe, and who even knows how the Chinese feel about all of it. There's also internal dissent we've taken note of—

—Right now, I own your Silicon Valley. Not directly, of course. But it's true. I've got my finger on the switch. The nucleite switch. All I have to do is flip it off. Stop dealing with the middlemen who supply to you. Then what? Bye bye computer chips. Bye bye mobile phones. Bye bye to all the grease, all the lubricant that keeps your economy running smoothly. Now wouldn't that make you look bad? If you'd just simply acknowledge our sovereignty, Prez, we could cut out the middlemen. Start doing business directly. Now wouldn't that be a nice arrangement, benefiting everyone?

—Mrdok, the political reality will not allow that to happen. Now we are fully prepared to launch—

–Now you listen here. I'm a reasonable man. So are you. Let's do things the adult way, shall we? I might be new at statemaking, but it doesn't take a great genius to know that the best way of dealing with a potential enemy is by neutralizing them. Am I right, Prez?

–We are not going to grant you sovereignty, Mrdok. There is no earthly way we could ever even *begin* to convince our allies—

–A peaceful solution. To a problem, let us say, that you don't even have to be *publicly aware* is a problem. You can spin the optics on this in any number of directions, Prez. The public is dumb. They don't care. They'll go along with anything.

–If we were to come to blows over this, Mrdok—

–There we go. Rallying the war cries again. How very American of you.

–Oh we don't have to go to war, Mrdok. We have more than physical weapons in our arsenal. Let me check this folder I have here on my desk... Settlers Landing, the world's first surveillance-free state? How many of your settlers are still buying that...

–Look. You can leak whatever nonsense you want. No one will believe you. We've got our own media machinery, which has been highly effective. And, yes, the weapons to back it up.

–Just the notion of sheer *size*, Mrdok...

–Hey. It didn't faze Cuba, did it?

–Do you really want to compare yourselves to them? Look, we don't even have to fight you directly. You have a, what is it, a quarter population of disenfranchised natives who are, as we say, not pleased with the status quo...

–You do whatever the fuck you think you have to do. My offer is crystal clear. We look forward to welcoming you in Olde Colonia some day, Mister President.

Click.

20.

–COCO, WHERE IS my... ?

Never mind, he found them.

The crystalline presence of day. The sun always shining here. The sun's been shining on Bobby constant—his whole life it seems. First California, then a brief stay in the Mediterranean, now this. An entire biography narrated by sunshine. Well, almost.

They chose, or were assigned, one of the smaller houses in the hills. Isolated by a field. He looks through the window. There's Jaco playing with some of the local kids, showing off his drone. Bobby almost wants to go out there. Somehow he always winds up looking out windows. Where's Coco?

Usually there's a lighter in the pack, now it's not there. Look around the mess of a house, what day does the maid come? What day does any of this happen? Some eggs in the frying pan they must've made then forgotten to eat.

–Coco!

He calls her name into the depths of the darkened house, the wine-dark house, no one is awake to answer. Goes outside. Jaco far away enough or too preoccupied with his new friends to see him standing out there, unlit cigarette hanging out of his mouth like some creepy bastard, the neighborhood perv.

Switch to vaping like Coco did ages ago. That's what he keeps telling himself he should do. Did for a while, but then as soon as someone lights a cigarette, he wants one. It's like the smell triggers it.

Goes back into the living room to where his phone's charging.

The state of not-knowing. That's the purest state, place where mystics depart from. Bobby's no mystic. But he's pretty sure he knows what it is to occupy that zone. That perennial place where you can transmit an inner buzz into whatever objects you touch and, doing that, in a sense, like, *animate* them.

These are stoned thoughts. What others are there? Bobby can't know. He can't even remember what it feels like to be on heroin anymore. When he first got the treatment, he remembers distinctly feeling like it's somehow different from smack. In what ways, he couldn't enunciate. Well, not at first. At first, before the first of the infinite adrenaline rushes kick in, it's like, okay, you're feeling *something*. Then, a few minutes later, you're like *fuck*. A ride you're never gonna get off of. Because you're too busy getting off. Ha.

Then you sort of get used to it. The high becomes like background static. Go through the daily motions, inside it's a cycle of endless explosions. And it gets to where you can control it on the outside, so no one can tell. No one knows how very good you are feeling. It is a violent tranquility. Seething yellow proof of violence.

Upstairs, she's left the bathroom door open. The master bathroom with the walk-in closet inside. The mile of shoes, all Coco's. Pumps every color and design, a sneaker section, the boots. Coco lying at the end of a pile her head resting on a folded-up blanket the phone glued to her ear. She says some words in Italian into it.

–Hey babe, ventures Bobby. Are you hungry? Cos I was thinkin…

She looks up, squints at his form. Coco went on it first. She was gonna do it on the sly, but it's not something you can really hide from others. Meaning, not the ones close to you. They're gonna notice the change—especially if they have any experience with drugs themselves. (Oh but it's not really a drug. LOL.) She announced it to him matter-of-fact. It's not like they both hadn't been considering it from the moment they stepped foot on the island. It's not like either of them had ever seriously cleaned up, either. They didn't really have to. There was a glamour in being high all the time, especially when you can get the good stuff. Coco had demonstrated this to Bobby. It wasn't the lifestyle he'd been living in Catalina, the kind of life they were living together in Europe. In Cali, it was shooting shitty dope, having to turn somersaults in order to get it, living in a rat trap of his own creation that he couldn't even be bothered to keep clean. In Italy, Corsica, all the places they went on the continent, it was fine powdered cocaine, pharmaceutical grade stuff all the way, blue pills chopped fine with razors, maids to pick your underwear up off the floor, marble tiles to keep your bare feet cool. Not a single bead of sweat upon your forehead, at least not one you could feel or otherwise notice. He could have gone on like that into old age, he would have been fine with it. But Coco grew restless. She'd wanted a change. And so there they were.

She pushes the red button without saying goodbye to the caller. Must be an awfully good friend if she can get away with that.

–You want the chicken parmesan-uh?

–Who was it on the phone?

–You know-uh. Famiglia.

She's been working on this deal with the Sicilians for, what, eight months now. It's not that Bobby minds her doing a little business on the side. It would just be nice if she were willing to divulge a detail or two now and again.

She lifts herself up off the floor.

–Can we, like, maybe collaborate on this, Coco?

She lifts the vape to her mouth.

–You don't-uh know-uh these guys-uh. Eets our culture, Bobby-uh. Even eef you speak Italiano, wheech you don't-uh, you steel would not able to get the way they are playing the game-uh. I'm sorry, baby, eet ees just-uh…

Her voice trails off, then refinds itself.

—Or how about the eggplant parmigiana. Eet ees more heathy-uh.

Frosty cloud of vape sauce comes peeling out of her grin. Bobby sits on the floor.

—I just feel like, once my brother gets wind of this—

—He ees not going to find out-uh.

—Okay, so like he's not really a businessman. But Lilbig is like on top of his shit. You know, he's had to be, managing that hip-hop empire for so long…

—What empire? Coco gives a derisive little cough-laugh.

—Coco. You can't be serious. He was like one of the biggest rap stars.

—Was-uh. And look at heem now-uh.

She hates to see him this way, getting all out of shape. She'd globbed on to his insecurities within seconds of first talking to him in rehab, she knows what his weaknesses are and she knows how to override them. How to trot those fears out of him when she has to and put them on display so that, seeing them, he'll feel confronted and shut his mouth back to zero so that she can move on with her own order of business. Her allegiances shift out of necessity. She loves Bobby, but she also gets bored with it at times; not with Bobby, but with the fact of their love, which comes to feel like a burden when they're not fucking or otherwise satisfying each other. Truth is, being on Viutex can make relations with other people near intolerable. You really have to work on it in order to make it work. Most of the time, working on it consists of going off on your own. Not giving the other person space. Giving yourself that space. Viutex clearly wasn't designed with the aim of the patient's maintaining cordial relations. More like launching them into solo orbit.

She had asserted her intention so surely and calmly, Bobby had thought in his mind, okay, fine, let her go on it first—that way I can see what it does, make sure *I* want to be on it. Though he was like ninety-nine percent sure he was going to follow. And so he did, without paying much attention to what it had done to Coco.

—He's still a huge star. In a way. He's just waiting for the scandal to die down, so that he can go back to recording…

—You believe thees bullsheet-uh?

—Coco. The deal is, I'm in business with him. Him and my brother. Eventually they're going to find out…

It is true that, in their minds at least, the trio is meant to have an exclusive monopoly on the black market trade of Viutex, which they exchange for a certain quantity of marijuana from Pembroke each month to sell on the island semi-legally, through a network of deliv-erymen. It is also true that no such monopoly can exist for long. Coco is certainly aware of this. So are the people who know Coco. At his most paranoid moments, Bobby wonders whether this was behind her plan all along to relocate here. So scared of the idea, he would never dare voice it aloud.

–Alora… Eggplant parmigiana?

She brushes past him, putting a full stop to the discussion. It will be out of his memory in a few minutes anyway. Another of the pleas-ing effects of the treatment.

She owes some people favors back home, is all. What the hot rapper fuck and the nihilist punk brother fail to realize is the short-term nature of the business they're getting into. This Viutex shit isn't a new commodity; it in fact poses a huge threat to the larger narcotics trade. The cartels, mafias, gangs, they're all going to want to see it die. Will do whatever they can to make it die. Because it threatens to put them all out of commission. There is no such thing as a repeat customer for Viutex. Unlike with, say, a heroin addict, who you can drain for years until they finally manage to croak—with every addict thus being a potential source for tens of thousands or even millions over a prolonged period, Viutex is a one-fix trick. Not only that, it also robs dealers of their potential clientele for heroin and other val-uable substances. Sure, you can make it expensive as fuck; but not *that* expensive, since those who could afford to pay an exorbitantly high price are the same who could then come to Settlers Landing and get the legal treatment under proper medical supervision and thus reduce the risk of killing themselves—and would naturally prefer to do so. So, in summary, what you were then left with was a medium-priced commodity that potentially ate up your clientele base for other commodities, created no repeat customers; all you could really do to push it in order to maximize your return is to try and get every single person on the face of the earth on it.

Still, there was some small potential for Viutex, but you needed someone with experience to manage it. Someone who had a plan and a means for putting it to good use. Coco knows the right people, and so she's handling this in her own way.

21.

LUCIA TRIES HER best to maintain the tradition of Sunday dinner, but with the boys grown and treading different paths, there are times she begins to regret this insistence. Still, for the sake of her husband. Though at times it seems as if he doesn't really care, she knows deep down inside he does. They are his boys too, and while he might be way past that point where he is able to empathize or even begin to understand—let alone follow the conversation when it is being led by either Vincent or Prince—she reckons that their occasional presence serves as a substitute normality that in itself at least partially makes up for everything else that might be going on.

—You put avocado in this? Vincent now spits out. Don't you know avocado cause moobs.

Lucia puts down her fork at this new word.

—What is moobs?

—Don't you know, ma? Man boobs. Moobs. Avocado got this fat in it that make men boobs grow.

Father says what the hell.

—Let me guess, now speaks Prince. This some shit you picked up hanging out with them white people in the town.

—I don't *hang out,* Vincent scowls. They pay me. Which's more we can say for you.

Lucia says now stop it. She knows what's about to happen. Been through it so many times now, she hardly have the patience anymore.

Prince isn't gonna respond directly to that jibe cos he knows in fact it is true but so what. Instead he'll sort of drive around it, like one does with a small dead animal lying in the middle of an empty road, so's not to bloody the tires.

—Point is, I still know who I is. What I is.

Father's fork shriek against the plate, causing Lucia to jump up all startled.

—How is things going on the *Lives,* mama?

Vincent says this all regal-like with an eye on Prince, like he be bein the dignified one in this scenario by evading the inevitable exchange of tonalities.

—You mean on the show or at work? That white lady keep buggin me on both.

This reignites Prince's interest.

—Buggin you like how.

—Chasin me down. Actin like we friends. I can't tell what it is, if she be lonely or want somethin from me. What that may be, I can't even fathom.

—Vincent can tell you. He an expert on the quasis by now. Aint you, Vince?

Father tells the boys to shut they mouths then goes back to munchin.

–By the time we get it figured out it's gonna be much too late to wait much longer.

–Now what's he sayin.

Prince got the dead weight of everyone's eyes on him now. Lucia break it with continuance.

–Every day now it's will you run lines with me Lucia, let's us go get a coffee Lucia, let's meet us in the makeup trailer Lucia, can you be in my movie Lucia—

–Wait. What movie?

Now dad's interested.

–You didn't hear? Them quasis is startin they own movie studio.

–Krstal is, to be precise.

–So-called first lady.

–Ha. First lady of what.

–She startin a *movie studio?*

–That's what she say.

–What the hell wrong with our own movie studio?

–Guess it aint precious enough, ha. She gonna bring in Tom Hanks or some shit.

–Not precious enough for her fancy quasi-elite ass.

–She is bringin in a director. From *Holly*wood.

–Holly... What the hell? Here in Sagosia?

–That's what they say.

–Well. I can *almost* see it.

–By the time you do, you's gonna be blind.

–Prince. Don't talk to your older brother in this way.

–Yeah Prince, Vince has to verbalize his agreement now aloud. Your brother who got a job. Who give some of his hard-earned money to support this family each and every.

–What this family *need.* Now it's Prince puttin down his fork—is loyalty. Someone to be loyal *to.* Not someone who's crossin over.

A reference to Vincent working in Olde Colonia. He's doin something there for the new government, it seems. No one is sure what. Vincent don't like to talk about it. Seems he aint allowed to. Actively discourage deep questioning with his words. It aint nothin too serious, truth be told. He just somethin like a messenger. Or so it seems. To some.

Father bangs his fist upon the table, says enough of this bull. Father otherwise mute so he easy to ignore, his TV powerlessness.

–This is the part where Prince gonna tell us all how to think? Prince, who barely got hisself an eighth year education?

Prince don't have much respect for father. Don't got much respect for anyone except Prince. All his moanin about the Sagosians and they heritage. They condition. The way Vincent sees it, it's all a foil. A foil so Prince can talk more about hisself.

–Why she can't get a Sagosian director. What the hell's the matter with this quasi woman.

There he go.

–Man, Sagosia only got one real director. He busy on the show. He's not gonna go round directin no movies. Mom can tell you that too. Right, ma?

–I don't know what the hell, Lucia sighs. Guess I could use the extra work, though. The extra money it's gonna bring in. We don't know how much longer the show's gonna last. Times is changin. That much for sure.

–That's what I'm fuckin sayin, Prince goes. They got one white lady on the show now, what's gonna be next. They takin over, the quasis. Year from now, it's gonna be all white people on the TV. You mark my words. We too lazy, that's the problem. We just sittin back doin our thing like it's still twenty-five, forty years ago. Out fishin and walkin around doin nothin. Meanwhile, they stealin the ground out right from under our feet. This aint even our island no more.

–Prince, says Lucia now. Why don't you hush up and let us digest our dinner for once.

Prince smacks his lips and looks down at his plate.

Later they out back, Vince and Prince, drinkin makin marks. Got a little bit of grass Vince brought. They smoke that too. They got they ligand wrapped with duct tape at the bottom on a long stick they take turns wieldin and they surface splayed out on the ground, this time it's this real thick paper Vincent brought back from Olde Colonia this afternoon, this long ass roll of it he got strapped to the back of his scooter it look almost like a diagonal sword from faraway and he a knight come ridin against the wind.

–There aint no strife in this life worth makin violence out of.

Vincent imbues these words with a calm. He wants to get all truce-like so as to placate the Mom who just don't want to listen to it no more, this constant bickering between the two of them always threatening to erupt into shouting or worse. Vincent won't let it get to the point of violence. Out he goes out the door when he feels the arguin is about to turn violent. Someone has to be man enough to leave. Prince, for all his constant runnin away when he was a kid. Now he wants to stay all the time. Stay and fight.

The quasi-elites brought with them to the island a whole lot of changes, some of them real obvious, but one of the more puzzling and mysterious ones was a change in seasons, in seasonality. See, before there was always mostly two seasons, which Sagosians like to call dry and wet. Hard for outsiders to fathom, because it wasn't what those words imply. It's always humid in Sagosia, so there aint no real thing as dryness, not the desert dry some people like them from California'll normally associate with the term. Dry season in Sagosia is when the storms aint supposed to come. They in the midst of it now. Wet is a like a polite way of sayin they get their asses whupped with these hard ass megacanes near all the time that part of the year. Since the quasis got here, at any time could the sky turn all turgid and gray, get to where a pseudotropical depression was about to swallow the whole island, be it season wet or dry. When even the weather can't be predicted or relied upon no more. Just think of what it does to all the fishermen out there, trapped at sea. All those fishers out there in the night, when it's so much easier to catch, and then suddenly a storm's upon you, and you don't even know what or where or what you're made of anymore. That's the thing Prince is thinking about now as he peers up at the moonless night. The changing weather and how lost they all is fast becoming because of it.

They both shirtless and drinking rum. Prince has the stick now and starts stabbing the ink in little slashes on the paper. His marks aint never controlled enough to attain elegance, Vincent feels, but he's long refrained from voicing his criticism out loud, lest it lead to another fight, more proselytization.

Prince and his newfound cause. Aint nothin in his early life give any sign he out to turn out this way. Sometimes to Vincent it's like theys brains is formatted different.

—You feel it yet? Prince now says to his older brother. He's stepped back from the surface, the markstick all wobbly in his hand, like he about to get a recommendation from some sacred force as to where to put it next.

—Feel what? You mean the weed?

Vincent grown out of believing in the trance effects of the mark-making process and brother Prince know that too well. Still, he always botherin on about it.

—What I feel is a little buzzed from the rum. That's all. And by the looks of it, it's what you startin to feel as well.

Prince now open his eyes and in em Vincent can see his inner jackal about to barge right out dodgin every gun aimed its way and any bullet that might spill forth.

–What I feel is the spirit of Yang Zhu entering full force into my blood. My soul. Which is what the ritual supposed to do.

Prince now directs that threat to Vincent with his eyes. Vince sighs.

–If that's the case, then I don't think you'd be able to really speak about it. Possession don't give one much space, much cause for talkin.

Now Prince hold out the stick to his brother to take it out of his hands. Almost put it down on the ground out of anger and walked out. Stopped himself; to lay the ligand stick on the ground is deeply unallowed, a supreme offense to the very deities they all supposed to honor as Sagosians. Bein Sagosian aint nothin to do with a nation; it's a spiritual condition; it be they blood. The stick hang from a hook on a woodbeam beneath the enclosed porch out the back of the family trailer. Little light inside so's they can see. The trailer that aint been knocked down in some thirteen storms, even though the rest around them has fallen one by one. And Vincent don't believe that aint got nothin to do with the interference of Yang Zhu, deity that reign over them all, giver of self and life? How Prince be protectin them all through his devotion?

Vincent take the stick and commence makin his own marks upon the paper. He got a fluidity to his runnin style that yeah arouses a little hit of Prince's envy. Cos he don't get how Vincent can mark like that with eyes opened or closed no matter and say he don't feel a goddamn thing. And if he really don't feel a thing then the offense is all the greater cos it mean he inauthentic, that he's not being led to do this by their ancestral spirit, that he doin it on his own; that it art instead of the experience that religion brings. There aint no hereticism in Yangist belief, but that don't mean there aint no ways of tarnishin the sacred. Prince beginning a list of those ways.

Prince just don't know where his brother's superiority done come from. That's the big mystery. Suspects it might have somethin to do with bein the first born, but that one will have to remain forever an unknown. Cos Prince'll never decode the pressures and hardships and luxuries of bein born first. Protected himself near constant by never bein around to observe. Going down into this deep shelter where the birds is all at. Prince remembers it as a kid, this old underground storm shelter near Baldheaded Mountain, all stocked up with canned food and provisions that could last a century, always told they could play down there but don't do nothin don't touch the food or provisions, in back of an old abandoned house he and his gang used to play at. Till of course they finally burned it down one sodden night. Rain came quick and put out the flames, reducing the house's skeleton to ashes, like a corpse in a morgue. Dry warmth of the flames bein the chief thing always draw Prince in, that and the spectacle from afar, not too far though, a short distance. Distance enough... They'd lit up the house but not the shelter, which was at a ways a distance from the house, built into the ground, nestled in a slit between those two testicular boulders at the base of Baldhead. Something about putting on fire something that was beneath the ground scared him, or not scared him but made him feel nervous. Never had to use that shelter, maybe some day they would. Maybe it was the influence of all those hellfire sermons Father always had on on the TV at home, him dozing in front of them constant, the background hum of the trailer, something else to run away from. Friends all forgot about that shelter, but Prince didn't. Used to go down there all alone to play. Even added to the canned food some candy he used to steal from the store, thinkin if the day ever came he needed to hide out that'd be the perfect place to do it. Like ever since he was young he was expecting the day to come that something like this would come to happen.

He had to come upon his own language, his own way of bein in the world. Some rationale behind all the fires, all the destruction that he carried out for reasons he himself couldn't fathom, it was all just rooted in impulse until he got to the age where he realized he had to make it all mean something if it were to work, if he were to continue with it. Or to find some other craft with which to set his mind right.

It was when he was first starting to articulate these thoughts to himself that the Devolution happened. That's how people like him, Sagosians who were awake to the reality of what was happening, that's how they liked to refer to it. When the quasi-colonials got kicked out, when they were replaced by this new breed, Mrdok and his quasi-elites. Suddenly it all was different. It's not that they hadn't resented the quasi-colonials. But they were a benign presence on the island, outnumbered, and they had been here so long, there was no question of their imposing their will on the quasi-natives. But it all changed when the quasi-elites got here and started talking about how all this was theirs. That this was a country now. When it never had been before. Not Sagosia. It wasn't even a colony, not what Prince could recall. What it was was a home. Him and his family and all the Sagosians, their ancestors who had landed here so many centuries ago. And now it was being claimed by someone else. It was real simple, the situation. And it was continuing to deteriorate. And then there was folks like Vincent. Not even sitting back and watching it happen. They were participating. They were making the process go forward by marrying themselves to the quasis.

—You can at least tell me something, Prince now says.

—I can try, Vincent says.

—What is it you do? The big mystery.

Vincent sighs.

—It aint no big mystery.

—It is, though.

—Look, you know the story. They started to come here, I's the only real fixer on the island. I aint nothin special. I just did things, simple things, where no one else bothered.

There emerges an itchiness in Vincent's person when topics related to his work arise. The only people who ask much is family. Prince especially. No one else seems to much mind. People is busy with they lives. Prince busy with everyone else's.

—You just on your fancy motorbike all the time. Goin.

—Yeah. Cept sometimes, I drive other vehicles.

—A messenger.

—I guess. You can say that.

—Workin for the Settlers' government.

—Yeah.

—… When you could be workin for your own people.

Prince stabs the paper with the brush.

—You got yours and I got mine, Vincent says.

—Vince. You aint got much of nothin.

Vincent finds this pretty funny. From the kid who aint never earned a farthing not once in his life. Even now, when they's money to be made.

—If it aint for me, man…

—Yeah. I know. This family be starvin.

—Dad can't work. Mama's soap don't never pay next to nothin. She do what she can do. It's always been up to me. Long as we all know. That's somethin you still can't see.

—I see it. That's my callin. To see things. Maybe it don't earn nothin. But there is other duties in this life besides makin money. Mine is protection. To protect, not just this family. But our people.

Vincent doesn't respond right away. He makes a spectacular cursive medley of tangles right below Prince's latest verticals.

Confidence. Like he showin his little brother the right way to mark-make.

–We a culture, man. A people. I got that. You don't need to preach to me. You know where you take it the wrong way, Prince?

–Vincent.

–No. I'm fixin to tell you. You know where it is you go wrong?

–Do one thing for me.

–It's where you get fucked up, where you start tailin off in a direction I can't follow…

–One thing.

–You inventin a history that didn't exist before. Our people. You tryn to turn it into a religion. That's not who we is. We never was that.

–Come to the temple.

–See? There we go.

–Just once.

Now Vincent's turn to stab the surface with his brush.

–No.

Responding to the airing of these words, Yang Zhu opens the skies up above them. They just stand there ignoring it, looking at each other, like the staring contests they had as little kids, only now, neither of em really wants to win. Vince and Prince. Two brothers in the pouring down rain.

22.

–WHAT DO YOU mean by *the alphabet of reason?*

Birchfield swallows, looks down at his hands. He hasn't done a Q&A in how long—or a reading, for that matter—and now he remembers why. He takes a sip from the glass of water set before him, wishing it contained vodka.

–Um, well… Keep in mind, the poem was written, what, more than thirty years ago. So, I think back then, I was probably, um, under the influence of Derrida. You know, I think *Of Grammatology* had just come out… Well, the English translation had just come out, and you know, up in Buffalo, a lot of us were reading it… So, um, I think what I was trying to say with that line, was like, to find a, a uh, grammatology of rational thought, you know, and so I simplified that thought into *alphabet of reason,* to like, make it clear to the reader who perhaps wasn't yet prepared to dive full in to Derrida, who can be quite tough to read, but you know, could still kind of, well, *feel* the sentiment that Derrida was trying to evoke... If that makes sense?

The horn-rimmed spectacles asking the question looks puzzled. Well, fuck, he's allowed. He's a *poet,* for chrissake.

—Any more questions? Gordina steps up to the mic.

Baldheaded Mountain will be the title of the poem, he's decided. Well, at least he's come up with a title. He'll write it, present it to G, then get the hell off the island and never come back. The sooner the better. Even if it winds up being a transcription of gibberish. Who the fuck cares? Anything to get back to upstate at this point.

The crowd buzzes murmuringly with that post-reading wakefulness as it becomes aware of the wine and crackers on the table behind. Birchfield speaks awkwardly with Gordina behind the mic, calculating the distance between his position in the back of the bookstore and the way to the exit. The hornrims come up to him. Birchfield hopes the grumble of his stomach isn't audible.

—I just wanted to introduce myself. Well, you probably already recognize me.

What the hell is *with* people on this island, anyway? What, they think they're all household name celebrities who are instantly recognizable?

—Anyway, I'm Doctor Schlitzkii from the international hospital.

—Oh, uh. Pleased to make your acquaintance. And, uh, thanks for that, that excellent question. I wish I had a better response, but...

—It's quite okay, Mister Birchfield. I can only imagine, having to improvise on the spot like that. Truth be told, I'm something of an amateur when it comes to poetry. So much of what you said was lost on me, I'm afraid.

—Oh, uh... I could hardly mean... I mean, I don't like to, uh... What's the word I'm looking for? I'm not talking over your head, I hope...

The good doctor smiles with the irony of the self-elected superior man.

—I won't beat around the bush, Mister Birchfield. Though, as a poet, I'm sure you must hate expressions like that—it's a cliché, isn't it? Anyway, what I want to communicate is that I think I might be able to help you.

—Uh, help me? Like how?

—Mister Birchfield, correct me if I'm wrong, but I believe you have a medical condition.

Birchfield laughs nervously.

–Which is to say, uh, what? I don't think… I'm actually feeling quite fine today, I mean…

–The way you stumble over your words when you speak. You often forget words. I could tell, just now, during the question and answer session, because you kept looking up at the ceiling when you were trying to recall a word, as though the ceiling might have the answer written on it. But it doesn't, does it, Mister Birchfield?

–Doesn't what?

–The ceiling does not contain the lost words you are searching for.

–Uh, I don't quite get what you are saying… What you want me to say…

–Aphasia, Mister Birchfield. It can afflict… individuals like your-self. Individuals with certain, well, shall we say, preexisting conditions…

Now Birchfield starts looking around the room for Gordina, a person he is otherwise eager to avoid. She is across the way, stuffing squares of cheese in her mouth as she discourses with some heavily Botoxed woman in a lavender smear of a dress. He tries to wave at her to come rescue him, but she's too deep in conversation to notice.

–I mean, I don't intend to pry into your medical history, the doc-tor continues. But I may have seen your file back at my office. Just standard protocol for anyone coming to the island, I'm sure you can imagine—we're a small island, we have to make sure the people are protected. You have, I believe, been diagnosed with this condition before, correct? Before arriving here on Settlers Landing, I mean.

Now the waiter is bringing over a tray of glasses. Finally. Birch-field immediately swipes a flute of champagne off it. He downs half the glass and stifles a belch.

–I think now is probably not the time or place, Doctor, uh…

–Schitzkii. I'm a specialist in the Viutex experimental division at the international hospital. Perhaps you are familiar with—

–Oh yes, I've heard all about it. Uh, … Kind of hard to avoid the topic if you spend any amount of, uh, time here…

–Well. I have some good news for you. If you want to come in and speak about it, I suspect you might be a candidate. We've seen some major improvements in patients with all kinds of speech disor-ders once they—

–Gordina!

Finally the bitch arrives. She smiles widely. Charmed that he has called her over.

–So, uh, how do you think the, uh, the, the the…

—The reading! It went marvelous, my darling. Simply marvelous. I really feel that this night will go down in our island's cultural history. Thank god I had the idea to bring in a film crew and a photographer to document it. And I see here you have met with our famous Doctor Schitzkii.

—Yes, the doctor was just saying… Asking, really, um, about…

—Well, I must say, this in itself could be considered yet another fortuitous moment in our island's fascinating intellectual history! Oh my, perhaps I'm getting a bit tipsy from the champagne. But really, it's just divine that you two are finally getting to meet. Why, here we have a world famous doctor crossing paths with one of the truly great poetic visionaries of our time!

Birchfield turns in an effort to worm his way out of the impending conversation.

—Oh Collins, where are you off to? Haha, like many an artistic genius, Collins is very modest when it comes to praise! Aren't you, Collins?

—It isn't that, I…

—Well, what is it, then? Has the eel caught your tongue?

—I am feeling, uh… unwell, Gordina. That reading really took a lot out of me. I need to go back and, uh, have a, a rest now…

Birchfield composes himself the best he can under the circumstances.

—I was just saying to Mister Birchfield, my office is always open to him.

—Oh, I see! Talking business at a poetry reading. Shame on you, Doctor Schitzkii. Well, I'm not the least bit surprised. I don't want to butt in, but if you are in fact feeling unwell, Collins, I can remind you that you are fully covered under the Settlers Landing healthcare plan. Considering how expensive it is in the US, you might want to take advantage while you're here. Even if there's nothing wrong and you just want to go in for a check-up and a chat. And Doctor Schitzkii here is one of the finest, not just on Settlers Landing, but in the entire world, really.

—I'll keep that in mind.

—Oh, I want you to, Collins.

Gordina now puts her hand on the side of Birchfield's face. Birchfield flinches away from it. And so she moves even closer.

—Collins. Perhaps it's the champagne talking here, darling. But I want you to know… I, well, we all here on Settlers Landing, we care for you dearly. I know that times have not been easy for you—I can see the strain you are under. A mere mortal like me cannot even begin to fathom the burdens of artistic genius. But I want you to know, I will do everything in my power to support you, to nurture you. You are, after all, our poet laureate. *My* poet laureate. You are— She now slips her hand in his (not an easy task given that her hand is far larger than his)—a pet project of mine. And, I have to admit… You are snaking your way into the depths of my soul, Collins. Collins… I'm… not the kind of woman who likes a lot of onions in my broth, if you get what I'm saying…

–Not really. I, uh… It's time for me to leave.

Birchfield swiftly puts down his half-empty flute then maneuvers his way past Gordina and the doctor. On his way out, he smiles and nods at the few doddling remainders as he finally makes it through the exit and into the night.

–Make sure you get him into your office this week, Gordina says under her breath to the doctor, then makes her way back to the crowd stewing around the poet's books on display up front.

23.

AFTER BIRCHFIELD'S POETRY reading, I meet up with Krstal at the Laundry Bag, Settlers Landing's premiere (meaning, in this instance, one and only) gay bar. We stand at the bar, wearily regarding the assortment of sodomists and sapphists scattered about, performing their salacious movements. Someone's faghag is smearing her gruesome tits across the dance floor and pretending as though it were the first time. Then there are the real women, namely Krstal and myself, leaning against the bar, sipping our fine cocktails, retaining at least a bit of sophistication for the rest of the denizens to admire. Settlers Landing has a diminutive homosexual community, one that is rather transient. Among the tiny clique of regulars—which does include a couple of quasi-natives, though the vast majority belong to the ruling class—the crowd consists of a multilayered patchwork of tourists bouncing around to the canned house music being spun by the resident DJ, who has assumed the pseudonym of Diana Rrhea. A tattered rainbow flag forms the backdrop against which miniscule heart-shaped reflections from the crystal ball traverse their orbit.

Krstal and I are far too busy discoursing on local show business and cultural matters in our roles as local celebrities to really pay all that much notice to the crowd, when, suddenly, out of the corner of my retina, and to my utter surprise, I am flabbergasted to spot Wim

Hofmeister, the critically and commercially acclaimed photographer. Wim walks right over to us, as though drawn in by my gaze.

–I thought this was supposed to be a gay bar, he sniffs.

–Oh, it is, honey, Krstal retorts with a snort.

–Doesn't look like it to me. Not like the bars we have back in Berlin. Where's the darkroom?

–Oh, we don't allow those kinds of spaces, I now speak up, slowly overcoming my starstruck state. We are a small island, after all, so there is the need to prevent disease from spreading.

–Honey, trust me, you've come to the right place, says Krstal. You're surrounded by so many cocksuckers right now, you might as well be in hell.

–As saddened as I am by the prospect of disrupting the flow of this charming conversation, I just want to say that I'm a *massive* fan of your work, Wim. I especially love your random snapshots of your London squatter friends from the '90s blown up to epic proportions in an effort to endow these rather slight subjects with monumental significance. For me, your oeuvre really elevates irony to a plateau that few contemporary artists have managed to attain, and even fewer connoisseurs are able to gauge. I'm actually the Ministress of Culture here on Settlers Landing. It is a *monstrous* honor to have you here with us. If you'd be interested, I'd love to arrange for you to give an artist's talk at our National Library—

–I don't want to talk about my work tonight, baby. I just want you to fist me.

–...

–If there's no darkroom here, let's just go back to my hotel. Come on, man.

–First of all, I'm not sure what gave you the impression that I am or ever once was a *man*—

–It's cool. I'm actually a big supporter of the trans community. Though it's usually FTMs I have sex with, I'm open. Are you pre-op or post-op? Not that it really matters. I'm not one of those transphobic gays who's just too good to slide his big Belgian saucisse inside a non-cis hole. I consider myself more than just an ally. I'm really one of you, in a lot of ways. You know, I've thought about changing my gender too, over the years. I'm more gender fluid than anything. In my opinion, all those cisgendered neoliberal fags who discriminate against the genderqueer community should all be herded away into camps, so that their homonormativity might be contained. They certainly don't deserve to get fisted by a hot femme top such as yourself.

Krstal's belt of laughter unfurls through her nose.

Wim pinches the behind of a queeny quasi-native who saunters past.

—You so cray-zee! s/he squeals.

—You know who he is, right? He's a famous photographer!

—I know, gurl. I had him last night!

—I'm really into femmes lately, Wim continues. Don't ask me why. It probably has to do with this new level of political awareness I've attained. You know, as an artist, I'm always very sensitive to everything that's happening around me…

—He's coked up, Krstal now whispers into my ear.

—… Of course I was always firmly in the Masc4Masc camp before. I mean, we never called it that, of course—we had a different language for things back then. But you can't just ignore the new reality that surrounds you, that surrounds us all…

—Well, you can here, I now chance to interrupt. What I mean is, that is one of the splendid pleasures of dwelling on an island. We are able to ignore all the unpleasantries—not just the political reality, as you deem it, but every aspect of reality that doesn't suit us—and essentially build our *own* reality, and the sovereignty required to protect it. In a way, you could even regard our president as an artist of sorts; his ultimate project is really *world creation*. You know what, Wim? I would *love* to introduce you to our poet laureate. He just gave a reading tonight—it's a shame you missed it. He was exhausted, so he didn't come out with us tonight, but, with figures like him and of course our founding senator Lil Bigfoot, Settlers Landing is manifesting quite the artists' colony!

—Well, what about me? pouts Krstal. I'm an artist too, you know!

—Right, how could I be so blind? This is our first lady, Krstal Mrdok, better known as the star of *Lives of the Innocents*. Perhaps you're already familiar with our soap opera?

—It's no longer a soap opera, G. It's a *streaming serial.*

—Right. I almost forgot…

—Well, I just got here. And unless it's on Netflix or FaNN, I wouldn't have seen it. I'm far too busy with work, as well as my political concerns. Which really are one and the same… And Lil Bigfoot is highly problematic, just to let you know. I mean, he is Black. But he's also a predator. I'm not even sure we can really consider him Black anymore. I mean, he's really kind of lost that privilege, in my opinion… Really, I'm not even Masc4Masc anymore. I just want to make that clear. I've been trying to feminize my own appearance. I'm not sure if you can tell in this light, but I'm wearing makeup right now. I *hope* you can tell. I only fuck femmes now. That's all I like.

Trans are okay, too. Only femmes and trans can fist me. No one else. Especially not any cis white males.

—Aren't you yourself… ?

—Don't say it. Do not say those words. I am, but that doesn't mean I need to hear the words. I certainly don't *embrace* it in any way. You don't need to *shame* me.

—Yes, I've always found denial works much better in these circumstances. Krstal rolls her eyes.

—Yes! Exactly! How did you… Was that a reference to my new series? My solo exhibition last fall at Hamburger Bahnhof. *Woke Denial,* it was called. In all lowercase letters…

—Well, like I said, on our island, we have our *own* reality. And by that, I mean we actually *own* it.

—I mean, what's happening in the States right now, it's *crazy*…

—Yes…

—I'm thinking of running for European parliament this year. It's the least I can do, to try and fight the power.

—But you do such a good job with that in your work. Surely a life in politics would rob your many admiring fans of further—

—I don't care, man. I mean, my art is my life. And vice versa. You know what I'm saying?

—What brought you to Settlers Landing, Wim (if I might deign to call you by your first name)? I ask because it's my ministry that's responsible for issuing artist visas. Surely I would have known before you were coming, had you applied for one…

—Oh, I'm not here on an artist's visa. I came on a journalist's visa.

—Oh really?

—Yeah. I'm on assignment for the *New York Times Magazine.* I don't normally do photojournalism that much anymore—not that I have anything against it. I just don't have time, what with my hectic exhibition schedule. But this is an issue that really means a lot to me. So I *made* time to come and do it.

—I am so touched to hear that! This New Country endeavor has inspired countless individuals internationally, though very few as talented as yourself. Still, here we are, five years later, endlessly arranging these press junkets. I think it's safe to say, the international media can't get enough of our little isle!

—This Viutex thing, man. So evil. I think it has the potential to become like AIDS four point oh.

—I… Excuse me?

—I mean, the opiate crisis is bad enough on its own. I myself was hooked for a number of years. But not everyone has the privilege of being a famous artist who can afford to stay in the world's second most expensive rehab resort in Greece (even if it wasn't me who paid for it, but one of my collectors.) I've been sober now for almost seven years. Well, besides the crystal and G and coke and occasional bumps of K. No heroin, though, I'm proud to say.

—It seems you are a bit confused, Wim. You see, Viutex is not a drug. It's a pain management system that is fully effective, with no known side effects—

—These poor people. They become all like strung-out, on a permanent nod. The Viutex Victims. That's going to be the name of the feature. Minimal text, you know. Just a paragraph in the beginning, explaining everything, packed with facts and statistics about the situation. The rest is just going to be a twenty-five page spread of my photos. Just simple portraits of the people, trapped in this, this *hell*, this hellish state they can never get out of.

—I just find it odd that you would describe, what is clearly a state of *perennial relief*. As *hellish*. I also highly doubt that our highly esteemed medical professionals would ever concur with this definition of hell. May I ask who is your editor at the *Times*?

—It doesn't matter. All that editorializing—it won't even be necessary. My photos really speak for themselves. I already started, before I even got here. I was shooting Viutex victims in Europe who came back. Even went to the US to shoot some. That vacant look in their eyes. The way their auras radiate this... this *grayness*. It's macabre, man. It's like a form of living death. This Viutex stuff, man—it's even *worse* than heroin. I'm fully convinced of it. At least with heroin, you can eventually get off of it, you still have that capability...

The more he keeps talking, the more I become aware of the ultimate futility of trying to infuse him with a reasoned perspective on the issue. Having worked with Mrdok now for however many years, a recurring theme has been the controversy garnered by virtually all of his philanthropic initiatives. Sadly, we are living in an era in which the generally ill-informed masses' contempt for the rich and powerful often overwhelms their understanding of these individuals' ultimate worth to society, which of course lies in their generosity. Just as Viutex's benefits greatly outweigh the insignificant complaints of a pesky minority, Mrdok's overextensive gregariousness would be awarded the Nobel Peace Prize were we to live in a world that was indeed noble.

In this case, however, it is no longer our president's honor that need be defended, but that of our country—and our country's economic interests, to be yet more exact. As a proud and fervent activist for all things Settlers Landing, it is hard for me to sit back and stomach such attacks, even if they are issuing forth from the mouth of a contemporary artist I have long admired.

–I'm just not ashamed of who I am anymore, Wim's ramble continues. We fistees, we have to get organized. We need political representation. We need reparations, for all those years of—

I look at Krstal, judging that she must be correct in her assessment of his cocaine ingestion.

–Well, not to rip the needle off the record and allow the scratch to tear the ear, grate the nerves—oh, wherever it was I was going with that metaphor… I haven't slept for many a night, sleeplessness being something of a general problem for those of us unaccustomed to the heat and humidity of these pseudotropical climes…

I find it prudent to resume this narrative without the aid of any further dialogue.

To accelerate the matter that now must be taken into my own hands, I agree to take Wim back to my living quarters on the pretext of engaging in that reprehensible activity that he is so eager to explore and that my current manicure forbids, even if some tiny and currently severed part of my former being could have fathomed once desiring it. Along the way (for it is but a short walk from the Laundry Bag to my faux loft in the newly restored hip artists' quarter in downtown Olde Colonia), he continues to ask me questions of a disgustingly personal nature to which I give vague responses at first, when I bother to answer them at all. Until, the thought occurs to me, why not? What does any of it matter now? Why not let loose, Gordina, let your actual hair down, now that you have quite a lot of it and on your head rather than your back? Why not have a bit of fun for once?

At which point I begin to fabricate a series of increasingly outlandish anecdotes—oh yes, I too am a proud radical queer so-called, why prior to my transitioning, I was known among other things as West Texas's pederastic pedant, a stalker of teenage boys who would frequently show up outside their windows in the middle of the night dressed in women's stockings with no underwear on at all underneath so that I might intimately feel the synthetic fabric crowding my genitals, that I would also often smother domestic animals and leave their carcasses on the front porch of those I most admired, until eventually the local authorities caught on and I was very nearly lynched by a group of current and former Klan members alongside parishioners of the local religious community to which I then belonged…

I nearly have to stop myself at one point from laughing out loud at these ridiculous and outlandish fabrications, which Wim not only believes, but appears to be nodding his head incessantly in a show of support, which I can so hardly believe until it occurs to me that, like many a cokehead I have encountered in the past, he is not even really paying attention to a word I am saying, but just waiting for a pause in the conversation so that he himself might resume his own incessant monologuing. Not being a drug user myself, I have always had trouble comprehending the semiotics of that humorless way coke fiends have of accepting every thing being said to them at face value while at the same time scarcely listening to any of it. Wim now numb-noddingly acquiesces as I swipe my thumbprint over the electronic sensor that opens the door to my loft.

His intention is to head straight for the bed, but I manage to barricade his way before his unshowered body attempts its imprint in my mattress. By this point in the evening's proceedings, I am nearly sick to my stomach just having to endure his deluded liberal agendicizing, and now, he is leaning in and I can smell his acrid dehydrated breath upon my face. He is trying with all his might to insert his snaking tongue into my mouth, until I am able to use all of my strength (for he does tower over me) to get him to sit in the armchair. I need to prepare myself, I tell him, mustering the best seductive tone I can manage, and instruct him to stay seated and wait and not to follow me into the bathroom.

Since my transitioning, I have come to understand well why the bathroom so often serves as a refuge for those of us belonging to the fairer sex. It is because there are unfortunately so few places in the world where a woman might feel simultaneously a sense of safety and protection while being surrounded by all of her most precious possessions and feminine accoutrements. Allow me to clarify my usage of a few of those adjectives, lest I be accused of trafficking here in crude clichés and stereotypes. When I say safety, one automatically assumes I am speaking of some physical threat which women are allegedly so frequently subject to; while I do not deny this, I myself have never personally encountered such threats, leading me to hypothesize that perhaps the threat of physical violation to women is somewhat exaggerated or else overstated. What I mean is safety from a different sort of threat, which is no less demeaning, the threat of indifference to our presence and our potential contributions to the discourse. Here, in the safety of the powder room, there is no expectation that we are meant to play a role that is more often contrary to the ones we wish to, that we perceive ourselves playing. Here, we find ourselves in a universe of proxy objects, of nonanimate substitutes that come to fulfill us in place of the human actors we must otherwise contend with.

After replacing my mascara, I remove the nail file from the topmost shelf. As it so happens, I had just that morning sharpened my nail file, because its blade had grown dull with frequent usage since I had taken to practicing the fine art of manicuring upon myself. As nail files go, it was not ideal; for it was lacking the gleam I would have preferred; its rendering in forged steel imbues the blade with a lackluster matte grayness that would certainly fail to attract the eye of a Collins Birchfield or any similarly gifted wordsmith who might be prone to viewing the instrument as not merely a utilitarian device for beautifying the hands, but as a symbol for justice, a sort of updated substitute for the scythe. Well, I would soon be rid of it all the same, and so I grip it in my hands and return to the living room, where Wim now stands next to the armchair where I'd previously left him. He has removed his pants and underpants in the interim. A ginormous Prince Albert, gleaming silver with the width of a coffee mug, pulls his elephantine penis in the direction dictated by gravity.

—I just remembered, I now pause before my guest, President Mrdok actually has one of your works in his collection. He has it hanging in his house, here in Settlers Landing. It's a C-print, I believe, of what appears to be a nightclub. Probably one of your Berlin clubs, only it's after the party—the floor is littered with empty plastic cups and cans and cigarette butts and packaging, you know, all the standard nightlife detritus. What I love the most about it is the color saturation: the floor is painted this red-violet that nearly approaches magenta, though with these splotches of deep purple that infer spillage of some sort. A small square-shaped ceiling light pours in sun from above; the effect is quite, well, heavenly, if that doesn't imbue the image with too much of a spiritual interpretation.

—Well. *Infernal Nocturne,* that one's called. That's an edition of three. It's from my early period. I didn't even know he had one. My gallery never told me.

Wim hovers now closely with his lips threatening to brush against mine. He moves in about a centimeter closer, and as I feel his warmth, I wrap my left arm around his shoulder and jam the blade of the nail file deep into the approximate location of his small intestine.

—That's because he got it off the secondary market, you pathetic little shit.

After a few subsequent repetitions of this movement, I let go the ruined instrument and allow the famed photographer to drop to the floor and attain mortality. I then order Siri to dial my colleague in the Ministry of Death.

–Karen? Sorry to wake you. I'm afraid we have another for the morgue.

–Is he...

–Yes. At mine. No paperwork necessary on this one.

–I'll fire up the furnace and send the limo right over.

Click.

24.

ONE NIGHT, MRDOK dreams he still has his hand. His right one, the one taken away by the gorilla. How did it happen, this unprecedented return? In the dream, he is woken up, in his suite in the presidential palace where he often sleeps when he is too tired to return home, it is just like any other morning. He looks down and he not only sees it is real, the hand, he is also able to feel it for the first time in however so many. It is as though the hand has never left him. He calls Gordina in to his bedroom, says hey, look at this. Gordina can't believe it either. She is one of the only ones who knows what Mrdok's original hand looked like. In truth, it is not so different from the fake one; the doctors did a fine job in its manufacturing. It is not as though Mrdok has any anxieties over his possession of an artificial limb. His hand is so real that only those closest to him even realize that it's not his real appendage. In the dream, it is more a sense of never having lost it. The potentiality, what it might feel like, were that event never to have taken place in real life. Going around, being able to feel things in your hand when you hold them; regaining that lost sense of touch. Then he is on a beach somewhere, but not one that he has been to recently, a beach on Settlers Landing, he somehow knows, but not one that he actually recognizes, there are only two beaches proper on Settlers Landing and this is neither Cove Beach nor Elias Shores. But a beach. It is an empty beach and he is facing the sea, watching the calm waters, it is that hour just before dawn just as the tide is starting to come in. He turns around and behind him is a blue beach towel and the artificial hand is lying in the middle of it. He looks down just to make sure his right hand—the real, original one—is there, like it always should have been—and in the dream, somehow always was. He begins to wonder if he just dreamed losing it—that incident with the gorilla on the island so many years ago, was it even him? Was it another person? Another Mrdok? Because, in a sense, it was. A dream within a dream.

It is one of the first times Mrdok has dreamed since relocating to Settlers Landing. Or, if not the first time, one of the first times he's remembered his dream the following morning. Because usually, he is so exhausted at the end of these long turgid days, he collapses into a comalike state. Not that he often remembered his dreams before he came here. Not to say he has no real dream life. Mrdok's dreams and his reality are very very close to one another. There is no need to separate them out, as is the situation for most people inevitably in a lower station of life.

He reaches down to pick up the artificial limb. He thinks to himself, I should keep it—maybe I will need it again some day. He turns around and the ocean behind him has disappeared. No more world. No more Settlers Landing. Wait, what's happening, he thinks to himself. Where did Gordina go? Gordo! He calls out. The day Gordo got his/her sex change, he'd gone to the hospital to visit. He didn't know what to bring, Krstal said flowers, but Gordo wasn't really the type who liked flowers—at least not to Mrdok's knowledge. Though maybe now that he was a different person, a she, he would be. Mrdok wasn't sure. And so he got the flowers anyway, or else had them delivered to his office, so that he could bring them to the hospital. Had Rick bring him. Rick wanted to go too. Said something like, now that he has a cunt, let's see if he's still a cunt. That made Mrdok crack a smile, even though he knew he shouldn't laugh at things like that. Not anymore. He's a head of state now. Shut up, Rick, he told him, and then they went into the room.

Gordo, Gordina he was now called, had been awake for at least an hour already. His/her hair was already long by this point, when she was still a guy she'd been wearing it tied back in a ponytail, now it fell around him/her. To Mrdok, he could almost believe he was a woman… Meaning, like a biological one. Not one that had been turned into one.

She smiled at the sight of Mrdok, frowned at the sight of Rick.

–I see you've survived.

–Congrats, said Rick. Wanna show us your new gash?

Mrdok slapped Rick in the ribs.

–Rick's just doing what he does best, being an asshole.

–Yes. Well. I would never expect otherwise.

She looked pale and weak.

–How are you feeling?

–I feel… As though I have been revived, to be quite candid.

–Well, you have… The anesthesia wore off.

–As though… The person inside me, the person I truly always was, is just now awakening.

–That's great. When do you think you can get back to the office?

The nurse came in with a tray. A bottle of spring water, sous vide salmon, an asparagus salad—Mrdok recalled that a shipment of asparagus for the quasi-elites had just landed that morning.

–I should be back on my feet by tomorrow morning at the very latest. I assure you I—

–Oh no you don't, said the nurse. The doctor has prescribed bed rest for at least a week.

Gordina rolled her eyes at the nurse and ordered her to bring something for her guests.

–Don't you see our *President* is here?

Mrdok said not to bother, that they wouldn't be staying for long.

–Hey Gordo… says Rick.

–It's *Gordina.*

–Gordina. There are only two kinds of women in this world: pros and cons. Which one are you?

Mrdok roars with laughter. This gives Gordina permission to laugh too. Laugh at herself laughing.

–Seriously. Why do you want to be a woman?

Gordina stares out the window.

–Enough, Rick, Mrdok said. Let's let the new lady get some rest.

Rick was the first out the door. Right before Mrdok crossed over the precipice, Gordina yelled out for him. Mrdok turned around.

–Mrdok, I just want you to know… And this is perhaps more the aftereffects of the anesthesia and the painkillers and whatever else is in this IV bag. But I just want to be the one to reiterate, Mister President, that… that… What you have done here, on this island, is so extraordinary. And that, it has been my honor to serve… And that, I do believe, were we to ever have to go to battle, to defend ourselves against, against, let us say, outside forces that do not, cannot understand our inherent superiority… That, that I believe we *will* be victorious, Mrdok… Here and evermore…

Mrdok had left the room not long after that. But the strangeness of those words stayed with him for some time after. At that point, there was no conflict whatsoever on the horizon, not even remotely. While they had already begun to assemble their own army, it was simply a formality, in Mrdok's mind, when you're starting a new country, just in case the quasi-colonials across the way in Pembroke started to get any fancy ideas. Like a symbolic army.

In the dream, he turned around, the ocean was gone, and it had been replaced with a battlefield. It was an empty battlefield—there weren't any soldiers on it—but it looked like every battlefield you would see in those old war movies about World War I or whatever—Mrdok had seen enough of those to know what it is he was looking at—and he turned back around again to see the field continued and to confirm that he was in fact alone, standing there with his artificial hand in his hands. And so he started to walk, walk back toward what he thought would be the direction of Olde Colonia, though it was more like he was floating, because he didn't have that feeling of his shoes in the muddied earth that denotes crossing a field.

The night before, he had had to go to a dinner with Barb at Eat This, the boutique diner in downtown Olde Colonia, an exercise in culinary irony, as the décor matched greasy spoon realism to the haute cuisine of an imported French chef and with prices that forbade all but the quasi-elites from eating there. They were entertaining the visiting wife of an investor in the nucleite scheme. She spent most of the night regaling them about her recent travails flying commercial, trying to smuggle back into Singapore eight hundred thousand dollars in jewels and a box of Crispy Crème doughnuts. She had shown off one of the pieces, a gold and sapphire ring, which Barb had coo'd over, and Mrdok had wondered whether Barb was being sincere or just playing some role, since, though she wore jewelry, nothing this gaudy or fancy he had ever seen on her. He made a mental note to ask her later whether this was really her taste, for if it was, maybe on her next birthday he should consider getting her something along those lines…

He was running across the empty battlefield, and suddenly, he looked down and the artificial hand had disappeared from his hands. He stopped running and turned around. He must have dropped it somewhere on the ground behind him. Now he had to go back and look, to try and find it.

Suddenly, he was standing at the entrance to a cave, and he had that woman's ring in his hand. Which meant, in the logic of the dream, that the artificial hand was inside the cave. Strange, because in waking life, he couldn't recall there being any caves in Sagosia, on Settlers Landing. Though, now that he thinks about it, there must be, somewhere in the hills surrounding Baldheaded Mountain, perhaps nestled in the crags of the mountain itself. At the entrance to the cave, there was this rock, about hip height, in the shape of a rhinoceros head—horns and everything. Something about the head told him don't go inside this cave. And yet he also knew, somehow, that his artificial hand was inside there. What was he to do. He started sweating profusely in his sleep at this point, he knew it, because when he woke up, he was all wet.

So he goes inside the cave to get the hand. He knows he has to, and he also knows that he shouldn't go. And so, in such circumstances, the hand is forced, to employ an unfortunate turn of phrase. Unfortunate, because what happens is, when he goes inside, he feels around in the darkness, but the hand is not there, his precognition has been betrayed, and when he emerges from the cave—the rhinoceros head now having mysteriously disappeared—he is without his hand again. Without the real one and the artificial one. He looks down and there is just a bloody stump that looks identical to that mangled hunk of flesh that was left after the gorilla took his hand off, and he woke up covered in sweat, and it's a dream he still remembers and still hasn't figured out what to do with.

25.

–THIS IS GORDINA Orlanda. May I please know who's calling?

–You know goddamn well who this is.

–I'm afraid—

–You should be afraid. You little prick.

–I—

–This is Joanne. Your soon-to-be ex-wife.

–Joanne… How *odd* for you to be calling.

–What the hell do you mean it's *odd?*

–Because we're not supposed to be communicating directly. That's what the lawyers are for.

–You son of a bitch.

–Joanne. I'd appreciate it if you'd use gender-appropriate insults—

–This was supposed to be a simple, civil divorce. Now you've gone and—

–Hold on, Joanne. What exactly is the issue?

–Your *lawyer.* Just contacted *my* lawyer. What's this about, Gordon? You're *suing* me?

–First off, it's Gordina. Gordon is dead now, Joanne. Secondly, while I was not *privy* to the conversation between our lawyers, I do not believe *sue* is the correct verb to use in this case. As far as I know, we have reached out to your team with an offer to *settle*—

—You. Left. *Me.* Gordon. I can't even—How *unreasonable* this all is. I have to wonder if I am living in reality or if this is all a nightmare—

—I believe the situation is quite clear, Joanne. We were married. You committed adultery. Now we are getting a divorce. Now, according to the laws of our state, the state where we were wed, adultery is a crime, and I am therefore entitled—

—What does this even mean, that I *committed adultery*? You were the first to come out as gay, Gordo, even before *my* relationship with Dot came to light—

—Yes, but the point is, I did not engage in any illicit affairs *while we were married.* Did I, Joanne? That's how you and I are different. I might have had issues with my sexuality—issues that, I might now add, have been fully resolved with my gender correction surgery—but I did not *act out* on those issues in quite the way you did, by engaging in your sapphic activities with the mail lady.

—What are you—What are you even saying? What is it that you think you're *entitled* to, Gordon?

—If you call me that name one more time, I swear, Joanne, I will end this call. Do you understand that? Joanne? Joanne? What is my name, Joanne?

A deep sigh on the other end.

—Gordina Orlanda.

—And what is the correct pronoun to use when speaking of me in the third person?

Another sigh.

—Well, what is it? What is my *pronoun,* Joanne?

—She. Her.

—*Wrong.*

—… Him? He? It? I don't know, I thought…

—It is *Gee.* Gee is me.

—Gee?

—Yes. I've adapted the pronoun Gee. That is how you are meant to refer to me with others when you are not referring to me directly by name. Surely that is in the paperwork the lawyer sent over. Or else my lawyer must have informed your lawyer—

—Gee? What does that even mean, Gord-, Gordina? Gee, as in, golly gee willikers?

—Gee as in me. As in, I have become *enlightened,* Joanne, in a way you likely never will be. I *deserve* my own pronoun. I'm entitled to it.

I've worked for it. My entire life. And if you're not willing to accept—

–Why are you doing this? This has nothing to do with whether I accept you or not. We are way past that point. *We are getting a divorce.* I thought, we have been over this numerous times, it was all going very civil, we had a clear agreement on the way things would go. And now, suddenly, you're *punishing* me, and I don't even know why…

–Oh, Joanne, I see no reason to get so emotional. This is simply part of the *process.* I know you are not accustomed to dealing with lawyers, it is a rather new experience for you. But I have to go through this all the time, hence my calm, I suppose.

–But this isn't one of your business deals. There is nothing for you here to *win.* You have way more money, more property, more *everything* than I do, than I have ever *had.*

–That may or may not be true, Joanne. In a sense, it is *all* business. May I remind you of who bought the house in Connecticut? Who purchased the cars? Everything in your life, that you take for granted—

–So what is this, you're going to take the *house* away from me? Is that what you're trying to—

–Well, again, Joanne, I really think we should leave this to the lawyers to settle. But if that were to be your offer—

–My *offer*?! What, to, to give the house to you? You don't even need it. You're not even living in this *country* anymore.

–No, I'm not. But I could liquidate the property. I could certainly use the assets. We all can, here on Settlers Landing. We are, after all, still in the process of building—

–Turn on your camera. Now, Gord-, Gordina.

–Why?

–Because I want to see your face. I need you to look me in the eye and discuss this with me.

–I believe we have to switch to video call in order to do that.

–Fine.

. . .

–Oh Gor-, Gordina. Look at your makeup.

–What?

–Your eye shadow is… You're doing it all wrong. Hasn't anyone shown you how to do makeup yet? I mean, if you're going to do this…

–If I'm going to do what, Joanne.

–This… Whatever it is you have done to yourself.

–That I've *done to myself*?! Have you not read my book, Joanne?

—You'll have to forgive me. Your actions of late haven't given me a lot of motivation—

—Well I hope at least you have a copy in the library. In my book I explain in detail my decision to transition. If I could take the liberty to quote from the book for a moment: *Binary and cisgendered people tend to cling to the ideal of a unitary sense of self that is simply not sustainable in today's increasingly globalized capital infrastructure. In transitioning, I was simply accepting a part of myself that was always there, buried deep within the capitalist realist segment of my soul.* If you had actually taken the time to read it, you might have actually learned something valuable and wouldn't be in such a pitiable state.

—Gord-, Gordina. Stay focused! We are talking about our divorce, not your gender. Now, I live a simple life here in, in Connecticut, me and Dot, we're not even, she's barely talking to me now because I think she is just getting sick of all this, hearing me complain about what, how we're divorcing and the uncertainties of the future. So you have already successfully taken *that* aspect of my happiness away from me. And now you are, what, you've hired some aggressive lawyer who is threatening me with an adultery suit if I do not—what is it I am supposed to give up? What do you want from me?

—You know, I think I really would prefer to let the lawyers handle this. But, if I am to be frank, Joanne, all of your assets are really *my* assets. I mean, objectively speaking.

—I have been working, practically since the day we moved up here!

—Oh, your little librarian job. Right. Does that actually pay anything? I mean, do you really think you can sustain, what, the bills on the house, the maintenance, the cleaning lady, the car? What are you planning on doing, Joanne? Especially now that you might have to pay me damages for the, well, for the damage you have done to our marriage?

—Damage *I* have done? It was *your* decision to get divorced. You were the one who first brought it up.

—I'll admit it was an *idea* I was *toying with* at the time.

—No no no. It was *not* an idea—

—But I did not go out and commit *infidelity* against you, Joanne. That is just not in keeping with my character. You can ask anyone, I am sure Mrdok would be willing to testify on my behalf—

—Oh, now, why am I not surprised that his name is suddenly coming up? Is he the one who's behind all this? Did *he* tell you to do this to me? Are you using *his* asshole lawyers? Or did you actually go out and get one for yourself who dreamt up this, this touching scheme?

–Not that it matters, but in case you are curious, both Mrdok and I have been working with Marty Hynek's firm for a number of years on any number of initiatives—

–See, I knew it.

–Look, Joanne, all your lawyer needs to do is propose a settlement. I am sure, Marty is an honest man—as lawyers go—I am sure that he will be willing to accept nearly anything your lawyer proposes, with some minor adjustments, of course—

–I. Am. Not. An. Adulterer.

–But you are, Joanne. You are. It's time you finally admit this to yourself. Now, to be honest, for the reasons that I just told you, to be completely realistic, you're going to have to get a second job anyway—

–We will countersue you. It's the *man* that's supposed to be supporting the *woman* in these divorce settlements—

–But I am not a man, Joanne.

–Yes. I think now, I can finally see that. Both literally *and*—

–I mean, it would be ideal if you could move in with Dot. Then the two of you could pool your resources—But then that would be proof that you've committed adultery, wouldn't it? Hmmm. I can see how that might put you in a quandary. Maybe you could move in with her *after* the settlement has been resolved—

–Dot doesn't want to be with me anymore. Don't you get that?

Now the tears begin to fall.

–Do you not get it, Gord-, Gordina? My life is falling apart. I'm going to lose the house, even if you don't take it out from under me, which you are probably going to do, and you're right, I *can't* survive on a librarian's salary… What am I, why does it have to be this way?! *Why?!*

–Oh Joanne. This is simply business. Which is distinct from life. You must learn to separate your emotions. Otherwise you are never going to survive on your own in the real world.

–If you really loved me, if you really *cared,* you would find a way to support me. Not drag me down. You have more money than, I don't know, than everyone I know put together. And yet you are coming after *me*. Why, pray tell, why are you doing this to me, Gordon? After everything we… Why?!

–Joanne. There you go with the name thing again. Look, if it helps—I know Gordina can be quite a mouthful—if it helps, I am going to give you permission to address me by my pronoun. Okay?

You can just call me Gee when you want to address me by name in conversation—Joanne, what are, what are you doing? Joanne. I would prefer it if you'd put that thing down, I... Is that a toy?

Gunshot.

–... Joanne?

26.

SO AS TO quell any rumors and suspicions floating about, I thought this might be an opportune moment to insert this brief commentary on the nature of Mrdok and Krstal's marriage. Since they remarried, Mrdok and Krstal do not actually have carnal relations. It is more an arrangement in the classical sense of the term. As marriage always was, going back centuries, before this modern notion of love came to pollute what was once a very beautiful (in its crystalline purity) formal designation of alignment, of property and wealth and power relations. To say *they have a classical marriage,* a statement that is repeated quite frequently in the press, is thus both honest and, for the less than historic minded, perhaps a tad duplicitous (though that's their fault, really.)

I was as shocked as anyone. Though the divorce with Mrtol was indeed inevitable—last we heard, she is withering away in some rather dreary low-rent apartment somewhere in the lower regions of New Jersey, no doubt fermenting in bourbon and gin—the choice of Krstal, who herself just happened to be going through her own divorce at the same moment in time, certainly wasn't. Whatever sentimentalities Mrdok possesses are hidden somewhere very deep within the man, in a region to which even I have scant access. Trashy, nouveau riche, Southern, calculating—all adjectives that have oft been deployed by others in rendering Krstal's character and that Mrdok himself is well aware of. (And likely wouldn't deny; rather, this composite picture lends her an ultimate knowability that makes her easy to get along with.) Yet the thing that drew him back to her was something far greater than either desperation or loneliness (or, less pressingly perhaps, the need to fill in the mother figure role for little Jaco.) What I myself witnessed is the evolution of a true and strategic friendship between the two. Despite (or, perhaps more succinctly: thanks to) the current and enduring sexlessness of the arrangement, Mrdok ultimately prefers her long-term company to that of any of his mistresses. Mrtol once had class, it is true—far too much of it, as it turned out. Krstal, on the other hand, has never had any. Hence, her enduring charm. Her penchant for saying exactly what is on her mind—which tends to be bluntly honest and often lacking in wit—is precisely what appeals to Mrdok's own sense of the usefulness of brutal truth for slaying his enemies and frightening his friends into becoming even closer to him.

I think I speak for all the women in Mrdok's life when I unambiguously assert that he could have found no more appropriate domestic partner to assume the important role of First Lady of Settlers Landing.

Naturally, the couple moved in with little Jaco to the house that everyone coveted. It encompasses the greater part of seventeen acres, and includes three guesthouses for the live-in staff, a swimming pool, tennis court, horse ranch, as well as a wide empty field from which the stars might be counted deep into the night. Still, in spite of the grandeur, I could not help but find it a slightly unbecoming choice on Mrdok's part. He is, after all, someone who prefers to *build*. Settlers Landing is but the most logical progression of this building impulse that he is constantly stoking and nurturing. Still, he has lent to the residence—its interior, mostly—his own specific taste through a series of upgrades that habitually removed the old world dustiness that Nelson had so steadfastly amassed. These hauntings of nostalgia hold no appeal for a man of Mrdok's sentiments, and his eagerness to see them removed comes as no major surprise to that select few of us who have known him well over the years. To begin with, there was the implementation of silver fixtures throughout the manor. All the dirty antique brass door knobs were removed and replaced with gleaming silver claw-shaped appendages designed by one of Italy's foremost silversmiths (a second cousin removed, it turns out, from Mrdok's daughter-in-law-to-be.)

Of course, Nelson took with him all the antiques and paintings of his illustrious lineage, leaving the floors and walls largely bereft. Mrdok thus was readily able to install a number of his personal furnishings selected from his other properties, as well as works from his personal art collection, curated in part by yours truly. The interior décor is still in many ways an ongoing work in progress, as with much else on the island, but its splendors are rich and varied in accordance with the person and inclinations of the patriarch whose presence honors its gilded halls.

27.

—THERE ARE TOO many trees here. We don't need so many.

—Too many trees. That's a problem.

—So let's knock some down.

—How many?

—Well. One thing is clear. Trees *can* be useful. I'm talking from a military perspective.

—What do you mean?

—You can hide behind them. In them, even.

—They provide cover.

—That too.

—So you're saying we *do* need the trees?

—Can we get the Minister of the Environment in on this?

—Very funny.

—We don't need him. *I'm* the Minister of Chill. This is *my* department.

—The thing is, some of these banyan trees are well over a millennium old. Older, even.

—How long is that?

—Millennium, he said. Thousand years.

—So what about we get them out of the way, but then toward some, some productive final end. Like using the wood to build houses.

—For the quasi-natives?

—For instance.

—They'll get blown down.

—Naw. This wood. The wood on these trees. It's… solid. Rock hard. Steady.

—Steady?

—Not like concrete, though.

—I thought the construction had already began. That we were using concrete.

—Has it?

—Well. We're on our way at least.

—Our way toward what?

—Autonomy. Sovereignty. Freedom.

—I thought we had already attained all those things.

—There's an argument to be made…

—A see-through argument…

—I think just the trees along the northeastern coastline.

—Those are *precisely* the trees that protect us, though. They act as a barrier against, against any invading power coming from the sea, who would want to target Olde Colonia—

–What *invading power* are you contemplating here, anyway?

–I don't know. Pirates…

–Pirates?! Don't be ridiculous. There aren't any pirates in the Brown Sea.

–There could be. There is, there is *dissent*. Not far away.

–This is the twenty-first century, man. We need to protect our *airspace*, first and foremost. Why all they need to do is send some powerful drone in—

–Our airspace *is* protected. You know that.

–I'm still interested in the question of who these pirates, so-called, might turn out to be.

–Anyone. Any number. I mean, come on. I think we all know that the president has a lot of enemies.

–The SunEye guys, for example.

–Who're they?

–You wouldn't have heard of them, you're too young. But they were a big thing, a big company, back in the day. He took them down. Not intentionally. At least I don't think so. But knowing Mrdok, who knows? What happened was, he bought a plane from them, then took it to Cuba. The US government, turns out, didn't like it all that much.

–I think the Cubans—

–The Cubans, something went wrong there, too. They ended up confiscating the plane from him for a time. He got it back, though. I'm not sure how.

–But how come—

–So the blame for the whole thing, I guess the plane was still registered under SunEye's name. The US government imposed this massive fine. To be fair, they were on their way down anyway. I'm sure a lot of those guys still have a lingering distaste for the president, though. How could they not?

–Sore losers.

–But so what? They don't exist anymore. How could someone like them be construed as a threat to our national security interests?

–The company might not be around. But those guys are. They could be wanting revenge.

–Revenge?

–Sure. Why not. Good ol' vengeance. Why, it's as American as fat jokes, Jesus, and institutional racism!

–I'd think Brussels, the Europeans, might be more of a problem… From what I've heard…

—The Europeans, the Australians, the Americans. It could come in any direction. At any moment. That is why we *need* the trees.

—But you're missing the fundamental point.

—Which is?

—The trees are in the way.

—I don't think…

—Look at the southern part of the island.

—You mean…

—Pirate's Bay. Where all the trailers are.

—The quasi-natives?

—Yeah.

—There are no trees there.

—See? Now you're starting to get it.

—I don't think…

—What *I* think we could do, is we move the quasi-natives, their trailers, whatever, to the northeast pocket of the island.

—Where the trees are.

—Yes. That would enable us to *cut down* the trees, thereby satisfying our concerns—

—While still providing the guard that we need.

—Precisely.

—So, the quasi-natives take the place of the trees. To protect us from attack in that direction.

—Why would it come—

—Because, it's obvious. That's where Pembroke is. It's the nearest land to us.

—And where they are now. The quasi-natives. That's the place…

—… Where we put the trees?

—No. You idiot. That's where we build it.

—It?

—What? What it?

—Headquarters. Home base.

—Home base? You mean where, like, a new presidential palace?

—No. We could centralize. The gray building. The function that, that… the *gray building* serves now… Could also go…

—But, what is the earth like there?

—Soft. As in most places. Away from the mountain, of course.

—Because it would have to all be underground. Not visible from satellite.

—Of course it would be.

—So: *military* headquarters.

—Headquarters for military. For… for… our, uh, *observation post—*

–Surveillance, you mean?

–What the fuck are you doing? Did you know I could fire you for even saying that word out loud? Watch your fucking mouth, man. I'm serious.

–Hey, lighten up. I thought your New Year's resolution was to be more zen about shit.

–Not when it comes to national security. It's my ass on the line here, too, you know. Everyone's asses.

–But they're gonna notice… The satellites will pick up when we're building. We would have to… conceal it somehow. Under a canopy of some sort.

–We could connect it to the nucleite somehow.

–Yeah! Like a refinery…

–Business as usual.

–That's all Mrdok's ever been about.

–We'll even put the logo on the canopy.

–That'll do the trick.

–We want to make sure…

–But what will we tell them? The quasi-natives?

–That it's for their own good.

–Hahaha. Like, *come be human shields!*

–Shut the fuck up. That's not what's going on.

–Of course not.

–We care. About our people. They're our people as well.

–Sure they are.

–We tell them it's for their own good.

–That we're gonna build something better for them.

–But are we?

–We have no choice.

–They're not gonna like it.

–Well why the hell not? One spot is as good as any other.

–Because so many of them still rely on the sea. Fishermen. They've been around Pirate's Bay for, how long?

–They'll still be close to the sea.

–Dude. You and I both know, that's a shitty bit of coastline. The quality of the water… There's not even a beach there.

–So we'll build them one.

–You really think Mrdok's gonna go for that? It's a lot of money, and no profit to be made. A beach for the quasi-natives! I mean, what the fuck?

–Well, we have no choice.

–Maybe we build like a bus network. To get them around the island.

–The trick is, we have to keep them out of Olde Colonia. Except, of course, for the ones with permission to enter…

–I mean, who would want to live there? They're gonna be right under the airport. With all those planes coming in, night and day.

–They will learn to accept it. There's a new order to things now. I think they're starting to get it.

–How do you know?

–I just know.

–You ever fuck with a quasi-native? Have you ever even *spoken* to one?

–Sure.

–Who?

–My maid.

–Ha.

–Ruthless.

–Pigs. You're all a bunch of pigs.

–Yeah? So? Oink oink.

28.

ON THE WESTERN gulf, the island's finest beach, with its ruby-colored sands, has been given the name Elias Shores, after Mrdok's seldom used first name. It was not his original idea to do so. At first it was just going to be Mrdok Beach. It was Gordina who made the suggestion of going with something subtler, softer.

Elias Shores is officially a private beach. Which means, in essence, that its use is restricted mainly to the quasi-elites, those recent transplants to the island working in the upperest echelons. A clubby atmosphere pervades.

Today is one of the rare occasions that the hard-working president has taken time off from his tireless schedule for some well-deserved R&R, and all the public relations that go with it. He smiles and waves at the crowds who greet him as he makes his way down the seaside promenade.

Those out there paragliding, what might they now see? The smiling inevitability upon the shoreline. Mrdok, drunk on his earned autonomy. Him seeing them back. And beyond… The sea and its endlessness—all those illusions of infinity.

—Well, I couldn't *believe* she would do something like that, it simply wasn't in her nature. To think someone who would actually kill themselves just for me—well, I have to admit, there is a *bit* of ego gratification in there. But still…

—See? There's a silver lining to every shitstorm, Gee. Now you don't have to go through with the lawsuit in order to get all your money and property back. It's gonna save you enormously on the legal costs.

Viutex patients—medical tourists—also have the option of purchasing a day pass to Elias Shores from the Settlers Landing International Hospital. Today, a certain number of them seem to have congregated to offer the president a visual treat of bikini'd bliss. As he inspects the ladies' upper halves, Gordina yammers on, oblivious to these delights.

—Well, it is true that it leaves me a lot more time to focus on myself. So I really do not need the distractions of a legal battle… I know I'm not *quite* there yet. But progress, indeed, has been made, if the registers I attained on last week's recording are any indication…

Gordina has been taking singing lessons, with the intention of launching a side career as a mezzo soprano in the Settlers Landing Opera House, currently under construction. It started out as vocal feminization sessions after her operation, but as her coach, Madame Zolyakova, was a former professional opera singer in her native Siberia, Gordina suggested they take the sessions a couple steps onward in that direction.

—I've actually been composing an aria. Just in my head, of course—I'm not quite at that level yet where I can read music, let alone write it… Oh, I haven't dared share it with the madame, either… I want to wait until it's complete. I could sing you a few bars, perhaps? Right now, my aspirations are more modest. Madame assures me that if I maintain discipline, I might be prepared in time to play a small role in the inaugural production of *Don Giovanni* this autumn. Well, modest goals for now, at least!

—You look so pretty, Gee! screams out a voice with a thick midwestern US twang from a group of tourists they pass. Just like Caitlyn Gender!

Even Gordina has her fans here.

From the sushi shop along the promenade, the summer's international R&B slow jam is grooving sultry through the speakers. A throaty alto detachedly emotes:

I will give you a call when I'm desperate

But you might be waitin a real long time
Cos I gotz enough menz for the present
And your broke ass aint even got fourteen dimes

Yeah I'll give you a call when I'm desperate
But baby don't you stay on the line
Cos you aint got a Benz or a Tesla
And you don't have a compatible starsign

Suddenly, a frizzy headed woman with a can of pepper spray manifests from the crowd of tourists before them. Spritz! Mrdok screams, falls to the ground, holding his face in his hands.

Gordina instinctively grabs the woman by her hair and commences beating her in the face with her Fendi handbag.

The woman screams. Gordina screams. Mrdok screams.

The president's plainclothes security detail, who'd been trailing them the entire time, trail over.

–Mister President! Are you all right?

–Don't worry, we caught the entire thing on—

–Sssssssssshhhhh.

Gordina stops her beating of the woman to hold her finger to her lips.

–I mean to say… We witnessed the entire thing with our very own eyes and no one else's.

–Yes, says the other guard. This being… the opposite of a surveillance state. Whatever that's called.

29.

PEOPLE BEGAN TO move here, which eventually became a problem. Or *try to move*, I should say—we were largely able to prevent such a cataclysm from getting underway via legislation and other proactive measures. But the issue of border security continued to vex us.

To be rather more precise, we faced a statist problem as well as a domestic one concerning the movement of peoples; a national one and a capital one. I shall focus on the latter for now.

History has taught us that as nations develop, so do their capital cities. So often have we as an enlightened species witnessed these maudlin hubs transform themselves into harbingers of disease and pollution by the influx of peripheral immigrants and other unfortunate souls who, though perhaps bearing no ill intention or innate fault of their own, nevertheless accelerate the city's decline by the committing of certain irreversible biological mistakes. While some cities have sought unique solutions to these problems—one thinks of Paris with its designation of *les banlieux* as a structuring device for the lower classes, or perhaps megalopolises such as Los Angeles which have merely absorbed neighboring towns and cities as a means of essentially decentering and de-cluttering themselves—others continue to suffer the rather remorseful conditions of the cosmopolitan malaise well into the century we currently so bravely occupy. To get at the root of the problem, we really have to harken back to the European city of the nineteenth century, where the average life expectancy was just twenty years old, where just walking down the street, one had to endure the daily risk of having the diseased contents of a chamberpot dumped upon one's head from above, where infanticide was so widespread that many new mothers gave up before even trying and abandoned their newborns to foundling homes where one third would perish before attaining adolescence, where all sorts of thievery and raping and pillaging and rip-off artists plied their disreputable trades.

Of course, two centuries have passed since then, as has the evolution of so many great capital cities, a number of which I have been fortunate to have traversed alongside Mrdok. Now that we find ourselves in the rather startling position of having to develop our own capital, a certain number of prerogatives corresponding to such factors as demographics and geography have commenced dictating the proceedings.

If I were pressed to select one word to sum up the needs and ideals imposed by the urbanization process, it would have to be a four-letter one beginning with the letter F: that is, flow. Flow of air, flow of capital, flow of human needs: it is this word that recurs again and again in our president's correspondence with our various senators and evolving citizenry.

Paris with the effect of rain. All those intersections of urban life, those crossings actual and symbolic of boundaries seen and depicted by Camille Pissaro from the safety of his hotel window on the Place du Théâtre Français in the waning years of Haussmann's century.

History as a double-edged sword with which one might either accidentally or intentionally stab oneself or others. The challenge being, of course, to fully absorb its lessons while simultaneously ignoring the fact of their occurrence, so that one doesn't become so mired down in principles so as to delay or else evade the actualization of processes.

Whether one wills it intentionally or more often than not no, a dialectic between center and periphery emerges upon its own restless accord. In the American model, we see a great exodus from the cities into the periphery by the upwardly mobile middle classes; in the European city, the reverse process occurs, Paris again being the most evocative model, where the ruling classes take occupancy of the *centre* to ensure its preservation, pushing the poor to the outskirts (though, it should be said, providing them with gainful employment oftentimes in the city center and the discounted public transportation with which to attain it.)

In our own Olde Colonia, an approach was underway that unwittingly, though advantageously, combined both European and American models. I have come to think of it as the doctrine of the expanding center. In truth, prior to our arrival, no strict perimeters had been drawn to delineate the city limits. Traditionally, what was called Olde Colonia referred to the smattering of buildings surrounding the main axis in the city center, which, to be fair, could best be described as a town center. Of course, central—or, as some wistfully called it, *downtown* Olde Colonia had to be both maintained and further developed into the urban sphere that a lifelong cosmopolitan like Mrdok could recognize as such. At the same time, many of the city-town's classical residences had been built in the hills forming the barrier between Olde Colonia and Baldheaded Mountain; it was here where many of our senators and affiliated quasi-elites took up residence in the vacated mansions of the former quasi-colonials. Then, to the north, the residence of Lil Bigfoot, who had expressed his intention to build his own property early on, and beyond that, the wharf, so vital in our country's transport and commerce.

Municipal decisions are ultimately made out of necessity. A utopian society cannot be attained with the stroke of a magic wand— building a castle requires time and patience—and it was thus that the decision was reached to delineate city borders and, in order to protect the capital and its interests, to erect an invisible wall around it, while making its boundaries known to all. Manned with guards at each of its entry points, only those citizens who had attained electronic clearance would be permitted to enter the capital with an app on their smartphones. This included a broad swath of Settlers Landing society, including Olde Colonia residents, government employees, military, those employed in the city's burgeoning service industry—in short, anyone who had a true and verifiable purpose for being there. Miscreants were to be kept out, as were tourists and visitors, who had to apply for special temporary permits in order to enjoy the capital's streets. This was all done not just to ensure residents' comfort, safety, and well-being, but in the spirit of rational and just nation-building.

It is true that the decision was difficult to fathom for a certain contingent of the quasi-natives, who felt that they were being barred entrance to what many still regarded as *their* capital and *their* own island. But it is, in my opinion, silly that it would garner such resistance. All we were doing, really, was concretizing, in dual interests of law and order, a practice that had long held sway on the island. It was also not our fault that many of the quasi-natives who would have liked to apply for an entrance permit did not have the mobile phones that were necessary to support the app. With a new regime comes new rules, like it or not. And with the recent attack on Mrdok at the similarly protected Elias Shores, we were newly aware of the importance of maintaining safety and security for those of us recently arrived and in vulnerable positions of power. Olde Colonia was no longer merely a city or a town, the pseudo-center of some colonial backwater; it was now our nation's capital.

Olde Colonia with the effect of rain. When staring at the face of the future, it is never a good idea to spit in it. Perhaps it is true that you cannot force evolution from above. But it never hurts to try.

In the dialectic of center and periphery, the challenges of flow can be difficult for outsiders to discern. When it came to national security, our borders, it was fairly easy to control who came in and who didn't. The problem was, we had an indigenous, quasi-native population that was here before us, that we had to control. We had to discern who the outsiders were, and alert them of their status, so that they would come to understand their place. We did not, it must be stressed, bar them entry as a matter of course. Those who wanted to could also apply for temporary permits to enter the city—for example, to go on shopping excursions on those occasions when they found themselves with capital to spend—though first, they had to submit to a rigorous security protocol that included a background check, a financial assessment (so as to prevent anyone from entering the city in order to beg or otherwise harass our citizens or to try and claim benefits that they did not in fact earn, the law being very clear on these matters but still difficult for certain of the quasi-natives to fathom), and the payment of a small fee to compensate for these services.

Indeed, the evolution of a certain contre-société was, I suppose, bound to happen sooner or later. It is still in its evolution, but appears to be chiefly taking the form of a sort of crude nativism among some of the rowdier and more youthful quasi-natives. Owing to the dual misfortune of having been raised in a global backwater and with a rather inferior educational system, it is easy for bizarre ideas and conspiracy theories relating to the past to spread among these people.

Culturally, there is nothing really much in the way of a heritage to speak of for the quasi-natives, sad to say. With all the talk of Nelson Rodgers of the glories of the markmaking, etcetera, fascinating as it might have been, what it really amounts to is a typically British and colonialist romanticization of the exotic other's drunken ditherings in a state of moral disrepair. Which is not to say that their race is in any way inferior to anyone else's, but that the wantonness with which they as a people might best be characterized hardly possesses the attributes that civilized people normally refer to when they speak of a thing called culture. And as for their mythical origins, well, the very fact that their name requires that particular prefix (quasi-) communicates rather clearly that any blood-and-soil ties that they may assert are clearly the product of illusion and not reality.

I suppose some might consider the institution of the border system around the capital to be the catalyzing moment for the establishment of this contre-société. There was further resentment, however, in what some began to perceive as a certain slowness in the new government's promised construction of housing for the quasi-natives, most of whom were dwelling in a sprawling trailer park in the south of the island, just north of Pirate's Bay and to the west of Cove Beach. Baldheaded Mountain formed the symbolic border between this hinterland and the realm of the city and the more prestigious center and northern part of the country, which, by wont of our economic success, was beginning to encroach upon the quasi-natives—or so they felt. While I cannot personally speak of the delays in construction with any great knowledge, as it is outside my personal sphere of influence—my office is with the president and the ministry of culture, whereas Senator Brunnei oversees all housing-related matters—the complaint seemed to have to do with the fact that despite the promises, it appeared our government was dragging its feet on the construction of housing, as the flimsy trailers had been designated as temporary, makeshift housing by the former quasi-colonial government, who didn't seem to care much for the inhabitants, a charge now being leveled at us. What these individuals seem to lack in their understanding is an appreciation that the building of infrastructure requires both time and a prioritization of projection based on the immediacy of need. When we inherited the

island, our airport was barely functioning; we had to rely on the rather weak port of Pirate's Bay, with its rotting docks and vestitures
more suited to the quasi-native fishermen than for the supply and
cruise ships we intended to bring in, hence the need for constructing
our own wharf on the more geographically advantageous northern
tip of the island; the upkeep and renovation of certain buildings in
the town center, including a number of buildings where key government business is daily conducted; the renovation and building of new
homes for the government employees in the hills surrounding Baldheaded Mountain; the repair of Yarmouth Road, the key stretch
connecting the city to Cove Beach and the closest thing to a highway
that exists on the island; and the buildings in the west of Elias Shores,
required as a private luxury alternative to Cove Beach with its inferior
waters on the east side of the island. I know that the building of
quasi-native housing was meant to feature somewhere on that list,
though am unsure of its exact positioning. I am quite sure that Barb
intends to embark upon the project any day now, especially given
that the Elias Shores resort project with the Saudis has reached its
inevitable zenith, which of course the quasi-natives could thank President Mrdok for, were they even aware of his omnipresent concern
for their well being.

Tragic as it may sound, in order to continuously maintain the surveillance-free status that our country enjoys and is enshrined in our
constitution, the limiting of entrants to the capital and its environs
became key to maintaining this freedom shared by all citizens and
staff of Settlers Landing—whether they be quasi-elites, quasi-natives,
new settlers, or those visitors who venture in increasing numbers to
enjoy our fair shores.

30.

–FRIZZY HEADED FUCKIN bitch.

–Yeah. What's the idea?

–Keep your hands *off* of me!

–You're in the hands of the Settlers Landing Royal Security Apparatus...

–*Royal.* Give me a break.

–We can do whatever the *fuck* we want with you. You're under
our jurisdiction now. Got that?

–Get away from me, onion breath.

–Don't make me use this. I really don't, more than anything, want to have to use this right now. But I will use it. To crack your skull. If you make me.

–He will. You can trust me on that one.

–It's pathetic. Treating a fellow American this way.

–I'm not American. He's not, either.

–Not anymore, we're not.

–Bullshit. We're all Americans. Stuck on this island, this pseudo-tropical hellhole. We're all here for the same reason—just the extent of our desperation varies a little bit. How much is he paying you, anyway?

–Enough.

–We're the ones asking the questions around here.

–So start asking them.

–Why did you attack the president?

–Shouldn't we get her name first?

–Good idea. Yeah. Tell us your name, prisoner.

–My name is I want to speak with a lawyer.

–Ha. She's hilarious.

–What I'm sick and tired of—

–What *I'm* sick and tired of is this sense of a future. Having one.

–Oh yeah. I'm sick of that, too.

–See? I *knew* you guys were on my side.

–Well. You'd be wrong there.

–What?!

–We're here to guard you.

–To interrogate you.

–Not be your friend.

–Don't get us wrong. Settlers Landing is a wonderful place to make friends.

–Yeah. Just look at us. We didn't even know each other before we came here. We're great friends now.

–See? Isn't life beautiful?

–But you ruined it…

–Yeah.

–When you attacked our president. For yourself, I mean. Not for us.

–What I did, I had no choice in the matter.

–Meaning?

–It was done out of raw instinct.

–The how hardly answers the why. That's what we're going after: the latter.

–All I did was spray him in the face with pepper spray.

–That would be the what.

–So now we have the what and the how. Still no why.

–I wanted to express myself. To express my anger.

–Well I think *that* might have something to do with—

–You think it's a democracy here. But it really isn't.

–Do you know what she—

–Let's take a sample of something.

–Like what?

–Her hair, for instance.

–Let me reiterate: you do not *touch* me.

–What would be the point of that?

–I don't know. For evidence, I guess.

–Evidence?

–Yeah. We need scientific evidence. She's a suspect.

–I guess that makes sense. But she's more than a suspect. We saw her do it.

–What she has done is really so awful, I just don't know what we're supposed to do next.

–I suppose there will be a trial.

–A trial.

–Sure. Isn't that how they normally do things?

–I don't know. This is the first time I've ever arrested anyone, if I'm being completely honest.

–So what are you gonna do now? Throw me in jail?

–We don't have any jails on Settlers Landing.

–An ideal society has no need for prisons.

–So then let me go.

–Ha. Yeah right.

–Frizzy headed fuckin bitch.

–I am not a bitch.

–What are you then.

–I came here. To get treatment.

–A Viutex patient, then.

–One of those.

–So: not a bitch, just a junkie. I should've known. Look: she's starting to sweat. Oh shit. I hope she doesn't start puking and shitting.

–Now why would she do that.

–That's what they do, when they start going through withdrawal.

–Who?

–Junkies, you idiot. My Uncle Benny was a pillhead. Then a heroin user. Tried to quit cold turkey. It was a mess.

–You're not gonna shit or puke, are you?

–Just don't touch me.

–We're not—

–Ouch! It hurts!

–I barely *brushed* you...

–We're just trying to get you to sit up, ma'am.

–I told you not to fucking touch me. It fucking hurts.

–Hurts where?

–Hurts all over.

–See? She's already gone into withdrawal.

–Can you tell us why you're here, ma'am? Where you're from?

–Why are you calling her ma'am now?

–I'm American! Just like you... And I came here to get *help*!

–Funny way you have of going about it.

–I mortgaged my house and my car to get here. It's my *second* mortgage on my house. Second fucking mortgage. And the fucking doctor told me...

–What?

–That it's *still* not enough.

–Not enough for what?

–To get the Viutex treatment. You retard.

–Hey. That's not nice. My brother is retarded. He's also a good person.

–I didn't know you had a brother.

–Sure as shit do.

–And so, wait. You didn't have enough to pay for the Viutex. And so you go and spray our beloved president in the face?

–Yeah. What kind of logic is that?

–We're patriots. We might not know how to properly arrest and interrogate someone. But that doesn't mean we're going to just sit back and let you rape our country while we watch.

–Dude. You make it sound kind of hot.

–Well I'm sorry but that wasn't my intention. Not at all!

–Why do you want to go on the Viutex anyway, lady?

–Can't you see? She's a junkie. Like all of them.

–Yeah. But junkies aren't supposed to be on Viutex. I read that article. It's supposed to be people suffering from real pain. From genuine pain. Our doctors don't allow it to be used as a drug substitute.

–You idiot.

–What?

–That's just a fucking ruse.

–What is.

–Pain relief. The people going on that shit are *all* junkies. Or else medicated up the wazoo when they arrive here.

–Hey. I take medication.

–Yeah. So do I. But we're on a different kind of medication. Ours is for PTSD. The ones who come here to get on Viutex are all hooked on opiates.

–How come no one explained this to me yet? I thought I was supposed to be part of the Ministry for State Security here and no one even told me.

–There's the official line and the unofficial line. Both are true, I guess. But each in its own special way.

–I don't know how many competing lines of truth I can handle anymore…

–Well you'd better get your shit together, man. We're about to start interrogating this prisoner.

–What the fuck are you talking about? Number one, she's about to start shitting herself. Number two—

–Shouldn't that really be number two?

–Fuck you… I'm not going to shit… Just get me my purse. It has my, my medication in it. Get me my purse, *please.*

–Why? So you can spray *us* in the face? I don't think so.

–She wants her stuff. Her pills. Her junk. Her morphine. Her heroin. Whatever it is she's on.

–She has *that* stuff on her? Then she should be *doubly* arrested.

–Get. Me. My. *Purse.* You fucking *imbecile!*

–Hey. Don't talk to him that way. That's my brother. My non-retarded one. My brother-in-combat. He fought for his country. Just like me. We both fought. So that people like you could stay at home and do your drugs. We fought for your freedom. You'd better show us some respect. Or else we'll blow your ass up. Just like we did to those goddamn Arabs.

–Bro, calm down. Did you take your meds today?

–I'm fucking sick of this shit, yo. Everything we've done for this country. These ungrateful fucking civilians—

–Dude. Listen. We haven't done jack shit for *this* country. Not yet. That's not our country anymore. Settlers Landing is our country. And she's not a citizen. She's a foreigner. A foreigner who attacked our president.

–So you're saying she's like… like… one of them… them Arabs?

–Yes. I am. That makes her a terrorist. From the standpoint of combat. Of the battle we now find ourselves in. She's worse than that, man. She's… she's… the enemy.

–Hm. You're right. So do we kill her now or later?

–For now, we let her shit herself. We'll interrogate her once all the drugs are out of her system.

–Nooo! Give me my stuff, you assholes. My stuff…

–Get her purse… What's in there?

–You know what this is? It's the same stuff my Uncle Benny was on. Heroin.

–Pleease. I'm getting sick. I need… just a little bit. Or else I'm going to die.

–You should have thought of that before you turned to terrorism. Kiss your drugs goodbye, bitch.

–Nooo! Nooooo! Nooo!

–Dude, why did you just flush all of it?

–It's illegal.

–That was *evidence,* man. Don't you get it? We're… well, not police—Settlers Landing doesn't have police, we have no need for it. But something *like* police.

–I'm dying! I'm gonna die.

–Shut the fuck up.

–We're the ones who decide who's dying and who's living around here.

–Yeah. You fucking *illegal.* Fucking *terrorist.*

–Let her suffer. Let her stew in her own shit for a while.

–Enjoy your withdrawal. Bitch.

–Turn the lights out.

… Screams resounding.

31.

HOLDING A GOVERNMENT post does open one up to all sorts of attempts at graft and leverage maneuvering, I have come to find, even when consigned to the rather modest department of Ministry of Culture. One concession I have elected to make rather reluctantly was out of friendship to Krstal. Who is, after all, the first lady of our fair nation, and thus deserving of, at the very least, a listening ear whenever Mrdok is too occupied to offer either of his. Krstal's request, her point of insistence actually, was one Billy R. Spack.

Krstal's master plan, it seems, is to expand the current meager offerings of the Settlers Landing Film Studio and turn it into a pseudotropical rival to Hollywood. Although I have been blessed with twenty-twenty vision, I have yet been forced to strain my eyes in order to perceive what it is, exactly, Krstal perceives in Billy and his films. Billy is a twenty-seven-year-old graduate of the film program at the University of Southern California, having been discovered by Krstal on the basis of his thesis film, which I was painfully made to sit through in the pitch proceedings.

The plot of the film, which is meant to be an ironic nod to the sci-fi B-movie genre, involves a contingent of alien scientists, some time in the future, locating the brain of a human dictator from some period in the past—perhaps Mussolini or Hitler, though I believe it was a fictionalized name given to the brain for some artistic reason or another. The aliens, who now roam the Earth in place of the human race, which has become extinct, one day discover the brain hidden away in some laboratory. It is labeled clearly with the dictator's name taped to the jar, and it is clearly a humanoid brain, floating in formaldehyde. They know this, as these are quite clever aliens—when they see a human brain, they know what it is they are seeing, even though they have never seen a human in the flesh before, even though their anatomy is doubtless quite different from ours, which is made apparent by the rather unintentionally humorous lizard-like costumes in which the actors playing them are costumed.

At first, the aliens assume the brain with the dictator's name affixed to it is what humans regarded as a joke—the aliens do not have a firm grasp on the subject of humor, which is alien to their species, though one of the alien doctors is on hand to give a brief explication of the concept. At this point, the evil alien scientist comes into conflict with the good alien scientist. The latter wants to leave it alone, while the former wishes to open the jar and perform some tests to determine whether the brain actually came out of the long-deceased dictator's skull. The aliens confer, and the evil scientist wins out among his peers. The good alien scientist takes the moral high ground and marches out of the room, refusing to have any further involvement with the proceedings. The evil alien scientist and his cohort immediately begin their experimentations upon the dictator's brain. Until unwittingly, they make the brain come to life. The brain is pulsing like a heart, the alien scientists are puzzled because they have never encountered this before—a living human brain. They do not know what to do with it, and so one of the aliens suggests they feed it. Feed it? replies the evil alien scientist. Why, that's ridiculous.

How do you feed a human brain? Just as he's saying these words, he brushes his hand up against the brain, which has grown to three times its normal size in the course of their conversation, which they were too involved with to notice, and a mouth-like fold has opened in the center of the brain as it sucks the evil alien scientist's left hand (which more resembles a claw than a hand, though a hand is what it is) up into its brainness, its brainsphere, whatever it is meant to be. The alien quickly pulls it back to reveal a bloody stump, screams, alien blood is squirting everywhere, everyone screaming, it resembles human blood close enough for viewers to recognize it as such, though it is more of a deep purplish hue—to make it more alienlike, one presumes? In panic and chaos, the alien scientists retreat into their nearby space ship in an effort to save themselves and to repair the evil alien scientist's missing appendage, leaving the evil dictator's brain behind them. Well, that was a mistake, for then the dictator's brain goes on a mad rampage in the laboratory. First, he breaks into the room where the cryogenic remains of Earth's remaining humans have been stored. He rips open their skulls and eats their brains, completely decimating the upper portions of their bodies, so that he might expand himself. (All except for one, though that will not be revealed until later on in the film…) With each human brain consumed, the bigger the dictator's brain gets, the more ravenous and uncontrollable his appetite, until he has morphed into a gigantic brainball bouncing through the deserted streets of this post-apocalyptic Earthscape with a ferocious boing that can be heard echoing from miles around, much as the footsteps of the tyrannosaurus rex must have echoed in the pre-apocalyptic era. The aliens, meanwhile, have been thrown into full-on crisis mode. How do they deal with, destroy this monster? They go through a variety of destruction devices that they know through their intense study of humanology had been effective during that era: nuclear missiles, poison gas, poison atmosphere, poison water, bombs, fire, hydrochloric acid, all kinds of bullets—but nothing seems to work and every attempt to destroy the dictator's brain results in the loss of alien life or else a severe injury. A protocol is issued among the aliens to abandon Earth once and for all, and so the aliens all board their spacecrafts and fly right off into the multiverse away from the gigantic mess they've made of the planet—all, that is, except for the good alien scientist, who is determined to stay behind, defeat the dictator's brain, and reclaim Earth once and for all for his species.

The good scientist, in his wanderings, one day encounters a human creature, a young female specimen named Molly Glumly, who had somehow been microwaved out of her cryogenic state while the evil brain had been busy maniacally desecrating all the other human brains back at the lab. Once he informs her who and what she is, for she hasn't been alive for a great many centuries and so needs to be brought up to date (a key moment of heavy-footed exposition in the film, rife with a series of illustrative flashbacks narrated by the good alien scientist), the alien scientist and Molly realize they must put their genetic differences aside if they are to defeat this horrible abomination. They have to work together, and it won't be easy; between them, they only have two brains, while the big dictatorial brain now consists of millions.

Molly's proposal is to combine what each of them does best; she will wear a slutty negligée in order to lure the dictatorial brain into an amorous setting which will actually be a space ship; once on board, she will shut the door, and the good alien scientist and his comrades (whom she rather dimwittedly expects to be suddenly and inexplicably summoned back to Earth) will then blast the evil dictator brain into outer space. The good scientist, of course, must scoff at this idea, informing Molly in the most non-condescending way he can muster that humans know very little about the multiverse, that in fact, were he dispatched into that realm, the possibilities are high that he would expand his current spree into an intergalactic rampage, possibly destroying the entire galaxy in due course. Plus, there are no spacecrafts left on Earth; the good alien scientist has been all but abandoned here by his fellow specimen.

Just as they are contemplating these measures, a horrific boing is heard somewhere in the distance, signaling the bouncing brain's arrival. Molly screams helplessly, humanishly. They run into an abandoned factory to seek shelter. The building turns out not to have been a factory, but a former drug treatment center. The aliens who were in control of it didn't know what use to make of it, so they had turned it into a laboratory for the study of dead junkie brains. The refrigerator of dead junkie brains is discovered by Molly in the back area. Once she alerts her intergalactic sidekick, the good alien scientist comes up with the brilliant idea of feeding the big dictator brain with the brains of junkies who died of heroin overdoses. If the toxicity level in the brains is still high enough, it might just be enough to stone the big brain into oblivion. They set about frantically testing the toxicity levels of the brains, discarding those that are too low and piling the really high ones on to a gigantic silver brain platter. They sprinkle the brains with glitter to give them a festive look, then set the brain platter at a way's distance from the laboratory and await the big brain's bouncing arrival.

Boing, boing, boing goes the dictator as it smells its diseased dinner rotting around the corner. Upon its discovery, the dictator gobbles up all the brains in one fell swooping munch. Afterward, the big brain doesn't feel so good. It leeches and leans, until finally opening its mouth to burp and winds up barfing brain matter instead.

Molly and the good alien scientist watch all this from behind an overturned Earthmobile. When the big brain attains the highest plateau of catatonia, they emerge with giant pitchforks in hand and proceed to decimate into tiny pieces all the little brains comprising the big brain. Then they smash the little brain bits with their raw toes until they've smeared all the concrete of the abandoned city with dead dictator brain matter.

Lying back in an exhausted state in some fallow field, having finally defeated the big brain, Molly and the good alien scientist look into each other's eyes for the first time. Being the last representatives of their respective species left on this abandoned planet, it is time for Molly to teach the good alien scientist a lesson. After she frees her ample bosoms from the tiring constraints of her metalloid undergarments, a projective foreshadowing displays the pair's procreative endeavor resulting in the creation of a brand new, half-human half-alien species, with which to repopulate the barren planet. Humanity, so-called, is thus left with some semblance of hope as they kiss and the credits begin to roll.

While all the queasy metaphorage was obvious enough, this Billy R. Spack could not resist putting the proverbial maraschino cherry upon the whipped cream of the sundae by endowing this dubious piece of cinematic art with the title, *Allegory of Fascism*, in an effort to endow the putrid morass with art school credibility, I suppose. Outside of some rather third rate film festivals, this *Allegory* had barely been screened anywhere when a screener made its way into Krstal's inbox via one of her film industry contacts in Los Angeles. I myself, being the wellspring of hope I have always aspired to be, do not possess the *profondeur* of cynicism required to assert that Billy's invitation to Settlers Landing might be attributed to the fact that he was the only director to respond to it. The First Lady did, after all, choose him, and such regal choices must be respected in our delicate system.

Needless to say, although he is some twenty-seven years her junior, Krstal threw herself into carnal relations with the so-called maverick director. This occurred seemingly within hours of his arrival on our fair island—very likely a reflex left over from Krstal's era in Hollywood, where this was the sole means by which an actress in her situation might hold out any hope of getting cast in a project. I'm curious as to whether it occurred to her that—she now being a producer—such machinations were hardly necessary. Though, given her amorous proclivities, it is not inconceivable that this endeavor was motivated by more earthy emotions as well.

The matter of taste, I suppose, is another entirely. When it comes to the cinematic arts, I myself am more partial to the European masters like Rosselini, Rohmer, and Riefenstahl—as Ministress of Culture, the idea of inviting a rather untested talent, if that not be too strong a word, engaged in the rather dubious task of B-movie revivalism, was somewhat difficult to digest. But again, given Krstal's positioning in the island's administrative structure, as well as the need to rapidly build up a film industry with which to promote ourselves overseas—not to mention the difficulties we encountered when trying to attract more well-known names—we eventually bent to the task and welcomed the relatively untried newcomer into our folds— with the first lady accomplishing this task in a rather more literal sense.

Of course the executive producer of their first project is meant to be our president, Mrdok, and here he is now discussing their first pitch. Krstal will co-produce, and also play the female lead. There is some disagreement about what the first project will be, with Billy having just finished his five minute pitch for a sequel to *Allegory of Fascism*, with Molly and the good alien scientist, having successfully repopulated the Earth, now having relocated to a nomadic existence on a floating ship in outer space, where a full-on cosmic war is underway between their fledgling team of neoearthlings defending themselves against the cruel plottings of the evil alien scientist, who has apparently been infected with that crude human emotion known as envy.

—I don't fuckin get it, Mrdok now says. You want to make a sequel to a movie that no one has seen? What's the, what's the, uh…

—Justification, I interject.

—Yeah. What, uh, Gee just said.

Billy R. Spack sits there in his New York Yankees baseball cap looking through his thick square-framed glasses at the adults before him, trying to gauge the room's temperature so that he can figure out some way to win this argument.

—Well, I don't mind doing a sequel. Lord knows I've done a fair amount of those, back in the day. What I don't feel just right about is the role. I know it would be impossible to cast the original actress, seeing as how she was tragically maimed filming that topless rock climbing scene, but I just don't know if I could endure another surgery right now, which we can all agree I'll need if I'm going to do that role—

–Krstal, says Billy, I believe in you as an actress, okay? I believe you can play almost anything.

–True, she says, but I would rather play someone else. At least for this first role.

–Yeah, says Mrdok. We need to make a splash with this shit. No offense, but if I'm gonna put this much money into a thing, I like to—

–I know exactly what you're going to say, Mister—

–He doesn't like to be called mister, I interrupt. He would be pleased if you'd address him as president.

–Just Mrdok's fine. Look, kid, tell me some of your other ideas. I don't want the full monty. Just give me, uh, like, the pitch in miniature. We're short on time here.

–Well, I have this one other screenplay completed, *The Traci Lords Story,* about—

–I know who Traci Lords is.

–I don't know that I'm the right age for that one…

–Well, neither was she, at the time…

–What about something with animals in it? I like animals. I feel like that's a challenge I can live up to.

–Yeah. Like, what, a python, maybe?

–I don't know about snakes. That could be dangerous.

–We could have a handler on the set. A snake handler.

Just then, Senators Lallyburt and Barb enter the room.

–Hey Lallyburt. This sounds like something you'd be into: snake-handling!

–Wayuhl ah do deklayuh. Is this heyuh the movie di-rectuh?

–No, Lallyburt, deadpans Barb. He's just competing in a Spike Lee lookalike contest.

–I actually don't know much about snake-handling, says Billy.

–Well I've got a snake you can handle right here.

–Oh Mrdok, stop. This is serious. We're losing focus now. We need to figure out what my first project, I mean *our* first project, is going to be.

–Well, if we *are* going to do a movie about snake-handlers, we need to bring Taggerston in on this. Lallyburt could introduce you. They're good friends.

—Weyuhl. Ah wutunt say we wuz the beyest of friyends. Though we do share many of the same beliefs.

—Yeah, says Mrdok. That's why they decided to leave the US. Because the government was putting chemicals in the water to turn all the amphibians gay.

—Your beliefs are a steaming crock of shit, says Barb.

—That's yo opinion, says Lallyburt.

—It's actually not. My opinion is actually far worse.

—So this is no longer a pitch session, complains Billy. More like a creative brainstorming session. I think we should end it right here. Too many voices in the room.

—Weyuhl who in sayum heyuhl do you think you are?

—No offense, man. It's just not my process. I'm used to doing this stuff alone, or with my own small team. I'm an auteur, you see. I went to USC.

—A whuht?

—An artiste, Lallyburt. You wouldn't understand. They don't got those in Texas.

—I happen to agree, Billy. These people are businessmen, not artists. Let's go back to my studio and brainstorm.

—Oh is that what they're calling it nowadays?

—Nice to see you too, Barb. And if you'd like to join the production for a producer credit, we'd love to have you on board.

—Something about religion isn't a totally bad idea. It would give us a chance to engage the quasi-natives.

—Yeah. Give it a local flavor.

—So why don't you two go and storm brains, says Barb. We've got some matters to discuss with the president. Issues concerning, uh, national security, shall we say.

Billy and Krstal usher themselves out.

—Mrdok, it's time we finally discussed this matter of—

—I know what you're about to say.

—When is Ma coming in, Mrdok?

—I don't know his schedule. Have you talked to his people?

—His peypuhl. Ha. Whuht peypuhl.

—Because I really think he needs to be here for this conversation…

—Look, Barb, I appreciate your concern, your wanting to know all the particulars, I really do. And I do, as well.

—I think you *do* know all the particulars, Mrdok…

—Yeayuh. What she sayed.

–… and that *some* of the particulars—perhaps a *great deal* of them—are not being communicated to us.

–Transparency is my middle name.

–Brynn is his middle name, actually, I deign to interject.

–Gee, could you go wait outside, please?

–I most certainly cannot. I need to be here to record minutes.

–This is a meeting I don't think anyone is going to want to have records of.

–Ahll dune teyuhl you won thang. Them Saudi boiz aint no one to play with. You mark mah word.

–What's he talking about?

–Your whole plan to screw over the Saudis on the resort deal.

–Well that's not exactly what's happening here.

–And that's not really what I said, Barb, just to clarify, I interject. I would call that a very crude summary of my remarks—

–What the hell were you doing talking to her about the Saudi deal? Wait a minute here. What is this? An ambush?

–Mrdok, you know I would *never*—

–It's not like we get all of our information from your tranny-in-chief over here, Mrdok.

–Yeayuh. Them Saudi boiz is mah family's good freyends. You screw them Saudis ovuh boy youh done screwin mah peoples ovuh too.

–Look, I'm not clueless when it comes to your family's dealings with the Saudis, okay? But at this moment, we have to think of our national interests.

–Which, inevitably, are your interests. Or so I'm starting to believe.

–Enough of the cynicism, Barb.

–Apparently all the cynicism in the world isn't enough for you. You know I have other investors who are in on this, as well, Mrdok. If this deal goes belly up under some fictive regulation that you're just going to invent out of thin air, then how in the hell are you going to expect me to maintain *my* reputation, to draw *more* investors and build *more* projects on this godforsaken—

–Enough. Your point is well taken. Okay. I didn't want to get into this today. But as I see you've got your panties crawling up into your cameltoe, then I might as well tell you—tell you both. I think Ma has been double-dealing us with the Saudis.

–Double-dealing.

–I'm almost completely sure of it. Which is why, I've been trying to rope him in here for the longest… He's just not… He's not taking my calls right now.

Lallyburt and Barb look at each other.

–Oh Mrdok…

–How much access does he have?

–What do you think? When he's not here—which he's not, obviously, most of the time—I have no rope on him. He's basically a free agent.

–Wayuhl whuht about our peypuhl out theyuh?

–Out where, Lallyburt?

–Out *theyuh*. You know. The world.

–We can't follow him *all* the time. Our resources are tied up here. Most of them, at least.

–You're not kidding, are you, says Barb.

–The thing is, I don't know what his motives are. That's the toughest part. You know me. I'm the king of rotten deals, Barb. I can usually spot these things from a mile away. But I've been working out the arithmetic, crunching the numbers, trying to see the psychology behind it. He's a total loose cannon.

–So you're…

–So my move to screw over the Saudis, as you put it. It's not really that. What I'm trying to do is screw Ma over, to put a stop to his, his double-dealing. *Through* the Saudis.

–But do them bois know thayuht?

–Of course not. Because then they'd tell him.

–How exactly is he double-dealing us, though?

Jaco now enters the room.

–Jaco? What are you doing here?

–Dad, I have a question for you. Did Jesus have a skin disease?

Lallyburt starts coughing and choking.

–Whuht in the sayuhm heyuhl…

–Not that I'm aware of, Jaco. At least it doesn't say anything about it in the Bible. Well, not that I remember. Lallyburt here's the real expert—

–That is *blas*phemy, sun. You are gonna go—

–Gee, could you do me a favor? Jaco, could you go with Gee in the other room for a minute? Daddy needs to finish up some important bus—Wait, who brought you here anyway? Is Rosalita here with you?

–Because I saw a picture in my art history textbook. We were looking at it today, in class. He was on the cross and his skin had all

these bumps on it. It was just like Krstal after she had her last surgery.

—Well, son, I don't know. Maybe Jesus had a facelift, too.

—*Blas*phemy!

—You said you were going to take me to meet the soldiers today,
Dad.

—Did I? Did I say that, Gee? Was that in the schedule?

—It is. I can move it, if you need me to...

—No, I can, just wait... Gee, would you mind? Jaco, Aunt Gee's
gonna take you in the other room while Daddy finishes up in here—

—Never mind. I'm going.

—Barb, where was I?

—The double-dealing. So-called. What's going on with Ma,
Mrdok?

—I don't think he's doing it directly. He has to be using a middleman.

—A middleman?

—Weyuhl, ifn ah wasuh fixin to screw someone, ahd do the sayme
thang. That way it aint comin fruhm you.

—It's the only way. He's using a middleman to tell the Saudis he's
gonna dick us over, let the cash wash through our bank, then use the
derivatives to pay out—

—So you're, in a sense, sweeping the rug out from under his feet,
by canceling the deal, appearing to screw the Saudis, but actually—

—Look, we write them an IOU. This piece of real estate we're
sitting on, I mean, there is an infinite number of deals we can eventually—

—And so then Ma gets pissed and leaves on his own accord. Is
that where we're going with this?

—Well, that's how it's been engineered. In my mind, at least.

—I would have appreciated you telling us this from the beginning,
Mrdok.

—Well I'm sure you can also appreciate the delicate arithmetic
that's gone in, that is still going into the whole—I mean, it's more
like calculus, Barb. One wrong move, one small word leaks out of
the island—

—But where, ultimately, does this leave us with the Saudis? I need
to know. Lallyburt needs to know. You can't just go—

—I just told you, Barb. The IOU. We can even issue it as a bond,
if it makes them feel better. Lallyburt, you can work your behind-
the-scenes magic, talk to your brother, get the Saudis to go along
with it, can't you?

–Ah dun told you, Merdek. Them Chahneeses. You caint trust em. Ah dun told you, and look where we now at.

–Ma's not Chinese, Lallyburt. He's from Taiwan.

–Same dam thang.

–Lallyburt, says Barb. Just shut the fuck up. Call your brother, call your cousin, call whoever the fuck and tell them to talk to the Saudis. Let them know what's going on, what's *really* going on, so that they don't feel like they're getting burned, pull whatever the fuck, crash an airplane into one of our buildings. Can we resume construction then, Mrdok? That's what's important now, for me.

–What about the other investors?

–If you're gonna underwrite this—if the *government* is underwriting this—then it's safe for us to write them *all* IOUs. Wouldn't you think?

–Well, Barb…

–Just yes or no, Mrdok. Because it's a fucking embarrassment for all of us, when we have an entire project, our biggest yet, that's just sitting there for the world to see in a state of half completion. You've got journalists here crawling up the wazoo. They're not buying the official line anymore.

–Resume construction then. We underwrite everything. Tell the Saudis the resumption of construction is just a PR stunt. Once we've got Ma out of the way, we'll figure out how to bring them back into the fold.

–He won't go quietly into the night.

–Eventually he won't have a choice.

–Chrahst. Ahm in mah office the restuh the afternoon, tryn to figure this mess on out.

–Bye, Lallyburt.

The president pushes a button on his console. The voice of Merrill, former porn star turned secretary to the Diamond Office, affirms itself through the speaker.

–Tell Rosalita and Jaco, tell Jaco his father, the president, is busy. That he loves him very much, but he has the whole nation to worry about. I really have to get this… Tell him we'll take him to meet the soldiers on Wednesday. No… Wait, on Sunday!

–Sunday it is, the voice affirms.

–Barb…

He calls out to her as she is about to make her escape.

–What?

–You know, you seem so uptight lately. I know it's been a while. Don't you miss this?

He stands, cradles his bulge.

—Fuck you, Mister President.

The door slams behind her. It is immediately reopened by Gordina, who comes sauntering toward Mrdok's desk.

—Hey Gee, he says, sitting back down, how much am I worth?

32.

ROBINSON SWERVES TO avoid hitting the fur-coated piglet that has made its way out on to the thinness of the twilit avenue, being chased by a woman whose thin wrists are weighted down by diamond bracelets and wearing upon her head what looks like a fan but must be some kind of fashion statement Robinson's eyes, stare as they might, just can't decode. The lady calls after the piglet but the piglet doesn't want to return, its name is Brooklyn and it has a fifty thousand dollar mink stole wrapped around it, or at least Brooklyn is what the lady keeps yelling at it, and Robinson slows against the curb to watch the show while awaiting his passenger's arrival. He hopes the poet remembers their little rendezvous, he forgot to get the guy's number so this is all rather twentieth century of them, and he's turned off the Uber app for the night so who knows what kind of calls he could be making at this, well, what is nearly always peak hour on the island, given that he is the only one of his kind here.

—Brooklyn! How can you *do* this to me when you know I'm wearing Valentino?

Her filet-fattened husband stands in tux on the pavement with Cuban cigar half-raised to his lips regarding the scene, trying to neutralize the facetious smile forming into the surrounding Botox where the lines should be and beads of sweat inevitable on this particularly humid night-to-be. Then he takes out his phone to selfie himself with cigar hanging out of his gobbet and the most insincere peace sign Robinson has ever seen two fingers make.

The poet's body goes past in the rearview mirror and there follows the opening of his left back car door.

—Sorry, I'm not late, am I?

Robinson nods at him in the rearview.

—Why don't you come sit up here with me?

He gestures at the passenger seat.

—Oh, uh, sure, I uh…

He slams the back door a bit too hard, causing Robinson to wince at the wear-and-tear prospect.

—It's funny, because nobody else seems to know about this talking dog. I was asking Gordina, people around the pub all day. You're the first to, to really know anything about it right here. I'm so, I mean… I hope… Do you think it's really real?

—Real as rain, singsongs Robinson as he gently presses the button to lower his window halfway in the hopes of getting out the boozestink that has accompanied Birchfield into the seat next to his.

—And… to get this straight… he speaks in Sagosian? Or English?

—English, man. Only the old ones, the fervent nationalists… They's the only ones who still speak Sagosian.

—Can you speak it?

—I don't speak it. No.

An air of melancholia pervades this response that Birchfield doesn't want to touch. And so he turns to the passenger side window to stare out of, clouds creeping in to engulf the night. Robinson notes these clouds at the exact same second, though with his regard comes a hint of worry, since the combination of cloud and humidity frequently infers the oncoming of a storm. Though he will soon find out, from the mouth of the dog himself, whether this possibility is imminent, and the potential severity thereof. For this dog knows things that no human creature can determine—not even the weatherman on TV.

—So, uh, you must make a fine living, being the only Uber driver on the island, Birchfield now trying to change the subject.

Robinson takes this as his cue.

—In case you ever wanna buy some marijuana. I mean, I know you a poet. I mean, I know some people. I can help.

—Really? There's weed here?

—Yeah, man. There is now. Wasn't before. But, well. It's a thing here, man. You want to buy?

Birchfield considers it. It used to help him write, when he was a kid. Who knows. But probably not the thing for the aphasia.

—I'll take a raincheck. But I've got your number. Maybe I'll change my mind.

Silence was descended from a long line of Sagosian terrier that traces its ancestry to the South China Sea; these dogs were trained by the Fujian pirates to attack and kill rats and small rodents that were an essential part of their diet;

also to protect them in military battles against rival pirates but especially all representatives of law and order that attempted to enthrone them. Theirs is a medium-sized breed marked by a profound soldierly grayness, like that found in the Russian blue breed of cat. Unlike that feline, however, their eyes are not blue but a green lined with yellow, eliciting a poetic field, though more likely the embedded reflection of the sea that they were bound to stare at for the centuries that required their evolution. His ancestors were all on the boat, and when the East Asian pirates joined their cohorts in Sagosia, they were let loose to wander feral throughout the island, forming a number of dog colonies that were never properly tamed until the English came and made a partially successful attempt to institute veterinary systematicity, which helped domesticate many, but not all, of the clans. Silence's mother and father met when the former came upon the latter humping a tree trunk late one sultry summer eve. The bitch was domesticated, walking along the beach leashless with her owner that night, when she smelled a scent accompanied by a noise toward the brush upon the shore that intrigued her so much she was forced to disobey her owner's command to halt in order to go investigate. It was the perfect moment, since she had been in heat of late, and so by the time her breathless human finally caught up with her, she was already on her haunches for her new husband, whose wolfish growl at the owner served as a strong enough warning to stay away until he was finished with the quarter-hour's business.

–So do you want to watch Silence with me, Robinson? the poet now asks. I mean, I understand if you have other, you know, your Uber thing to pursue. Don't let me keep you. It's just that, you know, none of the quasi-elites—

Robinson can see the reason why he's asking. It don't take a great scientific mind to understand. He's scared. This is not something that the folk in the city would normally attend. Hell, they didn't even know about it when he asked them. Shows how little the quasis know the local culture.

Robinson has a high-pitched laugh. Startled—himself even—it's the first time anyone's ever heard it.

–Yeah, I'm goin, I'm goin. You don't have to worry, we can go in there together.

What is a Greek amphitheater doing all this way? Birchfield wonders as they make their way past the arches after having put their 10 SL entry fee through the slot of a small wooden hut. But that is exactly what it is: built here on the west coast, though in a state of centuries-battered decay—clearly the genesis of some pirate who had chanced to visit that ancient kingdom and sought to replicate it here so far away.

A hush descends upon the few hundred spectators as the dog is trotted out nonchalantly by a dreadlocked quasi-native calmly holding it by its leash as though it were just another domesticated creature with the burden of needing to be guided by some human presence. The dog sits placidly with tongue awag out of its happy mouth and patiently waits for the black-shirted stage manager to adjust the mic stand so that the microphone parallels his visage exactly.

Then his voice rang out—like that of a middle-aged man, with the standard Sagosian accent—that patchwork patois, here deployed in the ancient craft of rhetorical flourish.

There's a place I like to go when there's no place for me
A little pocket of coast hidden along the deep Brown Sea
Where I might sit to regard the world's slow collapse
Without the uncertainties that might yield a perhaps
Master takes me there when he needs a read on the weather
To determine wither the wind (it is always toward the nether)
When you live in a state of blindness, as most of us do
In a land devoid of reason, where we might stare into the blue
And hope to find some semblance of a truth long gone
Humans and their identity, when all they really need is a song

There is a madness in time and wandering through it
Like the peach trees and banyans when abused by rain
The maudlin nights upon the capital's streets lined with shit
Ruled over by an emperor long gone insane

When walked down those streets on occasion to do my evening task
I witness beneath the glow of the streetlamps adorned women and
      men abask
I wonder what happened to all those rulers of old
Probably covered in dust, fungus, and mold
On another isle far away from here
Drowning their sorrows in endless pints of beer
While our quasi-elites take their wretched place
Scattered flowers in need of some fine vase
To keep them contained lest their ambitions overflow
That is a process I'm sure you all know
As humans yourselves who dwell on this land
You know well its glories, against storms you've taken your stand

As we all must are we to survive
Until a moment ago, the question of whether you will thrive
Might have never occurred
But now, I give you the word
Every single human's got a fascist in the brain
It grins at he who drives the train
Off the rails and into the dark never
So that from life we may perpetually sever

The soul's a myth and so's the body
The sun's a hole, the moon's all rotty
The trees with bark the shade of a leopard
The fields without sheep but still craving a shepherd

When a heart gets substituted for speech
There are no longer words for a sermon to preach
There are only the gods in the skies that control us
With remote controls like for the TVs that once stole us
When we're not making marks or listening to dogspeech
Man preys on man, the picture's absurd as a slug's leech

You were probably expecting another weather report
I can tell you're doing a fine job holding down the fort
Doing what you can to get by and endure
Never mind your limited capacity to be sure
About who holds the reins like my owner up here
To the leashes you all wear without being clear
About who and what you're serving or bothering to ask why
I'll tell you for certain: the answer's not in the sky

I once sang a song that no one knew
A song of a revolt, till resignation grew
Now we've run out of time, without gauging the truth
The island's no longer mine or yours, it belongs to an uncouth
Set of bastards who know our divisions
In which they shall make multiple incisions
Till we no longer know each other
A son will be severed from his mother
Fathers and uncles will tear each other apart
Civil war is a most ignoble art

There's a thing or two you might do to not make this occur

Whatever you do, do not further abjure
Hands don't get weary when they have a sword to hold on to
Rich men don't get hungry after a plate of fondue
Take back the life that was taken from you
Don't make my rhymes turn to bark
Or suppose my prophecies a lark

The rocks on this isle, old as time
Look away, the world is mine
And yours as well if you want a piece
Of the wheel, just don't forget the grease

Now if you'll excuse me, folks, I've got a date
With a real fine bitch, she will not wait
She craves a bone I'll bury deep
Within her folds and then we'll sleep
Exhausted from our mortal dance
The life of a dog's full of romance
But also jaundiced dreams run dry
Sometimes we see our owners and cry
At their gallant mistakes in trying to be honest
You'd think every Sagosian was born a monist
Unable to gage the heady fullness of life
Folks, it's about much more than the avoidance of strife
Every day we don't die is a gift from Yang Zhu
The chance to serve ourselves, to get drunk and screw
But we can't do that when we've all turned to slaves
So honor your ancestors; don't piss on their graves!

Silence gets up and leads his master off the stage once he is done. The crowd stirs a bit, but doesn't know what to do with itself on such occasions, how to be a crowd, and so rather than clap or otherwise allude to its self-consciousness, a quiet murmur resounds as though awaking from a collective trance. A slow dispersal toward the entry points. Though some, the young in particular, sit behind as their elders rise. Quiet nods communicate future meetings. There are no goodbyes here.

Making their way to the car, Robinson can't fathom out a reason for Birchfield's tears. Whether they might be tears of joy or else an erotic epiphany of sorts that Robinson just don't have the right pervert devices for measuring, the rightness of the things Silence was saying rather put the Uber driver in a mood best called pensive;

which is why the tears just don't fit in with this scheme, which he just ascribed to everyone else present in the amphitheater—it *was* the overwhelming mood at the end...

Quasi-native psychology having its cultural specificities. How disappointed Freud would be to be greeted with certain of these truths. Were he suddenly woke from the grave and reminded of all the places he forgot to visit. A map of the Earth with one of those long wooden pointer sticks stabbing at this archipelago of the long forgotten, of the never-to-be-colonized-again... Emotions squeezed out like salt from the pores of the skin, to be cleansed by the rival salts belonging to the sea, that were once a part of other beasts once alive, long perished to add texture to the groaning morass that offers a meek definition of ground against liquid. There has never been anything here even approaching the delusion of grandeur that allows for individuality to take a nosedive into the sort of neuroses that would enable the evolution of an entire medical industry. Madness has existed, for sure; but its manifested aberrations have rarely sought out dominance over, say, the need to go to the bathroom, eat, masturbate... Paradise is no setting for a bathrobe or even an evening gown.

Tears dry, thankfully the sky hasn't broken. Yet. The poet opens his mouth halfway along the journey back to town. Robinson anticipates some words, but they don't come for a minute or three. Just that hanging open, until finally they coalesce into the sole meaningful sound heard since Silence spoke.

—I thought... I mean, are you available as well, tomorrow, in the morning?

Robinson checks his rearview mirror. He has the feeling he's being followed, but there are no lights behind him. Convinced there were a few seconds ago, he wonders where the other vehicle might have gone, since there hasn't been a turn-off now for quite a while.

—Where do you need to go? he says.

—I have an appointment, says the poet. A doctor's appointment.

33.

THE CELEBRATED BELGIAN photographer Wim Hofmeister has disappeared from the island of Sagosia (Settlers Landing), the disputed territory in the Brown Sea. Mr. Hofmeister had gone there on assignment for the *New York Times* for a photo essay on the controversial medical treatment known as Viutex, which critics say reproduces the effects of heroin on a long-term basis, turning patients into what one doctor has described as *basically zombie.*

Mr. Hofmeister is only the latest in a series of high profile disappearances from the island, which was either purchased or forcefully taken over by the entrepreneur Elias Brynn Mrdok five years ago and has since attracted a large number of celebrity inhabitants, such as the disgraced hip-hop artist Lil Bigfoot, currently on the FBI's most wanted list for allegations of sex with underage women. The former Australian Prime Minister Sanford X. Foster also disappeared from the island more than a year ago. Australian authorities claim that they have been in regular contact with the fledgling government and police force on the island, but have been actively prohibited from entering the island themselves to conduct their own investigation.

Sagosia, as the island was formerly known, was an overseas territory of the United Kingdom until it was acquired by Mr. Mrdok. While the terms of the island's purchase have never been made public, sources say that it was forcefully acquired by the eccentric entrepreneur via a highly engineered hostile takeover of Sagosia's national bank that essentially denuded the island of its assets and forced its remaining British residents to flee to the nearby semi-autonomous island of Pembroke. Since taking over, Mr. Mrdok has declared national sovereignty over the territory and, in a highly publicized ongoing campaign, has renamed the island Settlers Landing. Mr. Mrdok's project has involved the participation of a number of billionaires who have since relocated to the island in what some have described as a high-profile pyramid scheme. In addition to conducting medical tourism, chiefly with its Viutex treatment which has been deemed an illegal narcotic virtually everywhere else in the world, the island's economy has benefited from the discovery of nucleite in its nearby waters. While the environmental effects of offshore drilling are still not known, critics contend that the native populace has been slow to benefit from the changes brought by the new residents, and that a significant number of the native population is discontented with the new quasi-government's failure to fulfill many of its initial promises, citing a number of delayed housing and infrastructure projects, and that the great riches that the island is thought to be currently yielding have yet to trickle down to its original inhabitants, most of whom subsist well below the global poverty line.

As of this morning, Mr. Mrdok and his representatives have yet to respond to our requests for comment.

34.

From the *Journal of Flatulist Studies*, Vol. 9, No. 107, "Reviews," p. 197-198:

THOSE WHO MIGHT have known Gordina Orlanda in her previous embodiment as Gordon Abu Lary Whiteman, who notably took second prize in the millennial World Farting Championships held in the Finnish town of Utajärvi, are likely familiar with the artist's transitioning, documented in her best selling tome, *Man Enough to be a Woman, Woman Enough to be Gordina*. Disappointingly few of those pages were devoted to Ordina's vocational proclivities as a flatulist, but for those adherents of the form, she is widely celebrated as an icon. Early on, her sphincter's undeniable prowess was devoted largely to enriching the musical theatre craft, with often unusual choices, such as several lesser known Sondheim compositions as well as a memorable concert rendition of the fateful Pitchford-Gore musical version of Stephen King's *Carrie*.

But it was her steadfast refusal to hone in on the melodiousness cultivated by other, lesser flatulists, and her stubborn insistence on the essential percussiveness of the form that cut her from the cheesecloth, in some critics' eyes, of the neo-primitivist, bent on using her anus as almost a blunt instrument with which to excavate hidden tonalities within the compositions she attacked from below. Few of her competitors in the field had the gall to use their rectums in this rather deliberate fashion; even fewer could compete with her sustained attack on the supposed purities of the Western tradition of the form, as Orlanda was one of the earliest adapters of the notoriously difficult *heppiri-otoko* techniques from Edo-era Japan, which viewed the anal cavity as a sounding horn for neo-Confucian social harmony, and often imbued its flatulist iterations with a Shintoist restraint that can come across as understated to untrained Occidental ears.

Indeed, legions of lesser, mainly cis-male farters in the ultra-competitive field have often grudgingly kotowed, whether publicly or privately, to Ms. Orlanda's diva status. So it should come as no surprise that since transitioning, Gordina Orlanda has pursued vocal training while simultaneously carrying her natural talent into a newly emergent state. In her recent performance of *Don Giovanni* at the newly inaugurated Settlers Landing Opera House, which I was privileged to attend, Ms. Orlanda has broken new wind by combining both of these talents into a singular performance.

Her depiction of Donna Elvira as a gassy seductress, well-equipped to use that powerful fulgent horn beneath her hoop skirt to spew her bitter disdain at having been scorned by the titular nobleman, certainly alters conventional understandings of the character as a victim of seductive forces beyond her understanding. With her fartations and queefings in full effect, Donna Elvira, as depicted by Orlanda, instead comes across as a feminist force of nature, adept at using her fanny as both flower and firearm.

While some of the audience members seemed all too eager to dismiss Orlanda's rectal resonances as mere novelty or else as decorative appendage to the operatic performance, there were also those of us who recognized that we were witnessing the ripping of an entire new form. There were even moments seemingly orchestrated for the ears of the flatulist connoisseur alone. The wind cut at the commencement of the Mi Tradi aria, for instance, with its pickled brashness culminating in a multihaired tenacity, evinced a nod to the Irish braigetoire tradition, with its spud-fueled bass inflections. Crepitationary stylistics aside, the most lasting contribution of Gordina Orlanda's to the ever emergent flatulist tradition will likely be seen as her provocative act of transmitting this fart form into the operatic fold, thereby endowing it with an interdisciplinary aroma.

Orlanda's performance was not without pathos. But can we really dismiss such endeavors as pathos when they are so virulently sustained by technique? The debate seems to settle itself in the final moments of the above-mentioned aria, whose sung completion is then endorsed with a sustained note whose emittance encompassed nearly a minute and a half, a gravity-defying feat that can only inspire awe among the more athletic plowers of the field (here, we must note the efforts of UK-based flatulist Mister Methane, whose attempted reinterpretation of Queen's Bohemian Rhapsody tragically resulted in a fulminant defecation.)

Having been absent from the stage for more than a decade, Gordina Orlanda's performance must be seen as more than just a triumphant return to a discipline for which she was seemingly born: that artful promulgation into the surrounding ether of what prominent fartologist Ji Dawson, in his legendary study *Blame it on the Dog,* sagely identifies as three-fifths nitrogen, one-fifth hydrogen, one-tenth carbon dioxide, and small amounts of methane and oxygen. Positing the body's potentiality for singing out of two, possibly three orifices in harmonious simultaneity, Orlanda's haunting emanations of *crepitans ventus* can ultimately be seen as a performative gesture of queer temporality, wherein the transsexed body's irruptive phallocracies and perceived failuretics are ultimately rehabilitated in a highly politicized project of what postcolonial flatulist scholar Aram Beck Rhinehart has deemed the post-aromatic ecological axis, wherein ass soundings are ultimately detached from their scent and thus enabled to attain political agency through the autonomy encapsulated in the collectivity inherent in their iterative eruptions. In this quasi-idyllic *fartocracy,* that is in many ways mirrored by the utopian aspirations of the Settlers Landing project (in which Orlanda has been ordained Ministress of Culture), the deficiencies of the current world order are both ruthlessly rejected and ultimately embodied, launching the fartee into an orbit in which the neoliberal nightmare of digestion-as-death cycle might be transformed into a recovery of selfhood, of unity in multiplicity. At least those were the thoughts that first came to mind when I exited the opera house that night and took my first whiff of fresh air, as the night breeze of the Brown Sea washed over me and my fellow viewers, in a state of transfixation— and trans-fixation, the stunning aftereffect of Orlanda's fluttering and effervescent phenomenology of fartation.

35.

THE PASSAGE WAS uncannily smooth this time, like a six-hour slow slide over a patch of thick ice. Harry's done it, what, at least six times by now, but it's usually rough, riding against the wind each and every voyage. Today there is no wind and that means calm before the storm. Harry knows it well. What that means in local translation… he figures time is about to tell him.

The building Nelson Rodgers has now taken to dwelling in resembles a shabby West Palm Beach motel last renovated some two decades past, if ever. Not even an elevator to take you up to the fourth floor, you just have to make your way up an outdoor concrete staircase with chipped paint railings, specks of birdshit and bubblegum blackened with age.

The front door a faded pale yellow, paint chipping. Paint chipping everywhere, it seems, as though chipped paint were the defining feature of the overall design.

Harry knocks.

—Who's it? calls out the muffled voice of broken despondency.

—The one you're expecting, Harry's inevitable reply.

The door cracks open but with no face on the other side to greet. Harry pushes it ajar. Nelson already at the other end of the dim hallway, walking toward the light at the end of the room.

Harry moves past the cardboard boxes, some empty others half full of document binders, one filled with broken wood, the likely remnants of some ancient chair or other piece of furniture preserved for sentimental value alone, piles of suitcases, a brass Buddha statue. On the wall, a poster with a blown-up photograph of a flea, a cartoon bubble coming out of its mouth saying *Forgive me!*—that one came with the place, Nelson tells Harry when he sees him observing it. The kitchen opens on to this living room, and inside, Harry can discern an ancient toaster oven sitting on a stack of old *Guardian* newspapers, an electric water kettle, likely the only thing in that kitchen that's ever been used, and on the floor, a bunch of rolled-up carpets.

–I see you're still moving in.

Five years on, Harry believes the correct term for it would be *clinical depression.*

–I know it doesn't look like it—half of Nelson's on the sun-drenched balcony, the other half in the shade-drunk interior—but I'm doing quite well.

–Well that's good to hear. I mean, you seemed to be before. It's just… Well, this is the first time I've been treated to a glimpse of how you *live,* if that's the right word for it.

–This is all temporary, Harry. I think you of all people should realize that. Now tell me. How are our friends on Sagosia doing?

–Funny you should mention that…

–Well why else would you be back here so soon?

–I think we could say they've seen better days.

–Yes. Then again, most of us have.

–Why don't we go out on to the balcony, Nelson? Seeing as how the seating options in here are… rather limited.

Outside, Harry gets a direct hit of all that Vitamin D3 cascading orange goodness.

–This table—Harry knocks on the wood with his knuckle—made from a six thousand-year-old banyan tree. Of all the things I was able to bring with me…

–Well don't get all sentimental on me *yet.* I come bearing good news.

–Oh?

A most skeptical vowel intonation that was. But Harry goes on undeterred.

–It seems like our friends want to have you back.

–… Our friends?

–Yeah. You know. The usurpers.

–Well. They're maybe *your* friends. Certainly not *mine*…

–Come on, Nelson. This is pretty good news, don't you think?

–No. It's not.

–I thought you'd be… I don't know. Maybe a *little* excited…

–How stupid do you… What kind of a *fool* do you take me for?

–Is there not, potentially, something that you want *embedded* in that offer?

–I can't even begin to put together the pieces of what you might be inferring—

–I'm talking a homecoming, Nelson.

–You're talking, what, walking into the jaws of death, I believe. Would you like some tea, by the way?

–I don't want any of your English tea.

–You'd better take something. You're not going to leave here with anything you came for.

The expected fulminations. Everything going perfectly according to Harry's plan.

–What I did was I told them you had infiltrated their visa office here.

–… You did what?

–So now they think—

–What on earth are you talking about, Harry?

–I. Told. Them. You are secretly running the Settlers Landing visa office. That you have infiltrated it—not directly, of course. But with your people.

–Why would I bother doing such a thing as that?

–Put two and two together, Nelson. So that you could get whoever you want over there. That you can—even more importantly—keep those who you don't want out. So that you can, in a sense, stage a coup.

Nelson opens his mouth as though to laugh but it is only a choking sound that comes out.

–Now I feel sorry for you.

–Why is that, Nelson?

–Because you are doing these things, clearly, in the hope that I will go along with them. That I will become a part of your little, what is it that you're doing, this, this, *masquerade*…

–Hey, I'm looking out for *both* of our best interests.

–Ha! It is hard for me to fathom that a word of truth has been uttered from your jaws since the moment you walked in here. Do you want tea? I'm making tea for myself. If you're having some, speak up now.

–I don't want any tea.

He really doesn't. Harry hates tea. Never could fathom why any-one would want to drink it. He's not even that much of a coffee drinker, truth be told. Have a cup every now and then, but not the type that needs to pour gallons down their throat in order to start the day.

Nelson rises and speaks to Harry behind his back as he makes his way into that cave that was once a kitchen.

–I'm going to have one cup. One cup of tea. And by the end of it, you'll be gone.

Don't get your hopes up, Harry thinks but doesn't dare utter out loud.

–Tell me something, Nelson.

–What.

–… Nothing.

–Well, what in the bloody hell is it, then?

–Were you ever married?

–No. Why would I want to go bothering about with that for?

–So it's true, then.

–What.

–That you're one of them… aristocratic old English homosexu-als.

–I never said that.

–Well what is it then? All those years on that island and you never got any nookie?

Nelson sips his tea contemplatively.

–I hardly suffer from the afflictions suffered by most men.

–What does that even mean?

–Oh, forget it. You're not worth the bother.

–You can open up to me, man. I'm from a different generation. Young people now, we're like fine with gay people. I mean, we're practically required to suck at least one dick before we even graduate from—

–I refuse to be intimidated by you. Just as I refuse to be intimi-dated by that Mrdok and his ridiculous cohort. They'll get his sooner than I ever will. The quasi-natives, the good people of Sagosia, they hate him far more than I do.

–Yes. And they're also without resources.

–The fall of man.

–… What?

–This whole story. This thing we're living through. It reminds me of the ancient myth. The fall of man.

–The fall of man? I haven't heard this one.

–Really more of a Biblical trope. Genesis, chapter three... Surely you've heard of Genesis? I don't know what they teach you these days in America, probably very little of any bloody use...

–We don't learn the Bible. We have separation of church and state. Although of late it's been withering.

–But surely you've heard of original sin? You don't have to be entrenched in Calvinist doctrine to know that one. Anyway. It gives one pause to think. The quasi-natives, what they must be going through right now...

–Suddenly you care so much for them.

–What do you mean.

–When you were vice consul...

–That was never my official position.

–When you, okay, whatever. When you ruled over the island, when you embodied British presence. You didn't seem to give much of a, how do you people like to put it, you *didn't give a toss* for them.

–Have your bloody CIA cronies not bothered to inform you about my academic work? If anyone could be said to have an abiding, deeply profound knowledge and interest in the ways of the Sagosians, well... I can't think of any other person, really...

–How modest of you, Nelson. But here's the thing. I'm afraid you don't have much of a choice in the matter.

–And I suppose you're about to tell me why that is.

Says it in a way to make clear how utterly bored he is with the entire situation, how indifferent to its outcome. To emphasize how much of a favor he is now doing Harry by even entertaining him in his dwelling hole.

–Because I don't, either. I have to go back there, whether I like it or not. And I can't go back empty-handed.

–Buy them a nice gift. Something hard to come by in Sagosia. Oh, I quite forgot—they have everything there except for dignity and integrity, don't they? Which aren't so easy to come by in material form.

–You can save your poetic witticisms for the boat ride over. I'll welcome the entertainment. It's not exactly a fun smooth passage.

–I. Shall. Not. Go.

–You. Don't. Have. A. Choice. Really. This is the American government you're dealing with now. You really don't want to fuck with them.

—Oh bugger off. I am a British citizen.

—You're not anymore, Nelson. You're in limbo land. You have been for some time now.

—What are you—

—You might as well accept this helping hand. Reaching down to, to pull you up out of this. Look at the way you're living, Nelson. Is this really the life you anticipated for yourself at this age? A stately old queen like you?

—And so what exactly are you promising? You're going to, what, somehow return everything that's been lost to me?

—I'm not the one to make you empty promises.

—Who is? Your Uncle Sam?

He will indulge these displays of irony and sarcasm, Harry, because he has also given his fair share to his interrogators and all the other men and women and others who have handled him these past months, years. He can also feel empathy. He knows that the ordeal that Nelson will undergo will be something akin to his. And Nelson is, what, twice his age, if not more…

—From what I gather, it's gonna be like a three-part exercise. All very well choreographed. We have the best intelligence in the world, after all. Even your MI5 relies on us. Can't even scratch their own goddamn pale asses without making a call—

—Three-part exercise. What on bloody earth are you saying?

—Okay. First, it's probably going to be jail. A very, very comfortable jail. See—

—Wow. You've bloody well won me over. Let me just get to packing—

—They don't have official jails on Settlers Landing. What they have is a, it's like a high-end detention center. For elites. Like—

—Political prisoners, I believe is the term for it.

—Yeah. Something like that. There's not torture, you get very good meals—

—Will you get on with it, then? What is part two? Chemical castration?

—Part two is likely—very likely—to be some sort of public statement. Along the lines of, showing your support for their project, for what Mrdok is doing there. Saying that you, the British government, you have no intention to get involved—

—I do not speak for the British government.

—A concession, of sorts.

—A humiliation. Of sorts.

–Whatever. Call it what you want. And then, the third thing, which is very exciting… We are going to knock that bastard out of power. He is going to be out of there, and—

–And the old Sagosian system and regime restored?

–… Almost! But not exactly.

–You want to know something interesting about the Sagosians?

–Why not.

–They don't have a word for goodbye in their language. Because it's such a small island, there is no way you aren't going to see the person again. In fact, it's likely you'll see them within the hour. So there's just no need for such a concept, let alone a word to denote it.

–I always learn such fascinating facts from you, Nelson. So have you started to give some thought as to what you want to take with you? We can allow one suitcase. A *big* suitcase.

–You dire prick.

–Come on. I thought you'd be in on this. What happened to the spirit of vengeance?

–It fades away with age.

–I don't believe that.

–Now I see how limited the Bible was. In its understanding of man. Our species. What it is truly capable of.

–How is that?

–That the fall of man would be supplanted by the rise of the middleman. A new species, risen to overtake the old.

–We've got them by the balls. They're paranoid. They're convinced that the island is crawling with spies. With *your* spies.

–I will not sacrifice myself.

–I thought I was clear that you did not have a choice in the matter. I have come here to take you back. I'm just trying to make this as painless as possible.

–And if I scream?

–You and I both know you don't have it in you.

Nelson stares out there. Down on the harbor another passenger boat was coming in, this one loaded with likely daytrippers from Croatoan, the closest island to Pembroke that is not Sagosia. Beyond that, Sioua, another island. Beyond that, yet another island. It's a whole chain of tiny islands, this part of the Brown, and Nelson has been to most of them, and he used to be able to elucidate well their idiosyncrasies and numinosities to the rare voyager who was curious to listen, but so few come round anymore that have the same anthropological interests as he once did. They all come now to preen and exploit then leave. Nobody cared, the dialect the Siouans spoke that bore some similarity to that nearly extinct patois of the Roanokeans, and since arriving here, Nelson had crossed that threshold of hope that might have once sustained these esoteric interests. Nobody cares. Nobody ever cared, except for he, Nelson, and he'd be gone soon, and what then? Now, he really just wanted to be left alone. But a part of him still clung to that idea of fate indoctrinated in him as a boy so long ago.

Now he looks back at this young man, this boy, who has come to deliver it to him.

—You're pathetic. I hope you realize that, Harry.

—I might have noticed it once.

—How long will the whole process take, might I ask?

—It'll all be over in a couple months.

—By whose guarantee?

—By no one's, of course. This is a classified operation. Surely you don't need me to spell that out to you, Nelson. You're a clever guy.

—If any of it goes wrong…

—Are you saying you don't trust me?

—Oh bollocks. Your own people don't even trust you.

—That may be true.

—Just give me one moment out here. To myself.

—I can't go any—

—You don't have to leave the bloody apartment. Just go inside. I want a last moment alone out here, to take in the view. Before I submit to, to prison, or whatever it is I'm meant to…

—Well. As long as you don't jump.

Nelson looks at Harry's shadow descending. He looks back out at the harbor, to the idiot passengers, the tourists and their ilk alighting upon the concrete, being absorbed into the hawkers, the cheap eateries and ticket offices and car rental storefronts. Then he looks down at the crumpled tea bag in his cup and he wonders if he'll see this, any of this, ever again.

36.

—DO YOU THINK you deserve this?

—What?

—This life you're leading. The island even.

—You were the leader of an island yourself once.

Dildonic pewterage of light cascading through the barred windowsill. The thrush of amber maybes that sift through the cracks of this makeshift prison wall, grayness of interior matching grayness of exterior—pale offerings of a natural world still staining the memory crags.

—I was the *lawfully elected* leader of a country recognized by others as such.

—So many fine words. And nobody to hear them. How sad.

—You're somebody. You're hearing them.

—But I'm not, you see. Times two.

—Then what are you doing standing there talking to me then?

Standing there in gray uniform drabness, a world awash in gray, no markings to identify neither role nor name. Decision was taken long ago to reduce the signifying of the policing presence to bare discernment. No excuses to be made in the channeling eyes of the unseen all-controlling.

—You never told me how you arrived here.

—Suddenly you're interested.

—You might say that.

The captive moves silently across the cell, inserting his foot into the square of light upon the floor like it's some kind of pond, then quickly removing it back into the safety of shade.

—From the moment we both… *occupied* this situation… I've been listening.

—An interesting way of putting it.

—Maybe I want to know something only you can tell me.

—About? For instance?

—I don't know. Australia. For instance.

The captive sighs all the mothball-laden misery out of his lungs like a crude melody sung by a tone-deaf prairie creature.

—I arrived here like most people in my position do. To the tune of a promise.

—I hear you.

—I had to check it out, at least.

—You and our president go way back.

—Your president.

—He's yours, too, now, it seems.

—Ha.

—Was it he who personally invited you here?

—The irony.

—You fucked his wife. Ex-wife.

—Is that what you think?

—Word on the street. Is it true or not?

—What word? What street? What does it matter?

–Matters to him at least.

–So then why doesn't he come here and talk to me about it?

–Maybe he will.

–He would have by now. If that were his true intention.

–It has to be something more than that. You're obviously a criminal.

–By whose definition?

–By the laws. Of this island. This… country.

–I don't think *you* even believe the words you're uttering now.

–If I didn't, why would I be saying them.

–How did *you* come here?

–I was recruited.

–Recruited?

–You bet.

–From your… glorious army.

–America's army. True.

–Which… I imagine you were kicked out of. What is the word? Discharged.

–What is it to you, mister? At least I've… regained my ground. My position. Unlike you. Mister… *Ex*-Prime Minister. Now prisoner. Under *my* guard.

–So you were *recruited*. As was I, in a sense.

–No, you were *lured* here.

–Give me a break. We were both *lured* here.

–Don't try that with me. Thinking, what? You're going to establish comradery? Please. I've been *trained,* you know.

–Trained to kill.

–Trained to *guard*. Among other things.

–What will you do when they come for me?

–Who?

–The soldiers of *my* country.

–That boat has sailed. Don't you get it? No one's coming. They've forgotten you. They don't care.

–I don't believe you.

–It's true.

–I've been trained too, you know.

–Trained how?

–In how to be a hostage. The leader of every country in the free world is. We're the most vulnerable, most valuable targets.

–Really. What is it they teach you?

–Well. One of the things is not to believe it when they say no one's coming for you.

–Ha.

–That the way has been blocked.

–Those were rules written for a situation as it existed back then. Not this situation.

–… You may be right.

–Of course I am. The sooner you admit it to yourself…

Phone vibrates. He looks at the screen, reads the message, puts it back in his pocket.

–What is it?

–Nothing that concerns you.

–Is it your wife? Are you married?

–I said it didn't concern you.

–Barbra Browneye. That's what we used to call her. Used toshave down there, don't know if she still does. Probably too busy. Maybe gets it waxed.

–You know I can't protect you in these circumstances. When you speak this way.

–Had the cutest little butthole. Would wink at you from under her meat flaps, when she'd lie on her back. That's how she got the name. Barbra Browneye. I had her, I think Mrdok had her… Hell, the whole free world had her. Look at her now.

The guard smirks.

–Free world.

–Well, what?

–Nothing, it's just… You've said it, what, like twice now.

–That's where I come from. You as well. We're both a great distance from it now.

–You especially.

–I'm somebody.

–And I'm not?

–No. You're a hired gun. That's all.

–And that's not *somebody*? In what? Your illustrious book?

–Illustrious. Now that's a big word for a US soldier.

–You're a bunch of convicts. That's who you descended from. Castoffs. Criminals and lowlifes who were castigated, thrown out of society. It's your lineage, not mine. And *I'm* the one who's a nobody?

–So you know your history. A little bit of it, at least. What, did you read the Wikipedia entry on Australia or something?

–I know what a nobody looks like. It's not me.

–Answer me this. What did they tell you I'm in here for?

–… They didn't tell me.

–I don't believe that for a second.

–No. Really. They don't tell me such things. It's not *my* job to know them.

–It is not your job…

–That's right.

So self-satisfied, the guard, in this simple declaration, again the captive is flooded with doubt so strong it is much the same gradient as the faith that fills the Christ fanatic at those moments when the threat of an encounter with mortality is at its peak.

–What is your job, then?

–My job is to guard you. To serve my country.

–As though those two things were somehow related.

–I took an oath.

–They actually make you do that bullshit here?

–Stop laughing. If you keep laughing, I will stop talking, I will cease all communication with you.

–So your job is to simply… as you say, guard me. Though I'm behind bars, and there's surveillance—

–There is no surveillance on Settlers Landing.

–There's no… Wait.

–Settlers Landing is the twenty-first century's premiere surveillance-free state.

–You're telling me that camera right there, across from my cell—

–It is not an actual camera.

–What is it, then.

–It is an idea of a camera. Even in this, the one and only high-security detainment center, we respect the rights of all Settlers Landing citizens and visitors—

–It is a prison. Why don't you call things what they are? You're saying that there is no digital, electronic, whatever surveillance—

–No. There's not. There's just me. Surveillance of the human sort. If you can call it that. Which I wouldn't. I'm a guard. That's all.

–What is this then?

Gesturing at the camera.

–I don't know what it's doing there. Maybe it's just there to trick you.

–To trick me?

–Into believing there's surveillance.

–You're incredible.

–I can tell you one thing. If you want.

–Yes. Do go ahead.

–The food that you're getting…

–Yes?

–Is much better. Than what the other prisoners get. Than what I get, even.

–Well I haven't had any complaints about the *food*…

–No you haven't. You're probably used to it.

–To what.

–This kind of luxury treatment. Gourmet cuisine.

–Are you saying…

–You're being treated like a VIP. Like a distinguished guest.

–Tell me what it is the other prisoners get to eat then.

A silence now engulfs that vast space between them and then eventually unfolds throughout the larger darkness. Silence like a clown spectacle filled with somersaults and intentional tumults and the muted reverence that serves as the respondent come too late to the task of smothering the words that inevitably must follow.

–There are no other prisoners.

–But you just said there were.

–I didn't.

–What do the other prisoners eat, then?

A reverberation that startlingly resonates throughout that humid gray dimlit concrete wall ceiling'd structure following the guard's banging something unseen and probably unseemly against one of the bars.

–I take that to be a weapon of some sort.

–Believe me. You don't want to find out.

–So wait then… If I am indeed a VIP. That means it is your job to *protect* me.

–That's never what I was told. I am here to *guard* you.

–What if I were, when you're not looking, when you've drifted off to sleep, as I've notice you so often do… What if I were to, accidentally, *injure* myself… or do something worse… What would then happen to you?

–There was one other.

–One other what.

–One other prisoner. A girl. Woman.

–And what happened to her.

–She might still be around. Somewhere. (If she's lucky…)

–Did you guard her as well?

–Sometimes.

–Was she also a… VIP?

–Haha no.

–What's so funny?

–Because. She was a lunatic.

—A lunatic?

—She attacked our president.

—Oh?

—It wasn't anything very serious. Just sprayed him with some pepper spray.

—She was… a local? A citizen, as you'd probably call it?

—A tourist. Medical tourist.

—That Viutex stuff.

—Probably. I didn't ask.

—I didn't fuck her.

—Who?

—The president's ex-wife. Or current wife, for that matter. Any of his wives.

—Well that's your business then.

—So let me see him. To clear up the matter.

—Ha.

—When am I going to see him?

—That's for him to determine.

—This violates every international law known to… To modern diplomacy. I have done nothing. I am being held against my will here. And for reasons unfathomable. Reasons never even *communicated*—

—You are an enemy of the state. Of our nation.

He thinks he can almost hear the wind blowing out the window, but cannot be sure. The window up high a thin squiggle that only lets in a thin ray the length of a day.

—Describe the architecture of the building we are in.

—Why?

—I need a sense. Of where I am.

—It's a state secret.

—At least some semblance.

—I'm not good with words. Anyway, there's not much to describe. Nondescript, is what I'd call it. Behind a gate, with a guard to lift the barrier and let you in if you present the proper documentation. People coming and going. That's all you see from the street. The same concrete grayness you see in here.

—So it serves other purposes, this building. It is not just a prison.

—I cannot tell you that. But from the street, it would raise no… suspicions. It just looks like any other drab government building, where boring bureaucratic business takes place.

—Is that what this is? Boring bureaucratic business?

—In a sense, yes. Until…

—Until what?

–Until the time comes when it is meant to become something more.

–What is that supposed to mean?

–When the instructions come from on high.

–When it is decided what on earth he intends to do with me.

–That too.

–And where will you be? On that day?

–I will be right here. Guarding you.

–Just like you did with that girl.

–No, says the guard. That was different.

–Different how?

The guard now looks at his prisoner with a regard bordering on sympathy, though not quite attaining.

–Different in a way you cannot know.

37.

IN QUALI ECCESSI, o Numi, in quai misfatti
    orribili tremendi
    è avvolto il sciagurato!

Pffffffrrrrp

    Ah no! non puote tardar l'ira del cielo,

Pffffp

    la giustizia tardar.

pfffp

    Sentir già parmi
    la fatale saetta,

Pfffrp

    che gli piomba sul capo!

Pffffffrrrrpppppffffp

    Aperto veggio
    il baratro mortal! Misera Elvira!

Pfffrp

    Che contrasto d'affetti, in sen ti nasce!
    Perchè questi sospiri? e queste ambascie?

Pfffrp

> Mi tradì, quell'alma ingrata,
> Infelice, o Dio, mi fa.

Ffffrrppt

> Ma tradita e abbandonata,
> Provo ancor per lui pietà.

Pffffrp

> Quando sento il mio tormento,
> Di vendetta il cor favella,

Pffrp

> Ma se guardo il suo cimento,
> Palpitando il cor mi va.

Pfffffrp pffrp frp pfffffffffffffffffffffffffffffffffffffffffffff

38.

THE NAKED MAN standing silent and placid before company headquarters at a certain hour each morning. The naked man who is no longer there, but his presence felt. An animal contains the knowledge that, just as it desires to kill and eat all those tender, fleshy beings lesser than it, so there must exist some larger being that sees it as its prey. Animals know this—there is always something potentially bigger out there, out to get you.

Cuba is useful in a way, as a model. Cuba: a tiny fish swimming just below a giant whale. The whale being the U.S. The land of freedom and big cars and the cheap oil needed to make them go. Place where there's no standing in line to receive rations. The Koreas have a similar dynamic going on.

That rogue employee who refused to be fired. Harry Hull. Followed us here, all the way to the other side of the void. And all for what? Well. For a lot, it turns out.

We realized, of course, that he had been sent here. Nobody comes and pulls a stunt like that on their own volition, standing there naked every day. Hiring him, sending him on this mission, was our way of buying time. So that we could determine what it is we were ultimately going to use him for. How to get the information we wanted out of him...

Swimming in the little duck pond. Two fishes, one a golden orange, the other deep dark hue of red-orange. Like to blot out the sun.

When you stare at them down there, chasing each other around, looking for their school. There is nowhere to swarm to. One day, pretty soon perhaps, a net reaches in, yanks you right out of the water, into who knows what choking lack of H20. You are wandering. Night doesn't care about your screaming eyes, how yellow you have become through these past few fears. Doubts hanging above you like chains you can grasp and pull yourself across the abyss to that other cliff where yet more uncertainties stew in the sleet driftage. Antique bottle rack with hanging bits of flesh belonging to an animal you cannot name for it resides thus far only in your dream, which makes no sense to anyone dwelling in the outside world, and anyway, you have no one left around you to explain such dreams to. You used to, to be sure, and yet where have they all gone? Chased away, into the sewers perhaps. You go online, to the sex sites, to look for a face you might recognize, a person once known. All that's there is a gallery of empty rooms; magical membranes in your eyelash. I myself have promulgated myself into serpentry at times. On the Chaturbate webcam, a man in a gorilla suit with crotch cut out revealing turgid micropenis. Where he is, it is wintertime. A season that no longer exists. Not where we are, where the fruit flies are able to multiply in peaceful nightstained airlessness. Place where the white collar proletariat packs its cheap suitcase and heads off into dereliction. Ratholes and collateral debt obligations, no-fee low financing, the mental geology of non-unionized collapse. Close that screen and go into another room, which features two kittens playfighting and not a single string of porn. The dingless transmission that takes place as fabrics fornicate gingerly and enunciate the holy rot before being given a screwless opp to satiate. Mock faciality let it ever be, let the flowtrap slam its doors behind you as you inch your way ever closer to the human target assigned by the forces beyond your immediate disposal. Factory forces, really, that have clamored on to you, in exchange for some molten negotiated release you know full well isn't worth the signature affixed to it, and yet honestly you can't fathom out any other way, so why not. Go forward, into this deep dark smear, these shadow cravings taste a lot like night and yet they are markedly indifferent to your hornful aspirations.

Flotilla across the still-moving waters. Galloping upon the sea, those horses moving toward the next body. Between devices, the standing nature of battle. Zoom in to a platform. A young man stands towering over an older man, their rival heights attune to the fluid duress, the lapping that is beneath them, and yet toward the horizon is where they look. They could be father and son and yet they are no such thing, they are merely a pale imitation of the life that has become. They are prisoner and captive, though in a way both prisoners of a reality too captive to entropic rhythms to ever embalm. The sea is beneath them, they are above this understanding, they stand there in agreement with their rival selves and they are each enveloped in separate notions of what it means to play a certain role in a combat operation both are too weak to ever claim victory over…

They are thinking about whatever it is they are thinking about, and a mammoth squid swims beneath them, munching on an octopus that will soon explode in the grip of the larger creature it can only gaze at from its remaining eyes, gaze at and experience what it is to be eaten—an experience so many of us crave but are so seldom able to engineer into being: the sultan and his little dance around his fears, the spaghetti western producer mainlining indifference into the colored spectrum of unaccented dub mistresses, the reality artist so-called drawing a picture of a mouse's face on to a name tag to be worn upon the chest before entering an over-air conditioned room populated by dolts and scourges adrift in the narrative tributaries of their own squander.

Ever sprung, ever pruned, ever collapsed in to wonder.

39.

WHAT I AM, as a matter of fact, is a good American. Because a good American, in my book, is a good employer. And what I'm doing is giving a job to all these army generals coming back from the wars of the past years—Iraq, Afghanistan—all these guys coming back from those shithole countries who can't find work, whose own country shows no appreciation for all the hard work they've done protecting America's freedoms. I take them and I say, you know what, guys? The rest of America might not realize your worth, those sons of bitches up in Washington might not have time for you. But I, Mrdok, I have time for you. And I'm going to put you to work, in the most exciting mission you're likely to experience in a long time. I am offering you a passport to a dream. That dream is Settlers Landing.

That Mrdok, what a wit. He knew how to lay it on thick when need be, America the beautiful, apple pie and fireworks farted out red white and blue from the stainless steel ass of the livid reincarnation of Uncle Sam himself. Maybe a microtad better than the propagandaspeak Gordina and everyone else was giving her, but still. Orangie Ambrosia now knew the real story. And once she told it, it was going to make her career.

She calculates in her mind that she is just crossing the six-week threshold of her stay when she literally trips over it. She had one too many drinks at the Wet Nasty where she had finally been granted an interview with this turd Mrdok and he spent half the night arguing with her and the other half ogling her tits. Now she is wobbling her way back to the hotel when she dives her arm into her purse for her phone thinking she might have forgotten it back at the bar and then, feeling some unpleasant wetness in there (for she had stashed the uneaten portion of a peach cobbler from her dessert that night at Eat This in her purse and the lid of the plastic container that contained it had managed to loosen itself), startles her hand right out and, flinging it across the night, her faux pearl bracelet goes flying right into the sunflower display beside the park bench on the intricately (some would say disturbingly so) manicured street corner where she now finds herself. Uttering the word *fuck* aloud, she knows she is too unsteady on her feet at this point to embark upon the task with much in the way of balance, and so she casts her handbag aside and goes stumbling as gently as possible into the flower display, trying her hardest to step *around* the flowers rather than *on* them, not that there is anyone around to witness and take offense at her actions on the deserted streets of Olde Colonia at this ungodly hour, when her foot hits what feels like a piece of plastic or metal that is clearly not supposed to be there and sends her face first into all that florae. She lifts herself up with a brand new *fuck* and steadies herself on her knees, brushing the soil off her hands, and that is when she sees the broken remnants of the thing she had tripped over having landed on the pavement whence she just came: yellow and green shards the same shade as the flowers though clearly not made of the same material.

Orangie holds a green shard in her hand, trying to gauge the reality of this strange material, what its utilitarian purpose might be. A black circle she pries apart with her fingers, what is, it is unmistakable: it is a lens. She digs in to the flowers: all fake, all plastic. All with lenses embedded: cameras. The entire, wait. A wall of cameras in front of her, recording.

Plastic: a synthetic, thermoplastic, solid, hydro-carbon based polymer. Though oftentimes plastic is attributed to any synthetic material of a similar composition, one that is not necessarily thermoplastic. Whereas nucleite: allotrope of carbon that consists of planes of carbon atoms arranged in hexagonal arrays with the planes stacked loosely; a dry lubricant, substitute for lead. Though then there is nucleite-reinforced plastic, which is a composite plastic made with nucleite fibers; a substance marked by light weight, stiffness, sturdiness, strength, perhaps best encapsulated by the tennis racket.

Orangie Ambrosia stands now suddenly sobered by the realization that she is surrounded—not by any animate source, she is as alone as she was just a minute before on those 3 a.m. streets of the emptied-out capital. But that she is and has been all along observed, monitored, every movement of hers taken cognizance of by the hidden technology surrounding. That all the new settlers who settled here out of paranoia with the existing orders, the surveillance states at home that threatened their ability to make their money grow or else just afforded them the basic privacy they believed to have been lost, that this Edenic state of things promised has never really materialized. And how they were brought here: that she got from Harry Hull, former hacker from Mrdok's Belle Encoding enterprise: algorithmic design meets data harvesting, yielding total control over human targets known as settlers; combined with *this* discovery, well. What we have here, Miz Ambrosia now realizes, is a whole new type of colonialism that the world has never before seen: *algorithmic colonialism,* she'll call it. She will go home, not home, back to her hotel, gather her things, perhaps first check under the light fixtures for bugs, in old spy movies that's always where they're planted... She will write the story on the plane, it will be a bombshell, it is the key to everything, she now realizes: *Fake Flowers,* she'll call the story, or no, perhaps *Flowers of Sagosia,* no, too poetic, her editor will never go for it. Editor rarely accepts her titles anyway. What matters is content, the bottom line: that under the illusion of some supreme libertarianism, free from the supposed withered claw of intervention, the entire populace is unwittingly being remote controlled into a form of submission that no sovereign has been yet able to manage. This changes everything. It will bring Mrdok, the entire project, down for good, down to the place where he truly belongs.

A shot now rings through the hollow beige nocturne, and it is Orangie who goes down in the artificial foliage. It is the first gunshot ever to sound upon the island but, for certain, not the last.

For here is another. Another shot crackles and down Brynn Street comes running a young Sagosian, his eyes all ablaze from behind the medical face mask concealing his lower features. Doesn't even notice the dead journalist in the artificial foliage, he keeps running and running until the night eventually catches up with him.

INTERLUDE

A REAL BAD STORM

Scene One.

Upon a yacht at sea. Noise of thunder and lightning.
Enter a Captain and a Boatswain.

CAPTAIN.   Yo! Boatswain!

BOATSWAIN.   Captain! What do I do?

CAPTAIN.   The marines! The marines! Get the fuckin marines! Tell em we're all gonna die if they don't get their fuckin shit together!

BOATSWAIN.   Aye aye, Captain!

Enter Marines.

BOATSWAIN.   Yo, men! Get to it! You—take in the topsail. You—grab the captain's whistle. Blow it till your fuckin brains liquefy and leak out of your ears if you have to.

MARINE.   What's that going to accomplish, sir?

BOATSWAIN.   Fuck if I know. Just do it, officer!

MARINE.   Aye aye, sir!

Enter Ma, Barb, Lallyburt, Mrdok, Gordina, and other quasi-elites.

MA.   Pardon me. May I ask who's in charge here?

BOATSWAIN.   Get back down below deck, mister, if you know what's good for you.

MRDOK.   I don't know that you heard the man. He asked a simple question: Who the fuck is in charge up here?

BOATSWAIN.   You're making things worse.

GORDINA.   Well, I think it might do you a bit of good to calm down.

BOATSWAIN.   Sure. And let us all drown.

GORDINA.   Just remember who you have on board here. This *is* the president.

BOATSWAIN.   I'm more concerned with saving myself right now, lady—or whatever the fuck it is you're supposed to be. Unless the president has some powers that I'm not aware of, that can put a stop to a megacane that's about to blow this motherfuckin boat to smithereens. And if he doesn't, then frankly you might both want to consider bending over and kissing your sorrowful asses goodbye. Cos the way it looks now, none of us is gonna survive this non-figurative shitstorm.

Exits.

GORDINA.   Well, with that kind of attitude, he certainly doesn't have what it takes to be a successful settler. I'm so sorry you were subjected to that heinous display of theatrics, Mister President. As soon as we get back home, I'll be sure to arrange his execution on grounds of treason.

Exeunt.

Boatswain reenters wearing binoculars and starts shouting.

BOATSWAIN.   Lower the topmast, you imbecile! Lower! Lower! Jesus fuck, bring her to the main sail.

The sounds of puking and screaming from below deck.

BOATSWAIN. God, these annoying rich fucks. Where are my god-damn pills?

Reenter Lallyburt, Gordina, and Mrdok.

BOATSWAIN. Oh god, you again! What, did you not understand me the first time? What was I speaking, pig Latin? Or wait—did you come up here to throw yourselves into the sea? Please! Do us all a huge favor. Go ahead. Kill yourselves. I don't mind. We could do without all the extra weight on board.

LALLYBURT. Who in thuh sayuhm heyuhl er you callin fat, you yankee sunuvabiyutch?

BOATSWAIN. Actually, I take that back: don't jump in all at once. We don't wanna cause a tsunami.

MRDOK. Scum like you doesn't even belong to the human race. You're just another brand of toilet paper that happens to have legs.

GORDINA. Which, I can personally guarantee, will be in shackles the moment this storm ends!

BOATSWAIN. Yo, lay her a-hold now! Set the mainsail *and* the foresail! The wind's blowing us in the direction of the sea again, oh fuck!

Enter Marines all wet.

MARINES. Shit! It's all lost! There's no hope! Say your prayers, boys, we're all gonna die!

BOATSWAIN. What the hell are you waiting for—Christ to come back and shit on a cracker? Get back out there, motherfuckers! We're not dead till we're floating!

GORDINA. How curious—Barb and Ma are downstairs meditating. I had no idea Barb was into that kind of oriental mysticism. She must have picked it up whilst living in Japan. Maybe we should go join them?

LALLYBURT.   Ah do not tayke paht in that kahnda devul worshippin activity.

MRDOK.   Look at them! They're all drunk! All of them! And the ones who aren't are crazy. Fuck. Whose idea again was it to recruit our army and navy from that cheapo private security firm?

GORDINA.   He's obviously proven he is not worthy to serve in our illustrious armed forces. He'll be court-martialed and tried for treason upon our arrival back in Settlers Landing. If the sea doesn't swallow him first, of course.

MRDOK.   I don't want to die with all these fucking assholes!

LALLYBURT.   Ahma fixin to go'n see ifn ah can pray this dam storm away!

Mrdok and Lallyburt descend below deck. Gordina pukes all over her tits.

GORDINA.   Oh, god! How am I going to clean this up? It simply can't be over! After all we've sacrificed to get us to this vulnerable phase of our sweet evolution. If only Collins were here to look after me, or to at the very least immortalize this moment in verse! No, actually that would make our national epic a tragedy, which is certainly not what we were going for… I can't even get a signal on my phone to call him—no Wi-Fi, even! Godforsaken storm, spare us— or, at the very least, the grand genius at our helm!

Scene II.

Back on the island. Before Nelson's cell.
Enter Nelson and Harry.

HARRY.   Did you engineer all this?

NELSON.   I'm afraid you overestimate my faculties, dear boy.

HARRY.   Because if you did, all I gotta say is one thing: I'm impressed. Everything is destroyed! Well, just about everything outside of Olde Colonia, that is. But the capital got it bad, too…

NELSON.   Well it's not like I can control the weather.

HARRY.   No. You can't. But you must certainly have had an *idea*. When we were crossing over…

NELSON.   Well you've lived on islands long enough yourself.

HARRY.   I have. But I'm not a meteorologist. I'm not…

NELSON.   Look. I might know things. A thing or two. As has anyone who has lived on this island for any length of time.

HARRY.   Yet you stayed silent… You tricky son of a bitch.

NELSON.   Your smile betrays your tone.

HARRY.   Ha.

NELSON.   I have a feeling you're smiling for other reasons, though.

HARRY.   Maybe I am, Nelson. Maybe I am.

NELSON.   Where are they?

HARRY.   That's what we're trying to figure out at this precise moment.

NELSON.   Are they dead?

HARRY.   Lots of people will be. That much is for certain.

NELSON.   You're going to get me out of here, right?

HARRY.   I am working on it.

NELSON.   When will it happen?

HARRY.   Soon. Soon enough. But today, I have a visitor for you.

NELSON.   Who?

HARRY.   It's a surprise.

NELSON. Life is apparently full of them.

HARRY.   Well, if anyone has the right to voice such a sentiment…

NELSON. What if I were to say I have a surprise for you?

HARRY.   I would be… well, surprised. I am very hard to surprise, Nelson. I know almost everything there is to know at this point.

NELSON.   What if I were to tell you that I'm your father?

HARRY.   I wouldn't believe you.

NELSON.   As well you shouldn't.

HARRY.   I know who you are. Who you used to be, at least…

NELSON.   And who you are…

HARRY.   Well. Or who I will become. But that remains to be seen. Doesn't it?

NELSON.   I didn't take it for granted, Harry. You have to understand. But I did allow myself to get distracted. That's a thing that can
never be forgiven.

HARRY.   Indeed. Your nose was in your books. You wanna know
how many books Mrdok's read? You wanna take a guess?

NELSON.   I even offered to help him. In the beginning. That's the
absurd bit. At first I thought his intentions were... Well, I didn't
know it would turn out like this.

HARRY.   You and your romanticization of—

NELSON.   Oh, cut it out, Harry. You wouldn't understand, either.
The position I was in—my scholarship, my studies were *bigger* than
this tiny little island. So he went behind my back, with this Ma Lin
person, who apparently no one has even seen—

HARRY.   Oh, he exists, all right.

NELSON.   I don't doubt that. He and Ma, they took over the bank.
That's how they did it. Stole the island right out from under me, from
under *us*. Suddenly, the ground beneath my feet, what I had known
my entire life. Suddenly none of it belonged to me anymore.

HARRY.   You don't need to tell me all this, Nelson. We both know
what Mrdok is capable of. But there are also things he isn't...

NELSON.   Something you maybe don't know. Or you think you
know, but you actually don't. Do you not realize how I got out of
here? The quasi-elites, they have their narrative. That, finding out
about the, the usurpation, the *sabotage*, I just calmly packed my bags
and left. But it wasn't that simple, Harry. I thought... They tried to,
to bring me in. Presumably to where I am now. But I thought the
worst. I was pretty sure they were going to kill me. I escaped, Harry.
And you know who helped me? It certainly wasn't the other Brits,
the quasi-colonials. The few stragglers, they got out of here the minute the news about the bank takeover got out. No no, it wasn't
them. It was the quasi-natives. They're the ones, they... It was Vincent, who worked for me ever since he was a lad. It was a rotten
carcass of a boat, I would have drowned had I tried it on my own.

But he was able to get me to safety, to Pembroke. It was the quasi-natives who saved me, Harry. The Sagosians.

HARRY.   What a beautiful story. See? Colonialism aint that bad after all!

NELSON.   Oh, shut up, Harry. What do you know? You're just a stupid Yank.

HARRY.   Looks like our visitor just arrived.

Enter Prince.

NELSON.   Is that… ?

PRINCE.   You seein right, old man.

NELSON.   You're… How's Vincent?

PRINCE.   In a compromised position. We don't talk no more.

NELSON.   What about the storm?

PRINCE.   It's bad. But it worse out there than over here, on the island.

NELSON.   Do you think…

PRINCE.   I doubt they dead. But anyway, it don't matter. Cos they will be soon enough.

NELSON.   And your brother?

PRINCE.   I just told you. He aint part of our fold.

NELSON.   You know how much he means to me.

PRINCE.   Why you bring me here today?

HARRY.   Why don't you two figure that out for yourselves? I'm going to take a nap.

Harry falls asleep.

NELSON.   You were always burning things, if I recall. We almost had to commit you at one point.

PRINCE.   And now you be wantin my fire.

NELSON.   Well, I guess that's one way of putting it…

PRINCE.   The storm aint completely over, you know. It's gonna hit us again.

NELSON.   How many men does he have out there?

PRINCE.   You mean this building?

NELSON.   I mean his army in general.

PRINCE.   Three, four thousand. Tough to know the exact numbers.

NELSON.   And how many are you?

PRINCE.   You mean us Sagosians?

NELSON.   No, I mean the ones who are with *you*. The ones who are in this to fight.

PRINCE.   Maybe seven hundred fifty.

NELSON.   And does anything about those numbers sound off to you?

PRINCE.   My man Temwen is takin care of the west coast, from where they set off from. I got a text just before I comed in here. Said he saw the Barbra lady come crawlin back to shore.

NELSON.   So that's one we know who's still alive. And did they nab her?

PRINCE.   I told them not to even let her know they was there.

NELSON.   I see. You're not the same firestarter you used to be.

PRINCE.   I growed up. I found out who I is, what I meant to be doing here. I learned what it is to attain the spirit. The spirit of Yang Zhu.

NELSON.   Whose lesson is self-preservation. The body...

PRINCE.   It's about *xing*.

NELSON.   Yes.

PRINCE.   It's understandin what people is, Nelson. And who we is, as Sagosians. And payin tribute to that, through our rites. In our temple. Which is here. On our land...

NELSON.   ... which is under threat. And your brother?

PRINCE.   You keep askin. And I keep tellin: he done sold out to them.

NELSON.   I don't believe you.

PRINCE.   That's why he can't be no brother of mine no more.

NELSON.   Yet there are certain facts you can't evade. You both have the same mother. The witch.

PRINCE.   She aint no witch, old man. She just play one on TV.

NELSON.   But you must want to protect her, at least. Isn't she being sucked into Mrdok's nasty games, alongside your brother? Doesn't family mean anything to you?

PRINCE.   Family one thing. Faith a whole other.

NELSON.   What if I were to offer you my help?

PRINCE.   What you say?

NELSON.   Say I can get you weapons. Not just Kalashnikovs, gre-nades, AK-47s—the greatest hits of guerrilla warfare. What if I could also get you some twenty-first century kind of weapons? Real weapons. They're going to be coming at you with drones, with sonic warfare, all kinds of things you and your little ragtag team probably haven't even heard of. *Psychological* warfare.

PRINCE.   We done already become victims of that. I mean my people. Sagosians. Question for me what the outcome be. I know what you thinkin. You thinkin this gonna be returned to the status quo you know. But my people aint thinkin that. We thinkin revolution. We thinkin of takin things back to the way they was years before. I mean, centuries before. You get what I'm sayin.

NELSON.   Well, Prince. You know I have always been a man of my word.

PRINCE.   No you aint. No white man is. Look at you now. There behind bars. If anyone be in the position to be helpin someone else out… I think you got things mixed up.

NELSON.   Fair enough, then. Let's just say we are helping each other. Uniting against a common enemy. A perfectly legitimate arrangement. Why, allied nations do it all the time.

PRINCE.   So we a nation now? Sagosia is?

NELSON.   In my personal opinion, it always was. We were always just visitors upon it. Long-term visitors, to be sure. But visitors nonetheless.

PRINCE.   And you can do all this from behind this cell?

NELSON.   Oh I'll be out of here soon enough. You need not worry about that.

PRINCE.   Just the weapons. We don't want no Brits comin in here fightin beside us. We aint needin that kinda *help*, so-called.

NELSON.   Oh I can assure you. I am acting out of strictly personal interest here. The Royal Army will not be involved.

PRINCE.   Hmmm. So where these weapons at?

NELSON.   Harry will assist you with the practicalities. But let him sleep it off first—he's been going at it full throttle since we touched down just before the storm. In the meantime, go entertain our friends, you and your men. I trust you've already made preparations for a rather nice banquet.

Prince exits.

NELSON.   Harry, wake up! Time to bring me the other brother!

Harry goes and fetches Vincent.

NELSON.   Vincent! So nice to see you after all this time. I take it you've been here before? This building, I mean.

VINCENT.   Officially? No. Unofficially…

NELSON.   Now now. No need to be putting on airs around your old boss, is there now, Vincent? You and I go way back. Why, when you were just a boy…

VINCENT.   What are you doin back here anyway, Nelson? The outcome bein what it is…

NELSON.   I can see the confusion writ large across your face. I can't say I blame you. How could I? You saved my life…

VINCENT.   I didn't have to. I didn't want to see you die.

NELSON.   … I don't blame anyone at this point. We could say you're all beyond blame.

VINCENT.   I have to go eat dinner soon.

NELSON.   It's already the supper hour, is it? Hard to tell what time it is in here. They feed you well, I take it? I just saw your brother, Vincent.

VINCENT.   Ha. Prince?

NELSON.   Do you have another brother of whom I am unaware?

VINCENT.   He lucky he aint in there behind bars with you.

NELSON.   You and I, we go way back, don't we? But I didn't raise you to, to… become this way. To become a slave.

VINCENT.   Ha. You didn't?! What did you raise me to become, then, Nelson?

NELSON.   Your brother has gone and grown a conscience on us. What are we to do?

VINCENT.   Forget him, Nelson. He know not what he do.

NELSON.   Confusion seems to run deep in your family. A trait that, sadly, can be quite easily exploited. What does your mother the TV star think of this whole mess?

VINCENT.   You leave her out of this. Leave *both* of theys out of it.

NELSON.   To have given birth to such an ungrateful monstrosity of a son. Who has now gone and, what? Riled up an entire army. I don't suppose you have had anything to do with that.

VINCENT.   Nelson. I warning you right now…

NELSON.   You're what the Americans would call an Uncle Tom. But deep down, people who play such roles are themselves mired in confusion, Vincent.

VINCENT.   You don't need to take professor airs with me, Nelson. You might've done helped me good when I was a lad. I aint no lad no more. I got my own vision on things.

NELSON.   And where exactly has it led you? Into the tiger's mouth.

VINCENT.   What options did I have, Nelson? What options did I ever have?

NELSON.   Do you know what's about to happen, Vincent?

VINCENT.   What other options did I have other than to be a servant of whoever was gonna help me the most? All I doin is takin a salary. I don't get caught up in none of the nonsense. I might not have no freedom. But aint no one in this life got freedom. No one. I'm just as unfree as no one else. As youse behind those bars.

NELSON.   What's going to happen is that Australia is going to sail their fleet on to the island sometime in the very near future. It could be a question of days, it could be a question of hours. It's hard to tell exactly when. But it is a certainty. And then there are the corporate thugs who run the US, who have their own reasons for wanting to destroy Mrdok. And that's just the beginning… I mean, I don't want to talk too much about what's happening offstage. But with that girl-friend of Bobby's bringing in the Mafia on their whole illicit Viutex trade, well. The island's defenses can only hold so well, particularly when there's such a shoddy infrastructure with which to shield it.

VINCENT.   You know who I'm workin for? And you're tellin me all this stuff?

NELSON.   I'm telling you for your own good, Vincent. At least your brother still has some fight left in him.

VINCENT.   He don't want you around, either. My brother will burn your ass to the ground.

NELSON.   What does it look like out there? Right now?

VINCENT.   I don't know. I haven't been home yet.

NELSON.   So you're actually living in Olde Colonia?

VINCENT.   What's it to you?

NELSON.   I can't imagine the trailers—

VINCENT.   I talked to my mom. Over the phone. They's fine.

NELSON.   Well that's good.

VINCENT.   … but everyone else's trailer gone.

NELSON.   Bloody hell.

VINCENT.   You act like you surprised. How many times this happened on *your* watch? And now you come back here. Like you some
kind of savior.

NELSON.   The difference now is, Vincent, that *I* had a plan in store
for situations like this—

VINCENT.   Yeah. A great plan: more trailers.

NELSON.   Well at least I had a plan. Do they? Do they really? How
many storms have there been—

VINCENT.   Not many.

NELSON.   Not many. Not any like this. There hasn't been a storm
this bad in probably five hundred years. I know what's going on out
there, Vincent. Right now they're all in shock. But it's going to turn
to chaos in a matter of days, hours maybe. Once they see that there
is no help in sight for them. Once the quasi-elites all retreat to the
city and commence building their wall around it—if they haven't
started already.

VINCENT.   Now's the time for me to go.

NELSON.   Oh, have you been contracted to help them with the
construction, then? Go, then, dear uncle. That's my new name for
you.

VINCENT.   Screw you.

NELSON.   See you in Pembroke, Vincent. That is, if you make it
out of here alive.

Vincent goes.

Lilbig rapping from the balcony of his house.

LILBIG.   Come on up on these ruby red sands
            Come on girl and take dese coal black hands
            For a walk trew dis poet's park
            Don't worry baby I guide you through the dark
            To the room where the bed is and there aint no ghosts here

neither
Dese goddamn waves done washed away all the ether
And da bad vibes that were disruptin my prior flow
'm about to put a bullet in da ass of a son who done stole
my dough

Barb wanders in all disheveled from the shipwreck.

BARB.   Wow, that's such great music, I'm distracted. Wait… I was drawn in by that… But was it all a song? Where the hell am I? Storm blew out our Wi-Fi it seems, I can't even get the Uber driver to take me home. How long have I been walking now, an hour? Fuck. If only this were a dream. I don't even want to think about the state the capital is in right now. Thankfully my house is far inland enough— Here's that music again. Could it be Lilbig emceeing?

LILBIG.   Full fathom five the fucker lyin on da ground
    Own it like a pair of nukks yanked from da lost n found
    Pow pow in da face till I make you shit yo pants
    Yo granny lend you Depends but it's covered in ants
    Yo moneymaker's itchin, girl, you can't earn yo fix
    Get da Viutex solution, on yo knees, and suck dis—

BARB. ..I wonder if Ma liked rap music. Probably not. Doesn't seem like his thing. Anyway, he's dead now. With his daughter, probably, the lesbian, in hell. There with my son… At least that's what Lally-burt would say. At least I'll never have to see that redneck cowboy again…

Enter Harry and Nelson.

NELSON.   Finally I'm out of that hellhole. Took you long enough.

HARRY.   How does it feel to be free?

NELSON.   I wouldn't know.

HARRY.   Holy… *Who* is *that?*

NELSON.   Well, if it isn't Barbra Brunnei. Real estate wonder of the Far East.

HARRY. Daaaamn. I mean, I'm not normally into older chicks. But this one…

NELSON. She looks more lost than I am.

HARRY. Hey babe. Wanna help me spawn a new civilization?

Barb slaps Harry in the face.

NELSON. Why do I feel like that's going to be the first of many?

BARB. Get me the hell out of this, this wherever the hell we are. Get me to Olde Colonia. That's an order! I'm a senator.

NELSON. Does it look as though we have a car, my dear?

BARB. I know this one, the pervert who would always stand outside our offices exposing himself for breakfast every morning. But who the hell are you?

NELSON. Just an Englishman visiting, my dear.

BARB. Do either of you have proper clearance to enter the capital?

NELSON. We're just coming from there. I'm afraid it's all quite in disarray. Your soldiers don't even know who's rightly in command or what they should be doing. We managed to slip in right past them, nobody even checked our security apps.

HARRY. Where are you coming from, you sweet thing?

BARB. We were on a yacht at sea when the storm hit. As far as I know, I'm the only survivor. Swimming thirty laps a day for the last fifteen years, I guess it saved me in the end.

NELSON. Who else was on board this illustrious yacht?

BARB. Let's see… President Mrdok, Gordina, Senator Lallyburt…

HARRY. And they're all dead?!

BARB. Seems that way. Ma Lin, head of our national bank…

NELSON.   Oh how tragic.

HARRY.   Luckily the fairest of them all has been spared.

BARB.   Look, you little pipsqueak, I could be your mother…

HARRY.   And you could be the MILF of my dreams.

Barb slaps Harry anew.

NELSON [*Aside.*]   Clearly they've already fallen in love. [*To Barb:*] Look, I think the time has come for me to be honest with you, my dear. I am not, in fact, a tourist on your island. I am Nelson Rodgers, if that name rings a bell.

BARB.   Oh, you… What the hell are *you* doing here?! Security!

NELSON.   You can call all you want, my dear. The nearest soldiers are about three miles away, nestled between the boulders at the base of Baldheaded Mountain trying to figure out who's in charge among the survivors. They cannot hear your cries from here.

BARB.   I swear, if you try *anything*. You have *no idea* what kind of people I have access to—

NELSON.   Relax. I am not going to hurt you.

BARB.   Harry, get over here and protect me.

HARRY.   Does that mean we're, like, a thing now?

NELSON.   You've seen him naked, so at least you've seen the goods in advance. I know it doesn't look like much. But, given your current circumstances, my dear, there's one thing I can assure you of: He's your best bet.

BARB.   What do you mean?

NELSON.   Mrdok, Ma. Lallyburt. All the senators. Well, the ones who actually *do* something. (In that regard, we can forget the rapper for now.) They're all dead. Gone. Have you given any thought to what that means?

BARB.   … That I'm the next President!

NELSON.   Oh does it? And what if I were to tell you that you were about to get some visitors on the island? Visitors that, shall we say, you were never expecting, and most likely do not want to see arrive? How would you handle this, this *rapidly evolving* military crisis, Madame President?

BARB.   I would say…

NELSON.   Oh, and that storm we just had? It's left the scrappy homes of the quasi-natives in a state of total disrepair. The majority are now homeless, wounded, desperate, wanting… Above all, eager to know where those new homes are you promised them so long ago. Well, guess what. That's not all. Another storm is coming. One that is bound to be even worse than the one that just destroyed the island's entire coastline, not to mention a number of homes in the hills surrounding the capital where you live. The capital itself isn't looking so great, either.

BARB. [*Regally, presidentially:*]   What this island needs…

NELSON.   Has Mrdok even informed you about all the threats he's been sitting on? Why, look at your position on the map, Madame Brunnei. The archipelago surrounding is, shall we say, rather thin. Erase all those islands, which it is easy enough to do, and you are surrounded three ways: You've got Australia, the US, and Europe all coming at you at once. Which is precisely what is about to occur. Indeed, it is hard for such an alliance to resist when they are able to see you quite clearly at your weakest.

BARB.   And so you are saying…

NELSON.   I've got Europe and Australia on speed dial. Harry here is, well… It seems that after his last misadevnture with your former president, may he rot in pieces, he was recruited by a certain intelligence agency in the US in exchange for his freedom, so-called…

BARB.   Wait. This is a coup!

NELSON.   It is not a coup if it was never a real state to begin with, my dear. Be reasonable. What on earth was someone with your business savvy doing involving herself with someone of Mrdok's perilous ilk to begin with?

HARRY.   Not to mention someone so sexy.

This time, Barb restrains herself from slapping him.

BARB.   Okay, now that it seems I'm about to die, I'm a little less turned off than I was before. But not by much.

HARRY.   Does that mean I might have some hope of actually hitting this fine piece?

NELSON.   What I would suggest is that the three of us hunker down and come up with a plan. A transition plan, we might call it. Which does involve, well, we can *perhaps* call you Madame President... For now, at least.

BARB. [*Aside.*]   I barely trust either of them. But what can I do? Until I get back to the office, I might as well go along with it. [*To Harry and Nelson:*] Gentlemen, let's just call me Madame President-in-Waiting for now, until we have a better idea of where this is all going. Now do any of you have any idea how we might get back to Olde Colonia, whatever might be left of it?

HARRY.   No, my lady. But you do.

Harry presses an iPhone into her hand.

BARB.   What's this?

HARRY.   It's one of the only phones on the island that's working right now. Connected to a satellite that I am uniquely controlling.

BARB.   And who the hell am I supposed to call?

NELSON.   The one in possession of the other working phone, my dear. Your faithful servant: Vincent.

ACT II..

Scene 1.

Another part of the island.

Enter Ma, Lallyburt, Mrdok, Gordina, Rick Stewart, Merrill, and others.

GORDINA.   Well, just think. It could have been far worse. At least we escaped with our lives! It's a shame about Robinson, though. It will be hard to find another quasi-native we can trust to serve as the nation's Uber driver.

MERRILL.   The boatswain? That wasn't Robinson!

GORDINA.   It wasn't? Gosh. They all look the same to me.

MA.   Can you please stop talking?

LALLYBURT.   Mah dam ear's bout to fawl raht awf. Ifn ah hafta hear wun mo thang bout that thar wig he dun lawst…

MA.   Wigs and Uber drivers. My god. When just look at the state of this island!

LALLYBURT.   Ah do deklayuh. How in the sayuhm heyuhl re we gonna rebiyild awl thiyuhs meyuhss? Specially when we aint got Barbra Bruen nd her connexions.

GORDINA.   Might I utter just one more word?

LALLYBURT.   You jest dam seyuhd mo than wun, fanny pack, ifn ah remembuh how to count.

GORDINA.   Mister President, just listen to how these senators are heckling me! As the Ministress of Culture and Personal Assistant to the president of our fair nation—

MRDOK.   Just shut up, Gordo!

GORDINA.   It's Gordina.

RICK.   This constant insistence on the stupid name. What a little bitch!

MERRILL.   I take offense at that term.

RICK.   What? Bitch?

MERRILL.   Precisely.

MRDOK.   That's because she's a whore!

MERRILL.   Now that's a name I've never minded.

MRDOK.   Although, to be fair, she's more like a *former* whore.

RICK.   Well at least we've got one real woman among us. In case we need to, you know. Repopulate the island.

MERRILL.   Sorry, hun. That boat has sailed. I had my tubes tied ages ago, back when I was still in the industry.

LALLYBURT.   She's as barren as thiyus dayum ahland noyuw.

MRDOK.   How much am I worth? How much am I worth?

GORDINA.   Oh, you need not worry. Surely this minor catastrophe hasn't had any effect on our nucleite interests.

MA.   Let us hope not. I am rather sure I can still hear the drilling from afar. Though perhaps that's just the ringing in my ears from the yacht wreck.

GORDINA.   Here is everything advantageous to life.

RICK.   I must say. You are looking a lot more womanly since the wreck. It is as though a whole new you has been excavated from the ruins of your former self!

GORDINA.   Bitch.

MA.   If the nucleite is preserved, not all is lost.

MRDOK.   Can someone *please* just figure out a way to get us a car?

LALLYBURT.   We hahdly even no wheyuh we ah.

GORDINA.   Weird that my dress doesn't smell bad at all. See! That's proof that the nucleite isn't polluting the water at all… Actually, this is the same dress I wore to the funeral of Mister Ma's daughter.

MERRILL.   Gee! Don't bring up such dismal memories! The situation is bad enough as it is.

MA.   You cram these words into my ears against the stomach of my sense.

RICK.   What's he saying?

MERRILL.   Must be one of those Chinese proverbs.

MA.   I feel like I've lost two daughters now.

MRDOK.   How's that?

MA.   With Barb's death. We really bonded, after my beautiful daughter passed away. She also lost her son, a queer, to suicide. We had so much in common. I don't know how I would have gotten through it without her wise counsel. And now she's gone. Gone!

MERRILL.   Honey, I'm pretty sure she's still alive. When we were all busy drowning back there, I saw her battling the waves with a mean breast stroke. Something tells me she made it to shore before the rest of us. She's probably on another part of the island right now, thinking the same thing: that *we* didn't make it.

RICK.   And that *she's* now queen of the island!

MA.   There's no way. She couldn't have made it. I saw her go down.

MRDOK.   We've *all* seen that pretty lady go down…

RICK.   Haha! Good one, boss!

LALLYBURT.   Weyuhl. Ah guess this means the resort project is dam finished theyuhn. Ah caint even imagine what it's a-lookin lahk raht bout nayow.

MERRILL.   What are your ears stuffed with, tumbleweed? I just said I think she's alive!

MA.   Will you all please stop? You're just making it worse. Let the dead rest.

LALLYBURT.   Ah do hope n pray that in the moment befo the Lawed Gawd dun took her away, that she dun repented. Othuhwahz, it's hard for us to no whethuh shes in Heaven raht nayow ouh the othuh playce. Though puhaps that othuh playce is weuh she maht prefer to eynd up, seein how it's lahkly where her son iyus raht nayow.

GORDINA.   Lallyburt, you really are only making the situation worse by uttering such remarks.

LALLYBURT.   Ifn Reverend Billy is stiyuhl alahv, we cayn have im blessuh when we dun fahnd the corpse.

MRDOK.   What are you, some sort of spiritual surgeon? Cut my hair!

GORDINA.   Oh, Mrdok! What a wit!

LALLYBURT.   Weyuhl, ah do deklayuh. It seems lahk the only re-mainin senatuhs re raht heyuh. Xceptin for thuh neegrow.

GORDINA.   Yes. As we await the rescue mission, perhaps now is the time to convene a meeting on how we will resume our governorship of the island once all this is passed.

RICK.   Oh Gee, why don't you just take over?

MRDOK.   Good one, Rick!

GORDINA.   What are you saying, Rick? Are you inferring that I'm incapable? I'll have you know that unlike you, I actually have a title here on this island!

RICK.   Oh yeah! Ministress of Culture! So what are you gonna do, Miss Thing? Turn this into an artists' colony?

GORDINA.   Ideally, a society should evolve to the point wherein it no longer requires such distractions as arts and culture. I do see that day coming, coming quite soon, for our humble little island nation, gentlemen. And when that day arrives, we will all be the better for it. Because we will also be a classless society by then. No more us against them, quasi-natives versus quasi-elites...

LALLYBURT.   Nd how in thuh sayuhm heyuhl would you do that?

GORDINA.   Well, after expelling all the undesirables, I would begin by building a wall. A very big wall.

RICK.   We already have a wall!

GORDINA.   What we have now is merely a virtual wall. One that wraps itself around the capital. It has been highly effective to date. But do you really think, in this new chaotic state, that a walless wall is going to do the trick? No no no, gentlemen. What I'm talking about is the need for a sea wall. One that would ensconce and protect the entire island from what are, after all, pirates, when you get down to it. To keep all undesirables, all the rapists and murderers and drugs dealers and ideological degenerates, far far away from our sweetened utopia...

RICK.   Keep dreaming, sweetheart.

GORDINA.   A walled-in world that would see the final and total triumph of us quasi-elites! No more bastard class trying to bring us down.

MRDOK.   I don't think I'd want to live in such a world. Just imagine how boring life would be if we all didn't hate each other.

RICK.   And I don't want to live in a world governed by some blow-hard tranny!

LALLYBURT.   Weyuhl. Ah don't know bout yall. But ahma thankin if we start walkin nayow, we maht dun reach Olde Colonia bah nahtfawl.

MERRILL.   Hey. Does anyone hear that?

RICK.   Sounds like… hip-hop to me.

MERRILL.   … Could it be?

MRDOK.   I haven't seen Lilbig in days, now that I think about it.

GORDINA.   Rap music always makes me rather sleepy, I must confess. I don't know why.

MRDOK.   Go ahead and take a nap. It's gonna take us a while to figure out what to do next anyway.

All sleep except for Ma, Lallyburt, and Mrdok.

MA.   Well, that was fast. I wish rap music also had such an effect on me. I need a cure for my insomnia.

MRDOK.   Maybe now would be an opportune moment for you to tell us where the hell you've been these past few months.

MA.   Excuse me?

MRDOK.   You know the rules, Ma. Or do I have to spell it out for you? There's a residency requirement. Ten months out of the year. *Especially* for senators. We need you to set a good example…

MA. Actually, suddenly I am very tired. Guess those funky rhythms do the trick after all!

Ma falls asleep.

LALLYBURT. Weyuhl ah do deklayuh…

MRDOK. Fuck!

LALLYBURT. Must be the teymperachur.

MRDOK. Oh there's something in the air all right.

LALLYBURT. Weyuhl it aint havin no effect on me. Mah ahs er wahd opun.

MRDOK. Just look at them! I mean, how could someone in *my* position even *consider* sleep right now? Maybe it's for the best. I'm thinking, Lal, I don't know what's gonna happen until I, well, understand what happened. One thing is clear, though. I'm thinkin it's time you took on… more of a role around here. If you catch my drift.

LALLYBURT. Ahma startin tuh thank you're a little sleepy aftuh awl. Yourah soundin lahk somewun who dun took an Ambien piyuhl bout thirty minutes befowuh. Er you sure no one dun slipped you wun when you werent lookin?

MRDOK. I'm wide awake. And I suggest you be as well.

LALLYBURT. Whuht n thuh sayuhm heyuhl er you tryna say, Merdawg? You tryna put a crown on mah heyuhd?

MRDOK. Well, you know, this isn't really a monarchy, Lal. But what I think we can both agree on… is that… a *certain person*… cannot be trusted.

LALLYBURT. You aint need say nuthin further on 'n thayuht. Ah no exactly hoo yer tawkin.

MRDOK. Something else you might *not* have realized. I have it on good authority. That Barb's alive.

LALLYBURT.   Whose authawrity maht thayuht be? You got a dahrekt lahn to owuh lawed up in heaven abuv?

MRDOK.   Maybe I damn well do. If that is indeed the case: then where does that leave us with the Saudis?

LALLYBURT.   Oh lawed. Wah don't *you* tell *me*, Merdawg?

MRDOK.   Well what's that supposed to mean.

LALLYBURT.   Sumtahms ah don't know which role you enjoy playin mowuh. Doubtin Thomas or Jewdas Iscariot.

MRDOK.   I've never read the Bible, Lallyburt.

LALLYBURT.   Me n Barb nevuh believed fer one rattle uhvuh rattlesnake's dick yo story bout Ma and the Saudis. We dun new all along you was ether in on it ouh else you wuz jest coverin fo him fo some othuh inexplicable. So it's really been you and Ma tryna screw me and Barb through to thuh Saudis all along. Aint that thuh godfersaken truth now, Merdawg?

MRDOK.   Farthest thing from it, Lallyburt. Maybe you do need some rest. I can see this sun is burning up what's left of your brain cells. I know damn well how important the Saudis have been to your family's interests all along. I would never even consider doing something that would jeopardize that relationship—because that would then put us all in jeopardy. We have very few friends in this world, Lallyburt. And we need every damn one we can manage to hold on to at this point.

LALLYBURT.   Whuht ah wanna no is wheuhs owuh dam army when we need em.

MRDOK.   They're on their way, Lal. You don't have to worry about that. What I'd rather you *worry* about, is how to bring the Saudis *in* on—

LALLYBURT.   Merdawg, ahv had enuf of them Saudis today, mmkay?

MRDOK.   I am thinking a whole new position for you in my cabinet. Minister of Defense. How does that sound?

LALLYBURT.   Sounds lahk you dun jest went n lawst a sack uv youh mahbles.

MRDOK.   Why? Because I'm perceptive? Isn't that a quality most desirable in a leader? Any leader? Come on, Lally. I know it's hard to get the Texas out of the cowboy and so forth, but what I'm attempting to give you here is a very simple gift: the gift of leverage. On a scale you've never... Why, with my brains and your connections... Well, do I have to spell it out for you?

LALLYBURT.   Oh am afeard ah awready no the werds that're bout to cum pourin raht outa that hurtin soul uv yers.

MRDOK.   Hurtin soul? Well you get points for originality there. But really, Lallyburt, tell me one thing: Where exactly in the human anatomy is the soul located? Have they ever been able to find it? Because, you know, I'm a big believer in medical science, believe it or not...

LALLYBURT.   Nd ahma believuh in mah holee sayvyuh Jaysus Aych Chrahst.

MRDOK.   Right you are. And which your Saudi pals most definitely are not. But you know who they're going to come to worship even more than Allah? You, Lallyburt. You. Because you, my friend, are about to turn this little paradise into the world's biggest third party for the armaments industry. And I'm gonna have nothin to do with it! It's all gonna be you. Our Minister of Defense. Which makes you, pretty much, the number two guy on the island—although make sure that never gets translated into *Chinese*, if you catch my drift...

LALLYBURT.   Hm. Weyuhl. Ah do arpreciate un offuh. But raht nayow? Its jest un offuh. Tiyuhl we ken get back to drah layund...

MRDOK.   We're on dry land right now, Lallyburt. Have been for at least an hour. Maybe four. Fuck knows what time it is.

Gordina's phone rings. She wakes up and takes the call.

GORDINA.   Hello? Wait… My phone's working, everybody! Everybody! Check your phones! It's… Oh. Okay, then. I see… Well. I will discuss this matter with the president…

MERRILL.   Who is it?

GORDINA.   It was… I don't know.

RICK.   What the fuck do you mean, *you don't know*? Wait. How come his, her… *its* phone is working? Is everyone else's phone working? Mine isn't. What's going on here?

GORDINA.   It was… the representative of an organization. Of sorts. Apparently they have taken Olde Colonia…

ALL.   What?!

GORDINA.   I'm sure it's just a misunderstanding!

LALLYBURT.   Whuht misunderstandin?

MRDOK.   Who the fuck was it, Gordo? What's going on?

GORDINA.   The young man—or it sounded like a young man—that is, a cisgendered man of young age—identified himself as a representative of the Sagosian Yangist Liberation Home Front. If I got the name right (it's quite a mouthful)… It could also have been the *Young* Sagosian Liberation Home Front. I couldn't quite tell because of the accent…

RICK.   Quasi-natives?

MRDOK.   Fuck.

GORDINA.   They say they've captured Olde Colonia.

MA.   Well where is our army?

MRDOK.   That's precisely what we're about to find out. Gordo. Call them. Right now. Everyone else. Bunker down. It's going to be a long fuckin night.

MA.   Is that the only call you've received? Did you hear from Barb? Why don't you try calling Barb first, Gee?

MRDOK. [*Aside, to Gordina:*]   Why in the *fuck* does he care so much whether Barb is alive or dead?

GORDINA.   I'm on it, boss, I'm on it.

Scene Two.

Another part of the island.

Enter Vincent on the phone. A noise of thunder.

VINCENT.   No, of course I haven't seen him for days. Not since the storm. What? Well, how am I supposed to know what he's been up to? Yeah. Yes, he's my brother. No. No, we haven't spoken in weeks. You know who's behind this? I think? Nelson Rodgers. Wait. You didn't *know*? How could you not… He's here. On the island. That's right. Well, he was in the pri—In the *detention center*. The gray building. You know. Whatever… This is a secure line. This is… What? Oh fuck. I think I see, it must be one of his *spies*. Definitely not a quasi-native, and I've never seen him on the island before. I'm gonna go sort this thing out.

Enter Miki.

MIKI.   I only just got here, and what a storm! Sounds like another one's about to hit. Everything fucked! Now how will I ever find Gordo, the love of my life? I came all this way just to find him. Good thing he told me the name of the island when he was blackout drunk that night in Tokyo so many years ago… I haven't been able to get him out of my mind since. But first thing's first: How will I ever find this stupid hotel? God, I *hate* booking.com! Such lousy customer service. Whenever you call, nobody ever picks up. And mailing—forget it! God, everything is so fucked up here. I wasn't expecting it. It wasn't reported on the news. Then again, it *is* pretty remote here. And what's that fish-like smell? It stinks of fish everywhere! Could it be I got off on the wrong ferry stop? Oh I'll ask this guy, he looks local. He'll be able to tell me for sure where I am. Maybe even where Gordo is. It's a small enough island, I imagine. But those storm clouds… That would really suck if another one were to hit right after this last one. Looks like it's done a ton of damage already. I sure hope Gordo's okay.

Enter Makiko playing electric guitar accompanied by a drum machine blaring a blastbeat. She sings a grindcore song in cookie monster grunt vocals.

MAKIKO. Soon you all will die
      I'll fuck you in the eye
      Inject maggots in your brain
      Until you go insane

MIKI. Wow, this chick must be Japanese!

MAKIKO. I am the hunter, you are the hunt
      Pull the guts out of your cunt
      Stuff your femur down your throat
      Make you lick a llama's scrote

MIKI. [*Speaking Japanese:*] That's a really great song.

MAKIKO. [*Speaking Japanese:*] Oh, thanks. God, finally, someone I can talk to. You know I haven't spoken a word of Japanese since I landed on this island five years ago.

MIKI. [*Speaking Japanese:*] Do you often walk around with a mobile PA system and drum machine playing grindcore? Or is this just like a one-time thing?

MAKIKO. [*Speaking Japanese:*] I'm just trying to get some practice done. Never a minute of silence to blast through on this fucking island it seems. Now that I have my moment, I won't let it slip past me.

MIKI. [*Speaking Japanese:*] Amen, sister!

VINCENT. Well, that was too loud for me. I prefer the sweet melodies and chaotic intergenre mixes of hyperpop.

MIKI. Oh, you startled me! I saw you back there, but then when she started playing, I forgot all about you.

VINCENT. Damn. My ears are still ringin.

MAKIKO. [*Speaking Japanese:*] Don't talk to him. He's one of the quasi-natives.

MIKI. [*Speaking Japanese:*]   What are quasi-natives?

MAKIKO. [*Speaking Japanese:*]   They're like the Koreans or the Chinese. But worse. A docile people.

MIKI. [*Speaking Japanese:*]   I'm actually Japanese American. So racism kind of offends me.

MAKIKO. [*Speaking Japanese:*]   Oh, I'm so sorry. I had no idea. Your Japanese is so good.

MIKI. [*Speaking Japanese:*]   Well, thank you. But as much as I'm enjoying this conversation right now, I'd better go find Gordo.

MAKIKO. [*Speaking Japanese:*]   You mean Gordina?

MIKI. [*Speaking Japanese:*]   Who's that?

VINCENT.   I'm sorry, little man. Would you mind telling me who you are and what you're doin on the island? Times are a bit chaotic now, so… I kinda need to know.

MIKI.   Oh, so sorry! My name is Miki. And you are?

VINCENT.   Vincent.

MIKI.   Hi there, Vincent. Would you like some Japanese whisky? I brought some with me from home.

VINCENT.   I only drink when I makin marks.

MIKI.   What is that?

MAKIKO. [*Speaking Japanese:*]   It's like calligraphy, only they don't know that that's what it is. They use long sticks and black ink to draw on the ground.

MIKI. [*Speaking Japanese:*]   So you speak English?

MAKIKO. [*Speaking Japanese:*]   Understand it. Refuse to speak it.

MIKI. [*Speaking Japanese:*] Why is that?

MAKIKO. [*Speaking Japanese:*] My boyfriend is American. The only way I can stand him is if I don't have to communicate with him.

MIKI. [*Speaking Japanese:*] Sounds like a very complicated relationship!

MAKIKO. [*Speaking Japanese:*] Yeah. I guess. Not really.

MIKI. [*Speaking Japanese:*] Do you want some whisky as well? [*In English, to Vincent:*] We're opening the bottle, man. You might as well have some.

Vincent assents and downs half the bottle in a single gulp.

MIKI. Whoa.

VINCENT. Sometimes I want to think there's no such thing as oxygen.

MIKI. Well why would you ever want to think such a thing as that?

VINCENT. It would somehow make life easier, wouldn't it?

MIKI. That actually makes a lot of sense. Life *would* be a lot simpler without any oxygen...

MAKIKO. [*Speaking Japanese:*] What's he saying?

MIKI. [*Speaking Japanese:*] He is tired of life.

MAKIKO. [*Speaking Japanese:*] Alcohol often makes words like that come out of the mouth.

VINCENT. Man, you're right, this shit is good.

MIKI. Yes. Japanese whisky is the best.

VINCENT. Man, you should fuckin. You should sell some of this stuff here. Right here. On this island. On Sagosia.

MIKI. Sagosia? I thought this place was called—

VINCENT. Let me show you around. What is it you said your name was? You friends with her? With the… Maybe you two related. I guess you both Japanese?

MIKI. I don't know her. We just met. I'm actually looking for—

MAKIKO. [*Speaking Japanese:*] Well, if you're gonna let him show you around, I hope you brought plenty of whisky. They're all drunks, you know. Can you give me another swig of that, before he disappears with the entire bottle? It reminds me of home. Is it single malt?

MIKI. [*Speaking Japanese:*] It's actually a pure malt. Karuizawa.

MAKIKO. [*Speaking Japanese:*] No shit. How old?

MIKI. [*Speaking Japanese:*] Seventeen years.

MAKIKO. [*Speaking Japanese:*] Mind if I stick with you and the savage for a little while?

MIKI. [*Speaking Japanese:*] Actually I am looking for someone. Maybe you could help me find him.

MAKIKO. [*Speaking Japanese:*] Him? You are talking about the transvestite, right?

MIKI. [*Speaking Japanese:*] No, haha. He might be gay, but he's no transvestite. His name is Gordo.

MAKIKO. [*Speaking Japanese:*] Not anymore it's not. But okay. He works for my boyfriend's father. So does the savage.

Thunder cracks.

VINCENT. [*Drunk.*] That sounds like it could be another megacane. A tropical storm. Dust devil. Electric storm. Tropical cyclone. Sea storm. Nor'easter. A hurricane. Typhoon. A coastal storm. A tornado. An extratropical storm. A mild-to-wild weather disturbance. A thunderstorm. A squall. Firestorm. Tropical depression. A hypercane. Or a medicane. A megaburst. A gale. A derecho. Bomb cyclone. A real bad storm.

MIKI. You'd better lead us to shelter.

VINCENT. Thass what I do. I lead people.

MIKI. Lead us to safety then. Or at least help me find my hotel.

MAKIKO. [*Speaking Japanese:*] Just look at him. He will lead you to the nearest bar.

Exeunt.

ACT III.

Scene One.

In bed.

BARB.   You remind me of someone.

HARRY.   I would love to know who.

BARB.   I don't want to say right now.

HARRY.   Why is that?

BARB.   It's painful. That's why.

HARRY.   Come on, baby. I know something that will take all that pain away.

BARB.   Ah. The wonders of youth.

HARRY.   I'm not *that* young, you know.

BARB.   Young enough to accomplish the Olympic feat of fucking a woman twice within the hour.

HARRY.   It's been at least two since we did it last. So what do you say? Are we getting married?

BARB.   Harry. Don't be ridiculous.

HARRY.   Well, I just—

BARB.   Look. I appreciate all that you and Nelson are doing. Indeed, I think the three of us may potentially work well together, as strange as it is for me to hear those words coming out of my mouth, and come to broker a deal—

HARRY.   Why are you talking business when the only business *I* want to be getting down to right now—

BARB.   Enough. Don't be callous. This is a simple, one time fuck. That's all. Although I do have to admit… You're a lot better than I would have expected.

HARRY.   Well. It's also true that you bring out the beast in me. You're about to do it once again, matter of fact.

BARB.   I need to get to my office. Whatever's left of it.

HARRY.   Yes, Madame President.

BARB.   Harry. I think it's a little premature to be calling me that. Don't you?

HARRY.   Not at all. As Nelson said—

BARB.   Nelson doesn't have any authority on this island. He's just a pretender at the moment.

HARRY.   Barb. He's the person who can help you. Who can help *us.*

BARB.   There is no us.

HARRY.   But I think there could be. Don't you?

BARB.   That's it. I'm leaving.

HARRY.   Fear of commitment. That's not a quality we look for in a leader.

BARB.   Ha. Who is this we?

HARRY.   The agency I represent.

BARB.   The agency. How intelligent can this intelligence agency be when—

HARRY.   Watch it, Barb.

BARB.   Look. You're a nice kid. Aside from what you represent, which really has nothing to do with me or my interests.

HARRY.   Only it—we—has—have the potential to put you on that throne. Isn't that what you want, Barb? Isn't that what you've worked for?

BARB.   No. It has nothing to do with anything I've worked for, or any agenda I will be working for. Now if you'll please let me leave—

HARRY.   We have the potential to make your life very good. To resolve certain, certain *conflicts* you are currently grappling with. To, to *legitimize* everything going on here. Now that Mrdok's out of the way—

BARB.   The chain of command falls to me. Yes. That is true. But do you know what else is true, Harry?

HARRY.   What, babe?

BARB.   That I don't need you, or Nelson, or any of your shady vested interests telling me that. It's in our constitution. Which I helped to write.

HARRY.   Which we can ratify like—

Harry snaps his fingers.

BARB.   Ha. You know something?

HARRY.   What, babe?

BARB.   Just shut it, Harry.

She kisses him and leaves. Harry picks up the phone.

HARRY.   Nelson? It's working… I mean I think we're in love.

Scene Two.

Another part of the island.

Enter Vincent, drunkenly wielding the bottle of Japanese whisky in his hand, Billy Ray Taggerston III, and Collins.

BILLY.   Well Vincent, I'm glad you called this meeting today. It was unexpected, but…

COLLINS.   I think it makes… a certain amount of sense. We are, uh, the spiritual foundation of the island, in, like, uh, some sense.

BILLY.   Yes. I represent the Word of God. He represents the Soul of Man.

COLLINS.   Uh, yeah. I agree.

BILLY.   I mean, you know I arrived here before Mrdok did? Right?

COLLINS.   I didn't know that, no.

BILLY.   Mrdok and I go way back, actually…

COLLINS.   Oh? I can't say I ever, uh, met the guy. Man. President. I was brought here by Gordina actually… You know the Ministress of—

BILLY.   He was a bastard. A liar. I think we can all agree. You too, Vincent. I for one am glad he's dead—God rest his soul. I mean, I know he's been your employer, in a sense, Vincent, but as we say in show business—

COLLINS.   You're involved in show business? I, uh, thought you were…

BILLY. Well. As Administrative Assistant to Our Lord Jesus Christ, I must play a public role, until of course He returns, at which point I may retire.

COLLINS. Ah, okay…

BILLY. So what's the poetry thing like? Is there any money in that?

COLLINS. I, uh…

VINCENT. Enough. I brought you two gentlemen here today to show you something.

BILLY. Oh, I'm sorry.

COLLINS. Go ahead, then, Vincent…

Vincent wields his stick and proceeds with the making of marks.

COLLINS. Impressive.

VINCENT. You've never seen this before?

BILLY. I have.

VINCENT. You wanna tell him what it is I'm doin?

BILLY. Markmaking. A Sagosian tradition. I mean. Among the quasi-natives.

COLLINS. Markmaking…

VINCENT. It is part of our culture. For some, it's a spiritual practice…

Enter Prince with a machine gun.

PRINCE. Put down that stick, brother.

VINCENT. Prince. What the *fuck* are you doing?

PRINCE.   I say, by the word of Yang Zhu, drop that stick right now or else I'll shoot it out of your paw.

VINCENT.   All right.

Vincent drops the stick. Prince reaches down and catches it before it is allowed to touch the ground.

PRINCE.   It be a story old as the night was black before the quasis moved here and gave us theys wonderful gift of light pollution. People move to a place, discover it, so-called, and by doing so, they ruin it. Ruin, especially, the peoples in that place. They natural habitat. I's readin this story about a national park in China yesterday on the internet before the storm blew out all the power. This park where theys got wild monkeys. The monkeys used to forage for their own food. Then the people started to come visit. They think it's cute to feed the monkeys. Well then what happens? The monkeys, they get dependent, start eatin food that aint theys natural diet. Forget how to forage for theys own food. Don't even teach their babys no more how to forage. So the young generation gets ruined. Has all these diseases now like diabetes never used to have before, all these forms of cancer. And the next generation. And the one after that.

BILLY. [*Aside, to Collins.*]   This is what we call a sermon in my line of business.

PRINCE.   Monkeys is similar to humans in a lot of ways. But they aint us. We aint them. You know one of the things that make us different? Our ability to stand up. To say no, we aint gonna take that no more.

VINCENT.   You jest go away, Prince. Don't you start no trouble now.

PRINCE.   We already in trouble. Brother. Have been for quite some time. You could a done your part, at least taught me that when I was a kid. That's what older brothers are supposed to be for. But naw. You led by givin me the great counter-example. Showin me what happens when there's no life left in a person. Cos they had the life sucked out of them, and now theys puppets. Like those monkeys in China, dancin for those people so they can get one of them processed snacks, with all they calories and unnaturals, they done come to subsist on.

VINCENT.   Who gived you the gun, Prince?

PRINCE.   Now as my brother over here was just tellin you. Mark-making. For some, it's just culture. Like my brother over there. See how pretty his marks is? How profound and insane that style is?

COLLINS.   Well, uh, yes, I'd say it's quite expressive…

PRINCE.   Oh, hear that, Vince? The quasi like it. Vincent's heart be beatin outside his chest now.

VINCENT.   You gonna deny it's our culture, Prince? Now I don't even know the game you playin. You confused. You need help.

PRINCE.   What else is our culture, Vince? You gonna dress up in pirate costume, go dance around in front of the quasis, drinkin rum? Is that what you do on those weekends when you stay away from home three days straight, me and mom don't know where you been off to, not a word when you return?

VINCENT.   I aint never said I aint Sagosian. Never said that.

PRINCE.   Markmakin, my quasi friends, that aint *culture*. That's a *spiritual practice*. You get it? We Sagosians. We *spiritual* people. Our deity be called Yang Zhu. He the one we worship. He the one who led us here to find Sagosia. He the one who taught us to make marks. Makin marks is how we communicate through Him. How we express the will of our ancestors. Past and future alike, wrapped up in our individual styles. Style aint *culture*. Style be *spirit*. And the reason why you don't get that from my brother is that he done lost his spirit.

BILLY.   I'm a spiritual person myself, young man. Like you, I am even regarded as a spiritual master of my faith.

Prince raises his gun.

PRINCE.   And I be thinkin we've reached the time for you to get *your* faith off this island.

VINCENT.   Hard to think we comin from the same mother.

BILLY.   Yes. I know her. The soap opera star. On the show, she is almost like a witch, right? She has special powers. In Christianity, witches are regarded as a bad thing.

Prince cocks the gun.

PRINCE.   Now you're gonna be talkin trash about my mother?

VINCENT.   Put the gun down, Prince. The one you wanna kill is Nelson.

PRINCE.   Now why would I do that?

VINCENT.   History, bro. Think back on it. To kill the tree, you need to cut the roots. Who the one brought all these white fools to the island to begin with? You think it's the quasi-elites. But you're not thinkin back far enough. It's the quasi-colonials. *That's* when it all began.

PRINCE.   You speakin for yourself now, Vince? Or are you speaking for your master?

VINCENT.   I'm speakin as your brother. I tryin to reorient your head. Cos it's clearly in a state of confusion. Confusion regardin your own place and how you might fill it. Brother, I's the one who taught you how to markmake when you was, what, but a decade old. Then you breaked away from the markmakin for a long time—you was runnin wild, startin fires everywhere. You growed a little bit, the quasis comed, suddenly you return to markmakin, which you had no real interest in before. Suddenly it all different now. Suddenly you got a *spiritual connection.*

PRINCE.   You're right that it wasn't born in me. How could it be? I had everything that was Sagosian beat out of me—

VINCENT.   Prince. I know what's happenin. You and your gang. You think he's gonna help you, that man. Nelson Rodgers. I can imagine the things he promised. But he's just gonna lead you down into a hole. You gonna wind up in that cell that you rescued him from. Or someplace even worse.

PRINCE.   That man practically raised you up. Now you trashin him.

BILLY.   Well I have an idea of how we might resolve all this in a reasonable way, gentlemen: let us pray.

COLLINS.   Or, uh, how about a poem? That might be, uh, less controversial…

VINCENT. [*Ignoring Billy and Collins:*]   If you gonna start a revolution, do it yourself. Don't form no alliances with no foreign powers.

PRINCE.   You ever heard of a useful idiot? Come from Comrade Lenin.

VINCENT.   *You* the idiot, Prince. *He* usin *you.*

PRINCE.   We'll see in the end, won't we? History is written by the victors.

Exits.

VINCENT.   Cept when it gets writ by the victims.

Exits.

COLLINS.   Well, uh, I myself am on the side of culture.

Scene Three.

Another part of the island.
Enter Ma, Lallyburt, Mrdok, Gordina, Rick, Merrill, and other quasi-elites.

GORDINA.   I can go no further in these heels. My ankles are killing me!

MA.   Young man, it's not your ankles that are going to kill you, but these native terrorists, if we do not get to Baldheaded Mountain and meet up with our army in time.

MRDOK. [*Aside to Lallyburt.*]   He's scared shitless, isn't he? This can only work in our favor.

LALLYBURT. [*Aside to Mrdok.*]   Yeahyuh. And ifn thar's rully a wawer goin awn, awl we need is wun stray bullet tuh pierce hiyuhs skull. Blayme it on theyuhm quasi-naytive terrorists. Ah thank ah can arraynge thayuht.

MRDOK. [*Aside to Lallyburt.*]   Now *that's* my Minister of Defense!

Suddenly some quasi-natives from the Sagosian Yangist Home Liberation Front appear and place a huge banquet before them. Nelson also enters and watches hidden from afar.

RICK.   Holy fuck! What's all this?

MRDOK.   This looks even better than the food at Eat This! I wonder who the chef is?

GORDINA.   Well, I am famished, actually.

RICK.   When are you not?

GORDINA. Shall we just call it serendipity and dig in? Or need we exercise some caution, given that there apparently is a civil war that's about to break out.

LALLYBURT. Weyuhl, boiz. Ah say we offuh up a prayuh to Jaysus and dig raht own iyuhn.

They feast.

RICK. Man, this goose sure does taste good. But these trimmings are like the most unhealthy thing you can eat.

MRDOK. I always thought that was dick.

RICK. Actually, did you know that in Beijing there's a restaurant where they only serve penis? All kinds of animal penis is on the menu. From humdrum sheep and bull and hog all the way up to endangered species—if you're a VIP, you can actually order tiger dick.

MRDOK. Well well. A nation of dick-eaters. No wonder we were never able to crack the Chinese market! No offense, Ma.

MA. We do not eat penis in Taiwan.

MERRILL. [*Aside:*] By all accounts his daughter didn't.

RICK. No, I'm the one who's sorry, Mrdok. Had I known, I wouldn't have even tried with those guys from Beijing.

GORDINA. We all know how much your manhood means to you.

MERRILL. Even when there's not much of it to speak of.

They all laugh.

MRDOK. God, this is good. Is this what they normally eat? The quasi-natives?

GORDINA. Perhaps we should consider integrating their culinary flavors into our own national cuisine. You know, that's something we haven't thought of yet. It could give Settlers Landing a distinct advantage. Why, we could add culinary tourism to our roster of cultural endeavor!

NELSON. [*Aside:*] See? I always felt that Gee had the potential to become a compassionate colonialist like me.

MA. Am I the only one who's noticed that they have all disappeared? All the quasi-natives? Does no one find that odd? Why would they lay this banquet out for us and then just go away without any explanation in the meantime?

LALLYBURT. It's sayfe. Theyuh jest servin theyuh mastuhs, Ma. Wah you don't hafta fret. Ah no yer a heathen, but you can reyst ashured ah dun blest this food with a prayuh to the lawed. Eat up, Ma!

MRDOK. Can someone please get the man some chopsticks?

MA. No, thanks. Somehow I don't have much of an appetite.

RICK. Must be all that talk about eating dick!

MERRILL. I see that hasn't stopped you from stuffing your mouth.

MRDOK. Hey, you two, get a room!

Thunder and lightning. Prince bursts in on the scene and overturns the table, sending food flying everywhere.

PRINCE. Hands up, motherfuckers! I hereby declare all you to be prisoners of the Sagosian Yangist Liberation Home Front! Surrender now before I kill your shit! Get that food out of your mouth, quasi-elitist honky. The time has come for you to understand and accept your fate. Your so-called nation is a nation of lies. A nation of bullshit. You didn't come to this island with good intentions. You comed here to stole it. You've been fuckin feedin us a hive of crap since the day you set foot. That you was gonna build us houses, no more trailers, new roads, jobs, healthcare. All bullshit. All you've done is pollute our waters, built up your cozy little capital, and enriched yourselves while neglecting us. When you're not motherfuckin *enslavin* us.

GORDINA.   I just want to interject that we *have* made some progress on the cultural front, at least.

ALL.   Shut up, Gordo!

GORDINA.   It's Gordina.

PRINCE.   Now that you've stuffed your pig faces, it's time for dessert. A dish best served sweet. Only you don't get to eat it. It's us, the Sagosian people, we the ones who gonna enjoy this…

MRDOK.   Gordina, quick! Your phone! Call the army! Tell them to get here fast!

PRINCE.   Don't you even try it, motherfucker. You know how come his phone get connected again? It's cos of us. We be monitorin your calls, all your movement. You know how we do that? It's the technology you done brought here! That we now stole from you!

MRDOK.   On a second thought… Throw that phone as far as you can—Here, give it to me.

Mrdok grabs the phone and throws it offstage.

PRINCE.   You've already heard the news. Olde Colonia's in our hands. You know what? I've decided I'm gonna be a bit lenient. I'm gonna let you all go, figure out a way to get off this island. I don't know why. My comrades, they all think I should kill you. Big part of me wants to. But what good's a bunch of dead quasis on my hands? Yang Zhu teaches us that war and killing is too much trouble. Instead, one should just stay at home, tend to one's own needs, while ignoring all the bullshit. I'm gonna take a page out of his book this one time. You motherfuckers have one day to get off this island and never be seen again. I don't care how you do it. But from what I hear, there is still a couple yachts left that didn't get smashed in the megacane. Better make your way to the wharf. Hint: it's that way.

Prince disappears in a cloud of thunder.

NELSON.   Good job, Prince. You scared the bollocks off them. They don't know what to do! They're fully in my powers now. The rest of this should be easy enough.

Exits.

GORDINA.   Well, Mister President. I rather hate to be the one to ask, though such is my role here, I'm afraid: What are we to do?

MRDOK.   This is totally fucked. I would think this were a dream or a bad Netflix series if I wasn't sitting here staring at your ugly fucking faces. Fuck! This is all your faults! Why did I hire you idiots? You're all fired! Wait, I don't mean that… I mean, yes I do! I mean… Fuck.

LALLYBURT.   Cum own, Merdawg. We don't even no if hes fer reyuhl. It could all be blustuh. Ah do deklayuh, we oughta stiyick to the original playuhn. On towuhds Baldheaded Mountin, where our army's awaitin!

RICK.   Yeah, I could do that.

MERRILL.   What he says.

MA.   What choice do we have. Really.

Exeunt Ma, Mrdok, Rick, and Lally.

GORDINA.   Oh honey. Now that it's just us girls, let's be honest: the men are all worked up. We need to go talk some sense into them.

MERRILL.   What kind of sense are we talkin?

GORDINA.   Let's get off this island!

MERRILL.   I'm with you on that.

GORDINA.   Then go! Stop them! Use your, ehm… *natural charms* if you have to!

MERRILL.   Are you talking about my tits? They're about as natural as yours, honey.

Exeunt.

Act IV.

Scene One.

Before Nelson/Mrdok's house. Enter Nelson, Barb, and Harry.

NELSON.   Well well well. I see you two are getting along just fine. How is he treating you, Miz Brunnei? May I call you Barb?

BARB.   If you really have to.

NELSON.   Ha! I always admired a sharp tongue on a female.

BARB.   Since you've clearly never had one applied to any of your bodily organs...

NELSON.   Replete with a splash of irreverent filth thrown in for good measure. I can now see what Mrdok sees in you.

HARRY.   Let's get down to business. My organization has managed the weapons shipment. The Sagosians are now armed.

NELSON.   If this plan were to go any smoother, I would think supernatural magic were at work. Surely *something* must have gone wrong since we last met?

HARRY.   If it did, then I certainly would have found out about it.

NELSON.   And you, Barb? How are you feeling about the wind's latest directional sway?

BARB.   Oh, I'm about as indifferent as they come.

NELSON.   Well. That makes one suspicious.

HARRY.   Which part of the phrase *You are our queen* leaves you feeling so ambivalent?

BARB.   Well, to name one, that you say it with my cunt in your mouth.

NELSON.   A woman of your age should find herself fortunate to be granted a romantic liaison with such a well-connected young stud.

BARB.   I'm not sure what that statement reveals more: how little you understand women or how little you know about me. I don't approve of this little revolution, so-called, Nelson. No matter how stage managed it happens to be.

HARRY.   But it is necessary, my love, to instill you on the throne!

Enter Prince. Nelson shushes them.

NELSON.   Would you two excuse me for a minute, please? [*To Prince:*] How is everything?

PRINCE.   I did everything we agreed. They know where they at. They have twenty-four hours to leave.

NELSON.   And of course they won't.

PRINCE.   Naw. But we gived them their chance. Didn't we?

NELSON.   As much of one as they're bound to get. Time to bring your people in.

PRINCE.   Right now?

NELSON.   Yes. The moment's right, I feel.

PRINCE.   Okay. I go get them.

Prince goes offstage then returns with the cast of Lives of the Innocents. *The play temporarily turns into an episode of the soap opera enacted by the cast.*

KRSTAL-AS-LYNETTE MERRIWETHER.   My life here on Port Matthews is so ideal. But why oh why oh why do I keep losing my memory? Could it be early Alzheimer's? I must make an appointment at General Hospital as soon as possible. Maybe I will be eligible for that Viutex treatment I keep hearing so many miraculous things about!

Enter Rae-as-Maria. Krstal screams, lifts a Greek statuette.

KRSTAL-AS-LYNETTE MERRIWETHER.   Aaaaaahhhh! *What* are you doing in my house? Who are you?

RAE-AS-MARIA. [*Possessed.*]   Here I come at the throat of the world in order to slit it…

KRSTAL-AS-LYNETTE MERRIWETHER.   Aaaaahhh! Aaaaaahhhh! Aaaaahhhhhh!

Breaks the statuette over Rae-as-Maria's head, but it has no apparent effect.

Enter Lucia-as-Hornby.

LUCIA-AS-HORNBY.   What is it, Madame Merriwether? Oh no, Maria! Possessed? Not you! I musta done messed up my magic again. Shoot!

KRSTAL-AS-LYNETTE MERRIWETHER.   What are you *talking* about, Hornby? What's the matter with her?

LUCIA-AS-HORNBY.   She done… swallowed the wrong medicine.

Rae-as-Maria lunges for Krstal-as-Lynette's throat.

LUCIA-AS-HORNBY.   Mblagerthonic fentoponaphy! Away, spirit!

Rae-as-Maria snaps out of it.

RAE-AS-MARIA. Where is I? [*Rubbing her head where Krstal-as-Lynette broke the statuette:*] My head sure do hurt.

LUCIA-AS-HORNBY. You in Madame Merriwether's house, Maria. Musta been sleepwalking again. Here's some aspirin for that headache.

RAE-AS-MARIA. Sleepwalking?! Me?! Wait… This lady sure does have some nice stuff. What's this?

KRSTAL-AS-LYNETTE MERRIWETHER. That's a china dog, Maria.

RAE-AS-MARIA. A china dog? It come all the way from China?

LUCIA-AS-HORNBY. Now you don't trouble your pretty little head about that, Maria. You get out of Madame Merriwether's house right away, afore trouble gets launched.

Enter Martinique dressed as a zombie.

KRSTAL-AS-LYNETTE MERRIWETHER. Oh my god! Who is *that* horrid creature? Is everyone on this island possessed?

MARTINIQUE. I am you. You am I.

KRSTAL-AS-LYNETTE MERRIWETHER. What? What's she saying? Can you speak English, please?

MARTINIQUE. I am you. You am I.

KRSTAL-AS-LYNETTE MERRIWETHER. Hornby, please help me! I'm so confused now! Please get all these crazy possessed people out of my house!

MARTINIQUE. I am the demon corpse of Anesthia, sister of Hornby.

LUCIA. [*Aside:*] They done got another actress to play her? [*In character.*] Anesthia! Oh my! But you supposed to be dead. You *is* dead.

RAE-AS-MARIA.   Oh how I wish this would stop. I don't want to be on drugs anymore.

LUCIA-AS-HORNBY.   But Maria, you aren't on drugs. You were under my magic spell. Now you've snapped out of it.

KRSTAL-AS-LYNETTE MERRIWETHER.   You know magic, Hornby? How come you never told me?

MARTINIQUE.   It's cos she don't want you to know, witch.

KRSTAL-AS-LYNETTE MERRIWETHER.   Who are you calling a witch? You have no right to call me that. No right at all. I know what my rights are. I pay my lawyer a handsome fee so that he can assure me of my rights each and every day. I have rights and you don't. Because I can afford them and you can't.

MARTINIQUE.   Nice try, Lynette. Only you not Lynette no more.

KRSTAL-AS-LYNETTE MERRIWETHER.   What do you mean I'm not Lynette? I know full well who I am. I am Lynette Merriwether, heiress to the Merriwether beef jerky and wax paper estate of the American Virgin Islands.

RAE-AS-MARIA.   … Say what?

KRSTAL-AS-LYNETTE MERRIWETHER.   My parents taught me from a young age to never be ashamed of where I came from. Rather, they taught me to be ashamed of where everyone else came from.

MARTINIQUE.   Witch! You aint Lynette no more. Lynette's maybe the body you're occupying right now. But your body been occupied by the spirit of Anesthia.

RAE-AS-MARIA.   But I *am* on drugs. I just haven't told anyone yet. It's a secret I've been hidin for so long now. Just afraid to let everyone know.

LUCIA-AS-HORNBY.   Oh, Maria. You've already been to that expensive rehab. When you could have just stayed in Port Matthews and taken the much less expensive Viutex cure!

RAE-AS-MARIA.   That's what you all think. I did go away for some time. But I didn't actually go to rehab.

LUCIA-AS-HORNBY.   You didn't?!

RAE-AS-MARIA.   It pains me to have to admit it now, but since I've been confronted, it's a reality I can no longer escape…

LUCIA-AS-HORNBY.   Where did you go then, Maria?

RAE-AS-MARIA.   I ran away with your husband, Hornby.

LUCIA-AS-HORNBY.   My husband Northrop? But I thought he was dead!

RAE-AS-MARIA.   No no no. He's still alive. He didn't want to leave you, but he had to. He found out that his twin sister, who no one knew he had because he was ashamed of her because of her moral deficiencies (she drank alcohol to excess, you see), his twin sister had been kidnapped by a government official living on a distant island, an island where they have communism. So, because I was having me an affair with him behind your back, which was really just because I've been on drugs, not because I actually like him, together we went to negotiate his sister's release, but because they're all communists there, he wasn't allowed to leave and was forced to change his name and become a worker. They let me leave, because we weren't married. But he had to stay, because he was related by blood to a person who had been converted to communism living on that island.

KRSTAL-AS-LYNETTE MERRIWETHER.   Oh my god. That is so awful.

RAE-AS-MARIA.   It is true. That island is terrible. You can't even get drugs there. Your husband, last I heard he is working in a factory under a new identity.

LUCIA-AS-HORNBY.   Maria, you slut! How could you commit this act of adultery against me?

Slaps Maria in the face.

RAE-AS-MARIA.   I'm so sorry, Hornby. I didn't want you to know. I was taking drugs at the time, so my reckless behavior is something I am not really responsible for. Since then, I have found God after watching Billy Ray Taggerston III's popular TV program. He has helped me mend my ways. Now I've been sober for three hours. Until I woke up here, in this strange white lady's house. Now I don't feel so sober no more.

LUCIA-AS-HORNBY.   But my husband Norbert! Is he okay?

RAE-AS-MARIA.   He seems to be doing all right. Though he is awfully unhappy there. Communism sure is bad.

LUCIA-AS-HORNBY.   Well, anything is inferior to the system of governance we have here on Port Matthews.

KRSTAL-AS-LYNETTE MERRIWETHER.   I didn't know you were married, Hornby.

RAE-AS-MARIA.   We all have secrets here, Miss Merriwether. Why, it's the nature of Port Matthews people. We don't like to tell outsiders our business. Let alone ourselves.

KRSTAL-AS-LYNETTE MERRIWETHER.   But I'm not an outsider. I've been living here for five whole months!

LUCIA-AS-HORNBY.   You're still an outsider to us, madame. Oh, how it pains me to say it. But it is the truth.

KRSTAL-AS-LYNETTE MERRIWETHER.   But what's this nonsense about the spirit of your dead sister occupying me? If your dead sister is standing right here in front of us, how could she also be inside me?

MARTINIQUE.   I am the body of Anesthia. But you are the spirit of Anesthia. We must have Hornby perform an exorcism, so that her spirit will be transferred back into my body. Then I can finally rest.

RAE-AS-MARIA.   Oh. That makes sense.

LUCIA-AS-HORNBY.   Sister, I can see it is truly you. And I have noticed Madame Merriwether having these odd spells every now and then. I know what I must do: Tonight I will make the water of the sea disappear.

RAE-AS-MARIA.   Oh shoot. That means a tsunami.

KRSTAL-AS-LYNETTE MERRIWETHER.   But I'm confused. How are you going to do that?

RAE-AS-MARIA.   Hornby here she control the weather on this isle.

KRSTAL-AS-LYNETTE MERRIWETHER.   She does?! My goodness, Hornby! It seems like I learn something new about you at every minute! I'm so glad I hired you!

LUCIA-AS-HORNBY.   I've gotta do it in order to take care of you, Miss Merriwether. That's my job, why I've been sent here. What will happen is first the water will disappear. It will then come back in a big wave, which looks like a tsunami, but you are the only one who will notice it, because the water is going to target you. But once all that water splashes over you, while I admit it will hurt or even feel like you're drowning for a few minutes, you don't have to worry. Once you're out of it, you will be cured, and no longer have these violent spells where you try to hurt people. Then I can finally go and find my husband on the island of communism, maybe even put a spell on the leaders there so that they can learn the principles of the free market and join the developed world.

RAE-AS-MARIA.   I'm sorry I did it with your husband, Hornby. Will you ever find it in your heart to forgive me? Or are you going to put a spell on me, too?

LUCIA-AS-HORNBY.   Oh you don't have to worry. I forgive you and, anyway, I only do white magic. It's just that sometimes I get the recipes to the spells slightly wrong and the magic turns a kind of shade of gray.

RAE-AS-MARIA.   In that case, could I just ask you for one favor? Could you put a spell on me, to help me get off the drugs?

LUCIA-AS-HORNBY.   Honey, the best cure for that isn't magic, but modern medical science. You need to make an appointment at General Hospital to get on the Viutex treatment now.

KRSTAL-AS-LYNETTE MERRIWETHER. [*Suddenly overcome with the spirit of Anesthia, lunges at Lucia-as-Hornby. In Anesthia's voice:*] No, sister! Don't do the exorcism! Let me stay in this white lady's body! I will *kill* you!

Krstal starts choking Lucia as Hornby. Dramatic music. Rae-as-Maria screams and grabs the china dog and smashes it against the wall for some reason.

Screen fades: To be continued…

Credits roll.

NELSON.   That was just a TV show. Not to be confused with real life. Believe it or not.

HARRY.   Well. That wasn't quite what I had in mind. But an interesting entertainment, nonetheless.

BARB.   I for one can't *wait* to find out what happens on the next episode. I'll be sure to tune in.

NELSON.   Well, not to get too meta about it. But in a way, the show is a lot like reality. For many years, it has served as a kind of parallel reality to life here on Sagosia… Oh, I nearly forgot. While all this was going on, Vincent was off with Mrdok's sons Stevo Rey and Bobby planning an assassination. My own.

HARRY.   Well. That sucks. Are you completely sure about that?

NELSON.   I suppose I should go do something about it. Of course, it would have been nice had your CIA cronies informed me. Though I guess their concern is solely for American lives.

BARB.   Well, that *is* the American way. As far as I've come to understand it.

NELSON.   Anyway, why don't you two go have sex again while I deal with my impending assassination attempt?

HARRY.   Sure, we can do that.

BARB.   You'd better make me come this time!

Harry and Barb exeunt.

Enter Prince.

NELSON.   Prince, have you set up that meeting with your brother?

PRINCE.   He on his way. With his boys. They all pretty high right now. Should be easy to thwart theys tryin to kill you.

NELSON.   Good. Now's the time to go get Lilbig out of his McMansion. Bring him here, so that we can have the moment of truth revealed. Then we'll see who gets killed!

PRINCE.   I go, I go.

Nelson hides behind a banyan tree.

Enter Bobby, Stevo Rey, and Vincent.

VINCENT.   Sssshhh! Be quiet! We near his house!

BOBBY.   That's my Dad's house. Not Nelson's.

STEVO REY.   Yeah. But Nelson's occupying the house. That's what Vincent's trying to say. You dumbass.

BOBBY.   You're the dumbass.

VINCENT.   Youse need to both shut up and concentrate on the task at hand. Remember: Nelson the usurper. If you want the island to come back under youse control, no matter what happened to your father, youse need to get rid of him.

Vincent hands them both pistols.

VINCENT.   Now, soon as he come to the door, aim your pistol and shoot. You got it?

STEVO REY.   Yeah. We think so.

BOBBY.   Shut the fuck up. You don't speak for me.

STEVO REY.   You shut the fuck up.

VINCENT.   You *both* need to shut the fuck up. And shoot.

Vincent rings the doorbell. The sons raise their guns.

Lilbig appears at the door. The sons drop their pistols.

STEVO REY.   Shit.

BOBBY.   Dude. What is this?

VINCENT.   Don't look at me. As far as I know, we at the right address.

LILBIG.   How come yall been avoidin my Black ass.

BOBBY.   What are you talking about, man? We… I mean… *Stevo Rey* maybe, but like…

LILBIG.   You and your girl, too.

STEVO REY.   You know, man, there was like this real bad storm. Everything's in chaos now.

LILBIG.   I'm talkin before the storm, you dumb honky ass motherfucker. You think I don't know what's goin on here? What kinda game you playin?

Lilbig pulls out his own two gats, aims them at the brothers' heads, while simultaneously kicking their pistols away.

STEVO REY.   Whoa, Lilbig, what are you doing, man?

LILBIG.   Get inside this house right now. We bout to talk this shit on out. Lilbig's finally gonna get some answers. The truth is finally gonna hit da air.

Exeunt.

ACT V.

Scene One.

Outside of the gray building.

Enter Nelson and Prince.

NELSON.   It seems as though everything is going remarkably according to plan. What time is it?

PRINCE.   Six. You said this'd all be done by now. That the revolution'd be finished.

NELSON.   It sort of is, isn't it? That storm was such a blessing; it really destroyed everything! What more could you want in a revolution? How's Mrdok and his people doing?

PRINCE. We rounded em up before they got to Baldheaded Mountain and have imprisoned em inside this building.

NELSON.   I know all that. My question was: How are they *doing*?

PRINCE.   Mrdok, Ma, and Lallyburt all seem distracted. The rest are depressed. The one called Gordina is cryin. If you went in there and saw how pathetic they all looked, you'd probly be cryin yourself.

NELSON. Do you really think so?

PRINCE. Least I would. If I was a quasi.

NELSON.   You know what? Go get them out of the cell. Bring them out here. It's time for me to finally confront these bloody bastards.

PRINCE.   I'll fetch em then.

Exits.

NELSON.   Once I finally have the island back, I can go back to being a good person like I always was. Having to play the punisher is not a fitting role for a gentleman such as myself.

Reenter Prince, followed by Mrdok, attended by Gordina; Ma and Lallyburt, attended by Merrill and Rick.

NELSON.   Are you really all that taken aback to see me here, Mrdok? Well, you shouldn't be. This was my island all along, don't you know? As much as it is Prince's, and his brother Vincent's. Why? We were all actually born here. To enunciate the most obvious fact. We have a *deserved* place here. We didn't just come upon it one day and decide all this was ours for the taking. Such a concept is clearly difficult for a man like you to fathom. A man with no real roots, a man with no connections, human or otherwise, to much of anything. And you, Ma Lin: scum, enabler. Beneath the false flag of philanthrophy. All of you, in fact. Broadcasting your good intentions so as to conceal your real ones. The entire world can see it. They only pretend to believe your pathetic spiel, until they are able to get what they want from you. Of course, you're not the only ones who have put your filthy money into this disreputable venture. There's the Texan cowboy over here, he of the oilfields and the murdering Saudi shiekhs. Don't think I've forgotten you! I'm just saving you for last, because you're too stupid to realize you're being used by all the others.

I have nightmares. Every night. I have been for so long now. Ever since I was forced into exile. Usually my dreams are centered on this place. Not this wretched building you've constructed, this place where I was kept when I was first brought back here. Where I just threw you, for my momentary mild amusement, that quick jolt of revenge I needed to get through this, to attain some sense of retribution. Petty emotions that you drench yourselves in day in and day out, and that I've always been above... No, I don't need those. What I need, all I need, in fact, is release from these nightmares. One, a recurring one, is of a rare breed of donkey that you have imported on to the island. I know you haven't done any such thing, but I thought I'd share the nightmare with you, so that you might understand how perverted I've become. The ass, the donkey, has pink skin and dark blue leopard spots, and a tail like that of a common housecat. The weird thing is, in my dream, I only ever see it from behind. I never know what its head looks like. It might not even be a donkey at all, but something about it just seems to signify, in my dream logic: donkey.

Do you know what this recurring nightmare means? I don't. And you know what? I don't care, either. All I know is that since I've been back here, the strange nightmares have stopped. Even when I was locked up in that prison from which you were just freed: no more nightmares. This island is the only place in the world where I can get a good night's rest. And you have robbed me of that. And no man, or woman, or whatever the hell it is you've become, Gordina—no being has the right to do that to another being.

It is true that, unlike most of you—Gordina perhaps being a slight exception to this, I don't know—unlike most or even all of you, I have led a rather reflective existence. A privileged position this puts me in, to be sure, this island existence. Fate seems to have slapped me on this floating slab of land for this explicit purpose: to reflect.

Do you know what it is that makes us as a species less highly evolved than we tend to believe we are? Just one thing: it is our uncertainty. Our uncertainty, constant, is the very thing that both motivates us and withholds us from evolving onward, from being the masters of the universe we so often deceive ourselves into believing we are. For proof of that unyielding uncertainty that haunts us, one need look no further than mankind's yearning for abstraction. We are so embroiled in abstractions—whether they take the form of gods, political ideals—even money, Mrdok, is an abstraction—money and power both... That's what abstraction is: false solutions to our yearning for certainty. All of human nature and history can be understood in an instant by grasping this fundamental principle—mankind's lack of certainty, its miserly grabbing at some fundamental abstraction it might hold on to, to serve as the key for unlocking it all—truth or whatever you want to call it. If we could just do away with this poisonous sense of certainty altogether, then, and only then, might we truly evolve as a species. But I frankly don't see that happening. Certainly not with the representatives of humanity I now see before me.

And you, Gordina, with your urine-tinged envy. You, deep down, imagine yourself to be the heroine of this narrative. You are anything but. You are little more than the sycophantic elephantine pillow for this ever falling man. You provoke the world's vomit with your fawning idolatry, the idiocy of your florid defenses of this one-dimensional creature's near-numinous putridities. To you and the rest of this gallery of ghouls I say: put all your hopes away! This isle, which was never your own, is now being returned to its rightful owners.

Prince. You are now like a son to me. At first it was your brother. But we can't always control the direction in which this river called life persuades us. Now, you have taken his place in so many ways. And, well, what else can I say? To my great surprise, you have turned out much better than your brother. More useful, at least. I hear the boatswain is now awake and the unharmed yacht has been found. Go fetch Robinson, have him drive these losers to the harbor. I don't want to lay eyes on the lot of them ever again.

Prince raises his gun, opens fire. Nelson drops to the ground, dead.

GORDINA.   My my. I wasn't expecting that!

MA.   Serves him right, I must say. For all of the *terrible* things he just said about my philanthropic endeavors, which have opened so many gates around the world.

GORDINA.   Not to mention our beloved president, who has devoted his entire life to the selfless endeavor of philanthropy.

Prince cocks his gun again. Commotion.

PRINCE.   Shut the fuck up! I got somethin to say that none of youse is gonna wanna hear. But I got to say it anyway. It's my role now. My spiritual path. In this island's affairs…

MA.   He's a madman. A madman!

PRINCE.   Oh, am I? Is this the moment I tell you that a couple of the peoples in our midst has been plottin against you? *Sir?* Are you in the mood, now, to be enlightened in that way?

MA.   What is he talking…?

MRDOK.   Whatever he's saying, it's bullshit.

PRINCE.   Oh no it's not. And I got the recordin to prove it.

MA.   What recording?

MRDOK.   He's clearly lying. There are no recordings. There is no surveillance here on Settlers Landing.

PRINCE.   The world's first surveillance-free state. Isn't that what you call it? Which is true, in a sense. If what that means is that the surveillance comes for free. I see a pattern emergin here. Been seein it for some time, actually. Fore you even arrived here. Back when this was still a place where a man could hold his head up high. Where he didn't need to *earn* no respect. Wasn't even such a thing as respect. A low concept, if there ever was one.

MERRILL.   Now I really don't understand what he's saying.

RICK.   You wouldn't, honey.

PRINCE.   I think everyone here knows that this place got more surveillance than China. All the hotel rooms bugged. Even got bugs under the mattresses of near everyones house in the hills outside Olde Colonia. Cameras, too.

LALLYBURT.   Whuht in thuh sayuhm heyuhl? Thar aint no bugs in mah hayuhs! Ah dun had thuh exterminatuh in layuhst munth!

PRINCE.   Oh but there is, you redneck fuck. Practically got bugs up your ass. Wouldn't surprise me.

MA.   Sir, whatever it is you want. You must understand, we've endured a lot in the last twenty-four hours. As you know, there was a terrible storm, just awful. We were out at sea when it happened, and we very nearly drowned. As a matter of fact, we lost a beloved senator of ours. Perhaps you know her? Barbra Brunnei? Why, she has been—*had* been—working on a number of housing projects that were meant to directly benefit you people. Surely you can at the very least join us in mourning this great loss.

PRINCE. Hm. That's real sad. You know what else is sad?

MERRILL. No. Tell us!

PRINCE. I done lost my brother.

MERRILL. Oh no, sweetie. Did he die in the storm as well?

MA. Apparently a lot of quasi-natives suffered huge losses. Such a tragedy, and one, I am sure, that our president will come to rectify in very good time.

PRINCE. Fuck no. I didn't lose him in the storm. I lost him long ago. I lost him the moment your foot touched down on the island. The very first day you comed to see…

MERRILL. I'm confused. Who is he talking about?

MRDOK. Wait a minute. Are you saying Vincent is your brother? I had no idea he even had a brother.

PRINCE. Or a family. Or a life outside of servitude. But he do.

GORDINA. We can assure you, young man, Vincent is very much alive. Why if you'd just—

PRINCE. Not to me he aint. He's deader than this colonial son of a bitch lying on the ground right here. Just as dead as youse all about to be real soon. But first, I got a little treat for you all to watch. Temwen!
     Temwen enters holding a widescreen TV. Prince removes a remote control from his pocket and turns it on to reveal a surveillance porn starring Harry and Barb.

MRDOK. Hot! Oh fuck… Wait a minute. Is that…

RICK. That's Barb, man!

MRDOK. I *know* it's Barb, you fuckin moron. I mean, the guy. That's… You know who it is.

GORDINA. Oh my. That's Harry Hull, isn't it?

MERRILL.   Oh my nasty goodness.

MRDOK.   How in the greasy fuck did that happen? Gee?!

GORDINA.   Oh I can explain. At least… Well, maybe I can't, actually.

LALLYBURT.   Oh mah lawed. Lucifuh has dun took ovuh this heyuh ahlund. Itsuh goddam moduhn day Sodom and Gumorruh.

PRINCE.   Filmed on your own special hidden cameras, Mister President.

MA.   Well, it's wonderful news! It means she's still alive… Doesn't it?

GORDINA.   How deeply unhappy we all are.

LALLYBURT.   Whah n thuh sayuhm heyuhl wud you say sumthin lahk thayuht, Gee?

GORDINA.   Well, because it's true. We're still alive and we're victims of this situation and we're all terribly unhappy now.

RICK.   I'm not unhappy.

GORDINA.   That's because you're not human.

RICK.   Well at least I still have my dick! Which is more—

MRDOK.   Enough, Rick. For all I know, this video could have been from a year, three years ago. How do I know—

GORDINA.   It's not, boss. Look at the date and time stamp at the bottom.

MRDOK.   … Oh. Do we have any coke left, Rick?

RICK.   We snorted it all up before the storm, boss.

MRDOK.   Some coke right now would be awful nice.

MERRILL.   Forget it. There's no more coke left.

MA.   Barbra's alive! It's so wonderful!

MRDOK.   Why in the hell do you care so much whether Barb is alive or dead, Mister Ma? Can you answer me, once and for all: Why is this such a thing for you? What have you and Barb been plotting behind my back?

PRINCE.   Like you and the cowboy been plottin behind the China-man's back.

MRDOK.   I'm warning you…

Prince raises his gun.

MRDOK.   Okay. So never mind.

MA.   Is it true, what he says? Have you been plotting against me?

LALLYBURT.   You dun been screwin us ovuh, is whut's been hapnin.

MA.   I can't understand him when he speaks. Could someone please translate that into either English or Chinese?

MRDOK.   What he's saying is that it's *you* who are screwing *us*, Ma. You know. With the Saudis.

MA.   Mrdok, I… Do you *really* want to discuss this here?

LALLYBURT.   Wahs he actin all suspicious lahk alluva sudden?

MRDOK.   I have no idea, I…

MA.   Because, if I air certain details about what you're alleging. I don't think it's going to bode well for you.

LALLYBURT.   Wah in thuh sayuhm heyuhl—

GORDINA.   Look, this is official state business, ladies gentlemen and all others, we are under duress here, with a gun literally being pointed at our heads—

PRINCE.   Since it's me with the gun, how about I just state it all out for you. Ma been doin behind the scenes with the Saudis on the resort deal. This great resort, that's supposed to bring soo many jobs and soo much fortune to the island. That's gonna make everyone here rich, richer than they already is. And then have the wealth trickle down on us, the Sagosians. And make us all happy that you've done come and ruined our lives. That was supposed to be the plan on the resort, right? Least how it's been publicized to the world. Then your President Bastard over here decided it wasn't gonna happen. Said he was gonna screw the Saudis, take a big chunk of they investment on some flimsy pretext, let the construction that'd already started go to rot. Least that's what he announced to Barb and the cowboy, who were meant to be semi-equal partners on the whole mess. They also made theys investment too, didn't theys? Ceptin the Saudis and Ma go back even further than the cowboy and his family do. Ma, who might as well be the real president, so-called, of this entire bullshit fake country, since it's he who organized the hostile takeover of the bank from the quasi-colonials, it's he who controls the damn bank— he the one who went to the Saudis with his own investment proposal, subvertin the original deal to use theys money instead to invest in— get this—a laundromat chain in the Philippines and his native Taiwan; quite an interestin investment for a buncha oil billionaires to make, but I'll leave it at that.

MA.   The deal, so-called, has nothing to do whatever with the resort, and it's a perfectly legitimate business in spite of whatever you might be implying. Taiwan has a very serious laundry shortage problem, has been plagued with one for years. It is part of my philanthropic mission in my home country to make sure the economically disadvantaged have clean clothes to wear!

LALLYBURT.   And so Merdawg was iyun own it with Ma Liyin thiyuhs hole tahm?

MRDOK.   Nope. The whole time, Ma didn't know this, but I was trying to do *damage control* behind his back with the Saudis, while pretending I was in on the deal, only secretly trying to protect *you*, Lallyburt, by deceving Ma and pretending to go along…

Enter Barb and Harry.

BARB.   Christ. You mean they're all alive?!

HARRY.   Don't look at me. I had no idea, babe, I swear.

PRINCE.   Welcome to the party, Madame President.

MRDOK.   What does he mean, *Madame President?*

BARB.   We all thought you were dead, Mrdok. I was just trying to keep the country going…

PRINCE.   … Yeah. By forging an alliance with this here dead quasi-colonial motherfucker.

MRDOK.   Barb?

BARB.   Why… He's lying. I would never.

GORDINA.   Could it be that we're all on Ambien right now?

MA.   Oh Barb! How happy I am that you are still alive. Please save me from all these terrible accusations that are currently being directed against me!

BARB.   Why? What have I missed?

MA.   At every step of the way on this resort project, I have been fully transparent with you. Am I right?

BARB.   When I can get in touch with you, sure…

MRDOK.   You mean to say you've been in contact with Ma this whole time?

MA.   Oh Barb. There's no sense in hiding it anymore. It's all coming out.

BARB.   What is?

MA.   We have to tell them.

BARB.   … Tell them what?

MA.   That you and I both knew the resort project would never come to fruition—we decided even before Mrdok did. Look, Barb has been funneling money in Japan for years from the Yakuza, helping them fund all sorts of escapades, including a joint construction venture they had with some politicians in the KMT in Taiwan with whom I've had some common business interests, okay? We both ran up a certain amount of debt when one of the leaders of that project was executed by a rival gang and the project had to be put on hold indefinitely. To help pay off the debts without having to reach too deeply into our own pockets, we thought we'd get some Saudi involvement, set up a fake resort and shower it with a big PR blitz to make it look realer than real, while whispering in Mrdok's ear that it was fake but that there'd be a big payout to him in the end, so that he'd go along with it. The only person who really lost anything, in material terms, was Lallyburt. Lallyburt, I'm sorry, we did take your investment, I'm not sure when we'll be able to get it back, but the good news is, you haven't lost face with the Saudis. Given your family's long-term investment in the oil fields—

LALLYBURT.   Wah you dam lyin cheatin slant ahd coolie. Ifn we wuz in Texus raht nayow, ahda hav mah dam shotgun out fastuh thayuhn uh sinnuh renouncin homosexuality and miscegenation on thuh Judgment Day.

MRDOK. [*Aside:*]   And what *none* of them realize is that *my* underworld connections back in Chinatown in the US of A trump *all* of their fuckin—

Gordina suddenly shrieks.

GORDINA.   Collins, darling! You're alive!

Prince ushers in Collins and Billy Ray.

LALLYBURT.   Ayund thuh good Revrend Billy! Prayse Jaysus!

BILLY.   Thanks, everyone. I just want to say that it's because of your prayers and financial contributions that we were able to overcome the gale winds of Satan. We sought refuge in the TV studio-slash-church on the outskirts of Olde Colonia, which thankfully wasn't harmed, so we should be able to resume broadcasts as soon as we get these evil revolutionaries out of the capital.

Prince fires a warning shot into the air.

BILLY.   I mean… Just kidding?

GORDINA.   I'm so sorry you had to be dragged into this, dear Collins. Though, I suppose, it will make for wonderful material some day…

COLLINS.   From what I understand, the boatswain is still alive…

GORDINA.   Oh, also?

COLLINS.   I would like to go with him. I think my time here on the island is finished.

GORDINA.   Heavens, no! I cannot allow that. I mean… This is only a momentary setback, dear Collins. We're going to get these beasts out of here very, very soon, take them out and drown them in the middle of the Brown Sea, then build a huge wall to protect our private utopia. It's going to be so impressive! Surely you haven't finished our national epic yet, have you?

COLLINS.   It seems your national epic is finished in more ways than one, Gee.

PRINCE.   That's right, that's right. In the words of Yang Zhu: Governing the world is as easy as turning your palm around.

He does just that and backhands Gordina, whose wig goes flying off. Gordina shrieks and runs to retrieve it.

PRINCE.   Don't you still have some people missing, Mister President?

MRDOK.   Not that I can think of. At the moment. Though it's Gee who usually looks over all that for me…

PRINCE.   What about your family?

MRDOK.   Oh, right. Well my wife, Krstal, is off making movies now with her young director who just moved to the island… What was his name again, Gee? Anyway, they were unable to join us on the yacht trip today—which is probably for the best—for them, at least…

PRINCE.   And your sons? Remember them?

MRDOK.   Oh, right. Well Jaco should be fine. Rosalita looks after him during the day, and I know our home is stormproof, because Nelson let that slip before we decommissioned the property from him.

PRINCE.   This dumbass motherfucker. [*Into his phone*:] Yo, Temwen. Bring those motherfuckers over here.

Temwen enters with Bobby and Stevo Rey in tow, followed shortly behind by Lil Bigfoot.

MRDOK.   Sons! You're still alive! How worried I've been about you.

STEVO REY.   Fuck you, Dad.

GORDINA.   Stevo Rey. Is that any way to speak to your father? After all he has done for you? The multitudinous ways in which he has *enriched* you over the years?

BOBBY.   Fuck you, Dad.

GORDINA.   And you, Bobby! All the fancy rehabs he paid for. And the brilliant scientific discovery he made in your honor: the Viutex cure for lifelong addicts like yourself!

BOBBY and STEVO REY.   Fuck you, Gee.

LILBIG.   These motherfuckas been treatin you real bad, Mrd. I don't know what else to say.

MRDOK.   My sons? How could they be cheating me? I never thought either of them'd be smart enough... Do you know anything about this? Barb? Lally? Gee?

LILBIG.   They been tradin yo Viutex shit on the black market to other islands.

PRINCE.   An activity you aint no stranger to neither, big rapper. Let's keep it real, as youse like to say.

LILBIG.   Man, that went out of style back in the two thousands. When you last listen to hip hop, my brutha?

PRINCE.   I aint your brother. You with them, that makes you my enemy. Speaking of brothers... Temwen! Go bring Vincent here.

Temwen ushers in Vincent, bound in chains.

PRINCE.   Well well well. Brother o mine. Fish done just fell right out of your skull and into your lungs.

BARB.   What's he saying?

VINCENT.   That an old Sagosian sayin. It means your true face been revealed. Somethin like that.

PRINCE.   You know what my brother Vincent here done? He tried to organize the assassination of Nelson Rodgers.

MRDOK.   Well good for him! I'm proud of you, boy.

PRINCE.   Oh, he your boy all right. Mister *President*. He done a real fine job bein your boy. In ways you might not even fathom. Do you know it was your sons over here he persuaded to kill Nelson?

MRDOK.   I don't think my sons have been trained in shooting. Have they, Gee?

GORDINA.   I'm unaware if they have.

MRDOK.   But even so. I'm sure they were just doing it to defend the nation.

GORDINA.   Yes! For our nation's protection and honor!

MERRILL.   The strange thing is something tells me they didn't do it for that reason.

PRINCE.   That's very perceptive of you, Miss Former Porn Star.

Enter Miki and Makiko.

MIKI.   Oh, why look at this crowd! Here I was thinking we were all alone on this island. I should be able to find Gordo here. Excuse me, has any one of you seen a man named Gordo Abu Lary Whiteman? He's corpulent, sweats a lot, has greasy hair, and has won my heart. I'm here to make him my husband.

Everyone laughs. Gordina steps forward, her wig on sideways.

GORDINA.   Miki, what are you doing here?!

MIKI.   Gor… Gordo? Is that you?

GORDINA.   I am not Gordo anymore, Miki. I am afraid I cannot be the person you want me to be. I have changed my gender. Not only that, I have fallen in love with our poet laureate. [*To Collins:*] You might as well hear the truth now, Collins.

COLLINS.   Um, I, uh… I'm afraid I will not be, um, available to make that kind of commitment. I'm, uh… What's the word I'm look-ing for?

RICK.   Disgusted? Mortified?

GORDINA.   Shut it, Rick, before I have *you* put on trial for crimes against culture.

PRINCE.   Speaking of show trials, I think it's about time for some executions.

TEMWEN.   Finally!

MA.   Kill these Japanese tourists first! They've been sent to this island as spies, haven't they, Barb? They're not tourists at all! They're a common enemy, out to disrupt me and Barb's new investment scheme! Whether you are quasi-native, quasi-colonial, quasi-elite, quasi-human, whatever, we can all agree: Kill the Japs now! Before they destroy everything we've worked for!

MRDOK.   Guys, I have a vision. I'm going to remodel time on the island. Gee, get this down… Instead of Sunday through Saturday, each day of the week—no: every day of the year—is going to have its own name. Three hundred sixty five names of days for an entire year.

RICK.   Three hundred sixty six for leap year?

MRDOK.   Exactly. Therefore, in a sense, every single day will be a holiday, with a different reason to celebrate.

GORDINA.   Oh Mrdok. You're such a genius! I'm going to see to it that this goes into effect immediately. As soon as we get out of this hostage situation.

PRINCE.   You're not going to.

MAKIKO.   We can help you remodel time on the island. I happen to be an expert in this area. Not to mention your daughter-in-law. If that means anything to you…

MERRILL.   The Japs are drunk. I just noticed.

RICK.   Where did they get the booze from? I want some!

MAKIKO.   We're drinking Japanese whisky. But since you all are saying such horrible things about us, we're not going to let you have a single drop.

BOBBY.   I didn't know Makiko could speak English.

STEVO REY.   I didn't either. And she's been my girlfriend now for nearly ten years! You learn all sorts of things during a revolution.

BARB.   I guess this storm has brought out an interesting side of each and every one of us. A side that might help us better understand ourselves, and perhaps even build a lasting peace here on this island.

Prince cocks his gun.

PRINCE.   Okay, so who wants to die first?

VINCENT.   No, brother! Can't you see? A peaceful resolution is right around the corner.

PRINCE.   It can't be. Not when you have the quasi-elites. We cannot have even one measly quasi-elite dwelling on this island. The people will not stand for it.

VINCENT.   Suddenly you speak for the people.

PRINCE.   I don't. Yang Zhu does.

GORDINA.   And you are the voice of this Yang Zhu?

PRINCE.   Yes. If you don't believe me, we can all go to the temple right now and ask Him. He will tell you the correct answer.

VINCENT.   What I object to, above all, is the use of violence inherent in your conception of Yangism, brother. If you want to have a revolution, fine. But let it be along political grounds, culture. Let's change the system here, make this a real democracy, not the fake one that they're proposing. We can run for office. *You* can run for office. But you won't be taken seriously as a politician if all you want to do is kill people.

RICK.   Yeah. Unless you're President of the United States.

PRINCE.   What you say, brother, amounts to treason. There can be no collaboration whatsoever with those who have enslaved us. Neither past, present, nor future.

VINCENT.   You sure didn't mind forging an alliance with Nelson Rodgers when he was still alive. Was only a few minutes ago, too.

PRINCE.   I wasn't forging an alliance, you imbecile. I was manipulating him into believing we were forging an alliance. I was using him for my own ends. Our own ends. The endgoal being the bloody triumph of the total Sagosian revolution.

VINCENT.   Brother, Yang Zhu didn't believe in war.

GORDINA.   There is indeed a tension here between orthodoxy and liberalism well worth exploring.

MERRILL.   If only to be able to watch the resulting explosion as mere captive spectators.

MRDOK.   *Captive* being the operative word here.

VINCENT.   Because Yangism, in its originary conception, was against *all* forms of collectivization. Which means Prince's efforts here… Well, the implications certainly don't bode well.

MERRILL.   We need an outside expert on this.

BARB.   Bring back Nelson Rodgers from the dead.

Nelson pops up.

NELSON.   It is true that Yangism would seem to preclude any such manifestations of collective will. However, Yangism as it has been lately practiced on the island—what with the revival of ceremonial rituals in the temple and so forth, seems to indicate an interpretative split from the originary doctrine. An inevitable process in the evolution of oblations, with parallels in the Protestant split, Sunni and Shi'ite Islam, etcetera.

MERRILL.   Nietzsche was right, then. Everything is cyclical, isn't it?

GORDINA.   Which, one might argue, makes renewal all that harder to attain.

MA.   If it is the sort of renewal meant to be awash in bloodshed…

PRINCE. Yang Zhu was not against war, per se. He was just against participating in it himself. 为我. We are thus not breaking from the doctrine. We are merely waging war on his behalf.

MERRILL. They should build a memorial to every dream ever had by each individual human. Then this planet would be filled with dream monuments. Dreams are the only things worth commemorating. All other statues can be safely knocked down and destroyed.

HARRY. Oh I like that!

MRDOK. Me too. Too bad it isn't practical.

BARB. Neither is starting a new country. That hasn't stopped some of us.

NELSON. If we look at what your ancestors were doing around the time that Yang Zhu was actually proselytizing, they were producing a pottery devoid of imagery and ornament. While over in Europe, the adornments of ornamental iconography, rigid in their two-dimensionality, ruled the aesthetic universe. But in China, in their unadorned purity: the true image of godlessness.

VINCENT. It sounds like you're talkin about the pottery of the much later Song Dynasty, Nelson. Yangism had its roots in the Warring States period, when the Hundred Schools of Philosophy flourished.

GORDINA. I agree with Vincent. A medievalist really ought to keep their thoughts to themselves. Lest they contaminate the poisonous modernity for which we have all fought in violent earnest.

RICK. Go back to being dead, Nelson. When we need more colonialism, we'll call you.

Nelson dies again.

VINCENT. Anyway, the point I'm trying to make is that the secular interpretation of Yangism is worth preserving. Not the extremist version that my brother wishes to spread. Yangist extremism will be the end of this island. It will be the end of all Sagosians, too. Can't we learn to compromise, brother?

PRINCE.   Tell that to the impoverished people called the Sagosians who now rely on this faith because it is the very last thing they have left, everything else having been destroyed.

VINCENT.   Maybe then you should explain to them Yangism in its historical context. Its emergence coincided with the first pangs of a post-agrarian moment in Chinese history, when material things and the first stirrings of culture were making themselves felt. Therefore, the emergence of a hedonistic philosophy of some sort was rather inevitable; though the fact that it did not survive speaks for where China ultimately arrived at. (Go to China today, no one's heard of Yang Zhu. Laozi, Chuangzi, okay. No Yangzi.) In the context of its adaptations by the Yangist pirates who were the forebears of the current day Sagosians, the anarchistic elements of the philosophy really came to the fore…

As the two brothers have been debating, the quasi-elites managed to sneak off and escape. Now they notice, though it's clearly too late.

VINCENT.   Wait… Where'd they all go?

PRINCE.   Ahh shit.

EPILOGUE.

Spoken by Mrdok and Nelson's corpse.

MRDOK.   Now I must confess: this Brown Sea affair's an excremental mess!

NELSON.   Maybe it's all a dream, I don't know.

MRDOK.   Come on, Nelson, let's do some blow!

NELSON.   Maybe I never existed to begin with. This isle, all its spirits. But to finally put an end to these panegyrics—

MRDOK.   Or at least no more hysterics!

NELSON.   … let us at least admit to what our charms have prevented us from attaining. That is, to give in to what makes us human—

MRDOK.   Without explaining. Because to explain is to deny what has yet to be overthrown. All the strength I have left is my own.

NELSON.   And what will you do with me? Bury me in the sea? I am afraid there is no satisfactory ending to this play. All the hopes of your audience have long run away.

MRDOK.   I think they are happy that you're dead and gone. Though I'm a bit sad that you can no longer serve as my pawn.

NELSON.   You have a few others you haven't yet thrown away. No doubt you'll put them onstage in some sequel to this play. Still, there's a thing that can't be evaded, it will remain long after this act has faded: Truth isn't something that can be tapdanced around. Nor retrieved from the lost and found. The forces you've unleashed are beyond your knowing. From off this island you'll soon be going, likely in a state similar to my own. That is: permanently lodged in the non-living zone.

MRDOK. I love how you think such threats reach my head. For all you know I'm already dead. The world I live in is not limited by fear; it is clearly not a world you could ever domineer.

NELSON. And yet I am fine with this absence of living. Looking back, I only have one misgiving: that I lost my dear Sagosia to such a reckless fool, who has turned the place into a real cesspool.

MRDOK. All those things we have been offered as part of the world and all the things the world has failed to offer us. Being keen to hold on to what you have not been offered is called a sin. I will not allow this world to reign me in! Endurance is a lost art, with the remnant scent of a stale fart. But now I must prepare for my next act; we're going to war, now that's a fact. I'll blow these quasi-native asses away with the soldiers in my pay. I'm unafraid of what comes next, because, after all, I've already written the text.

PART TWO

PHANTOM LIMB

THE WATERS OF the Brown Sea are shit brown. Not golden or russet, but a definite mottled sense of uncleanliness. Home of the giant storied but never-before-seen Feces Monster, capable of swallowing entire naval brigades whole, farting out their digested remains in the form of smoke as it swims along in search of its next bit of diseased prey. The sands of Cove Beach by contrast somehow manage to retain their pristine appearance, counter-intuition seeming to protect these shores. Though, who really knows for sure—certainly none currently damned to dwell upon them, in the shadow of the submerged unseen.

At first, it was just the translucent jellyfish washing up on shore in alarming quantities. Jellyfish being harbingers of evolution and the change of climate… some say they will outlast the human race, just as they preceded us… Then, shortly after their abrupt turning—from crystalline to the purest evocation of excrescence—the waters brought with them an array of dead fish floating. Trout, marlin, salmon, snapper, barracuda at first, then even bigger roamers of the eternal blue—dolphin and whale and sandshark. All those dead eyes staring at the gray clouds hovering over, eyes that'd frequently burn those clouds with their rays and cause all sorts of meteorological damage and/or damnation to come spewing forth, disregarding all human cares and concerns, let alone needs (for what is the definition of human need according to the barren cruelty of Nature?), let the rains come and let a wind stir up to push those rains ever harder down. Brown people'd then rush to the shores where those brown waters were pushing those silver punished fish, scrap them up hurriedly into baskets and plastic bins hurriedly made and prepared, then dash back to their makeshift dens to haphazardly clean them with boiled water and roast over trash-fueled fires, feasting on toxicity as explosions in the sky above and in the surround whistled into booming ejaculation, the half-starved populace by now too accustomed to to be startled by.

A whole army of Ahabs; Mrdok can afford it, even though he's not one himself. More importantly than army (ground control), he needed a navy fleet to constantly patrol the island, the seas surrounding, keeping it secure. And an air force, to make sure they don't try to enter from above. The Ahab Army. He thought he had it. Until it became clear he was no longer in control. And that's when the real battle started...

After the explosions quieted down for long enough—according to some mysterious rhythm everyone learned to sense—rush outside to see which limbs had come detached from which bodies, which bodies come detached from which names... Battle-scars and mutilations seek to enunciate themselves beneath dim patch of sunlight while the lone squawkings of some soon-to-be-extinct commentarying invisibly from above.

Decommission that general, bring in another that tells you the things you wish to hear. It doesn't matter, anyway, not when depression sets in. For a day or so, then another day'd come to rouse him out of it, give him new hope toward resolution. Mrdok is going to run full straight ahead into the jaws of the future screaming his fucking head off like a banshee or Michael Jackson with his hair on fire. Anyone who isn't along for the ride *deserves* to die.

Here's to the unending we all wish you could be here to enjoy. Precarious postcard of doom in front of your mottled ego face, grinning out at the world of dumb dervish saintliness unwhirling, we aren't the world.

One would think eating mutant fish would cause all kinds of cancerous outbreaks, but the Sagosians seem immune, even strengthened, as though the nucleite were some mineral enhancement long lost to mammalic nutrition now rediscovered for a posthistoric species. Though it is also true that sickness and hunger left unchallenged that dividing line meant to separate. And when the men started returning to shore at the end of the day with empty nets, the collective intuition of a whole new form of desperation waved its tall finger at them through the night air. Soon, there would be no such thing as sunrise. That is, no one had the strength or will to be up for it. Too dangerous, as when one or other of the enemies (for it became too complicated in this mazelike war structure to determine who the good guys, as traditionally conceived, might be, and so the vast majority of Sagosian civilians were prone to take zero side in the infernal debate) liked most to strike, and since they have long run out of reasonable targets, anything resembling a structure might come to ideate a rational substitute. They were all living mostly in caves and dugouts of their own shovelage round the lone mountain and its rugged gangraped hills, drawing straws when supplies run out to determine who'd next undertake the suicidal journey to which shore. To bring back more carcinogenic wastage with which to nourish themselves until they were unlucky enough to themselves become wastage in some muddled exchange of crossfire or else burnt ants in some drone-led aerial bombardment.

Lucia's managed to turn herself into quite an effective runner. Part luck, of course, but mainly her skill on those blades, she manages to time it right so that she dodges all explosives raining down… Course, there's a certain science to bombing a moving target that can be difficult, if not to master, then to execute under a state of blurred vision. Mouse dives into a hole: where did it go? How to access the hidden tunnel. Requires infiltration, an ally to strap on the ol' mouse costume, squeak and bend in a convincing mouselike manner. The word for *paranoia* in the Sagosian language is etymologically similar to the word for *beholder*. A fanatical lingering inheritance of that post-colonial stinkstain—the domain for those, that is, unwary enough to trace its buried roots to the source. Too many have been killed or otherwise destroyed to make much of that inheritance. Production on *Lives of the Innocents* has halted for the first time in even-history-herself-knows-not-when. At night you can finally make out the constellations, reminding those old enough of the Way Back When—save for those times, past and present, when the burning fires, their flames and the smoke produced by them, polluted that view.

And still, the waves continue to crash, undaunted. Undaunted and oblivious to the wreckage they are literally up against. The storms, lesser in intensity perhaps than that Great One that launched this seemingly endless tempest upon the blighted shores, come and go, as though to provide a temporary soundtrack or else alternating moodscape to the battle scenes. There is no true war without nature's loving involvement. At home, colorful lights of the chandelier in the entrance parlor rumbling. A home like all others that has had to be abandoned for the hastily dug shelters below. Task that took up so much of the SL Home Army's resources they were ill-prepared when the first Australian chopper broke through one of those gray clouds hovering.

Melt your eyes into the sea, soldier. That way you will finally be able to see… something? Perhaps not. Even the lens on those binoculars, fogged-up, seeming to ignore certain truths. It's the Great Layering, the unfathomability of the godless wonder you have learned to pray to, in the absence of any higher hope. Of getting out of here, whole and unsevered, for instance; of seeing mom and the kids you left behind, on what was sold to you as a brief Get Rich Quick mission, to make up for all that had been lost on home shores, all that was promised and never made good on; you can no longer even remember the plane and boat trips that brought you here, wasn't so long ago but now feels it, crowded and stinking in those windowless tubes with your fellow soldiers. Uncertainty is truth in action. War was never on the list of promises. This is the post-storm prefix, pulpy and ready to get unfried. Watch as your new best friend loses his head right next to you. One day literal, the next one figurative. An enemy on two fronts: the natives, quasi-, on the ground right in front of and in back—on all sides actually, and in the skies, some foreign enemy, or foreign so-called, an amalgamation of nations one of which you might have once belonged to, the intelligence, so-called, is not too clear. Bicycle chains ripped from spokes, wrap them round the wheels of this makeshift tank, try to get them over the hill up ahead. Shots ringing out, the eerie echo of a grenade just past exploding in the chambers of your fallow ear—the one still in command.

Look through the spotting scope at the territory you once occupied. Rugged terrain and the enemy's flag squirting its breastmilk all over. Bombs you've never seen or heard of before, bombs that do things besides exploding you have yet to understand, for it is the nature of progress that every war that is fought is a whole new war, one that annihilates all past lessons. Collins Birchfield, war poet, intuits this well. And since receiving the Viutex treatment, the verses flow from the tips of his fingers in an unending spool, without mind's burdensome interference.

> bomb reigns down on subterfuge
> you can imagine yrself glistening out of spite
> the enlightened toilet bright

He doesn't doubt his inheritance, there is no longer space for such doubts within him, no more stuttering confusion frothing the mouth of his innate talents. His mission clearly enunciated, the men keep him safe in one of the tanks, and when they cannot, he is evacuated underground or else into one of the makeshift caves burrow'd into Baldhead, whence his masterpiece-in-progress takes its name. And from there the spillage can resume unfettered. Like the very late (extremely late) modernist he has lower-cased himself into being— gigantism being the implicative corollary to minimalist inference—

those lines shoot spirals into the blithering cascades of brown. Poetry even to be found in the nucleite stainage left behind!—for this, an idiosyncrasy, can certainly not be left unnoted, unmemorialized by the master's ever quibbling pen.

A hammering at the shores of someone else's brilliant flight. Distance, distance. People, civilians, the lost ones who arrived here last, uncertain of their status, all becoming yet dumber with each ray of the setting sun. Bitch dog barking at predawn. No one left to be sure—or so it would seem at most hours close to this one. Soon, optimism goes, we will melt into collective determination. Soon, the hidden world will reemerge to announce its fitness from beneath the cruel batterings. Gelatinous folds of fabric held together by a sudden wind. Insert your legacy here to make sure it still fits.

And yet, oddly enough, it goes on. In one mercifully or mercilessly preserved sliver of the island, a roughly halved section of what was some distant moment ago known as Elias Shores—located more precisely and ironically upon the grounds of the abandoned-then-rapidly-developed resort, the last legs of a makeshift tourism industry have been given space to kick. Largely the daredevil dangerously overconfident dwindizens of Gen Next, clued-in via a series of cleverly psycho-engineered app algorithms that led them here, that made spending their unearned income in a war-torn island paradise seem, not just cool, but urgently necessary—beneficial, even, to themselves and some freedom effort so-called that most could barely articulate, let alone comprehend. Free from the hassles of nuance, they selfie their suntans to the soundtrack of explosions in the far-off-enough-to-impress-but-not-to-endanger, a distance agreed-upon for the benefit of all, since each of the warring entities appears to have some stake in the enterprise. Until a winner is fathomed out of the wreckage, best not to drop any wrenches in the machinery.

There's Bev speaking in her mirrored reflection on her phone screen, the self-selected leader of this campaign. And the official mistress-in-chief, nay, first lady, having married Mrdok in the bunker—this time no suicides followed the ceremony—perhaps history doesn't repeat itself after all... Twas, though, hastily arranged, after Krstal's ongoing carnality had become the talk of the underground, Bev showed up as if on cue to fulfill that face-saving mission. Oh she knew not to show up empty-handed alright. Those glued-together papers on Belle Encoding that she'd fished out of the trash back in Manhattan all those years ago and finally found a use for—well, they wouldn't be enough on their own to seal the deal. She knew she had to have a duty-free purpose wrapped pre-arrival like a bird reads cues from the first peelings of a season. By the time she made her landing, she knew she'd be far too useful to be ignored. But she'd have to make her usefulness known in, like, an expansive way.

–Mrdok. This *entire island* is Instagrammable.

That had been the rich substance of the influencer's post-coital pitch. Not just let's sell the world on the sunshine and relatively unpolluted stretch of beach real estate. She was going to go out there and grab content that, frankly, no one else was foolish enough to venture toward—and certainly not with an iPhone as one's sole weapon.

Yeah. To Mrdok, she was Anywoman—one look at her was enough to awake the unflinching rage of all his insecurities and wildest desires of possession, desires that could never possibly be fulfilled because of the type of man that Mrdok *really* is—this, his tragedy *and* his raison d'être. Part of the time, sure, he managed to fool himself into thinking he was something greater, somehow more *virulent* than the man he actually was. Because his imagination in this regard (his desirability) is largely limited to issues of virulence—a natural side effect of warfare.

Mrdok had to purchase some additional data in order to algorithmize them to come here—there was a generational stopgap on the Belle Encoding stuff they'd brought over, his programmers were really in need of more in order to make the gag really effective. And it was a worthwhile investment, as Elias Shores now ranks as the premiere item on any search engine search for *dark tourism*. Siilky came all the way from Silicon Valley to deliver the thumbdrive. Even though she had a slight harelip, there was something undeniably boner-inducing about her appearance, she was like one of those late 90s punk chicks Mrdok had always fetishized fucking but were too damn smart to ever want anything to do with him, those chicks from that Suicide Girls website or the riot grrl bands, yeah, her blonde hair with streaks of green braided down either side, she wore these huge round black circle sunglasses framed by a leopard print so as to hide her eyes from he and Bev the entire time they were talking even though they were indoors, she kept the meeting brief because she had heard that Mrdok doesn't have the attention span for long meetings. For this meeting, he would have… She had masterminded the theft by spiking the joint with spice she had offered to the CEO of one of the big five Silicon Valley companies at a tech conference in Brazil, she had made her way into his hotel room as a representative of CWC, Chicks Who Code, a made-up nonprofit sure to justify his titillation. While he was passed out, she'd hacked into his laptop and stolen the data and had been on the lookout for up and coming overseas content producers to vend it to. Bev seemed right because she was operating in some dubious legal realm that always spells safety for individuals of Siilky's proclivities. Siilky allegedly invested the profits in plastic surgery, sorta fixed her harelip and got new tits and enhanced her eyelids, a new name and new identity, and a private island of her very own, where she is said to be running a rival empire of online securities fraud, somewhere far out of reach in the Red Sea… Where, nobody knows, Mrdok hears of her activities from time to time and a certain shade of envy floods his earlobe, and yet he is okay with this mild gain even though a part of him knows that were he not so out of his element right now—well, if he weren't having to dwell in an underground bunker, if his sole source of UV light weren't an artificial lamp that Gordo'd brought in and that Mrdok now sits in front of for fifteen minutes each day to absorb all the D3 needed to stave off the paralyzing depression that threatens to take over—he might have a piece in Siilky's game, as well, his profits might, who knows, be doubling or tripling or otherwise maximizing themselves, which reminds him, when Gordo comes in, he really must ask him again how much he's worth, whether the sale of crypto war bonds to the overseas networks has resulted in the spike he's been long predicting…

Topless sunbathing in a g-string. Watch on yr monitor upon the temporary throne. The chocolate dinosaur of happenstance just came out of your ass. Finally—relief! This morbid constipation ever since the war began. To have this pulled out of you, temporaneity. What you don't realize is that, in the pants curled round yr ankles, you just pocket-dialed Barb.

–Hello?... Mrdok?

Pfffffffffffffrrrrrrrp. Splt. Sprrt. Pfff.

–You're fucking disgusting. Don't ever call me on this line again, you imbecile!

Click.

Mrdok, unharmed by the awareness, puts his iPad down to wipe. Difficult with one hand, bull balls out of the way. But promises have been made that the kidnapped appendage will be rescued from the bearded smellful rebels at any hour, confidence further boosted by the news of a new and even better item in current manufacture in M's private medical laboratory not far from his bunker's entrance. He had to admit it was a masterpiece of felonious engineering, that snare. One night he'd drunk himself into a red wine stupor, passed out just before midnight fully clothed in bed, he awoke and the hand was gone. They had somehow managed to infiltrate the bunker. Gordo fired the remaining quasi-native staff they still had en emploi, he wanted to do a further investigation though Mrdok insisted that he not; he was embarrassed, not many people knew of the artificial limb, he didn't want word to get out—best to keep the investigation private. It was clear that it was The Other Side who had taken it. Made him hate them even more. Time to really punishfuck them in this war. The message was passed to the generals and colonels, it's time to take things up a notch, though of course they were not told why. Nobody really knows about the missing hand now except for a select few, Mrdok rarely appears in public because he doesn't want his disfiguration known…

Till the hand regained, testicles to contend with. A mild frustration, but within the past few days, he's sort of gotten used to the stump once again. And noticing the testicles in a new way.

The trade-off indeed worth it—for everyone. Krstal gets to pursue her love unhidden while making future potential film festival favorites, Billy R. Speck boning his leading lady which makes him feel like a genuine auteur. And Mrdok, Mrdok getting laid again at precisely the moment when he had to go underground, when a piece of puss'd become a process to procure. At least *something* good has come out of this war. One less thing for Gordo to have to fret over as he runs among tunnels. And yes, it is Gordo and pronoun he/him once again—for our Gee made the decision to retransition for the war effort. Some might chalk this up to a mere scarcity of hormones. There might even be some truth to that assertion, given the dearth of life-giving supplies in a more general sense that all of the remaining dwelling quasi-elites have unluckily been forced to endure, though Gee himself would insist that the decision was all practical and no medical. That he feels it is only right to be a man in a time of war—or a partial man, to be honest, court eunuch—and that his manshape standing beside Mrdok somehow strengthens the tower when it is most in need of support.

Scroll down. The morning's rich array of content roasting next to the coffee. Bombed-out remnants of the Greek amphitheater where Silence the talking dog, long a casualty of some stray shell, once delivered his oracles to the sunbaked fired masses all stinking of sweat and sea congealed. (Rumor floating that Bev has hired a PR company to train a new dog to do the same trick, though at press time, this was yet to be confirmed.) The rock once composing now split apart like the spikes sticking out from the back of a stegosaurus. The tan rigid formations of scorched earth and a lonely white cloth draped upon an ear-shaped boulder all lopsided diagonal and threatening to turn over, is it a filth-splattered robe or a towel or some other garment, an oversized dustrag abandoned to those abusive elements. Not a green leaf or other parcel of foliage in sight, but some tank tracks in the mud alongside some casings and fuselage bearing traces of the bombardment. Beneath all this in the text box, Bev's misspelled tag *#givepieceachance*.

Mrdok starts to chortle, his chortle erupting into a bellow. Laughter so hard it is a struggle to lift himself off the porcelain throne, but he eventually makes it to the sink, after washing his hand he lifts his watered-down glass of morning bourbon to dry lips and turns the bedroom TV on to Christ's administrative assistant.

–Now, ladies and gentlemen brothers and sisters boys and girls, we can finally *taste* the flavor of Armageddon. And how, *how*, I might ask you, shall we *begin* to *describe* the taste?... Well. There is only one word: bittersweet. Oh—that's right. Armageddon tastes bittersweet! We all knew it was a-coming, didn't we? We all knew that the evils of this world we were all drenched in, that they would some day bring all of God's wrath and fury come rainin down upon us here. And we knew, too, that we, the denizens of this isle, the *settlers* of Settlers Landing, that *we* would be the ones to first feel those dreaded raindrops. For that's what those bombs are, ladies and gentlemen boys and girls sinners and winners: they are raindrops of God's inner private fury turned outward. And the planes dropping em and the drones buzzing about are the electronic clouds containing God's all-seeing eye. He has multiple ones. He is an eyeful being. And He is using those eyes to determine who shall perish and whom He shall *save*. The Final Reckoning is now upon us. And it don't matter how much money you have, your status in this sinful new society that's been built, or even what you once aspired to, back when we could all still aspire. All that matters is that you repent by turning your back to this evil, corrupt war that nobody understands, that we can't even tell who's winning and who is being defeated, that you all turn your attention to the only Real War that is happening, for that battle, ladies and sinners and former breadwinners cast down by the Satanic forces that have taken control of this isle, that *battle* is *spiritual*. It is a Holy War we are fighting, and *that*, I repeat: *that*, is the only war effort worth supporting. To secure your place in Heaven today, on that great battleship of righteousness, go to the website flashing across your screen right now, if your Wi-Fi is down, take your credit card to the nearest phone you can find, God will *protect* you from the rain of bullets—

Mrdok makes a mental note to have this clown killed—that is, if the quasi-natives don't get to him first, have him placed before a military tribunal firing squad for crimes of spiritual pollution or whatever charge they'll inevitably trump up.

Martin sits before the glowing screen, drooling near dumb in that illumination, one of the few left still to watch. He and Lucia alone in their miniscule single room bunker—still a luxury compared to where most of the remaining quasi-natives have been destined to endure this—thanks to their son's gilded patronage. Martin the father—he, too, a fisherman once. Like most of the men on the island. Those sodden olden days, when to be out in a boat frying beneath the deadly rays while you wait patiently for the nets to come up—when that was as complicated as life promised to get. Before shapeshifting into this devolution of himself: this pile of formless sludge, mute and matte in front of the Preacher's televised tirades. Been watching the Preacher ever since his first fateful arrival on the isle, all those years back. Martin was one of his first converts, so-called. Set up to be a receiver of those missives by none other than chance, the unchallengeablity of that place time and all its events has put before him, there in that armchair. Take the armchair away, there'd be no more Martin. He has grown into it. When he was a young man, there was no TV. Not on the island, at least. Father used to get him up every morning five o'clock. As the sun rose before them, they'd gather their nets, the day's supplies, gather them on to the boat and head paddling out. Never gone too far—wasn't until a few years into it that his father got one with a motor—a whole lot further, a whole lot more catch, a whole lot less work… That world when all the men, nearly everyone, was a fisher. He and Lucia met, fell in love, married. Then he had his own sons. By that time, the world was growing fast obsolete. Separate directions: Martin, the world; both his sons; even he and Lucia eventually. She managed to stay part of the world, Martin couldn't bear its changes. She'd appear from time to time on the screen in front of him. Sometimes he couldn't understand the words she was saying. He felt dumb in front of everything he could not comprehend. Dumb in front of this world that was no longer his. TV moved in, faith provided the answer to his loneliness. He has geriatricized prematurely, molding himself into the TV, the Preacher's words. They bathe him in a sort of glassy light. Vincent thought giving him the Viutex treatment would make him somehow come alive again. But it didn't make much of a difference. He talks even less now. Much less to say, though a lot more to feel. Still, doesn't feel the need to communicate it with any of them, his family. Now, the Preacher's words reach him different. Now, it's like the words go directly into his veins, course through his body. He has become addicted to them in a way whereas before they were more like just the soothe of a diversion. Benumbed patriarch of the fallen world, found salvation in the televised spiritual forecast. He stopped talking, period, after the Viutex. Now no one, not even Lucia, who brings him his meals before the TV, gives him sponge baths and gets him to stand up two or three times a day, not even Lucia knows what he's thinking anymore, if he even is thinking…

Solar panels, electrodes, batteries. Just some of the many numbered electronic products that benefit from nucleite and its high conductivity—not to mention drones, which have played such a vital role in the war effort, really serving as the advance guard—not to denigrate our soldiers' valiant efforts at battling the detested and ever detestable enemy fighting for its freedom, so-called. Nucleite, it is believed by many in the scientific community, is the second or third oldest material in the universe—its exact positionality an endless topic of debate for those natural historians of ancient matter whose vision has become tunneled from staring too long into powerful microscopes. Some of the grains extracted from beneath the bed of the Brown Sea have revealed isotopic compositions, clearly inferring a birthdate that predates the solar system, formed in the ejecta of exploding supernovae or perhaps the discarded outer envelopes of prehistoric stars having given up their lives before being damned to shine upon men.

Before the accident, the Settlers Landing nucleite mine was yielding a respectable thirty thousand metric tons a year.

In 1897, the Bessel brothers of Dresden became the first to introduce a commercially successful froth flotation method for the extraction of nucleite. Froth flotation being one process for the separation of minerals from gangue by taking advantage of differences in their hydrophobicity. The ground ore or pulp is mixed with water to form a slurry and the desired mineral is rendered hydrophobic by the addition of a surfactant or collector chemical (although some mineral surfaces are naturally hydrophobic, requiring little or no addition of a collector; nucleite is not one of them.) The slurry (or *pulp*) of hydrophobic particles and hydrophilic particles is then introduced to tanks known as flotation cells that are aerated to produce bubbles. The hydrophobic particles attach to the air bubbles, which rise to the surface, forming a froth. The froth is removed from the cell, producing a concentrate (or *con*) of the target material, while the waste is excreted into a separate tank—mirroring, in a sense, the human digestive process.

A further development, known as the Cattermole process of 1902, emulsified the pulp with a small quantity of oil, subjected it to violent agitation followed by a slow stirring, which coagulated the target minerals into nodules which were then separated from the pulp by the forces of gravity. This became known as agitation froth flotation, which Settlers Landing would adapt, using the radical and untried method of using sea water—the waters of the Brown Sea being remarkably lower in saliency compared to other seas and oceans—as slurry. In addition, the engineers made another innovative decision by positioning the froth flotation cell on the water; so that the flotation cell was itself floating, floating in the sea... A mad genius idea: rather than being attached directly by some column to the bottom of the sea from which the stuff was being extracted, the bottom of the flotation cell utilized wind energy to produce a blowing pressure beneath, incredibly fast powerful blasts that served as a virtual column.

What these engineers neglected to anticipate were the cyclonic winds that accompanied the last megacane, winds that destabilized the cells and then destroyed them, spewing forth all that raw nucleite and gangue and slurry.

Re the spillage. It is true that much of this precious resource has now been lost. Even in wartime, discussion continues as to how to renew this key contributor to the economic sector. One idea floated, if that is not putting it too distastefully, has been to redirect local expertise to the alternative manufacture of nuclear nucleite; a sort of cush alternative to the real stuff.

Nuclear nucleite—that is, the utilization of nucleite as a neutron moderator in the nuclear fission process—is not without its own spillage controversies. The two major accidents to date being the Windscale fire of 1957 as well as the more storied Chernobyl disaster of 1986. Though in both incidents, despite the bad name it has earned as a result, the nucleite reactors were little to blame. Experimentation was at fault in the former incident. An untested annealing process for the nucleite was tried out. This caused overheating in unmonitored areas of the core, leading to the fire's ignition. It was not the nucleite monitor itself that ignited but rather those canisters of metallic uranium fuel within the reactor. By the time the fire was put out, it was revealed that the sole areas of the nucleite moderator to have incurred thermal damage were those that had been close to the burning fuel canisters.

When it comes to Chernobyl, the moderator again bore no responsibility for the primary event. Rather, a massive power excursion during a mishandled test caused the catastrophic failure of the reactor vessel and a near-total loss of coolant supply. As a result, fuel rods commenced their swift melt, flowing together in an extremely high state of power, causing a small portion of the core to reach that state of prompt criticality so relied upon by nuclear weapons and leading to a massive release of energy. The reactor core exploded, the building housing it flew to pieces. The massive energy release during the primary event superheated the nucleite monitor, and the disruption of the reactor vessel and the building that contained it allowed the superheated nucleite to come into contact with atmospheric oxygen. The nucleite moderator was thus set ablaze, releasing a plume of highly radioactive fallout into the atmosphere over a very widespread area... In a word, clearly nucleite was the falsely accused.

Nucleite's safety, its innocence lies in its unfettered purity. It might aid certain processes in which part of the world sees reflections of its very downfall. But the material itself, in either its natural or synthetic state, is but a tool in these processes. And, detached even further from them in one's mind, can be viewed in its purest state as a commodity. It is this pure vision that protects, so-called, certain interests, so-called... Even if there is no such thing in this world as an innocent actor.

At this point in the game, Mrdok favors abandoning nucleite altogether and turning toward the comparative simpler extraction of ilmenite from those stretches of Elias Shores that are pearly white rather than ruby red. He's gotten Abe, Minister of the Environment and still-current commodities broker, on his side, too. But some of the senators are still stuck on nucleite. And so the conversation has stalled for now.

The storm hit, and then the war, and then another storm, and then the resumption of the war, until there was almost nothing left building-wise near any of the coasts. Even the houses inland and part of the capital, re-named Mrdokia, suffered the wanton destruction.

—If pressed to describe myself, I would say I'm a low-carb pescatarian with a medium-high following on social media.

Bev livestreams and insta-tags and blogs while Monsieur de Broqueville already put an EU tariff on nucleite from Settlers Landing, which he and the rest of the civilized world so-called still insist on calling Sagosia, long before the war began and so perhaps the spillage was all for the best since selling the stuff was to become even more of a hassle than producing it.

Inside the barracks, Unit 307, the *commando unit*, SL Home Army. Portrait of dilapidation here. Spring sunshine my ears don't hear, they are ringing with the whir of gear, explosions not too distant, some of them right near. First Lieutenant Dorita Vandross calls in her ragtag assemblage of what's left. Deep in this makeshift bog where saintly wiles go to ploy, ringing angularity of cleavage must be staved off in order to guard the remaining weaponry. Lt. Dorita unpacks a pistol from the depths of her bra, sets it on the mess table, orders Second Lieutenant Bevis N. Domerider to clean it. Lt. Domerider is an excellent pistol-whip and an even better pistol cleaner, having learned the trade as an infantryman in Afghanistan all those years back. His second specialty is digital warfare, but there's not much use for that here, since the rebels have taken the war offline, and have even proven themselves adept at shooting down spitfire drones. How they do it, no one can figure out; they must have some sort of night vision gear provided by the Chinese or some other foreign actor who've involved themselves in the project of the Home Army's defeat. Mulling this over for too long instills a hopelessness best left in the recycling bin of the uncontemplated.

She peruses the dead list in front of her, taking her munchings from a plate of makeshift sushi that's been assembled—mainly the cleansed ingredients of what was found washed up after last night's battle. They've constructed a kinda-sorta base by piecing together the trailer wreckage in the south and have been able to hold the lower part of the island now for some seven weeks, the Enemy having taken control over the upper five-eighths of the land territory. But their hold is slipping even further. Lt. Vandross, with her calm mind, has been promoted after the second-in-command, Sgt. Wellington, fell full throttle to PTSD paranoia that the dwindling supplies of medication suddenly failed to stymy. He's locked up now, in the same bunker with the POWs they've managed to capture, the ones they haven't bothered to kill yet and are still pressuring, so-called, into giving information. Information that is still not forthcoming… Nothing useful at least… Rife with the misunderstandings that hornily accumulate in the boglands that this nation's inner recesses have become in their bombed-out state of apocalyptic abandonment, Thanatos has left his skidmarks all over the horizon…

It is a multiplicitous Enemy, for what was once a civil war has now been enriched with troops from seemingly all over. Daily reconnaissance missions filled with speculations as to who they're truly fighting, what to target and where and when. The quasi-native rebels being engineered into real soldiers by the Australians, the British, the

Belgians, the who… Even some Americans, or maybe that is just a rumor.

The one thing that truly disturbs the otherwise indomitable spirit of the Liberation Army is that the Home Army has occupied the Temple, which is being used as a guardpost. From his lookout point on the middle shaft of Baldheaded Mountain, Prince now stares through binoculars at that temple longingly, a true possession that has been struck from the roster. He lowers his binoculars and submits to time, because it is all he can do at this point. In this decimated pelted landscape, the lone Bible is that of asymmetrical warfare, and it hasn't been written down, they must all rely on Prince's honed instinct; raw as it is, it has also gotten them this far. And so maybe… Thing is, he's never sure of his direction—not literal direction, just his metaphysical instinct seems to be out of whack at key moments—and his underlings tend to intuit this. It takes its toll on troop morale—hard to fight hungry for an ideal one is too foam-mouthed to properly enunciate—but if they can get back the temple, that will truly be something. A victory on more than one front.

Prince had arrived at his doctrine through a cursory study of various revolutionary movements throughout history. In particular, he was taken by the template developed by Cuba in their revolutionary war. Under the command of Che Guevara and Fidel Castro, the Cubans defined asymmetrical warfare in opposition to what they deemed academic or traditional warfare, a tactic inevitably relied upon by the enemy. The Cuban revolutionaries were, of course, equal part fighters and intellectuals, deploying their Marxist analytical instincts toward the art of war in a way that the larger and more seasoned army sergeants could readily dismiss as idealistic baloney. The Cubans' onslaught was indeed rooted in a kind of schoolless approach to combat: knocking the enemy off his feet at that precise split second when he did not realize he was standing. It was all, Prince gathers, about *feeling*, knowing the enemy from within his skin. Knowing the trappings by which they had been educated—even never having had access to that education himself, his Yangist instinct honed into a discipline others'd call recklessness, especially each time a soldier lost… But fuck those traitors who express doubt out loud, they will be dealt with in full severity later on, once their services are no longer required.

Pseudotropical twilight breezes juiceless through the banyans, the eagleless sky. On the streets of what was briefly known as Mrdokia, Liberation Army soldiers patrol in pairs through that diamond night. They've managed to reignite the streetlamps, at least, to ensure a clear vision of the mottled state. Prince, it is known, has already been drawing up plans for a new city, a new capital, once the war has finally come to an end and the island is returned to the Sagosians. To build their own nation, their own capital; their own army and a system that is based on rightness, fairness, the Yangist way... The Yangist way as interpreted *correctly*, that is, as interpreted by Prince himself, and with the island's defenses secured. The glow of those soldiers in their green fatigues, moving across the brown spot of night.

–Fuck that. I'm goin to Canada when this all over.

Jersey chewin on a fern, walkin his patrol alongside Bora, second lieutenant.

–Canada? Why the fuck?

Bora don't understand much about the entertainment industry, never has, he bein a part of the fisherfolk, the poorest of the poor. Jersey, the fancy director, he joined the war effort because he occupied too high a position in the world that was Sagosian cultural life. As director of *Lives of the Innocents,* he had no choice but to take a stand—not like he could hide behind apoliticism like some of his actors done did. That's not to say he much believed in the fight that was goin on.

–They say that they offerin refugee status to all Sagosians who manage to get out of here. They don't help you escape, you got to get there on your own. But once you hit they land, you a Canadian.

–And what the hell you gonna do in *Canada?*

Bora can't even place it on a blank map.

–Man, Bora, you don't know nothin do you. Canada in *desperate* need of soap opera directors. They fuckin soap industry been in decline since at least the 1990s. All they talent done got taken away by the Americans. They's prime territory now for a soap opera revival. And I gonna lead it.

Another explosion. The soldiers duck down. How much am I worth?

Inside the temple, Home Army third-in-command Nihil Donaldson peering through the telemetric scope.

–Holy shit! I think that one just hit near the capital. Woo-hoo!

He takes a celebratory hit off the meth pipe.

–Pembroke's been turned into a fucking US military base, from what I hear, says fourth-in-command Ernest McAnally, chewing on one of his PTSD pills. That's the place where all their drones are now originating from. I don't think there are any actual US soldiers on *our* island. They're remote controlling the whole goddamn thing from over there, all the help, so-called, they're giving to the animal Yangists. But Pembroke, man. Gotta feel sorry for those desperate fucks. Whatever autonomy *they* once had sure as fuck's been lost.

Ignore the implication that even if the Home Army does manage to win the war, they'll have the Americans pawing as the eternal wolf at the door. Unless the war effort then extends to Pembroke... And then on to the other islands?

–Fuckin Americans, says Nihil, smoke pouring out of his rotten frown. Makes me hate these quasi-native bastards even more.

Nihil reckons he's got more to fight for than anyone here. Fuck America, he'll never go back there. Never since they took his badge away after that shooting. Wasn't even his fault; Jesus made him do it.

–Gross, Nihil.

–... What?

–You don't even realize? Are you that high, man? You just let one go. Fuckin stinks in here now.

–I can't help it! America makes me fart!

Nevermind the *order* of the hierarchy—what bugs Lt. Vandross is that she can hardly gauge the *size* of the hierarchy, the weight of the boulder they are now upholding. It goes something like this: First the Australians declared a proxy war, supposedly in retaliation for the imprisonment of their ex-Prime Minister (who never, apparently, apologized for fucking Mrdok's ex-wife—apparently in Australia adultery isn't recognized as a sin!), while also simultaneously investing a three-quarter share in the Elias Shores resort, promising a quarter of that share to the Yangist rebels in the event that they're victorious. (Little are they aware of Prince's intention to nationalize all industry minutes after declaring victory...) They were soon joined by the Americans, whose interest and involvement actually commenced many moons ago following SunEye's dissolution after the Cuban plane incident, its disgruntled exec Louis Farquahson—or *Fart Moccasin* as Mrdok has taken to calling him—had pooled his personal resources into the formation of a new lobbying group in Washington padded largely with retirees from FBI and CIA and various other intelligence agencies with connections reaching all the way up to the very top, whose sole intent seemed to be the plotting of Mrdok's fall. Then, unbeknownst to even the quasi-natives themselves (let alone the SL Home Army), they are being aided further by a disgruntled faction of Chinese. Which would be directly related to the, in retrospect, rather elegant con job performed by Yeh and No all those evenings ago in Hong Kong. For—as Mrdok and his fellow quasi-elites are bound to find out sooner or later—Viutex was, in pointed fact, *not* the invention of Doctor Yeh. Rather, the good doctor stole the formula from the Chinese, in coordination with the North Koreans, in an exercise funded by Lallyburt, whose hands turned out to be much larger, his pockets much deeper than Mrdok had previously gauged.

–But what do we do with the hand?

They're keeping it in a black light-illuminated aquarium beneath a miniature statue of Yang Zhu watching over it night and day. Temwen's concerned about the probability of a factionalist split soon emerging within the revolutionary folds if a strong decision doesn't stake itself into the ground within another twenty-four or forty-eight max. Already, the appearance of Prince's waffling imprecision in the matter has made a nasty mark on internal optics.

–Goddamnit Temwen if it aint the sixth time this week you asked me the damn question. We aint doin nothin with the hand now cept keepin it safe. Safe till the right moment arrives. We gonna use it as a tool, tool for negotiation. It's gotta keep right—

–But what *kinda* negotiation?

Temwen clearly just wants this war to end. In that he might be inferring the general consensus, and Prince gets that all right, he wants it all to end too, nothing more than that, but if it don't end the way they've all been *fighting* for it to end, then it will mean THE END painted in a much darker shade than the rest are currently conjuring in their fidgeting malawares.

The answer, of course, bein he don't know. But it has to be the kind of negotiation that's gonna bring him down to his knees. Sodden bastard done destroyed so much of life there aint even much left to it. Except some mild feeling of victory. The real battles already been fought, now they at a stalemate for, what, seems like months now. And they still in the temple, the most annoying feat of all. Prince he can't even be standin in the same room as that hand because if he sees it, wants to destroy it up, slash it into pieces right then and there. It up to Temwen to keep the hand safe in whatever hidden chamber. Maybe the grotesque certainty, his knowledge of where it located be destabilizin his brain.

–... We might not know who our enemies on this earth are. But we do know who our Savior is. That is a thing that is *most* certain. And we know who our enemy down below is, oh yes ladies and gentlemen creatures human and not, fair-headed warriors fightin the good fight for the sal*va*tion of our *nation* and for the human souls contained therein...

Now he can't hide the sweat come dripping down his forehead. The sweat glistens translucent beneath those lights, and if you hone your eyes in on it, you can perceive greens and pinks of reflection, the effect being similar to boring into uncut crystal or diamond. He doesn't bother to hide it at a certain point, does away with the handkerchief as a prop, he knows the precise moment when sweat must be introduced as a signifier, just the texture needed to maintain the viewer's gaze upon whatever must be sustained of this current sermon. He's been going at it for some seven hours now. Since *Lives of the Innocents* had to go off the air, he has a lot more time to preach his word. And it gets delirious at times, this stream of conscious blarble, and it gets repetitive, and it gets to the point where he froths into a sort of sacred tongue of holy nonsense. And he has to wonder who out there is still watching, because he is rather isolated himself in that studio because he cannot return to the bunker anymore, it is just not safe to travel, and so he stays there, the studio has become his bunker, his safe place, and he hasn't seen the sun in weeks now, the only glare comes from those studio lights cast by the skeleton crew remaining, quasi-native sellouts though that's not how they see themselves of course, more like people who just made a simple decision based upon solid economics, who view *taking a stand* as something that only those with privilege can afford to do.

Time is a key element in asymmetric warfare. And this is where both sides are now. Prince knows that strategic patience is anathema to the enemy's broiling paranoia.

They've arranged to meet at the shore beneath the three-quarter moon. Lucia sees Vincent up ahead and drops the blades she's carrying, almost a maternal reflex, to begin running toward him, then she turns round to pluck them out of the sand and commence her running till she reaches her son's strong vanilla-scented vein-valiant arms. She stifles an urge to cry as she peels her way out of his grasp and they retreat from the sea's bronzed lappings to the safety of tree coverage where they sit in silence a while till one of them figures out a way to break it.

–Do Prince know? she asks.

–That we meeting? Doubt it. But I lost communication with him a long time ago, mama.

She nods into the breeze, understanding. Understanding what a broken family is—attained that understanding a long time ago. This beckoning toward remembrance—will she go there?

The bag next to the rollerblades.

–Brought you something.

Unfurls.

–Where'd you get beer? Mama…

–Sssssshhhhh.

–I can't drink now even if I—They won't let me.

–Hush now. You drink one with me. We share one.

Lucia cracks open the can.

–Soon as we finish this war, I want you to come back and live with me. Wherever it is we will be. Me and your father… We build a new home together. Maybe it won't be like it used to be.

–Mama I don't see this war ending anytime—

–Hush I know that. Here, drink. Truth is, we don't know how long your father. It's not like it used to be, son.

–They still bringing you weekly provisions in the bunker? You need anything—

–We wants our sons back, is all. Your father *needs*. He even more of a ghost of his self than he was five years ago. Back when you knew him.

Half-moon shivers on the sea that is gray now in the dark of near morning.

–We could send a nurse in…

–You know there's no point to that. He on his way out. Truth is, a part of me glad. Since you and Prince gone, it's the sole reality I got to confront each day. Specially since no more *Lives of the Innocents*. It's draggin me down. Even more than the everything else.

Bird erupts. Some half-baked mating call. (Knowing it is not to be answered…)

–This battle, ma. Do you understand it? What it's all about?

–I know enough not to involve myself witit. Howmi supposed to feel? With two sons on either side.

–Well. It's a little more complicated than that, Mama.

–I know I know. Your brother started it. That's what you're about to tell me. And you just goin with the side that pays you…

–We're the ones protecting you now, Mama. You and dad. Surely you understand that. It aint Prince sittin here drinkin this beer with you now, is it?

Now he does have a point there, and it's not like Lucia hasn't reckoned with it and its full throttling force of implications like any mother in her position inevitably would. The unfairness of it all, she had to let it wash over her. There's no chapter on personal survival in any of the manuals of parenthood. Where one is forced to choose between which of the children that is gonna keep you alive…

It wasn't intentional, Prince's abandonment. Even Vincent knows this, scarce the chance there is of him ever admitting it.

Shakespeare, perhaps never having had a brother himself, was obsessed with brotherly rivalries, allowed them to form the basis of nearly all his tragedies—the important ones, at least. Great drama in the grand unfolding of what is essentially a rivalry with the mirror; man extending himself outward, externalizing those bits of himself he never wishes to confront so as to annihilate them. This, utter madness, is what it means to become a ghost. Having devoted a lifetime to the evasion of ever having looked at yourself too crudely and closely.

–Prince my son, she says. But to be honest about it, he hard to know right now.

Overly mild understatement, Vincent swallows it with the last of the beer.

–We'll meet again after the next storm, he says in lieu of contradicting her.

–Like always, her reply, because, under circumstances such as these, there is little to be asserted that hasn't been before.

–Do you know how hard it is to wipe with one hand? Especially when you got balls like this?

Mrdok waving the stump around in Gordo's face. It is rather disgusting looking, and so Gordo, having gorged himself at lunch today owing to the sudden availability of starches and meats long absent from the settler diet, must struggle to choke back the vomit. Look away in a way that doesn't seem too obvious or revealing of disgust, so as not to offend the ever offendable.

–I can assure you that great progress is being made in engineering the new—

–I don't want the new one, Mrdok sniffs. I can't trust it—How do I know these people really know what they're doing? Getting a new one means having to relearn how to use it… I want my old one back. That's the one I understand how to use.

Is it night or day? It is hard to tell the hour inside the bunker, thus clocks everywhere. You learn to ignore them. You don't want to be haunted by the truth every time you look up. And so the perpetude of sleeplessness sets in. A key factor in feeling that demon rise within you each day, at each hour that you suddenly find yourself waking up, not having remembered ever going to sleep.

Sing a song that's an ode to annihilation. Breathless blow the days right past us. They teach us how to sing, how to be one with the righteousness we have long preached, the something we were surely all born into. Screens of a divided night torn asunder by technologies ill-facilitated ill-understood, a knife could do the trick so much easier, we are fathomless ourselves and cannot hold in the splintered lessons imbibed, let alone pass them via standard means of digestion. Lists of deadened eyes and arms, battle scars, phantom limbs asserting their floating place amongst the carnage. Vegetable wants and needs and withered fleas. A dream that just, well, what? Aches in front of your face each day, sends you into spasms of spasming lust. Each time a comrade fallen, a vow to kill three more quasi. Till your mind becomes preoccupied with arithmetic, it overrides strategy, days like this one you don't even know which battle you're fighting, shots ring out and is it our command or theirs, febrile beckoning the wanton calibration, reload your rifle and shoot, shells fall out kid runs round to collect for the victorious war museum in progress, everyday life a new chance to get shot in the face, by now you've seen too much you no longer get paranoid, everything has trained you into honing those primitive animal instincts the rest of us are trained to overcome in an existence deemed civilian; to harness the animal the gateway path back to a salvation marked by original goal, days like this difficult to discern. Fervid beckoning into silence as an answer. Sound as warfare.

Lilbig still detached from the rest—his bunker under his house in the north. Still, got his weed and his comics, got his girl, got his studio built, he don't give a shit about the rest, at this point he just lookin for a way off this island first chance he get. Problem is, he still has to find extraditionless territory, all dat bullshit back in da US, not to mention the wrath of the baby mamas and all theys chile support suits. After all da shit these bitches done pulled on his ass all those years back, he aint givin no coins to no bitch, and that's a fack, Jack. You don't like that shit, go up there on da rooftop, let them commando muthafuckas blow yo ass to shit.

GOWANUS POLYAMOROUS KETO PALEO PESCATARIAN: Stevo Rey! Haven't heard from you in like *years,* man. What have you been up to—and, most importantly, can fans expect a new Mormons album this year?

STEVO REY: Things've been hectic in my world, okay? I moved from one island, where I'd been based for many many years, to another one far far away.

GoPoKePalP: That would be Sagosia, I'm guessing?

SR: Settlers Landing, man.

GoPoKePalP: But that's not really the *woke* name of the island, is it?

SR: Look, I'm not gonna get into politics, mainly because it bores me. I'm just living for my art out here, you know what I'm saying?

GoPoKePalP: Must be hard living for your art when a war's going on around you. How are you holding up? I guess you're in a safe place?

SR: Oh I've never been in a safe place. Not since I was a young child. I've always been pretty much living on the edge. It's a wonder I evaded getting arrested so many times in Tokyo. But yeah, I'm safe from all the violence that's going on out there. If that's the question you're asking…

GoPoKePalP: I imagine all that brutality must be, like, a huge artistic inspiration for you.

SR: You know, the new Mormons sound has been going in a couple different directions of late. I'm still harnessing the raw power, the harsh noise that all my hardcore fans still love—still crave, really. But I've been combining that with the local indigenous Sagosian sound, on the one hand, while also bringing this hip-hop element into it.

GoPoKePalP: That brings us to your collaboration with the notorious Lil Bigfoot.

SR: Yeah. I suppose it does.

GoPoKePalP: How did that collaboration come about?

SR: Serendipity. Pure, evil, green serendipity, my friend. We both happened to wind up exiled on this island around the same time. It aint that big of a place, it was inevitable we'd one day meet. Two musicians, even though we're occupying vastly different fields, I guess we just had to put two and two together, and this new strain was born.

GoPoKePalP: You've released a couple tracks online already. Is there a full album in the works?

SR: You know, we've decided to kick it old school. In a way, I've been involved with convergence culture going way back, once I started to integrate traditional Japanese noise into my own sound. Now, we're kind of doing the same, what with the Sagosian shit thrown in to the hip hop/noise mix, but we're also doing it in terms of the old school technology. Me and Lilbig are going to release all our stuff on cassette for now on.

GoPoKePalP: Awesome, dude. I love how the cassette has been undergoing a revival of late. How will the cassettes be distributed?

SR: We haven't thought that far in advance. Maybe we'll just have them for sale at the record shop in Mrdokia.

GoPoKePalP: Where's that?

SR: It's our nation's capital, you dimwit. Oh wait, maybe you haven't heard. It used to be called Olde Colonia. It got re-named a few months back, around the time the war started. To clarify things.

GoPoKePalP: What is it meant to clarify?

SR: You know. I'm not a political person in any way, but it does make sense. I mean, my father has done a lot to help these people since he took over here. You have to give him that. I'm not going to get into it, but I think his record speaks for itself.

GoPoKePalP: I noticed you've deleted your blog which was pretty harshly critical of your father.

SR: Let's just say we came to an agreement. It was time to patch things up. I wouldn't really be here if it weren't for that. For him. Plus, blogging's over, man. I mean, who has the time to read blogs anymore?

GoPoKePalP: How's your father doing these days?

SR: I think he's doing an admirable job coordinating the war effort. It's awful that he has to devote his time to a cause like this when he could be using his energies to do more productive things. Like building up this island's economy, helping the locals. But a very small proportion of the quasi-natives apparently weren't happy with all the good results he was getting. You know, what can I say. There are loonies everywhere, I guess.

GoPoKePalP: You seem a lot more mellow than last time we spoke.

SR: You change and evolve over time. That's what it means to be an artist.

GoPoKePalP: Can you tell me more about the Sagosian sound you integrated into your latest collab with Lilbig, *Yr Face is Like the Skull I Saw on TV*?

SR: Sagosian music has a certain swagger to it, like a lot of pseudo-tropical island sounds. But it's not at all lazy. There's a pertinent backbeat that upholds it, a little like in reggae, where just as you think you're sliding down, that snare drum kicks in to pick it back up again. That kind of rhythm, what's amazing about it is that it's able to sustain itself for a really long time—I mean, traditional Sagosian songs, they can be nine, ten, sometimes even fifteen minutes long. So we just kind of jet ski over those kinds of rhythms.

GoPoKePalP: Somehow it's rather buried in the mix, wouldn't you say?

SR: You can hear it if your ears are trained.

GoPoKePalP: What would you say to your critics who claim that this is cultural appropriation?

SR: Man, that argument is already so dated. Just like blogs. And anyway, it stands no bearing in fact. If anything, we've all become rather integrated into the local culture down here. My wife is even learning Sagosian. She might not be able to speak English, but she can say a few words in Sagosian. I dare you to find any other quasi-elite musician on this island who's that well integrated.

GoPoKePalP: We're speaking of Makiko, of course, front woman of Derogated Necroplastic Gore Hooker.

SR: Right-o.

GoPoKePalP: How's she adjusting to the life down there? Any chance of you two collaborating at some point in the future?

SR: We made a vow never to collaborate early on in our relationship.

GoPoKePalP: Why is that?

SR: So as to keep things pure.

GoPoKePalP: Is that machine gun fire I hear in the background or one of your new tracks?

SR: We've become numb to it here. I barely hear it anymore.

Vincent buzzed in to the bunker. Mrdok stands there anxiously.
—That's my man! The man I've been waiting to see. How goes it, my man?
—We're getting a little closer to it, Vincent hesitates. I don't want to make any big promises, Mister President.
Mrdok grunts softly.
—Well that's not exactly what I'm paying you for, Vincent. I'm actually paying for big promises. And big results.
—Intelligence is limited because... Well, you wants me to say it? They got control of most the island right now. They even up above your very head.
—You think I don't know that? They can't get down here.
—Yet. And let's hope it stay that way.
—Vincent. I truly believe no one knows this island better than you. Its ins and outs. Hidden nooks and crannies. All those little holes and artificial caves in Baldheaded Mountain we're about to—
—It's not about geography anymore, sir. It's about penetrating the opposition to the extent that we can find what they've done wit your hand.
—I don't understand why you can't meet with your brother.
—Yes you do. He knows I'm compromised. He knows I workin for you.
—Vincent. You met with your mother last night.
Vincent shoots his suspicion down to the floor through his eyes.
—How you know that?

–Come on, Vincent. If there's anything we've got on our side, it's not weaponry. Intelligence is how you win a war, my friend. Raw, pure intelligence. How the hell you think I've gone this far in life?

There is a savageness that comes through in these claims of purity. Vincent has heard it before when he's spoken to Mrdok. It reminds him of something, some former shade of himself long ago lost. It's like, Mrdok, being here so long, has taken up that shade that he cast off. That he has all the resentments and savageries alike of the slave boy character that life has cast him in. And he, in turn, well, hasn't quite attained the sophistications he still perceives in the quasi-elites. But they, in turn, will never attain the depths of his knowledge of his own self—the lost parts and the parts still there that are getting hardened as each day cascades past.

Ilmenite is ultimately the most cosmetic among minerals. It's the white stuff added that makes you want to buy. Anything gleaming is a moneymaker in this world, from the Americas to China, Black Africa included. Gleaming white is a form of mental security, the pure signifier of certainty in a world that has none. What cannot be stipulated can at least be bought. Actually, the irony being that it's magnetic black in its titanium iron oxide form, black at the moment of its extraction. But is used as the main source in titanium oxide, the very thing used to turn everything we most desire sparkling white—imagine sunscreen a different color. Or paper. Titanium oxide being the sole thing practically it is sought for. All this sand here we have on the island—surely we can turn it into something. That being Mrdok's logic. But he is in the midst of a stand-off now with Bev about it. Bev who argues that it's not worth it to disturb the beach, which is the island's main selling point at this precipice. There's no other way to make money, except for the sale of crypto war bonds to a shrinking pool of offshore investors. But what if just a small, teeny tiny section of the shoreline were to be used in this way. There must be a means of accompanying both the algorithm tourists and the desire of investors, surely. True dilemma for our times, that hour when Jupiter and Saturn collide. Bev lights a purple candle next to Mrdok's bedside and asks the stars for the return of his artificial limb. In exchange, she will extract a promise to get what she wants from him. Like all Mrdokian promises, however, she has learned to place it in the refrigerator.

Elsewhere, the post-apocalyptic landscape has been put to excellent use in *Uncle Sam*, latest magnus opus of the island's other Billy. Billy Buttfuck, Mrdok has taken to calling him, as anyone who's stuck it in one of his wives after him deserves a cruel moniker. In this work,

Spack is clearly harnessing the propagandistic tendencies of the 1980s gore genre as it was manufactured in the good ol' US of A at the height of its Cold War penis prowess, yet this time, infused with a potent dose of new century post-ideological spay-and-neutering, in order to meet the Ministry of Culture's demand that all artistic works be invested in promoting the war effort. In a screenplay collaboratively authored with the film's co-star Krstal Mrdok, Billy R. Spack, like any artist viewing the new constraint as a perimeter of the commission (since funding inevitably accompanied the provision) that might be transformed into a creative beacon, did exactly that, virtually producing a new genre in the process: horror agitprop. One might go so far as to say that just as the golden age of US horror cannot be detached from the Reagan doctrine, so this new hybrid Spackian emission shall forever be tied to the Mrdokian enterprise of island communism for global elites, insert trademark symbol here.

As the film opens, the camera pans over a desolate smoldering landscape seemingly devoid of all animal, mineral, or human life (filmed shortly after a surprise air raid attack by the American-backed Australians that essentially annihilated the suburb-in-progress that had been developing between Mrdokia and the Greek amphitheater.) America has entered the final phases of World War III in the fictitious Middle Eastern country Islamisbad, and is on the losing side. The war was clearly a last ditch effort at maintaining imperialist control over the region's dwindling oil supplies, which the US has long ago run out of, and is currently being run under the cabal of an elite institution of Zionist commodity traders known as the Global Liberal Insurrectionist Bank, which has sought to maintain the US's hegemony by issuing loans with enslaving interest rates to countries it has previously bankrupted through other means (not limited to dirty warfare, the sale of dubious capital gains investments, and corporate takeovers of local energy and mining initiatives.) Hovering over GLIB is the demonic apparition of its leader, Sam Wahlbergson, popularly known as Uncle Sam, his zombielike appearance being attributed to his being 142 years of age, having formerly been the CEO of a life extension company whose technologies can only be afforded by the top zero point zero one percent. When it appears that GLIB is losing the war against the ragtag resistance, Uncle Sam undergoes robotic enhancement surgery, so that when he emerges, with all his soldiers slowly killed off one by one, he alone becomes the lethal killing device, annihilating all Islamisbad insurgents using every inventive goreful method, radiation and spikes and bullets and hooks and rays and unseen psychological warfare gadgetry all emanating from his scary undying body—until the final stand-off against a buff radiant feminine warrior, played by Krstal, who has similarly undergone robotic enhancement that allows her to transform herself into various minerals as a protective shield, until the final showdown, which takes place inside a cathode ray tube (which one US academic critic was quick to identify as a sort of literalist application of Kosslyn's cathode ray tube theory to cultural memory), unfurls over a seat-gripping twenty minutes, and concludes with both protagonists hovering somewhere between death and life, allowing for the inevitable follow-up sequel…

Proud was Speck that he had, in his mind, remained true to the neo-Marxian principles he had so thoroughly digested at film school in California, while simultaneously producing a work that had pleased his patron, whose value system ran totally counter to his own. Because of its ultimately ambiguous message, the film was maddeningly promoted by certain sectors of the quasi-native revolutionaries, who saw in the film's villain a clear evocation of Mrdok and the other quasi-elites' nefarious ambitions, rather than the critique of the American Enemy that the filmmaker ostensibly intended. Outside the island, critics would consider this combination of political indefinability with a revival of straight-to-VHS aesthetics as one of the defining characteristics of Slollywood.

Panning out to the real, actual war: the Cuban methods deployed early on met with almost immediate success—driving the battle out of the capital and into the difficult terrain of Baldheaded Mountain, for instance. Most of the soldiers in the Home Army were used to fighting in flat desert territories, so the minute they were led into the mountains to go against the Liberationists, bad things began to happen to them. Unlike the Home Army honkies, the Liberation Army could also slip smoothly back into quasi-native civilian life as soon as they finished an ambush. This put to a challenge the Home Army's original intention to consider quasi-native civilians on the same level as their quasi-elite equivalents. And in so doing, the Liberation Army was winning increasingly more support from the quasi-natives, especially when the nucleite spill turned the sea into a holocaust for the fish, which had been the quasi-natives' chief economic commodity going back centuries before either the quasi-elites or quasi-colonials arrived…

—But according to our research, it seems that most of your soldiers were, in fact, hired from a private security firm. Not exactly *recruited* in the way you imply.

What pisses Mrdok off the most about the journalist on the screen in front of him is that she is so damn ugly and that her self-righteousness makes her even uglier. It is bad enough that so much of his days now are eaten up with this kind of interview from the enemy's media machinery. They could at least have the common decency to send him an attractive emissary from their stinking uncomprehending world. The brute ugliness of the specimen serves as a further insult, in Mrdok's estimation; she wasn't even a three.

–I am trying to build a civilization here! Mrdok screams, frothing. He has to remember to keep his right stub lowered so that she won't see. Tell me, what the hell do *you* know about building a civilization? I bet you haven't even gotten out of that ergonomic chair you're sitting in for half a year or even longer, by the way your body looks. Which is why you're jealous of people like me, who actually manage to go out into the world and, well. To *create* a new world. And, in doing so, solve a lot of this world's effin problems!

–Okay, I'm going to do you a favor for a minute and ignore all the sexist things you just said about my body, which are anyway going to do you plenty of damage once I upload this thing. What I want from you now is a coherent answer to the following question: What about your total and utter disregard for the spiritual beliefs of the quasi-native Liberation Army you are currently fighting?

–Oh, don't give me that shit. Those people are *terrorists*, pure and simple. Just because they bring religion into it—are you going to sit here and tell me that these people who use some bullshit spiritual justification for waging a campaign of war and destruction—they have killed *so many* of our soldiers, many of whom have fought *your* wars for you, not just ours—you're telling me that their bullshit so-called religion has any bearing whatsoever in this war? Their religion is just an excuse to terrorize the good people that our government has been installed to protect.

–But would you not agree that Yangism—which, after all, is mentioned in the full name of the opposition army—is a valid religious practice, and that since it represents the faith of a tiny minority which your war has put under threat, you are, in a sense, committing genocide against these people by—

–Enough.

Click.

It's quite a departure he's taken from the no-media days of Tony Fatballs. When nothing appears in the press about Settlers Landing for a couple of weeks, Mrdok begins to grow nervous, reckless. He has Gordo reshuffle his entire PR staff like a deck of cards. Everyone is suddenly keen to please, and so the game shifts from cards to darts, with each of the dozen staffers trying to land a story in a major media outlet—dreams of hooks keep them awake at night, until they are no longer darts, but, like much of the quasi-natives formerly, fishermen in the ocean, competing to nab the biggest shark. Finally, all metaphors fall apart as does the game when not a single email is responded to, nary a single phone call vibrates Merrill's device. Not even *Private Islands Magazine* wants to talk anymore, and so he is forced into these interviews with these self-elected imbeciles on the fringes of discourse. And yet it is better than the nothing he otherwise faces—much better than having to continue to fight this battle alone and in the dark…

–Gordo, how much am I worth?

Some say the United States' actual contribution to the Liberation Army's efforts amounted to no more than fifty grand, which would nevertheless be a big assist. Marty the lawyer parachuted in to give it to them while simultaneously delivering a US court summons to Mrdok from Mrtol, a lawsuit for what it deemed *causing permanent psychosomatic damage over a fourteen-year-marriage*. A court summons received, naturally, by Gordo and immediately ripped into shreds.

–Naw, man. The 1990s were like stylistic reruns of the entire twentieth century to prepare us for the brave new internet age. The decade was perfectly understated in its ruthlessness. America was in its decline, but no one realized it yet. Perestroika clearly wasn't working, China was cracking its steel knuckles, Mother Russia was scratching her hairy balls. The world was awash in cheap oil, drowning us in our own putrid stores of need, periodic states of recession revolving…

Some aging hipsters are conversing in the smog white interior of the Wet Nasty relocated from Mrdokia to Elias Shores, fake smoke coming out of their vapes as scroll feeds compete in the mind annihilation game.

–I don't know, dude, I think the 90s were more like a warm-up for the global awareness we were all bound to attain in the 2000s anyway. It just took us a little longer to get there cos of Bush and stuff, but today, we're like so much more *aware* than we were, so much smarter than our parents' generation.

–Remember the hypertext novel? What ever happened to that shit?

–Dude, I don't know. I think it was kinda overtaken by a postliterate kind of, like, digital nomadism that people like us sort of like embody…

Some would say the conversation has been elevated somewhat thanks to the Wet Nasty's removal to Elias Shores. Since the overall patois in the olden days was more along the lines of *Your t-shirt has a genital on it* and *Wait, are you telling me your daughter can fit an entire avocado up her poo-tang?* But there are those still likely nostalgic for the glamour that the Olde Colonia/Mrdokia location once proffered, not to mention the cocktails, which were infinitely—

Suddenly three mustachio'd men in sweatsuits through a burst of machine gun fire decimate much of the premises at the moment of entry.

Lt. Vandross only asleep, what, must be an hour, suddenly awoken by some private whose face she immediately recognizes but can't assign a name for. Beating in her chest tells her it must be something grave.

—Shots emanating from the western corridor.

—And?

Blinking into the dim silver'd light.

—Could be a distraction game. Sergeant says we need to be alert, lest they're leading us into another ambush.

At this hour? Fuck. More likely than not.

—Wait. The western corridor. Isn't that the Italians?

—Right.

It's the general consensus, at least. The Mafia having infiltrated via the Elias Shores tourism scheme. That goddamn racket. Lt. Vandross isn't alone in her resentment of it. Letting strangers on to the island, virtually no security clearance, this is what it leads to. The Italians—no one is completely certain whether they're Camorra or Mafia or some other clan—let in by the president's daughter-in-law Coco—some shady deal involving Viutex—seemingly the minute the Home Army became aware of the Italians' presence on the island Coco disappeared. Bobby's been desolate, virtually comatose since then, refusing to go outside his bunker or see anyone.

The Italians, it is believed, aren't actually fighting on the side of the Liberation Army. But they're definitely fighting against the Home Army, for reasons that remain murky, but are inevitably tied to Viutex or Coco or likely both.

It will be a couple more hours before they get word that it was the Wet Nasty that was attacked. The First Lady is rushed into Mrdok's bunker via armored Hummer. Gordo receives the report that the Mafia is out to take over the entire Elias Shores project, hold it for ransom until SL gives up the entirety of its Viutex operation to them.

—Ilmenite?!—Abe, exasperated—No no no. Just no. I mean, what are you talking, a fuckin *toothpaste factory*? I'm sorry, Mrdok. I didn't get into this to, to invest in, what, one of those banana republic, Caribbean clichés... You might not have any reputation left in the outside world. But some of us still do.

This kind of blatant disrespect took some time to get used to, but he's getting there. They're peeling off, one by one. Barb, run off with some CIA nab. Not sure she's even still on the island anymore—if she is, no contact for weeks now. Ditto the cowboy. The fuckin cowboy. Dug his shares so deep into some Saudi oilfield, it's a wonder the Jihadists haven't joined the offensive. Maybe they have. At this point, the intelligence is all mottled, he doesn't even know who they're fighting half the time. Leave it to the military men, those who know more than he does in these areas. Commander-in-Chief, he doesn't even pretend that role like the American president has to. If you try to run a war like you run a business, he knows, they'd be annihilated in a second. Sometimes you just have to trust people who are dumber than you. Was that also one of Tony Fatballs's lessons? He can't even remember at this point.

One day Mrdok's home, once the home of Nelson Rodgers, simply floated away. It was the darndest sight, the few stragglers still around to watch—mainly quasi-natives employed as security guards and gardeners, not yet having faced the music that they would be living in holes for the next year or longer. They were still out there, and so they could see the day that the waters came and just wrapped themselves around the base of the entire estate and then slowly dragged it out into the beyond so distant (for they were quite far inland) you had to have a very powerful drone to follow. Which of course none of them did, although one or two of the more athletic members of that entourage deigned to chase it on foot for a while, until it became clear where it was headed. That house and all the treasures belonging to it: could it still be floating out there, or is it at the bottom deep down, like some forlorn shipwreck, awaiting the crazed ambitions of some deep-sea diver to come ransack its sea-preserved goodies? Mrdok of course has heard the story, but can't bring himself to believe it was a tsunami. After all, it was just his house that was washed away... How could not Barb's or anyone else's, none of his storied neighbors? Who, by the way, are just as blacklisted in virtually every sphere of the carved-up planet as he by now, why not their houses alongside his? Or at least some partial damage. But no. They are all probably, the ones still standing, invaded now by the barbarian enemy, who knows what kind of infections those *people* bear, maybe it's best his house isn't there to have been polluted, when the war's all over he wouldn't be able to go back and live in it anyway, knowing all the disgust and damage, the sex and wastage they've like to have inflicted upon it… No, it had to have been a targeted fuck-you operation by one of the foreign enemies, the Americans most likely, only they have the technologies available at their disposal, but who knows, could have been the Chinese as well, at this point nothing is surprising, he can see it in his mind: the laboratory development of some wet substance that resembles water but is actually sticky and noxious enough to fistfuck gravity and yank the foundations of an entire colonial mansion out of the ground and drag it away, perhaps it was a drone affair, had the idiots who reported all this to him looked up at the sky they might have seen some hovering overhead controlling the whole thing, instead they could only look dumbfounded right before them and watch as the president's own residence got yanked away and taken to who knows where. No, there is no water that can do that, Mrdok cannot believe it, even if he had seen footage of it it is not something he could overcome. He understands nature well enough, having had to submit to it now all these years, the mysterious forces it put on his welcome mat each morning, but there are some things even nature that old whore can't come up with herself, certain things that only men can do when they're manipulating her.

Run away from the moment, Mrdok, before it catches you.

He is bored now and listless and so he stares at the stub at the end of his right arm. He usually avoids looking at it, so as not to cognate its existence whatsoever, now he has no choice, he is alone, Bev is not here, Gordo is off running his errands. White and knobular, matte beneath this cruel fluorescence he has demanded now more than once be changed to something softer, it is as though nobody listens. That fucking gorilla he had the pleasure of watching getting shot in the head after it happened. The gorilla looked into his eyes from behind the bars of the cage. He looked right into them. It wasn't a cold expression, but it was resigned. The ape knew exactly what it was he had done, Mrdok could read that quite clearly in its dispassioned gaze, it knew that its life was about to be shortened. Mrdok stood there staring, they were waiting for the gunman to arrive, and he asked the zookeeper whether this was one of those apes that knew sign language. The zookeeper told him no, that it was just a common ape, that it might understand some things, but not enough to communicate them to humans. So all Mrdok had to go on were the eyes at the moment. He wanted to say something to it, but there were other people in the room, he'd feel stupid doing that—uttering words aloud to some animal. Then the ape did something strange. He raised its finger and pointed to its mouth and smiled. He rolled his lips around that smile as though he were showing his teeth off to his captor. As though he were mocking him. The ape then crinkled its nose and farted. An extremely large rectal explosion that shook the cage. At that precise moment, the gunman arrived. Let that fart be the thing's last words. The ape fell down at the first shot. It doesn't take a lot to kill the thing you hate the most.

On the red sands of Elias Shores, the air smells like Scotch tape. Explosions that aren't fireworks alight the sky in the near-far, as a thin crowd of feminine and femme-identified human creatures fattens itself out in a standing-squatting ceremony along the beachhead.

–By the power invested in me by the Holy Church of Our Settlers Landing Incorporated, I now pronounce you two… wife and wife.

The two brides look at Billy. The Afrikaner with the sapphire nose piercing scowls like she wants to impale him on some neo-colonial dildonic spear, while her Dalmatian dreadlocked paramour's more skeptical scowl questions his assertion earlier that afternoon that he had no ties or allegiances whatsoever to the patriarchy, by which he presumed, in his relative political innocence, that she was referring to the Catholic Church.

–Oh shit, I'm sorry… I don't have the script here in front of me, he flusters, then pulls out his iPhone and scrolls down to find the correct wording. I now pronounce you… post-gender polyamorous vegan co-op partners for all eternity.

The Dalmatian leans in to kiss the South African, who puts her hand up.

–Please, says the Afrikaner. Don't invade my safe space right now.

–I totally understand, replies the Dalmatian, clearly touched. And I admire you so much more now than I did before for canceling me in front of all our guests before I could make that vile assault.

–You do understand that I will have to find new ways to punish you this night.

Undoubtedly it will involve a plentiful supply of almond milk and a catheter tube… But Billy doesn't have time to contemplate that at this moment. The armored Range Rover waits in the beach parking lot to take him back to his TVLand bunker. In the island's New Economy, he has had to stoop to taking these wedding gigs whenever he can get them, as barely any funds are coming in through his TV sermons these days.

–It safe to go now, Robinson? he asks the driver upon entering the vehicle.

Robinson checks the app.

–That light in the sky you just saw maybe five minutes ago, he says. Landed just to the West of Baldhead. That was one of the Home Army's. The Uber app is telling me that if we go around the base of the mountain, especially avoiding Yarmouth Road, we can then go along the Cove Beach route toward Mrdokia, round the capitol building and the presidential palace—or what used to be the presidential palace, I guess, not sure why they still have it on the map here—that we can get there around nine, give or take.

–So that's… Shit. An hour and a half just to get back?

What the Uber app can't and won't tell you, of course, is that the longer you're out, the more danger you've put yourself in. It is difficult to find a way to monetize danger. It can be done, Mrdok has several of his own programmers affiliated with the Elias Shores project working toward that specific goal. Maybe, when he figures out a surefire way, he can take it and sell it to those Silicon Valley bastards once the war finishes up.

–It should be illegal to feel this good. In most places, it is…

One of the thoughts that entered Birchfield's mind the day he woke up after receiving the Viutex treatment.

> middle-aged men having done their tours
> now in a new land to do it once again
> whispering calm quotes from the bible
> as they finger their AKs
> the pseudotropical wind is less dry
> than the desert's, says one
> when i ask what's the diff
> fighting here and afghanistan
> both proxy wars for some purpose
> that remains obscure to our civilian eyes
> needs guys like us to fight those guys
> guys with much less fight in em
> than we might've once had before

–Seems the shrapnel cauterized when it was making its way through his body, broke a rib upon entry, then burnt a hole through his left lung, came out of his back here…

The surgeon drones on. But the patient feels no pain—they use Viutex here on all of them, so they at least feel wonderful—better than most have ever felt before in their entire lives, hanging on—in the moments before it dawns on them that maybe death isn't so bad after all.

> soldier lying up in his bunk at night
> studying a sagosian language primer
> he's been newly stationed to the intelligence unit
> i don't have the heart to tell him
> most of the sagosian soldiers no longer speak sagosian

One soldier shot himself in the mouth with his rifle and still hasn't managed to croak. There isn't a lot of romance to war at this precise moment, Birchfield will have to write some tragic poems that Gordo will likely consider unpatriotic, maybe dock his pay.

This direct voice, free of all artifice—where'd he get it? His poems were never like this before. Shell-shocked, on the magic V, the words just flow out of him like complete thoughts—it's like he doesn't have time, certainly no longer the ability to make the kind of art that was his practice before. He's been reduced, in a sense, to this blanket reportage. At least I am writing, he tells himself. Yeah… That's something. Hard to ornament your verse when you are hardly on anything resembling a winning side. Keep that thought to yourself, buck.

> they live in holes dug in the ground
> next to the dead
> the living keeping the dead company
> while the dead keep the living alive
> sleep beneath them at night
> safety blankets, cos the
> corpses still wearing their bullet-
> proof vests
> preacher billy said i just have to
> pray to find the salvation i so need
> at this cold-blooded hour
> and like a miracle he gets it the next day
> when a grenade goes off
> where he is sleeping
> pieces of his body flown around
> the landscape can be seen at first
> like a beautiful flower garden
> it has a soldier's name attached to it

> the reds and purples and flesh
> from a distance can be seen
> as roses, azaleas, or a succulent
> that needs no further nurturing
> liquid or otherwise

He doesn't bother giving the sections titles or numbers or even revising. He doesn't want to stem the flow. Terrified, in fact, of damming this river, this unending. He doesn't want to go back to the way he was before, unable to form words, unable to know even what it is he is feeling, how to translate that experience into the form that is, after all, meant to be his art.

> the vultures arrived around the same time
> as the tourists but with different plans
> why do fish in a pond swim in circles, one might ask
> because we all desire to be led
> even vultures have a leader
> that will take them over the seas
> to find the feast of flesh they so crave
> created by man as though to whet their palate
> the insatiable hunger displayed by these creatures
> as they go to work on a fallen soldier
> and me, past that point where i am able to protect
> how harsh the awareness hits
> the pen is not truly a weapon

This, of course, is, not a lie, there are no lies in art, but an embellishment—maybe you can call it that, yes. No vultures ever came within a thousand mile radius of the Settlers Landing coast, there was just no way, they are desert creatures, unsupported by the Pseudotropics. But maybe metaphor is better here than embellishment—it is the poet's art form, after all. And, in his mind, it delivers a clean break from that previous charge he had leveled against himself, that of reportage. The point being, of course, to communicate with the reader the gravity, the amount of death being confronted here on a daily basis.

Now he's in the decapitated forest, forest of decapitations, battle underway, just between the two boulders at the base of Baldhead, dodging bullets, chasing poems.

—Birchfield what the fuck are you doing? a command sergeant screams out over the noise of the cascading carnage. Retreat, civilian, retreat!

He has a helmet and a bulletproof vest on, he keeps running, it is his job to be here. And he runs and runs, dodging the falling rain of bullets, dashing away from the throne grenades in the moments just before explosion, runs and runs until the fear overtakes him.

When it gets too dangerous to be on his feet, the poet crawls across the ground torrents of fire dashing just above his head and oh shit, this might be a bit too much after all… Yes, certainty overrides, what has he gotten himself into now, the closest shelter is he knows not where, when all of a sudden, amidst the shell casings landing around him, he feels the ground sinking in a kind of promising way, no this is what, is it a fold, it is something like a door. He presses all of his panicked body weight down on to it and falls six and a half feet, landing on the padding that still hasn't been sweated off his alcoholic belly.

The children look up from their game at the noise of the new arrival.

—Who in the hell is that? says Wessel.

A glint of recognition in Jaco's eyes.

—I think I know that guy. Hey, aren't you the poet?

Birchfield rises carefully, inspects the damage of his lower torso. Doesn't seem to be anything too pained or broken. He dusts off the patches of wood and dust and deadened leaves and allows himself back on to his feet. Eyes adjust to the dimness, till the three figures clarify before him. One of them is the son of the president.

—Jaco… What on earth are you, you *doing* down here?

Jaco's eyes widen.

—These are my friends. We've been down here for a long time now.

—Who the hell are you? Alexander echoes his sister's interrogation.

—I know who he is, says Jaco. He's the poet.

The children are dressed in their everyday clothes, like they had just left the school or playground. Remarkably clean and well-fed, in appearance at least immune to the effects of the war blaring ahead up above, it is as though he is meeting them in a dream.

—We came here to look for my drone, says Jaco. We never found it.

—Your drone?

—Yeah, says Alexander. He had this really cool drone. At first we'd just fly it in his backyard. But one day we flew it too far. Then the war started.

—We were up there looking for the drone, Wessel goes on to explain.

—Then we found this, Jaco finishes.

—Do your parents, does, what's her name, Rosalita know where you are?

—Rosalita's dead. At least that's what we think.

—We haven't heard from Rosalita for a long time.

—She wasn't picking up her phone when we called. And then our battery died.

—But how are you… how are you surviving down here? How are you *eating*?

Jaco signals over to the shelf, where about half a million cans have been lined up.

—My favorite is the minestrone. So hearty!

—Wessel likes the alphabet soup.

—That's cos I can write my name with it once.

—You hungry? There's also some beef jerky…

And like that the poet sputters, a feeling as though he is about to, I don't know, have a heart attack or shit or something, and then—a boom, splat—he feels nothing no more—he spontaneously combusts, is splattered among the children.

—Oh shit, says Alexander, cupping a huge chunk of poet flesh off his cheek and flinging it splat on to the concrete, careful to avoid getting any on the carpet adorned with traditional Sagosian markage.

—There goes another, deadpans his sister, who was lucky enough to have ducked the splatterage.

—This is like, what, the third one this week? remarks Jaco, half-pensively. I don't get it… Why do they always explode once they're down here?

—Maybe it's something in the air down here. Something the grown-ups are like allergic to.

—Naw. It's cos they like givin us something to do, a chore. Something to clean up. Adults always like to do that to kids.

—My parents never made me do any chores.

—That's because your parents were hardly ever around.

—That's not true.

—Where are they now then?

Good question. Jaco reckons one of em'll turn up eventually, one of these days. Hopefully not to explode on them. That would be a little uncomfortable, not to mention gross.

–Where are your parents, then? Jaco now retorts.

–We've been over this before, says Wessel.

–Probably dead, says Alexander.

–Anyway, you know the rule. We got to finish the game now.

–Right.

They're playing a board game that Wessel invented. It's called Warzone. They don't have dice, so it starts out with a round of paper-rock-scissors to determine who goes each round and how many paces forward. Through a series of tunnels and barricades artfully sculpted out of recycled soup cans and snack wrappers, each player's glass figurine moves across a mapscape battlezone obstacle course. The endpoint is a simple hill, where the winner gets to simply glare out at all the surrounding carnage still ensconcing the grappling seekers down below.

–Loser has to clean him up. And patch up that goddamn hole before they find us.

–It's not gonna be me this time.

–It's been you the last two times, Jaco. Face it. You're on a losing streak.

–Shut up. My dad's the president.

–That don't mean anything down here. Fuckface.

–Board up that ceiling. Before the next one falls down. That's the last thing we need right about now. Another fuckface exploding adult in here.

What the children didn't, couldn't realize is that the mystery of the self-combusting adults lay in the Settlers Landing International Hospital, where all of the victims had received the latest doses of the Viutex treatment. Having run out around the start of the war, the good doctors attempted to fabricate their own version, as a face- and money-saving gesture. This counterfeit version, however, was burdened with, shall we say, certain deficiencies. The combination of certain substitute substances had turned these adults into walking timebombs. It takes time, naturally—sometimes up to seven months before they go off. Unfortunately, some of the Home Army soldiers have also had this scarily diluted version of the Viutex treatment and have a tendency to explode on secret missions on enemy territory, drawing attention to the survivors, who are then immediately bombarded by the Liberation Army's increasing prowess.

Uncle Sam: He never dies, He only cries…

Look at the landscape. Then lick it. I'm weary from all the lessons. Still some sky left. Maybe a chance. What the clouds seem to promise. Living face.

—You don't know what it means to be an island, Mrdok told the Prime Minister of Australia over the horn shortly before the war got declared. Australia was joining in on the Brussels anti-nucleite measure, which was going to further complicate SL's export of the mineral, clearly a retaliatory measure for the misunderstanding with the ex-Prime Minister, who by that point had been released from Settlers Landing unharmed and returned to Australia, where he had taken up a new prestige post as executive director of one of the country's premiere cultural institutions, the AC/DC Museum in Canberra.

—Perhaps that is so. But we *do* know what it means to be a continent, mate, the Prime Minister had replied. And unlike you, we also know how to deal with our Ab...

... And when the warring brothers finally do meet, it is in the back of Robinson's car.

—What is it, brother?

—Surprised you still call me that.

—We all brothers here. In Sagosia. What is it?

—I here to make a trade.

—A trade?

—A trade.

—Lemme guess.

—I don't think you have to.

—You damn right.

—What I have to do to get it.

—You aint gettin the hand. That's our favorite treasure of em all.

—You already got enough—

—We don't have even halfa what we want. We want it all, is what we want.

—I can only help you if you help me.

—So that's what you offerin? Help? That all?

—Don't be dumb, Prince.

—You the dumb one. Look at where you is and where I at right now. Then you can fathom out who the dumb one be.

—Give da man his hand back. You do that and I can get you somethin valuable. More valuable than you can see.

—You don't even know what it is I want.

—I think I have an idea.

—What then.

–The temple.

At that, Prince has to shut the fuck up for a minute. If they could get control of the temple… The symbolism alone could make them win this war in a heartbreak of an instant…

–You get me the temple I get you whatever you fuckin want, Prince says quietly staring through the tinted windows into the bombscape surrounding.

–Well okay, then. There's a message coming into your sector to-night.

–How that?

–The usual means.

Robinson grunts from the driver's seat. In want of any Uber rides, he'd become a gopher going tween the two zones near every day. A double agent, to be sure, and both sides knew it, though he was too valuable for now to be disregarded. Any one of these days somebody'd shoot him, once his usefulness had worn off.

You don't have to go to Harvard to learn how to make your own napalm. These days, they're cooking it up in the kitchens of the quasi-elites' houses. All you need, really, is gasoline and a thickener of some sort. The Sagosians like to use those styrofoam packing peanuts—easy to get, since they form the lining in all the guns and drone ship-ments from the Saudis—so a matter of pure recycling. Prince once picked one of those little foam nuggets up to investigate closer, found a Made In USA engravement on it. It didn't take long for him to complete the arithmetic. Lallyburt selling the Saudis the guns that were being sold to the Sagosians purchased with money provided by the Americans.

Of course, Prince adds his own special ingredient to the recipe. Grinds high-grade magnesium pills in a blender into a powder, then slathers that into the mix. When lit, it gives the exploding napalm a bit of an extra spark. Others might not notice it, but Prince certainly does. It's that Zoroastrian influence that their pirate forebears had brought to Yangist ritual, this love of the light that burns you. Born in him at such a young age and his brother not, genetic inheritance being the farce of randomness it happens to be. Watching, for the first time, the napalm alight an entire unit of Home Army soldiers, it gave him a hard-on.

It's relatively hard to die in the developed world, Mrdok now re-alizes. Same realization the soldier had long ago… When Private Corporal Din Danils dreams, he almost always dreams of Afghani-stan. Sent on a mission to shadow Lieutenant Temwen of the rebel army. *Shadow*… That's the word that was attached to the assignment.

Came to realize that they wanted more than just to gather intelligence. Eventually, he was going to have to kill the guy. And so he watches him now, from behind the tower they've built, and when that position gets too hot, he retreats to the meeting point behind the boulder late at night, when the patrols are loosened. Because in the geometry of the war that's evolved, it's the Liberation Army now that owns the night—the Home Army doesn't dare to attack. Darkness being no longer a cover, just a threat...

Even finds time to dream on these nights when he's dispatched to enemy territory. He can't help it—a side effect of the PTSD medication he was prescribed—minutes after taking a pill, he'll just zonk out for a little while, come to gripping his rifle, still undiscovered. He hears Temwen's voice speaking in his ear piece. They're saying something about the temple, taking it. The temple that belongs to us now...

–Have sympathy for the underdog. Their teeth are much sharper than ours.

–A quote worthy of Heraclitus!

–Hairy clitoris?

All advertisers have long ago pulled out, so in lieu of commercials, Gordo came up with the brilliant idea of gathering together all the Settlers Landing celebrities to record an uplifting charity single, the video of which could be played in half hourly rotations, so as to keep up troop and civilian morale throughout the heat of battle.

First comes Bev in string bikini sipping a cocktail on Elias Shores:

> You woke up one morn in our beautiful land
> To find the time had come for you to take a stand

... Fade to Krstal, hair piled atop her skull in a high top perm, in recording studio with headphones on, croaking her verse accompanied by autotune in a Virginia Slims-inflected alto into a mic adorned with the silver-orange colors of the Settlers Landing flag:

> What we need now is a strong state
> Or else we'll all die, and that won't be great

As she commences giving the microphone a blowjob, fade to Lilbig rapping in front of the Colt painting in his home recording studio.

> Lonely drones in the sky go zoom

> Big fat bombs in the night go boom
> All you soldier muthafuckas real cool
> Kill them rebels then we'll kick it ol' school

For the filming of the video, all of the participants were given 1980s haircuts—not as a nod to this style of inspirational song-video, but because irony has now been made an official cultural policy of Settlers Landing in a movement passed by the remaining Senators proposed by the Ministry of Culture in the early days of the war effort. Though Serious Irony, an irony devoid of humor, it should be said—it is meant as a new kind of irony that the world has never seen before—an inspirational irony. Lilbig sports a flat top; after he turns around, you can see the letters *SL* have been shaved into the back of his skull in lightning lettering.

Lallyburt the Cowboy pictured atop a horse crooning his contribution beneath the high Texan noon:

> Well our freedom is under threat
> And a war is what we get
> But we can win
> If we only kill them right!

After, Stevo Rey, with wavy pompadour, autotunes out his verse—

> We're gonna shoot em down like pigeons
> And institute our own new religion

then turns the knob on his soundboard to emit a split second of white noise with which to signature his contribution—for those soldiers who are white noise fans…

The Shell-Shocked Choir, comprised of decommissioned soldiers no longer psychologically fit to serve, intones the chorus while performing the simple choreography, swaying interlaced with sidestepping, left to right and right to left. Sometimes a sway and a sidestep combined. You can't do much else when you have thirty-seven middling celebrities jammed on to a small stage and have to fit all their egos.

> We aren't the world
> We are an island
> We come together singin' hand-to-hand
> We stand defiant

> We aren't the world
> We are an island
> But it is still a geographical land mass
> So please don't slight it

The song, composed jointly by Collins and Gordo beneath the steamed pressures of sexual tension, has multiple choruses in order to address both the multiple concerns of the songwriters as well as the songwriters' own warring expressive proclivities, resembling on paper something closer to an epic than a song, though a wily length was needed to accompany all the disparate celebrity voices and to maintain the anthemic length thought to satisfy soldiers' inspirational needs… Oh, here comes the bridge:

> Stand on your feet
> Listen to the beat
> Of the hearts
> That are attacking
> For youuuuuuuuuu

Wearing a bouffant wig, Gordo steps forward with an oversize headset mic strapped round his waist, turns round, and emits a solo of carefully nurtured operatic flatulence as his contribution to the song's unfurling.

At the end of the song, Mrdok appears with a public service announcement:

—Hello. You might recognize me as President Mrdok. But deep down inside, I'm a citizen of Settlers Landing just like you. If you love our fair island nation as much as I do, you will do everything in your power to support the war effort. Well, I'm here today to tell you that there's a way you can do that—and get rich in the process. By purchasing our very own decentralized crypto currency, the Bang-Buck, we guarantee a rate of return of one hundred percent once the war is over. Why are we doing this? Of course we don't need the money! What we need is your patriotism, to give our soldiers the energy they need to keep fighting. It doesn't matter how much or how little you buy. Even if you only have a dollar, that's enough to make our men and women in uniform holler. And, once this war winds down, you will be eligible to sell your BangBucks back two-to-one. That's right. Double your money. And, for those who buy fifty thousand or more, we will not only double your money, but give you Settlers Landing citizenship at the hour we declare victory against these Yangist terrorists who are threatening to take control of our island. Interested in learning more? Download our app today, SLapp. You can use it to book your vacation on Elias Shores, buy BangBucks, or make your own unique contribution to the war effort by purchasing a download of the song you just heard...

Sometimes, those rare moments when he is fortunate to find himself alone, Gordo will flatulate to himself to be reminded of the past. Entrenched in that bitter nostalgia, he entertains himself with episodes of his journey, culminating in that late great moment on-stage at the Settlers Landing Opera House, when he/she had finally trained his mezzo-soprano to accommodate the trembling vibrato of his other orifice, the glory... Will those days ever return? It is hard to know now. To maintain morale, best to lie to yourself about the way the war is actually going. Not bad faith, per se, he has a duty, a role to play. That columnar support structure M so heavily relies upon as his formerly tall stature begins to slope diagonally...

Not everyone will get to come out of hiding when the war is over, imagining for a moment it ever will be... Lilbig knows the Mafia's after him now, his share of the Viutex export biz, after his stash and his connections to be sure, but once they secure those through some inevitable process of torture, he figures, they'll just silence him. All cuzza that fuckin Italian bitch from Bobby. As for now, what can he do? At least he got his girl Shelley down here with him to cook and to clean and to service him when needed, though at fourteen, she gettin kinda old. She'll be havin her baby real soon, they just got to figure out a way to rebuild that heliport so that they can get offa this damnation isle...

The ghost of Tony Fatballs hovering.

–Let me tell you about something called the Grand Overcoming, Mrdok. You get, maybe, three chances, three chances tops to be something in this world, before the world takes its turn—and when it does that, it defeats you. And when I say it defeats you, I mean that's it—you're finished, there's no coming back. Pay attention to the interstices—those little cracks and ledges so insignificant from way up high, where you're standing, those little fuckers that you step right over. Vassal sieves of fortified hopes, little graves where people have deposited all those secrets that are the very thing they've kept living for. Those little crags hiding cemented fabrics—because, true to all life, they've been encrusted with the codings that other peo-ple—big, powerful people—have written on to them, that tattooed all these realities into their skin before they even had a chance to be aware of the fact that they *had* skin. Questions… We can ask ourselves questions, sure. As your voice of counsel, at this particular moment. I would advise you *not* to ask any questions. No more questions, Mrdok. Because the more questions we ask, the further we are led astray. The most potent thing that anyone in your situation can do is to act. Act like the world has cauterized you—which it, in a sense, has. What's going on now is… It's the milking of the galaxy, essentially. All these lives you lord over, that you know nothing about. I know I'm not supposed to be talking to you like this. But I'm going to go ahead anyway. Just… Put yourself in the position, for a moment, of the Enemy. You know, the big one, the one we're all up against right now. Try to think of what *they're* sacrificing. They're sacrificing things you've never had to, to even *conceive of* giving up. And they're doing it in, well, their own dignified way. Not that I would ever call, uh, terrorism, violence, *dignified.* Maybe that's the wrong word for it. But they're putting up a, a god honest fight. And they're, well. They're winning, at least in a way, in a way that we're not. Think about them.

We require the cogent, at time painful recognitions and lessons that experience brings, lest we learn anything. Those who don't have it are often discovered to be shrouded in the eternal faux ecstasy of narcissism. Tragedy… Mrdok had some, but not quite enough.

Mrdok's perfectibility. We can't all be strangers to ourselves, one way or another, though many of us try it at least one point in our lives, usually a period of crisis—cloying toward attainment of that outside perspective that, of course, you can never fully reach—and if you could, then what would it be—voilà, death: the answer.

Intuition a burden under these circumstances. To distract himself from this troubling state of handlessness, he's gone back to one of his old hobbies he's had to neglect the past few years in his new role as national leader: mapgazing. Mapgazing in a kind of daydreamish sort of way: of other islands, other worlds: never to concede any kind of defeat out loud, that's been ingrained in him since the Tony Fatballs years, but at times pragmatism comes gnawing at his intestines and in order to scare it away, he'll submit for a little while to that perchance to dream… What island to go to next, should the need for escape become somehow unavoidable. Of course he doubts it ever will, and no one has to know anyway. Atolls away from here and others close by, places he could skip and jump and dance to, imagine Gondwana welling back up to the surface—submerge yourself into dry continental land… So many blank spaces left on this earth, sometimes he closes his eyes and puts his finger down in the middle of a map and yells out before looking where it's landed *I'm going there next!*

Bobby lies in bed, looking up through the skylight—his bunker specially designed with one, little bulletproof window to stare up at a patch of sky. Most days he can hardly see anything, it quickly gets covered with foliage from the forest floor. Once a soldier even stepped on it, didn't even notice and kept walking—though Bobby's not sure if it was one from Our Side or Theirs, or if it even mattered. He spends most days staring up, and today it's clear enough for him to see the rain clouds, the hydration that starts coming down.

… At first the sound was like bottle rockets. Ones you used to do off as a kid, back when you ran things in the neighborhood. That was what you thought during basic, when you first heard the blast. Blast that'd come to shatter your eardrums one day, land you shell-shocked at the hospital in Kabul. When the road exploded in front of your eyes. All bits of gray and green shit splattered against it, in front of your face. Red, from your buddy's arms getting blown off. MacAlister, he got blown up right in front. They were collecting his body parts in a bucket after that… This Temwen fuck. Why kill him? He aint a A-rab, this aint no Desert Storm. Where the fuckin blasts define you. These other fucks, they don't know nothin either. Want to send an innocent white boy to get destroyed. MacAlister like you, a back-to-backer. What other choice they give us? Sent home to the swamp. Fuckin Bougainvillea. Bougainvillea, Louisiana. Aint nothin there. First it was Memorial Day that pissed you off. The fuckin veterans parade. All those fuckin hypocrites out there, honor our troops, they won't even give you a deal on a goddamn SUV with mileage higher than a fuckin. Than a fuckin bald eagle they aint even got squawkin in their daytime overhead. Fuckin. Fuckin Deep South, they called it. The Deepstate name for it. The stewage. Where an honest man could starve. Every time you hear a shot, them hunters and such, takes you right back. You forget where you is, you think you back there, those fuckin gray lights in the desert night. When you outside in the cold just waitin, some fire in the sky up ahead. Or old codger Linthrope, now that old motherfucker was actually *in* Desert Storm. That night when he went out to take a pee, the only thing that saved his life is he sat down on the toilet cos he was too tired to stand. Next thing you know you're coughin up shrapnel in some tent somewhere. So the only thing you can do to stop the panics is to join the boys in the woods. Less for the political junk they was always spewin, more just an excuse to feel protected again. To feel useful.

Cos you only feel protected when you're holdin a 107 in your hands. They said the country's under attack. All these fuckin wetback scumlords comin in from the borders, tryin to steal our land right out from under us. I say, okay, whatever. Just give me a weapon, boys, I'm in control. Trade some desert dryness for some fields and forest, why not. Aint no fuckin Lieutenant Danils out here, out here I'm just your fuckin brother, okay? Cos out in the desert the only thing that matters is the man fighting next to you, you might get detached from the rest of your unit for a few hours, hand in hand it's survival. Out in the bayou it's all your brothers who are fightin side by side because we got political armageddon that's about to come rainin down, the Mexicans on one side the US government on the other. Soldier for hire, fuck that, I'm takin shit into my own hands. You fuckin squawk too loud you're likely to get your head taken off, I'm the man who'll do it too. Cos you can be the hunter or the hunted. Important to understand that. You must be one or the other. It's up to you to decide which it is you are going to be. If you the hunted, then you got to turn the game around, boy. Become the hunter once again. Cos they *will* kill the shit out of you. And when you get to seein so many people die, it's not a spiritual thing, death. It's the thing that takes care of you alright. But you're right here on earth. Not in the skies. LEGALIZE FREEDOM. That's what the banner said, back home when we were preparing the good fight. Shooting up old broken down cars in the bayou. All the places you've been. The crackling sound that a 107 makes, you take to lovin it. That's your weapon, boy. You got to treat it right. Cos it might not be today. It *will* be tomorrow. When they come. We've got to defend what's ours. Our constitution, our right to hold these goddamn weapons in our hand. Our right to overthrow this government once it stops standin for the people and starts standin for some forces we can no longer honor. Them politicianspeak cruel and insincere as an enemy's touch. Like them bastards usin the Koran as justification for their killing. Blowin themselves up in a fuckin teahouse or shop with women and children in there. From your observation post, start to notice what's really goin down here. Days you can remember where you are, startin lose some sense of that too. You in the employ of another evil emperor, just like you was in the fuckin desert, when they was usin you to impose their will and get the oil from the A-rabs. At least in the swamp you're useful. Are we in the swamp now? It's the humidity that confuses you, nights like these. Fuckin fleas buzzin in your ear. Get so angry, wanna smash something, wanna aim your weapon at the sky and shoot out those stars overhead. Same stars that the president starin down. Stare so hard, make the new sky come, make the sky fall apart. Take the initiative, soldier. Can hear MacAlister's voice right now and those words and understand what they really mean. That the time has come to finally destroy what's been aimin to destroy you all these years, in a finality that'll be lastin. In the end-times that spell relief…

Sewn into the light, the violence. The rain coming down, and with it, the announcement of a new day. Day that presents access as a barrier; as a burden. The rain gasps in a way that somehow signals relief, an end to all suffering.

NO I SAID gross and then get the fuck off of me no I mean it like I just said no omigod are you deaf like a million times no and he just kind of slid off more like shook himself off of me the fat pig and then smirked and said since when does no not mean yes wanted to kill him at that point the fucking bastard but then that was mixed with like another feeling and so I spread my legs like go on back in I mean fuck those were the days I was doing so many crazy things I was totally on the rebound but doing it in an unhealthy way I now realize like going on dates with these sleazy guys I never should have I remember was I wearing my dolce and gabbana halter top M had bought for me after what was it like the second or third breakup goddamn yes I was that was it so weird who knew the clinic would have a waiting room though I have to say like so far this is definitely the nicest bunker I have been in in this whole stinking war anyway like way overdue for some injections and all this sun has been leaving its marks on my skin okay doctor lets start with the crows feet around the eyes god do I even like have to point it out its like the most no-ticeable cant even remember when was my last treatment I swear oh yeah cheap bullshit this what my life has turned out to be like I totally dont even care anymore ill just fuck anything any old ugly bastard didnt even feel anything inside what was wrong with me but that was before the reconciliation when my life attained new purpose see these lines in my forehead thats right it was the forehead I got done last time yeah totally it was like five needles or something but now but now doctor slopowski is saying eight needles holy shit is that really what its going to take and his stuff its not cheap either god knows some of the girls here its like what in the hell are they pump-ing into their faces look like a frickin space alien when its all over if you get the cheap stuff and too much of it your face is not going to look good are you sure youre ready sez the doctor and im like ready as im ever going to be I remember of course the first question you have before the first time does it hurt I think I like even googled it and of course theres no dancing around it yeah it hurts totally hurts

like a goddamn bitch but its like you just have to know what youre
going into beforehand and be totally committed no I said when mom
asked me no of course im not doing it for him mom im doing it for
me for chrissakes what you think id go through all this pain christ its
not like hes even going to notice I mean the point is you kind of dont
want them to notice not that im ashamed or anything bev okay here
it goes okay that one was fine I like didnt even feel the needle just
slid directly into the pore wow doc youve got the magic touch oh
god I blanched the instant I said it sounds like im flirting did he look
at me weird hard to look up move my eyes ha no its more like an
after effect of the last fillers and botox but that was like four months
ago god girl its been a while better not let it go this time motherfucker
ouch ouch ouch that hurts wanna scream but cant do it dont want
to fuck up doctor slopowskis work fuck I mean dont want to fuck
up my face its the last thing I need for it to be my fault after all it
took to persuade M to fly doctor slopowski here just to do this kept
saying why not just let doctor soukowski do it doctor soukowski I
said the disbelief in my voice that hed even suggested it yeah doctor
soukowski is good he said operated on gordo or maybe it was gordina then I cant remember okay first of all mrdok im getting botox
not a sex change its like two completely different things second thing
is I dont care how well it worked for gordo I am not about to let
some sketchy foreigner guy with a russian accent inject botox into
me for all I know and then he interrupted me to say hes a slav just
like your slopowski and im like first of all no doctor slopowski is
from LA second he is polish and then he sez he is also a naturalized
citizen of our fair nation and im like dont give me that crap mrdok it
is not like youre giving an interview right now I am like your wife
okay how many is it now that was just the second shot sez the doctor
im like fuck but out loud im like alright sometimes you just have to
faze out sucks you cant use your phone in these situations this is like
when you need the distraction the most sometimes it takes like forty
five frickin minutes fuck thats like forty five minutes without checking my phone that is like the longest I have gone this entire year
without checking my phone except for those times when I am asleep
ouch shit ouch felt that one you cant say anything you cant scream
eyes start to water fuck its like the time that little girl quasi native girl
I had styled for a shoot on my insta the time she stepped on a
landmine and the next time I saw her her legs were gone it was like
so sad she had such beautiful long legs too definitely had model potential but now that potential was like wasted all gone it was so sad I
had to lock myself in the bathroom and watch my tiktok feed for like

seventy minutes or something to make myself forget so I wouldnt tear up because I dont want to eff up my mascara get bags under my eyes especially when im so long in between treatments and at that point it was uncertain when doctor slopowski could even get here because of the stupid war at that point it was a question of like where do we even land the frickin plane thank god hes here now M sez its getting too expensive to fly him here every time im like mrdok I need him here at least every five months or else my face will just frickin fall right off and what happens then that means the face of settlers landing is literally gone thank god we finally got it figured out and now its like you have to mom taught me that trick to deal with pain like the kind of pain you have no choice but to endure actually theres like a couple things you can do one is like its hard to describe what did mom how did she put it you like neutralize it by like totally focusing on it like almost like using your mind as a laser to like zap it out and then another is kind of the opposite like to ignore it and think of pleasant things a picnic no thats dumb I love my mother so much but at times M doesnt like her dont have to be a brain scientist to figure that one out or a plastic surgeon either for that matter a separate place where no one else really wants to go oh that was it put yourself in your favorite place and for most people they dont like automatically know what their favorite place is and so that sends you off on a sort of head trip where youre like what is my favorite place and then youre off thinking of all the places youve ever been to and then youve forgotten the pain ouch until you think of it again god was that was that my eyelid that was your right temple doctor slopowski sez oh right I think another good way is to do it kind of the opposite like to be totally present but not in your body just focus on the details of the room around you like I have my eyes closed now but I can remember the purple trim on the walls the wallpaper with the yellow sunflowers who chose that for the medical bunker its kind of oh I bet it was gordo he likes all that flowery stuff so tacky signifies safety and warmth or something to him I guess it makes sense it is supposed to be a refuge from the war zone like the quasi elites who use it dont want to be reminded how ugly the fields up there have actually gotten because of all the carnage they want to fantasize some pseudotropical paradise like how the island was when they found it and who can blame them then theres the purple leather of the operating table underneath me a different purple from the trim on the walls like this one looks more like I hate to say it the head of a dick sure that was probly Gs idea too ooh gross I mean who knows I know nothing about his her sex life does he even have one just try to get that thought out of my mind right now before I barf all over doctor slopowski I think the longest needle ive ever had is the one that went into my butt I mean actually when angeline asked me does it hurt getting botox its more like the first time that after weirdness feeling where its like heavy in places a heaviness where youve never had and thats when you remember duh bev you just got botox yesterday or whenever its like a small stinging sensation right when he takes the needle out like now though I guess some people when theyve gotten it enough they dont even feel *that* anymore like look at krstal cant even move her neck anymore let alone her face that sex crazed bitch tho who was it the conversation they had with her in her first year here as first lady no honey of course we dont fuck meaning M of course mrdok and I have an *arrangement* dont you see like she would put it out in the open like that with people she was drunk at the wet nasty not even quasi elites like tourists journalists even and G in the corner watching it all seething of course reporting it all back to M verbatim if the bar was too loud for the microphones in the table to get it like I think that even counts as treason here but M he was busy with far more important things im sure krstal and her botoxed vagina omigod im just kidding but maybe I mean at her age vaginal rejuvenation surgery a total necessity except some women I heard they actually get tighter down there as they age like having a lot of babies also makes it much stronger theres one thing you dont need to worry about now bev I mean even finding a surrogate after the war is gonna be a *process* assuming M even wants to do that I mean all the problems with his kids now does he really want another but I mean honestly look at who the wives were their mothers I mean if I raise it this kid is gonna be like awesome but I think what mom meant like her pain advice was more like menstrual stuff childbirth and thank god ive never had that the bad cramping I mean I know a lot of girls get it mom sez its genetic she never got it that bad either thank god for moms genes then even I dont think it was ever about botox though yeah like its more a stinging pain in the aftermath followed by numbness as your muscles in those areas go to beddy bye would you mind closing your eyes while I do this yes of course I mind it makes me nervous to close my eyes on an operating table but no I say I dont mind at all being a good patient always saying yes to men it is not a good way to go forward not that id define myself as a feminist as such not at all I wouldnt be married I guess if I was so many other women these travelers here the girls at the wet nasty they talk like these things make any real difference and if they did its like they cant bring themselves to understand how a man works dont want to but like if you dig guys and actually want to do something then you kind of have to get how they think how they operate I mean I know its disgusting in some ways one woman is not enough for them they always have to have a lot of women all the time and its not like they will ever say no if one tries to seduce them even an ugly one just for the experience the chance to stick it in some new chick see how it feels I guess its just the nature of having that thing protruding you always want to stick it in inside something someone but then its like jealousy on these girls part the ones who claim they just dont understand men because the horniness we feel as well I mean maybe were not as horny as them but biologically I mean I need it too like the last time M did it to me it was my idea to take a shower together and I know he thinks I havent seen the blue pills in the medicine cabinet how else can he get it up anymore but that time in the shower I mean it was the first time since the hand disappeared he put the stump up me and oh my god the way he did it so fast I swear how many times did I cum like three I was wetter than a 12 year old at a justin bieber concert thats what M said afterwards and I had to laugh my whole body shaking just couldnt look at his face I was too embarrassed that perverted demented grin like a little boy I just figured out a new way to get a woman off wonder if hes tried it with any of those whores his other wives probly I mean how could you not want it all the time have to take the hand off then I know he doesnt like to so much thicker than what hes got down there then he tried and I was like no immediately no you are not about to put that thing in my butt mrdok I mean its bad enough with a penis but a stump no way but then he put it in my ass anyway even as I was saying no I needed a break I had already come but what was I to do hes my husband for chrissake so I just let him ram it up me and of course first it hurt but then I sort of got into it after I stopped crying I guess anal is okay once in a while M telling me that time he was on the bus in london and he overheard this girl I was on me bob so I let im do me up the shit-uh the way he did it in that perfect trashy british accent I almost died laughing could even feel my face muscles moving for the first time in like three months but I think another thing is they do get more and more perverted with age I mean now the things M wants to do I think it also has to do with the fact hes so stressed because of the war and stuff its like I would be too but can we think of another way to work our stress out but again you have to understand guys thats just how they are like all these women coming forward okay of course im not saying its a bad thing but take some initiative girl like sexually harass the men back lol I cant believe I just said I mean thought that well your mind kinda goes crazy in these situations that is when he wants sex at all I mean its not like in new york when we were going at it all the time night and day once even in his office with gordo in the next room taking calls in the middle of the day me laying face down on his desk he wanted like every porno position he had ever seen and truthfully I think we did it all that afternoon back then it was normal but now its like if there is anything weird that comes to mind he wants to try it like removing my tampon with his teeth like I dont even like it when im on my period but what am I supposed to say hes my husband its not like I *have* to submit every time I just feel bad times like this when theres so much stress for him saying no

but god bev stop thinking all the time about sex so gross especially here on the table like what if I get all flustered and doctor slopowski notices bet he has a big one oh god bev stop it think think think well some girls more yves st laurent girls I myself am more gucci not that im vulgar about it but when mrdoks your husband you cannot just go around looking like some withered old dustrag there should be no such thing as limits in this life I overheard barb saying to that texas cowboy before they all disappeared whatshisname god I wonder how old *she* is before she left think hes gone too not sure then again I have no real reason for knowing its not like I have anything to do all the senators its a matter of national security whether they are here or not no one tells me these things I am just like the face of the island can barely understand anything that guy sez half the time its embarrassing im like what sorry im a staten island girl we talk normal english where I come from and omigod the entire left side of my face is like frozen now I can really feel it its like a botox high lol couldnt even smile if I wanted to usually when youre getting a procedure done the doctor will like ask you do you want a smile or resting bitch face because especially if youre getting some in the dimple area its important like some people prefer to have a permanent smile on their faces so the doctor asks them to smile during the injection others prefer more serious but then like you cant smile risk looking like melancholy everywhere you can I asked M he said a constant smile is too american we need to set ourselves apart this is a new world and yet I get what hes saying but what about my insta my tiktok you have to look at things from like a proper PR this century perspective course I guess you could fix it put a smile on in post in photoshop or whatever they use mrdok sometimes hes too stuck in the last it really worries me like the 90s are like the most over thing ever omg he like doesnt even look at any of his social accounts probly doesnt even know the passwords just has gordo do it all for him I was too embarrassed to even tell him in the first week my insta had like 90k followers more than his I mean im just the wife here if you want to be a proper world leader mrdok but he never knew which is better and ouch fuck damnit what the effin fuck dont flinch doctor slopowski sez dont flinch or youre going to ruin this fill so I chose not smiling because like for one thing I think my IRL social skills are good enough developed so that I can make a joke or like a laughing noise if I want people to know im amused the other thing is you can like totally do way more things with not smiling in a way it is even like whats that word like provocative because just think about it sexy for one you can do sexy *nobody* smiles when theyre doing sexy unless its like a half smile at most the other thing of course is a serious look which in terms of selfies it can express so many things like not just seriousness but smartness also or like having an inquisitive nature like for those selfies when youre looking at art or something or just looking into the lens you know having a me moment ive heard that if the doctor is really good like a filler artist almost they can capture any facial expression there is even subtle ones like freeze it okay not like permanently unless you consider six months to be permanent you have to get further treatments it melts away your expression after a few months but omigod now that I think about it botox is really like the photography of the twenty first century or like the sculpture really its like an art form because you can do so many things with it its like art but it also solves a problem I mean im partly convinced thats one of the reasons M got sick of me the first time in new york I hadnt had any work done in those days and okay so sure I was like what six seven years younger than I am now still there were like lines there my forehead especially and my bum was like sooo flat like oh my effin fuck like I just had no booty whatsoever finally my girlfriend desirée was just like okay girl aint no man gonna wanna go wit no flat booty chick you gotz to get you a booty girl and I was like omigod how is it I never even thought of this before I was so immature I am cringing now and not just from the sting either like if someone tagged a photo of me from behind showing my butt from those years I would like DDB detag defriend and block immediately my pre bo-toxed butt is for no one to look at how did mrdok ever how did ernie for that matter omigod ernie glen gallagher now if thats not a wet blast from the havent thought of him in like what a decade even longer the guy who took my virginity it was so awkward talking about my first with angeline she was like did you cum im like no of course not how many girls actually cum the first never mind that it was also over in like five seconds heard hes working at a gas station now at first he was gonna go into the army but they didnt take him for some reason I forget why omg mental note when this is done check my list of followers see if I can find him what if I dont think he ever actually I think I came once but it was so long ago fucked me like an animal fucked me stupid his was really long too but not that thick tid was his name tid boyle he had like a llama dick is the only way I know how to describe it or what I think a llamas dick would look like not that ive ever seen one well okay maybe once when I went to the san diego zoo that trip to the west coast M should totally build a zoo here once the war ends omigod I could build a whole photo concept around that one god maybe I should get procedures done more often im like so full of ideas whenever im laid out on the table by the way sez doctor slopowski are we doing ze butt today no I tell him just cheeks eyes forehead I am seeing some creases in your neck my darling are you for certain you only have me here maybe twice a year who knows when ze next time will be if zey cannot land the elicopter oh god youre right okay so do my neck too can you just warn me before now getting it in the necks a bitch on a pain scale of one to ten its like fifteen skins more sensitive there I guess I mean it is like a severe pinch like beth hollowell did to my tit once in high school think it was the left one omigod how I squealed it was in gym class supposed to be a joke but it hurt so bad im pretty sure there was some menace she was going with bobby singleblott at the time and I think he liked me maybe she suspected but I would never date bobby he was soo not my type and anyway I would never two time a ho I mean yeah I did it with mrdok but that was the first time in my life and it was special circumstances for one thing I didnt even know he was married the first time we met so its not even my fault he quote unquote forgot to tell me as it would transpire I mean its hard for people to believe now but he was actually on the DL in those years he wasnt a big celebrity big world leader influencer the way he is now he totally gave me the idea he was just this humble guy rich okay I got that when he brought me the chanel bag and the second date I was like holy mother of frick is this fake he just laughed and said no its not fake ernie glenn gallagher my first but wait who was the first who made me cum now I cant remember god I remember tid boyle I guess it was tho it wasnt like an intense orgasm where youre shaking all over some girls even squirt I saw it online of course when I was watching with mrdok thats so gross I said is there like something wrong with her but of course M was turned on I mean its kind of gay if you think about it they want a woman to do what they can do but then its not really a woman is it but I guess thats porn for you its like women acting sexually like men in front of the camera like that animal form of sexuality I mean I guess some women have it naturally still even then I think we express it in different ways we were talking me and angeline and angeline was like guys always cum the first time and girls never do really we should count the first time we cum with a guy as the actual loss of virginity im like that is such a good idea angline is like so smart she could always figure out what was trending like WEEKS before I knew she has her finger on the finger on the clit M would say and then the third time our third date time we actually fucked is when he gave me the dolce and gabbana bracelet watch the one with the multicolored gems and no this ones not fake either he joked and omg I knew I was in love like no guy before had done such nice expensive things for me ever not even llama dick who mightve made me cum once or twice god why is it so hard desirée sez it helps if he has a thick one I was like really I always thought it was length that mattered she just looked at me like gurrl that look I always know to mean I should shut my mouth right then and there to avoid looking like a dumbass desirée is like smart AF tho so I often have to shut my mouth around her which reminds me I should really get M to import more black talent to the island like especially if the reality show deal goes thru it will look so bad if all the people on it are like white trustafarians I mean lets be honest like go google it if you dont have people with like contrasting features your reality show is going to be a bust unless it is like one of the all asian ones where its supposed to be like that but I dont even know if its happening at this point G being vague on the details im really gonna have to wrestle that one out of that bitchs hands like if there is going to be a settlers landing reality show it is going to be *my* project and nobody elses I already have ideas on how to style it and who id want I mean we also need to cast some quasi-natives or else the optics would just be like wrong like I think vincent could be good for it as long as I dress him and I mean he could do with some slight skin work just the sun spots on like his forehead and shoulders but that can all be done with a laser otherwise he looks great I mean what a body and he hardly ever works out must be all that manual labor he did when he was younger still does I guess though not fishing aint no one round here doing fishing no more omigod that could be like an episode or at least part of an episode where like the quasi-natives have like this sad nostalgia childhood trauma about how hard it was being fishermen both the hard work of their parents and them being drawn into it YES child labor but ultimately it has a happy ending because theyre all gainfully employed in the service industry now with like a government that actually cares about them see I think M would love that too definitely G doesnt have such good ideas for him its just some like vanity project and anyway its not even his her whatever generation like wtf dude talk about someone who should be consulting with doctor slopowski I think he barely sleeps and you can tell not just the bags under his eyes but how like manic he is always about everything like theres a difference between being high energy and being like a total maniac like if youre going to retransition its great and all like it's your journey your narrative you have every right to whatever but just *complete* the process surgically I mean he didnt even take the time to remasculinize his facial features shit maybe I should say something about this to doctor slopowski like stage a beauty intervention ouch there goes the frickin needle in my neck the bubbly stiffness follows at least its over soon and I am not like dying over here and his skin omfg gurl we need to talk about the skin we are like in the pseudotropics where it is humid AF how in the hell is his skin dry as like an old dust rag thats a good description actually his entire manner he is like an old dustrag and he seriously thinks hes gonna manage the reality show like well give him a producers credit or something but he wont actually do anything or well like hire someone just to listen to his quote unquote input feedback whatever the word is just so he feels like hes being heard what would a good title be I mean the obvious thing would be something with settlers in the title like the new settlers or just new settlers no thats awful maybe something like settlers empire or maybe something with landing in it like landing on you settling on you thats kinda cute I dont know titles are like the hardest thing ever maybe I should talk to M about it tonight sometimes he has really good ideas for this sort of thing usually I dont like him to see me right after a treatment but tonight theres a red alert I have no choice but to sleep in his bunker its not really safe anywhere else I am like so ready for this stupid war to be over with like how much longer when are these rebel idiots just going to give up I mean like really they stand no chance whatsoever of winning I mean we have like trained soldiers whove fought in wars and stuff what do they have like most of their people have never even left this island im not trying to be mean they just need to face the facts anyway its none of my business really im just here to make it all look glamorous and I mean like it totally is if you are like brave enough to endure it all as long as you dont look too long at like the body parts in the landscape or the bulletholes I mean every country has its drawbacks thats exactly what I told whatshername when she

was interviewing me for her youtube channel all these influencers
hard to keep track of still it was an important platform generated a
lot of hits and likes and she has more than a hundred thousand followers last I checked probly more now unless theres a scandal those
numbers keep going up up up its like a whats the word bull market
thats right gotta respond to lindsay PRs email as soon as this is done
where to send my complimentary loreal gift basket last weeks loreal
shoot with the amputee male soldiers in makeup cradling their guns
like little babies in the bomb shelter so cute totally went viral our
stats just shot through the roof thats the key edgy enough to generate
mass buzz while also drawing attention to the cause like all the comments we got so heartbreaking kill those quasi bastards liberate
settlers landing I mean we have the entire world on our side if my
facebook feed is any indictator all my social in fact I wonder whats
in the gift basket though I hope more liquid eyeliner im running low
sucks its so hard to get supplies as soon as the war is finished elias
shores will be lined with boutiques prada gucci dolce alexander wang
comme des garçons dior vivienne westwood hermes yves st laurent
lancome loreal then we will have one designated pop up store where
we will invite different influencers from around the world to curate
their own products for short periods say one to three months my
idea of course ill be the one to select them based on strict criteria like
their stats and whether the image they promote really fits the settlers
standard of beauty and freshness I mean the concept here is fashion
forward pseudotropic island lifestyle the three Bs beach beauty botox
speaking of which doctor slopowski when the war is over what about
opening your own clinic here on elias shores I do not want to leave
ze hills of beverly he sez then he sticks a needle into my lip so I cant
respond if I could talk I would tell him look this is going to be so
much more glam than beverly hills like it already is in a way but hes
old too maybe he doesnt even understand social media I should ask
if he has a daughter maybe omg I bet she looks so good like if your
dad is a plastic surgeon you have it made you like dont even have to
go out of the house make a mental note to search for slopowski on
insta after this maybe I can find her or a wife even these beverly hills
guys always have younger wives like if I could get his wife or daughter on board and like invite them to come here and do something I
bet he would relent I mean I have been kind of pushing for this but
in a passive way to add plastic surgery to the list of medical tourism
you know theyre doing well now or they were before at least with the
viutex treatments but if we could really get botox in there like we
could overtake korea thailand places like that as world class

destinations for beauty or even offer like combined packages viutex and botox together maybe call it like viutox or botex like combine the two words somehow biuvox lol I dont know I mean now that I think of it there will probly also be a big domestic market once the war finishes all the wounded soldiers who need to get cleaned up and like face transplants and stuff it is not going to be easy I should mention this to doctor slopowski I mean he might up for more of a like challenge

I mean I already looked kinda great today when I looked at myself in the mirror on the way over but now im gonna come out of this looking even better I mean mrdok if he even notices he doesnt really pick up on the details but still im sure hell love it even if he doesnt really realize the reasons why but really my goal in life is to have tits like kim one day you have to have a really good surgeon for that not totally sure if doctor slopowskis the one to do the work havent really looked at his tit portfolio yet thats why I havent said saying anything dont want to be forced under the knife just one procedure at a time thats always been my philosophy like I wonder if a female doctor would be better the male doctors theyre more likely to put a bigger implant in because thats what they want even if it looks fake like theyll even force the issue like you have to get this size sweetie I hate that a female plastic surgeon is more likely to go for naturalness even if you say you want big I mean I want bigger its important im doing a lot of bikini shoots now you know you cant really sell settlers landing without cleavage an increase in volume but not like porno titties one surgeon I consulted with in ze hills of beverly as doctor slopowski calls it said he thought I was full enough then kind of licked his lips in a gross way I was there for another reason to try and get my backrolls lipod out but I know what theyre all thinking their motivation they like to stick their thing in between and hump the cleavage fold feels good to them and we have to lay there and pretend to like it try not to laugh is more like it like what would the female equivalent of that even be like rub our clits on their nipples ooh gross no of course not there is none how come girls are not capable of such perversion well lets not get too philosophical its only filler I mean last procedure for a while girl so enjoy the pain while it lasts youll be missing all those needles soon enough dynamic wrinkles are more my problem static wrinkles not so much like im still in my twenties so dont really have to deal with static wrinkles yet this is like partly for dynamic wrinkles then partly preventative filler more the idea as I discussed with doctor slopowski before is to totally freeze those lines so that the static wrinkles dont develop so thats why you totally have to get these regular treatments or else everything ive worked for is just going to go for naught and then ill wind up some old bag that mrdok will probly divorce because thats the thing this island is going to be full of beautiful women I mean beautiful people in general so its like fine you have to accept that your man is gonna fuck around but its not like you have to encourage it so many women in the old days they would get married and then just like give up on themselves I find that so demeaning like you have to be your very best you all day every day because nothing in this life can be taken for granted I mean take mrdok he has already had like how many wives none of them were able to keep him and I mean at the end of the day its their fault at least partially like you have to take responsibility for this stuff thats part of what being a woman is is to take that responsibility at least over things you can control and master like your appearance for one dont let yourself go girl that would be my advice to like any of my friends on their wedding day cos you never know when your mans eye is gonna wander mmkay its like a ring is no guarantee it is a promise not a commitment you need to be devoted to yourself first and foremost so if you wanna call that feminism then okay im totally a feminist I mean its my philosophy of feminism at least which is why im here right now botox isnt like just a surgical procedure botox is empowerment maybe if mrtol had had some she would still be a part of mrdoks life she definitely needed it from what I hear because she was an alcoholic and alcohol totally damages the skin and im sure krstal feels exactly the same way with all of her vaginal rejuvenation surgery

ouch the fucking pain just concentrate on being in the moment bev the buzz of the air conditioner the feel of the organic paper beneath your back and the purple leather beneath that yeah feel that purple penis power lol not the feel of the needle going into your skin the sound of doctor slopowskis like labored breathing kind of phlegmy like I dont think he smokes but he probly vapes yeah its definitely more the sound of a vaper than a smoker like hes not hacking but theres something there that is more like chemical or something but really must repeat these creases and crows are not who I am these creases and crows are not who I am botox gives you the best version of yourself an injection of confidence is what it is never give up on you girl especially the version of you with filler in it that is my motto my philosophy or whatever should be at least I think that should actually go in my bio line on my insta yeah cos what im really here for is to inspire other women say you know what you can look like me if you just put a little effort into it I mean if you can afford the injectables I mean sure we cant all be married to billionaires fair enough but you can like use your imagination or something I mean wealth is something that you feel on the inside it doesnt really matter if you actually have it yeah sounds good I should like record this or something like me and my mom werent particularly rich when I was growing up I mean we got by didnt starve but I always felt like rich on the inside even when I couldnt really afford to shop at dolce and gabbana every day and then one day I got to be rich on the outside as well and look at me now getting beverly hills injections on my very own private island well okay it is not *my* island per se and its not really private its a country okay but im first lady now if thats not something to inspire young girls I dont know what is like being rich is all about being a good enough person in like that you ultimately just like *deserve* it pretty soon your followers go up and youre getting all these sponsorship offers like even if I divorced M tomorrow I could probly live really well on my social alone I mean I dont know if it would work as well in other countries where you have to like pay taxes and stuff but here id like have my own empire not that id ever think of divorcing M he is like the love of my lifestyle if not the love of my life speaking of mom its not like ive become a diva dont know where that accusation comes from I mean my motto has always been keep it real just because my reality has become different so much bigger than hers I mean thats the nature of celebrity you either deal with it or you drift away like the last time we talked it was all I never hear from you anymore you communicate more with your social media followers than you do your own mother im like mom thats sort of my job like what am I supposed to do cut them off then fade into oblivion I mean get real I mean its sad like we were always a team I tried I offered to bring her out here shes afraid of the war im like mom the war is frickin far away like ten miles from here you dont understand like some girls who have like a soldier fetish will go on tinder hoping to hook up and their profiles dont even show half the time theyre so far away like we have an agreement in place on both sides that the war wont ever come here elias shores is off limits it is like totally safe at least like ninety five percent of the time those italians blowing up the wet nasty was a total fluke like they werent even supposed to be a part of the war those guys and anyway it was almost a good thing cos we were able to relocate the wet nasty in a much better much more well designed location and I brought in this really good interior designer from los angeles who has been on all these reality shows where he goes in and redesigns celebrities homes and we even filmed the whole thing so we can use that footage for our own reality show some day I mean yeah its sad that some people happen to have lost their lives but those guys who died werent really a big part of the community I mean combined they had maybe 450 followers on insta and in total and they both followed way way more I mean I would never say these things out loud I dont mean to crap on the dead but thats just sad like in this day and age I mean get with it if youre not particularly good at posting its fine there are like professionals you can hire who will take care of that for you I mean I am totally going to transform elias shores into like influencer central like were gonna require so much more bandwidth its not even funny today my horoscope suggested I find a water moon a water moon will show you how to be kinder that is what you need right now im like wtf first of all a water moon who do I know thats a water moon secondly what do you mean by im not kind enough already like im one of the kindest people I know even though I dont always know what to do in like every IRL situation I get myself into id say im still pretty kind with an emphasis on pretty of course lol I mean I like so many different peoples posts and really diverse too like I especially try to like the posts of POCs and LGBTs and like I follow the instas of every single one of our soldiers even if their posts arent always the most exciting or I dont get them like as the first lady of settlers landing I totally believe in our troops I mean you might say I am their biggest cheerleader I take selfies with them all the time whenever I see one of them when im like doing a photo shoot in the field like nobody treats their fans or followers better than I do I think I am the queen of kindness or at least I will be if doctor slopowski ever finishes im like how much longer is this going to take do I have to like start paying rent just to lay here like if the water moons whoever the heck they happen to be dont realize I am kind enough already I really do not want to spend anytime whatsoever actually I wonder if angeline is a water moon it would fit certainly not krstal lol I guess water moons theyre like super emotional people cancer pisces scorpion am I forgetting one make a mental note to google it if I ever get off this operating table I dont think krstal has felt anything since what like the 70s probly did a ton of blow then must have done some severe surface damage I mean I dont mean to be mean but she is mean so why show her any sympathy I mean not mean exactly more like self centered in a way that is almost like distracting see I look for ways to be more *present* all the time especially when im with other people god I am thinking being away from my phone this long is really starting to drive me mental like what do people even do toody doo ooh la la im so bored im even making up songs making weird

sounds now in my mind like how much longer OUCH FUCK want
to scream out but that ones in my cheek dont want to mess it up like
its almost like the doctor was responding telepathically to my
thoughts of anger boredom with his needle like could he actually hear
me who knows doctors are smart you have to go to college for like
ten years or something to become a plastic surgeon maybe they teach
you how to read peoples thoughts based on their facial expression as
well but seriously is my face expressing anything at this moment its
swollen as fuck I mean of course not maybe the eyes then I thought
about getting colored lenses I just couldnt decide which color theyre
hard to get here like thats one thing we desperately need a really good
eyeware store like luxury brands only prada is the best especially for
men like if youre not gonna get laser you have to get prada that
should like be a law like seriously I want that written into the settlers
landing constitution omg like eyeware laws that would be so cool like
we would get so much press for that if we actually passed it like the
headlines would be island nation passes prada law make a mental
note to email mrdok about it as soon as I get off this operating table
OM frickin G that one right between the eyes blinking now blinking
fast eyes water feel my face getting flushed as fuck its like going to
the brow bar only worse like the last time I got my eyebrows done
the girl just totally ripped them right off heard her shriek when she
did it which of course is like the most alarming thing ever because
you think to yourself omg like did she just totally deform my brows
but she said after it was more like a shriek of pleasure like for some
reason she almost gets off on doing it but then she got all serious
and she was like but girl you have a really strong browline I do have
to say and she had like *no idea* that I had had injectables because the
stuff at the time I mean at that point I was actually flying to hollywood almost every month from manhattan but thats just the kind of
person ive always been I was telling the girl interviewing me the other
day like I just like to take the initiative like when I was 10 I knew I
was fat and so I just decided one day I stopped eating it took a while
for my mom to notice one day shes like beverly how come you are
not eating and I was like stop mom I dont want to talk about it and
that was it she knew she couldnt stop me I mean I slimmed down to
like 90 it only took me a month and a half or something now im
older and taller my ideal weight is like 105 and now I mean I hardly
have to worry I am like the queen of the sample size I mean thats the
one good thing about not being able to get pregnant ill never have
to worry about cellulite well okay never say never like I never even
want to consider in vitro or whatever its called because then you end

up like on that show where that woman winds up with quadruplets im like wtf like that is beyond human that is when you become like a cow and I mean that both literally and figuratively I mean its sad when youre that pregnant when you get that blown up like the woman was saying I was pregnant in places where a woman is not even supposed to be pregnant like her entire body had babies ballooning out of it and im sorry but when that happens girl you can never get in a bathing suit ever again not even a one piece just like a bathing suit in general because between the stretch marks and the cellulite it is just over for you and on the show even after the plastic surgery and all the injectables I mean to be honest im surprised they even aired that episode because even after all the surgery she still didnt look that good okay that is mean to say even to think so yeah you cant get pregnant bev and so I made the decision to just focus on me instead stay focused on your body girl stay positive and dont let any haters demean you that is like my philosophy of life in a nutshell and I dont care if the entire world knows it either because if there is one thing I am then it is proud mmmmkay I would totally smack my lips right now if there werent three needles going into them at once lol

but omg what about the time when you were the school slut thank god it only lasted a week but still it was so humiliating I was dating who was it at the time must have been tid the llama dick guy and he was in line at the cafeteria when he pulled out his wallet to pay and out fell a condom like woopsy it was a magnum of course he needed one tbh and who was it that saw whoever he was in line with well anyway by the time lunch was over half the cafeteria the entire school knew about it we were dating at the time they all knew that and so it was obvious that we were having sex still nobody was supposed to know back then it was still like a taboo thing like it wasnt a catholic school per se but it was majority catholic and so pretty strict when it came to sex and stuff and of course with guys its like congratulations bro youre getting some but with girls everyone turns to look at you like youre easy suddenly girls are distancing themselves from you they dont want to be your friend the guys are all harassing making fun of you even though they all secretly want to do you because they think youre easy so that just increases the pressure omg so much social pressure these were the days before social media became such a thing thank god they could have really destroyed my life thank god the scandal didnt last long but I think thats because my personality is just so nonoffensive I mean one thing I will say this makes me sound so old but I just feel that guys were a lot less perverse back then I mean I guess part of it is that when youre at that age you just feel so lucky to be doing it that *any* girl really will be doing it with you that you dont want to push your luck like they must have a lot of traumatic experiences with getting blueballed too they dont want to say the wrong thing so that the girl will be like no lets stop now I mean I have to admit I was guilty of that when I was like fourteen one of my first boyfriends sam bailey always making out on the couch in his rec room had to be careful that his mother didnt come in I would let him eat me out tho loved it in fact it felt so good never came tho probly didnt even know what coming was back then but still let him suck my titties too but I wouldnt really do anything back to him I didnt want to put it in my mouth because I thought it was gross at the time and fucking of course it was out of the question I was like way too young he would always beg me but I was like no no way just dry humping on the couch while we were making out hed get so hot I think one time he pulled out just the tip of it and asked me to kiss it and I was like okay fine I did it for like one second but just a dry kiss no tongue of course but then fast forward to mrdok the time he asked if he could just jerk off on my face didnt want to fuck or something I was like ew gross no never like he wanted to get the stuff all over it but its good for the skin he said I dont care if it is I dont want your nasty jizz on my do you know how much it costs how much I spend each month on skin care products to have it all ruined but sperm has a lot of protein in it he said and that gave me pause ive never heard that but I made a mental note to like ask my dermatologist about it at our next appointment of course I totally forgot about it until now if its not putting their thing between your tits then its something gross like that seriously I think these guys watch too much porn at least thats what desirée said and I happen to agree like usually I dont mind if its something really degrading then maybe like id never let them pee on me maybe not even in the shower there have been guys whove tried its like where does that even come from the thing is the older they get the more things they want to try in sex and its like cant you just calm down for five minutes I think they get bored with doing it the normal way and so then you have to seek out new ways of doing it almost like how mrdok had to come out here to find a new country the old one just wasnt good enough

omfg what was that explosion so frickin loud I am shaking thank god not a needle in my face when that happened it sounded like a bomb I swear to god we are all going to be so triggered by this by the time it finally finishes I mean not just soldiers can get PTSD civilians also glamour in a warzone maybe that would be a good title for the reality show or just warzone glamour and it can be me doing the voice over during the opening sequence like in life beauty thrives even in the most unexpected of places but nobody said it would be easy let me be your guide an animated rain of bullets me in a bikini emporio armani of course then there could be me in like a cute nurses outfit caring for our wounded soldiers or like giving them skincare tips because even if youre an amputee or something no matter how bad your wound happens to be you can still take care of your skin thats my philosophy or motto or whatever its called like anyone can take care of themselves have to think about when the next procedure on my butt will be whether I should just get implants or keep going on with injectables butt was my first big procedure even before I got anything done in the face desirées advice it was but also that plastic surgery reality show where the girl was like theres a revolution in beauty thats going right into my booty I just thought that was soooo cute I was like yes sister I am with you and truthfully I havent looked back since no need to keep looking better and better like if I wind up winning an emmy or something for the reality show like the first person I will thank in my acceptance speech will be doctor slopowski even ahead of mrdok no thats not true dont get carried away bev everybody in LA goes to him then theyd totally know youve had work done not that its anything to be ashamed of still I mean im pretty sure they all go to him all the big name actresses and stuff not that hes ever told me client patient confidentiality or whatever its called but still you hear things theres always been rumors I mean thats how these surgeons survive the industry is tough you get recommendations direct from friends who look good whose opinions you respect on the one hand and then theres the rumor mill where its like so and so goes to this one and so then of course you want to look like her and so you go I mean true happiness is looking your best and saying fuck the rest that should be my motto I mean I could really have one for my twitter bio line one for my insta another for my tiktok now theyre all the same and I mean on the one hand it makes sense for establishing a brand but then it also makes it all a little bland hey I made a rhyme there I should be a poet lol yeah I mean since the other poet disappeared the one who is like supposed to be writing our national epic or whatever it is maybe I could undertake that too lol no not really its not like I can rhyme all the time ooh just made another one lol anyway im sure gordo is like heartbroken apparently they had a thing tho tbh I have no idea who would actually want to do it with gordo I know thats mean to say I mean think but come on girl I mean it could be worse the skin at least theres no sun damage thats because he probly hasnt gone outside since like the 1990s not like krstal who has like submitted herself to the california sun for what decades now I mean when you live out there even if you religiously slather yourself in 50+ sunscreen every single day youre still going to get some sun damage theres just no way around it its like florida but worse she could be like a hot milf if she tried a little harder I mean I guess billy already sees her as one or else he just sees it as like a power couple dynamic situation whatever not like its any of my business but her face if she had started much younger like I am doing right now preventative botox then she would have far less aggressive facial expressions or at least be more conscious of her facial expressions all the time not give away so much of course botox wasnt even invented back then lol like if you get botox enough times you can actually train yourself to move your face less and the less you move your face of course the less lines youre going to get like if you could just paralyze all your facial muscles you could pretty much stay young forever and look like youre 20 even when youre 90 sad because for krstal its too late I mean anyway tbh I think she does get hers from doctor soukowski who lets be honest is just not as talented with the needles as slopowski is thats why in my first consultation with slopowski we decided on botox without a smile because I mean we want to avoid the accumulation of expression that leads to static wrinkle formation like in a way its self discipline to be completely blank all the time which is not to say you cant have a personality you totally can but personality is separate from your facial expression you can like crack funny jokes all the time just dont laugh at them yeah like the best thing is to have a deadpan sense of humor like in that way mrdok has been very helpful because he is like the most deadpan person ever I mean sure he does laugh all the time too but not all the time but he laughs a lot but still it doesnt matter really cos hes a guy I mean most guys dont worry about lines and wrinkles and stuff like that like especially now when hes the president and has much more important things to deal with just like every american president sez this job ages you I mean it is aging mrdok sure but mostly like in the way I was thinking before like he gets more perverse in sex things and stuff like that he could probly use some lipo especially the back fat but im not I mean its not my place to say tho maybe for the neck I could give him one of those silicon patches I use they are like really helpful in smoothing out those wrinkles or get not botox but some of those sugar threads injected into his skin to start producing more collagen because hes at that age I mean krstal too tbh even more shes like way beyond it I am totally going to start with the sugar threads the instant I hit 30 like on my 30th birthday or something like ill admit it I did research how to do your own botox at home just in case something like the absolute worse happens doctor slopowski cant come here anymore I mean tbh I would rather learn how to do my own rather than let doctor soukowski do it what are you crazy home botox god if the doctor if anyone for that matter could hear these thoughts right now then again were all going a little crazy right now isnt that the truth the stress of everything going on M probly feeling it most of all I mean he really has the most pressure to deal with if I was him I dont even know how I would deal I mean all the political crap having to run a war all the pressure and then keeping up a media profile as well like I honestly dont know how he does it well I do I mean he has G to do half the work no thats mean but still being cooped up in that bunker all day how many months has it been now I think like nine no eight no god I dont even know anymore if I had my phone here maybe he sits in front of that sun lamp G brought him for like half an hour every day the only way he can get light you need some to get you energy its the UV rays that are so damaging but the lamp of course doesnt have those it is just really really bright but in like a safe non skin damaging way at least he doesnt have to worry about what he wears anymore except when he like does an interview over skype or whatever even then he jokes with me that he doesnt wear any pants like a suit on top but then hes naked with his thing hanging out down below even plays with it while hes giving the interview haha even the one time when he had me blow him while he was talking to I think was it huffington post or the leader of germany one of those anyway he maintained an ice cool composure throughout the whole thing dont know how he did it I think he wanted to test himself to see if he was capable I mean all the blowjobs I have given in this life I was like why not though it was hard to open my mouth I remember because I had had a procedure done what like three days before so there was still that stiffness I was like mrdok I will only do it during the time of the interview if I do it too long it will cause lines or even my botox to rupture I said that even though I dont think thats a real thing still it sounded good and then he was like dont worry baby I only need five minutes youre better than any professional and I had to laugh like it sounds disrespectful but it was actually really funny like of all the weird places and situations ive given guys blowjobs before in a car of course but I guess every girl has done that in an office of course then in like an elevator when it was just the two of us and it was one of those old ones that didnt have a camera but then that time when we were in hong kong he wanted to do it in an alleyway outside it was like the middle of the night we were both drunk AF but even then I was like no mrdok lets just wait till we get back to the hotel wed been drinking cocktails in that place on that hill since like what time at first he was talking like he wanted to find a girl for us to have a threeway with and im not totally against the idea but then he was like no actually I just want to watch you two and like jerk off to it and I was like no effin way like I had to draw the line there I mean I asked angeline once have you ever with a girl and she was like yeah in college once its no big deal havent you and I was like no maybe its because I never went to college lol but even if I had I dont think I mean its just not my thing I dont have anything against it its not like the idea disgusts me but I also just dont really get off on it I mean I think if me and M were to have a threeway I would maybe like make out with a girl but beyond that I dont know like I just dont think I could go down on another woman dyke out like that I could maybe let her go down on me that wouldnt be so bad but I mean even to make out with one there are limits like they would have to look really really good im not about to make out with no skank of course in the dressing room of omg what was it so embarrassing forever 21 when I actually used to shop there well what can I say it was like another lifetime I mean it really was who did I blow in the forever 21 changing room it must have been mark koopler who I went out with for like thirty seconds right after high school well what can I say I think he probly wanted to do it it was in front of the mirror might have even filmed the part of me blowing him but we didnt do it that day because I was on the rag I mean I didnt want to get blood all over the clothes I wasnt even planning on buying them in the end even if I was going to buy them thats like double the reason not to like that would be so embarrassing hi I would like to buy this and theres like a huge bloodstain on it like oops like first of all you could never get it out so you wouldnt want to even actually take it home anyway I guess the alleyway was the most daring like an outdoor scenario no there was also that time at the beach but I mean I dont know if it counts really because it was a private beach after all so it was just me and M no one could see like when I told desirée about the hong kong alleyway she looked at me like gurl and im like stop slut shaming me that is so not okay like gay guys do stuff like that and even worse all the time but omg that is like the one thing I am missing is a gay best friend a gay best friend is like the accessory of the century it is almost like if you dont have one you cannot be a real influencer or at least taken seriously as one if I cant find any gays here I might just have to invent one that I like refer to but he doesnt appear on camera because hes shy or like we only talk on social or something because hes in another country like canada or some place and cant come to settlers right now is canada even a country lol like yeah that would give me something new to talk about too and then I could get more gay followers like I already have the rainbow flag in my bio line but its not really enough I mean definitely we could audition one for the reality show omg make a mental note to scroll through insta look for like really fashion forward gays who would be like adventurous enough to come here like if I had a co host or something that would like take things to the next level like yass queen and all that god gotta learn the lingo maybe I should start watching whats that reality show with all the drag queens on it omg I have a frickin rainbow flag on my bio line I should be watching it already thank god no one really knows its so weird there arent more gays here I heard there used to be a gay bar in mrdokia back when it was still called olde colonia or something like that it was really popular too we should totally open one on elias shores and like turn it into more of a lgbt friendly destination like im sure we could market it if we get the right data I think rick is handling the algorithms now for all the elias shores projects the pink dollar is really hot right now but ill have to check with M as soon as these frickin needles stop going into my face omg this is taking so much longer than it normally does I wonder what doctor slopowski is like even doing not old homos like G either like we dont want it to be like a sex destination for old queers like thailand or something I mean who knows if hes still even a homo anymore gordo who knows what he is I wonder if he actually got it taken off his thing I mean gross like I dont even want to think about G and a dick right now like barforama like what was mrdok thinking when he was starting out like hmm for an assistant I think I ought to track down the worlds biggest freak lol I guess there are some things I dont could never understand I mean theyve known each other forever but still what a mess and gordo what was he thinking too like when he was a kid about to go off into the world like hmm I think I will just become the worlds biggest freak weirdo like use all these fancy words so that no one can ever understand what the heck im saying and then like act all weird all the time I mean its more than just socially awkward he makes like everyone in the room embarrassed to be there and like he isnt even aware of like the level of mortification he arises in all the people like im sure thats probly why people like barb and them left the island or that probly has a lot to do with it like screw this they just didnt want to deal with gordo anymore or gordina as she was probly known then well until the start of the war when everything got all shot to hell apparently krstal was trying to teach him her whatever how to do make up right after she transitioned it was like a total mess I mean how you go from being a guy to like learning how to blend ill never know I mean there are youtube channels where you can learn this stuff but thats like beyond him her it they are way too old for it at this point like whats youtube like it wouldnt surprise me if he actually had to ask someone that im not even kidding I mean its not enough to be weird he is just SAD tho tbh mrdok is starting to get sad as well not in like a pathetic public way more on a private level like I think this war is starting to take its toll not on like his health or his appearance but on his investments like yes and I mean that ultimately is what is making him sad like he is no longer going to be the worlds fifth richest man or whatever if the war doesnt get straightened out soon like the other night when I got back to the bunker and he was just laying there all silent the tv going and so I was walking around doing my normal nighttime routine you know make up removal moisturizer all that and hes not saying a word the entire time or like just giving one word answers when I would ask a question and finally im like what is it mrdok whats wrong and hes like nothing and I turn to him and im like mrdok you are watching rednecks hunting alligators in a swamp on tv like somethings wrong this isnt like you what is it and he just turned away from me put his head into the pillow and started to cry like bawling like a baby like omfg I had never seen him do that before it was like scary I didnt even know what to do like am I supposed to play the mommy role now he is always the strong one its me if anyone who is weak I mean now that I think about it a part of me is glad not that he was sad and crying of course but just that it exposed this like whole other dimension to him that I didnt even know existed before I mean how much longer can it go on this way thats a really a question you have to ask yourself at times not that its one I would ever voice out loud in front of mrdok but I mean even desirée she was writing me on insta the other day and she was like I dont know about this war thang girl and I was like you mean my war thong lol because I actually had a thong with like the neon orange silver and green and purple colors of our national flag because I made a support our troops post where I just wore the thong and I was topless but of course I didnt show my nips you cant do that on insta so I was just holding my breasts in my hand cupping them with my expressionless face I got like a ton of likes for that post I think more than any other in my entire insta history like more than 75k comments and when mrdok saw it he was like take it down and I was like what no way he was like take it down and I was like why and he was like I do not want other men and then he stopped himself because he knew he was starting to sound like all possessive and I hate that in a guy and then he corrected himself he was like it is not becoming for a first lady and its not just my opinion gordo thinks the same dont you gordo and gordo is standing right there of course he is not going to disagree with anything M sez and I was like SEETHING on the inside I was like mrdok when I came here we both agreed that this would be my job and that I would have total control over it so like why are you trying to control me now and he said im not babe but this has to do with our marriage and it has to do with MY image as well and I was like mrdok this has nothing to do with our marriage and certainly nothing with your image I mean how could it like you arent even in the frickin photo or mentioned in the post like if someone were to tag him or something then I could see how that would be an argument even though I could just go and untag him in that case that still didnt happen tbh I think he didnt like some of the comments like some were pretty crude and in the end we came to a compromise where I would just turn the comments off on that particular post and then after a day of tenseness it was like over I think he just forgot about it tbh but then what can you do it wasnt like it was our worst fight our worst fight definitely the one where I wound up getting smacked I mean I kind of asked for it I think I called him a crip or an amputee I made some kind of reference to it like I was pulling out all the things I know he hates like being called elias I just wanted to hurt him and so well I got what I asked for then he hurt me I was livid with rage like he knows how much time and money I have spent on this face for him to risk fucking it up like that thank god there was no real lasting damage to it but I talked to angeline after and she was like girl are you going to leave him I mean even then I was like no no way but then I thought about it and what would I do if I actually left him like the ideal would be if the country were developed enough I could still live here like I base myself in elias shores have like a condo there or something and he is just in mrdokia but of course I dont think it will ever be like *that* developed I mean the islands not that big I would have to go somewhere else and thatd be scary angeline was like you guys have a prenup right and I was like no whats that and she was like girl she couldnt believe I would marry a guy who is like so rich and not even have a prenup in place tbh the thought never even occurred to me probly because I didnt even

know what a prenup was when I married him lol do now but its a
little too late I mean I guess you could say that those papers I glued
together about belle encoding I mean I still have those I refused to
give them up and the fbi would love to get their hands on not that
id ever but I guess thats like a prenup in its own way anyway thats
one reason he would never leave me or at least never get divorced I
mean let him fuck around thats what a man does but still stay married
places I could go I mean definitely back to nyc live with my mom for
a while wouldnt really want to stay there for long probly LA like I
think I fit in there maybe start my own make up line or like own a
chain of fitness studios that has always been a dream of mine like in
LA you wouldnt even need to spend the money on tanning beds
because all you have to do is go outside lol not that wed ever attract
low class clientele like that who wanted to damage their skin it would
be like a high class fitness studio with like pilates instructors and stuff
and wed serve like zen tea and all of that anyway its just an idea not
that it will ever be necessary because elias shores is going to be like a
life long project of mine and anyway im like the happiest ive ever
been right now

what I had for lunch today lets see half an apple cut into quarter
slices fat free sugar free gluten free yogurt and a single leaf of butter-
head lettuce havent eaten a carb since I got here how else are you
going to maintain this figure bev I mean for realz like the time I
stopped eating when I was a kid well time more like times it was like
what two or three mom was relatively fine with it once she knew it
was when mrs browning the stupid school guidance counselor
thought she would call god such a do gooder like I had a whole entire
plan and she disrupted it made me watch those stupid educational
films where like an anorexic girl winds up in the hospital being fed
through a tube like hello I am not anorexic I am on a diet okay then
I showed her the web forum where I got the diet from she read it all
interested like but then at the end I saw her kind of get this skeptical
look and like nod her head and she was like that is anorexia nervosa
and I am like omfg did you not just read it it explicitly sez they do
not endorse anorexia whatsoever like and the person who wrote it is
like a trained physician a dietician I think is what it is called you have
to have like a medical degree to do that kind of work write that kind
of article and mrs browning is like no beverly I am afraid this is not
sound medical advice and I am like what do you know you are just a
stupid guidance counselor you are not a doctor like so many of these
people working in schools public school think they are so smart but
theyre actually not like if they were really that good they would

actually be working in the private sector thank god when me and mrdok have our kid it will never have to go to a frickin public school like having been through it myself I like totally dont believe in it anymore at least not anywhere in the city of new york anyway mrs browning was just jealous because she was old and well lets face it she never had my figure thats why you could tell in the beginning she was reading the article with like great interest you could tell by looking at her face she was thinking hmm maybe I should try this diet as well and the truth is she should have because she had those cow hips that like you cant cover up with anything you wear like she had been neglecting herself for years was like what when youre that age everyone seems so old she was probly like forty but she looked sixty and on top of that she was divorced I will never let myself wind up that way like that barb woman too tho of course she is rich enough she can like hire someone whenever she gets horny I guess its optimal when youre that age and rich AF but at least barb has managed to stay thin through it all not only that I always always envied her that cartier watch she has on all the time it is like a conversation piece for sure like you can wear almost anything like jeans or sweats and as long as you have that on you are going to look great thats the thing about jewelry about accessories in general it can either totally stand in for an overall look or it can totally destroy a look if youre not extra careful about it like gold for instance thats one thing me and mrdok totally have in common we are both silver people like gold just doesnt do it for us for him I think its something financial thats like too deep for me to understand for me it is more like overload in blingness like you have to be subtle and understated or else people are going to think youre just showing off I know I know it totally sounds like there is something wrong with me when I say it like desirée just gives me that look and is like girl how can you not like the bling but im like honey I do like the bling silver is bling too silver and diamonds and amethyst amethyst has always been my favorite precious stone like this ring that I have on now that mrdok gave me is pure silver with an amethyst stone I almost came when I saw it I was like where did you find this and he was like starting to tell me and I was like nevermind just kiss me and then I think I got on my knees and blew him right there we were in his office in the bunker but I didnt even care if anyone came in at that moment I was so happy I would have sucked him off in front of the pope even I think I even swallowed the stuff at that moment I didnt even care thats how ecstatic I was like im sorry jewelry just does something to me drives me insane even more than a man does A is for amethyst and armani B is for balenciaga and bmw and botox and the bahamas my favorite place in the world except for settlers landing of course C is for chanel and for cartier and for christian dior D is for dolce and gabbana of course E is for ecstasy which me and mrdok took together that one time it was like totally insane I think we danced until like 7 oclock in the AM and then we fucked for like twelve hours more F is for facebook and ferrari and for fredericks of hollywood which makes like the best push up bra ever G is for gucci H is for hermes I is for instagram and my iphone of course like if I ever get it back J is for j lo who is like my favorite star of all time and I guess justin is maybe second place even though he is starting to get a bit fat gross K is for kim kardashian who is like the one person who has done more for women in this century than any other L is for lamborghini for louis vuitton and the love of my life M is for mercedes benz and for mrdok of course N is for the needle going into my left jaw right now which hurts so fucking much but will be so so worth it in the end what is O for O is for the orgy that M always sez he wants to have but I would never do something like that just because I think its unsanitary and gross like lots of guys different things going in me after theyve already been in other women in the same room that means youd also have to taste other girls vajayjays in your mouth when you suck on the guys things like again that is just a fantasy that only guys can get off on no girls would ever go for that unless they were like seriously horny in like a perverted sort of way oh and omega watches I guess P is for prada and for porno which I never particulary liked tho I know mrdok watches it cos sometimes he makes me watch it with him when he wants to do it and even imitate some of the things were seeing on the screen like I cant half the time I feel too silly or self conscious or even if its one of those tricks like the one where the girl squirts like a man does when shes coming im like I dont even know how they do that like is it pee or what whatever it is its gross but then I think porn is good in some ways like angeline and I were talking about it once and she was like yeah dont you get it its for ugly guys and im like what do you mean and shes like its for guys who cant get laid but also she had heard about this one guy who was like butt ugly and knew he would never be able to get a hot chick and so he trained himself using porn and im like what do you mean he trained himself and she was like he started watching porn with fat ugly girls in it and it got to the point where he could get turned on by them so that way he could start dating all the fat ugly girls no one wanted in real life and he finally met one that fell in love with him and then they got married and lived happily ever after im like is that for real and angeline was like yeah totally my cousin maureen told me about it she even knows the guy went to high school with him or something and im like okay so porn is inspiring in a way it really does help people Q is for queer which is like a category that I am so supportive of R is for rolex like if you dont have at least one I dont even want to talk to you S is for settlers landing the best country ever T is for tiffanys and for tesla U is for the USA who were fighting right now and will never win though im sure we will make up one day cos that is like the country that I was brought up in and that my mom still lives in and I want her to be okay but seriously after the war M sez we will eventually establish diplomatic relations with them whatever that means but I think its like a good thing V is for valentino which I only wear on like super formal occasions because tbh I think most of their pieces are for like much older women though I do respect the brand and all the classical elegance it stands for W is for the wet nasty which is only like the greatest bar ever okay so maybe the new new one isnt so so great but we cant market it that way of course it has to be like new and improved even if its not but I have thought of some improvements just to make the general atmosphere like sexier not sexy like in a gross sexual way but like just a place where people could come to and feel at home in a luxury sense X is for the extraordinary way my life has turned out like who wouldve thought a girl from staten island I say this on my blog all the time couldve come this far this is just proof that if you like really stick to your dreams you can accomplish all those and more one day like your life can be Xtraordinary too and I really mean that im not just saying it because it sounds good Y is for yves st laurent of course like where would I be without you Z is hard there arent really a lot of brands that start with Z I mean im sure there are some but I would have to google it which of course I cant do right now because this annoying doctor is still sticking needles in my face now hes getting up really close I can like feel his breath underneath the needles when he moves away im like how much longer is this going to take doctor and he whispers at me that I just need to be patient that true beauty is worth waiting for and im like okay whatever you say oh wait zenith there are zenith watches thats one luxury brand though tbh theyre not my favorite swiss okay so not the worst in the world but I much prefer cartier or rolex its just personal preference I guess but anyway ill put it on the list because I cant think of anything else for Z maybe I should actually do this as a blog post like the alphabet according to bev that would get like so many likes and reposts probly I am a tastemaker after all I mean one idea were still toying around with I mean should I do it is to like leak a sex tape I mean paris did it kim did it its kind of a sure path to stardom thing is im pretty sure mrdok wouldnt want to be in it so we would have to either find one from when I was in high school like I think we made two or three but I would have to track down one of those guys and see if they would be up for it like if I even had one of the files then it was on an old phone I probly dont even have anymore and this was before the cloud so really wed have to like ask one of the guys if they still had theirs and were willing to share it with me or just like leak it themselves I mean tid for sure if its true hes actually still working in that gas station he could probly use the money tho am not sure if hed want the publicity like maybe hes married now or something and doesnt want his wife to find out then again she might find it pretty cool I mean I know a lot of women would be proud especially a dick that big like thats all mine girls stay away lol or else if all those files have actually been deleted it then we could actually stage like a fake sex tape from years ago would have to find a guy to do it with and get mrdoks permission his blessing I mean but im sure hed understand if it was going to be a huge benefit for us in the end hed probly just want to watch the filming of it lol maybe even hold the camera himself omg I mean we could do it in a tasteful way like nothing too gross it would have to tittilate if thats the word but like I dont want to be on film doing anal or something like that it would just be like me blowing the guy and then doing it with him that is all leaking it is the easy part tho you want to do it in the right way like I heard the same agent whos working on the reality show deal is also really good at leaking sex tapes and stuff so we could ask his advice or he could just do it for us I mean this could also be beneficial help us with the war effort we could use the money we get from it to like buy more weapons and stuff

but ultimately I mean its about doing it in a way where you stay true to yourself like I would only do a sex tape if its going to be life affirming in some way speaking of which I hope we can get some oysters flown in this week we havent had any for like omg almost a month O is for oysters I am like starving for some oysters and the great thing about them is they have so little fat only like three grams like a lot of people when theyre trying to lose weight will turn to chicken but oysters actually have half as many calories so its like a great alternative but anyway there is like so much going on right now makes it hard to even hold down like a proper diet like OM on the motherfuckin G if I have to eat one more avocado M sez its cos bobby is like addicted to them lived in california for too long so he put in an order for like a million of them I have nothing against avocados per se but like seriously enough is enough the chef comes up for a new use for one at like every meal but I mean you can only disguise an advocado for so long and anyway it is high time we get a new sushi chef in as well like sugimoto has been here for half a year already I am getting sick and tired I just want a change like all mrdok has to do is pick up the phone call barb get a recommendation for a new one or like maybe someone not even from japan but who is like really good at doing fusion sushi I heard of one he like does things with vegan cream cheese sounds yummy omg I am like getting hungry now will go to the eat this bunker directly after gonna stuff my face lol no not really hard to eat after botox you have that frozen stiff face feeling all over but maybe if I chew softly or really ill probly wind up just getting a smoothie or something some froyo something soft you dont really have to chew eat this has done nice things with their new interior I have to admit theyre like independently managed I havent met the guy who did the revamp yet it might even be the owner who I also dont know I saw some photos of the old space in mrdokia where they had like the 50s diner memorabilia but only high class stuff and a hopper painting that was supposedly real they got it right though because on the booths and seats they used real leather dyed bright red not like the fake pleather youd see at most nyc diners but its the same waitresses who all have russian accents for some reason M sez theyre actually all from the ukraine I asked him once how they all wound up here and he stayed silent on that one then I pushed him again and he was like youll have to ask ali the owner hes from kyrgyzstan via moscow im like okay you already lost me nevermind anyway its probly best I dont eat for a few days have a photo shoot on wednesday scheduled it so that the botox should have settled by then this time we want to do something a little edgier so mrdok is gonna be in it as well dressed like a sort of old fashioned 1970s gangster pimp with like huge sunglasses a jigolo suit smoking a cigar and like a kalishnikov rifle propped to the side whereas im gonna be in my armani bikini the one we had custom made with the colors of the national flag on it I kind of want the huge gucci sunglasses with the bling encrusted but theres kind of an argument going on right now between me and the stylist about that she claims that the reflection of the diamonds clash with the colors on the bathing suit I have seen the test photos I have no idea wtf shes talking about it looks totally fine to me I showed mrdok he feels the same way like what is this stylist smoking and can I get some too lol no but seriously she needs to like loosen up get the stick out of her butt or else

I will totally have mrdok fire her and have to find someone else like seriously I am not even joking maybe I should try getting filler in my nipples not today I think ive had enough injections at this point lol but maybe next time doctor slopowski visits our fair island I thought it sounded weird at first but then I saw some and its really not it actually can look really good like make your nipples a whole lot perkier what is gross is the time I was researching plastic surgery online and I came across the page about penis implants I was like oh my nasty goodness that is beyond beyond in the words of angeline like what is even the point I guess its for guys who cant get it up and even the little blue pills the one mrdok takes dont help or else just feel like really self conscious about their size well I guess some guys do need it lol god so awful like can you imagine dont know who im talking to here lol we are nearly done now sez doctor slopowski and im like thank god but I dont say that out loud I just say oh okay even tho it has been like what now four hours feels like in reality probly just like one I hold my watch up cartier okay so its been like 45 minutes omfg I bet I have like a million texts emails comments to reply to well thats the rest of my day for me hopefully will get thru most of it at lunch but whatever good excuse tonight to have my face turned away from mrdok will be having to reply to things like all night but god thinking of blowjobs I remember I didnt even know what one was until the fifth grade there was this boy black boy in our class reginald hall was his name he was so gross but in like a funny way people said he was actually like 14 but had been held back so many times whenever the teacher left the room he would sing all these gross perverted songs that were like hilarious one of them went she swallered it the whole thang now my big dick tracy dont feel the same and at first I was like whos dick tracy and then this girl karen who sat behind me laughed and was like hes talking about his thing and im like what thing omg but in retrospect it was like so cute how innocent we all were back then and then once I remember he even pulled it out in class I was like omfg like even at that age he had a big one like I guess most black guys do have I ever well duh of course you never forget that its like what do they say once you go black but I mean it wasnt that great its not like I have to have it every single time when I was working in that bar in the east village that one summer this guy used to come in all the time think he was a medical student at nyu was he cute hell yeah and he was so charming the way hed flirt with me I mean I had never considered dating a black guy before but then I was like come on bev dont be racist give it a shot and was the sex good I mean yeah it was okay was it big I mean sure tho not the biggest ive ever had to be completely honest like probly a good eight inches but ive definitely had bigger than that did I cum yes because I mean even tho he wasnt the biggest he definitely had skills he was one of those guys who would only get off if the girl gets off first he was like a real gentleman now that I think about it what ever happened I mean the sex was good we got along okay but there was no real chemistry I think the conversation kind of lagged like he was studying to be what was it an optometrist whatever that is think it has something to do with the eyes and like ive always had really good 20 20 vision thats like something me and mrdok both have never even had to consider contacts or laser surgery tho I do like to get colored contacts from time to time just to vary my look a bit so anyway there wasnt a lot for us to talk about he was also kind of not a jock but one of those people who liked to talk about football all the time and I have to be honest I know nothing about football except who some of the hotter players are lol but of course he wasnt interested in that like I think it was just one of those things that kind of faded over time we didnt have to break up because we were never really dating seriously it was more like a friends with benefits type of situation you know you go thru those when you are younger just trying to find your way thru life there is totally nothing wrong with it like if I have a kid and she turns out to be a daughter im going to be just like open with her about things like that like when shes eleven teach her how to put on a condom with her mouth because you can never learn birth control at too young an age I mean some girls start menstruating now when theyre 9 or 10 think its mainly in like the midwest places like that where they have less access to organic food because if you eat a lot of factory farmed meat then you get all these hormones like some girls even grow beards and not even like persian and greek ones like average american girls and it comes straight from the food thank god all the beef we get here is organic grass fed its shipped in from I forget where but anyway definitely not america the meat there sucks now hes examining my face cupping my jaw in the palms of his hands kind of prodding I think you just need a little more volume to fill our your left jaw line then I think we are done for now sez doctor slopowski and im like finally but I just say meekly okay and then lay back and like prepare myself for another needle god ive never been penetrated so much in one day lol thats such a funny joke I should try to remember that one for mrdok later he will like laugh his ass off I totally love the way he cackles too at first it really got on my nerves like who is this guy with this *grating* laugh sometimes even makes like the pig snorting noise at the end of it

probly because of all the coke he used to do its like done some damage to his nostrils lol jk but seriously at first it was like the most
annoying thing ever now ive gotten used to it I find it kind of charming thats the thing like when you really love a person then you even
start to like their flaws after a while too bad I dont have any lol well
not any physical ones at least certainly not after this lmao but can
you imagine getting your period at the age of nine that means you
could actually get preggers which I mean I dont want to get gross or
mean but a lot of those girls out there they then go and let like their
cousin or someone do it to them and then thats exactly what happens
I mean weve all seen it on TV enough times to know that it is real
then of course they refuse to get abortions because like their religion
wont allow it or something and they have like inbred kids with so
many problems like america is so messed up right now we are like an
edited version of america with all the bad elements taken out of it
like no teen underage pregnancies no tanning salons like if anything
you can get a really good professional spray tan done here no violence except for the stupid war of course but that will be all over
soon what else only organic meat and vegetables of course all dairy
not that id ever actually eat dairy except for like yogurt if that even
counts as dairy probly not too healthy like the only milk I take is
almond or soy sometimes pea milk no cellulite it is strictly forbidden
except for krstal lmao no jk there is no body shaming at all on settlers
landing we welcome all types tho of course it helps if you are photogenic I mean especially now when were really still in the pilot phase
I mean no one ever said it was going to be easy but mrdok and I
together we are really launching something that is almost like a revolution here a beauty style wellness revolution I mean I can totally
see like midnight yoga sessions on the beach omg we totally have to
get someone from that like im sure we can find one of the soldiers
who also does yoga like that would be even better if the yoga instruc-
tor had a back story like he came here to fight for freedom and then
once he won the war he ended up staying and now he like leads people on a quest for like spiritual freedom thru yoga omg I am starting
to tear up just thinking not that this person actually exists lol but we
could sort of like find someone and turn them into that thats what
were about like giving people new futures just like mrdok really had
to start from scratch when he came here I mean we all did his is really
like a narrative of constant reinvention or like whats the word reten-
tion something like that but seriously thank god this is the last needle
going in a bit deep well its my jawline it makes sense but still hurts
like a bitch ass motherfucker you just have to think you are going to

look so good after this it is thoughts like that that really help me get through it I mean the future is so bright for me I just have to figure out what do I want to do next like do I want to launch my own perfume line or like something more unique like an eyeware line or maybe just simple things like that navel piercing I always wanted I mean on my stomach it would be like sexy af have to ask Ms opinion first like he can be weirdly conservative about such things we are finished now bev how do you feel sez doctor slopowski and im like im good I sit up can I have a mirror please he sez yes of course and brings me the hand mirror I shriek he sez what what is the matter omg my fucking eyebrows I look like motherfucking doctor spock from star trek what the fuck has he done to me my lips are swollen they are like sticking out bigger than my nose I turn to him and he is giving me this fucking ugly smile that ive never seen suddenly I realize he has a gap he is like missing his bottom two front teeth how the fuck did I never notice this before I look back into the mirror and omigod the degree of damage the heaviness of my forehead and then look at the cheeks I scream out why did you put so much in the cheeks I look like a motherfucking chipmunk what do you say sez doctor slopowski you say you want bigger cheeks no I never said that I said I want I cant even finish talking it is going to even out he sez and then you will have nice smooth contour lines and im like stop talking please and it is hard for me to talk because of my fucking lips my lips he sez do you like them I think they are very sexy now just the kind of lips that really talk to a man look at the neck there are little bumps like areas of swelling there what the fuck have you done I am the best filler man in ze hills of beverly he screams you know not what you are talking your neck looks fine now it was ugly neck before now it is beauty beautiful neck omg what are you even saying what have you done I thought you used the expensive stuff what is this he sez this is the very best saline that you can get and he brought it all the way here I should be happy now no more lines in your forehead no more wrinkles no more crows eyes and it is true I do not have lines and wrinkles but I also look like a mutant like omg like one of those botched plastic surgery episodes am I dreaming now or what this cant be real I throw down the mirror no I scream no no no no NO

CHAPTER THREE

—I THINK WE'RE getting to the point where...
—Where what?
—Don't make me say it. I really don't want to say it.
—Say what. You're acting all gay... Don't, then.
—But I have to. Mrdok. There is a... a madman running around out there. In the tunnels.
—I know.
—One of our own.
—I know, I know.
—Who knows how many he has killed already.
—Well he hasn't killed us. We're safe in here.
—Yes. Quite... For now.
—You heard anything from Bev?
—I'm afraid we've lost contact.
—Fuck.
—I'm sure she's doing all right.
—What makes you...
—She's in one of the secure bunkers, after all.
—She is, isn't she.
—I just think. Well, I'm at a loss. Perhaps we might conjure... a, uh... a PR offensive?
—PR offensive? What do you mean?
—Well I'm not talking about surrendering. Certainly not that.
—Oh there's no need to surrender. We're definitely winning.
—All right.
—There has never been a time when we weren't winning. You of all people know that, Gordo. You've been with me longest.
—Of course I do. I mean, what an amusing thought: to think otherwise.
—It's just one rotten apple.
—Yes.
—Forgot to take his meds. Or whatever.
—Are those gunshots?

—Now you're being paranoid.

—I'm sorry. I thought I heard…

—We wouldn't hear them. Even if they were right in front of the door. Not only is this bombproof, bulletproof. Heavy artillery-proof. It's also soundproof. Meaning: they can't hear what goes on in here. But we also can't hear what's going on out there.

—Yes, of course.

—So don't let your imagination carry you away, Gordo.

—Oh I wouldn't.

—Because I need you here, present, more than I ever have before.

—I am *most* present. I can assure you…

—Good.

—I have been doing research.

—Good… What kind of research?

—Well. I thought it might be useful. To see if there were any such thing as, ah, a *precedent*. For, uh, situations such as these…

—… And?

—Well, it is a most unusual set of circumstances. Certainly nothing in the *Art of War*…

—GPS wasn't invented back then, back when the guy wrote the *Art of War*, Gordo. The question I've been asking all morning, all night—I don't even know what fucking time is it anymore—the question I'm asking is: are we tracking him? Have we been able to pinpoint his exact movements?

—An excellent question, if I do say so myself. A sure indication of your perceptiveness and your leadership skills.

—Then why in the fuck have I not been able to get a straight answer out of anyone?

—It seems, in all honesty… Well. It seems like we've been cut off from the central command.

—Why is that.

—A number of reasons. For one—and please don't get angry with me, I'm just leveling with you now, Mrdok. For one thing there was something of a morale crisis.

—A morale crisis?

—A crisis of morale.

—Why? We pay these guys well, don't we?

—We do indeed.

—Ungrateful little shits.

—… It seems that for some—for a certain small contingent—our generosity has been rather underappreciated.

—You know what it is you're saying, Gordo.

–Well. I would hope I do… To make such a. Such a serious charge.

–You're saying it's mutiny. High treason.

–And I do regret having to make such a charge. But honestly…

–That means we'll have to execute them. Like, how many are we talking?

–Well we don't know an exact number. The evidence is all anecdotal at this point. It is rather difficult to carry out a proper investigation under. Under these rather… strenuous circumstances.

–I mean, we can give them a chance to redeem themselves. By, by catching this sniper. This madman who has been allowed to… who has been turned loose on us. I mean… I still don't get it. We're sure he's one of ours.

–Yes. We've identified him. I have his folder.

–He hasn't been… I don't know… *corrupted* by the other side?

–He's just gone commando, that's all. I mean… Perhaps we—I mean *I*, of course—perhaps I should have done a more thorough job of vetting these soldiers before we hired them.

–Well did he have a history of mental illness?

–Well, yes. But most of them did. That's how we were able to get them so cheap.

–I thought you said we were paying them well.

–Oh we are, we are indeed. Considering… And, really, Mrdok, most of them suffer, in various measures, from the same affliction. But all the evidence I've read suggests that PTSD is treatable with medication. You certainly don't see any of those others running around doing this. It is precisely as you said: just one bad apple.

–Enough to spoil the whole batch.

–Not at all.

–Coming for *us*.

–I know it might be hard to garner any optimism in moments such as these—

–Gordo nobody has even been able to come and do my fucking laundry in a week. This is bad. This is like really really bad.

–But we mustn't give in to despair.

–We also can't totally evade it. Now can we. Given the circumstances…

–They're bound to catch him. Very, very soon.

–Well get them to hurry the fuck up.

–I'm trying.

–Don't just *try*, Gordo. You've got to *incentivize* them.

–An excellent idea, boss.

–So do it.

–It is hard to know with what, though.

–What? What do you mean?

–What to incentivize them with.

–With money, of course. Ever heard of money? You fat fuck.

–Well. That brings us to a rather pertinent point I've been… eager… or, perhaps, *anxious*… to bring up with you.

–… And? That is?

–There is the tiny issue of our shared collective wealth.

–Speak English with me, Gordo.

–Well it's a term you invented, Mrdok. In our publicity materials. The recruitment of new settlers, to be precise…

–Right. Our alternative taxation scheme. Stored in our national bank, where we keep all our assets. I don't see how that has anything to do with—

–Mister Ma. He has… absconded with those funds.

–Hahaha. Good one! You fat fuck. And Barb was always claiming you have no sense of humor!

–I'm afraid I am being quite serious, Mrdok. My duties preclude me from joking about such weighty matters.

–… What the fuck are you saying to me right now, Gordo?

–… I am saying that the Settlers Landing National Bank, for all intents and purposes, is no longer in existence.

–You've gotta be. Get him on the phone. Now. This instant.

–Mrdok. Do you not think we've been trying to get a hold of him? For weeks now?

–Well where in the fuck is he.

–Where is he? Where is Barb, Mrdok? Where is Lallyburt for that matter? Where is—Okay, I'll stop now. Mrdok, stop doing that. Mrdok…

–CHRIST!

–Well, let's just be constructive about it and think of it as a momentary setback.

–A momentary setback?! What are you, fucking—When did this happen?!

–Does it really matter at this point, Mrdok? Does it?

–How are we even paying for everything at this point?

–We've had to dip into the organization's assets.

–You mean… You're using my offshore accounts?

–That's the protocol.

–The protocol.

–Yes. The protocol that was put into place. Were… a situation along these lines to one day develop…

–I want. This fucking bastard… I want his entrails on my desk. I want to play with his fucking entrails! And… and for his goddamn yellow chink skin to be made into a fucking valise—

–We're going to find him eventually, Mrdok. A shark that big can't stay hidden for long. The question is…

–What?

–Well. How do I put this? There's not a lot we can do, Mrdok.

–What the hell do you mean?

–I mean the way the whole thing was structured. The documentation and all of that… He *was* the director of the bank, after all.

–On paper!

–Yes yes. On paper. But, in the end, that is sadly all that matters. Is it not?

–I really can't believe what I'm hearing right now. After everything I've—all the support I have shown you over the years? All the support I gave you through all of your little fucking… gender problems or whatever the hell they were? For you to go and, and turn around? And talk to me this way? You are lucky I—

–Please, Mrdok, I fear you are misunderstanding, that you have misunderstood my tone. Never once did I intend—

–Then you need to fucking support me on this! Okay?! I mean, I thought I could *trust* you, Gordo! Do I have your loyalty or don't I?

–You have my unwavering, my undying—

–Good. Then shut the fuck up and do what I say. Don't tell me things I don't want to hear.

–I'm terribly sorry.

–Good. That's better. Now we're getting somewhere. Finally. It doesn't matter anyway. Between the Elias Shores project and the medical tourism, we're gonna have more fuckin capital—And don't forget the crypto war bond scheme! The BangBuck!

–Well…

–Well what?

–Crypto *is* crashing at the moment. I mean, not just the Bang-Buck… Even bitcoin is—

–Well. *They* don't have to know that, do they? The people. We just need to keep emphasizing its *eventual* worth.

–Yes. Let's do that… But then there's the matter of our currency. As you know, we're also being attacked by our enemies on the economic front. They've been printing, in droves, counterfeit versions of our currency abroad in the hundreds of thousands, as an attempt to devalue it. And, well… It seems as though it is working.

–What the fuck are you telling me?

–I take it you haven't read the latest reports.

–What reports?

–The ones Rick had sent in for you.

–The ones from Thursday?

–Mm. I believe these are more recent. Let me check.

–I don't feel like reading a bunch of shit right now. Just summarize it for me.

–…

–Bulletpoints. You know. Just the important shit.

–Perhaps we should save it for later, after you've had a bit of rest. I don't want… I don't want to provoke you again, so soon—I'm afraid I would be disobeying your previous commandment not to tell you things you do not wish to hear.

–Oh my god. That was like five minutes ago, Gordo. Keep up with the program.

–I'm—

–I'm not gonna yell anymore this morning. Or this afternoon—whatever the fuckin time is now. Don't worry. Better you lay it on me now. I need to hear all of this shit so that I can come up with a plan.

–Well. Okay… You're already well aware of the Viutex shortage, I presume?

–Right. I thought that there had been. Some kind of, I don't know. Medical solution to that. That had been manufactured…

–You are aware, of course, of the reasons behind the shortage…

–Remind me again. Something about the North Koreans fucking the Chinese. Or the Chinese fucking the North Koreans. I forget who fucked who. They're all a bunch of commies with small dicks anyway…

–Doctor Yeh, it seems, was not completely forthright in his self-presentation as the inventor of Viutex. Rather, it appears as though he actually stole the formula from another Chinese inventor…

–Yeah. That's right. I remember now. And the big fuckin to-do is?

–Well, that gained the ire of the Chinese government. And so it seems they began covertly aiding the enemy forces…

–Yeah yeah, what government isn't at this point.

–Okay. So then I think we can both agree that the Viutex deal was a set-up.

–I thought you said there was something new in the report, Gordo. Something I don't already know.

–There is. It would seem… How it pains me to say this… It would seem that Lallyburt was somehow covertly involved in the orchestration of that deal.

–… This is what Rick has unearthed?

–Yes. If his information is correct…

–I don't understand.

–Do you remember that Hong Kong trip? Lallyburt was there. We ran into him. Uncanny, the coincidence, n'est-ce pas?

–He was drunk off his ass. I ended up taking his whore off him…

–That you did. Well. According to Rick's findings—I don't know how to say this…

–No. Couldn't be.

–I'm afraid—

–Are you fuckin tellin me I got honeypotted?

–I don't know that that's the case. I think it's more… She was just there to ensure you'd wind up going where they wanted you to go.

–My morning wake-up call.

–Something like that.

–So wait: Lallyburt's in bed with the North Koreans?

–It could be that No was just a middleman on the deal, just brokering for the commission. At least that's what I'm wont to believe. We think Lallyburt was more on the Yeh side of the transaction. Someone in the organization also clearly leaked to him our potential interest in him as a senator for the island project, back when it was just another item on the day's agenda…

–So someone from the organization was clandestinely collaborating with that redneck fuck?

–I'm as confused as you are, Mrdok. But I think—

–And let me guess. No one knows where Lallyburt is at this moment, either.

–He's been off the island for months. We think he left when the war started to get bad—around the time the central admin began moving into the bunkers…

–Well then Ma must have also had some involvement in the deal.

–We don't know exactly. Though there is some likelihood… It's more a matter of connecting the dots. An ongoing process, if you will.

–So what does this have to do with the shortage?

—It doesn't. The shortage is chalked up to typical... well, wartime shortages. Only the information about Lallyburt's involvement—potential involvement, I should say—is new.

—What do you mean potential. Did the cowboy assfuck me or not?

—... It seems highly likely he was involved. Based on what I read in the report.

—So Lally, the Asians... Barb's disappeared, she must have some involvement in this shitshow as well, am I wrong? She's a Jap, a part Jap. Jesus, I've got the entire Asia fuckin me down here with their tiny fuckin pricks.

—She certainly had some involvement with the Saudi issue. But we haven't been able to find any links between the Saudis and the Chinese. Not yet at least.

—Well. We all know the Saudis screwed me. Screwed us, I mean.

—How it ended up in the end. Well, this is my understanding of it. I believe Barb did coordinate this with Lallyburt, as well. But the Lallyburt family connection with the Saudis was already there, of course... So now, we are buying weapons from the Saudis at an inflated price, weapons that the Saudis have acquired from Lallyburt...

—A beautiful story, isn't it? Let's move on to a cheerier topic. What's going on up there now?

—Since Lieutenant Vandross defected, third-in-command Nihil Donaldson has taken over. It seems Lieutenant Donaldson has some rather... eccentric ideas when it comes to defeating the enemy.

—Has he managed to pull off any ambushes? You got some footage for me?

—He is employing... well... we might call it alternative methodologies.

—Such as?

—Man-eating plants, for one.

—... What?

—Apparently he was doing some heavy research into carnivorous vegetation—an area in which I certainly don't have any expertise, so I can't really comment on the feasibility of the plan. Though I know he asked for a quarter of a million for seeds, which he had dispersed to the enemy territories at night through the use of wind energy, some powerful windmills that he had covertly installed on the outskirts of Elias Shores.

—Are you fucking shitting me right now?

—I'm... not.

—Because if you're fucking shitting me, I swear to god, Gordo. I will have your ass fucking court-martialed and… No. No. I don't even have to do that. I'm President and this is a time of war. I can just have you fuckin executed right here, right here in front of me if I get even the faintest whiff—

—I have never lied to you, Mrdok. You know that. I never will. Please. I beg of you. Get some rest. I'm worried about you. We all need… We need your clear head, clear vision, now more than ever.

—Oh shit. We're doomed. How the fuck did my entire life wind up being controlled by… by *idiots*. Just… How?!

—Perhaps now is the time for us to… Not *consider other options*. I would never employ such, such fatalistic jargon, haha. You know me, Mrdok, it's simply not my style. Though… Since we're both stuck here for the time being… Perhaps we might make the most of it by, uh… Well, by playing a sort of verbal game.

—Spit it out. What are you thinking.

—Well, you know me, I hardly think at all. I'm just the messenger really, the one who transmits what others around me happen to be thinking… And I do feel at liberty to tell you that we received a message this morning.

—A message?

—Yes. From. From the rebels. Well, to be precise, *you* received a message. A message from Prince.

—Uh huh. And what is it the little prick wants?

—It seems he is offering to meet with us. Well, to meet with you.

—Well aint that something.

—Do you want me to read this?

—Just give me the juicy bits.

—It seems he is making you an offer.

—He's making *me* an offer?

—An offer to… to *exit with dignity*. His words, not mine.

—To exit what? This country?

—I believe he's referring to the war. But, yes. Such an exit, I imagine. Would also entail you leaving the country.

—Gordo. Tell me something.

—Sure.

—When you… had your surgery.

—My gender reassignment surgery?

—Yeah.

—What about it?

—Did you cut it off?

—I don't think…

–I'm just curious. Always wanted to know. I could've asked the doctor, at the hospital, of course. But at the time, it slipped my mind, I guess. I mean, I was quite busy. It was in the early days, you'll recall.

–I would rather not... convey that information. If you don't mind...

–I'm just curious. It doesn't make any real difference. But... I'm wondering if I'm dealing with, like, a dickless guy right in front of me. Because, in case I am... I mean, I don't really know what that means.

–I can assure you that we have much bigger things to worry about than my gender identity and the current state of my genitalia, Mrdok. If we're not going to take this meeting with Prince, then I feel we need to formulate some sort of punchy response—

–What is it?

–I just got a text message. On my phone.

–Oh yeah?

–Corporal Danils...

–Who the fuck is that?

–The one who's gone commando. The one on the rampage.

–What about him? They catch the crazed fuck finally?

–Unfortunately not. He was spotted in the northeast corridor...

–Fuck. You're kidding me.

–Close to Bobby and Stevo Rey's bunkers.

–What the—Well if they know where he is, that means they can get him, right? I mean what are they waiting for?

–I'm afraid it's not that simple. He's... heavily armed, Mrdok.

–Where the fuck did we go wrong.

–At least he's being tracked. Now... That's something.

–Exit with dignity. Some fuckin balls this little quasi-native fuck. Who does he think he's dealin with anyway?

–They *are* rather poorly educated...

–Yeah. That's right. And most of them love me, too. It's just a measly few... psychotic brats.

–Again, the lack of appreciation for your generosity is disdainful...

–Yeah... Because, I just want to say, if you *did* cut it off, Gordo. Kudos to you. I mean, that takes some balls. Literally. Like, even if I was suffering from that gender dysmorphia, or whatever it's called. I don't think I could ever take it that far. I just don't have it in me.

–I feel that, given the circumstances, a more optimal utilization of our time would be for us to decide—

–But wait, so does that make you like a trans man now? Like, one of those guys with no dicks? I saw a porno with one of those recently. Guy had a fully functioning vag. Got fucked and everything in it. By a guy with a huge dick, as well. It was pretty hot. I mean, if you just focus in on the pussy, of course. The rest of it—the flat hairy chest and the beard and all that—the rest of it I didn't too much care for… Now I suppose for gays it's kinda the opposite.

–I'm texting Mark now. I'm ordering an extra security detail for Bobby. I believe Krstal's not far from that corridor either, shall I order an extra detail for her as well?

–What do we know about this fucking. What's this maniac's name again?

–Danils. Private Corporal Din Danils.

–What a name. What do we know about him.

–Born in Fort Jackson, Wyoming. Raised in Louisiana. Swamp country. Two tours in Afghanistan. Was part of a meth-dealing anti-government militia in the bayou territory upon his return to the States—

–I don't want to hear banal shit like that. I wanna know like what triggered it. What pushed him over the edge.

–I don't know that anyone has a surefire answer to that question. We've interviewed his superiors, I do know that. He was trusted enough at at least one point to have been sent on a special mission. It was presented to him at first as an intelligence gathering mission, but it was just a ruse—he didn't have the training for it. The man is a killing machine. What they wanted was for him to take out the number two man in the rebel army.

–And? I take it he didn't succeed.

–I suppose they overestimated his capabilities. Or underestimated them… One of the two. According to what Sergeant McAnally told us, everything was going fine and according to plan, until one day he returned from a reconnaissance mission and commenced aiming his gun in the wrong direction.

–Just snapped. No warning signals or nothing.

–No one knows what, if anything, triggered it. First he shot and killed his bunkmate, a Muslim from Texas. Which makes some sense, given that Danils had served two turns in Afghanistan—probably that style of prayer or perhaps just the Arabic facial features triggered something in him. But then apparently he grabbed a semi-automatic and walked into the mess hall… Fifty-three of our soldiers lost their lives that afternoon. Then he disappeared.

–Though not completely.

–Not completely, no. But they lost track of him for a couple hours. But he'd leave a trail of bodies in his wake. See, he was given a silencer for his weapons. It was needed to carry out the rather dangerous mission that, well… he ultimately did not succeed at. He *is*, after all, well trained, well armed. He's been roaming the hallways and corridors of the underground city for days now, treating it as though it's his own private jungle. Our army is now essentially fighting a battle on two fronts.

–Let's not get too dramatic now, Gordo. He's just one guy. They should be able to take him out.

–They're trying.

–None of the surveillance cameras has been able to get any footage of him?

–Oh Rick didn't tell you? He's managed to disable most of them.

–Of course he has.

–Whenever he passes by one, he shoots it. We've amassed quite an array of footage of him pointing his gun into the lens and the screen going black.

–How are people getting from point A to point B?

–Right now they're not. The corridors are off-limits to everyone who's not military. Everyone has to work from their dwelling bunkers. Going anywhere is… inadvisable.

–I mean… The optics on this. It just makes us look… inept. Has this gotten out?

–I was checking all the news sites this morning. There's nothing.

–Good.

–We might want to brace ourselves, however. If it goes on much longer, I'm afraid it's inevitable.

–We should start thinking of ways to spin it then. So that we'll be prepared.

–Well I think it's quite clear. In line with your philanthropic inclinations over the years, you hired your army from a private security firm that specializes in giving jobs to veterans with PTSD… America has turned its back on these heroes, you believed in them and opted to give them a second chance…

–Yeah. And we were givin them free medical treatment over here and everything… I mean, we were, weren't we?

–Indeed. Well. Almost free…

–This is America's fault, really. I mean, if you really think about it…

–Yes. They might have even, might have *engineered* this conspiracy. In their, their evil little campaign against us.

–Well do you have any evidence that suggests that?

–I'm sure we could find some.

–Great. Get on it… But why wasn't he taking his meds?

–Well we're not sure that was what was at issue. PTSD is tricky. I took the liberty of doing some research…

–… And?

–Would you like me to tell you what I've found?

–No I want you to show me your man pussy. Yes Gordo of course I want you to fucking tell me, you fucking fat fuck.

–The symptoms tend to arise rather uncontrollably, involuntarily, mysteriously, making the disorder difficult to diagnose and hence treat. They vary, according to both the nature and degree of the trauma. But cognitive behavioral therapists generally tend to group them into four categories: intrusive memories, avoidance, negative changes in thinking and mood, and, finally, changes in physical and emotional reactions.

–In the interviews we did, did any of his superiors notice any of these things in him in the lead-up to all this?

–Some did, but they only thought it was some minor variance of the symptoms they themselves were wont to experience now and again. The important point being, I suppose, that PTSD doesn't usually lead men to go off on killing rampages.

–It was apparently more severe than theirs.

–Yes. That would be one reading of it.

–Those symptoms you mention. Those are all just things that you witness from the outside. They don't really tell me what the person is going through on the inside.

–Whatever trauma the person experienced—and in his case, it no doubt relates to his previous experiences in combat—he reexperiences in the form of flashbacks. It is as though he cannot get out of it. Especially if he is exposed to sensory stimuli that reignites memories of the traumatic experience; and, well. Here he has gone from one combat zone to another. So of course…

–Yeah. I get that. But what about his doctor? We have any word with his doctor here?

–I did interview Doctor Soukowski about it personally, as I had to visit the doctor for my own reasons. He had difficulty recalling, since he sees so many patients in the military. But he was able to dig through his files. All he said was that he had suggested the Viutex treatment to the patient, but that Danils refused.

–So he was given other medication instead?

–He was just given a refill of the Zoloft he was already on.

–Everyone's on that.

–Well, a lot of our soldiers. Yes.

–So that proves it was a conspiracy then.

–It does?

–Well it's certainly likely. If we manage to catch him alive, we can interrogate him. Find out if he has any connections to the CIA.

–A most excellent plan… Though a part of me doubts whether he can actually be caught alive. Desperate situations call for desperate—

–Yeah. I know. I mean I wanna see the fucker dead more than anyone. You can trust me on that shit.

–Well. In one way or another…

–Goddamn monkey.

–Pardon?

–I mean if what you're saying is PTSD. I've probably had it too. Some version of it. That ape. The one that took off my hand. You know I used to have dreams. Nightmares. I've had my pain, my struggles. I mean, he just came right at me. Mauled me. You don't even have time to think in a situation like that. Nightmares. I mean, like apes coming at me in my dreams. Even sometimes during the day, when I'd be awake, I'd get to thinking of it. These… these ape attacks. That's what I started to think of them as. Like what. Would one come and, and tear off my other limbs, one by one? It's just that it happened so fast. The way it happened. It was so unexpected. And cruel, in its fastness. Its unexpectancy. One minute you're, you're there, everything's normal. You're fuckin around a bit. But everything fine. You're all out in the world, fearless. Next minute, your fucking hand's gone. I mean, nothing prepares you for that. Nothing. It more than just debilitates you. It like mutilates you on the inside too. There were nights I didn't sleep. Nights I didn't do nothing but sweat. And my wife. Treating me like I was half the man I once was. Nothing she ever said, of course. She would never be that blatant about it. Just the way she'd look at me. Even, sometimes the look I'd catch her, even sometimes after I'd gotten the new one. The fake hand. The artificial. Which, I mean, let's face it, in many ways is even better than the original hand. The real one. I mean, I could afford the very best. It didn't take long for me to figure out how to use it, either. The technology was all based on muscle memory. See, you've probably heard of that phenomenon known as the phantom limb. Where you still feel the thing even when it's gone. I forget whether there's a scientific explanation for it. Doesn't really matter if there is. The point is, you never lose the feeling. It never goes away. It stays right there with you. Like, even now, when I just have this stub right here. If I look away and try not to think about it, I'll swear to god I still have a hand. Like I'll still be able to feel it there. The fingers and everything. So anyway, it was melded to that phenomenon, the technology. I remember the first time, the first day I got it, after the doctor's office, we went and had tacos. And I was able to pick that taco up and put it in my mouth like it was nothing. Krstal was so amazed. They let me kill it, though. The gorilla that did this to me, ran off with my hand. I mean, I was spurting blood all over the place. Lost consciousness, when I came to they had my, my stump wrapped in a shirt, I was spurting blood, they got me to the nearest clinic, some little shack of a place—I mean, we were in the middle of nowhere, you've got to remember. Wasn't like advanced state of the art. They could save my life, but that's all they could really do. So anyway, once I was sufficiently recovered. They let me do the honors, so to speak. They were going to have to put it under anyway, they had had so many problems with it over the years, this was just the pudding in the... How do you say it? Like the tipping point. Gizmo was its name. Shot it right between the eyes. Gizmo the big dumb gorilla. I never bought into that Jane Goodall crap, how they're these peaceful loving creatures. Our closest ancestors on earth or whatever. Naw. They're savages. They're mean, they're angry, they hate us. If you had got it near a gun, it would have shot me too. Right between the eyes. Thing is, I had never even shot a gun before. It was my first time. That's the amazing. I didn't even need to practice. It's like I was born to shoot a gun. It was just one shot, but it gave me this indescribable feeling. I shot him with my left hand, by the way. That's the lucky part. I've always been left handed. So the ape bit off my right. Took it without a fight. It was so fast, it's not like I just gave it up to him. More like I never had a chance. That's the traumatizing bit. The thing that'd give me the sweats, keep me up at night. Of course, seeing another gorilla, forget it. I couldn't go to the zoo anymore—not that the zoo is ever a place I would regularly go to. Stinks. Sometimes, as a kid, the Bronx Zoo or whatever. Not that often, though. More in my travels, if I had to go to a place where there would be, it didn't even have to be full grown chimpanzees. Even little, fuckin monkeys. Because of the association. To me they were all the same. Damn nasty, excited and mean little fucks. No, not me. I'm not connected to them. Maybe billions of years ago. But we're so divorced from that now. I don't care if they all go extinct, to be honest. The world needs to evolve too, you know. Not just animals, humans. The entire ecosystem needs to be upgraded. And that upgrade entails loss. The discarding of certain obsolete softwares that have no use anymore. That's how I see it. Kill all the monkeys. Hahaha. Kill the apes and the chimpanzees. Kill the orangutangs. Those fuckin nasty ass baboons. Jaco's never seen one. I told Mrtol when I married her, we can take the kid anywhere, but never to the zoo. He also didn't know about my hand until he was eight or so. Like most people. He just wasn't aware of it. The artificial one was just too damn good. Well, so much for that. Wonder what he saw when he was looking at me. Dead eyebrows staring him down. That metal piece I was holding in my claw. Or if he even remembered who I was. That I'm the one whose hand he got. The one he mauled. I mean, we're all going to fucking, we're all going to die here, aren't we? Isn't that what this is all about? Gordo? The no light at the end of the tunnel scheme? Hahaha. Maybe we should, should call the preacher in here, that Billy Ray Taggerston fuck, see what he has to say about it all. You know the funny thing is? That fuck. I saw him, the day the ape took my hand. He was there selling peanuts. Can you believe that shit? That guy just keeps popping up in my life like you wouldn't believe. If I were the truly paranoid sort, I'd think he was put on my path intentionally, you know. Like *he* could be CIA. Of all people. I mean, why the fuck not. They've put weirder cats in motion. Haven't they? Sold me the bag of peanuts I was feeding the goddamn gorilla. Fucking Gizmo. But you know what helped me? What helped me, get over that, that PTSD, if that's what in fact it was? It's just the simple fact, that he's dead and I'm still alive. That I caused its extinction. Hahaha. But I guess it's still somehow present in my life. Gizmo I mean. That's why I can never get rid of the fear. Like even when I see one in a film. *Planet of the Apes,* forget it. Can't watch it. Or if I hear the sound, a screeching monkey. It just... You know. It actually gives me pain. Pain in my stump. Moments like those. You don't feel the limb. You just feel the pain in those moments. Getting all panicky. It's an ugly feeling, Gordo. And nobody knows it. Just me. Not like there's a fuckin, there's someone that could relate to something like this. So yeah. I can understand. Whatever that soldier went through, in Afghanistan or whatever the fuck it was. And, I'm sorry to have to say it, but now he's become like the ape to me. Something I have to kill. Hey, I wonder if the ape had some trauma too. Who knows. Maybe that's why he took my hand off. He was in captivity. Maybe some fuckin, fuckin poacher or something had killed its mother. I don't know. I guess we all play both roles in life. Hunter and hunted. The goal, of course, is to minimize the second, try to stay true to the first. But anyway. It happened a long time ago. This kind of pain, it fades. This sniper fuck, runnin around out there. He needs to man up. Get over it. I'm over it. At least I don't get the nightmares. Not anymore. Not for a long time. Well, that's not true. Since the artificial hand got kidnapped, got stolen away, it's been coming back, but in a limited way. The worst was, I think it was last week, maybe two weeks ago. I got up one morning, I had slept terribly. I got up and I looked in the mirror, and for a second, maybe a split hair of a second, I could swear it was the ape, Gizmo, staring back at me. Like I had… like I had somehow morphed into him. Or else he had replaced me. Say, whatever happened to Vincent?

–Vincent? Well. Nothing good has come of that one, I quite fear…

–I thought he was brokering a deal. To get the hand back…

–Yes. We all thought he was. He did have it all mapped out. And then it went wrong. Terribly, terribly wrong. Well, from a strategic vantage point…

–What happened exactly.

–He was in talks with his brother. What they wanted, the rebels, more than anything, was that temple. You know. It rather holds quite a lot of spiritual significance to them. They almost thought that if they could win the temple back, it would be the equivalent to winning the war…

–So why'd he give it to them?

–This was the price of the hand, Mrdok. He didn't want to. Though now, it all seems rather…

–Are you inferring…

–Well, no one knows for sure.

–You're saying—

–I don't know.

–You're saying that he's secretly working with his brother? While working with us? Fuck. How many double agents are on this island right now anyway?

–Well. The only prominent one really was Robinson, the Uber driver. But everyone knew about him. And anyway, he's been dead for a long while now. Caught up in some crossfire after giving Taggerston a ride back to the studio one night after a wedding on Elias Shores…

–Fuck it. Never liked Uber anyway. Too much, too much mobility… Our people have their own cars. Or they should. If they're patriots…

–You know, there's this whole trope that recurs throughout the history of literature. That of the noble savage. Well, it's an ideal, really. An ideal masquerading as a trope… I remember being quite taken with it, quite fascinated by it. Oh, these were the early days, back when I actually had time to read! It comes and goes over time, recedes into the background at those moments when we run out of use for it. Though somehow it's always there—he's always there—standing tall—even when he is temporarily retired to the back of the room. Like a mannequin or a history painting, his presence always manages to enunciate itself, oftentimes in spite of our very worst fears. I know you are not fond of reading, Mrdok, though I am sure you are familiar with the idea nonetheless. For it has woven its way rather mercilessly into our culture, into popular consciousness. The reason why, I think, is that there is something in our nature—that of civilized man, I mean—there is something there that we do not particularly like. And it is difficult for us to admit this to ourselves. Because on the surface, well, it would appear as though we have everything. Especially men like us; men like you. Men who enjoy such exalted status, it is only natural that we should seek out our polar opposite. To find in him all those things that we are embarrassed to admit we are lacking… Plotting, plots. The entire nature of benevolence. An image of nature that is somehow pristine, unblemished by all the corrupted needs and wants we have developed over the course of our evolution—our version of civilization where the flaws can be complained about endlessly and yet readily glossed over in the field of daily action.

—We told him that in Mrdokia, there would always be a place for him.

—Even took care of his family, as well. It wasn't enough for him, was it? See, it is our fault, in a way. We ourselves fell for that noble savage ideal, the way that countless other visionaries before us have. It is almost… a trap. Something that has been laid before us, to entrap us.

—Yes. By the CIA…

—Or worse. Our own fears. Our own… dare I say it? Our own ambitions.

—You're saying we but you really mean me.

—I mean we are controlled by forces outside of ourselves, Mrdok. What led us here was, well. In a word, Vincent. I think, had we never met him that day, had he not been so welcoming when we first came here for that scouting visit, that—

—I would have found another place.

—Yes, but maybe not—

–The noble savage has nothing to do with it. I don't give a fuck about the noble savage. Never have. None of these people. I never saw any romance, any purity, in how they lived, in what they are. Don't flower over things, Gordo. You do shit like that all the time. It's counterproductive. They're savages. That's all. You give them one chance to fuck you over, and they will. Well, the thing with Vincent is. We may have given him many—many chances to fuck us over. And he didn't. And so we thought we could trust him. That's what made him clever. We thought, we were willing to give him the benefit of the doubt. Like, this guy is really really clever. And he's on our side! The whole deal was just so sweet, we couldn't see how rotten it actually was on the inside.

–But are they collaborating… is still the question.

–It's not worth answering. They might as well be. He's disappeared, Vincent. Who knows. Maybe he died. Maybe the fuckin sniper got him. Maybe he is the fuckin sniper. Who can tell anymore. I mean, the way things are goin now—

–But there must be ulterior motives. Strategically, I mean in terms of military strategy, there is no great reason for them to have that temple. Is there? I mean, I've been over this countless times with the generals.

–The generals. The colonels. All those fuckin bastards. They're CIA too. Probably.

–Who? You mean *our* generals?

–The rebel army, certainly. With their shipments of weapons and guns and food coming in every day… Why haven't we been able to stop one, just one of those measly shipments? Huh? Answer me. Why?

–The reason why is plain enough, Mrdok. While our intelligence skills might be overdeveloped, our military logistics department is, well… rather underdeveloped. At least at the moment. We've replaced the woman who was heading that department. Hopefully with the infusion of fresh blood, we might manage to turn a corner.

–Turn a corner.

–Yes. To… to emerge anew. And afresh.

–Those are terms you'd use to describe a military operation. A *military logistics* operation. You're certainly not much interested in the life, are you.

–What do you—

–I just now realized that. You're not. Not at all.

–Maybe that's because I've *given* so much of my life… No. I won't say that. I won't say that.

–Gordo.

–Yes, Mrdok.

–I want you to tell me everything you know. Everything. About Vincent.

–Mrdok. I know far less about Vincent than you.

–How is that? What do you even *mean* by that?

–I mean that you and he are nearly the same person. Or that, rather. You have rather become one another.

–You're saying I'm the noble savage now?

–I'm saying he was never noble to begin with. And you, well. You certainly are a man possessed of, what I might call savage instincts. They have helped you get to this particular place in life…

–They have been my downfall then. So-called. They have led me to, to this. This new plateau. That of failure.

–You mustn't be so hard on yourself, Mrdok. There's still so much that can come of this. There is so much more yet to be built.

–I've returned to mapgazing recently.

–A quite admirable hobby.

–You know: where can we go next? All that.

–Yes. You see: there are always other places. There is always that. No need to draw perilous conclusions!

–Perilous conclu… Gordo. There's a fuckin psycho right outside our door. Would that not fit the definition of a, of a fuckin perilous conclusion to you? It's only a matter of time before he holds hostage someone who… someone who has the capability of opening that door and coming in here. And putting us both out of our fuckin misery. And what, when that happens. What will I defend myself with? This fuckin stump I've got right here?

–I feel, have felt, that Vincent was on our side all along. There came a moment when his priorities shifted. I don't know if it had to do with family. Certainly I don't think it had anything to do with the brother, wanting to help the brother out. I think it might be more rooted in the parents. His father, he and Prince's father, has not been well for some time.

–And we took care of him, the father! Both the parents! We're *still* taking care of them! Are we not?

–We won't be able to take care of them much longer. Not without… Not without an infusion of capital.

–For now, I want a freeze. I don't want *any* of my personal assets to be threatened by this. Understand?

–Yes. I understand.

–We've done a lot for *all* of them. Not just his parents.

–You mean…

–You know. The unoriginals.

–Aborigines. Quasi-natives. Is I believe how they like to be called.

–Yeah. Like I said. The unoriginals. Good name for them. It's what they are. Get it? Unoriginal.

–I think the prefix ab- actually means—

–Shut up, Gordo.

–Okay.

–Just shut the fuck up for once.

–I'm shutting.

–He got Prince the temple; he did *not* get the hand in return. Therefore he is collaborating with them. I don't know, I don't know why you keep trying to sketch in some gray area where there is none. Facts are facts, Gordo. You need to finally learn that.

–It is true I learn more and more from you each day.

–That's great to hear. So then that means you are now in a position to advise me.

–Well. I don't know if I'd take it that far—

–Okay. So one question. One simple fucking question: Do I take the meeting with Prince?

–That would depend on whether you already know what you want the outcome to be. I believe that's a piece straight from Tony Fatballs's toolkit? Only take a meeting if the desired outcome is clear, articulable, and foreseeable?

–I think the only one who sees a clear outcome in this circumstance is Prince. Whether it's my surrender or my death. They're both the same, actually. And to him. He's not even sophisticated enough to tell you the difference between the two.

–There's a rumor that they had live geese flown in last week. For some… some outlandish feast they were preparing… I don't know why I just thought of that.

–No. Live geese?

–This is what I heard. It is unclear whether they procured it on their own. Or whether it was a gift from, from one of the parties that is aiding them. I don't know, are there many geese in Australia? I guess that would be the obvious—

–Where did it come from, Pembroke? One of the Seashells?

–It must have come in from Pembroke, yes. That general direction.

–And we're sitting here eating… We're sitting here eating this shit? And they're feasting on goose?!

–Perhaps I shouldn't have—

–You definitely shouldn't have mentioned that… Why did you mention that?

–Perhaps it was to convey a certain sense of… of gravity. I suppose.

–That fuckin temple. We should've, should've *firebombed* it when we had the chance. When it was still in our possession.

–Well we didn't want to do that. To do so would have alienated a large part of the abor—, of the quasi-natives. At the time there was the thought that we still could get them on our side.

–Wouldn't that be ironic? If it were one of our own that ultimately killed me?

–Please don't speak that way, Mrdok.

–I just think it would be the funniest fuckin thing.

–I think it is best if you try and refrain from breaking any more furniture. It is getting difficult to find replacements. And we don't know when we'll be able to get a carpenter in here.

–I like to slam things, Gordo. Inanimate objects. It's my only reprieve—

–I'm just saying because Bev—She asked me to intervene in moments like these. And I believe you also supported her in that motion.

–Bev. Poor Bev.

–Well she just doesn't want to be seen right now.

–I know.

–Apparently her last appointment with Doctor Slopowski did not go according to plan.

–I know. Have you seen her?

–She won't see anyone.

–Well. It's just Botox. I mean, it goes away after a while, doesn't it?

–The effects are indeed temporary. Though they can last up to several months.

–Like how many?

–Around half a year, I suppose?

–I'm gonna have to wait half a year to have sex again?

–I'm sure she'll pull through. Her, her morale is low at the moment. Though she'll get used to it. If worse comes to worse, we still have Doctor Soukowski here. He is known for performing marvelous corrective procedures—or so I am told. Though the issue at stake now of course is our ability to move people from place to place. Like, how we will get her from her bunker to yours, even… Well, it will be done, of course, when she is ready, when you are both ready for it. But it will require a thick detail...

–You know what the thing is? The temple wasn't even that important to the people until a few years ago. Hardly anyone ever went in it. Vincent told me this. The only time was on special occasions. Or if like someone hit a windfall. They would leave offerings to the sea there from time to time. Not even to Yang Zhu—to the gods of the sea. Half of these illiterate morons don't even know who Yang Zhu is. Just go there to leave things, out of ignorant superstition. Fishermen, for instance, fishermen would use it, go in there to give thanks whenever something auspicious, when they had like a huge catch at the end of a day or something. Fruit and bottled water. Burn some incense. The barest inference of ritual. Other than that, it was abandoned. Rotting. Then Prince and his little degenerate friends discovered it one day. Probably bored out of their minds. Thought, hey, this is a new kinda, kinda den we can use, a place from where we can plan shit, how to fuck shit up. And we went and gave it back to them. Look at us now.

–I have learned quite a bit about them, since we got here. Certainly more than the rather paltry information we were given on that first visit by Nelson Rodgers. Who knew that the markmaking had an ulterior motivation all along? One that Nelson himself couldn't even figure out. And to think: he wrote a bloody dissertation on the topic! Something so, so *burningly* obvious... Well, it just goes to show you he never truly deserved to be a part of this place after all.

–The Capitol Building.

–Yes. The Capitol Building. Where we discovered the marks. All over the floor, the walls. They even managed to get them on the ceiling. It's telling that they did not destroy the building. They could've easily bombed it. Would have sent a powerful message.

–They bombed it with their ink instead.

–Yes. Filled it with their strange writing. How odd. Until we began to decipher what it was. Thankfully we had a couple good cryptologists. Both dead, from what I understand. Lost in battle. Separately. A tragedy—I mean, particularly for our intelligence unit... In Sagosian belief, there is a direct connection between the marks and the land. The two are inseparable. Without the marks, there is no land here. Without the marks, they believe that the sea will eventually well up, take the island back.

–Crazy as it sounds, it starts to make more sense to me.

–Me as well. Maybe it's... So the writing, the markmaking all over the interior of the Capitol Building. Well, it would be useful here to have a Vincent on our side, to help us interpret it. They all know what it means, even if we don't.

—It's, like, the written version of the Sagosian language?

—Not quite. It's its own language. You can interpret it. But you cannot speak it. At least that's what our cryptographers concluded, after conducting their study. They also consulted Nelson's tome, I do believe. It's their own private mythology, the marks. A personalized way of expression. Looking at the marks, they can tell who made it. Almost like animals, like dogs who can recognize the scent of a rival creature's territory.

—They are animals.

—Well. Even a dog knows how to express gratitude. They are something worse. But they are interesting beasts, after all.

—So the writing on the building… it's a kind of curse.

—We can view it more as a, as a reclamation, I think. They think it's theirs now.

—So maybe, uh. Maybe we tell them to give it back to us. Like, we arrange a trade.

—A what?

—You know. Like we gave the temple back to them. They need to give the capitol back to us.

—I don't see that happening…

—You know. This meeting or whatever.

—So I interpret that to mean you *are* considering now taking the meeting with Prince?

—So then here's a question: What came first: the landscape or the marks?

—Definitely the landscape. It was here before they, the Sagosians arrived and started making their marks.

—Yeah. But would *they* buy into that? And how does it all tie in with this Yang Zhu?

—Just as, I suppose, the Australian aboriginals have their songlines which tie them to the land. I think it's the same with the Sagosian aborigines, the quasi-natives. Though whereas the Australians' is spoken or sung, the Sagosians' is, well. A form of writing. A writing that is a mapping in both a, a physical sense and a spiritual one, as well. Because the markmaking is ultimately a spiritual practice.

—But Yang Zhu. Wasn't he all about ego? Like, my way or the highway?

—Well. I'm sure they, meaning Prince and his lot, would say that's a crude bastardization of the idea. But like a lot of what happens when Chinese philosophy is transformed into religion—Taoism being the obvious example here—the original ideas are lost and superstition of a sort seems to take over... And, what's happening here, as we all know, is really crass politicization of these spiritual ideas which have no real substance to begin with!

–What if we're wrong, though? What if... What if those marks have the power... What if they've put a curse on us, Gordo? Like they've written all over us? What then?

–You don't truly believe in such things. Do you?

–I don't know what to believe anymore... What are we ever gonna do about Bobby?

–He is in a slump, I'm afraid. I'm not sure the Viutex is helping anymore.

–That little bitch. Evil cunt. I feel somewhat responsible.

–Why, Mrdok?

–Because I knew her even before he did. I should have known what kind of person she was.

–Those were different times, though. Completely different circumstances.

–I remember, all the fun we used to have in Venice. Fuck, man. Venice. Maybe after this I'll just go back to my palace for a little while.

–I don't think anywhere in Italy would be an optimal hiding place at this point...

–One day she took me to, to where was it? The Palazzo Grimaldi. Surprised I can even remember the name. I remember the sculpture, though. The most beautiful fuckin thing. She showed it to me. It was... An eagle eating an angel.

–*Ganimede rapito dall'aquila.*

–What's that?

–Ganymede raped by the eagle. The sculpture to which you are referring. I remember it well. Descending from the ceiling in the Palazzo Grimaldi.

–Yeah. Civilization's a beautiful thing.

–You know, it's full of these, these violations. These rapes. Why, the very name Europe. You do know the story of Europa and the bull, correct?

–Will I never see Venice again?... Gordo?

–I think... I'm not sure. If we could somehow establish some form of contact with Coco. Try to figure out what on earth she's—

–Should we sell it then? The Venice palazzo? I mean, if we can't ever go back there...

—Well never say never, Mrdok. Though I imagine we can have it assessed, determine whether the market conditions are optimal in Venice at the moment. I could add that to my list of—

—I bought that place for Krstal, you know. Maybe we should check with her. Check to make—

—I don't think she even remembers it, Mrdok. She was there, what, one time? And it was years ago…

—Yeah, you're right. She has better things to worry about. Like boning that pencil dick… What are they up to now, anyway? You heard anything?

—Making a movie. If you can believe that…

—I imagine that's on pause at the moment.

—It must be.

—What's this masterpiece supposed to be.

—I have the details here, let me bring it up on the iPad… Oh yes. *The Trees Have Testicles*. The Sagosian banyan tree is supposed to play some sort of central role in it, I gather. Mister Spack has described it as a necro-phallic crypto-accelerationist remake of Wes Craven's *The Hills Have Eyes*…

—And what role does Krstal play in this one?

—Well shall I read you the summary?

—Why the fuck not.

—It says Shot in the caves of Baldheaded Mountain on Settlers Landing and the forest forming its base, *The Trees Have Testicles* is a bald parable of nature's rancorous intentions in the face of global calamity. When a middle-aged lesbian couple, both veterans of the San Fernando Valley pornographic film industry, and their three teenage children find an unbelievably cheap vacation package to a remote desert island that none of them had previously heard of, little do they know what awaits them as they are descended upon by the occupiers of that island, the descendants of shipwrecked slaves who turned to cannibalism to sustain themselves and have maintained the habit over generations, now offering cheap vacation deals through popular travel websites in order to lure their victims to the island…

—And Krstal?

—She plays the main lesbian. The one who survives in the end.

—Good for her. It fits. I mean. She always was a survivor.

—I guess production has been put on hold.

—Of course it has.

—Vincent's mother is in the production as well. She plays the matriarch of the cannibals. In the end of the film, Krstal's character is able to seduce her, they have an onscreen erotic tryst, and just as she is bringing the cannibal lady to the cusp of orgasm, Krstal impales her with the sharp point of a rose murex… It was meant to be the opening film at this year's Sitges Film Festival, though they've had to give up the slot.

—And Stevo Rey. We'll probably never see that one again.

—You know, I always thought Stevo Rey would have eventually emerged as an overachiever much like you, his father, were it not for the weather he wore within: his narcissism, that is. By the time he finally arrived here, on Settlers Landing, what had he done, really? He had been wandering through a perpetual Hardonville for most of his conscious life, extending his adolescence into a smoky realm of hapless dissidence and pathological self-pity. He wore his privileged skin like the disease he perceived it to be, never really coming home, rarely registering anyone else's presence in the dim rooms he occupied. The word he uttered most often was Oh. It made others feel like he was listening. When often, he wasn't.

—You missed something earlier, in your little speech about the Sagosians and markmaking. I remember Krstal telling me about it. I just remembered. I think it was… whatsername… the mother of Vincent, that actress she always works with on the soap. The markmaking is also a form of navigation. That's what they believe. That, the Chinese side of their ancestors at least, that that's what led them here, to this island. They were making marks on the ship as a means of, of determining… their GPS coordinates. And that's how they got here. And that's one of the reasons they still practice it.

—Well. It does make for compelling reading material at least, doesn't it?

—I feel the need to warn you
Bout those dark alleys in my mind
Think I forgot to mention
I am not the marryin kind

—Is that a Belle and Sebastian number?

—No. Just one that I made up just now.

—Well, quite snappy, if I do say so myself. Perhaps you might consider going into the biz with Lil Bigfoot!

—Where the hell is that Black motherfucker anyway?

—Holed up in the bunker beneath his house. The corridors don't extend to ours. He doesn't want to be in contact…

—We all know why that is.

—Well. There are many reasons. But yes. Chief among them is. Little Shelley.

—How far along is she now?

—She might have given birth. By now. Who knows? Someone actually gave her parents my email address. I had to redirect all their emails to my spam folder.

—I mean, we've got government agencies coming after us…

—Yes. But he's been problematic from the beginning.

—Have we… Have we explored the option…?

—Of what? Of selling him? To the Americans?

—For extradition…

—The negotiations did not go well. They weren't willing, for instance, to pull out their funding of the enemies. That was the main thing we wanted. We were even willing to sell her back to her parents. Though the terms weren't as good, obviously. They had very little they could offer us. And anyway, it would have caused strife here between him and us. And it seems she doesn't want to go.

—She doesn't? I thought he was basically holding her hostage.

—Well, it's the Viutex. I mean… Whatever willpower she might have once had…

—Anyway, we have no leverage now, do we. Zero leverage.

—That topic of conversation seems to have died.

—What are going to do with him if…

—He doesn't seem to have much interest in governance. Never really did. He still has his role as senator. So he will continue being…

—What if we win?

—…

—Gordo… What if we win?

—… I believe… we haven't thought that far in advance. At this point.

—…

—Excuse me, I should take this.

—Who is…?

—Yes? Yes? Yes, it's Gordo. I… What? Okay. I'll check it right now.

—What is it?

—An email came in.

—Yes?

—Encrypted.

—Well who is it from?

—I'm checking now… They didn't want to say over the line…

—What is it? You're shaking.

—My god. Mrdok! We… We might have… I might have just found a way out for us!

–What? What is it? Is it… did we get some valuable intelligence? Or… or did we win the battle?

–No no no. It has nothing to do with that. It's… Wait, I'm reading… It's… It's an offer! For a… for a loan!

–… What are you—What do you mean, a *loan*?

–From… Oh my god. The International Monetary Fund. Is offering us a loan! A loan, Mrdok! A loan!

–… What?

–They are offering us a chance to become a member nation. And upon doing so, we will be able to access funds—

–You have got to be shitting me.

–I am not! We will then be able to access billions of dollars in funds for rebuilding and restructuring our—

–Give me that fucking iPad.

–Mrdok. Please. Don't—Mrdok, no!

–It's not broken.

–Oh dear. But the screen is… The screen is smashed. Mrdok, what ever is the matter? This is good news. We've just been, been formally recognized! Our sovereignty! Not only that, they are willing to, to *help* us, to support us in the war effort—

–It's a fucking insult, Gordo! Do you not get it?! They're fucking laughing at me! Making fun of us!

–I… But it came through, through Rick, through our office—

–We are *not* one of those shithole countries! Those shithole countries, with, with some corrupt money-grubbing leader, with no economy, no worth, no nothing. We are the fuckin greatest country in the world, the greatest country that this fuckin lousy century has managed to produce so far! Okay? You fuckin understand that, Gordo? Because clearly you don't. Clearly you think—Do you even understand how they operate, the IMF? They're fuckin, they're trying to *buy us out* with one of their loans. Do you not understand that, Gordo? I mean, really. Your fuckin head. I wonder where it is sometimes. I wonder what's got into it. A bunch of shit, clearly. I mean, fuck. If anyone needs to be loaded up on Viutex, it's you, Gordo. Might fuckin, might bring some sense to you. Fuckin World Bank. Fuckin IMF. I bet it was fuckin, I bet it's Ma who's behind this! Ma or Barb. Or Lally, for that matter. Maybe it's all of them! They're off, fuckin, laughing their asses off. Probably off in DC right now. Fuckin. Getting sucked off by a bunch of lobbyists. Fuckin CIA lackeys. IMF. Let me see that.

–I think it's best if I handle the iPad for now, Mrdok. Until you… Until you decompress.

–I—Fine. Take the fuckin faggoty ass fuckin iPad. I don't fuckin care anymore.

–I just thought… I'm sorry, Mrdok. I thought it… Well. I thought it was something.

–It's not, Gordo. It's not anything.

–I understand that now. And I'm sorry.

–You know what?

–No… I don't… I can't say I know much of anything anymore. Let alone the… the right words to say.

–I think I'll take that meeting with Prince.

–… Really? What, what for?

–No reason. Just to… Just to hear what he has to say.

–Do you think that's advisable?

–I don't know. I have no one left to advise me. I never did, really.

–You were always peerless. You've always been… inadvisable. In all your worldly wisdom…

–With instincts like mine…

–You're right. There is little need.

–And so my instincts are telling me now…

–I will tell Rick to arrange the meeting.

–No decisions. I won't even say anything. I'm just gonna sit there. I'll sit there and listen.

–I'll make sure that is communicated.

–God I can't stand this anymore! No fuckin, no fresh air. No oxygen. No pussy. No nothin. What the fuck can I—How can people stand this?

–Perhaps we will… We are lost. Perhaps we will be lost to history. Like the lost colony.

–What's that.

–The lost colony. Don't you know? It was in the early days, when the English were first attempting to form a settlement in North America. On Roanoke Island, off the coast of North Carolina. The English first arrived there in 1584. They were shown around by two Native American Indians, Manteo, from the Croatoan tribe, and Wanchese from the Roanokes. At the time the area was controlled by two tribes: the Croatoans and the Secotans, who were affiliated with the Roanokes. They were often at war with each other, and perhaps one of the points of conflict was their attitude toward the settlers from afar. The Croatoans were largely friendly to the English settlers, while the Secotans were hostile. Perhaps this had to do with the personalities of the tribal representatives. Manteo and Wanchese became the first Indians to visit England. They spent a year living in

London before returning home with the settlers. Manteo, for his part, was fascinated by everything English, learning the language and adapting to the new technology, their way of being. Wanchese, on the other hand, grew increasingly hostile. When he returned home, he urged his tribe to resist colonization at all costs. The first attempt to settle was made in 1585, with Ralph Lane at the head. The colonists were essentially dropped there by Sir Richard Grenville, who then returned to England in order to bring back supplies. A sense of desperation took over as Grenville's return was delayed, and the supplies began to dwindle. The colonists relied upon a local tribe for their food supplies. Lane got the idea to attack the tribe in an effort to gain more food supplies, killing the chieftain in the process. Well, the end result was that the colony's primary food source was then cut off. So when Sir Francis Drake stopped off in Roanoke, fresh off of his attack on the Spanish colony at Saint Augustine, the colonists climbed aboard his ship and returned to England. Grenville eventually returned with the supplies, only to find the colony abandoned. Grenville then returned to England, leaving fifteen soldiers behind to guard the fort. All of them were either killed or driven off in an attack by the Roanokes that Wanchese himself personally led. In 1587, the English made yet another attempt to settle Roanoke Island. This time they were led in their quest by John White, an artist and mapmaker who had been on Grenville's original ship. By this time, the Secotan tribe and their Roanoke dependents were filled with hostility, yet the Croatoan tribe, headed by Manteo, remained loyal and friendly, even after the English mistakenly killed Manteo's mother. The English baptized Manteo in the Anglican church and appointed him the representative of all natives in the region, even though it was only the Croatoans over whom Manteo held any real sway. As head of the colony, it was now John White's turn to return to England for supplies. And so off he went, leaving the colonists in that rather fraught atmosphere, in the expectation that he would be back with all their much needed foodstuffs and materials in three months' time. Well, England, at the time, was under the threat of an invasion from Spain, and so all of its ships were put in use to defend the English Channel. This effectively prevented White from returning to Roanoke until 1590. By the time he arrived, all of the colonists had disappeared.

—Where did they go?

—No one knows. Wanchese and Manteo also disappeared, as though they had been specters all along. As though they had never existed to begin with. The only clue left behind was the word

CROATOAN which had been carved into a tree. This seemed to be the following of a protocol. White had instructed the colonists, upon leaving three years prior, that if for any reason they had to abandon the colony, they should etch into a tree the name of their destination, as well as a Maltese cross in the event they had been in danger. Croatoan was the name of an island to the south where the friendly tribe dwelled. But the weather turned poor, and White was unable to travel to the island to investigate further. He returned to England, and never set foot in the new world again.

–Gordo…

–To this day, no one knows what happened to the settlers. Nothing substantial of their whereabouts was ever uncovered. Gone without a trace… Some suppose that they fell victim to some new world plague that their immune systems were not equipped to fight. Other speculate that they were decimated in an attack by the Roanokes or perhaps the Secotans, that Wanchese finally had his way with them. Still, some others think that they integrated with the Croatoan tribe, adapted their ways…

–Gordo. Be honest with me. How much am I worth?

–… I don't…

–How much?

–I'm having difficulty now retrieving numbers, Mrdok… The connection is not ideal. The screen is cracked. The page isn't reloading.

–Fuck that. Just tell me. What was it the last time you checked.

–It was… I can't remember the exact number. A lot.

–A lot? How much is a lot.

–I don't know, Mrdok. It was. Rather a lot…

Then, upon further reflection:

– Perhaps even a bit too much.

TRAVIS JEPPESEN is the author of ten books, including *The Suiciders*, *Victims*, and *See You Again in Pyongyang*. His latest play, *Ghosts of the Landwehr Canal*, recently premiered at the Berlin Ringtheater, under the direction of Wang Ping-Hsiang. Jeppesen has contributed essays and reviews to the *New York Times Magazine*, *Artforum*, *Mousse*, *Wall Street Journal*, *The Believer*, *Review of Contemporary Fiction*, and other media. An accomplished art critic, he is the recipient of an Andy Warhol Foundation Arts Writers Grant. His calligraphic and text-based artwork has been the subject of solo exhibitions at Wilkinson Gallery (London), Exile (Berlin), and Rupert (Vilnius), and featured in group exhibitions internationally, including the 2014 Whitney Biennial.

BOOKS BY ITNA

Urban Gothic: The Complete Stories
Bruce Benderson

Crashing Cathedrals: Edmund White by the Book
Tom Cardamone

Aaron's Rod
D.H. Lawrence

Victims
Travis Jeppesen

The Virtuous Ones
Christopher Stoddard